£10.95 for £3.95

torn d/jacket

A

François Mauriac

OMNIBUS

A FRANÇOIS MAURIAC OMNIBUS

CONTAINING

The Desert of Love
The Knot of Vipers
The Frontenac Mystery
A Woman of the Pharisees

Translated by
GERARD HOPKINS

BIBLIOPHILE BOOKS
33 Maiden Lane, London, WC2E 7JS

THE DESERT OF LOVE
First published in French in 1925
First English edition published in 1949
by Eyre and Spottiswoode (Publishers) Ltd

THE KNOT OF VIPERS
First published in French in 1932
First English edition published in 1951
by Eyre and Spottiswoode (Publishers) Ltd

THE FRONTENAC MYSTERY
First published in French in 1933
First English edition published in 1951
by Eyre and Spottiswoode (Publishers) Ltd
Reprinted 1971 © 1971

A WOMAN OF THE PHARISEES
First published in French in 1941
First English edition published in 1946
by Eyre & Spottiswoode (Publishers) Ltd

This omnibus edition published 1984
by Bibliophile
Printed in Great Britain
by Richard Clay (The Chaucer Press) Ltd,
Bungay, Suffolk

ISBN 0 413 55240 3

THE DESERT OF LOVE

I

FOR years Raymond Courrèges had been cherishing the hope that one day he might run across Maria Cross, the woman on whom he had so ardently longed to be revenged. Often in the street he would follow some chance passer-by, thinking to have found her. But in the course of time the edge of his resentment had become blunted, so that when, at length, they did come face to face, he felt, at first, none of that joy shot with fury which such a meeting should have stirred in him.

It was only ten o'clock when he entered the bar in the rue Duphot. The coloured jazz-band was playing softly for the delectation of a solitary waiter. Over the tiny floor which, when midnight came, would be crammed with dancing couples, a ventilating fan was making a noise like a gigantic bluebottle. To the doorman, who said, with a look of surprise, "Don't often see you here as early as this, sir," he replied with no more than a wave of the hand, which conveyed a wish that something should be done to stop this intrusive bumbling. The man did his best to explain, confidentially, but without success, that the new system "absorbed the smoke without causing a draught." Courrèges gave him such a look that he beat a hasty retreat to the cloak-room. Up in the ceiling the ventilator droned to silence, as though a bee had suddenly alighted.

The young man sat down at one of the tables, thus breaking the immaculate vista of white cloths. A glance in a mirror showed him that he was not looking his best. 'What's the matter with me?' he wondered. God!—how he hated a wasted evening—and all because of that swine Eddy H——. He had had to dig the fellow out and almost drag him to a restaurant. During dinner Eddy had scarcely listened to what he was saying, and had excused his inattention on the ground of a sick-headache.

He had sat perched on the very edge of his chair, impatience in every line of his body, obviously preoccupied with the thought of some happiness to come. No sooner had he finished his coffee than he had taken eagerly to his heels—eyes shining, ears flushed and nostrils flaring. Raymond had spent the day in delighted anticipation of their dinner and of the evening that was to follow it. But, no doubt, Eddy had in prospect pleasures more stimulating than any offered by a mere exchange of confidences.

Courrèges was amazed to find that he felt not only disappointed and humiliated, but also sad. The discovery that the companionship of a friend to whom he attached no particular importance could show as thus precious to him, came as a shock. It was something entirely new in his life. Up to the age of thirty, being quite incapable of the selflessness demanded by true friendship, and devoting much of his attention to women, he had disregarded everything that was not an object to be possessed, and, like a greedy child, would have said, had he put the feeling into words, "I like only what I can eat." At that period of his life he made use of his cronies either as witnesses of his conquests or as recipients of his confidences. He looked on a friend as, first and foremost, a pair of ears. He liked, too, the feeling that he could dominate them and control their actions. Influencing others had become a passion with him. He flattered himself that he had reduced the demoralizing of his companions to a fine art.

Raymond Courrèges could have built up a big career for himself, as his grandfather the surgeon had done; his uncle, the Jesuit, and his father, the doctor, if only he had been capable of harnessing his appetites to work, if only his natural tastes had not led him to concentrate all his energies on the achievement of immediate satisfaction. But by now he was reaching the age at which only those who address themselves to the soul can set their dominance on a firm foundation. The best that Courrèges could do for his disciples was to assure them a quick yield in terms of pleasure. But the younger men of his acquaintance preferred to share their adventures with others of their own age, and his circle was growing thin. In the preserves of love there is no shortage of game, but we soon find that the little group of those in whose company we set out grows smaller year by year. Those who had survived the dark violence of the war had either dwindled into husbands or had their natures distorted by the pursuit of a calling. He noted their greying hair, their protuberant bellies, their bald pates, and hated them because they were the same age as himself. He accused them of having murdered their youth, of having betrayed it even before it had fled from them.

It was a matter of pride with him to be taken for a "post-war product"; and this evening, in the still empty bar, where the only sound was the muted thrumming of a mandolin (the flame of the melody rising, falling, flickering), he studied with fierce attention the image thrown back at him from the mirrors, the image of a face with a thatch of vigorous hair on which his thirty-five years had not yet set their mark. It came to him, as he pondered, that age would lay hands upon his life long before it touched his body. If it bolstered up his self-esteem to hear women say among themselves—"Who's that tall young man?" he knew that the keener-eyed twenty-year-olds no longer thought of him as forming one in their ephemeral group. Maybe Eddy had had something better to do than talk about himself to an accompaniment of wailing saxophones; on the other hand, he might be doing just that at this very moment in some other bar, laying bare his heart to some youth born in 1904, who would constantly interrupt the flow of his talk with "me, too," and "that's just what I feel. . . ."

A number of young men began to drift in. They had assumed expressions of self-conscious arrogance preparatory to crossing the floor, and were now, at sight of the empty room, visibly embarrassed. They gathered in a little cluster round the barman. But Courrèges had made it a rule never to let himself suffer because of the behaviour of others—whether mistresses or friends. True, therefore, to this principle, he set himself to stress the lack of proportion existing between the insignificance of Eddy H——, and the feeling of uneasy restlessness which was the legacy left behind after that young man's defection. . . . He was pleased to find that this weed of sentiment, when he tried to pull it out, came away without any difficulty. He wound himself up to the pitch of thinking how little it would mean to him, next day, to show his friend the door. He even contemplated without concern the possibility that he might never set eyes on him again. It was almost with a sense of gaiety that he thought: "I'll wash my hands of him once and for all." He sighed with relief, only to find that a sense of unease remained which had nothing whatever to do with Eddy. . . . Ah, yes, of course, that letter! He could feel it in the pocket of his evening jacket. No point in reading it again. Dr. Courrèges, in communicating with his son, made use of a telegraphic brevity of expression which was easily remembered:

> Staying at Grand Hotel duration Medical Congress. Available mornings before nine, evenings after eleven.
>
> Your father,
>
> PAUL COURRÈGES.

"Not if I know it!" he murmured, unaware that his face had taken on an expression of defiance. He held it against this father of his that it was less easy to despise him than the other members of the family. On reaching the age of thirty, Raymond had demanded a lump-sum down comparable to what his sister had received on her marriage. But in vain. Faced by the parental refusal, he had burned his boats and taken himself off. But it was Madame Courrèges who held the purse-strings, and he knew perfectly well that his father would have acted generously by him had he been in a legal position to do so, and that money meant nothing to the old man. "Not if I know it!" he said to himself once more, but could not, for all that, help catching the note of appeal which sounded in the dry little message. He was far less blind than was Madame Courrèges, who felt only irritation at her husband's undemonstrative nature and brusque manner. "He may be a good man, and he may have a heart of gold," she was fond of saying, "but what good is that to me if I never get a glimpse of it? Just think what he would be like if he was *bad*!"

Just because it was so difficult to hate his father, Raymond found these claims upon his affection hard to endure. He wasn't going to answer the letter . . . all the same. . . . Later, when he thought back to the circumstances of this evening, he remembered the bitterness of his mood when he entered the deserted little bar, but forgot what had caused it—the defection of a friend called Eddy, and his father's presence in Paris. He believed that his sour ill-temper had been born of a presentiment, and that a connexion existed between the state of his emotions, on that occasion, and the event which was fast approaching. He has always since maintained that neither Eddy nor the doctor were, in themselves, capable of getting him worked up like that, but that, from the very moment he had settled down with a cocktail, some inner voice, some clamour of the flesh, had warned him of the imminent appearance of the woman who, at that same moment, in a taxi which had already reached the corner of the rue Duphot, was rummaging in her little bag, and saying to her companion:

"What a bore! I've forgotten my lipstick!"

To which the man replied, "There'll probably be one in the ladies' room."

"What a foul idea! one might catch . . ."

"Well then, get Gladys to lend you hers."

* * * * *

She came into the bar. A "cloche" hat completely obliterated the top part of her face, leaving visible only her chin, that feature on which time sets the sign-manual of age. Forty years had, here and there, touched this nether segment of her countenance, drawing the skin tight and sketching a hint of sagging flesh. Her body beneath its furs must, one felt, be shrunken. As blind as a bull brought suddenly from its dark pen into the glare of the arena, she stopped short on the threshold of the glittering room. When her companion, who had been delayed by a dispute over the fare, rejoined her, Courrèges, though not at once recognizing him, said to himself: "I've seen that fellow somewhere—bet he comes from Bordeaux": and then, all of a sudden, as he looked at the face of the man of fifty, swollen, as it were, by the sense of its own identity, a name formed itself on his lips: Victor Larousselle. . . . With beating heart he resumed his examination of the woman who, quickly realizing that no one else was wearing a hat, had taken off hers, and was shaking out her freshly cropped hair in front of a mirror. He saw, first of all, a pair of eyes that were large and calm: next, a wide forehead, its limits sharply marked by the seven youthful points of her dark hair. All that remained of the legacy of youth seemed concentrated in the upper part of her face. Raymond recognized her in spite of the short hair, the middle-aged "spread," and nature's slow work of destruction, which, beginning at the neck, was busy invading the areas of mouth and cheeks. He recognized her as he would have done a road familiar to him in childhood, even though the oaks once shading it had been cut down. He calculated the lapse of time. The sum took him a bare two seconds. 'She's forty-four,' he thought: 'I was eighteen and she was twenty-seven.' Like all those who confound the ideas of happiness and youth, he had a consciousness of the passage of time which was ever active, strive, though he might, to keep it muffled. His eye was for ever measuring the sundering gulf of the dead years. He at once inserted in life's chronology every human being who had played a part in his existence. No sooner did he see a face than he could supply a date.

'Will she recognize me?' But would she have so sharply turned away if she had not already done so? She went up to her companion and seemed to be begging him not to stay, for he replied very loudly, and in the tone of a man who craves an admiring audience, "What nonsense! it's not a bit gloomy. In a quarter of an hour it'll be as tight packed as an egg with meat!" He pushed out a table not far from the one at which Raymond was leaning on his elbow, and sat down heavily. The blood had rushed to his face, sure sign of hardening arteries. But apart from that its expression was one of unruffled satisfaction. The woman was still standing motionless. "What are you waiting for?" he asked. Gone, suddenly, from the eyes, from the coarse and purplish lips, was all look of pleasure. In what he thought was a low voice, he said: "It's enough for me to like being here for you to start sulking—of course!" She must have told him to be careful, have warned him that he could be overheard, for his next words were almost shouted: "So I don't know how to behave, don't I?—What does it matter if they *do* hear?"

Seated not far from Raymond, the woman seemed to have recovered her composure. In order to see her the young man would have had to lean forward. It was for her now to avoid his eyes. He realized her renewed sense of security, and was made suddenly aware, with a quick feeling of terror, that the opportunity which, for the last seventeen years, he had so eagerly desired, might slip through his fingers. He thought that he was still, after all that time, determined to humiliate the woman who had so deeply humiliated him, to show her what manner of man he was—the sort that doesn't let a bitch get the better of him without hitting back. For years he had found pleasure in thinking what would happen when fate at last should bring them face to face, how he would skilfully contrive matters so as to ride rough-shod over, and reduce to tears, the woman in whose presence he had once cut so ridiculous a figure. . . . Doubtless, if to-night he had recognized not this woman, but some other trivial familiar of his eighteenth year—the boon companion of that distant time, the miserable usher whom he had loathed—he would, at sight of them, have found in himself no trace either of the affection or of the hatred which the callow schoolboy, now outgrown, had then felt. But, faced by this woman, did he not feel now just as he had felt on that Thursday evening of 19—, when he had walked in the fading light along a dusty suburban road smelling of lilies, and stopped before a gate whose bell would never again ring to the pressure of his finger? Maria! Maria Cross! Of the shy and grubby youth he had been then, she had made a new man, the man he was to be for ever after. How little she had changed! The same questioning eyes, the same radiant forehead. Courrèges reminded himself that his favourite school friend of 19— would, by this time, be heavy, prematurely bald and bearded. But the faces of a certain type of woman remain steeped in childhood until well on into maturity, and it is that quality of childhood, perhaps, that produces in us a fixation of love kept inviolate from the weapons of time. There she was, as she had always been, after seventeen years of passions about which he knew nothing, like one of those black Virgins whose smile the flaming fanaticisms of Reform and Revolution have been powerless to change. She was still being "kept" by this same man of substance who was noisily venting his ill-humour and impatience because the people for whom he was waiting had not yet turned up.

"I expect it's Gladys as usual who's making them late. . . . I'm always on the dot myself . . . can't stand unpunctuality in others. I suppose I'm odd in that way. I just can't bear the thought of keeping other people waiting—some sort of an instinct, I suppose—no use fighting against it. But good manners are a thing of the past. . . ."

Maria Cross laid a hand on his shoulder, and must have said again: "Everyone can hear what you're saying," because he growled out that he wasn't saying anything he minded people hearing, and that it really was a bit much *her* teaching *him* how to behave.

Her mere presence had the effect of delivering Courrèges bound hand and foot to the vanished past. Though he had always had a keen sense of days long gone, he had a hatred of reviving the memory of their details, and feared nothing so much as the shuffle of ghosts. But he could do nothing this evening to disperse the crowding procession of faces brought by Maria's presence to the surface of his consciousness. He could hear again, in memory, the clock striking six, and the banging of desk-lids in Upper School. Not enough rain had fallen to lay the dust: the light in the tram was too bad for him to finish reading *Aphrodite*—in the tram filled with workpeople to whose faces the exhaustion of another day had imparted a look of gentleness.

II

HE was a grubby brat. Much of his time at school he spent being turned out of the class-room, wandering about the passages or leaning against old walls. When he left it of an evening, and before he got to his suburban home, there was a long interval of time, spent, most of it, in the tram, which stood in his mind for freedom, for deliverance. At last he could feel himself alone, surrounded by indifferent faces and incurious eyes. Especially was this so in winter, because then the darkness, shredded only at intervals by scattered street-lamps and the glare of occasional bars, shut him away from the world, isolated him in a universe that reeked of damp working-clothes. Dead cigarettes dangled from sagging lips; faces seamed with coal-dust lay tilted back in sleep; newspapers slipped from hands gone numb; a hatless woman held up her novelette to catch the light of the lamps, her lips moving as though in prayer. But the end of the journey came at last, and, just after they had passed the church at Talence, he had to get out.

The tram—a moving Bengal Candle—lit up for a few brief moments the yews and naked elm branches of a private park. Then the boy heard the noise of the trolley-wheels diminish as he stood in the puddle-pocked road. His nose was filled with the scent of rotting wood and leaves. He turned up the lane that ran by the Courrèges garden wall, and pushed open the half-closed gate leading to the backyard. The light from the dining-room window lay across a clump of bushes where, in Spring, the fuchsias were planted, because they love the shade. At this point in the return journey his face took on the sullen look it wore at school; his eyebrows drew together till they showed as a single matted line above his eyes, and the right-hand corner of his mouth began to droop. Entering the drawing-room he threw a collective "good evening" to the occupants who sat grouped about a single niggardly lamp. His mother asked how often must he be told to wipe his feet on the scraper, and did he mean to sit down to dinner with his hands "like that"? Madame Courrèges, the elder, murmured to her daughter-in-law: "You know what Paul says: don't nag the boy unnecessarily." His very appearance seemed to start an exchange of bitter words.

He sat down where the light could not reach him.

Crouched over her embroidery, Madeleine Basque, his sister, had not so much as raised her head at his entrance. He was of less interest to her, he thought, than the dog. In her opinion, Raymond was the family's "running sore." "I don't like to think what *he'll* grow up into," she was for ever saying, to which her husband, Gaston Basque, would contribute his mite by adding: "It's all because his father's so weak."

She would look up from her work, sit for a moment with her ears pricked, say suddenly, "There's Gaston," and lay aside her task. "*I* don't hear a thing," Madame Courrèges would remark. But—"Yes, it's him," the young woman would repeat, and then, though no sound had reached any ear but her own, would run out on to the terrace and disappear into the garden, guided by an infallible instinct, as though she belonged to a species of animal different from all others, where it was the male, and not the female, who exhaled the odour that would draw his partner to him through the darkness. In a moment or two the Courrèges would hear a man's voice followed by Madeleine's gratified and submissive laughter. They knew that the couple would not come back through the drawing-room, but would use a side-door and go straight upstairs to the bedroom floor, from which they would not descend until the gong had been sounded twice.

The company round the dining-room table, beneath the hanging lamp, consisted of the elder Madame Courrèges, her daughter-in-law, Lucie Courrèges, the young couple and their four little girls, all with their father's reddish hair, all dressed alike, all with the same complexion and the same patches of freckles. They sat huddled together like tame birds on a perch. "No one's to say a word to them," ordered Lieutenant Basque. "If anyone addresses them, it's they who'll be punished. Now don't say I didn't warn you."

The doctor's chair remained empty for some considerable time, even when he happened to be at home. He would come in half-way through the meal, carrying a bundle of learned journals. His wife said, hadn't he heard the gong? and complained that with everything in the house at sixes and sevens, it was quite impossible to keep any servant for long. Shaking his head, as though to chase away a fly, he proceeded to bury himself in one of his journals. This was not affectation on his part, but merely a way of saving time devised by a man who was in a constant condition of over-work, never free from worries, and fully aware that every minute was precious. At the other end of the table, the Basques sat isolated and aloof, supremely indifferent to everything that did not directly concern either them or their little ones. Gaston would be explaining how he was pulling strings to avoid being moved from Bordeaux, how the Colonel had written to the Ministry . . . his attentive wife all the while keeping a watchful eye on the children and maintaining an uninterrupted flow of educative comment: "Don't you know how to use a knife?" "Don't sprawl." "Keep your hands on the table—hands, I said, not elbows." "Now mind what I say, you won't get any more bread." "You've had quite enough to drink already."

The Basques formed an island of secrecy and suspicion. "They never tell me anything"—all Madame Courrèges' grievances against her daughter could be summed up in that phrase—"they never tell me anything." She suspected that Madeleine was pregnant, kept a careful eye on her figure, and drew her own conclusions when the girl complained of not feeling well. The servants, she maintained, always knew everything before she did. She believed that Gaston had taken out an insurance policy on his life, but for how much? She had no idea what money they had come into on old Basque's death.

In the drawing-room, after dinner, when she grumblingly enquired whether Raymond hadn't any home-work to do, any essay to write, he made no answer. He would take hold of one of the little girls, look as though he were about to crush her in his great hands, toss her up over his head so that she could touch the ceiling, and swing the lithe little body round and round, while Madeleine Basque, like a ruffled and uneasy hen—though disarmed by the child's excitement, would exclaim: "*Do* be careful; I'm sure you'll do her some injury," and then, turning to the company in general, would remark: "He's so *rough*," at which, Grandmamma Courrèges, laying down her knitting and pushing up her spectacles, while her whole face crinkled into a smile, would at once embark on a brisk defence of Raymond: "Why, he *adores* children," she would say. "You can't deny that children are all he cares about . . ." for it was one of the old lady's convictions that he wouldn't be so devoted to them if he hadn't a heart of gold. "You've only got to see him with his nieces to realize that there's nothing really to worry about."

But did he really care so very much about children? The truth was he made use of anything that came his way, provided it was warm and living, as a weapon against those whom he called the "corpses." Depositing the young body on the sofa, he would, on these occasions, make for the door, rush from the house and stride along the leaf-encumbered paths.

Between the branches a lighter patch of sky guided his steps. Doctor Courrèges' lamp glowed from behind a window on the first floor. Should he go to bed without looking in on his father to say good-night? The three-quarters of an hour of hostile silence each morning were, alas! all that he could stand. Every day, early, the brougham set out, carrying father and son. Raymond got out at the Barrière de Saint-Genès, whence he walked, by way of the Boulevards, to school, while the doctor continued on to the hospital. For three-quarters of an hour they sat side by side in a smell of ancient leather, between streaming windows. The practitioner, who a few moments later, would be speaking eloquently, authoritatively, to his helpers and his students, had been vainly seeking, for months, some word that should provoke a response from this being of his own flesh and blood. How was he ever to succeed in blazing a path to this heart which was always bristling with defences? Each time he congratulated himself on finding a joint in the young man's armour, and began speaking to Raymond in phrases planned long in advance, his words seemed suddenly like the words of a stranger: his very voice, dry and mocking, had, he felt, turned traitor—no matter how hard he tried to make it sound natural. This powerlessness to give expression to his feelings was his habitual martyrdom.

It was only through his actions that Dr. Courrèges' kindness of heart was widely recognized, for they alone bore witness to the good that lay so deeply embedded in him that it was like a man entombed. He could never hear a word of gratitude without a growl and a shrug. Bumping along through rainy dawns beside his son, he was for ever addressing silent questions to the withdrawn and sullen face there at his elbow. In spite of himself he could not help interpreting the signs that showed upon that face as those of some dark angel—the deceptive sweetness, for instance, that he caught in eyes that were more deeply shadowed than they should have been. 'The poor boy regards me as his enemy,' thought the father, 'and the fault is mine, not his.' But he was reckoning without the sure instinct for those who love him which is for ever active in the adolescent. Raymond heard the unvoiced appeal, and never confused his father with the others. But he deliberately turned a deaf ear to what never found release in words. Nor could he, on his side, have thought of anything to say to the victim of shyness at his side, for the effect of his presence was to numb the older man with timidity, and so turn him to ice. Nevertheless, the doctor could not refrain, now and again, from remonstrating with him, though he always did so as gently as possible, and in terms of a friendship between equals.

"I've had another letter about you from the headmaster. Poor Abbé Farge, you'll really send him out of his mind! It seems to be proved without a shadow of doubt that it was you who passed round that treatise on obstetrics—I suppose you sneaked it off my shelves. I must confess that his air of outraged virtue seems to me somewhat excessive. After all, you're old enough now to know about the facts of life, and it's a good deal better that you should get them from solid, scientific books. That's the line I took in my reply. . . . But I gather, too, that a number of *La Gaudriole* was found in the newspaper rack in Upper School, and, very naturally, you are under suspicion. All the sins of Israel are laid to your charge. Better look out, my boy, or you'll find yourself expelled with the final exams. still a good six months off."

"No."

"What d'you mean—no?"

"Because I'm working extra hard and stand a good chance of not being ploughed a second time. I know their sort! They're not going to get rid of the only chap who's likely to pass. Besides, if they showed me the door, the Jesuits would snap me up in a jiffy! They'd far rather let me go on contaminating the others, as they put it, than run the risk of losing a good item in the school records. Think how triumphant old Farge'll look on Speech Day: thirty candidates—twenty-three 'Honours' and two 'Passes.' . . . Thunderous applause. . . . What a lot of swine they are!"

"No, my boy, that's where you're wrong." The doctor stressed those words "my boy." Now, perhaps, was his opportunity to penetrate the lad's stubborn heart. For a long time his son had obstinately refused to show the slightest sign of weakening. The glow of a trusting confidence showed through the cynical words. What should he say that might have the effect, without putting the boy on the defensive, of proving to him that there *are* men who don't resort to tricks and calculations, that sometimes the cleverest are those Machiavellis of high causes who wound us when they wish us well? . . . He felt about in his mind for the most suitable formula, and even while he pondered the problem, the suburban road had turned into a city street filled with the bright and melancholy radiance of morning and the jostle of milk-carts. A few moments more and they would reach the city limits, that Croix de Saint-Genès where once the pilgrims to St. James of Compostella had knelt in momentary adoration, and where now only bus inspectors leaned against the walls. Unable to find any suitable words, he took the other's warm hand in his, said in a low voice, "My boy," . . . and then noticed that Raymond, his head pressed to the window, was asleep, or pretending to be asleep. The young man had closed his eyes, perhaps for fear that they might, for all his efforts to the contrary, betray a weakening, a desire to yield. He sat there, his face fast shut to all approaches, a bony face that looked as though carved in granite, in which the only sign of sensitiveness was the vulnerable line of the eyelids.

Very gradually the doctor withdrew his hand.

* * * * *

Was it before that scene in the brougham, or later, that the woman sitting over there on the settee, separated from him by no more than a single table, so that he could have spoken to her without raising his voice, had come into his life? She seemed calmer now, and was sipping her drink with never a fear, it seemed, that Raymond might have recognized her. Every now and again she looked at him, only to look away almost at once. Suddenly her voice—and how well he remembered it!—rose above the babble of noise: "There's Gladys!"

The newly-arrived couple came over at once and sat down between her and her companion. They all started talking at once. "We were waiting for our cloak-room tickets." "We're always the first to arrive—well, anyhow you've come, that's the main thing."

No, it must have been more than a year before the scene between father and son in the brougham, that, one day at dinner (it would have been in the late Spring, because the lamp in the dining-room had not been lit), Madame Courrèges the elder had said to her daughter-in-law: "I know whom the white hangings in the church were for, Lucie."

Raymond had thought that one of those endless conversations was about to begin, full of trivial phrases that dropped dead about the doctor's chair. As a rule, they had to do with household matters, each of the women present rushing to do battle for her own particular member of the staff, so that the encounter became a squalid Iliad in which the quarrels of the servants' hall set the various patron Goddesses at one another's throat in the Olympus of the dining-room. Often the two families would set about disputing the favours of the daily sewing-woman. For instance: "I've arranged with Travaillotte to come to me next week," Madame Courrèges would say to Madeleine Basque, and then the younger woman would at once protest that the children's underwear needed mending.

"You always nobble Travaillotte."

"Well, then, why don't you fix up with old broken-nose Mary?"

"Broken-nose Mary is a much slower worker. Besides, she always insists on my paying her tram fare."

But on this particular evening, the mention of the white hangings in church had given rise to a more serious discussion. Madame Courrèges the elder had more to say.

"They're for that poor little boy of Maria Cross's, the one who died of meningitis. I gather she ordered an extremely expensive funeral."

"How very tactless!"

At his wife's exclamation, the doctor, who sat reading a journal while he drank his soup, raised his eyes. She, as usual when that happened, lowered hers, angrily remarking that it was a pity, all the same, that the curé hadn't managed to instil some sense of guilt into a woman who, as everyone knew, was a kept creature, who flaunted her shame all over the place, with her horses and carriages and all the rest.

The doctor made a gesture with his hand indicative of protest.

"It's not for us to judge: she's done *us* no harm."

"What about the scandal? I suppose that doesn't count?"

From the face he pulled she could see that he was saying to himself how vulgar she was. She made an effort to moderate her tone, though a few seconds later she exclaimed as loudly as before that women like that gave her the horrors. . . . The house that for so long had been the home of her old friend, Madame Bouffard, Victor Larousselle's mother-in-law, was now occupied by a slut. . . . Every time she passed the door it cut her to the heart. . . .

The doctor, speaking very calmly, and in an almost hushed voice, interrupted the flow to point out that the only person in that house to-night was a mother sitting by her dead child. At this, Madame Courrèges, with one finger raised, announced solemnly:

"It is God's judgment!"

The children heard the scraping sound made by the doctor's chair as he pushed it sharply back from the table. He thrust his journals into his pocket, and, without another word, walked across to the door. He forced himself to move slowly, but the family, all attention now, could hear him running upstairs four steps at a time.

"Did I say anything so very extraordinary?" Madame Courrèges addressed a questioning look at her mother-in-law, at the young couple, at the children, at the servant. The only sounds in the room were the scraping of knives and forks and Madeleine's voice: "Don't nibble your bread—stop playing with that bone. . . ."

Madame Courrèges, her eyes fixed on her mother-in-law, said: "I really think he must be ill."

But the old lady, her nose buried in her plate, seemed not to have heard. It was at this point that Raymond had burst out laughing.

"If you must laugh you'd better go outside! And don't come back till you can control yourself!"

Raymond threw his napkin on the floor. How peaceful it was in the garden. Yes, it must have been late Spring because he remembered the bumbling noise made by the cockchafers, and that they had had strawberries for dinner. He had sat down in the middle of the paddock on the still warm stone rim of a fountain which no human eye had ever seen spouting water. He noticed his father's shadow passing and repassing the windows of the first floor. In the twilight that poured dusty and heavy over this stretch of country not far from Bordeaux, a bell was tolling at long intervals because death had come for the child of this same woman who now sat drinking so close to him that he could have stretched out his hand and touched her. Since starting on the champagne, Maria Cross had been gazing more boldly at the young man, as though she were no longer afraid that she might be recognized. To say that she had not aged was an understatement. In spite of the fact that she had cut her hair, and that she was wearing nothing that trespassed beyond the winter's fashion, her whole body had somehow kept the lines that had been in vogue about 19 . . . . She looked young, but it was as though her youth had come to flower fifteen years ago and remained unchanged. She was young in the way that no one is young to-day. Her eyelids looked no wearier than they had done when she had said to Raymond: "Our eyes have a fellow feeling."

* * * * *

Raymond remembered how, on the day following the evening on which his father had suddenly left the table, he had sat very early in the dining-room drinking his chocolate. The windows were open on the dawn mist, and he shivered a little. There was a smell of freshly-ground coffee. The gravel of the drive crackled under the wheels of the ancient brougham. The doctor was late. Madame Courrèges, in a purple dressing-gown, her hair plaited and twisted in the way she always wore it when she went to bed, kissed him on the forehead. He went on with his breakfast without pausing.

"Isn't your father down yet?"

She said that she had got some letter to give him for the post. But he could guess the reason for her early appearance. When the members of a family live cheek by jowl, they get into the habit of never giving away their own secrets but of ever being on the alert to probe the secrets of others. The mother said of her daughter-in-law: "She never tells me anything, but there is precious little I don't know about her." Each person in the group claimed to know all about the others, while themselves remained inscrutable. Raymond thought he knew why his mother was there: "She wants to make it up." After a scene like that of the previous evenings, she would dog her husband's footsteps, seeking to be taken back into favour. The poor woman was always discovering too late that she had the fatal gift of habitually saying what would most get on the doctor's nerves. As in certain forms of nightmare, the more she tried to approach him, the further away she seemed to get. She could do nothing, say nothing, that was not hateful to him. Tangled in her clumsy efforts at tenderness, she was, as it were, always groping her way forward with outstretched hands. But whenever she touched him it was to bruise.

As soon as she heard the sound of his bedroom door closing,

she poured out a cup of steaming coffee. A smile lit up her face, which was marked by the traces of a sleepless night and worn by the slow dripping of laborious and identical days. But the smile vanished as soon as the doctor appeared. She was already on her guard, trying to read the expression in his eyes.

"Why, you've got your top-hat and overcoat on!"

"That is quite obvious."

"Are you going to a wedding?"

. . . .

"A funeral, then?"

"Yes."

"Who has died?"

"Someone you don't know, Lucie."

"Tell me who it is."

"The little Cross boy."

"Maria Cross's son? Do you know her? You never told me you did. You never tell me anything. Considering that we were talking at dinner of that hussy . . ."

The doctor was drinking his coffee, standing. He answered in his quietest tones, which was always a sign with him that he was exasperated almost beyond bearing, though well under control:

"Haven't you learned, even after twenty-five years, that I prefer to discuss my patients as little as possible?"

No, she hadn't, and insisted that it always amazed her to find out, quite by chance, in the course of a social call, that this or that friend of hers had been attended by Dr. Courrèges.

"It's so awkward for me when people look surprised. 'What,' they say, 'do you really mean to tell me that you didn't *know*?' and then I have to admit that you don't trust me, that you never tell me anything. Were you treating the child? What did he die of? I can't see why you won't tell me. I never repeat things. Besides, with people like that, what can it matter? . . ."

For any sign the doctor gave, he might not have heard or seen her. He put on his overcoat, calling to Raymond: "Get a move on; seven o'clock struck ages ago."

Madame Courrèges pattered along behind them.

"What have I said now? You suddenly put all your prickles out. . . ."

The door slammed. A clump of shrubs hid the brougham from view. The sun began to shred the mist. Madame Courrèges, talking disjointedly to herself, turned back towards the house.

Seated in the carriage, the schoolboy looked at his father with eager curiosity, anxious for confidences. Now, if ever, father and son might have drawn closer together. But the doctor's thoughts were far from the boy with whom, so often, he had longed to come to grips. Here was the young prey ready to his hand, and he did not realize it. He sat there, muttering into his beard, as though he had been alone: "I ought to have called in a surgeon. One can always try trepanning as a last resort." He pushed back his top-hat with its nap all brushed the wrong way, lowered one of the windows and thrust out his hirsute countenance above the traffic-encumbered road. At the city limits he said absent-mindedly: "See you this evening," but he did not gaze after Raymond's retreating form.

III

IN the course of the following summer Raymond Courrèges had his seventeenth birthday. He remembered it as a season of torrid heat and shortage of water. Never since then had the city of stone lain prostrate under so intolerable a glare, cluttered though his memory was with many summers spent in Bordeaux, a city protected by hills from the north winds, and close invested by pines and sand which concentrate and accumulate the heat—Bordeaux, so poor in trees, except for its Public Gardens, where, to the eyes of children parched with thirst, it seemed as though the last vestiges of green in all the world were being burned to cinders behind the tall and solemn railings.

But perhaps, in retrospect, he was confusing the sun's heat of that especial summer with the inner flame that was burning him up, him and sixty others of his age, who had their being within the limits of a yard separated from other yards by the back walls of a row of latrines. It needed the constant presence of two ushers to control this herd of boys who were dying into life, of men on the verge of being born. Responsive to the thrust of painful growth, the forest of young lives put forth, in a few short months, spindly and ailing shoots. The world and its ways had the effect of pruning the rank growth of these young scions of good families, but in Raymond Courrèges the action of the rising sap was fierce and uninhibited. He was an object of fear and horror to his masters, who kept him with his scarred face (because his tender skin could not endure the razor) as far as possible from associating with his fellows. The good boys of the school looked on him as a "dirty beast" who carried photographs of women in his note-case and read *Aphrodite* (disguised as a prayer-book) in chapel. He had "lost his faith." This phrase caused as much terror in the school as would, in an asylum, the rumour that one of the most dangerous lunatics had broken out of his strait-jacket and was wandering stark-naked through the grounds. It was matter of general knowledge that on those rare Sundays when he was not being "kept in," Raymond Courrèges hid his school uniform and his cap, with the monogram of the Virgin, in a bed of nettles, put on an overcoat bought ready-made at Thierry and Sigrand, clapped on his head an absurd bowler which made him look like a plain-clothes policeman, and hung about the more disreputable booths at the fair. He has been seen on the merry-go-round hugging a slut of indeterminate age.

When, in the pompous setting of Prize-Day, an attendant multitude of parents sat stupefied by the heat in the shade of leaves already shrivelled by the sun, and heard the head master announce that Courrèges had "passed with distinction," he alone knew what an effort he had made, in spite of the apparent lawlessness of his days, not to be ploughed. A single fixed idea had filled his mind to the exclusion even of the sense of persecution, so that the hours of detention, spent standing against the rough-cast wall of the playground, had actually seemed short—the idea of departure, of flight, in the first glow of a summer morning, along the high-road to Spain which ran past the Courrèges' garden, a road that looked as though it were weighed down by the bulk of its great flagstones, a relic of the Emperor, of his guns and of his convoys. He savoured in anticipation the heady delight of every step that should put a little more distance between him, the school and his depressing family. It was an understood thing that on the day he passed his examination his father and his grandmother would each give him a hundred francs. Since he had already got eight hundred saved up, he would thus be owner of the thousand which, so he thought, would enable him to travel through the world, miles and miles from his own "people." That was why he had spent the hours of detention working, untroubled by the sight of others at play. Sometimes he would shut his book and chew the cud of day-dreams. In imagination he could hear the scrape of cicadas in the pine trees along the roads which soon he would be travelling, could see the cool shade of the inn before which, tired out with travelling, he would sit in some unidentified village. The rising moon would wake the cocks, and off he would start again in the freshness of the dawn, with the taste of bread in his mouth. And sometimes he would sleep beneath a mill, a single corn-stook blotting out the stars: and the damp fingers of the early day would rouse him. . . .

But, though masters and parents had agreed in thinking him capable of anything, he had not, after all, taken to flight. His enemies, though they knew it not, had been too strong for him. Defeat comes to the young because they let themselves be so easily convinced of their own wretched inadequacy. At seventeen the most undisciplined of boys is only too ready to accept the image of himself imposed by others. Raymond Courrèges was blessed with good looks, but thought himself a monster of ugliness and squalor. He was blind to the fine contours of his face, and convinced that he could rouse in others only feelings of disgust. He was filled with a horror of his own person, and felt assured that he could never pay back in kind the emotion of hostility which he caused in those about him. That was why, stronger even than the longing to escape, he felt the desire to hide, to veil his face, to be compelled no more to wipe away the hatred of future enemies yet unknown. This youthful debauchee, whose hand the pupils of the Church School were afraid to touch, was no less ignorant than they of women, and could not conceive that he might be capable of giving pleasure if only to a slattern in the gutter. He was ashamed of his body. It never occurred either to his parents or to his masters that all his glorying in wildness and dirt was but the miserable bravado of the young which he assumed because he wanted to make them believe that he revelled in his own uncomeliness. His attitude was no more than the threadbare pride of adolescence, a sort of despairing humility.

The holidays that followed his examination, so far from opening a way of escape, were a period of secret cowardice. Paralysed by timidity, he thought he could read contempt in the eyes of the servant-girl who did his room, and quailed before the brooding look which, at times, his father turned on him. Since the Basques were spending August at Arcachon, he had not even the consolation of the children with whose young bodies, supple as growing plants, he loved to play so roughly.

As soon as the young family had gone, Madame Courrèges heaved a sigh of relief.

"It's nice to have the place to ourselves for a bit," she said, in this way taking her revenge on a remark of her daughter's to the effect that "Gaston and I really need a little course of solitude."

Actually, the poor woman lived for nothing but the daily letter, and could not hear the muttering of a storm without seeing in imagination the whole Basque family being dashed to destruction in an open boat. The house was only half-full, and the empty rooms weighed heavily on her spirits. Of what comfort to her was a son who spent his time running wild about the roads, and came back sullen-tempered and dripping with sweat, to dash at his food like a ravenous animal?

"People say, 'Well, you've got your husband.' My husband!—I ask you!"

"You forget, darling, how busy Paul is."

"He doesn't have any rounds to make, mother. Most of his patients are on holiday."

"Not his poorer patients. Besides, he's got his laboratory work, the hospital, and all those articles he has to write. . . ."

The embittered wife shook her head. She knew that her husband's active temperament would never lack employment, that never, till the day of his death, would there be a moment's pause in which, for a few brief instants, she might count on his whole and undivided attention. It never occurred to her that such a thing could be possible. She did not know that in even the fullest lives love can hollow out its little nest; that the harassed statesman will stop the wheels of the world when the moment comes for his mistress to pay him a visit. This ignorance spared her much suffering. Though she was only too familiar with the kind of love that dogs the feet of someone beyond the power to touch, someone who will not so much as turn his head to take a moment's notice, the mere fact that she had always been powerless to hold his attention for no matter how brief a while made it impossible for her to imagine that for some other woman the doctor might be a totally different person. She would have hated to think that somewhere a woman might exist who was capable of charming him from that incomprehensible world in which he lived, made up of statistics and observations, of blood and pus imprisoned between glass slides; and it was many years before she discovered that there were evenings when the laboratory remained deserted, when the sick had to wait in vain for the man who, when he might have eased their pain, preferred to stand motionless in a dark and stuffy drawing-room, gazing down at a woman stretched upon a sofa.

In order to contrive such secret oases in his days of toil the doctor had to work with twice his normal intensity; had to hack his way through every kind of obstacle that he might win as his reward those few moments filled with concentrated watching and impassioned silence, when to look was all the satisfaction he desired. Sometimes, just when the long-expected hour had almost sounded, a message would reach him from Maria Cross saying that she was no longer free, that the man on whom she was dependent had arranged a party in some restaurant on the outskirts of the city. When that happened he would have found the thought of life intolerable had she not added a postscript to her note suggesting another day. Then, in a flash, the miracle occurred, and at once his whole existence centred about the thought of the new meeting promised by her words. Though every hour of every day was filled with duties, he included in a single sweeping act of vision, like a skilful chess-player, all the possible combinations that might enable him so to arrange matters that, when the time and date arrived, he could be there, motionless and disengaged, in the stuffy and encumbered room, gazing at the figure stretched upon its sofa. And when the moment came and went at which, had she not put him off, he might have been with her, he was filled with happiness, thinking: "It would have been over by now, but, as things are, I still have that happiness in front of me. . . ." There was something then with which he could fill the empty days that lay between. At such times the laboratory in particular took on the quality of a haven. Within its walls he lost all sense of the passing hours, even of love itself. Absorbed in research, he felt freed from time, filling with work the moments that must be lived till, suddenly, the longed-for hour would come when he could push open the gate of that small house where Maria Cross lived behind the church at Talence.

Devoured by his obsession, he gave, that summer, less and less attention to his son. He who had been made privy to so many shameful secrets often said to himself: 'We always think that the happenings tucked away in newspaper paragraphs don't concern us, that murders, suicides and scandals are what come to other people, while, all the time . . .' And yet, all the time, he did not know that there had been moments in the course of that devastating August when his son had been within an ace of taking an irreparable step. Raymond longed to run away, but longed, too, to hide, to become invisible. He could not pluck up courage to go into a café or a shop. He would walk up and down a dozen times before a door before he could bring himself to open it. This mania made all flight impossible, though he felt stifled in his home. Many were the evenings when death seemed to him to be the simplest of all solutions. He would open the drawer in which his father kept an old-fashioned revolver, but it was not God's will that he should find the cartridges. One afternoon he walked between the drooping vines down to the pond that lay beyond the sun-baked paddock. He hoped that the weeds, the growing water-plants, might knot a tangle round his feet, that he might be unable to extricate himself from the muddy liquid, that his eyes and mouth might be filled with slime, that no one might ever see him more, nor he see others watching him. Mosquitoes were skimming the surface, frogs were plopping in the eddying shadows like so many stones. Caught in the weeds a dead animal showed white. What saved Raymond then was not fear but disgust.

Fortunately, he was not often alone. The Courrèges' tennis-court was a focus of attraction for all the young people of the neighbourhood. It was one of Madame Courrèges' grievances that the Basques should have involved her in the expense of having it made, and then, when they might have played on it, had gone away. Only strangers got the benefit of it. Young men in white, with rackets in their hands, moving inaudibly on sandalled feet, appeared in the drawing-room at the hour of siesta, greeted the ladies, barely bothered to ask after Raymond and went out again into the glare which echoed soon to their cries of "Play" and "Out," to the sound of their laughter. "They don't even trouble to shut the door," grumbled Grandmamma Courrèges, who thought of nothing but keeping out the heat. Raymond might have been willing to play, but the presence of the young women frightened him—especially of the Cosserouge girls, Marie-Thérèse, Marie-Louise and Marguerite-Marie, all three fat and fair and suffering from headache because of the weight of their hair, for they were condemned to wear upon their heads enormous structures of yellow tresses imperfectly secured with combs and always on the point of falling down. He hated them. Why must they always laugh so much? They were in a constant state of wriggling convulsions, convinced that everybody else was a "scream." They didn't, as it happened, laugh more at Raymond than at anybody else, but it was his particular curse to feel himself the centre of a universal derision. But there was one reason, in particular, why he hated them. The day before the Basques went away, he had found it impossible any longer to refuse to keep a promise he had made to his brother-in-law that he would ride a monstrous great horse that the lieutenant was leaving behind in the stables. He was at the age when no sooner was he in the saddle than he was seized with giddiness. Consequently, he cut a poor figure as a horseman. One morning the Cosserouge girls had come on him suddenly in a forest ride, clinging desperately to the pommel of his saddle. A moment later and he was sprawling on the sandy ground. He could never see them after that without hearing again the giggling screams in which, at that moment, they had indulged. Each time they met they took delight in reminding him of each circumstance of that humiliating fall. What storms does teasing, however harmless in intention, raise in a young man's heart in the springtime of life! Raymond was incapable of distinguishing one Cosserouge from another, but lumped them collectively within the orbit of his hatred, regarding them as a sort of fat, three-headed monster, always sweating and clucking beneath the motionless trees of that August afternoon of 19...

Sometimes he took the tram, crossed the blazing inferno of Bordeaux, and reached the docks, where human bodies, devoured by poverty and scrofula, were splashing about in the stagnant water with its iridescent scum of oil. Their owners laughed, chasing one another, and leaving on the flags the faint, damp outline of their feet.

October returned. The passage perilous had been accomplished. Raymond had passed the dangerous crisis of his life. It was written that he should be saved, and, indeed, he was already saved when, at the beginning of term, the new school books (he had always loved the smell of them) brought to him a sort of concentrated vision, as he stood upon the threshold of the year which was to initiate him into the study of philosophy, of all the dreams and systems that have beguiled the human mind. Yes, he was to be saved, though not by his own unaided efforts. The time was near when a woman would come into his life—that same woman who, this evening, was watching him through the smoky haze and crowding couples of the tiny bar, whose wide and tranquil brow no passage of time had had the power to change.

During the winter months through which he had lived before they met, his spirit had lain in a profound torpor. A sort of dull passivity had left him weaponless. Stripped of his old aggressiveness, he was no longer the eternal whipping-boy of fate. Once the holidays had passed that had tormented him with the twin obsession of escape and death, he found himself acquiescing in the expected conduct of his days. Discipline came to his assistance by making life a good deal easier. But he savoured even more intensely his daily journey home, the evening passage from one suburb to another. The College gate once left behind, he plunged into the secret darkness of the damp little lane which was sometimes filled with the smell of fog, sometimes with the hard, dry breath of frost. With the sky, too, in its many aspects, he became familiar—overcast, swept clear and corroded with stars, veiled with a covering of cloud that seemed to be lit from within by a moon he could not see. And then, in a short while, would come the city limits, with the same crowd of tired, dirty, submissive men and women waiting to lay siege to the tram. The great glowing rectangle plunged ahead into a land, half town, half country, carrying more lights than the *Titanic*, rumbling on between pathetic little gardens that lay submerged beneath the fathoms of the winter night.

At home he no longer felt himself to be the object of a never-ceasing curiosity. General attention was now concentrated upon the doctor.

"I'm worried about him," said Madame Courrèges to her mother-in-law. "You're lucky to be able to take things so calmly. I envy temperaments like yours."

"Paul is rather overworked. He does too much, there's no doubt about that. But he has a magnificent constitution, so I'm not really concerned."

The younger woman shrugged her shoulders, making no effort to hear what the other muttered half to herself: "He's not ill, I'm sure of that. All the same, he *is* suffering."

Madame Courrèges said, not for the first time, "Trust a doctor never to take care of himself."

During dinner she kept a watchful eye on him. How emaciated she thought his face looked when he raised his eyes from his place.

"It's Friday, why cutlets?"

"You need a good body-building diet."

"What do you know about it?"

"Why won't you go and see Duluc? No doctor can ever prescribe for himself."

"My poor Lucie, why have you made up your mind that I am ill?"

"You can't see yourself. Why, the mere look of you is enough to frighten one. Everybody says the same thing. Only yesterday, someone—I forget who—said: 'What *is* the matter with your husband?' You ought to take choleine. I'm sure it's your liver."

"Why my liver rather than some other organ?"

Her reply was peremptory: "My impression is that it *must be* your liver."

Lucie's impression to that effect was very definite, and nothing would induce her to give it up. Her comments buzzed round the doctor like so many flies, only far more irritating: "You've already had two cups of coffee—I must tell cook to see that the pot isn't filled. That's your third cigarette since lunch. It's no good your denying it. There are three stubs in the ash-tray."

"What proves that he knows he's ill," she said one day to her mother-in-law, "is that I caught him yesterday looking at himself in the glass. As a rule, he never bothers about his appearance, but there he was, peering at his face and running his fingers over it. It was as though he wanted to smooth out the wrinkles on his forehead and round his eyes. He even opened his mouth and examined his teeth."

Madame Courrèges the elder looked at her daughter-in-law over the top of her spectacles, as though fearful of detecting upon that puzzled countenance something more than mere anxiety, something more in the nature of suspicion. The old lady had a feeling that her son's good-night kiss had recently been less perfunctory than usual. Perhaps she knew what that momentary surrender to emotion meant. Ever since he was a young man she had got into the way of guessing the precise nature of those wounds which one person alone, the owner of the hand that deals them, can cure. But the wife, though for many years frustrated in her instinct of tenderness, had thoughts only for physical ailments. Each time the doctor sat down opposite her, and raised his clasped hands to his face with its look of suffering, she said:

"You really *ought* to see Duluc: we *all* think so."

"Duluc could tell me nothing I don't already know."

"Can you listen to your own heart?"

To this question the doctor made no reply. His whole attention was concentrated upon the pain at his heart. It was as though a hand were holding, and just faintly squeezing, it. Ah! who better than he could count its beats, for were they not the evidence of what he had just been through with Maria Cross? How difficult it was to slip a more than usually tender word, a hinted declaration, into a conversation with a woman who showed herself always so submissive, who insisted on regarding her doctor as an almost godlike creature, and forced upon him the dignity of a spiritual fatherhood!

He went over in his mind the circumstances of his most recent visit. He had got out of the carriage on the main road, opposite the church at Talence, and had walked up the puddled lane. So swift had been the progress of the dusk that it was almost dark before he reached the gate. At the far end of an untidy path a lamp threw a ruddy glow from the ground-floor windows of a low-built house. He did not ring. No servant preceded him through the dining-room. He entered the drawing-room without knocking. Maria Cross was lying on a sofa and did not get up. Indeed, for a second or two she went on reading. Finally:

"So there you are, doctor; I'm quite ready for you," she said, holding out both hands, and moving her feet so as to make room for him on the end of the sofa. "Don't take that chair, it's broken. I live, you know, in a jumble of luxury and squalor. . . ."

Monsieur Larousselle had set her up in this suburban villa where the visitor was liable to trip over tears in the carpet, and only the folds of the curtains concealed the holes in the fabric. Sometimes when he went to see her she said nothing. He was prevented from starting a conversation fitted to his rôle of suppliant lover—a conversation which he had made up his mind *must* take place—by the presence, over the sofa, of a mirror which reflected the image of a face eaten away by a mass of beard, of two bloodshot eyes dimmed as the result of constant application to a microscope, of a forehead from which the hair had already begun to recede when he was still a house-physician. Nevertheless, he was determined to try his luck. One of her small hands was trailing over the edge of the sofa, almost touching the floor. He took it, and said in a low voice: "Maria. . . ." Such was her confidence in him that she did not withdraw it. "I'm not feverish, doctor; really I'm not." As always, she spoke of herself. "Dear friend," she said: "I've done something of which you'll thoroughly approve. I've told Monsieur Larousselle that I no longer need the car, that he'd better sell it and get rid of Firmin. You know how it is with him, how incapable he is of understanding any delicacy of feeling. He just laughed, and said what was the point of upsetting everything merely because of a moment's whim? But I mean it, and I never use anything but the tram now, whatever the weather. I came back in it to-day from the cemetery. I thought you'd be pleased. I feel less unworthy of our poor dead darling . . . less . . . less like a kept woman."

The last two words were barely audible. The eyes which she raised to the doctor's face were brimming with tears, and seemed humbly to implore his approval. He gave it her at once, gravely, coldly. She was for ever invoking him. "You're so *big* . . . you're the noblest human being I have ever known . . . the mere fact that you exist makes me believe in the reality of goodness." How he longed to protest, to say: "I'm not the man you think me, Maria; only a poor, a very poor creature, eaten up by desire just like other men. . . ."

"You wouldn't be such a saint," she replied, when he tried to put these thoughts into words, "if you didn't despise yourself."

"No, no, Maria: not a saint at all: you don't, you can't know . . ."

She gazed at him with a fixed stare of admiration, but it never occurred to her to worry about him, as Lucie worried, to notice how ill he looked. The concentrated worship which was her tribute to him made of his love a despair. His desire was walled up within this admiration. He told himself in his misery, when he was far from her, that his love could surmount all obstacles; but as soon as she was there before him, deferential, hanging on his words, he could no longer deny the evidence of a wretchedness that was beyond all cure. Nothing in the world could change the nature of their relation. She was not his mistress but his disciple. He was not her lover but her spiritual director. To have stretched his arms towards her supine body, to have pressed it to his own, would have been as mad an act as to break the mirror hanging above her head. He knew, too, with horrible clarity, that she was waiting for him to go. The realization that she was an object of interest to the doctor was, for her, a matter of pride. Surrounded by the wreckage of her life, she prized very highly the intimacy of so eminent a man. But how he bored her! He, without having the slightest idea that his visits were a burden to her, did increasingly feel that his secret was becoming more and more obvious, so obvious, indeed, that only her complete indifference could explain her inability to guess it. Had Maria felt even a vestige of affection for him, his love must have stared her in the face. Alas! how utterly insensitive a woman can be when confronted by a man whom, otherwise, she may esteem and even venerate, whose friendship fills her with pride, but who bores her! Of this truth the doctor had some faint realization only, but it was enough to crush him.

He got up, cutting her short in the middle of something she was saying.

"I must say, you *are* a bit abrupt in your manner of taking leave," she remarked; "but there are so many other sufferers waiting for you. . . . I mustn't be selfish and keep you all to myself."

Once again he crossed the empty dining-room and the hall. Once again he breathed in the smell of the frost-bound garden, and in the carriage on his way home, thinking of Lucie's attentive, worried face—no doubt she was already getting anxious, and would be straining her ears for the sound of his return—said to himself: 'The great thing is not to *cause* suffering. It's quite enough that *I* suffer: I mustn't create suffering in others.'

"You're looking much worse this evening. Why *will* you put off seeing Duluc? If you won't do it for your own sake, you might at least do it for ours. You're not the only person concerned: it affects all of us."

Madame Courrèges called the Basques to witness the truth of her pronouncement. They emerged from the low-voiced conversation which they were carrying on, and obediently backed her up.

"It's quite true, Papa, we all want to have you with us as long as possible."

At the mere sound of the hated voice the doctor felt ashamed of the strength of his dislike for his son-in-law. 'He's really quite a decent fellow . . . it's unforgivable on my part . . .' But how was he to forget the reasons he had for hating him? For long years one thing only in his marriage had seemed to be precisely as he had always dreamed it would be—the narrow cot standing beside the vast conjugal bed, and he and his wife, each evening watching the slumber of Madeleine, their first-born. Her breathing was scarcely perceptible. One innocent foot had kicked off the coverlet. A small hand, soft and marvellous, hung down between the bars. She was such a sweet-natured child that they could afford to spoil her without fear of consequences, and such advantage did she take of her father's infatuation that she would play for hours in his study without making a sound. "You say she's not very intelligent," he would say; "she's much *more* than intelligent." Later, though he hated going out with Madame Courrèges, he loved to be seen in the company of the young girl. "People think you're my wife!" It was about then that he had made up his mind that the right man for her would be Fred Robinson, the only one, he felt, of all his pupils who really understood him. He already called him "my son," and was just waiting until Madeleine should have turned eighteen to conclude the marriage, when, at the end of the first winter after she had "come out," she told him that she was engaged to Lieutenant Basque. The doctor's furious opposition had lasted for months. No one could see any sense in it, neither his family nor the world at large. Why should he prefer a penniless young student, who came from heaven knew where, to a well-off officer of good ancestry with a brilliant future before him?

His reasons were too personal to himself to make it possible for him to discuss them. From the first moment that he had started to raise objections he felt that in the eyes of this dearly loved daughter he had become an enemy. He told himself that his death would have been a matter to her of rejoicing, that she looked on him now merely as an old wall that must be battered down so that she could join the male who was calling to her. Because he wanted to see precisely where he stood, because he wanted to be sure to what extent this child, on whom he had lavished all his affection, hated him, he had intensified his stubbornness. Even his old mother was against him and joined forces with the young people. Plots were hatched under his own roof to enable the lovers to meet without his knowledge. When, finally, he had given in, his daughter had kissed him on the cheek. He had pushed away her hair, as he used to do, so as to touch her forehead with his lips. Everyone said: "Madeleine adores her father. She has always been his favourite." Until the day of his death, no doubt, he would hear her calling him "Darling Papa." Meanwhile he must put up with this Basque fellow. But no matter how hard he tried, he could not help betraying the fact of his antipathy. "It really is extraordinary," said Madame Courrèges. "Here he is with a son-in-law who shares his views about everything, and yet he doesn't like him!" It was just this that the doctor could not forgive, this seeing all his most cherished ideas turning to caricature in the distorting mirror of the young man's mind. The lieutenant was one of those persons whose approval flattens us out, and makes us doubt the very truths for which, previously, we would have shed our blood.

"Really, Papa, I mean it. You must take care of yourself for your children's sake. You must allow them to take sides with you against yourself."

The doctor left the room without answering. Later, when the Basques had sought the refuge of their bedroom (so sacred was it held to be that Madame Courrèges was wont to say, "I never set foot in it: Madeleine has made it perfectly plain that she doesn't want me there. There are some things that don't have to be said twice: I can take a hint"), they undressed in silence. The lieutenant, on his knees, his head buried in the bed, turned round suddenly and put a question to his wife:

"Was this house part of your parents' marriage settlement? . . . What I mean is, did they buy it after they were married?"

Madeleine thought so, but was not certain. "It would be interesting to know, because in that case, should anything happen to your poor father, we should have a legal right to one-half of it."

He said no more for a few moments, and then, after a pause, asked how old Raymond was, and seemed annoyed to learn that he was only seventeen.

"What difference does that make? Why do you ask?"

"Oh, nothing. . . ."

He may have been thinking that a minor always complicates an inheritance, because, getting to his feet, he said:

"Naturally, I hope that your poor father will be with us for a long time yet. . . ."

In the darkness of the room the huge bed yawned to receive them. They went to it, just as twice a day, at noon and at eight o'clock, they sat down to table—when they were hungry.

About this same time Raymond woke in the night. Something that had a flat taste was trickling over his face and down his throat. His hand felt for the matches. He lit one, and, by its light, saw that blood was spurting from his left nostril and staining his nightshirt and the sheets. He got up and stood, petrified with fear, in front of the looking-glass, staring at his long thin body all speckled with scarlet. He wiped his fingers that were sticky with blood, on his chest, and thought how funny his smeared face looked. He began to play a game in which he was both murderer and murdered.

IV

THE evening was just like any other evening at the end of January, when, in those latitudes, winter is already on the wane. Raymond, seated in his workmen's tram, was jarred by the sight of the woman opposite. Far from being distressed at the thought that he formed but one anonymous unit of this human freight, he enjoyed pretending that he was an emigrant in the steerage while the ship drove ahead through the darkness. The trees were coral reefs, the people and the traffic on the road outside, denizens of the vasty deep. The journey, which, while it lasted, kept from him all sense of humiliation, was all too short. Not one of all the bodies round him but was as much neglected as his own, as badly dressed. When, as occasionally happened, his eyes met other eyes, he saw in the answering look no hint of mockery. All the same, his linen was cleaner than the unbuttoned shirt, say, of the man with as much hair on his chest as a wild animal. He felt at ease among these people. It never occurred to him that one spoken word would have been enough to conjure up the desert that separates classes as surely from one another as it does individuals. But such communion as might be possible was, no doubt, achieved by this contact, this shared immersion of a tram-car driving through the suburban night. Rough though he was at school, here he made no effort to shake himself free of the head that was bumping up and down on his shoulder, the head of an exhausted urchin of his own age whose body sagged in sleep, as loosely articulated as a bunch of flowers too lightly bound.

But on this particular evening he noticed, opposite, a woman, a lady. She was dressed in black, and was wedged between two men in greasy overalls. There was no veil over her face. He was to wonder, later, how it was that beneath her gaze he had not, at first, been conscious of that shy awkwardness which the humblest servant-girl could usually produce in him. He was troubled by no feeling of shame, no embarrassment—perhaps because in this tram-car he felt himself to be without identity, and could imagine no circumstances which might establish a relation between himself and this particular stranger. But the chief reason was that her expression was entirely devoid of anything that might have been taken for curiosity, mockery or contempt. But, Lord, how she stared! It was as though, absorbed in that concentration, she were saying to herself: 'The sight of this face brings consolation for all the tedium to which one is exposed in a public vehicle. Confronted by what might well be a sullen angel, I can forget the whole miserable scene. Nothing now has any longer the power to rasp my nerves. Merely to look brings me deliverance. He is like some unknown country. The lids of his eyes are a barren stretch of sea-sand. Two troubled lakes lie drowsing between their bordering lashes. The ink on his fingers, his grimy collar and cuffs, that missing button—all these things are no more than the earth that dirties a ripe fruit ready to fall from the tree, and only waiting the touch of a careful hand to gather it.'

He, too, feeling so safe because he had nothing to fear from this stranger, not even a word, since nothing had built a bridge between them, stared back with that tranquil intensity with which we gaze upon a distant planet. . . . (What innocence still clung about her brow. Courrèges, this evening, cast a furtive look at it. The radiance which bathed it owed nothing to the glare of the tiny bar, all to that intelligence which is so rarely found in a woman's face, though, when it is, how deeply it moves us, how convincingly persuades that Thought, Idea, Intelligence are words of the feminine gender!)

In front of the church at Talence the young woman got up, leaving with the men she was deserting only the fragrance of her presence, and even that had vanished by the time Raymond reached the end of his journey. It was scarcely cold at all on this January evening. He was not even tempted to run. Already there was a promise in the foggy air of the secret sweetness of the coming season. The earth was stripped but not asleep.

Raymond, intent on his own thoughts, noticed nothing that evening as he sat at table with his family, though his father had never looked so ill. Madame Courrèges made no reference to the fact. He mustn't be "pestered," as she said to the Basques as soon as he had gone upstairs with his mother. All the same, she had made up her mind to talk to Duluc without his knowledge. The room reeked of the Lieutenant's cigar. Leaning against the mantelpiece, Gaston said: "There's no doubt about it, mother: something's the matter with him." There was a military quality of command about the jerky brevity of his speech, and when Madeleine, taking an opposite line to her mother, remarked: "It may be only some temporary upset . . ." he interrupted her.

"No, Madeleine, it's serious. Your mother is quite right."

The young woman had the temerity to argue. He raised his voice:

"I say that your mother is right, and that should be enough for you!"

Up on the first floor Madame Courrèges the elder knocked gently at her son's door. She found him seated with a number of books open before him. She asked no questions, but sat knitting, saying nothing. If her silence, her reticence became more than he could bear, if he felt the sudden need to speak, she was ready to listen. But a sure instinct kept her from forcing his confidence. For a moment he was tempted to choke back no longer the cry which was stifling him. But to speak now would mean going so terribly far back in thought, would mean telling over one by one the beads of his misery up to the moment of to-night's discomfiture. . . . How could he explain the disproportion between his suffering and its cause? What had happened would seem so trivial. It was merely that when he had called on Maria Cross at the time they had arranged, the servant told him that she had not come in. The news had inflicted the first stab of pain. He had agreed to wait in the empty drawing-room where a clock was ticking—though less quickly than his heart. A lamp shone on the pretentious beams of the ceiling. On a low table beside the sofa he noticed an ash-tray filled with cigarette ends. 'She smokes too much . . . she's poisoning herself.' What a lot of books there were, but in none were the last pages cut. His eye took in the torn folds of the great curtains of faded silk. To himself he repeated: "Luxury and squalor, squalor and luxury" . . . looked at the clock, then at his watch, and decided that he would wait only another fifteen minutes. How quickly, then, did time begin to fly. That it might not seem too short, he refused to let his thoughts dwell on his laboratory, on his interrupted experiment. He got up, went over to the sofa, knelt down, and, after first glancing nervously towards the door, buried his face in the cushions. . . . When he got up his left knee made its usual cracking sound. He planted himself in front of the mirror, touched with his finger the swollen artery upon his temple, and thought to himself that if anyone had come in and seen him, they would have thought him mad. With the characteristic aridity of the intellectual worker who reduces everything to the terms of a formula, he said, "All men are mad when they are alone. Yes, self-control is active only when it is backed by the control imposed upon us by the presence of others." Alas! that one little piece of reasoning had sufficed to exhaust the fifteen minutes' grace he had allowed himself. . . .

How could he explain to his mother sitting there, eager for

confidences, the misery of that moment, the degree of renunciation it had demanded, the fact that it had had the effect of tearing him up by the roots from the melancholy satisfaction of his daily conversation with Maria Cross? What matters is not the willingness to confide even when we have a sympathetic listener, even when that listener is a mother. Which of us is skilled enough to compress a whole inner world into a few words? How is it possible to detach from the moving flow of consciousness one particular sensation rather than another? One can tell nothing unless one tells all. How could he expect this old lady to understand the music that sounded so deep down in her son's heart, with its lacerating discords? He was of another race than hers, being of another sex. They were separated more surely than people living on two different planets. . . . There, in his mother's presence, the doctor remembered his misery but did not put it into words. He remembered how, tired of waiting, he had just picked up his hat, when he heard the sound of steps in the hall. It was as though his whole life hung suspended. The door opened, but, instead of the woman he expected he saw Victor Larousselle.

"You know, doctor, you're spoiling Maria."

Not a hint of suspicion in the voice. The doctor smiled at sight of the impeccable figure with its full-blooded face and light-coloured suit, bursting with self-satisfaction and contentment.

"What a windfall for you doctors these neurasthenics are, these *malades imaginaires.* No, no, I'm only joking. Everyone knows what a selfless fellow you are. . . . Still, it's a bit of dam' good luck for Maria that she should have happened on so rare a bird of the species as you. D'you know why she isn't back? Just because she's given up the car—that's her latest fancy. Between ourselves, I really think she's a bit touched—but that's only an added charm in a pretty woman, eh? What do you think, doctor? Must say I'm very glad to see you. Look here, stay to dinner: Maria'll be delighted: she adores you. You won't? Well, at least wait until she gets back. You're the only person I can talk to about her."

"You're the only person I can talk to about her." . . . That sudden outburst of tormented words from this fat, resplendent man! 'This passion of his,' said the doctor to himself, as he drove home, 'is the scandal of the place. All the same, it is the one noble sentiment of which the fool is capable. At fifty he has suddenly discovered that he is vulnerable; that he can suffer because of a woman whose body he has almost certainly conquered. But that is not enough for him. Somewhere, outside his world of business and horses, there will henceforward be a finer principle of suffering. . . . The romantic conception of passion is not, perhaps, as silly as we think it.' Maria Cross! Maria! What misery not to have seen her! 'But even worse than that is the knowledge that she didn't even think of sending me word. How small a place I must occupy in her life! She can break an appointment without so much as a thought . . . I cram infinity into a few short minutes that for her mean nothing. . . .'

The sound of spoken words roused him from his reverie. His mother could bear the silence no longer. She, too, had been following the drift of her secret preoccupations, and was no longer dwelling upon her son's load of mysterious sorrow. She was back once more with what so constantly obsessed her—her relation with her daughter-in-law.

"I let her trample on me; I never say anything but 'Have your own way, my dear, do just as you want.' Nobody could say I provoke her, but she's forever throwing her money in my teeth; money! as though you didn't make enough! I know, of course, that when you married you had nothing but your future to offer her, and that she was a Voulassier of Elbeuf—though their mills in those days weren't anything like what they have become since. All the same, she could have made a better match, I realize that. . . . 'When one's got something, one always wants more'—as she said to me one day about Madeleine. But let's not complain. If it wasn't for the servants, everything would be all right."

"There are few worse things in life, my poor, dear mother, than having servants of different masters all living together in the same kitchen."

He touched her forehead with his lips, left the door ajar so that she could see her way, and repeated mechanically, "There are few worse things in life."

The next day Maria's whim about the car must still have been in the ascendant, because, coming home in the tram, Raymond saw the unknown woman seated in her usual place. Once more her tranquil gaze took possession of the childish face opposite, making the circuit of the eyelids, tracing the line where the dark hair met the forehead, pausing at the glint of teeth between the lips. He remembered that he had not shaved for two days, touched his skinny jaw, and then, in an access of shyness, hid his hands beneath his cape. She lowered her eyes, and he did not at first notice that, since he wore no suspenders, one of his socks had slipped down, revealing a patch of bare leg. Too nervous to pull it up, he changed his position. He was not, however, conscious of mental discomfort. What he had always hated in other people was their laughter, their smiles—even when suppressed. He could catch the faintest sign of a trembling at the corners of a mouth, knew only too well what it meant when somebody started to bite their lower lip. But the expression on this woman's face as she looked at him was something he had never met before, something at once intelligent yet animal. Yes, it was the face of some marvellous, impassive *beast*, incapable of laughter. He did not know that his father often teased Maria Cross about the way she had of adjusting laughter to her face like a mask, and then letting it fall again without the slightest hint of alteration in the imperturbable melancholy of her gaze.

When she had got out of the tram by the church at Talence, and there was nothing left for him to see except the faint dent in the leather of the seat which she had occupied, he felt absolutely certain that they would meet again next day. He could give no good reason for his hope, but just had faith in the event. That evening, as soon as dinner was over, he carried two jugs of boiling water to his room, and took down his hip-bath from where it hung on the wall. Next morning he got up a good half-hour earlier than usual, because he had made up his mind that henceforth he would shave every day.

The Courrèges might have spent hours watching the slow unfolding of a chestnut bud without even beginning to understand the mystery of the rising sap. Similarly, they were blissfully unaware of the miracle that was happening in their midst. As the first strokes of a spade may bring to light the fragments of a perfect statue, so the first glance from Maria Cross had revealed a new being in the grubby schoolboy. Beneath the warmth of her contemplative gaze a body, lovely, though ill cared for, had on a sudden stirred, as, in the rough bark of some forest tree, a spellbound goddess. The Courrèges had no eyes for the wonder, because the members of a family too closely united lose the power to see one another properly. In the course of a few weeks Raymond had become a young man careful of his appearance, converted to the use of soap and water, secure in the knowledge that he could be pleasing to others, eager to attract. But to his mother he was still an unwashed schoolboy. A woman, without uttering a single word, merely by the intensity of her watching eyes, had transformed their child, moulding him afresh, though they were incapable of detecting so much as a trace of this strange magic.

In the tram-car, which was no longer lit now that the days were lengthening, Raymond, at each encounter, ventured on some new gesture. He crossed his legs, displayed his clean and uncreased socks, his shoes shining like mirrors (there was a shoe-shine boy at the Croix de Saint-Genès). He had no longer any reason to conceal his cuffs. He wore gloves. There came a day when he took one of them off, and the young woman could not suppress a smile at sight of the over-pink nails on which a manicurist had been working hard, though, because for years he had been in the habit of biting them, it would have been better had they not as yet been allowed to draw attention to themselves. All this was but the outward sign of an inner, an invisible, resurrection. The fog that for so long had been collecting in the boy's most secret heart was thinning by degrees under the influence of that serious and still wordless gaze to which custom had already given a certain intimacy. Maybe he wasn't a monster after all; perhaps, like other young men, he could hold the attention of a woman—and, perhaps, more than her attention! In spite of their silence, the mere passage of time was weaving between them a web of contacts which no word or gesture could have strengthened. They felt that the moment was coming when, for the first time, they would speak, but Raymond did nothing to hasten its approach. Shy galley-slave that he was, he found it enough that he no longer felt his chains. For the moment, all the happiness he needed lay in this feeling of his that he had become someone entirely different. Was it really true that until this unknown woman had begun to look at him he had been nothing but a dirty little brat? We are, all of us, moulded and re-moulded by those who have loved us, and though that love may pass, we remain none the less *their* work—a work that very likely they do not recognize, and which is never exactly what they intended. No love, no friendship can ever cross the path of our destiny without leaving some mark upon it for ever. The Raymond Courrèges who sat this evening in a small bar in the Rue Duphot, the man of thirty-five, would have been someone quite different if, in 19— when he was just embarking on his philosophy course, he had not seen, sitting opposite him in a tram on his way home from school, Maria Cross.

V

IT was his father who first noticed the new man in Raymond. One Sunday, towards the end of that same spring, he was seated at the family table, more deeply buried in his own thoughts even than usual, so far buried, in fact, that he scarcely heard the noise which had started as the result of a dispute between his son and his son-in-law. The subject of the argument was bull-fighting, a sport of which Raymond was a passionate devotee. He had come away that afternoon after seeing four bulls killed, so as not to miss the six o'clock tram. But the sacrifice had gone unrewarded, because the unknown woman was not in her seat. He might have guessed as much, it being Sunday. And now she had made him miss two bulls. Thus was he busy with his thoughts while Lieutenant Basque was holding forth.

"I can't understand how your father comes to let you watch such an exhibition of slaughter."

Raymond's reply, "That's a bit comic, I must say: an army officer who can't stand the sight of blood!" started a real row.

The doctor suddenly became aware of what was going on.

"And what, may I ask, do you mean by that?"

"That you're just yellow."

"Yellow?—say that again!"

They were both on their feet. Every member of the family was now taking sides. Madeleine Basque, cried to her husband:

"Don't answer him! He's not worth it! What does it matter what *he* says!"

The doctor begged Raymond to sit down.

"Get on with your meal, and let us have no more of this!"

The lieutenant shouted that he had been called a coward. Madame Courrèges maintained that Raymond had meant nothing of the sort. Meanwhile, they had all resumed their seats. As the result of a sort of secret connivance they one and all set about throwing water on the flames. Family feeling made them view with extreme repugnance anything that might upset the smooth running of their little circle. They were a crew embarked for life in the same ship, and an instinct of self-preservation made them careful to see to it that no one should start a fire. That was why silence now descended on the room. A light rain had been falling, but the sound of drops on the steps outside suddenly stopped, and the newly released fragrance of the garden drifted in to where they all sat saying nothing. Someone remarked hastily that it was already cooler, and another voice replied that the rain hadn't amounted to anything, and would barely lay the dust. The doctor, with a feeling of bewilderment, looked at the tall young man who was his son. He had hardly thought of him at all for some time, and now scarcely recognized him. He himself had just emerged from a long nightmare. He had been caught up in it ever since the day, now long past, when Maria Cross had failed to keep her appointment, and had left him closeted with Victor Larousselle. The Sunday now drawing to a close had been one of the most horrible days of his whole life, but at last it had given him back his freedom (or so he thought!). Salvation had come to him as the result of an overwhelming fatigue, an indescribable lassitude. His sufferings had been too much for him. All he wanted now was to turn his back on the battle, to go to ground in old age. Almost two months had elapsed between the ordeal of his profitless vigil in the "luxury and squalor" of Maria Cross's drawing-room, and this hideous afternoon which had witnessed his ultimate surrender. Seated at the now silent table, he once again forgot his son, letting his memory recall each separate circumstance of the hard road that he had travelled. In imagination he could see once more its every milestone.

The intolerable agony had started on the very morning after the broken appointment. Her letter of apology had struck the first note.

"It was to some extent *your* fault, my dear, good friend"—Maria had written in the missive which he had read and re-read over and over again, in the course of those two months:

". . . because it was the thought of you that gave me the idea of turning my back on a hateful luxury which had begun to make me feel ashamed. Not having the car any longer, I couldn't get back by our usual time. Being without it meant that I reach the cemetery later, and that I stay there longer, because my conscience is clear. You've no idea how quiet it is there at the end of the afternoon, full of birds perched on the grave-stones and singing. I felt that my baby-boy approved of what I had done, that he was satisfied with me. I feel already rewarded for my action by having been allowed to sit with all those working-people in the tram. You'll think I'm becoming too romantic, but indeed it is not so. It makes me feel happy to be there with all those poor folk of whom I am so little worthy. I can't find words in which to tell you what that coming home in the tram means to me. 'A certain person' is ready to go down on his bended knees, so anxious is he that I should take back the car which 'a certain person' gave me. But I won't. Dear, dear doctor, what does it really matter if we *don't* see one another? Your example, your teaching, is enough for me. We are so closely united that mere physical presence has no importance. As Maurice Maeterlinck has so wonderfully written—'A time will come, nor is it far off, when human souls will be aware of one another without the intervention of any physical organ.' Write to me. Your letters are all I need, dear spiritual director!

M. C.

"Ought I to go on taking the pills and the injections? I've only got three doses left. Must I buy another box?"

Even had it not so cruelly wounded him, this letter would have aroused the doctor's displeasure, so eloquent was it of self-satisfaction and the pleasure that comes of sham humility. There was no secret of the human heart to which he had not been made privy, and, as a result, his tolerance, where his fellow-men were concerned, was almost unlimited. One vice, and one vice only, irritated him beyond bearing: the effort of the morally depraved to put a mask of beauty on their depravity. For him the last infirmity of the human creature lay in the ability to be dazzled by its own filth as by a diamond. Not that this sort of lie in the soul was habitual with Maria Cross. In fact, what had first charmed the doctor had been a power in her to see herself as she was, a refusal to embellish what was naturally ugly. One of her favourite themes had always been the noble example which her mother, a poor schoolmistress in a small country town, widowed while still young, had given her.

"She worked like a slave to pay my school-fees, and had quite made up her mind that I should go to a training college. She had the great happiness, before she died, of being present at my marriage, a happiness for which she had never dared to hope. Your son-in-law was well acquainted with my husband, who was a medical officer in his regiment. He adored me, and I was very happy with him. Left, as I was, with a child, I had scarcely enough to live on when he died, but I could have managed somehow. It wasn't sheer necessity that was my undoing, but something that is really much more hateful—the desire to cut a figure, the longing for the security that marriage gives. . . . What, now, keeps me from leaving 'him' is the fact that I am too cowardly to take up the struggle again, to work my fingers to the bone for an inadequate salary."

Often, since the time of those first confidences, the doctor had heard her deprecate herself, mercilessly pass sentence on her weaknesses. Why then had she suddenly fallen a victim to the detestable vice of self-praise? But what most hurt him in her letter was something quite different. His grievance against her came from the fact that he had lied to himself, that he dared not probe a far deeper wound, the only wound of which he could not endure the pain. Maria showed no desire to see him, could quite gaily envisage the possibility of their separation. Time and time again, while he was listening to some patient endlessly elaborating the details of his ailments, or to some floundering candidate humming and hawing over the definition of hæmoptysis, he heard an inner voice repeating that phrase of Maeterlinck's about human souls being aware of one another without the intervention of any physical organ. He must have been mad ever to have believed for a single moment that a young woman could feel the need for his bodily presence. Mad, quite mad: but then, what resource of reasoning can save us from the unendurable pain of knowing that the adored creature whose "being there" is a necessary condition of our continued existence, even of our physical existence, can resign herself with complete indifference (perhaps, actually, with a certain sensation of relief) to the prospect of never seeing us again? At such times we realize that we mean nothing to the one person who means everything to us.

During all this period the doctor made an effort to get the better of himself. "I caught him again the other day looking at himself in the glass," said Madame Courrèges: "that means he's beginning to get worried." What sight better calculated to bring tranquillity and the apathy of complete despair than that of his own face, with all the telltale marks left upon it by fifty years of exhausting work? There was only one thing for him to do—to think of Maria only as he might have thought of someone dead and buried; to await the coming of death, and hasten it by doubling his daily dose of work—yes, to drive himself without mercy, to kill himself with work, to achieve deliverance through the opium of forced labour. But he who showed so little mercy to those of his fellow-men who lived a lie, was still the dupe of his own thoughts: 'She needs me: I must give her what I would give any sick person.' He answered her letter with one of his own, in which he said that he felt it necessary to continue his treatment. She was perfectly right, he told her, to travel by tram, but was it necessary for her to go out every day? He begged her to let him know when he should find her at home. He would so arrange matters as to be free to come at the usual hour.

A whole week passed without a further word from her. Each morning he had only to glance at the pile of prospectuses and newspapers to see that she had not written. He gave himself up to a calculation of probabilities. 'I posted my letter on Saturday. There is only one delivery on Sundays. She can't have got it till Monday. Assuming that she has waited two or three days before replying, it would be very extraordinary if I heard from her to-day. If nothing happens to-morrow it will be time enough for me to start worrying.'

And then, one evening, when he came in from a particularly hard day, he found a letter.

"I regard my daily visit to the cemetery as a sacred duty. I have quite decided to make my little pilgrimage no matter what the weather. It is just when evening is falling that I seem closest to my lost angel. I have a feeling that he knows when I shall come, that he lies there waiting for me. I know it is ridiculous, but the heart has its reasons, as Pascal says. I am happy and at peace when I get into the six o'clock tram. Have you any idea what a workers' tram is like? But I feel no fear. I am not so very far removed from 'the people,' and though there may be an apparent gulf between us, am I not linked with them in another way? I look at all those men, and it seems to me that they are just as lonely as I am—how shall I put it?—no less uprooted, no less socially at sea. My house is more luxurious than their houses; still, it is nothing but a series of ready-furnished rooms. Nothing in it belongs to me any more than what is in theirs belongs to them. That is true even of our bodies. Why not call one day, very late, on your way home? I know that you don't like meeting Monsieur Larousselle. I'll tell him that I want to see you alone. All you need do when our interview is over is just exchange a few polite words with him. . . . You forgot to say anything about the pills and the injections. . . ."

The doctor's first instinct had been to tear the letter up and scatter the fragments. Then he went down on his knees, gathered them all together, and scrambled to his feet again with considerable difficulty. Didn't she realize that he couldn't bear even the proximity of Larousselle? Everything about the man was hateful to him. He belonged to just the same general type as Basque. The lips that showed beneath the dyed moustache, the heavy dewlaps, the stocky figure, all proclaimed a complacency that nothing could shake. The fat thighs below the covert-coat were expressive of an infinite self-satisfaction. Because he deceived Maria Cross with the lowest of the low, it was said in Bordeaux that he "just kept her for show." Scarcely anybody but the doctor knew that she was still the one great passion of his life, the secret weakness which drove him almost beside himself. The man might be a fool, but the fact remained that he had bought her, that he alone possessed her. Now that he was a widower, he would probably have married her had it not been for the existence of his son, the sole heir to the Larousselle fortune, who was being prepared for his august destiny by an army of nurses, tutors and priests. It was unthinkable that the boy should be exposed to contact with such a woman, unthinkable that he should inherit a name degraded by a *mésalliance*.

"There's no getting away from it," Basque was fond of saying —for he was deeply attached to all that made for the greatness of his native place—"there's no getting away from it, Larousselle's out of the top drawer all right, he's a gentleman through and through, and what more can one ask?"

Maria knew that the doctor loathed him. How, then, could she dare to make an appointment for the one time of the day when he would be sure to be brought face to face with the object of his execration? He went so far as to persuade himself that she had deliberately planned the meeting so as to get rid of him. After spending several weeks writing and tearing up a number of mad, furious letters, he finally sent her one that was both short and dry, in which he said that since she could arrange to be at home on only one afternoon, it must be because she was perfectly well and had no need of his ministrations. By return of post came four pages of excuse and protestation. She would, she said, be at home to him at whatever hour he might like to come on the next day but one, which happened to be a Sunday.

"Monsieur Larousselle is going to a bull-fight. He knows that I don't like that sort of thing. Come for tea. I shall wait for you until half-past five."

Never had the doctor received from her a letter in which the sublimities played so small a part, in which matters of health and treatment were not even mentioned. He re-read it more than once, and frequently touched it as it lay in his pocket. This meeting, he felt, would be different from all that had preceded it. At last he would be able to declare his passion. But, man of science that he was, and taught by repeated experiences that his presentiments had a way of never being realized, he kept on saying to himself: 'No, it's *not* a presentiment . . . my attitude of expectancy is wholly logical. I wrote her a churlish letter to which she has sent a friendly answer. Therefore, it is up to me to see to it that our first words shall give to our talk a tone of frankness and intimacy. . . .'

As he drove from his laboratory to the hospital, he rehearsed the coming interview; again and again asked *her* questions, again and again framed the replies he would have her make. He was one of those imaginative persons who never read novels because for them no work of fiction can ever be nearly so enthralling as the one they invent for themselves, the one in which they play the leading rôle. No sooner had he signed a prescription and found himself on the way downstairs from his patient's room, than he was back, once more, like a dog digging up a buried bone, with his fond imagined reveries. Sometimes he felt ashamed of yielding to them, but they served his ordinarily timid nature as a means of bending things and people to the all-powerful will he would have liked to possess. Scrupulous though he was in daily life, he knew no inhibitions of any kind in these adventures of the mind. He would gladly have countenanced the most appalling massacres, would, even in imagination, have blotted out every member of his family, if by so doing he could have created for himself a new and different existence.

During the two days that elapsed before his meeting with Maria Cross he did not, it is true, have to suppress any fancies of this blood-curdling kind, but that was because in the particular episode which he had invented for his pleasure it was unnecessary to wipe out anybody. All he had to do was to break with his wife, as he had seen many of his colleagues do with theirs, and for no better reason than that he found the thought of living any longer with her unutterably boring. At fifty-two a man may still hope for a few more years of happiness, even though they may be poisoned by feelings of remorse. But why should one who has never known happiness resist a chance of tasting even its make-believe? His continued presence no longer served to bring contentment to an embittered partner, and, as to his son and daughter, well, he had long ago given up all hopes of waking any feelings of affection in *them*. Ever since Madeleine had got herself engaged he had known only too well what the love of his children amounted to. . . . And Raymond? Surely when a person is so inaccessible there is no reason why one should sacrifice oneself in vain efforts to make contact?

He realized well enough that the imagined delights in which he was now indulging were altogether different from his habitual day-dreams. Even when, at a single imagined blow, he blotted out, in fancy, a whole family, he could still feel faintly ashamed, though not at all remorseful. What he was really conscious of on those occasions was a faint sense that he was making himself ridiculous. Such fantasies were purely superficial and did not involve the depths of his being. No, it had never occurred to him that he might be looked upon as a monster, or that he was in any way different from other men who, in his view, were all of them mad as soon as they were alone with their thoughts and freed from the control of others.

But, during the whole of the forty-eight hours which had got to be lived through until the appointed Sunday arrived, he knew he was clinging with all the strength that was in him to a dream that was rapidly becoming a hope. So obsessed was he by the anticipated interview with this woman that he could think of nothing but the words he had decided must pass between them. He occupied himself with putting the finishing touches to a scenario, the central situation of which could be summed up in the following piece of dialogue:

"We are both of us, Maria, at a dead end. There is only one alternative before us. Either we must die with our backs to the wall, or we must retrace our steps and—live. I know you can't love me, because you have never loved anybody. There is nothing for you to do but put yourself wholly into the hands of the one man capable of demanding nothing in exchange for his own devotion."

At this point he could hear in imagination the sort of protest she would make:

"You must be mad! What about your wife, your children?"

"They don't need me. When a man is buried alive he has the right, if he has the strength, to lift the stone that is choking him. You can have no idea of the desert that lies between me and my wife, between me and my son and daughter. The words I speak to them scarcely reach their ears. Animals, when their young have become full-grown, drive them out. More often than not the males do not even recognize them as their own. It is only human beings who invent sentiments which survive the activities of function. Christ knew this well when He said that those who followed Him must leave father and mother for His sake, who gloried in the knowledge that He had been sent to separate husband from wife, and children from those who had brought them into the world."

"You can't compare yourself to God."

"Am I not God's image in your eyes? Is it not to me that you owe your taste for a certain kind of perfection?" (But here the doctor would break off: 'Better keep metaphysics out of it.')

"But what about your position, your patients, the career of beneficent activity which you have built up? Think of the scandal. . . ."

"If I were to die they would have to do without me. No one is indispensable. And when I say die, I mean die, Maria. For I shall set the equivalent of death between me and the wretched hermit existence, so full of grinding labour, which I have been leading. With you I shall be reborn. What money belongs to my wife she shall keep. I can make enough for our needs. I have been offered a professorship in Algiers, another in Santiago. . . . I will hand over to my children what I have managed to save up to date."

The imagined scene had reached this point when the carriage stopped at the hospital. With his thoughts still far away, the doctor passed through the door. His eyes were the eyes of a man who is just emerging from some mysterious enchantment. As soon as his rounds were finished he returned to his day-dreaming, driven on by a secret hunger, saying to himself: 'I am quite mad . . . all the same. . . .' Among his colleagues there were men, he realized, who had made dreams like that come true. To be sure, their undisciplined lives had done something to prepare public opinion for the scandal of their break with the proprieties, whereas it was the opinion of the whole town that Doctor Courrèges was a saint. But what of that? It was just because he had got this reputation without wanting it that it would be such a relief to shed the tiresome load. Once free of it, he would no longer have to spend his time urging Maria Cross to act nobly, or in giving her edifying lectures. He would be a man with a woman to love. He would be a man strong enough to take by force everything he wanted.

At last Sunday dawned. On that one day of the seven it was the doctor's custom to attend only his most important cases. He was careful not to go near the consulting-room which he kept in town. It was always swarming with patients, but he used it only three days a week. He hated the ground-floor room in a building entirely given over to offices. He couldn't, he said, have written or read a line in it. As, at Lourdes, the most trivial little thank-offerings find a place, so, between those four walls, he had accumulated the various gifts showered upon him by grateful "cases." He had begun by hating the "artistic" bronzes, the Austrian terra-cottas, the composition cupids, the objects in porcelain, and the combined barometers and calendars. But gradually he had developed a kind of taste for the whole horrible museum, so that he was filled with joy each time that some more than usually hideous piece of "art" found its way into his hands. "Mind, nothing *old*," his patients would say to one another when discussing how best they could please Doctor Courrèges.

But on the particular Sunday which was to enshrine his meeting with Maria Cross, the meeting that was to change the whole course of his life, he had agreed to see, at three o'clock in this same consulting-room, a business man suffering from neurasthenia who could not manage to visit the doctor on any other day of the week. He had resigned himself to the necessity. At least it would provide him with an excuse for going out immediately after luncheon, and would occupy the few last moments before that fatal meeting so eagerly awaited, so deeply dreaded. He did not use the carriage, nor did he attempt to get into any of the overcrowded trams. Groups of human beings were festooned about their platforms, for there was to be a big Rugby match, and it was also the day of the first bull-fight of the season. The names of *Albagene* and *Fuentes* stared from great red-and-yellow bills. Though the spectacle was not due to begin until four o'clock, the gloomy Sunday streets, with their shuttered shop-fronts, were already filled with crowds making their way towards the arena. The young men wore boaters with coloured bands, or hats of light grey felt which they fondly imagined had a Spanish look. They laughed in a thick cloud of cheap tobacco smoke. The cafés breathed into the street the clean smell of absinthe. He could not remember how long it was since he had last wandered aimlessly through the hurly-burly of the city with no other preoccupation than to kill time until a certain hour should strike. To be thus unemployed was a very strange experience for a man who was usually so overworked. He had lost the secret of doing nothing. He tried to think of the experiment he had recently begun, but could see nothing with his inner eye but Maria Cross lying on a sofa with a book.

Suddenly the sun stopped shining, and the walking folk turned apprehensive eyes to where a heavy cloud was creeping across the sky. Someone said that he had felt a drop of rain, but after a few moments the sun once more came out. No, the storm would not break until the last bull had been put out of its agony.

Perhaps, reflected the doctor, things would not turn out precisely as he had imagined they would. But one thing was certain, mathematically certain: he would not leave Maria Cross without making her privy to his secret. This time he would put his question. . . . Half-past two: another hour to kill before he was due at his consulting-room. At the bottom of his pocket he could feel the key of his laboratory. No, if he went back there it would mean leaving again almost as soon as he had arrived. The crowd swayed as though in the grip of a blustering wind. A voice cried: "There they are!" In a procession of ancient victorias, driven by coachmen who had caught something of reflected glory for all their shabbiness, sat the glittering matadors with their *quadrillas*. It surprised the doctor that he could discern no baseness in the emaciated faces of this strange priesthood clad in red and gold, in violet and silver. Once again a cloud blotted out the sun, and they turned their thin profiles to the tarnished azure of the sky. He thrust a way through the crowd. He was walking now along narrow and deserted thoroughfares. His consulting-room, when he reached it, was as cool as a cellar. Women in terra-cotta and alabaster smiled down on him from columns of malachite. The ticking of a sham antique timepiece was slower than that of an imitation Delft clock which stood in the middle of the table, where a "modern-style" female, seated on a block of crystal, did duty as a paper-weight. All these various figures seemed to be singing in unison the title of a revue which had stared down on him from every corner or every street—*N'y a que çà de bon!*—including the bull in bogus bronze, his muzzle resting on the back of a companion cow. With a quick glance he took in the whole motley collection. Very quietly he said: "The human race could sink no lower!" He pushed open a shutter and set a dusty sunbeam dancing. Then he began to walk up and down the room, rubbing his hands. 'There must be no beating about the bush,' he assured himself. 'With my very first words I must make her realize how terribly I suffered when I made up my mind that she no longer wanted to see me. She will express surprise. I shall tell her with all the earnestness I can command that it is impossible for me any longer to live without her . . . and then, perhaps . . . perhaps . . .'

He heard the sound of the bell, went to the door and admitted his visitor. No interruption to this day-dreaming would come from *him*. All *he* asked was to be allowed to talk and talk. Neurasthenics of that sort seem to demand nothing of their doctors beyond a patient hearing. This one must have endowed the members of the profession with a kind of priestly aura, so eloquent was he in pathological confession, so anxious to display the most secret wounds of his soul. The doctor was once more, in imagination, with Maria Cross. 'I am a man, Maria, a poor creature of flesh and blood like other men. No one can live without happiness. I have discovered that truth rather late in life, but not too late—say it is not too late—for you to throw in your lot with mine. . . .' By this time his patient had stopped talking, and the doctor, with that air of noble dignity which had earned him such universal admiration, said:

"The essential thing is that you should believe in the power of your own will. If you refuse to regard yourself as a free agent, I can do nothing for you. Even the art of healing can be wrecked on the reef of a wrong mental attitude. If you persist in thinking of yourself as the helpless victim of heredity, how can you hope that I shall be able to do anything for you? Before going further I demand from you an act of faith. You must believe that it is in your power to control all those wild beasts in yourself that are not the real you at all."

The other kept on eagerly interrupting him, and all the time he was speaking, the doctor, who had risen and gone over to the window, pretended to be looking into the empty street through the half-closed shutters. It was with something amounting to horror that he noted in himself the survival of all these lying phrases which expressed nothing but a faith long dead. Just as we perceive the light given off by a star which has been cold for centuries, so those around him heard the echo of beliefs which he had ceased to hold. He came back to the table, saw that the sham Delft clock marked four o'clock, and hastily got rid of his patient.

'I've got plenty of time,' he told himself as he all but ran along the pavement. When he reached the Place de la Comédie he saw that the trams were being besieged by the crowds of people who were pouring out of the cinemas. Not a cab was to be seen. He had to take his place in a queue, and kept consulting his watch. Accustomed as he was to driving everywhere, he had left himself too little time. He tried to calm his nervousness. Even putting things at their worst he would be no more than half an hour late—no unusual thing for a doctor. Maria always waited for him. Yes, but in her letter she had said "until half-past five," and it was already five! "Just you stop pushing!" exclaimed a fat and angry woman, the feather of whose hat was tickling his nose. Inside the tram, which was packed to suffocation, he regretted that he was wearing an overcoat. He was sweating, and hated the thought of arriving with a dirty face and a strong smell.

Six o'clock had not yet struck when he got out in front of the church at Talence. At first he walked quickly, then, mad with anxiety, broke into a trot, though his heart was troubling him. A great storm-cloud had darkened the sky. In this ominous light the last bull must even now be bleeding. Between the railings of the little gardens branches of dusty lilac thrust out little begging hands, craving for rain. Under the warm slow drops he ran towards the woman whom he could see already, in imagination, stretched on her sofa. She would not immediately, on his entry, raise her eyes from her open book. . . . And then, just as he reached her front door, he saw her coming out. They both stopped. She was out of breath. Like him she had been running.

There was a hint of annoyance in her voice as she said:

"I *did* say half-past-five in my letter."

He took in her appearance with an observant eye.

"You're not in mourning."

She glanced down at her summer frock and replied:

"Doesn't mauve count as half-mourning?"

How different, already, everything was from what he had been imagining! Oppressed by a great weight of cowardice, he said:

"Since you had given me up, and probably have an appointment somewhere else, we had better put off our meeting to another day."

She spoke eagerly, quickly:

"With whom *should* I have an appointment? What an odd creature you are, doctor!"

She turned back towards the house, and he followed her. She let her skirt of mauve taffeta drag in the dust. When she bent her head he could see the back of her neck. She was thinking that if she had chosen Sunday for the doctor's call it was because she felt sure that the unknown boy would not be in the six o'clock tram. All the same, beside herself with joy and hope when he did not come at the hour named, she had run down the road, just on the off-chance, saying to herself:

'There is just one possibility in a thousand that he has taken his usual tram because of me. Whatever happens, I must not let such a chance of happiness slip.' But, alas! she would never know now whether the stranger had been struck with gloom when he saw that she was not in her usual seat. The heavy rain was splashing on the front steps as she hurried up them, and she could hear behind her the old man's laboured breathing. How importunate are those who do not touch our hearts, those whom we have not chosen! They are wholly external to ourselves. There is nothing about them that we want to know. Should they die, their death would mean no more to us than their lives . . . yet it is they who fill our whole existence.

They went through the dining-room. She opened the drawing-room shutters and took off her hat. Then she lay down and smiled up at the doctor, who was trying desperately to pick some shreds and tatters from the words he had so carefully prepared. She said to him: "You are out of breath. I made you walk too fast."

"I am not as old as all that."

He raised his eyes, as he always did, to the mirror that hung above the sofa. What! was he even now not familiar with his own appearance? Why was it that, on each occasion, he felt that stab at the heart, that sense of numb misery, as though he had expected to see his own youth smiling back at him? But already he was putting the usual question: "And how are we to-day?" in that tone of paternal concern, with that half-serious inflexion, which he always adopted when he spoke to Maria Cross. Never had she felt so well, and in telling the doctor so she felt a pleasure which to some extent compensated her for the earlier disappointment. No, to-day, Sunday, the unknown boy would almost certainly not have been in the tram. But to-morrow, yes, to-morrow he would be there: of that there could be no doubt, and already her whole being was turned towards the joy to come, the hope that, every day, was doomed to disappointment and rebirth, the hope that something fresh might occur, that the moment would come when he would speak to her.

"I see no reason why you shouldn't leave off the injections." (He saw reflected in the glass his skimpy beard and barren brow, and remembered the burning words he had prepared.)

"I'm sleeping well: I don't feel bored any longer—just think of that, doctor! And yet, somehow, I have no wish to read. I couldn't finish *Voyage de Sparte*; you'd better take it away with you."

"You still see nobody?"

"You don't really think that I should suddenly let myself get mixed up with all these men's mistresses, do you? I, who till now have always avoided them like the plague? In the whole of Bordeaux there is no one of my kind, as you must realize, nobody of whom I could make a friend."

Yes, she had said so often enough, but always, in the past, on a note of self-pity, never, as now, with peace and happiness in her voice. It was borne in on the doctor that her long and tapering flame would no longer point heavenward a flickering tongue, would no longer burn in a void, that somewhere, close to the earth, it had found, unknown to him, fuel on which to feed. He could not keep himself from saying with aggressive emphasis that though it might be true that she did not frequent the women, she nevertheless occasionally saw the men. He felt himself blushing as he realized that the conversation might, even now, take the very tone he had so ardently desired. Indeed, Maria did actually say with a smile:

"Don't tell me you are jealous, doctor! I really do believe you're going to make a scene! No, no, don't be frightened, I was only joking," she added immediately. "I know you too well."

It was obvious that she had been within an ace of laughing outright, that it had never even occurred to her that the doctor might really be capable of such weakness. A worried look came into her eyes.

"I haven't said anything to hurt you, have I?"

"Yes, you have."

But she failed entirely to understand the nature of the hurt he spoke of. She said that her feeling for him was one of veneration and respect. Hadn't he lowered himself to her level? Hadn't he sometimes deigned to raise her to his? With a movement as insincere as her words had been, she seized his hand and drew it to her lips. He snatched it away. Annoyed by the action, she got up, went over to the window, and stared out at the drenched garden. He, too, had risen. Without turning her head, she spoke:

"Wait till the shower's over."

He made no move, but stood there in the dark room. In all things a man of method, he employed the agonizing moments in rooting from his heart all desire and all hope. Everything was over, really over. From now on, nothing that had to do with this woman would ever more concern him. He had withdrawn from the battle. With his hand he made in the empty air the gesture of a man sweeping some obstacle aside.

Maria turned her head:

"It has stopped raining," she said.

Seeing that he still did not move, she hastened to add that it wasn't that she wanted to get rid of him, but wouldn't it be as well to take advantage of this momentary break? She offered him an umbrella which at first he accepted, only, a moment later, to refuse, because he had caught himself thinking, 'I shall have to bring it back: that'll give me a chance to see her again.'

He felt no pain, but only a sense of enjoyment in the tail end of the storm. His thoughts ran on himself, or rather on one part of himself. He was like a man who finds consolation for the death of a friend in the certainty that he has ceased to suffer. He had played and lost. No use crying over spilled milk. Henceforward nothing would matter to him but his work. Yesterday they had rung him up from the laboratory to say that the dog had not survived the removal of its pancreas. Would Robinson manage to find another at the Lost Dogs' Home? The trams swept by, crammed with an exhausted, singing crowd. But he had no objection to walking along these suburban roads filled with lilac and smelling of the real country because of the rain and the effect of the failing light. He was done with suffering, with beating, like a prisoner, against the walls of his cell. The vital force which had been his since childhood, but which the pressure of so many human creatures had led him to dissipate, he now took back, thrusting it deep, deep into himself. Complete renunciation. In spite of staring posters and gleaming tram-lines, in spite of cyclists bent double over handlebars adorned with bunches of faded lilac, the suburb merged gradually into open country, the bars gave place to inns full of mule-drivers preparing to set off by moonlight. Onwards through the darkness they would trundle, like so many corpses stretched out in the bottom of their waggons, their faces to the stars. On the doorsteps of houses children were playing with drowsy cockchafers. Never again would he kick against the pricks. For how long now had he been exhausting all his energies in this dreary battle? He saw himself by the light of memory sobbing (it must be almost half a century ago) beside his mother's bed on the last day of the holidays. "Aren't you ashamed of crying, you lazy little silly-billy?" she had exclaimed, not knowing that what had provoked the outburst had simply been despair at the thought of leaving her: and later . . . once more he made that sweeping gesture with his hand, as though he were clearing a space before him. 'Now, what have I got to do tomorrow morning?' he thought, inoculating himself, as with an injection of morphine, with the thought of daily duties . . . of the dead dog, of the need to start the whole business over again from the beginning. Surely he had tabulated a sufficient number of observations already to enable him to confirm his hypothesis? What a lot of time he had wasted. Through what thickets of shame he had been wandering! Convinced that the whole human race must be hanging on his every movement as he worked away in his laboratory, he had yet been willing to see day after day go by spoiled and empty. Science must be served with an undivided passion. It brooks no rival. 'I shall never be more than an amateur scientist.' He thought he saw fire burning in the branches and realized that it was the rising moon. He caught sight of the trees that hid from view the house which harboured that group of beings whom he had the right to call "my people." So often already he had been false to his vow, only later to renew it in his heart: 'From this very evening I will make Lucie happy.' He hastened his pace, impatient to prove that this time he would not weaken in his resolve. He thought of their first meeting, twenty-five years before, in a garden at Arcachon—a meeting engineered by one of his colleagues. But what he saw with his inward eye was not the betrothed of that distant time, not a pale and faded photograph, but a young woman in half-mourning, wild with joy because he was late, and hurrying to a meeting with someone else . . . but with whom? He felt a sharp stab of pain, stopped dead for a moment, and then broke into a run so as to put as great a distance as possible between himself and the man whom Maria Cross loved. The action brought comfort, ignorant though he was that each step he took was bringing him closer, though he did not realize it, to the unknown rival. . . . And yet it was on this very evening that, scarcely across the threshold of the room where Raymond and his brother-in-law stood at odds, he became conscious of a sudden burgeoning, a sudden rising of the spring sap, in the stranger whom he had brought into the world.

Those present had risen from the table, the children offering their foreheads for their elders absent-mindedly to kiss. This done, they went off to their rooms under an escort provided by their mother, their grandmother and their still more ancient ancestress. Raymond moved across to the French window. The doctor was struck by the way in which he took a cigarette from his case, tapped it and lighted it. There was a rose-bud in his buttonhole, an orthodox crease in his trousers. The doctor thought: 'How extraordinarily like my poor father he is!' Indeed, he was the living image of the surgeon who, until he was seventy, had frittered away on women the fortune he had amassed by the practice of his art. He had been the first to introduce into Bordeaux the blessings of antiseptic treatment. He had never paid the slightest attention to his son, to whom he habitually referred as "the young 'un," as though he had forgotten his name. One night a woman had brought him home. His mouth was twisted and dribbling. His watch, his notecase and the diamond ring which he wore on his little finger were all missing. 'From him I have inherited a heart capable of passion, but not his gift of pleasing—that is a legacy reserved for his grandson.'

He looked at Raymond, who was staring into the garden—at this grown man who was his son. After the day of feverish emotions just past he would have dearly loved to confide his troubles to a friendly ear, or, rather, to indulge in a burst of maudlin self-pity, to say to his child: "Why do we never have a good talk? Is it that you think I should not understand you? Is the gulf that separates father and son so unbridgeable? I have the same heart to-day as I had when I was twenty, and you are the flesh of my flesh. There is at least a good chance that we have in common the same set of tastes, antipathies and temptations. . . . Which of us shall be the first to break this silence that divides us?" A man and a woman, no matter how completely estranged they may be, can at least come together in the ardour of an embrace. Even a mother may take between her hands the head of her grown-up son and kiss his hair. But a father can do no more than the doctor did when he laid his hand on Raymond's shoulder. The boy trembled and turned his head. His father averted his eyes and asked:

"Is it still raining?"

Raymond, upright upon the threshold, stretched his hand into the darkness.

"No, it's left off."

Then, without looking round, he added: "Good night," and the sound of his footsteps died away.

About the same time, Madame Courrèges was feeling completely "bowled over" because her husband had just suggested that she should take a turn with him in the garden. She said she would go in and fetch a wrap. He heard her go upstairs and then come down again with unwonted speed.

"Take my arm, Lucie: there's a cloud in front of the moon, and it's difficult to see one's way."

"But the path shows white."

She leaned rather heavily on him, and he noticed that her body still smelled the same as it had done in the old days of their engagement, when they sat together on a bench in the long June evenings. The mingled scent of human flesh and summer dusk was, as it were, the very essence of their betrothal.

He asked whether she, too, had not noticed the great change that had taken place in their son. No, she said, he was still as surly, as sullen, as pig-headed as he had always been. The doctor pressed his point. Raymond, according to him, was now far less undisciplined. He seemed to have more control over himself. It showed, if in nothing else, at least in the care he was giving to his personal appearance.

"That reminds me. Julie was complaining only yesterday that he wants her to press his trousers twice a week."

"Julie must be made to see reason. Don't forget that she has known him ever since he was a baby."

"Julie is devoted to us, but there are limits even to devotion. It's all very well for Madeleine to talk: *her* maids do nothing at all. I know that Julie is difficult, but I do understand why she should feel annoyed at having to sweep the back stairs as well as the front."

A skinflint nightingale uttered three short notes. Husband and wife caught the hawthorn's scent of bitter almonds as they sauntered on. In a low voice, the doctor continued:

"Our little Raymond . . ."

"We shan't find it easy to replace Julie, and the sooner we realize that, the better. I know you'll say that she drives every cook we have out of the house, but more often than not she is in the right. . . . For instance, Léonie . . ."

With weary resignation he asked:

"Which of them was Léonie?"

"Surely you remember?—the fat one, not the last, but the woman who only stayed with us for three months. She objected to doing the dining-room. But it isn't part of Julie's work."

He said: "Servants to-day are very different from what they used to be."

It was as though some tide in him were suddenly ebbing, and drawing back as it receded all desire in him to confide, to confess, to abandon pretence, to let his tears flow.

"We had better go in."

"Madeleine is for ever saying that the cook is stubborn, but that's not Julie's fault. The woman wants us to raise her wages. They don't make as much out here as they do in town, though things are cheaper. If it wasn't for that they wouldn't stay at all."

"I'm going in."

"Already?"

She had a feeling that she had disappointed him, that she ought to have waited, to have let him do the talking.

"We don't often get a change to talk," she murmured.

From somewhere beyond the wretched fabric of words that she had built up, from somewhere beyond the wall that her vulgarity had erected, with ant-like patience, day by day, Lucie Courrèges could hear the stifled cry of a man who was buried alive, the shout of an imprisoned miner, and deep within herself, too, another voice replied to his, a sudden tenderness fluttered.

She made as though to lean her head upon her husband's shoulder, but guessed how his body would stiffen, his face take on an expression of hard remoteness. Raising her eyes towards the house, she could not resist saying:

"You've left the light on in your room!"

She regretted the words as soon as she had uttered them. He hurried on so as to be free of her, ran up the steps, and sighed with relief at finding the drawing-room empty, because it meant that he could reach his study without meeting anybody. Safe there at last, he sat down at his table, kneaded his care-worn face with both hands, and once more made that motion of sweeping something aside. . . . The dog's death was a nuisance. It wasn't easy to find animals for his experiments. With all the ridiculous nonsense that had been bothering him of late, he had lost something of his grip on things. 'I've been relying too much on Robinson . . . he must have miscalculated the time of that last injection.' The only solution would be to begin again. From now on Robinson must confine his activities to taking the animals' temperature, to collecting and analysing their urine. . . .

VI

A FAILURE of the current had brought the trams to a standstill. They stood all along the boulevards, looking like a procession of yellow caterpillars. It had needed this incident to establish, at long last, some sort of direct contact between Raymond Courrèges and Maria Cross; not but what, on the day following the Sunday when they had not seen one another, a terrified feeling that they might never meet again had laid hold on both, with the result that each had separately decided to take the first step. But to her he was a shy schoolboy whom the slightest thing might frighten; and how, he felt, should he ever summon up enough courage to speak to a woman? Although for the first time she was wearing a light-coloured dress, he sensed rather than saw her presence in the crowd, while she, for all her short-sightedness, recognized him from afar. There had been some sort of ceremony, and he was dressed in his school uniform, with the cape unfastened and hanging loose about his shoulders (in imitation of the cadets of the Naval Medical School). A few intending passengers got into the tram and settled down to wait until it started. Others wandered away in groups. Raymond and Maria found themselves side by side at the far end, close to the platform. Without looking at him, so that he might not think she was speaking for his benefit, she said in a low voice:

"After all, I haven't very far to go. . . ."

And he, with head averted and cheeks all flame:

"It might be rather nice to walk home for once."

It was then that she brought herself to look him full in the face. Never before had she been so close to him.

"We've been travelling back together for so long that we mustn't lose the habit."

They walked a short distance in silence. Furtively she looked at his hot and scarlet face, at the tender skin of youth scraped and sore from the razor. With a boyish gesture he was hugging to his body with both arms a well-worn portfolio crammed with books, and the idea that he was little more than a child became firmly fixed in her mind. This realization produced in her a sense of uneasy shyness in which scruple, shame and pure delight played an equal part. He, for his part, felt no less paralysed with nervousness than when, in earlier days, he had decided that only the exercise of superhuman will-power could induce him to enter a shop. Recognition of the fact that he was the taller of the two came as a staggering surprise. The lilac straw hat that she was wearing hid most of her face, but he could see her bare neck and one shoulder which had slipped free of her dress. The thought that he might not be able to find a word with which to break the silence, that he might ruin this precious moment, filled him with panic.

"You don't live very far away: I was forgetting."

"Not very far. The church at Talence is only about ten minutes' ride from the boulevards."

He took from his pocket an ink-stained handkerchief, mopped his forehead, noticed the ink, and put the handkerchief away again.

"But perhaps you've got further to go?"

"Oh no I haven't: I get out just after passing the church——"

Then, very hurriedly, he added: "I'm young Courrèges."

"The doctor's son?"

There was an eager note in his voice as he asked:

"He's pretty well known, isn't he?"

She had raised her face, the better to see him, and he noticed that the colour had gone from her cheeks. But even as the fact was borne in on him, she said:

"It really is a very small world. But you mustn't talk to him about me."

"I never talk to him about anything. Anyhow, I don't know who you are."

"That's just as well."

Once more she fixed on him a long and brooding look. The doctor's son! In that case, he must surely be just a very innocent and very pious schoolboy who would turn from her in horror as soon as he heard her name. It was impossible that he should not know about her. Young Bertrand Larousselle had been at school with him until last year. The name of Maria Cross must be a by-word among the boys. Less from curiosity than sheer nervousness he pressed her to disclose it.

"You really *must* tell me your name. After all, I've told you mine."

The level light touched to flame a basket of oranges standing in the doorway of a shop. The gardens looked as though they had been daubed all over with dust. At this point a bridge crossed that very same railway-line which once had been to Raymond an object of thrilling excitement because trains ran along it to

Spain. Maria Cross was thinking: 'If I tell him who I am, I may lose him. . . . But isn't it my duty to scare him away?' This inner debate was rich for her with pain and pleasure. She was quite genuinely suffering, but at the same time felt a vague satisfaction in murmuring to herself: "What a tragedy!"

"When you know who I am . . ." (she could not help thinking of the myth of Psyche, of *Lohengrin*).

His laugh was rather too boisterous. When he spoke, it was without restraint:

"Sooner or later we should have been bound to strike up an acquaintance in the tram. You must have realized that I made a point of always taking the one that leaves at six. . . . You didn't? Oh, I say, come off it! I often get to the terminus early enough to catch the one before that leaves at a quarter to, but I always give it a miss, just so as to see you. Yesterday I actually came away from the fight after the fourth bull in order not to miss our meeting, and then you weren't there! They tell me that Fuentes was on the top of his form in the last kill. But now we've broken the ice why should I care *what* your name is? There was a time when I didn't care about anything, but from the moment I realized you were trying to catch my eye . . ."

Had anyone else been speaking, Maria would have found such language atrociously vulgar, but in his mouth it had a delicious freshness, so that, later, each time she passed this particular spot on her journeys to and fro, she was to be reminded vividly of the sudden access of tenderness and joy that had been released in her by his schoolboy chatter.

"You can't get out of telling me your name. After all, I've only got to ask Papa. That'd be easy—the lady who always gets out of the tram by the church at Talence."

"I'll tell it you, but only on condition you swear never to talk about me to the doctor."

She no longer believed that the mention of her name would frighten him off, though she pretended to herself that the threat was real. 'Fate must decide,' she thought—because, deep down, she was quite certain that she held the winning cards. Just before they reached the church she asked him to continue his journey alone—"because of the neighbours" who would recognize her and start gossiping.

"All right, but not until I know . . ."

Very hurriedly, and without looking at him, she said:

"Maria Cross."

"Maria Cross?"

She dug the point of her umbrella into the ground and added, precipitately:

"Wait until you know me . . ."

He was staring, as though dazzled by the sight of her:

"Maria Cross!"

So this was the woman whose name he had heard whispered one summer's day in the Allées de Tourny, when he and his companions were going back to school after the break. She had just passed them in a two-horse brougham. One of the other boys with whom he was walking had said: "Really, women like that! . . ." And suddenly another memory came back into his mind. There had been a time when he was taking a course of medicated baths, which meant that he had to leave school at four o'clock. On this particular occasion he had overtaken young Bertrand Larousselle. He was striding along, his long legs encased in gaiters of undressed leather. Already, in spite of his tender years, he was a bullying and overbearing youth. The younger boy was, as a rule, accompanied by either a servant or a black-gloved priest with his coat-collar turned up. Among the "juniors" Raymond enjoyed the worst reputation of all the "uppers," and, whenever the two of them met, the pure and pious Bertrand would devour the notorious "dirty beast" with his eyes. It never even occurred to him that to this same dirty beast he was himself an object of mystery. At this time Madame Victor Larousselle was still alive, and many ridiculous rumours about her were rife in town and school. Maria Cross, it was said, had set her heart on marriage, and was demanding that her lover should turn his family out of doors. Others announced as a fact that she was waiting until Madame Larousselle should have died of cancer, so that she could then be married in church. More than once Raymond had caught sight of Bertrand behind the closed windows of a car, driving with his corpse-like mother. The women of the Courrèges and Basquefa milies, speaking of her, used to say: "Poor thing! With what dignity she bears her martyrdom! If ever anybody had their purgatory here on earth, it's she! . . . If *my* husband behaved like that, I'd spit in his face and just clear out. *I* wouldn't stand it!"

On the day in question Bertrand Larousselle was quite alone. He heard behind him the whistling of the dirty beast and increased his pace. But Raymond kept on a level with him and never took his eyes off his short covert-coat and cap of handsome English tweed. Everything that had to do with the younger boy fascinated him. Suddenly, Bertrand broke into a run, and a note-book slipped from his satchel. By the time he noticed his loss Raymond had already picked it up. Its owner turned back, his face pale with fear and anger. "Give it me!" he cried: but Raymond read out in a low voice the title on the cover—"My Diary"—and sniggered.

"Young Larousselle's diary—that ought to be pretty juicy!"

"Give it me!"

Raymond sprinted ahead, turned into the Parc Bordelais, and ran down one of the deserted paths. Behind him he could hear a miserable, breathless voice panting out, over and over again, "Give it me! I'll tell them you took it!" But the dirty beast, hidden from view by a thick shrubbery, was engaged in mocking young Larousselle, who, by this time at the end of his tether, was lying full length on the grass and sobbing.

"Here's your beastly note-book, your precious diary. Take it, you little idiot!"

He pulled the boy to his feet, wiped his eyes and brushed down the overcoat of English tweed. Whoever would have thought that the great bully could be so kind! The brat smiled his gratitude at Raymond, who, suddenly, could not resist putting into words a vulgar whim of curiosity:

"I say, have you ever seen her—this Maria Cross woman?"

Bertrand, scarlet to the tips of his ears, picked up his satchel and took to his heels. It never even occurred to Raymond to run after him.

Maria Cross . . . it was she now who was devouring *him* with her eyes. He had expected her to look taller, more mysterious. So this small woman in the lilac dress was actually Maria Cross. Noticing his confusion she mistook the cause.

"Please don't think . . ." she stammered. "You mustn't, really . . ."

She trembled in the presence of this judge whom she had viewed in the light of an angelic messenger. She saw no sign of the grubby thoughts of youth, did not know that spring is often the season of mud, and that this growing lad might be mostly composed of filth. She could not endure the contempt which she imagined him to be feeling, and, with a few hurried murmurs of farewell, was already beating her retreat. But he ran after her.

"Tomorrow, same time, same tram?"

"Are you sure that's what you want?"

She made off then, but twice turned her head. He was standing where she had left him, thinking, 'Maria Cross's got a crush on me!' As though he could not believe his good luck, he spoke the words aloud: "Maria Cross's got a crush on me!"

He breathed in the dusk as though it contained the very essence of the universe, as though he could savour it in every nerve and fibre of his exultant body. Maria Cross had got a crush on him! Should he tell his pals? Not one of them would believe it. He could already see before him the leafy prison where the members of one single family dwelt side by side, yet no less cut off from one another than the worlds which make up the MilkyWay. How inadequate, this evening, was that cage to house the stature of his pride! He skirted it, and plunged into a plantation of pines—the only one that was not fenced in. It was called the Bois de Berge. The earth on which he flung himself was warmer than a human body. The pine-needles left deep imprints on the palms of his hands.

When he entered the dining-room his father was cutting the pages of a journal, and saying something in reply to an observation of his wife's.

"I'm *not* reading—just looking at the titles of the articles."

No one but his grandmother seemed to have heard his "Good evening."

"So it's you, you young rascal!"

As he passed her chair, she put out her hand and drew him to her:

"You smell of resin."

"I've been in the pine-woods."

She looked him up and down with an air ot knowing tolerance, murmuring an abusive epithet as though it had been an endearment:

"You little horror!"

He lapped up his soup noisily, like a dog. How insignificant all these people seemed to him! He was way up above them, soaring in the sunlight. Only with his father did he feel that he had some connexion, because *he* knew Maria Cross, had been in her house, had attended her professionally, had seen her in bed, had pressed his ear to her chest, her back . . . Maria Cross! . . . Maria Cross! . . . the name choked him like a clot of blood. He could taste its warm saltiness in his mouth. The hot tide of it flooded his cheeks, broke from his control.

"I saw Maria Cross this evening."

The doctor fixed him with a stare.

"How did you recognize her?"

"I was with Papillon—he knows her by sight."

"Hullo!" exclaimed Basque; "Raymond's blushing!"

One of the little girls took up the phrase:

"Oo! Uncle Raymond's blushing!"

He made an ill-tempered movement of the shoulders. His father questioned him again, this time averting his eyes:

"Was she alone?"

At his son's reply—"Quite alone"—he returned to his occupation of cutting pages. Madame Courrèges said:

"It really is extraordinary how much more interested you are in that woman than in any other. What's so very odd, after all, in his having seen that creature in the street? In days gone by, when she was a domestic servant, you wouldn't have paid the slightest attention to her."

There was an interruption from the doctor: "My dear, she never *was* a domestic servant."

"Well, even if she had been," put in Madeleine, and there was a sharp edge to her voice, "that's nothing to be ashamed of—very much to the contrary, I should have thought!"

The maid having left the room with one of the dishes, she turned angrily on her mother:

"It almost looks as though you were deliberately trying to upset the servants and hurt their feelings! Irma has an extremely sensitive nature!"

"So I've got to handle the staff with kid gloves, now, have I? Really, no one would believe the things that go on in this house!"

"You can behave exactly as you like with your own servants: all I ask is that you shouldn't drive other peoples' away . . . especially when you expect them to wait at table!"

"You're not exactly tactful yourself where Julie is concerned, and you've got the reputation of never being able to keep a maid when you do get one. . . . Everyone knows that the only reason *my* servants ever give notice is because they can't get on with yours!"

At this point the maid came back and the altercation was interrupted. But as soon as she had once again returned to the pantry it was resumed in a series of whispers. Raymond studied his father with amusement. Had Maria Cross been a domestic servant, would *he* have so much as noticed her existence? Suddenly, the doctor raised his head, and, without looking at any of those present, announced:

"Maria Cross is the daughter of the woman who was head mistress of the St. Clair school when your beloved Monsieur Labrousse was curé there, Lucie."

"What? The harpy who used to plague the life out of him? Who preferred to stay away from Mass unless she and her girls could have the front seats in the nave? Well, I can't say I'm surprised: like mother, like daughter."

"Don't you remember," said Madame Courrèges the elder, "that story of poor Monsieur Labrousse's about how, when the Marquis de Lur-Saluces was beaten in the elections by a wretched little attorney from Bazas, she came round in the evening attended by the whole school, and stood under the presbytery windows jeering at him, and how her hands were quite black with letting off fireworks in honour of the new Deputy? . . ."

"A nice lot they were, I must say."

But the doctor did not wait to hear more. Instead of going upstairs as usual to his study, he followed Raymond into the garden.

Both father and son wanted to talk. Unknown to themselves some strong influence was forming a bond between them. It was as though they were harbouring the same secret. In just such a way do initiates and conspirators recognize and seek one another. Each found in the other the one being in the world to whom he could unburden himself of his precious obsession. As two butterflies, separated by miles and miles, meet at the spot that houses the odorous female, so had they followed the convergent tracks of their desires, and alighted side by side on the invisible body of Maria Cross.

"Have you got a cigarette, Raymond? I've forgotten what tobacco tastes like. . . . Thank you. . . . What about taking a turn?"

He heard his own words with amazement. He was like a man

who, having been cured by a miracle, sees the wound that he had thought healed suddenly open again. No longer ago than that morning, in his laboratory, he had been conscious of the lightness of spirit that comes to the devout penitent when he has received absolution. Seeking in his heart some trace of his recent passion, he had found none. How solemnly, and rather priggishly, he had lectured Robinson, who, ever since the spring, had been somewhat neglecting his work for a lady of the chorus.

"My dear chap, the scientist who really loves his work and is consumed with the desire to make a reputation will always regard the hours and minutes given over to sexual passion as so much time wasted."

Robinson had swept back his tousled hair, rubbed his spectacles on his acid-stained overall, and ventured a protest:

"All the same, sir—love . . ."

"No, my boy, for the real scientist, except in brief moments of purely temporary surrender, his work must always take precedence of love. He will, if he sacrifices it, always be haunted by bitter thoughts of the noble satisfaction he might have known if only he had been faithful to his vocation."

"It certainly is true," Robinson had replied, "that most great scientists do occasionally indulge their sexual impulses, but I know scarcely any whom you would call men of really strong passions."

The doctor understood now why it was that this acquiescent attitude on the part of his disciple had brought the colour to his cheeks.

Raymond had only to say, "I saw Maria Cross," for the passion he had thought dead to stir again. Alas! it was merely in a state of torpor . . . a single word could bring it back to life, provide it with the food it craved. It was already stretching its limbs, yawning and getting to its feet. If it couldn't embrace in flesh and blood reality the woman of its choice, it would find relief in speech. No matter what the cost, he *must* talk about Maria Cross.

Though they had been drawn together by a mutual desire to sing Maria Cross's praises, their very first words set father and son at odds. Raymond maintained that a woman of her emotional scope could not but outrage the anæmic susceptibilities of the devout. What he admired in her was her boldness, her limitless ambition, the dissolute life which he imagined her to have led. The doctor, on the contrary, insisted that there was nothing of the courtesan about her, that one must not believe what people said:

"I *know* Maria Cross! I was her best friend during all that time when her little François was so desperately ill, and I still am. . . . She unburdened herself to me. . . ."

"My poor dear father, what you mean is that she pulled the wool over your eyes. . . ."

The doctor controlled himself with an effort. His reply, when it came, was given with considerable warmth:

"You're quite wrong, my boy. She confided in me with quite extraordinary humility. If it is true to say of anybody that their actions bear no resemblance to themselves, it is certainly true to say it of Maria Cross. Incurable laziness has been her undoing. Her mother, the St. Clair school-mistress, got her to work for the entrance examination for the Sèvres Training College, but when she married an army doctor of the 144th regiment all that went by the board. The three years she spent as his wife were uneventful, and if he had lived she would have led an ordinary decent and humdrum existence. The only cause of complaint he had against her was that temperamental indolence to which I have already referred, because it meant that she didn't run his house well. He used to grumble a bit, she told me, when he came home of an evening, at finding that there was nothing for dinner but a dish of noodles heated up over a spirit-lamp. Her favourite occupation was to lie in a torn dressing-gown and slippers, reading all day long. People call her a courtesan, but you'd be surprised if you knew how little mere luxury means to her. Why, only a short time ago she decided to give up using the car which was Larousselle's present to her, and now she travels by tram like anybody else. . . . What are you laughing at? I don't see anything particularly amusing about that. . . . Stop it! it's getting on my nerves. . . . When she found herself a widow with a child, you may imagine how ill-equipped for work an intellectual woman like that would feel. . . . Unfortunately, a friend of her husband's got her the post of secretary to Larousselle. She was completely innocent of any sort of scheming, but—well, though Larousselle had the reputation of being a harsh employer, he never said a word to her, though she was always late at the office and was hardly ever up to time with her work. That alone was enough to compromise her, and by the time she realized the situation it was too late to do anything about it. The others treated her as the boss's little bit, and their hostility made her position impossible. She spoke to Larousselle about it, which was just what he had been waiting for. He had a small property close to Bordeaux for which, just then, he had failed, or perhaps not wanted, to find a tenant. He suggested that she should act as caretaker until she could land another job. . . ."

"And I suppose she found the suggestion all innocent and above-board?"

"Not at all. Obviously, she realized perfectly well what he was after: but the poor woman was saddled with an establishment far too expensive for her straitened circumstances, and, to crown all, the child was struck down with enteritis, and the doctor thought it essential that he should have country air. Finally, in view of the fact that she was already so deeply compromised, she just hadn't the courage to refuse such a windfall. She let herself be over-persuaded. . . ."

"You're telling *me*! . . ."

"Don't talk like that! You know nothing whatever about her. She stood out for a long time. But what was there for her to do? She couldn't prevent Larousselle from bringing his friends out to dinner. I realize that she was weak and irresponsible, that she ought to have refused to act as his hostess; but I can assure you that those famous Tuesday evenings were very far from being the hideous orgies of popular imagination. The only thing at all scandalous about them was that they occurred at a time when Madame Larousselle's health had taken a turn for the worse. I can swear that Maria had no idea that her employer's wife was in danger. 'My conscience was clear,' she told me. 'At that time I had not permitted Monsieur Larousselle so much as a kiss. There was nothing between us, absolutely nothing. What harm was there in my presiding over a tableful of fools? . . . I admit that the idea of dazzling them did go to my head. I enjoyed playing the bluestocking. I knew that my employer was proud of me. He had promised to do something for the boy.' "

"And you really swallowed all that? . . ."

What a simpleton his poor father was! But the thing that Raymond really resented was that the doctor should have diminished Maria Cross to the stature of a respectable, weak-willed little school-mistress—and thereby reduced his sense of conquest to nothing.

"She didn't yield to Larousselle's suggestions until after his wife's death, and only then from lassitude, from a sort of despairing apathy—yes, that exactly describes it. She used the phrase herself when describing the situation—a *despairing apathy*. She had no illusions, was perfectly clear-headed. She was not taken in by his assumption of the rôle of inconsolable widower any more than she was by his promise of eventual marriage. She knew too much about men of his type, she told me, to be deluded. As his mistress she was a distinct asset, but things would be very different if she were his wife! I suppose you know that he sent young Bertrand to the Collège de Normandie so that he shouldn't be exposed to contact with her? In his heart of hearts he thought her no different from the common-or-garden drabs with whom he was for ever deceiving her. Besides, I happen to know that their physical intimacy doesn't amount to much. I am convinced of that; you can take my word for it. He, of course, is mad about her, and he's not the sort of man to be content with having her just for show purposes, as is generally supposed in Bordeaux: but she is adamant. . . ."

"You're not going to tell me that Maria Cross is a saint?"

They could not see one another, but each could sense hostility in the other, though they kept their voices low. They had been brought together for a moment by the name of Maria Cross, and it was her name that separated them now. The man walked with head high: the youth kept his eyes fixed upon the ground and vented his ill-humour by kicking at a pine-cone.

"You think me a fool, but of us two, it is you who are the innocent. If you think only ill of people, you'll never get to know them. You have stumbled on precisely the right word. I know what Maria Cross has been through, and I know that somewhere in her there are the makings of a saint . . . yes, really, a saint. . . . But you could never understand that."

"Don't make me laugh!"

"What do you know about her? You've merely been listening to gossip. I *do* know about her."

"I know what I know."

"And how much may that be?"

The doctor stopped dead in the middle of the path where the chestnut trees threw a deep shade. He gripped Raymond by the arm.

"Oh, let me alone! It's all one to me whether Maria Cross does, or does not, go to bed with Larousselle—but he's not the only pebble on her beach!"

"Liar!"

Raymond was brought up with a shock. "Oh, look here . . ." he muttered. A suspicion had dawned in his mind, only to die out again almost at once, or rather to withdraw from his immediate consciousness. Exasperating his father might be, but he found it no more possible than did Maria to connect the idea of love with the rather neutral image of him which had been his since childhood. He has always seemed to him to be a man without passions and without sin, a man impervious to evil, incorruptible, living in a world far above the rather earthy concerns of other men. He heard the sound of his rather heavy breathing in the darkness.

The doctor made a violent effort to control his feelings. In a tone that was half-mocking and almost cheerful, he repeated:

"Yes, liar and humbug. All you want to do is to destroy my illusions. . . ."

And, since Raymond remained obstinately silent, he added:

"Go on, out with it. . . ."

"I don't know anything. . . ."

"You said just now—'I know what I know.' "

The boy replied that he had spoken without thinking. His manner was that of someone who has made up his mind to say nothing. The doctor did not press him. This son of his, so close that he could feel the warmth of his body and catch the smell he exuded as of some young and untamed animal, would never understand him.

"I shall stay out here a bit. Won't you sit down a moment, Raymond? There's a breeze getting up at last."

But his son said that he would rather go to bed. For a moment or two longer the doctor heard the sound he made as he kicked at the pine-cones, then he was alone under the dense and drooping leaves—alive to all the passionate melancholy flung heavenward by the sleeping fields. With an immense effort he rose from his seat. The light was burning in his study. 'I suppose Lucie thinks I'm still working. What a lot of time I've wasted! I'm fifty—no, fifty-three. What tittle-tattle has that Papillon boy been repeating?' He let his hands wander over the bark of a chestnut tree where he remembered that Madeleine and Raymond had once carved their initials, and suddenly, flinging his arms about the trunk, closed his eyes and laid his cheek against the smooth surface of the wood. Then he stood back, dusted the sleeves of his jacket, straightened his tie, and walked towards the house.

Sauntering between the vines, Raymond was still amusing himself by kicking a pine-cone. With his hands stuck deep in his trouser pockets, he muttered to himself: 'What a simple-minded old ass! there can't be many of his sort left!' Well, he at least would be equal to his opportunity; no one should lead *him* by the nose. He had no intention of prolonging his happiness through the dragging hours of this stifling night. The stars meant nothing to him, nor the scent of the pale acacia blooms. The assault of the summer darkness was powerless against this well-armed young male who was so sure of his strength in the splendid present, so sure of his young body, so utterly indifferent to all that it could not subdue and penetrate.

VII

WORK, the one and only opium. Each morning the doctor woke, cured of his obsession, as though what had been gnawing at his heart had been cut out by the surgeon's knife. He left the house unaccompanied (in fine weather Raymond did not use the brougham). But his mind raced ahead of him. Already, in imagination, he was at work on his experiments. His passion diminished to a dull throb which made itself felt as a threat rather than an actuality. Whether it would become more than that, would wake again into active life, depended upon him, and upon him alone. Let him but touch the sore spot, and the sudden pain would make him cry out. . . . But yesterday his pet hypothesis had been brought tumbling to the ground by one single fact—or so Robinson assured him. What a triumph for X., who had accused him before the Biological Society of using faulty methods.

One of women's curses is that they can never free themselves of the enemy who preys upon their vitals. And so it happened that while the doctor, intent on his microscope, was blissfully unaware of his own wretchedness and of the world outside the walls of his laboratory, a prisoner pent within the confines of his observations, Maria Cross, lying on a sofa behind closed shutters, could think of nothing but the moment when she would see Raymond again, of that brief flame which alone brought warmth and brightness into the dreary sequence of her days. But how disappointing the moment was when it came! Almost at once they had had to give up their plan of travelling together as far as Talence church. Maria Cross went on ahead and met him in the Park, not far from the school buildings. He was less forthcoming now than he had been on the occasion of their first exchanges, and his attitude of shy mistrust did much to convince her that he really was only a callow boy, though an occasional snigger, a sudden furtive glance, should have put her on her guard. But she clung to her darling theory of his angelic purity. With infinite precautions, as though she were dealing with an untamed and still unsullied bird, she, as it were, crept closer and closer, walking on tip-toe and holding her breath. Everything about him conspired to strengthen the outlines of that false image of him which she had constructed: the cheeks so prone to blush, the schoolboy slang, the still visible traces of childhood that hung like morning mist about the strong young body. She was terrified by what she thought she had discovered in Raymond, though it had no existence in fact. The candour of his glance set her trembling, and she felt guilty of having brought into that frank gaze a hint of trouble and unease. Nothing occurred to warn her that when they were together he wanted only to run away, the better to gloat on the thought of her and to decide what line he had better take. Should he hire a room? Papillon knew an address, but it was a bit too squalid for a woman of her type. Papillon had told him that one could get rooms by the day at the *Terminus*. He'd have to find out about that. He had already walked up and down outside the hotel without being able to summon up courage enough to make enquiries at the desk. There might be other difficulties, too, of a physical nature. Over these he brooded until he had made mountains out of molehills.

Maria Cross was playing with the idea of asking him to her house, but of this plan she had, so far, said nothing. She was resolved not to smirch, even in thought, this child of nature, this untamed bird. In the stuffiness of her drawing-room, in the drowsy heat of the garden, their love would burgeon into words, and the storm within her breast would find relief in rain. Beyond this point she would not let imagination go. The extreme of her permitted indulgence was to fancy the feel of his head pressed to her body. He would be to her as a fawn domesticated by kindness . . . she would feel the warm, soft muzzle in her hand. . . . She seemed to see before her a long, long vista of caresses. They must be fond yet chaste. She would not let herself, even in imagination, dwell upon a fiercer pilgrimage of love, upon that ultimate bliss of tangled forest undergrowth into which they might plunge and be lost to all the world. . . . No, no—passion must never be allowed to sweep them to such extremes! Not for all the world would she destroy the childish innocence which filled her with such feai, such adoration. How convey, without startling him into flight, that this very week he might take advantage of Monsieur Larousselle's absence on business in Belgium and venture into the stuffy and encumbered intimacies of her drawing-room? Surely, if she put such a thought into words, he would at once suspect some evil intention? What she did not know was that he took his pleasure of her with far greater satisfaction to himself when they were not together, that she was with him in fancy wherever he went, or that he possessed her, turned from her and possessed her, again and again, like a famished puppy.

At dinner the doctor kept his eyes upon him. He watched him greedily lapping up his soup, and saw, not his son, but a man who had said, speaking of Maria Cross, "I know what I know. . . ." What could that Papillon possibly have told him? It was no use deceiving himself. Quite obviously, someone of whom he knew nothing was monopolizing Maria's thoughts.' I go on expecting her to write, when it should be perfectly clear that she doesn't want to see me ever again. And if that is true, it means, further, that she has given herself to another . . . but to whom? Impossible to sound the boy any more than I have done. If I insist on his telling me what he knows I shall merely be betraying myself.' At that point in his ruminations his son got up and left the room, without deigning to answer his mother, who called after him: "Where are you off to?"

"He goes into Bordeaux almost every evening now," she said. "I know that he gets the key of the gate from the gardener, and comes in at two a.m. by the scullery window. You ought to hear what he says when I question him. It's for *you* to do something about it, but you're so weak!"

The doctor could only stammer: "The wisest thing is to keep our eyes shut."

He heard Basque's voice: "If he was *my* son I'd bring him to heel soon enough. . . ."

The doctor got up from the table in his turn and went into the garden. He would have liked to cry aloud: "My torment is the only thing that has any reality for me!" No one realizes that it is a father's passions, more often than not, that alienate him from his son. He returned to the house, sat down at his work-table, opened a drawer, took out a packet of letters, and settled down to re-read what Maria had written to him six months earlier:

> "Only the desire to become a better woman reconciles me to the necessity of living. . . . I care little that the world should know of my salvation, or that others should continue to point at me the finger of scorn. . . . Humbly I accept their censure."

He no longer remembered that, when he had read those words for the first time, such extravagance of virtue had filled him with despair, that the obligation to walk with her in so rarefied an air had been his martyrdom, that it was maddening to think that he was expected to show the way of salvation to the one woman with whom he would so gladly have gone to perdition. He thought how, reading this letter, Raymond would laugh; grew indignant at the fancy, and voiced a protest in a half whisper as though someone were walking at his side. "Bogus, you say? . . . bogus? . . . The trouble is that whenever she gets a pen in her hand she becomes too 'literary.' . . . But was that humility of tenderness when she sat by her dying child bogus, that acquiescence of hers in suffering, as though the mysterious heritage of faith had come down to her through all her mother's tedious rehash of Kantian principles? In the presence of that small bed beneath its load of lilies" (how isolated and alone the body of the dead child had looked, how silently it had seemed to be accusing her!) "she gave expression to her sense of guilt, beating her breast and groaning aloud that all was for the best, finding consolation in the thought that he had been too young to feel ashamed of her. . . ." But here the man of science intervened: 'The truth is rather more complicated. She *was* sincere in her grief, but, all the same, she got a certain amount of satisfaction out of her heroics—they gave her the excuse to strike an attitude.' Maria Cross had always had an appetite for situations of high romance. Hadn't she even gone so far as to play with the idea of having an interview with Madame Larousselle on her death-bed? It was only with the utmost difficulty that he had made her realize that scenes of that kind never "come off" except on the stage. She had given up the plan, but only on condition that he should undertake to plead her cause with the wife. Luckily, he had been able to assure her that she had been forgiven.

He went to the window, and, leaning out in the half-darkness, occupied his mind with analysing the various night sounds—a continuous scraping of crickets and grasshoppers, the croaking of two frogs in a pond, the intermittent notes of a bird that probably wasn't a nightingale, the clanging of the last tram. "I know what I know," Raymond had said. Who could it be that had caught Maria's fancy? The doctor pronounced one or two names, but at once rejected them. She had a horror of those particular men. But of whom *hadn't* she a horror? 'Remember what Larousselle told you in confidence that time he came to have his blood-pressure tested—"Quite between outselves, she doesn't really enjoy—you know what I mean. She puts up with it from me because, well, with me it's rather different. . . . It really was screamingly funny the first time I asked all these chaps to the house. They fluttered round her like moths. When a man introduces one to his mistress, one's first thought, isn't it? is whether one can cut him out. . . . Go ahead, my fine fellows, said I to myself . . . and, of course, nothing happened. They were all quite quietly kept in their place. No one knows less about love than Maria, and takes so little pleasure in it—and I'm speaking about what I know. She's as innocent as you make 'em, doctor, a great deal more innocent than most of the fine respectable ladies who turn up their noses at her." ' He had said, too: "It is because Maria is so completely unlike other women that I'm always terrified lest, some time when I'm not there, she may make some absurd decision. She spends her whole day in a sort of dream, and only leaves the house to go to the cemetery. D'you think it possible that she has been influenced by something she has read?"

'It may be something she's read,' thought the doctor: 'but, no; if it were I should have heard about it: books are my line of country. A book sometimes turns a *man's* life upside down, or so one's told, but does the same hold true of women? It's only life that really and truly affects them deeply, things of flesh and blood. A book?'—he shook his head. The word book brought "buck" to his mind, and he had a sudden vision of some wild young animal rearing at Maria's approach.

Some cats in the grass set up a prolonged miaowing. A footstep sounded on the gravel: there was the noise as of a window being opened. It must be Raymond coming back. A moment later the doctor heard someone in the corridor. There was a knock at his door. It was Madeleine.

"Not in bed yet, Papa? I'm worried about Catherine. She suddenly started a nasty hacking cough. I was afraid it might be croup."

"Croup doesn't come on suddenly like that. I'll be along in a moment."

Some time later, as he was coming out of his daughter's room, he felt a pain in his left side, and stood leaning against the wall in the darkness, clutching at his heart. He did not call for help. His brain was perfectly clear, and he could catch from behind the door the sounds of a conversation that had just started between husband and wife.

"I know all about his being a good scientist, but science has made him sceptical. He no longer believes in medicines. But how can illness be cured without them?"

"He assured us it was nothing, not even a false-croup."

"Don't kid yourself: if it had been one of his own patients he'd have prescribed something, but because it's one of the family he's not going to spend an unnecessary penny. There are times when it's an awful nuisance not being able to call in an outside man."

"But it's very convenient having him always on the spot, especially at night. When the poor old thing's no longer there, I shall never know what it is to sleep in peace, worrying about the children."

"You ought to have married a doctor, that's what *you* ought to have done!"

There was a sound of a laugh being quickly silenced by a kiss. The doctor felt the hand that was squeezing his heart loosen its grip. Very quietly he stole away. He turned in, found that he could not lie at full length without pain, and spent the night sitting upright on his bed. The whole world was asleep. The only sound was the fluttering of the leaves. 'Has Maria ever known what it is to love? I know she's had crazes for people—for instance, there was that little Gaby Dubois girl, she tried to make her break with young Dupont-Gunther, but that was a romantic passion. She must have had some apostolic ancestor from whom she inherits that taste of hers for saving souls. Who was it, by the way, who told me a lot of beastly things about her, in connexion with this same Gaby? . . . Can she be "one of them"? I remember other crazes of the same kind. . . . There may be a touch of it in her case. I've always noticed that an excess of romanticism . . . Dawn already!'

He lowered his pillow, and with many precautions lay down in such a way that his wretched carcase suffered no hurt. In a few moments he had lost consciousness.

VIII

"BUT what am I going to say to the gardener?"

In one of the deserted paths of the Parc Bordelais Maria Cross was trying to persuade Raymond to pay her a visit at home. In her own house there would be no risk of their meeting people. She urged him to agree, and felt ashamed of doing so, felt that, in spite of herself, she was corrupting him. How was it possible not to see in the unreasoning terror of a boy who had once walked up and down in front of a shop because he didn't dare go in, the indisputable evidence of frightened innocence? With that thought in her mind she hastened to say:

"But, Raymond, you mustn't think I want . . . you mustn't start imagining. . . ."

"It'll be so awkward if I run into the gardener."

"But there *isn't* a gardener: I've told you so already. I'm living in an empty house which Monsieur Larousselle had not succeeded in letting. He has installed me there as caretaker."

Raymond burst into a guffaw of laughter:

"A lady gardener, eh?"

The young woman looked down so that he should not see her face, and stammered out:

"I *know* appearances are against me. After all, people can't be expected to know that I accepted the situation in perfect good faith. . . . François had to have country air. . . ."

Raymond was familiar with this particular refrain. 'Talk away,' he said to himself, and broke in with:

"So I needn't worry about the gardener, but what about the servants?"

She reassured him on that point too. On Sundays she always let Justine, her only maid, go out. She was a married woman whose husband, a chauffeur, slept in the house so as to ensure there being a man about the place, which was none too well protected. The suburban road was not very safe. But on Sunday afternoons Justine and he always went out together. Raymond would merely have to enter by the front door and go through the dining-room on the left. He would find the drawing-room at the far end.

He dug his heel into the gravel with a thoughtful air. The creaking of a swing could be heard coming from behind a privet-hedge. An old woman was hawking stale cakes and bars of chocolate done up in yellow paper. Remarking that he had had no lunch, he bought a crescent and a chocolate praliné. As she watched him munching his meagre meal, Maria suddenly saw with perfect clarity the inexorable nature of her destiny. The desire that had come to birth in her heart had been pure and limpid, yet her every action had the appearance of a monstrous depravity. When, in the tram, her eyes had first found rest and refreshment in the young face opposite, there had been no trace of evil intention in her mind. Why should she have fought against a temptation that was so little suspect? A thirsty traveller has no reason to beware of the stream he happens on. 'I *do* want him to come to my house, but only because in the streets, on the bench of a public garden, I shall never succeed in probing his secret self. . . . But that doesn't alter the fact that, so far as appearances go, here is a young kept woman of twenty-seven luring a young boy into her web—the son of the only man who has ever believed in me and has never cast a stone. . . .' A little later, after they had parted, and just before reaching the Croix de Saint-Genès, her thoughts returned to the subject: 'I want him to come, but with no evil design, not the least in the world. The very idea of such a thing makes me feel sick. But he doesn't trust me, and why should he? Everything I do is double-faced: to me it looks innocent enough, but to the world, hateful, abominable. Perhaps the world sees more truly than I do. . . .' She spoke first one name, then another. If it were true that she was held in contempt for actions in which she had become unintentionally involved, she could remember others that she had done in secret, others of which no one knew but herself.

She pushed open the gate which, next Sunday, Raymond would unlatch for the first time, and walked up the drive which was overgrown with grass (there was no gardener). So heavily did the sky seem to sag that it was hard to believe the over-arching cloud would not burst with its own weight—it was as though the heavens had caught discouragement from a thirsty world. The leaves hung blighted from the trees. The maid had not closed the shutters, and great bluebottles were bumping against the bottom of the window frames. She had only just energy enough to throw her hat on to the piano. Her shoes left dirty marks on the sofa. There was only one thing possible to do —light a cigarette. But she was aware, too, of something no less habitual, the physical apathy that accompanied the activity of her imagination, no matter how wrought-up that might be. What an endless number of afternoons she had wasted. lying just here, feeling slightly sick as the result of over-smoking! How many plans of escape, of self-betterment, she had elaborated, only to see them fall in ruins! To bring them to fruition she would have had, first, to stop lying there supine, to do something positive, to see people. 'But even if I abandon all attempt to improve the external conditions of my life, I can at least refuse to do anything of which my conscience would disapprove, which might cause it to feel uneasy. Take, for instance, this case of young Courrèges. . . .' She had quite decided that if she were about to lure him into her house it was only because she wanted to indulge that sweet and harmless sentiment which had come to her, originally, in the six o'clock tram; that sense of comfort in another's presence, that melancholy pleasure of quite quietly letting her eyes take their fill—though here, in this room, she would taste it more intimately than had been possible in the tram, and at greater leisure. But was that really all? When the presence of another person thrills us emotionally, our imagination leaps ahead, though we may not always realize it, opening up vistas the very vagueness of which has something about them that is not wholly innocent: 'Very soon I should have grown tired merely of looking at him had it not been that I felt convinced that he would respond to my handling, that, sooner or later, we should speak to one another. . . . This room, so far as I can foresee, will witness nothing but motherly caresses and unimpassioned kisses, will hear nothing but spoken confidences. . . . Oh, come now, be honest with yourself! Admit that you *are* aware of the existence, beyond such innocuous happiness, of a whole region of the emotions, forbidden, it is true, yet open to exploration. There will be no barrier to break down. The field of action will lie open before you. You have only to work your way cautiously forward, to lose yourself in the misty distance as though by accident. . . . And afterwards? Who is there to forbid you the enjoyment of this delight? . . . Don't you know that you could make the boy happy? . . . Ah, that's where you begin to be the dupe of your own appetites. . . . He is the son of Dr. Courrèges, of the saintly Dr. Courrèges. . . . *He* wouldn't admit that the case was even open to argument. You once told him jokingly that the moral law within him was as bright and shining as the starry sky above his head. . . .'

She could hear the raindrops on the leaves, the tentative rumble of the storm. She closed her eyes, tried to fix her thoughts, concentrated her mind on the beloved face of the young boy whose innocence was wholly unsmirched (or that was what she wanted to believe), the boy who, at that very moment, was hurrying along in an attempt to outstrip the coming storm, and thinking: 'Papillon says it's always best to take the bull by the horns. With women of that kind, he says, brutality's the only thing that counts, the only thing they really like. . . .' With his thoughts in turmoil he looked up at the growling heavens. Suddenly he began to run, his cape flung over his head, took a short cut and jumped over a patch of shrubbery as nimbly as a buck. The storm was moving away, but it was still there. The very silence betrayed its presence. Maria had a sudden inspiration which she felt certain could not be misunderstood. She got up, sat down at her desk, and wrote:

> "Don't come Sunday—or any other day. It is for your sake, and for your sake only, that I agree to this sacrifice. . . ."

She should have left it at that, and just signed her name. But some devillish counsellor persuaded her to add a whole page more:

> ". . . You will have been the one and only happiness of a tormented and hopeless life. As we travelled home together all through this last winter, the sight of you brought me peace, though you did not know it. But the face that was your gift to me was but the outward and visible sign of a soul which I longed to possess. I wanted there to be nothing about you that I did not know. I wanted to provide the answer to your uncertainties, to smooth the path before your feet, to become for you someone who would be more than a mother, better than a friend. I lived in my dream of that. But it is not in my power to be other than I am. In spite of yourself, in spite of me, you would breathe the corruption with which the world has choked me."

On and on she wrote. The rain had settled in for good, and the only sound to be heard was that of falling water. The windows of all the rooms were shut. Hail-stones rattled in the hearth. Maria Cross took up a book, but it was too dark to read, and, because of the storm, the electricity was not working. She sat down at the piano, and leaned forward as she played. It was as though her head were drawn by some attraction to her hands.

The next day, which was Friday, she felt vaguely pleased that the storm had broken the spell of heat, and spent the whole day in a dressing-gown, reading, making music, idling. She tried to recall every word of her letter, to imagine the effect it would have on young Courrèges. On Saturday, after a close and heavy morning, the rain began again. She realized then the reason for her pleasure. The bad weather would prevent her from going out on Sunday, as she had meant to do, so that should the boy after all, keep their appointment in spite of her letter, she would be there to receive him. Stepping back from the window through which she had been watching the rain splashing on the garden path, she said aloud in a firm, strong voice as though she were taking a solemn oath: "Whatever the weather, I shall go out."

But where should she go? Had François been alive she would have taken him to the circus. It was her habit, sometimes, to go to a concert, where she would sit alone in a private box, or—and this she preferred—would take a seat in a public one. But on these occasions the audience always quickly recognized her. She could guess, from the movement of their lips, that people were talking about her. Levelled opera-glasses delivered her up, at close range and utterly defenceless, to a world of enemies. A voice would say: "When all's said, women like that *do* know how to dress—but then, of course, with all that money it's not difficult; besides, they've nothing to think about *except* their bodies." Occasionally one of Monsieur Larousselle's friends would leave the Club Box and pay her a visit. Half turned towards the audience he would laugh loudly, proud of being seen in conversation with Maria Cross.

Except for the Saint-Cecilia concert she had, even during François's life-time, given up going anywhere. This change in her habits had occurred after several women had insulted her at a music hall. The mistresses of all these various men hated her because she had never shown herself willing to be on terms of familiarity with them. The only one of them who, for a short while, had found favour in her eyes was Gaby Dubois. The girl, she had decided, on the strength of a brief exchange of talk one evening at the *Lion Rouge*, whither Larousselle had dragged her, was a "sweet creature." The champagne had had a good deal to do with Gaby's spiritual effervescence on that occasion. For a whole fortnight the two had met daily. With dogged determination Maria Cross had vainly tried to break the links that bound her new friend to her various other acquaintances. Then they had begun to see less and less of one another, and a little while later, during a matinée at the *Apollo* into which Maria had drifted from sheer boredom, alone as usual, and, as usual, drawing all eyes, she had heard, coming from a row of stalls just beneath the box where she was sitting, Gaby's shrill laughter. Other laughs had mingled with it, and odds and ends of insulting comment had reached her ears, though the voices had been kept low. "That tart who gives herself the airs of an Empress . . . —— who's always putting on a virtue act. . . ." It had seemed to Maria that all the faces in the theatre were turned towards her—and the faces were the faces of wild beasts. Then the lights had gone down, all eyes had been riveted on a nude dancer, and she had slipped away.

After that she would never leave the house without her little boy François. And now, even though a year had passed since he had vanished, it was still he alone who could tempt her out, or rather, that grave-stone, no longer than a child's body, though to reach it she had to walk along the special avenue in the cemetery marked "Adults." But Fate had ordained that on the way leading to the dead boy another, living boy, should cross her path.

On Sunday morning there was a great wind—not one of those winds that serves to dandle the piled clouds, but a roarer from the south with the smell of the sea, and driving before it a sweep of muffled sky. The note of a solitary tit only emphasized the silence of a million other birds. There could be no question of going out in such weather, which was a nuisance: but by this time young Courrèges would have had her letter. Aware of the extent of his shyness, she felt sure that he would obey her injunction. Even had she not written he would probably never have dared to cross her threshold. She smiled to herself as she conjured up a vision of him digging his heel into the gravel of the drive, and saying to himself, with that mulish expression which she knew so well: "What about the gardener?" While she ate her solitary luncheon she could hear the storm raging round the house. The flying horses of the wind galloped madly on, and now, their task accomplished, were whinnying and snorting among the trees. No doubt from the cloven turmoil of the deep Atlantic they had brought flights of gulls seeking the sanctuary of the river, and kittywakes that hold the air and do not settle. A livid colouring of seaweed seemed to tint the clouds of this suburban sky, a salty scud to splash the inland foliage. Leaning from her window that gave upon the garden, Maria had the taste of it upon her lips. No, he would not come: how should he in such weather, even if she had not sent her letter? Had she not been sure of that she would have known an agony of apprehension lest he might suddenly appear. Far, far better to feel that she was safe, to know for certain that he would not come. And yet, had expectation been wholly absent, why should she open the sideboard cupboard just to make sure that there was some port left?

At last the rain began to fall in a solid curtain shot with vagrant sunlight. She opened a book, but her eyes would not take in the sense of what she read. Patiently she went back to the top of the page, but in vain. Then, seated at the piano, she began to play, but not so loudly that she could not hear the sound made by the opening of the front door. She was overcome by dizziness, and just had time to say to herself: 'It's the wind, it must be the wind,' and, a moment later, though the shuffle of hesitating footsteps reached her from the dining-room—'It's just the wind.' She had not strength enough to get up from her chair. He was already in the room, awkward, embarrassed, not knowing what to do with his streaming hat. He did not dare to take a step forward, nor did she call to him, so powerless was she in the tumult of a passion that had burst its banks and was sweeping all before it, vengeful and frantic. In a moment it engulfed her, leaving no inch of body or soul unfilled, topping the peaks, drowning the roots, of her being. Nevertheless, when she did at last manage to speak, her expression was stern, her words no more than ordinary.

"Didn't you get my letter?"

He stood there dumbfounded. ("She wants to lead you up the garden," Papillon had said. "Don't let her put you where she wants you. Just stroll in on her with your hands in your pockets.") But, faced by what he took to be her anger, he hung his head like a schoolboy in disgrace. And she, tense and trembling with emotion, as though what she had caught in this stuffy trap of her over-furnished interior was a frightened fawn, could venture on no movement. He had come, though she had done everything in her power to keep him away. Therefore no remorse could poison this, her happiness. She could surrender to it wholly. To that destiny which had precipitated the boy into this room as food for her hunger, she swore that she would be worthy of the gift. Of what had she been afraid? There was nothing in her mind at this moment but love at its noblest. If that truth needed to be proved, proof lay in the tears which she checked, thinking of François. In a very few years he would have grown to be just such a boy as this. . . . She could not know that

Raymond had interpreted the face she made in her effort not to cry as a sign of ill-humour, perhaps of anger.

She said: "After all, why not? You did well to come. Put your hat down on one of the chairs. It doesn't matter if it's damp; it's not the first wet hat their Genoa velvet has seen. . . . I'm sure you'd like a glass of port now, wouldn't you? Yes, or course you would."

While he was drinking she went on:

"Why did I write that letter? Honestly, I don't know. . . . Women do funny things . . . and then, of course, I knew you'd come in any case."

Raymond wiped his lips with the back of his hand.

"All the same, I jolly nearly didn't come. I said to myself—she'll probably be out, and I shall look an awful fool."

"I hardly ever go out—since I've been in mourning. I've never talked to you about my little François, have I?"

François had come tip-toeing as though he were in very truth alive. Just so might his mother have kept him by her to break a dangerous tête-à-tête. But Raymond saw no more in her words than a trick designed to make him keep his distance, though Maria's only thought was to put him at his ease. Far from fearing him, she thought that she was an object of fear. Besides, this intrusion of the dead child was not of her contriving. The little boy had forced his presence on them. He had come as children do, when, hearing their mother's voice in the drawing-room, they enter without knocking. 'The mere fact that he is there proves, you poor dear, the purity of your intentions. What's worrying you? François is standing by your chair, not blushing but smiling.'

"It's rather more than a year since he died, isn't it? I very well remember the day of the funeral. Mother made a scene . . ."

He broke off. He would have unsaid the words if he could have done so.

"A scene, why? Ah, yes, I understand. Even on that day there was no pity in people's hearts."

She rose, fetched an album, and laid it on Raymond's knees.

"I should like to show you his photographs. No one but your father has seen them. That's him at a month old, in my husband's arms. When they're as young as that they look like nothing on earth—except to their mothers. Look at this one, with a ball in his arms—laughing. That was taken when he was two. *This* was when we were at Salies. He was already ailing. I had to sell out some of my tiny capital to pay for our trip. But the doctor there was kindness and generosity itself. He was called Casamajor . . . that's him, holding the donkey's bridle. . . ."

As she leaned over Raymond to turn the pages, she was quite innocently pouring oil on the flames, stoking the blaze. Her breath fanned the fire within him. She could not see the look of fury on his face. There he sat, the heavy album weighing down his knees. He was breathing heavily and trembling with frustrated violence.

"Here he is at six and a half, just two months before he died. He looks much better, doesn't he? But I can't help wondering whether I didn't make him work too hard. When he was six he read everything that came his way, even books he couldn't understand. Living as he did, all the time with grown-ups."

"You see," she said, "he was my companion, my friend"—because, at this moment, she could make no distinction between what François had been for her in actuality and what she had hoped he might become.

"Even then he used to ask me questions. What nights of torment I went through thinking that one day I should have to explain. The only thing that consoles me now is the realization that he went without knowing . . . that he never knew . . . that now he never will know. . . ."

She was standing upright, her arms hanging at her side. Raymond dared not raise his eyes, but he could hear the rustling of her movements. Struck though he was by her words, he had an uneasy suspicion that her grief was not altogether genuine. Later, when he was walking home, he said to himself: 'She was playing a game, and taking herself in with it. . . . She was running the dead-child business for all it was worth. Still, there's no getting away from it, she *was* crying.' He was shaken in the idea he had formed of her. In his youth and inexperience he had painted for himself a picture of "bad women" that was entirely theological in character and modelled on what his masters had told him, convinced though he was that he had successfully resisted their influence. Maria Cross hemmed him in like an army ordered for battle. On her ankles tinkled the bangles of Delilah and of Judith. There was no treachery, no trickery that he would have put beyond one whose glance the saints had dreaded like the glance of death.

Maria Cross said to him: "Come and see me whenever you like: I am always here." With tears in her eyes and peace in her heart, she went with him to the door, without even fixing another day for their next meeting. When he had gone, she sat down by François's bed, carrying her sorrow like a sleeping child in her arms. The tranquillity she felt may have been the result of disappointment. She did not know that she would not always be safe. The dead cannot help the living. In vain do we invoke them from the edge of the abyss. Their silence, their absence, seems to take sides against us.

IX

IT would have been far better for Maria Cross if this, Raymond's first visit, had not left her with an impression of security and innocence. She was amazed that everything had gone so smoothly. 'I worked myself up unnecessarily,' she thought. She believed her predominant feeling to be one of relief, but already she felt unhappy in the knowledge that she had let Raymond go without arranging for another meeting.

She was careful now never to go out at the times he might be likely to come. So simple is the squalid game of passion that a youth can master it on his very first adventuring into love. It needed no worldly-wise counsellor to persuade this one to "let her cook in her own juice."

After waiting for four days, she was in a fit state to lay all the blame for his silence on herself. 'I talked to him about nothing but my own troubles, and about François. It must have been terribly depressing for him. What possible interest could he take in my album? I ought to have asked him about his life. . . . I ought to have laid myself out to win his confidence. . . . He is bored with me . . . thinks me just a tedious woman. . . . What if he never comes back?'

What if he never came back? To such an extent did she worry over the possibility, that it was well on the way to becoming a torment. 'I may wait as long as I like, he won't come. I have lost my hold on him. He's at the age when young men don't suffer bores gladly. Better face it, the whole thing is over and done with. . . .' The evidence was too shattering, too terrible. He would never come back. Maria Cross had filled up the last well to be found in her desert. Nothing now but sand. The most dangerous of all things in love is the flight of one of the parties to the plot. The presence of the adored is, more often than not, an obstacle to passion. When she was with Raymond Courrèges she saw, in the first place, a young creature whose innocent heart it would be a crime to disturb. She remembered whose son he was. The last traces of childhood in his face reminded her of her own lost boy. Even in thought she could not draw near that young body save with a sense of ardent modesty. But now that he was no longer there, now that she feared she might never see him again, of what use was it any longer to mistrust the muddied waters of her heart, the dark confusion of her feelings? Now that this fruit was to be dashed from her thirsty lips, why deprive herself of the satisfaction of imagining the flavour she would never know in fact? Whom would she wrong by so doing? What reproach need she fear at sight of the headstone on which the name of François was engraved? Who was there to see her shut away in this house, without a husband, without a child, without servants? Madame Courrèges's endless lamentations about the quarrels of her domestic staff might be trivial enough, but how glad would Maria Cross have been to occupy her mind with such things? Where was there for her to go? Beyond the drowsing garden stretched the suburban roads, and further still the stone-built city where, when a storm bursts, one knows for certain that nine days of stifling heat will follow. A fierce and torpid beast seems to prowl, to growl, to crouch in a sky drained of all colour. She too, pacing like a beast the garden or the empty rooms, yielded (how else could her misery find an issue?) little by little to the fascination of a hopeless love, a love that could offer nothing but the wretched happiness of a self-consuming anguish. She gave up all attempt to put out the fire, no longer suffered from aimlessness and lassitude, since she had no thoughts now for anything but the blaze. A nameless devil whispered in her ear: "You may be dying, but at least you are not bored!"

What is strange about a storm is not its tumult but the silence, the torpor which it imposes upon the world. Maria could see the leaves lying motionless against the panes of the window, almost as though painted on them. There was something human about the drooping melancholy of the trees. It was as though they were conscious of their lifelessness, their numbed and sleeping state. Her mood was one in which passion takes on the semblance of a physical presence. She scratched at the sore place in her soul: she kept the fire in her heart alive. Her love was becoming a choking contraction which, had she so wished, she could have localized in her throat, in her chest. A mere letter from Monsieur Larousselle had the power to make her shudder with disgust. As to the idea of his making approaches to her, *that* from now on would be no longer possible for her to endure. He would not be back for another fortnight—time enough in which to die. She gorged her imagination on thoughts of Raymond, on certain memories that formerly would have overwhelmed her with a sense of shame. 'I looked at the leather lining of his hat, where it presses against his forehead . . . seeking in it the very smell of his hair. . . .' She yearned for his face, for his neck, for his hands, for all and each of them had become the incomparable signs and symbols of a secret reality which was filled to overflowing with delight. . . . How inconceivable was this new tranquillity at the heart of her despair. Sometimes the thought came to her that so long as he was alive nothing was lost; that maybe he would return. But as though there were something terrifying in the hope which such dreaming implied, she hastened to immure herself once more in an absolute renunciation, in the peace of mind that refuses to expect. There was for her a horrible pleasure in digging still deeper the gulf which separated her from the being whom she forced herself to see as pure. The inaccessible youth blazed in her firmament bright as the hunter Orion, and no less remote from her passion. 'I am already a woman burned up by life, a woman lost, while he has about him still the magic of childhood. His purity has set great spaces of sky between us, across which my longing refuses even to blaze a trail.'

All through these days winds from the west and south drew after them great tumbled ranks of cloud, legions of grumbling vapour which, just as they were about to burst in a torrential downpour, suddenly hesitated, turned round about the charmed and toppling peaks of æther, and disappeared, leaving behind them that sudden sense of freshness which comes when somewhere rain has fallen.

In the night hours between Friday and Saturday the rain at last set in with an unbroken sound of murmuring waters. Thanks to the chloral that she had taken, Maria, at peace with all the world, breathed in the scented air which, through the blinds, the garden wafted to her tumbled bed. Then she fell into a dreamless sleep.

Lying there relaxed under the early morning sun, she thought with amazement of all the suffering she had been through. She must have been mad. Why had she seen everything in such gloomy colours? The boy was alive: he was merely waiting for a sign from her. The crisis past, she felt once more clear-headed, balanced, perhaps even slightly disappointed. 'Is that all it was?' she thought. 'He'll come, and just to make doubly sure, I'll write. . . . I'm going to see him again.' At all costs she must confront her misery and the youth that caused it. She forced herself to contemplate in memory only a simple, inoffensive child, and was surprised to find that she no longer trembled at the thought of his head upon her knees. 'I'll write to the doctor telling him that I have made the acquaintance of his son' (but she knew that she would not). 'Why shouldn't I? What harm are we doing?' In the afternoon she went into the garden with its waste of puddles. She felt really at peace, too wholly at peace, so much at peace that she was vaguely frightened. The less she felt her passion, the more she felt the threat of nothingness. Reduced in stature, her love no longer obliterated her inner emptiness. Already she was regretting that her round of the garden had lasted only a bare five minutes, and made the circuit once again, following the same paths. Then she hurried back because the grass had made her feet wet. . . . She would change into slippers, would lie down, smoke, read . . . but what? She had no book on hand that really interested her. As she approached the house she raised her eyes to the windows, and there, behind the drawing-room panes, saw Raymond. He was pressing his face to the glass, amusing himself by squashing his nose flat. Was this rising tide of feeling in her, joy? She walked up the front steps, thinking of the feet that, but a moment before, had pressed them. She pushed open the door, her eyes fixed on the latch because of the hand that had rested on it, crossed the dining-room at a slower pace, composed her features.

It was Raymond's misfortune that he should have come immediately after the long train of days during which she had dreamed so exclusively of him, and suffered so much on his account. Seeing him there in the flesh, she could not fill the void between the endless agitation of her heart and the being who had caused it. She did not know that she was disappointed. That she was, her first remark soon proved:

"Have you just been to the barber?" She had never seen him look like this before, with his hair cut far too short, and shining. She touched the faint scar left above his temple by some blow.

"I got that falling off a swing when I was eight."

She looked at him, trying to bring into focus her desire, her pain, her hunger, her renunciation, and this long, lean youth who looked so like an overgrown puppy. A thousand feelings, all to do with him, surged up within her, and those of them she could retain grouped themselves, for good or ill, about the taut, congested face. But she failed to recognize the peculiar expression in his eyes that betokened the blind fury of the timid man who has decided to try his luck, of the coward who has screwed himself to the sticking-point. Never to her had he looked so much like a child, and she said with an air of kindly authority what, so often, in the old days, she had said to François:

"Are you thirsty? I'll give you some red-currant syrup in a moment: but you must cool down first."

She directed him to an armchair, but he chose to sit on the sofa where she had already lain down. He protested that he wasn't a bit thirsty:

". . . and if I were, it wouldn't be for syrup."

Her legs were rather too much exposed, and she pulled down her skirt. The action provoked a compliment:

"What a pity!"

She changed her position and sat down beside him. He asked her why:

"It couldn't be that you're afraid?"

His words made Maria realize that that was precisely what she was. But afraid of what? This was Raymond Courrèges, young Courrèges, the doctor's son.

"How is your dear father?"

He shrugged his shoulders and stuck out his lower lip. She offered him a cigarette which he refused, lit one herself, and leaned forward, her elbows on her knees:

"You told me once before that you aren't on very intimate terms with your father. That's natural enough. . . . Relations between parents and children are never easy. . . . When François used to hide his face against my knees, I always thought to myself—make the most of it, it won't always be like this."

She had misinterpreted the movement of his shoulders, the pouting of his lips. Just now he wanted to push the memory of his father into the background—not from any feeling of indifference, but, on the contrary, because the thought of the elder man had become an obsession with him since something odd that had happened two evenings before. After dinner the doctor had joined him on the path that ran between the vines, where he was smoking a solitary cigarette, and had walked beside him in silence, like a man who has something to say but does not say it. 'What's he after?' Raymond had wondered, indulging to the full the cruel pleasure of silence—that same pleasure which he gave himself on early autumn mornings in the carriage, with the rain streaming down the windows. Mechanically, he had quickened his pace, because he saw that his father had difficulty in keeping up with him, and was lagging a little behind. Realizing suddenly that he could no longer hear the sound of his breathing, he had turned his head. He could see the vague outline of the doctor standing there motionless on the path between the vine shoots. His two hands were clutching at his chest, and he was swaying on his feet like a drunken man. He took a few paces forward, and then sat down heavily between two of the rows. Raymond dropped to his knees and raised the seemingly dead face to rest on his shoulder. Only a few inches separated them. He had looked at the closed eyes, at the cheeks that had taken on the colour of dough.

'What's the matter, Papa, Papa, *dear?*"

The sound of his voice, at once beseeching and authoritative, roused the sick man as though it possessed some peculiar virtue. He tried to smile, but looked bewildered, and his words, when they came, were breathless.

"It's nothing. . . . I shall be all right. . . ."

He fixed his eyes on his son's worried face, heard in his voice the same note of tenderness that it had had when he was a boy of eight.

"Rest your head against me: haven't you got a clean handkerchief? Mine's dirty."

Very gently Raymond wiped the face in which, now, there were signs of returning life. The eyes were open, gazing at the boy's hair which the wind was lightly fluttering. Behind him was the dense foliage of a vine plant, and, further still, a yellowish sky full of growls and grumblings. It sounded as though it were emptying cartloads of stones. Leaning on his son's arm, the doctor returned to the house. The warm rain splashed their shoulders and their cheeks, but it was impossible to walk any faster. He had said to Raymond:

"It's this false angina—just as painful as the real thing. I'm suffering from a form of auto-intoxication. . . . I'll stay in bed for forty-eight hours on a diet of water . . . and remember, not a word about this to your granny or your mother."

But Raymond broke in on him with words of his own:

"You're not kidding me? You're *sure* it's nothing? Swear to me that it's nothing."

In a low voice, the doctor said:

"Would you mind so much, then, if I . . ."

But Raymond would not let him finish. He put his arm about the body that was shaking with its gasping efforts to draw breath, and his protest came in a sudden cry:

"What an old *idiot* you are!"

The doctor was to remember later the sweet insolence of the words, to remember it in the bad times when once again his child had turned into a stranger and an enemy . . . into someone whose heart was deaf to all appeals, who was incapable of responding. . . .

They went together into the drawing-room, but the father dared not venture an embrace.

"Let's talk about something else: I didn't come here to chat about Papa . . . we've got better things to do than that . . . haven't we?"

He thrust forward a large and awkward paw, but she caught hold it of before it had attained its goal, restraining it with gentle insistence.

"No, Raymond, no. You live too close to him really to understand. Those closest to us are always the ones we know least about. . . . We reach a point at which we can't even see what lies beneath our eyes. Do you know, my relations always thought of me as ugly, because when I was a child I had a slight squint. I was amazed, when I went to school, to find that the other girls regarded me as pretty."

"That's right, tell me nice little stories about when you were at school!"

His fixed obsession made him look prematurely old. Maria dared not let go of the great hand. She could feel it growing damp, and a feeling that was almost disgust took hold of her. This was the same hand whose touch, ten minutes ago, had made her turn pale. There had been a time when merely to hold it in hers had compelled her to shut her eyes and turn away her head; and now, it was just a flabby, clammy object.

"I want to show you what the doctor's really like, and when I've made up my mind I can be as obstinate as a mule."

He stopped her by saying that he, too, could be obstinate.

"Look here, I swore that to-day I wouldn't be played with. . . ."

He spoke in a low voice, stumbling over his words; so low, indeed, that it was not difficult for her to pretend that she had not heard. But she increased the space between them. Then, after a moment, she got up and opened one of the windows:

"It's stifling in here—just as though it hadn't rained at all! But I can still hear the storm, unless it's gunfire from Saint-Médard."

She pointed to where, above the trees, a dense, dark cloud showed a wind-tossed summit edged with sunlight. But he seized her forearm in both his hands and pushed her towards the sofa. She forced a laugh—"Let go!"—and the more she struggled, the more she laughed, to prove that this wrestling match was just a game, and that she regarded it as such. "Let me alone, you nasty little creature! . . ." The lines of laughter about her lips became a grimace. She stumbled against the divan, and saw, only a few inches away, the myriad drops of sweat on his low forehead, the black-heads on his nose. She could smell his sour breath. But the young faun strove to hold both her wrists in one hand so as to have the other free for what he wanted to do, and with one convulsive wriggle she freed herself. There was now between them the sofa, a table and an armchair. She was rather breathless, but again forced herself to laugh.

"So you really think, my child, that you can take a woman by force?"

He did not laugh, the young male humiliated and infuriated by defeat, touched in the most sensitive part of that pride of body which was already abnormally developed in him, so that it bled. All his life he was to remember this particular moment when a woman had found him not only repellent but grotesque. No matter how often he might be victorious in days to come, no matter how many victims he might subdue and make miserable, nothing could assuage the burning smart of this first humiliation. For many years, remembering this moment, he would bite his lips till the blood came, would tear his pillow with his teeth in the watches of the night. . . .

He fought back the tears which sheer frustrated anger had brought to his eyes—never for an instant imagining that the smile on Maria's face might be no more than a mask, never for an instant understanding that she was seeking, not to hurt an over-sensitive boy, but rather to keep herself from betraying by any sigh the sense of the disaster and the ruin in which she found herself involved. . . . If only he would go away! If only she could be left alone!

It was only such a short while ago that he had been struck with amazement to feel that the famous Maria Cross was actually within his reach. Again and again he had said to himself, 'This simple little creature is Maria Cross!' He had only to stretch out his hand, and there she would be, inert, submissive to his will. He could take her when and how he chose, let her fall and then pull her to her feet again—and now, the movement of his outspread arms had sufficed to send her dizzily spinning out of reach. She was still there in the flesh, but he knew with a sure knowledge that from now on he could no more touch her than he could have touched a star. It was then that he realized how beautiful she was. Entirely occupied in thinking how to pluck and eat the fruit, without for a moment doubting that it was meant for him, he had never really looked at her. And now, all he could do was to devour her with his eyes.

She said, gently, for fear of irritating him, but with a terrible fixity of purpose: "I want to be alone. . . . Please listen to me, Raymond . . . you *must* leave me to myself. . . ." The doctor had suffered because he felt that Maria did not want to have him with her. Raymond knew an anguish still keener—the certainty which comes to us that the beloved object can no longer pretend, no longer hide the fact that it is the imperative need of her being not to see us any more, that she has rejected us and spewed us up. We realize, then, that our absence is necessary to her life, that she is on fire to forget us. She would hustle us from the room were it not that she is afraid we might resist.

She held out his hat, opened the door, flattened herself against the wall, while he, once more the adolescent youth, filled with horror of himself, wanted only to vanish, babbled idiotic excuses, was paralysed with shame. But no sooner was he out on the road again, no sooner had the door closed behind him, than he found the words he should have thrown in the trollop's teeth. But it was too late! For years to come he was tortured by the thought that he had turned tail without so much as telling her what he thought of her.

While the boy, as he walked home, was voiding his heart of all the abuse with which he had been unable to smother Maria Cross, that young woman, having first closed the door and then the window, lay down. Somewhere beyond the trees a bird was uttering a fragmentary song that sounded like the broken mutterings of a man asleep. The suburban air echoed to the noise of trams and factory whistles. Drunken singing reached her from the Saturday streets. Yet, for all that, Maria Cross lay swaddled and stifled in silence—a silence that came not from without but from within, from the depths of her being, filling the empty room, invading the house, the garden, the city, the whole world. She lived at its airless centre, her eyes fixed on that inner flame which, though suddenly all fuel was lacking, burned inextinguishably. Whence, then, did it derive its sustenance? She was reminded how, sometimes, at the fag-end of her lonely evenings, a last flicker would sometimes start from the blackened ashes in the hearth where she had thought all life was dead. Eagerly she sought the loved face of the boy whom so often she had seen in the six o'clock tram, and could not find it. All that had reality for her was a little tousled hooligan, driven beside himself with shyness, forcing himself to overcome his own timidity—a vision as different from the real Raymond Courrèges as had ever been that idealized portrait which had given beauty to her love. Against him on whom she had bestowed the transfigured features of divinity she raged and fumed. 'Did I suffer the torments of hell and the ecstasies of heaven for a grubby little urchin like that? . . .' What she did not know was that it had been sufficient for her glance to fall upon this unformed boy for him to become a man whose dishonesties many women were to know to their cost, submitting to him as lover and as bully. If it were true that she had *created* him by virtue of her love, it was no less true that by scorning him she had added the last finishing touch to her work. She had let loose upon the world a young man whose mania it would be to prove to himself that he was irresistible, even though a Maria Cross had successfully resisted him. From now on, in all the amorous intrigues of his future, there would always be an element of unexpressed antagonism, a longing to wound, to extract a cry of pain from the female lying helpless at his mercy. He was to cause many tears to flow on many nameless faces, and always they would be *her* tears. Doubtless he had been born with the instincts of a beast of prey, but, had it not been for Maria Cross, their violence might have been softened by some touch of weakness.

How fathomless her disgust for this "hooligan"! Yet, the inextinguishable flame burned on within her though there was nothing now for it to feed upon. No human being would ever have the benefit of all this light, all this warmth. Whither should she go? To the cemetery where François's body lay? No, no; far better to admit at once that the dead body of her son was nothing now to her but an alibi. She had been content in her visits to the child's grave only for the sake of the sweet homeward way which she had trodden with another, a living, child at her side. Hypocrite! What could she do, what say, before that tomb? She could but cast herself upon it as upon some door she could not open, a woman damned to all eternity. As well might she fall upon her knees in the dusty street. . . . Little François was no more than a handful of ashes, he who once had been so full of laughter and of tears. . . . Whom did she wish to have near her? The doctor?—*that* bore?—no, not a bore. But what availed all her striving to attain perfection since it was her destiny to set her hand to nothing that did not turn awry, no matter how excellent her intentions? Many had been the glorious goals on which she had set her heart, yet in each of them only the worst part of herself had found its satisfaction. She wanted no one with her, nor yearned to find herself elsewhere than in this room with its torn curtains. Perhaps at Saint-Clair? Saint-Clair had seen her childhood. . . . She remembered the park into which she had crept as soon as the church-going family, so antagonistic to her mother, had gone away. Nature, it had seemed, was only waiting for their departure after the Easter holidays to break the coverings of all its shoots. The bracken grew high and rank, touching with formless, frothy green the lowest branches of the oaks. Only the pines swayed, unchanged, the same grey tops that seemed indifferent to the spring, and even for them a moment came when they, too, saw torn from their entrails the cloudy plenty of their pollen, the yellow immensity of their passion. At a turn in the path she would find, in those days, a broken doll, a handkerchief caught on a furze-bush. But to-day she was a stranger to that world. Nothing would greet her there but the sand on which so often she had lain face downward. . . .

When Justine came to tell her that dinner was ready, she tidied her hair and sat down before her steaming plate of soup. But because nothing must stand in the way of her maid's visit to the cinema with her husband, she was once again, half an hour later, alone at the drawing-room window. The fragrant lime had as yet no fragrance. Below her the rhododendrons already showed dark with coming colour. The fear of nothingness, the longing for a breathing-space, led her to seek some piece of wreckage to which she might cling. 'I yielded,' she thought, 'to that instinct for flight which comes over all of us when confronted by a human face made ugly by exigence and hunger. I convinced myself that the young brute and the young creature whom I once adored were different persons—but they were the same, the same child, only wearing a mask. As pregnant women wear a mask of fretfulness, so men, obsessed by love, have, too, close-moulded on their faces that look, so often hideous and always terrible, of the beast of prey that stirs within them. Galatea fled from what frightened her yet lured her on. . . . I had dreamed of a long pilgrimage of kisses along which, making scarce noticeable progress, we should have passed from the regions of temperate warmth to those of enervating heat. But the young buck was too headstrong. Why did I not surrender to his fumbling urgency! In my raped and ravished body I might have found peace beyond imagining, something, perhaps, even better than peace. . . . Maybe, where human beings are concerned, there is no severing gulf that kisses will not bridge. . . . But kisses of what sort?' Remembering the rictus of his grin, she gave vent to an "Ugh!" of disgust. A whole gallery of pictures forced themselves into her mind. She saw Larousselle turning from her with a muttered growl, his face suffused: "What *is* it you want? . . . You're just a lump of wood, not flesh and blood at all!"

What, if it came to that, did she want? She wandered about the deserted room, sat for a while by the window, looking out, elbow on sill and head on hand, dreamed of some mysterious, unvisited land of silence where she might have felt her love, yet not demand of it speech or sound, though the beloved would have heard it, would have understood the nature of her desire even before desire was born. The touch of hands and lips implies between two persons a physical separation. But so deeply interfused would they have been one with the other, that no grip and clasp of limbs would have been necessary, that brief encounter so quickly loosed again by shame. Shame? She seemed to hear the laugh of Gaby Dubois, the light o' love, the words that once she had spoken: "Speak for yourself, my dear . . . *that's* the only consolation I've got in the bloody awful life I lead. . . ." Whence came this feeling of disgust? Did it really mean anything at all? Was it something positive and personal? A thousand formless thoughts woke in her mind and disappeared again, as, in the empty sky above her head, the shooting stars and falling, burned-out meteors.

'Is not my lot,' thought Maria, 'the common lot of all womankind?' Without husband, without children, no one, indeed, could be more lonely than herself. But was this solitude more actual or more intense than the sense of isolation from which no family life, however happy, could have saved her—the sense of being alone which comes to all of us as soon as we learn to recognize in ourselves the distinguishing marks of that accursed species, the race of lost souls whose instincts, needs and mysterious ends we alone can interpret? A truce to such exhausting analysis! Pale though the sky might be with traces of the lingering day, with the promise of a rising moon, beneath the still leaves darkness was massing. Leaning out into the night air, drawn, almost physically absorbed, by the quietness of the vegetable world, Maria Cross yielded not so much to a desire to drink deep of the branch-encumbered air as to a temptation to lose herself in it, to feel herself dissolved and atomized, till the inner desert of her heart should become one with the emptiness of space, till the silence within her should in no way differ from the silence of the spheres.

X

MEANWHILE, Raymond Courrèges, having, as he walked the road, emptied his mind of all its foul abuse, and inwardly raging that he had not turned the flood on Maria Cross, felt an urgent need to spatter her with still more mud. Obsessed by that craving, he longed, as soon as he got home, to see his father. The doctor, true to his expressed intention, had decided to spend the next forty-eight hours in bed, eating nothing and drinking only water—to the great satisfaction of his wife and mother. The onset of his false angina was not alone in determining him to act in this manner. He was curious to observe the effect upon his own constitution of such a regimen.

Robinson had already looked in to see him on the previous evening.

"I'd rather it had been Duluc," said Madame Courrèges, "but Robinson's better than nothing: after all he *is* a doctor, and knows all about testing the heart."

Robinson crept cautiously through the house, keeping close to the wall, and furtively climbed the stairs, dreading lest he find himself suddenly face to face with Madeleine, though they had never been actually engaged. The doctor, his eyes closed, his head feeling empty but his mind curiously lucid, his body free from pain beneath the light encumbrance of the sheets, and screened from the blaze of the sun, found no difficulty in following the tracks made by his thoughts. Here for a moment lost, there recovered, tangled and confused, they stretched before him, and his mind nosed its way along them as a dog might beat the bushes while his master walked, but did not shoot, amid the undergrowth. Without the slightest sense of fatigue he composed whole articles, to the last word, so that all that was left for him to do was to set them down on paper. Point by point he answered all the criticisms that had been provoked by the paper he had recently read to the Biological Society. His mother's presence was sweet to him—but so, also, was his wife's, and that was a matter to give him pause. Brought to a standstill at last, after an exhausting chase, he was ready to acquiesce now in Lucie's company. He noticed with appreciative wonder how careful his mother was to efface herself, and so avoid all risk of conflict. Without a shadow of mutual recrimination, the two women seemed content to share the prey, now that he had been torn for a few brief moments from his professional duties, from his private research and from a passion which, for them, remained anonymous. He did not put up a struggle, but appeared to take an interest in all that they said, however trivial. His world had suddenly contracted to the dimensions of their own. He actually wanted to know whether Julie was really leaving, or whether there was a chance that she might come to terms with

Madeleine's maid. The feel of a woman's hand upon his forehead, his mother's or his wife's, gave him back the sense of security which he had known in the days of his childhood's ailments. It rejoiced him to know that if he was to die, he would not die in solitude. It seemed to him that death in that room, with its familiar mahogany furniture, with his wife and his mother forcing themselves to smile, would be the most normal, the simplest, occurrence in all the world; for would not the bitter taste of his last moments be disguised by them as always, in the past, had been the nasty taste of medicine? . . . Just to slip away, wrapped in the warm folds of a lie, knowing himself a dupe. . . .

A flood of light invaded the room. Raymond came in, grumbling that he couldn't see a thing. He approached the man lying in the bed. In his presence alone he could relieve himself of all the vicious hatred that he felt for Maria Cross. Already he could taste in his mouth the sour flavour of what he was about to vomit forth. The sick man said: "Give me a kiss." A great warmth of feeling was in the eyes which he turned upon his son who, two evenings ago, among the vines, had wiped his face. But the young man, coming straight from the daylight into the darkened room, could not make out his father's features very distinctly. There was a harsh note in his voice as he put a question:

"D'you remember our talk abour Maria Cross?"

"Yes, what of it?"

Raymond, leaning above the supine body, as though for an embrace or a murderous blow, saw beneath him two tormented eyes fixed upon his lips. He realized that someone else, besides himself, was suffering. 'I have known it,' he thought, 'ever since that evening when he called me a liar.' But he felt no jealousy. He was incapable of imagining his father in the rôle of lover: no, not jealousy, but a strange desire to cry, with which was mingled a sense of irritation and of mockery. The poor cheeks looked grey under the thinning beard, and there was a tightness in the voice that begged him to go on:

"Well, what is it you know? Don't keep me on tenterhooks: tell me!"

"I was misled, Papa: you are the only person who really knows Maria Cross. I just wanted to tell you that. Now try and get some sleep. How pale you look. Are you sure this diet is agreeing with you?"

It was with amazement that he heard his own voice saying the very reverse of what he had meant to say. He laid a hand upon the sad and arid brow—the same hand which Maria Cross had held such a short while before. The doctor found it cool, was afraid that it might be taken away.

"My opinion of Maria dates from far back. . . ."

At that moment, Madame Courrèges came back into the room. He put his finger to his lips, and Raymond noiselessly withdrew.

His mother was carrying a paraffin lamp (because in the doctor's weak state the electric light would have hurt his eyes). She put it on the table and lowered the shade. The restricted circle of illumination, the old-fashioned nature of its source, brought suddenly to light the mysterious world of rooms now vanished for ever, where a nightlight had been wont to struggle with a thick darkness full of furniture half drowned in obscurity. The doctor loved Maria, but he could see her with detachment. He loved her as the dead must love the living. She made one with all the other loves of his life, from boyhood on. . . . Feeling his way along the pathway of this thought, he now saw that one and the same sentiment had always held him in thrall down the years. It had always been like the one that had caused him the torment from which he had only just been released. He could feel his way back along the dreary sameness of that eternal pilgrimage, could have put a name to each one of all the passionate adventures most of which, like this one, had ended only in frustration. Yet, in those days he had been young. It wasn't, then, age alone that stood between him and Maria Cross. No more successfully at twenty-five than now could he have crossed the desert separating this woman and himself. He remembered how, just after he had left college, when he was the same age as Raymond, he had loved, yet never known a moment's hope. . . . It was the law of his nature that he could never make contact with those he loved. He had never been more conscious of that truth than in those moments of partial success when he had held in his arms the object so long desired, and found it suddenly poor and dwarfed and utterly different from what it had been in the agonies of his desire. No reason to seek in the mirror the reasons for that solitude in which he was fated to remain until his death. Other men—his father had been one such, Raymond would be another—can follow the law of their being into old age, obedient to the demands of their vocation of love. But he, even in his youth, had been obedient only to the call of his predestined solitude.

The ladies having gone downstairs to dinner, he heard a sound that came straight out of his childhood, the tinkle of spoons on china. But closer to his ears and to his heart were the noises made by rustling leaves, by the crickets, by a frog pleased at the coming of the rain. Then the ladies returned. They said:

"You must be feeling very weak."

"I certainly couldn't stand upright."

But because this diet of his was a form of "treatment" they were pleased that he felt weak.

"Wouldn't you like a little . . .?"

The sense of weakness helped him on his way of exploration into the distant past. The two ladies were carrying on a conversation in undertones. The doctor heard a name mentioned, and questioned them:

"Wasn't that a certain Mademoiselle Malichecq?"

"So you heard what we were saying? I thought you were asleep. No, it's her sister-in-law who's a Malichecq. . . . She's a Martin."

The doctor had gone to sleep by the time the Basques put in

an appearance, and did not open his eyes until he heard the doors of their rooms shut. Then his mother rolled up her knitting, rose heavily from her chair, and kissed him on the forehead, the eyes and the neck.

"Your skin's quite cool," she said.

He was alone with Madame Courrèges, who at once embarked upon a grievance:

"Raymond took the last tram into Bordeaux again. God knows what time he'll come in. He looked terrible this evening; I felt quite frightened. When he's spent the money you gave him, he'll run into debt, if he hasn't started already!"

In a low voice the doctor said: "Our little Raymond . . . nineteen already," and shuddered, thinking of certain streets in Bordeaux that were always deserted after dark. He remembered the sailor over whose body he had tripped one evening. The man's face and chest had been blotched with stains of wine and blood. . . . Somebody was still moving about upstairs. A dog in the stable yard started to bark furiously. Madame Courrèges listened intently:

"I can hear somebody moving about. It can't be Raymond as early as this. Besides, if it were, the dog wouldn't be making all that noise."

Somebody was coming towards the house. There was nothing furtive about his movements, indeed, he seemed to be going out of his way to avoid concealment. The shutters of the French window were shaken. Madame Courrèges leaned forward.

"Who's there?"

"An urgent message for the doctor."

"The doctor doesn't go out at night: you ought to know that by this time. Try Doctor Larue in the village."

The man, who was holding a lantern in his hand, was insistent. The doctor, who was still half asleep, cried out to his wife:

"Tell him it's useless. I didn't come to live in the country just in order to be pulled out of bed by night calls."

"It's out of the question. My husband only sees patients by appointment. He has an arrangement with Doctor Larue . . ."

"But, Madame, it's about one of his patients that I've come, a neighbour of his. . . . He'll come soon enough when he hears the name. It's Madame Cross, Madame Maria Cross. She's had a fall—on her head."

"Maria Cross? Why should you think he'd put himself out for her more than for anybody else?"

But at sound of the name the doctor had got out of bed. He elbowed his wife aside and leaned out of the window.

"Is that you, Maraud? I didn't recognize your voice. What has happened to your mistress?"

"She's had a fall, sir, on her head. She's delirious and asking for the doctor."

"I'll be with you in five minutes; just give me time to get something on."

He shut the window and started looking for his clothes.

"You're not really going?"

He made no reply but muttered to himself: "Where are my socks?" His wife protested. Hadn't he just said he wouldn't be disturbed at night for anybody? Why this sudden change of mind? He could scarcely stand up: he would faint from sheer weakness.

"It's one of my patients. Surely you see that I can't *not* go?"

There was sarcasm in her voice as she answered:

"Oh yes, I see right enough. . . . It has taken me some time, but I see now."

She did not yet actually suspect her husband. For the moment she was intent only on wounding him. He, confident in his detachment, in the fact of his renunciation, had no qualms on her account. After the long torment of his passion, nothing, he felt, could be less blameworthy, less guilty than his feeling now of friendly alarm. It never occurred to him that though he might, his wife could not, draw a comparison between the past and present states of his love for Maria Cross. Two months earlier he would not have dared to show his anxiety so openly. When passion is a flaming fire we instinctively dissimulate. But once we have given up all hope of happiness, once we have accepted an eternal hunger, an eternal thirst, the least we can do—or so we think—is not to wear ourselves out with pretending.

"My poor Lucie, you're quite wrong. All that is very far away now . . . quite, quite finished. Yes, I *am* deeply attached to the poor creature . . . but that has nothing to do . . ."

He leaned against the bed, murmuring: "She's right; I've eaten nothing," and proceeded to ask his wife to make him some chocolate on the spirit lamp.

"Where d'you think I'm going to find milk at this time of night? I don't suppose there's a scrap of bread in the kitchen, either. But no doubt, when you've seen to this—this woman, she'll make you a nice little supper. It will be well worth while having been disturbed for that!"

"What a fool you are, my dear. If only you knew . . ."

She took his hand and came close:

"You said—all that's quite finished . . . all that's very far away —then there *was* something between you? What was it? I have a right to know. I won't reproach you, but I want to know."

The doctor felt so breathless that he had to make two attempts before he could get his boots on. He muttered:

"I was speaking generally: what I said had nothing to do with Maria Cross. Look at me, Lucie . . ."

But she was busy going over in her mind the events of the past months. She had the key to it all now! Everything hung together: everything was as clear as clear. . . .

"Paul, don't go to that woman. I've never bothered you with questions . . . you must do me the justice to admit that."

He answered gently that it was not in his power to do what she asked. His duty was to his patient—she might be dying: a fall on the head might well prove fatal.

"If you keep me from going out, you will be responsible for her death!"

She loosed him, finding no more to say. As he moved away from her she began speaking to herself, stumbling over her words: "It may be all a trick . . . they may have fixed it up between them." Then she remembered that the doctor had had nothing to eat since the previous evening. Seated on a chair, she listened to the murmur of voices in the garden.

"Yes, she fell out of the window . . . it must have been an accident. She wouldn't have chosen the drawing-room one, which is on the ground floor, if she had meant to throw herself out. Quite delirious . . . complaining about her head . . . doesn't remember a thing."

Madame Courrèges heard her husband tell the man to get some ice in the village: he would find some at the inn or at the butcher's. He must get some bromide, too, at the chemist's.

"I'll go by the Bois de Berge: it'll be quicker that way than if I had the horse put in."

"You won't want the lantern, sir: it's as bright as day with this moon."

The doctor had only just passed through the small gate leading to the stable-yard when he heard someone running after him. A voice panted out his Christian name. He saw that it was his wife, in her dressing-gown, with her hair in plaits, ready for bed. She was too breathless to say more, but held out to him a piece of stale bread and a large bar of chocolate.

He went through the Bois de Berge. The clearings were stained with moonlight, though the full strength of the white radiance could not penetrate the leaves. But the great planet sat in throned majesty above the road, shining as though in a river bed cut for its brightness. The bread and chocolate recalled the taste of all his schoolboy snacks—the taste of happiness—at dawn, when he used to go out shooting, in the days when his feet were soaked with dew and he was seventeen. Numbed by the shock of the news, he only now began to feel the pain. Suppose Maria Cross were going to die? Who was it that had made her want to die? But had she wanted it? She could remember nothing. How completely knocked-out are those victims of shock who never remember anything, who smother up in darkness the essential moment of their destiny! But he mustn't question her. The important thing for the time being was that she should work her brain as little as possible. 'Remember, you are only a doctor attending his patient. There can be no question of suicide. When people have made up their minds to die, they don't choose a ground-floor window. She doesn't take drugs, or not as far as I know, though it's true that there was a smell of ether in her room one evening when I was there; but she'd been suffering from headache. . . .'

Beyond the area of his stifling torment, on the very edge of his consciousness, another storm was growling. When the appointed moment came, it would burst. 'Poor Lucie—jealous! what a wretched business . . . but time enough to think about that later. . . . Here I am. The moon makes the garden look like a stage scene. It's as puerile as a setting for *Werther*. . . . No sound of raised voices.' The main door was ajar. From sheer habit he went straight to the empty drawing-room, then turned and climbed the stairs. Justine opened the door of the bedroom. He went across to the bed, on which Maria was lying, moaning to herself, and trying to push away the compress from her forehead. He had no eyes for her body beneath the close-clinging sheet, the body which so often he had undressed in imagination. He had no eyes for her disordered hair, nor for her arm, naked to the armpit. All that mattered was that she recognized him, that her delirium was only intermittent. She kept on saying: "What happened, doctor?—what was it?" He made a mental note: amnesia. Leaning over the naked breast whose veiled loveliness had once made him tremble, he listened to her heart, then, very gently touching her injured forehead with his finger, he traced the extent of the wound. "Does it hurt you here . . . or here . . . or here?" She complained, too, of pain in her hip. Very carefully he drew down the sheet so as to expose no more than the small bruised surface; then covered it up again. With his eyes on his watch, he felt her pulse. This body had been delivered to him for cure, not for possession. His eyes knew that they were there to observe, not to be enchanted. He gazed intently at her flesh, bringing all his intelligence to bear. The clearness of his mind barred all roads of approach to his melancholy passion.

"I'm in pain," she moaned; "I'm in such dreadful pain."

She pushed away the compress, then asked for a fresh one which the maid proceeded to soak in the kettle. The chauffeur came in with a bucket of ice, but when the doctor tried to apply it to her head, she pushed away the rubber skull-cap and, in commanding tones, insisted on a *hot* compress. To the doctor she exclaimed: "Don't be so slow: it takes you an hour to carry out my orders!"

He was extremely interested in these symptoms, which were similar to others he had noticed in cases of shock. The body lying there before him, which once had been the carnal source of all his dreams and reveries and delight, roused in him nothing but an intense curiosity, a concentrated and enhanced attention. The patient's mind was no longer wandering, but she poured forth a spate of words. He noticed with surprise that she, whose powers of speech were normally so defective that she had to make an effort, and not always a successful effort, to find the right words for what she wanted to express, had suddenly become almost eloquent. She had complete command of her vocabulary, and seemed capable of calling on technical terms at will. 'What a mysterious organ,' he reflected, 'is the human brain. How extraordinary it is that it can develop its scope in this amazing way merely as the result of shock.'

"I never meant to kill myself—you must believe that, doctor. I absolutely forbid you to think that such an idea ever came into my mind. I can remember nothing. The only certain thing is that what I wanted was not to die but to sleep. I've never truly longed for anything in my life but peace and quiet. If ever you hear anybody boasting that he dragged me down to the point of making me want to kill myself, I tell you you mustn't believe it. Do you understand me? I pro-hi-bit anything of the sort."

"Yes, dear lady. I swear to you that nobody has ever uttered such a boast in my hearing . . . Now, just sit up and drink this. It's only bromide: it will soothe your nerves."

"I don't need soothing. I am in a good deal of pain, but I am perfectly calm. Move the lamp further away. There now, I've messed the sheets. But I don't care—I'll empty the drug all over the bed if I want to. . . ."

When he asked whether the pain was less acute, she replied that it was excruciating, but that it didn't come only from her injury. In an access of talkativeness she once more raised her voice and spoke in such an unbroken flow that Justine observed that Madame was "talking like a book." The doctor told the woman to go and get some sleep. He would sit up with the patient, he said, until daybreak.

"What other way out is there, doctor, except sleep? I see everything so clearly now. I understand what I never understood before . . . the people we think we love . . . the passions that end so miserably . . . now, at last, I know the truth. . . ." (The compress had grown cold and she pushed it away with her hand. The damp hair clung to her forehead as though she were sweating.) "No, not passions, but one single passion. It goes on inside us, and from a casual meeting, from the eyes and lips of some perfect stranger, we build up something that we think corresponds with it. . . . Only by physical contact, by the embraces of the flesh, by, in short, the sexual act, can two persons ever really communicate. . . . But we know only too well where that road leads, and why it was traced—for the sole purpose of continuing the species, as you would put it, doctor. We choose the one path open to us, but it was never designed to lead us to our hearts' desire."

At first he had lent but half an ear to this outburst. He made no attempt to understand what she was saying. What interested him was her irrelevant talkativeness. It was, he noticed, as though the physical disturbance she had suffered had sufficed partially to bring into the open ideas that had been lying repressed in her mind.

"One's got to love the pleasure of the body, doctor. Gaby used to say—it's the only thing in the world, darling, that has never disappointed me—but, unfortunately we can't, all of us, do that. And yet it *is* the only thing that makes us forget the object of our search, forget so far that it actually becomes that object. Stupefy yourself . . . that's easier said than done."

How curious it was, thought the doctor, that she should speak of sexual pleasure precisely as Pascal had spoken of faith. In order to quieten her at all costs so that she might get some sleep, he held out some syrup in a spoon. But she pushed it away, and once again made a stain upon the sheets.

"No, I don't *want* any bromide. I shall empty it all over the bed if I like: *you* can't prevent me!"

Without the slightest subtlety of transition she went on: "Always between me and those I have longed to possess there has stretched this fetid region of swamp and mud. But they didn't understand. . . . They always thought I was calling to them because I wanted to wallow in the dirt."

Her lips moved, and the doctor thought that she was muttering names, Christian names. He leaned over her eagerly, but did not hear the one name which would utterly have destroyed his peace of mind. For a few moments he forgot that she was his patient and saw only a woman who was lying to him. In an agony of misery he murmured:

"You're just like all the others. You want one thing, and one thing only, pleasure. . . . It's the same with all of us. It's the only thing we want."

She raised her lovely arms, hid her face, uttered a long-drawn moan. In a low voice he said: "What's the matter with me? I must be mad!" He renewed the compress, poured some more syrup into a spoon, and supported the sufferer's head. Maria at last consented to drink: then, after a moment's silence:

"Yes, I too, I too. You know, doctor, how sometimes one sees the lightning and hears the thunder simultaneously—well, with me pleasure and disgust are all confused, just like the lightning and the thunder: they strike me at the same moment. There is no interval between the pleasure and the disgust."

She grew calmer and stopped speaking. The doctor sat down in an armchair and watched beside her, his mind a confusion of thoughts. He believed that she was asleep, but suddenly her voice, dreamy now and at peace, rose again:

"Someone with whom we might make contact, someone we might possess—but not in the flesh—by whom we might be possessed. . . ."

Fumblingly she pushed the damp cloth from her brow. The room was filled with the silence of the dying night. It was the hour of the deepest sleep, the hour at which the constellations change their pattern in the sky so that we no longer recognize them.

Her pulse was calm. She was sleeping like a child whose breathing is so light that one gets up to make sure that it is still alive. The blood had once more mounted to her cheeks and gave them colour. Her body was no longer that of a sufferer: not now did pain divorce her from desire. How long must his poor tormented flesh keep watch beside this other flesh deadened at last to suffering? 'The body has its agony,' thought the doctor. 'To the simple, Paradise lies wide open. . . . Who was it said that love was the pleasure of the poor? I might have been the man who, his day's work ended, lay down each night beside this woman. But then, she would not have been *this* woman. . . She would have been a mother more than once. All her body would bear signs of the purpose it had served, the traces of a life spent in degrading tasks. . . . Desire would be dead: nothing would remain but a few grubby habits. . . . Dawn already! How long the servant is in coming!'

He was afraid that he would never be able to walk as far as his house. He told himself that it was hunger made him weak, but dreaded the treachery of his heart whose beats he could so clearly hear. Physical anguish had freed him from from love's sickness. But already, though no sign came to warn him, the destiny of Maria Cross was imperceptibly drifting away from his own. . . . The mooring ropes are loosed, the anchor raised: the vessel moves, but as yet one does not realize that it is moving, though in another hour it will be no more than a dark stain upon the sea. He had often observed that life takes no heed of preparations. Ever since the days of his youth, the objects of his affection had, almost all of them, disappeared with dramatic suddenness, carried away by some other passion, or, with less fuss and bother, had just packed up and left town. Nothing more was ever heard of them. It is not death that tears from us those we love; rather, it keeps them safe, preserving them in all the adorable ambiance of youth. Death is the salt of love: it is life that brings corruption. To-morrow the doctor would be stretched upon a sick bed, with his wife sitting beside him. Robinson would be keeping a watchful eye on Maria Cross's convalescence, and would send her to Luchon to take the waters, because his best friend had set up in practice there, and he wanted to help him with a few patients. In the autumn, Monsieur Larousselle, whose business often took him to Paris, would decide to rent a flat close to the Bois, and would suggest to Maria that she move there, because, by that time, she would have said that she would rather die than go back to the house at Talence, with its worn carpets and torn curtains, or put up any longer with the insults of the Bordeaux folk.

When the maid came into the room, even had the doctor not felt so weak that he seemed to be conscious of nothing but his weakness—even had he been full of life and vigour, no inner voice would have warned him to take his last long look at the sleeping Maria Cross. He was fated never to enter this house again, yet all he said to the maid was: "I'll look in again this evening. . . . Give her another spoonful of bromide if she seems restless." He stumbled from the room, holding to the furniture to keep himself from falling. It was the only time in his life that he had left Maria Cross without turning his head.

He hoped that the early morning air would sting his blood to activity, but he had to stop at the bottom of the steps. His teeth were chattering. So often in the past, when hastening to his love, he had crossed the garden in a few seconds, but now, as he looked at the distant gate, he wondered whether he would have strength enough to reach it. He dragged himself through the mist and was tempted to turn back. He would never be able to walk as far as the church, where, perhaps, he might find somebody to help him. Here was the gate at last, and, beyond the railings, a carriage—his carriage. Through the window he could see the face of Lucie Courrèges. She was sitting there quite motionless and as though dead. He opened the door, collapsed against his wife, leaned his head on her shoulder, and lost consciousness.

"Don't agitate yourself. Robinson has everything under control in the laboratory, and is looking after your patients. At this very moment he is at Talence, you know where. . . . Now don't talk."

From the depths of his lassitude he noticed the ladies' anxiety, heard their whispering outside his door. He believed that he was seriously ill, and attached no importance to what they said: "Just a touch of influenza, but in your anæmic state that's quite bad enough." He asked to see Raymond, but Raymond was always out. "He came in while you were asleep, but didn't like to wake you." As a matter of fact, for the last three days Lieutenant Basque had been in Bordeaux hunting everywhere for the boy. They had taken no one into their confidence but a private enquiry agent. "Whatever happens, he must never know. . . ."

At the end of six days Raymond suddenly appeared in the dining-room while they were at dinner. His face looked thin and tanned by exposure. There was a bruise under his right eye where somebody had hit him. He ate as though he were famished, and even the little girls did not dare to question him. He asked his grandmother where his father was.

"He's got a touch of influenza . . . it's nothing, but we were rather worried because of the state of his heart. Robinson says that he mustn't be left alone. Your mother and I take turns at sitting with him."

Raymond said that to-night he would relieve them, and, when Basque ventured to remark, "You'd much better go to bed: if you could only see what you look like! . . ." he declared that he wasn't the slightest bit tired, and that he had been sleeping very well all the time he was away:

"There's no shortage of beds in Bordeaux."

The tone in which he made the remark made Basque lower his eyes. Later, when the doctor opened his, he saw Raymond standing beside him. He made a sign for him to come closer, and, when he did so, murmured: "You reek of cheap scent . . . I don't need anything: go to bed." But towards midnight he was roused by the sound of Raymond walking up and down. The boy had opened the window and was leaning out into the darkness. "It's stifling to-night," he grumbled. Some moths flew in. Raymond took off his jacket, waistcoat and collar. Then he sat down in an armchair. A few seconds later the doctor heard his regular breathing. When day came, the sick man woke before his watcher and gazed in amazement at the child sitting there, his head drooping, seemingly without life, as though sleep had killed him. The sleeve of his shirt was torn, and revealed a muscular arm that was the colour of a cigar. It was tattooed with the sort of obscene design favoured by sailors. The congested patch beneath his eye had obviously been caused by a fist. But there were other scars on his neck, on his shoulder and on his chest, scars that had the form of a human mouth.

XI

THE revolving door of the little bar never remained still for a moment. The circle of tables pressed closer and closer on the dancing couples, beneath whose feet the leather floor-covering, like the wild-ass's skin, continually shrank. In the contracted space the dances were no more than vertical jerkings. The women sat jammed together on the settees and laughed when they noticed on bare arms the mark of an involuntary caress. The one called Gladys and her companion put on their fur coats.

"You staying?"

Larousselle protested that they were leaving just as things might get amusing. With his hands thrust into his pockets, unsteady on his feet, and his paunch sticking out provocatively, he went across and perched himself on a high stool. The barman burst out laughing, as did the young men to whom he was explaining with considerable pride the ingredients of a special aphrodisiac cocktail of his own invention. Maria, alone at her table, took another sip of champagne and put down her glass. She smiled vaguely, utterly indifferent to Raymond's proximity. What passion might occupy her mind he could not know. She was armed against him, separated from him, by the accumulated experiences of seventeen years. Like a dazed and blinded diver he fought his way to the surface, up from the dead past. But the only thing in the unclear backward of time that really belonged wholly to him was a narrow path, quickly traversed, between walls of clotted darkness. With his nose to the ground he had followed the scent, oblivious to all others that might cross it. But this was no place for dreaming. Across the smoky room and the crowd of dancing couples Maria gave him a hasty glance, then turned away. Why had he not even smiled at her? He dreaded to think that after all these years the youth that once he had been might again take visionary form in this woman's eyes, that image of the shy young boy in the grip of an impotent and furtive desire. Courrèges, notorious for his audacities, trembled with anxiety this evening lest, at any moment now, Maria might get up and disappear. Wasn't there anything he could try? He was the victim of that fatality which condemns us to play the rôle of a man in whom a woman makes exclusive, unalterable, choice of certain elements, for ever ignoring those others that may, too, be part of him. There is nothing to be done against this particular chemical law. Every human being with whom we come in contact isolates in us a single property, always the same, which, as a rule, we should prefer to keep concealed. Our misery, on these occasions, consists in our seeing the loved one build up, beneath our very eyes, the portrait of us that she has made, reduce to nothing our most precious virtues, and turn the light full on our one weakness, absurdity or vice. And not only that. We are forced to share in the vision, to conform to it, for just so long as those appraising eyes, with their single, fixed idea, are bent on us. Only to others, whose affection is of no value to us, will our virtues glow, our talents shine, our strength seem superhuman, our face become as the face of a god.

Now that he had become, under Maria Cross's gaze, once more an abashed and foolish youth, Courrèges no longer wanted to revenge himself. His humble desire went no further than that this woman might learn the details of his amorous career, of all the victories he had won from that moment when, shortly after he had been thrown out of the house at Talence, he had been taken up, almost kidnapped, by an American woman who had kept him for six months at the Ritz (his family believed that he was in Paris working for his exam.). But it was just that, he told himself, that was so impossible—to show himself as someone totally different from what he had been in that over-furnished drawing-room, all "luxury and squalor," when she had said, averting her face, "I want to be alone, Raymond—listen to me —you *must* leave me to myself."

It was the hour at which the tide begins to ebb. But those regular patrons of the little bar who left their troubles with their coats in the cloak-room stayed on. A young woman in red was whirling round ecstatically, her arms extended like wings, while her partner held her by the waist—two happy mayflies united in full flight. An American showed the smooth face of a schoolboy above a pair of enormous shoulders. With ears only for the voice of some god within him, he danced alone, improvising steps which were probably obscene. To the applause which greeted his efforts he responded awkwardly with the grin of a happy child.

Victor Larousselle had resumed his seat opposite Maria. Now and again he turned his head and stared at Raymond. His large face, of a uniform alcoholic red (except under the eyes, where there were livid pouches), had the look of a man eager for a sign of recognition. In vain did Maria beg him to turn his attention elsewhere. If there was one thing above all others about Paris that Larousselle could not bear, it was seeing so many strange faces. At home there was scarcely one that did not immediately bring to mind some name, some married relationship, someone whom he could immediately "place" whether publicly, as a person demanding social acknowledgment, or surreptitiously, as a member of the half-world whom he might know but could not openly greet. Nothing is commoner than that memory for faces which historians attribute only to the great. Larousselle remembered Raymond perfectly well from having seen him driving with his father in the old days, and from having occasionally patted his head. At Bordeaux, in the Cours de l'Intendance, he would have made no sign of recognition, but here, apart from the fact that he could never get used to the humiliation of passing for ever unnoticed, he was secretly anxious that Maria should not be left alone while he played the fool with the two Russian girls who were so obviously wearing nothing under their frocks. Raymond, acutely conscious of Maria's every gesture, concluded that she was doing her best to prevent Larousselle from speaking to him. He was convinced that, even after the lapse of seventeen years, she still saw him as an uncouth and furtive oaf. He heard the man from Bordeaux snarl: "Well, I *want* to, and that ought to be enough for you!" A smile lay like a mask on his unpleasant countenance as he picked his way towards Raymond with all the self-confidence of a man who believes his handshake to be a privilege. Surely, he *couldn't* be mistaken? he said. It was, wasn't it, the son of that excellent doctor Courrèges? His wife remembered quite clearly that she had known him at the time when the doctor was attending her. . . . He was completely master of the situation, took the young man's glass, and made him sit down beside Maria, who held out her hand, and then, almost immediately, withdrew it. Larousselle, after sitting down for a few moments, jumped up again and said without the slightest show of embarrassment:

"Forgive me, will you?—back in a minute."

He joined the two young Russian women at the bar. Though it might be only a matter of moments before he would be back again, and though nothing seemed to Raymond more important than to turn this short respite to the best advantage, he remained silent. Maria turned away her head. He could smell the fragrance of her short hair, and noticed with deep emotion, that a few of the strands were white. A few?—thousands perhaps! The strongly marked, rather thick, lips seemed miraculously untouched by age, and still gave him the impression of fruit ripe for the picking. In them was concentrated all the sensuality of her body. The light in her eyes, under the wide, exposed brow, was astonishingly pure. What did it matter if the storms of time had beaten against, had slowly eaten away and relaxed, the lines of neck and throat?

Without looking at him, she said:

"My husband is really very indiscreet. . . ."

Raymond, as sheepish now as he could ever have been at eighteen, betrayed his amazement at the news that she was married.

"D'you mean to say you didn't know? It's common knowledge in Bordeaux."

She had made up her mind to maintain an icy silence, but seemed astounded to find that there was anybody in the world—least of all a man from Bordeaux—who was ignorant of the fact that she was now Madame Victor Larousselle. He explained that it was many years since he had lived in that city. At that she could no longer keep from breaking her vow of silence. Monsieur Larousselle, she said, had made up his mind the year after the war . . . he had waited until then because of his son.

"Actually, it was Bertrand who begged us, almost before he was out of the army, to get the whole thing settled. It didn't matter to me one way or the other. . . . I agreed from the highest motives only."

She added that she would have preferred to go on living in Bordeaux:

"But Bertrand is at the Polytechnic. Besides, Monsieur Larousselle has to be in Paris for a fortnight every month, so we thought it better to make a home there for the boy."

She seemed suddenly overcome by shyness at having spoken like this, at having confided in him. Once again remote, she said:

"And the dear doctor? Life has a way of separating us from our best friends. . . ."

How delightful it would be to see him again! But when Raymond, taking her at her word, replied: "As a matter of fact, my father is in Paris at this very moment, at the Grand Hotel. He would be more than pleased . . ." she stopped short, and appeared not to have heard him.

Eager to touch her on the raw, to rouse her to a show of anger, he took his courage in both hands and proceeded to voice his one burning preoccupation:

"You don't still hold my boorishness against me? I was only a clumsy child in those days, and really very innocent. Tell me you don't bear me a grudge . . ."

"Bear a grudge?"

She pretended not to understand. Then:

"Oh, you're referring to that ridiculous scene . . . really, there's nothing to forgive. I think I must have been slightly mad myself. Fancy taking a little boy like you seriously! It all seems to me so entirely unimportant now . . . so very, very far away."

He certainly had touched her on the raw, though not in the way he had expected. She had a horror of all that reminded her of the old Maria Cross, but the adventure in which Raymond had played a part she looked on as merely ridiculous. Suddenly grown cautious, she found herself wondering whether he had ever known that she had tried to kill herself. No, for if he had he would have been prouder, would have seemed less humble.

As for Raymond, he had discounted everything in advance—everything except this worst of all foreseeable possibilities, her complete indifference.

"In those days I lived in a world of my own, and read the infinite into all sorts of nonsensical trifles. It is as though you were talking to me of some perfectly strange woman."

He knew that anger and hatred are but extensions of love, that if he could have roused them in Maria Cross his cause would not have been entirely hopeless. But the only effect his words had had upon this woman was to irritate her, to make her feel ashamed at the thought that once she had been caught out with such a wretched trick and in such paltry company.

"So you actually thought," she went on, "that a piece of silliness like that could mean something to me?"

He muttered that it had certainly meant something to him—an admission that he had never before made to himself, but now, at last, scarcely knowing what he said, put into words. He had no idea that the whole pattern of his life had been changed by that one squalid incident of his youth. He was caught in an uprush of suffering. He heard Maria's calm, detached voice:

"How right Bertrand is to say that we don't really begin to live until we've reached twenty-five or thirty."

He had a confused feeling that the remark was not true; that by the time we are beginning to grow up the future is wholly formed in us. On the threshold of manhood the bets have already been placed; nothing more can be staked. Inclinations planted in our flesh even before birth are inextricably confused with the innocence of our early years, but only when we have reached man's estate do they suddenly put forth their monstrous flowers.

Completely at sea, fighting his losing battle against this inaccessible woman, he remembered now what it was that he had so longed to tell Maria, and even though he realized increasingly as he spoke that his words were about as ill-timed as they possibly could be, declared that "our little adventure certainly hasn't stood in the way of my learning about love." Oh, very far from it! He was quite sure that he had had more women than any young man of his age—and women who had something to them, not just your common-or-garden tarts. . . . In that respect she had brought him luck.

She leaned back and, through half-closed eyes, looked at him with an expression of disgust. What, then, she asked, was he complaining of?

"Since, I presume, that sort of filth is the only thing you care about."

She lit a cigarette, leaned her cropped neck against the wall, and watched, through the smoke, the gyrations of three couples. When the jazz-players paused for breath the men detached themselves from their partners, clapped their hands, and then stretched them towards the negro instrumentalists in a gesture of supplication—as though their very lives depended upon a renewal of the din. The coloured gentlemen, moved by compassion, resumed their playing, and the mayflies, born aloft on the rhythm, clasped one another in a fresh embrace and once again took wing. But Raymond, with hatred in his heart, looked at this woman with the short hair and the cigarette, who was none other than Maria Cross. He searched for the one word that would shake her self-control, and at last he found it.

"Well, anyhow, you're —— here."

She realized that what he meant was—we always return to our first loves. He had the satisfaction of seeing her cheeks flush to a deep red, her brows draw together in a harsh frown.

"I have always loathed places like this. To say that sort of thing shows how little you know me! Your father, I am sure, remembers the agonies I went through when Monsieur Larousselle used to drag me off to the *Lion Rouge*. It wouldn't be of the slightest use my telling you that the only thing that brings me here is a sense of duty—yes, of duty. . . . But what can a man like you know of my scruples? It was Bertrand himself who advised me to yield—within reason—to my husband's tastes. If I am to retain any influence, I mustn't ride him on too tight a rein. Bertrand is very broadminded. He begged me not to resist his father's wish that I should cut my hair. . . ."

She had mentioned Bertrand's name merely in order to lessen her nervous tension, to feel at peace and mollified. By the light of memory, Raymond saw once again a deserted path in the Public Park in Bordeaux. The time was four o'clock. He could hear the panting of a small boy running after him, the sound of a tear-thickened voice: "Give me back my notebook." What sort of a man had that delicate youth become? Intent on wounding, he said:

"So you've got a grown-up son now?"

But she wasn't wounded at all; she smiled happily:

"Of course, you knew him at school. . ."

Raymond suddenly took on for her a real existence. He had been one of Bertrand's school-fellows.

"Yes, a grown-up son, but a son who can be at once a friend and a master. You cannot imagine how much I owe to him. . . ."

"You told me—your marriage."

"Oh *that*! . . . my marriage is the least of my debts. You see, he has revealed—but it's no good, you wouldn't understand. It was only that I was thinking how you'd known him at school. I'd so much like to have some idea of what he was like as a little boy. I've often asked my husband about him, but it's extraordinary how little a man can tell one about his son's childhood: 'A nice little chap, just like all the others'—that's as much as he can say. I've no reason to believe that you were any more observant. In the first place, you were much older than he was."

"Four years—that's nothing," Raymond muttered, and added: "I remember that he had a face like a girl."

She showed no sign of anger, but answered with quiet contempt that of course they could not have had much in common. Raymond realized that in the eyes of Maria Cross her stepson floated in an airy world far above his head. She was thinking of Bertrand: she had been drinking champagne; there was a rapturous smile upon her lips. Like the disunited mayflies, she, too, clapped her hands eager for the music to renew its spell about her. What remained in Raymond's memory of the women he had possessed? Some of them he would scarcely have recognized. But hardly a day had passed during the last seventeen years that he had not conjured up in his mind, had not insulted and caressed, the face which to-night he could see in profile close beside him. He could not endure that she should be so far from him in spirit. At all costs he must bridge the gap, and to that end he took the conversation back to Bertrand.

"I suppose he'll be leaving college very soon now?"

She replied with a show of polite interest that he was in his last year. He had lost four years because of the war. She hoped that he would pass out very high, and when Raymond remarked that no doubt Bertrand would follow in his father's footsteps, said, with some animation, that he must be given time in which to make up his mind. She was quite sure, she added, that he would make his influence felt no matter what profession he adopted. Raymond could not make out in what way he was so remarkable.

"The effect he has on his fellow-students is quite extraordinary. . . . But I don't know why I am telling you all this. . . ."

She gave the impression that she was coming down to earth, coming down a long way, when she asked:

"And what about you. What do *you* do?"

"Oh, I just potter about, in the business world, you know."

It was suddenly borne in on him what a wretched mess he had made of his life. But she was barely listening. It wasn't that she despised him—that, in its way, would have been something definite, but that for her he simply did not exist. She half rose from her chair and made signs to Larousselle who was still holding forth from his stool. "Just a few more minutes!" he called back. In a low voice she said, "How red he looks—he's drinking too much."

The negro musicians were packing up their instruments with as much care as though they had been sleeping children. Only the piano seemed incapable of stopping. A single couple was revolving on the floor. The other dancers, their arms still intertwined, had collapsed on to seats. This was the moment of the evening which Raymond Courrèges had so often sipped and savoured, the moment when claws are retracted, when eyes become veiled by a sudden softness, when voices sink to a whisper and hands become insidiously inviting. . . . There had been a time when, at such moments, he had smiled to himself, thinking of what was to come later, of men walking homeward in the early dawn, whistling to themselves and leaving behind, in the secrecy of some anonymous bedroom, a jaded body sprawled across a bed, so still, so spent, that it might have been that of a murdered woman. . . Not thus would he have left the body of Maria Cross! A whole life-time would have been all too short to satisfy his ravenous hunger.

So completely indifferent was she to his presence that she did not even notice how he had moved his leg closer to her own, did not even feel the contact. He had no power whatever over her. And yet in those distant years he had been hers for the taking.

She had thought she loved him—and he had never known. He had been an inexperienced boy. She should have explained what it was she wanted of him. No whim, however extravagant, would have rebuffed him. He would have proceeded as slowly as she wished. He could, at need, make smooth and easy the voyage of pleasure . . . it would have brought her joy. But now it was too late. Centuries might pass before their ways should cross again in the six o'clock tram. . . . He looked up and saw in a mirror the wreckage of his youth, the first sure signs of creeping age. Gone were the days when women might have loved him. Now it was for him to take the initiative, if, indeed, he were still worthy of love.

He laid his hand on hers:

"Do you remember the tram?"

She shrugged her shoulders, and, without so much as turning her head, had the effrontery to ask:

"What tram?"

Then, before he could reply, she hurried on:

"I wonder whether you would be so very kind as to bring Monsieur Larousselle over here and get his coat for him from the cloak-room . . . otherwise we shall never make a move."

He seemed not to have heard her. She had asked that question, "What tram?" quite deliberately. He would have liked to protest that nothing in his whole life had ever meant so much to him as those moments when they had sat facing one another in a crowd of poor work-people with coal-blackened faces and heads drooping with sleep. He could see the scene in imagination—a newspaper slipping to the floor from a hand gone numb; a bare-headed woman holding up her novelette to catch the light of the lamps, her lips moving as though in prayer. He could hear again the great rain-drops splashing in the dust of the lane behind the church at Talence, could watch the passing figure of a workman crouched over the handlebar of his bicycle, a canvas sack, with a bottle protruding from it, slung over his shoulder. The trees behind the railings were stretching out their dusty leaves like hands begging for water.

"Do, please, go and fetch my husband. He's not used to drinking so much. I ought to have stopped him. Spirits are so bad for him."

Raymond, who had resumed his seat, got up again and, for the second time, shuddered at what he saw reflected in the mirror. He was still young, but what good would that do him? True, he might still awaken love, but no longer could he choose in whom. To a man who can still flaunt the passing glories of the body's springtime, everything is possible. Had his age been five years less than it was, he might, he thought, have had a chance. Better than most he knew what mere youthfulness can achieve with a woman who has been drained dry, how magically it can overcome antipathies and preferences, shame and remorse, what pricking curiosity, what appetites it can wake. But now he was without a weapon. Looking at himself he felt as a man might do who goes into battle with a broken sword.

"If you won't do what I ask, I suppose I must go myself. They're making him drink. . . . I don't know how I can manage to get him away. How disgusting it all is!"

"What would your Bertrand say if he could see you now, sitting here with me . . . and his father in that state?"

"He would understand everything: he *does* understand everything."

It was at that moment that the noise of a heavy body crashing to the ground came from the bar. Raymond rushed across the room and, with the help of the barman, tried to lift Victor Larousselle, whose feet were caught in the overturned stool. His hand, streaming with blood, still convulsively clutched a broken bottle. Maria tremblingly threw a coat round the shoulders of Bertrand's father, and turned up the collar so as to hide his now purple face. The barman said to Raymond, who was settling the bill, that one could never be sure it wasn't a heart attack, and half carried the great hulking body to a taxi, so terrified was he of seeing a customer "kick the bucket" before he had got clear of the premises.

Maria and Raymond, perched on the bracket-seats, held the drunken creature in a sitting position. A bloodstain was slowly spreading over the handkerchief which they had wrapped round the injured hand. "This has never happened to him before," Maria moaned. "I ought to have remembered that he can't touch anything but wine. Swear you won't breathe a word of this to anyone." Raymond's mood was exultant. In an access of joy he greeted this unexpected turn in his affairs. No, nothing could have parted him from Maria Cross this evening. What a fool he had been to doubt his lucky star!

Although winter was on the wane, the night was cold. A powdering of sleet showed white on the Place de la Concorde under the moon. He continued to hold up on the back seat the vast mass of flesh from which came the sound of hiccups and a confused burble of speech. Maria had opened a bottle of smelling-salts. The young man adored their faint scent of vinegar. He warmed himself at the flame of the beloved body at his side, and took advantage of the brief flicker of each passing street-lamp to take his fill of the face that looked so lovely in its humiliation. At one moment, when she took the old man's heavy and revolting head between her hands, she looked like Judith.

More than anything she dreaded that the porter might be a witness of the scene, and was only too glad of Raymond's offer to help her drag the sick man to the lift. Scarcely had they got him on to his bed than they saw that his hand was bleeding freely, and that only the whites of his eyes were visible. Maria was worse than useless. She seemed quite incapable of doing the simplest things that would have come naturally to other women. . . . Must she wake the servants, who slept on the seventh floor? . . . What a scandal there would be! She decided to ring up her doctor. But he must have taken off the receiver, for she could get no answer. She burst into sobs. It was then that

Raymond, remembering his father's presence in Paris, had the happy idea of ringing him, and suggested to Maria that he should do so. Without so much as a "Thank you," she started to hunt through the directory for the number of the Grand Hotel.

"He'll be here as soon as he can get dressed and find a taxi."

This time Maria did take his hand. She opened a door and switched on the light.

"Would you mind waiting in here: it's Bertrand's room." She said that the patient had been sick and felt better. But his hand was still giving him a good deal of pain.

As soon as she had left the room Raymond sat down and buttoned his overcoat. The radiator was not giving much heat. His father's sleepy voice was still in his ears. How far away it had sounded. They had not seen one another since old Grandmamma Courrèges had died three years before. At that time Raymond had been in pressing need of money. Perhaps there had been something rude and aggressive in the way he had demanded his share of the inheritance, but what had really got under his skin and precipitated a rupture had been the way in which his father lectured him on the subject of his choice of a profession. The mixture of cadging and pimping by which he had elected to earn a living had horrified the elder man, who regarded such an occupation as being unworthy of a Courrèges. He had gone so far as to try to extract a promise from Raymond that he would find some regular occupation. And now, in a few moments, he would be here, in this flat. What ought his son to do—kiss him, or merely offer him his hand?

He tried to find an answer to the question, but all the time his attention was being drawn to, was being held by, one particular object in the room—Bertrand Larousselle's bed, a narrow iron bed, so unaccommodating, so demure beneath its flowered cotton coverlet that Raymond could not keep himself from bursting out laughing. It was the bed of an elderly spinster or a seminarist.

Three of the walls were quite bare, the fourth was lined with books. The work-table was as neat as a good conscience. 'If Maria came to my place, she'd get a bit of a shock.' She would see a divan so low that it seemed part of the floor. Every woman who ventured into that discreetly dimmed interior was at once conscious of a dangerous sense of being in some strange new world, of a temptation to indulge in activities which would no more commit her than if they had taken place in a different planet—or in the innocent privacy of sleep. . . . But in the room where Raymond was now waiting, no curtains hid the windows frosted by the winter night. Its owner wished, no doubt, that the light of dawn should wake him before the sounding of the earliest bell. Raymond was entirely insensitive to all the evidences of a life of purity. In this room designed for prayer he could see merely a cunning piece of trickery, a deliberate exploitation of refusal, of denial, designed to increase the delights of love by suppressing all obvious allurements. He looked at the titles of some of the books. "What an ass!" he murmured. These volumes that spoke of another world were quite outside his experience and gave him a feeling of disgust. . . . What a time his father was taking! He did not want to be alone much longer. The room seemed to mock at him. He opened the windows and looked out at the roofs beneath a late moon.

"Here's your father."

He closed the window, followed Maria into Victor Larousselle's room, saw a figure bending over the bed, and recognized his father's huge bowler hat lying on a chair, and the ivory-knobbed stick (which had been his horse in the days when he had played at horses). When the doctor raised his head he hardly knew him. Yet he realized that this old man who smiled and put his arm about his shoulder was his father.

"No tobacco, no spirits, no coffee. Poultry at lunch and no butcher's meat at night. Do as I say, and you'll live to be a hundred. . . . That's all."

The doctor repeated the words "That's all," in the drawling voice of a man whose thoughts are elsewhere. His eyes never left Maria's face. She, seeing him standing there motionless, took the initiative, opened the door, and said:

"I think what we all need is a good night's sleep."

The doctor followed her into the hall. Very shyly he said: "It was a bit of luck, our meeting like this." All the time he had been hurriedly dressing, and later, in the taxi, he had been quite convinced that as soon as he had said that Maria would break in with—"Now I've found you again, doctor, I'm not going to let you get away so easily." But that wasn't at all the answer she had made when, from the open door, he had eagerly remarked, "It was a bit of luck. . . ." Four times he repeated the phrase he had so carefully prepared, as though by stressing it he could force from her the hoped-for answer. But no: she just held up his overcoat and did not even show signs of impatience when he failed to find the sleeve. Quite unemotionally she said:

"It really is a very small world. This evening has brought us together after many years. It is more than likely that we shall meet again."

She pretended not to hear him when he said: "But don't you think it is up to us to put a spoke in fortune's wheel?"

He repeated the same remark more loudly: "Don't you think we might manage to put a spoke in fortune's wheel?"

If the dead could come back how embarrassing they would be! They do come back sometimes, treasuring an image of us which we long to destroy, their minds full of memories which we passionately desire to forget. These drowned bodies that are swept in by the flooding tide are a constant source of awkwardness to the living.

"I am very different from the lazy creature whom you once knew, doctor. I want to get to bed, because I've got to be up by seven."

She felt irritated by him for saying nothing. She had a sense of discomfort beneath the brooding stare of this old man who merely went on repeating: "Don't you think we might put a spoke in fortune's wheel?"

She replied with a good grace, though rather brusquely, that he had her address.

"I scarcely ever go to Bordeaux these days: but perhaps you . . ."

It had been so kind of him to take all this trouble.

"If the staircase light goes out, you'll find the switch *there*."

He made no movement, but stayed obstinately where he was. Did she never, he asked, feel any ill effects from her fall?

Raymond emerged from the shadows: "What fall was that?"

She made a gesture with her head expressive of utter exhaustion.

"What would really give me pleasure, doctor, would be to think that we could write to one another. I'm not the letter-writer I used to be . . . but for you . . ."

He replied: "Letters are worse than useless. What's the point of writing if we are never to see one another?"

"But that's precisely the reason."

"No, no. Do you think that if people knew they were never going to see one another again they would want to prolong their friendship artificially by corresponding, especially if one of the two realized that letter-writing imposed a dreary duty on the other? . . . One becomes a coward, Maria, as one grows older. One has had one's life and one dreads fresh disappointments."

He had never put his feelings so clearly into words. Surely she would understand now!

Her attention had strayed because Larousselle was calling for her, because it was five o'clock, because she wanted to get rid of the Courrèges.

"Well, *I* shall write to *you*, doctor, and you shall have the dreary duty of replying."

But a little later, when she had locked and bolted the door and gone back to the bedroom, her husband heard her laugh and asked what she was laughing at.

"The most extraordinary thing's just occurred to me . . . promise you won't mock. I really believe that the doctor was a bit in love with me in the old Bordeaux days . . . it wouldn't surprise me."

Victor Larousselle replied thickly through clammy lips that he wasn't jealous if that was what she meant, and followed up the remark with one of his hoariest jokes: "He's just ripe for the cold stone." He added that the poor fellow had obviously had a slight stroke. Many of his old patients, who didn't like to abandon him, secretly consulted other doctors.

"Not feeling sick any longer? Sure your hand doesn't hurt?"

No, he was quite comfortable.

"I only hope that the story of what happened to-night doesn't make the rounds in Bordeaux. . . . Young Courrèges is quite capable . . ."

"He never goes there nowadays. Try to get some sleep. I'm going to put out the light."

She sat in the darkness, motionless, until a sound of quiet snoring rose from the bed. Then she went to her room, passing, on the way, Bertrand's half-open door. She could not resist the temptation to push it wide. Standing on the threshold she sniffed. The mingled smell of tobacco and the human body filled her with a cold fury. 'I must have been mad to let him come in here! . . .' She opened the windows to let in the cold air of dawn, and knelt down for a moment at the head of the bed. Her lips moved. She buried her face in the pillow.

XII

THE doctor and Raymond drove away in a taxi. It was like the old days when they had sat together in the carriage with its streaming windows on a suburban road. At first they said no more to one another than they had used to do in that forgotten time. But there was a difference in the quality of their silence. The old man was sagging with weariness and leaned against his son. Raymond held his hand.

"I had no idea that she was married."

"They didn't tell anybody: at least, I believe and hope that they didn't. They certainly didn't tell me."

It was said that young Bertrand had insisted on the situation being regularized. The doctor quoted a remark made by Victor Larousselle: "I am making a morganatic marriage." Raymond muttered: "What dam' cheek!" He stole a glance in the half-light at the tormented face beside him, and saw that the bloodless lips were moving. The frozen expression, the features looking as though they were carved in stone, frightened him. He said the first thing that came into his head.

"How's everybody?"

Flourishing. Madeleine, in particular, said the doctor, was being splendid. She lived for nothing but her two girls, took them out to parties, and hid her sorrow from the world, showing herself worthy of the hero she had lost. (The doctor never neglected an opportunity of praising the son-in-law who had been killed at Guise, striving, in this way, to make honourable amends for the past. He blamed himself for having been wrong about him. So many men in the war had been surprisingly unlike themselves in death.) Catherine, Madeleine's eldest daughter, was engaged to the Michon boy, the youngest of three brothers, but there was to be no public announcement until she was twenty-two:

"You mustn't breathe a word about it."

The voice in which he uttered this injunction was his wife's, and Raymond caught back the words he had been about to say: "Why should anyone in Paris be interested?" The doctor broke off as though suddenly silenced by a stab of pain. The young man began silently to calculate: 'He must be sixty-nine or seventy. Is it possible to go on suffering at that age, and after all these years?' He became suddenly aware of his own hurt, and the consciousness of it frightened him. It wouldn't last . . . very soon it would pass into forgetfulness. He remembered something that one of his mistresses had said: "When I'm in love and going through hell, I just curl up and wait. I know that in a very short while the particular man in question will mean absolutely nothing to me, though at the moment I may be ready to die for him, that I shan't so much as spare a passing glance for the cause of so much suffering. It's terrible to love, and humiliating to stop loving. . . ." All the same, this old man had been bleeding from a mortal wound for seventeen long years. In lives like his, hedged about with routine, dominated by a sense of duty, passion becomes concentrated, is put away, as it were, in cold storage. There is no way of using it up, no breath of warm air can reach it and start the process of evaporation. It grows and grows, stagnates, corrupts, poisons and corrodes the living flesh that holds it prisoner.

They swung round the Arc de Triomphe. Between the puny trees of the Champs Élysées the black road flowed on like Erebus.

"I think I've done with pottering around. I've been offered a job in a factory. They make chicory. At the end of a year I shall be managing director."

The doctor's reply was perfunctory: "I'm so glad, my boy." Suddenly he shot a question: "How did you first meet?"

"Meet whom?"

"You know perfectly well what I mean."

"The friend who offered me this job?"

"Of course not—Maria."

"It goes back a long way. When I was in my last term at school, we got to exchanging a few words in the tram. I think that's how it all began."

"You never told me, though once, if I remember correctly, you did mention that some friend had pointed her out to you in the street."

"Perhaps I did . . . one's memory gets a bit hazy after seventeen years. Yes, it all comes back now: it was the day after that meeting that she first spoke to me—actually, it was to ask after you. She knew me by sight. I think that if her husband hadn't come over to me this evening she'd have cut me."

This brief interchange seemed to have set the doctor's mind at rest. He leaned back in his corner. He muttered: "Anyhow, what does it matter to me? What does it matter?" He made the old familiar gesture of sweeping away some obstacle, rubbed his cheeks, sat up and half turned towards Raymond in an effort to escape from his thoughts, to occupy his mind only with his son's concerns.

"As soon as you've got an assured position, my boy, hurry up and get married."

Raymond laughed, protested, and the old man was once more driven in upon himself:

"You can have no idea what a comfort it is to live in the middle of a large family. Yes, I mean it. One's all the time got to think about other people's troubles, and those thousands of little hypodermic pricks keep the blood flowing. D'you see what I mean? One has no time to think of one's own secret miseries, of the wounds that strike deep into the very roots of one's being. One gets to rely on all these family concerns. . . . For instance, I meant to stay in Paris until the end of the Conference, but I've suddenly decided to catch the eight o'clock train this morning. I just can't help myself. The great thing in life is to make some sort of refuge for oneself. At the end of one's existence, as at the beginning, one's got to be borne by a woman."

Raymond mumbled something about rather seeing himself dead first. He looked at the shrunken, moth-eaten old figure at his side.

"You can have no idea how safe I've always felt with all of you round me. To have a wife, children, about one, pressing in on one, is a sort of protection against all the undesirable distractions of outside life. You never used to say much to me—I don't mean that as a reproach, dear boy—but I don't think you'll ever realize how often, just as I was on the point of yielding to some delicious, maybe criminal, temptation, I would feel your hand on my shoulder gently guiding me back into the right path."

"How ridiculous to think that there are such things as forbidden pleasures," Raymond muttered. "We're completely different, you and I; I'd have overturned the whole apple-cart in next to no time."

"You're not the only one who made your mother suffer. We're not really so different. Scores of times I've sent the apple-cart spinning—in imagination. You don't know. . . . No, you *don't*. A few casual infidelities would have brought me far less sorrow than the long-drawn-out disloyalty of desire of which I have been guilty for the last thirty years. It is essential that you should know all this, Raymond. You'd find it pretty difficult to be a worse husband than I have been. Oh, I know my orgies never went beyond day-dreaming, but does that make it any better? The way your mother takes her revenge now is by being over-attentive. Her fussing has become a necessity of my existence. The endless trouble to which she goes. She never lets me out of her sight day or night. I shall die in the lap of comfort, never fear. We're not looked after now as we used to be. Servants, as she says, are no longer what they were. We've never replaced Julie—d'you remember Julie? She's gone back to her native village. Your mother does everything. I have to scold her, often. There's nothing she won't turn her hand to—sweeping out the rooms, polishing the floors."

He stopped, then, with a note of supplication in his voice: "Don't live alone," he said.

Raymond had no time to reply. The taxi stopped in front of the Grand Hotel. He had to get out, feel for his money. The doctor had only just enough time to do his packing.

These early hours of the morning, all given over to street-sweepers and market-gardeners, were familiar to Raymond Courrèges. He breathed in the dawn air, rejoicing in the well-known sights, remembering how he always felt as he walked home in the small hours, physically exhausted, his senses gorged and satisfied, happy as a young animal, wanting nothing but to find its burrow, to curl up and sleep. What a blessing that his father had decided to say good-bye at the door of the Grand Hotel. How he had aged! How he had shrunk! 'There can never be too many miles for my liking, between me and the family,' he thought. 'The further away one's relations, the better.' It came over him that he was no longer thinking about Maria. He remembered that he had a whole lot of things to do to-day. He took out his engagement-book, turned the pages, and was amazed to discover how vast the day had become—or was it that the things with which he had proposed to fill it had diminished in number? The morning?—an empty waste: the afternoon?—two appointments which he had no intention of keeping. He leaned over his day like a child over the rim of a well. Only a few pebbles to drop into it, and *they* wouldn't fill the yawning void. Only one thing could do that—going to see Maria, being announced, being welcomed, sitting in the same room with her, talking to her—it wouldn't matter about what. Even less than that would have sufficed to fill these empty hours and many, many more—even just to have known that he had arranged a meeting with her, no matter how far ahead. With the patience of a marksman in a butt, he would have shot down the days separating him from that longed-for moment. Even if she had put him off, he would have found comfort somehow—provided she had suggested an alternative date, and the new hope thus started on its way would have been enough to fill the infinite emptiness of his life. For life now had become for him nothing but a feeling of absence which he had got to balance by a feeling of anticipation. 'I must think the whole business out seriously,' he told himself, 'and begin only with what is possible. Why shouldn't I get in touch with Bertrand again and worm my way into his life?' But they had no single taste in common, did not even know the same people. Anyhow, where was he to find him?—in what sacristy run this sacristan to earth? In imagination he obliterated all the intervening stages which separated him from Maria, jumped the gap, and reached the point at which he was holding that mysterious head in the crook of his right arm. He could feel on his biceps the touch of her shaven neck, like the cheek of a young boy. Her face swam towards him, closer, closer, enormously enlarged as on a cinema screen, and no less intangible. . . . It struck him with amazement that the early wayfarers he met did not turn to look at him, did not notice his mania. How well our clothes conceal our real selves! He dropped on to a seat opposite the Madeleine. This seeing her again . . . that was the trouble. He ought never to have seen her again. All the passions in which he had indulged for seventeen years had, unknown to him, been lit to protect himself from her—as the peasants of the Landes start small fires to keep the greater fire from spreading. . . . But he *had* seen her, and the fire had got the better of him, had been increased by the flames with which he had thought to combat it. His sensual aberrations, his secret vices, the cold technique of self-indulgence, so patiently learned, so carefully cultivated, all had added fuel to the conflagration, so that it roared upwards now, sweeping towards him on a vast front with a sound of crackling undergrowth.

'Lie low, curl yourself up into a ball,' he kept on saying to himself. 'It won't last, and until it's over, find some drug with which to stupefy yourself—float with the current.' Yes, but—his father would know no lessening of *his* pain until the day of his death. What a dreary life he'd led! But would a course of debauchery have freed him from his passion?—that was the question. Everything serves as fuel for passion: abstinence sharpens it: repletion strengthens it; virtue keeps it awake and irritates it. It terrifies and it fascinates. But if we yield, our cowardice is never abject enough to satisfy its exigence. It is a frantic and a horrible obsession. He should have asked his father how on earth he had managed to live with that cancer gnawing at his vitals. . . Of what use is a virtuous existence? What way of escape can it provide? What power has God over passion?

He concentrated his attention on the minute-hand of the great clock away to his left, trying to catch it in the act of moving. By this time, he thought, his father must already have left the hotel. He suddenly felt that he would like to give the old man one last kiss. There was more than paternity between them, there was another tie of blood. They were related in their common feeling for Maria Cross. . . .

Raymond hastened towards the river, though there was plenty of time before the train was due to leave. Perhaps he was yielding to that species of madness which compels those whose clothes have caught fire to run. He was oppressed by the intolerable conviction that he would never possess Maria Cross, that he would die without ever having her. Though he had had his will of many women, taken them, held them for a while, abandoned them, he felt himself to be in the grip of the same sort of wild despair which sometimes overwhelms men who have never known physical love, men condemned to a life of virginity, when they face the horror of dying without ever having known the delights of the flesh. What he had had in the past no longer counted. Nothing seemed worth the having save what he would never have.

Maria! He was appalled to think how heavily one human being may, without wishing it, weigh in the scales of another's destiny. He had never given a thought to those virtues which, radiating from ourselves, operate, often without our knowing it and often over great distances, on the hearts of others. All the way along the pavement that stretches between the Tuileries and the Seine he found himself, for the first time in his life, compelled to think about things to which, up till then, he had never given a moment's consideration. Probably because on the threshold of this new day he felt emptied of all ambitions, of all plans, of all possible amusements, he found that there was nothing now to keep his mind from the life that lay behind him. Because there was no longer any future to which he might look forward, the past swarmed into his mind. For how many living creatures had not his mere proximity meant death and destruction? Even now he did not know to what lives he had given purpose and direction, what lives he had cut adrift from their moorings; did not know that because of him some woman had killed the young life just stirring in her womb; that;because of him a young girl had died, a friend had gone into a seminary; and that each of these single dramas had given birth to others in an endless succession. On the brink of this appalling emptiness, of this day without Maria, which was to be but the first of many other days without her, he was made aware, at one and the same moment, of his dependence and his solitude. He felt himself forced into the closest possible communion with a woman with whom he would never make contact. It was enough that her eyes should see the light for Raymond to live forever in the darkness. For how long? If he decided that, at no matter what cost, he must fight his way out of the dense blackness, must escape from this murderous law of gravity, what choices were there open to him but the alternatives of stupor or of sleep?—unless this star in the firmament of his heart should go suddenly dead, as all love goes dead. He carried within him a tearing, frantic capability of passion, inherited from his father—of a passion that was all-powerful, that would breed, until he died, still other planetary worlds, other Maria Crosses, of which, in succession, he would become the miserable satellite. . . . There could be no hope for either of them, for father or for son, unless, before they died, He should reveal Himself Who, unknown to them, had drawn and summoned from the depths of their beings this burning, bitter tide.

He crossed the deserted Seine and looked at the station clock. By this time his father must be in the train. He went down on to the departure platform and walked along the row of waiting coaches. He did not have to search for long. Through the glass of one of the windows he saw the corpse-like face etched on the darkness of the interior. The eyes were closed, the clasped hands lay on a spread of newspaper, the head leaned slightly backwards, the mouth was half open. Raymond tapped with his finger. The corpse opened its eyes, recognized the source of the sound, smiled, and, with uncertain steps, came out into the corridor. But all the doctor's happiness was ruined by his childish fear that the train might start before Raymond had had time to get out.

"Now that I've seen you, now that I know you wanted to see *me* again, my mind is at rest. Better go now, dear boy. They're closing the doors."

It was in vain that the young man assured him that they had a good five minutes before the train would start, and that, in any case, it stopped at the Austerlitz station. The other continued to show signs of nervousness until his son was once more safely on the platform. Then, lowering the window, he gazed long and lovingly at him.

Raymond asked him whether he had got everything he wanted. Would he like another paper or a book? Had he reserved a seat in the restaurant car? To all these questions the doctor replied "Yes, yes." Hungrily he fixed his eyes on the young man who had asked them; the man who was so different from himself, and yet so like him—the part of his own flesh and blood that would survive him for a few more years, but that he was fated never to see again.

THE KNOT OF VIPERS

". . . Consider, O God, that we are without understanding of ourselves; that we do not know what we would have, and set ourselves at an infinite distance from our desires. . . ."

SAINT THERESA OF AVILA

THE man here depicted was the enemy of his own flesh and blood. His heart was eaten up by hatred and by avarice. Yet, I would have you, in spite of his baseness, feel pity, and be moved by his predicament. All through his dreary life squalid passions stood between him and that radiance which was so close that an occasional ray could still break through to touch and burn him: not only his own passions, but, primarily, those of the lukewarm Christians who spied upon his actions, and whom he himself tormented. Too many of us are similarly at fault, driving the sinner to despair and blinding his eyes to the light of truth.

It was not money that this miser really treasured, nor, in his blind fury, was it vengeance that he sought. What it was that he truly loved you may discover who have the strength of mind, and the courage, to follow his story to the end, to that ultimate moment of confession which death cut short.

PART ONE

I

WHEN you find this letter lying on top of a bundle of securities in my safe you will be surprised. I might have been better advised to entrust it to my solicitor, with instructions to hand it to you after my death, or to leave it in that locked drawer of my desk which my children will almost certainly force before my body has grown cold. But for years I have written and rewritten it in imagination, and always, in my bouts of sleeplessness, have seen it staring at me from the shelf of a safe empty of everything except this single act of vengeance upon which I have been brooding for almost half a century.

You need not be afraid. As a matter of fact, any cause for fear that you might have had will have been dissipated before you read these lines. "The securities are there all right!" I can hear your raised voice in the hall as you announce the good news on your return from the Bank. "The securities are there all right!" you'll say to the children through the folds of your mourning-veil.

But you've had a very narrow escape! I had taken all the necessary steps. Had I so willed it, you would stand to-day stripped of everything but the house and lands. You can thank your lucky stars that I have outlived my hatred. For years I believed that it was the most vital part of me. But now, quite suddenly, and for the time being, at least, it has ceased to mean anything to me. I find it difficult in my old age to recapture the vindictive mood of earlier years when I would lie in my sick-bed, night after night, not so much planning the method of revenge (the delay-action bomb had already been "set" with an attention to detail which was a matter of considerable pride to me) as wondering how I might derive the maximum of satisfaction from its detonation. I wanted to live just long enough to see your faces when you got back from the Bank. It was merely a matter of not giving you authority to open the safe too soon, of waiting just long enough to enjoy the sound of your despairing question—"but where *are* the securities?" I felt that no death-pangs, however frightful, could spoil that pleasure for me. Of such calculating malice was I capable! And yet, by nature I am not a monster. How came it, then, that I was brought to such a pass?

It is four o'clock, and my luncheon tray is still standing on the table, with flies buzzing round the dirty plates. I have rung, but with no result. Bells never work in the country. I am lying quite patiently in this room where I slept as a child, and where, no doubt, I shall die. When that moment comes, the first thought of our dear daughter Geneviève will be to claim it for her children. It is the largest in the house, and has the best outlook. It has been earmarked entirely for my own use. You will, I hope, do me the justice to admit that I did offer to move out in Geneviève's favour, and would have done so had not Dr Lacaze expressed the opinion that the dampness of the ground-floor might be bad for my bronchitis. I have no doubt that I should have been as good as my word: but I should have harboured such a sense of grievance that the doctor's refusal to countenance the change was, perhaps, fortunate. All through my life I have made sacrifices, and the memory of them has poisoned my mind, nourishing and fattening the kind of rancorous resentment which grows worse with the passage of the years.

The love of quarrelling is, with us, a family trait. I have often heard my mother say that my father quarrelled with his parents, and that they themselves died without ever again setting eyes on the daughter whom they had driven from home thirty years earlier (she married and produced that brood of Marseilles cousins with whom we have never had anything to do). None of us ever knew the rights and wrongs of the squabble, but we took the hatreds of our forbears so wholeheartedly on trust, that, if I ran across one of those Marseilles cousins in the street, to-day, I should turn my back on him. But, after all, one needn't have anything to do with one's distant relations. It is a very different matter with wives and children. No doubt united families *do* exist: but when I think of the number of households in which two individuals live a life of constant exasperation and mutual loathing, for ever sitting at the same table, using the same wash-basin, lying between the same sheets, it is really remarkable how few divorces there are! They live in a constant state of mutual detestation, yet can never escape an enforced proximity!

Why should I have felt the itch to scribble on my birthday? I am entering on my sixty-eighth year, but no one else knows it. There are always cakes and flowers and little candles for Geneviève and Hubert and their children when birthdays come round. . . . If I have never, for years past, given you anything on yours, that is not because I have overlooked it. No, it is my form of revenge, and I get a certain satisfaction from it. . . . The last bunch of birthday flowers that ever came my way was picked by the crippled fingers of my poor mother. In order to get them, she had, in spite of her weak heart, paid one last, painful visit to the rose-garden.

Where was I? Oh yes, you will doubtless be wondering why I have been suddenly seized by this mania for writing. "Mania" is the right word. You can judge of its strength from the way all the letters lean the same way, like pine-trees under the impact of a westerly wind. Listen: I began this letter by referring to a vengeance on which I had long brooded but now renounce. There is, however, something in you, some part *of* you, that I long to overcome—your silence. Don't mistake my meaning. You have a ready enough tongue, and can talk about poultry and vegetables for hours on end with Cazau. With the children, even with the youngest of them, you can jabber, day after day, until I can scarcely hear myself think. Many's the time I have got up from the table with my head feeling as empty as a rotten nut, obsessed by business cares and worries of every kind, which I could not share with a soul . . . especially after the Villenave case, which led to my being recognized (to quote the newspapers) as a "great Criminal Pleader." The more tempted I was to believe in my own importance, the more determined did you seem to make me feel my insignificance. . . . But it's not that I am referring to now. The silence I want to get my own back on is of quite a different kind. It comes of your determined refusal ever to discuss our own affairs, our own utter failure to understand one another. Many and many a time, watching a play or reading a novel, I find myself wondering whether, in actual fact, there ever *are* lovers or married couples who have "scenes," who lay all their cards on the table and find relief in unburdening their hearts.

For forty years we have suffered side by side. In the whole of that time you have always managed to avoid saying anything that went below the surface, have always avoided committing yourself.

I believed at one time that this attitude of yours was deliberate, the expression of some fixed determination the reason for which escaped me. And then, quite suddenly, I realized the truth—which was that discussions of the kind I longed for just didn't interest you. So utterly alien was I from all your concerns, that you shied away, not because you were frightened but because you were bored. You became an expert at scenting danger, and could see me coming a mile off. If, sometimes, I managed to take you by surprise, either you succeeded, without difficulty, in avoiding the issue, or you patted my cheek, gave me a kiss, and made for the door.

I might have some reason to fear that, having read thus far, you will tear this letter up and read no farther. But somehow, I don't think that is likely to happen. For some time now I have caught you looking at me with a certain amount of surprise and curiosity. You may not be very observant where I am concerned, but even you can hardly fail to have noticed a change in my mood. I feel pretty well assured that, this time, you will not avoid the issue. I want you to know, you, and the rest of your brood, your son, your daughter, your son-in-law and your grandchildren, what manner of man it is who has lived out his solitary existence in your midst, and against whom you have closed your ranks; the overworked lawyer who has had to be handled with tact because he held the purse-strings, but whose sufferings might have been those of somebody living on a different planet. What planet? It has never occurred to you to try to find out. Don't be alarmed. I am no more concerned here to compose an advance Obituary of myself than to draw up a Brief for the Prosecution in the case of Me versus You. The one outstanding quality of my mind—which would have impressed itself on any other woman—is a terrifying lucidity.

I have never possessed the power of self-deception which is most men's stand-by in the struggle for existence. When I have acted basely, I have always known precisely what I was doing. . . .

At this point I had to break off . . . no one brought me a lamp, or came to close the shutters. . . . I sat here looking out at the roof of the bottling-shed, the tiles of which are as vivid in colour as flowers or the breasts of birds. I could hear the thrushes in the ivy on the Carolina poplar, and the noise made by somebody rolling a cask. I am fortunate in being able to wait for death in the one spot of all the world where everything is as I remember it, the sole difference being that the stutter of a motor-engine has replaced the creaking of the old bucket-and-chain well worked by a donkey. (And of course, there's the loathsome mail-plane which announces tea-time, and leaves its horrible smear across the sky.)

Few men are lucky enough to be able to find again in their actual physical surroundings, and within their range of vision, the world which most discover only if they have the courage and the patience to search their memories. . . . I lay my hand on my chest and feel the beating of my heart. I look at the glass-fronted medicine-cupboard containing the hypodermic syringe, the little bottle of nitrite of amyl, and such other odds and ends as might be needed should I have one of my attacks. Would anybody hear me if I called? You're all so insistent that it's only a *false angina*, not so much because you want to convince *me*, but because you'd like to believe it yourselves, and so feel justified in sleeping soundly at night. I am breathing more easily now. It is exactly as though a hand were gripping my left shoulder and keeping it rigid in a strained position, so that I may never be allowed to forget, for a moment, what's lying in wait for me. In my case, death certainly won't come by stealth. It has been snuffing round me for years. I can hear it and feel its breath. It treats me with patience because I make no effort to resist, because I submit to the discipline which its approach imposes. I am ending my life in a dressing-gown, surrounded by all the paraphernalia of incurable disease, sunk in the great winged chair where my mother sat waiting for her end. There is a table beside me, as there was beside her, laden with medicine-bottles. I am ill-shaven and evil-smelling, a slave to all sorts of disgusting little habits. But don't be too sure. In the intervals between attacks I am my old self. Bourru, the solicitor, who thought me as good as gone, has got used to seeing me turn up as hale and hearty as ever, and I can still spend hours in the safe-deposit vault, snipping off dividend coupons unaided.

I must manage to live long enough to complete this confession, to *make* you listen. During all the years in which I shared your bed, you never failed, each time I got in beside you, to say—"I'm simply *dropping*, I'm half-asleep already. . . ."

It was less my endearments than my words that you were trying to avoid.

True, our unhappiness began with the sort of interminable discussions which are the delight of young married couples. We were little more than children. I was twenty-three, you eighteen, and perhaps love was less of a pleasure to us than the confidences, the talks, in which we gave free play to all our thoughts. Like young children in their earliest friendships, we had sworn to tell one another everything. So little had I to confess, that I was driven to elaborate and embellish such squalid little adventures as had come my way, nor did it ever occur to me that your experience had been any fuller than my own. I never dreamed that, before I came into your life, you might have murmured another man's name to yourself, and in this belief I continued, until . . .

It was in this very room where I sit writing now. The wall-paper has been changed, but the mahogany furniture still stands precisely where it did then. There was then, as now, a tumbler of iridescent glass upon the table, along with a tea-set which had been won in a raffle. Moonlight flooded the matting, and the south wind, blowing across the Landes, brought the smell of heath-fires to our very bedside.

That night you spoke once more of Rodolphe—the old friend whom you had often mentioned, and always in the dusk of our room, as though you wanted to make sure that his ghost should be between us in the moments of our closest union. Have you forgotten? It was not enough for you now merely to mention his name.

"There are things, darling, I ought to have told you before we got engaged. I feel rather guilty about having kept them back—not that there was ever anything the least bit serious—so please don't start worrying. . . ."

I was quite easy in my mind, and did nothing to provoke a confession. But you forced it on me.So eager were you to tell me the whole story that, at first, I felt rather embarrassed. It wasn't that you wanted to ease your conscience: it wasn't that you felt you owed it me to make a clean breast of this particular chapter in your past—though that was the reason you gave, and that was what I think you really believed.

No, the truth of the matter was that you were revelling in a delicious memory. You could no longer resist the sweet temptation. Perhaps you suspected that the incident might constitute a possible threat to our happiness. However that may be, the whole thing was, as they say, beyond your power to control. The shadow of this Rodolphe hung over our marriage bed, and there was nothing you could do about it.

But I don't want you to run away with the idea that our unhappiness started in jealousy. Later, it is true, I was to become furiously jealous, but I certainly felt nothing remotely resembling that passion on the summer night of '85 which I am now recalling, the night on which you confessed that, while on holiday at Aix, you had become engaged to this unknown young man.

How odd to think that I should have had to wait forty-five years before explaining what I felt about it all! I am not even sure that you will read this letter. The whole thing is of so little interest to you. *My* concerns are, to you, sheer boredom. Very early on, the children began to come between us, so that you neither saw nor heard me, and now there are the grandchildren. . . . Well, it can't be helped. I am going to make this one last effort. It may be that I shall exert greater power over you when I am dead than I ever did while living . . . anyhow, at first. For a few weeks I shall once again occupy a place in your life. If only as a matter of duty you will read these pages to the end. That I *must* believe. I do.

II

AS I have said, at the time of your confession I felt no jealousy. How am I to make you understand what it was that it destroyed in me?

I was the only child of the woman whom you knew as a widow, or, rather, in whose society you lived for many long years without ever really knowing her at all. But even if you had been sufficiently interested to try to discover the precise nature of the bond uniting that particular mother and that particular son, I doubt whether you would have succeeded in doing so. *You* were one of the many component cells of a powerful and numerous middle-class family, one element in a hierarchy, one cog in a highly organized machine. You could not begin to grasp the extent to which the widow of a minor official at the Prefecture could be wrapped up in a son when he was all that she had left to her. She took pride in my school successes, and in them I, too, found all my happiness. At that time I was fully convinced that we were very poor. The evidence was all around me, in the narrow pattern of our lives, in the strict economy which my mother made the law of our being. Not that I was allowed to want for anything. I realize to-day how spoiled I was as a child. My mother's farms, at Hosteins, furnished us with a quantity of inexpensive food, and I should have been much surprised had I been told that it was of exceptional quality. Corn-fed chickens, hares, goose-paté, were not my idea of luxury. I had always heard it said that our land was of no great value, and, indeed, when my mother came into her inheritance it had consisted only of stretches of grassland on which my grandfather, as a child, had herded cattle. What I did not know was that my parents' first care had been to make it productive, and that at twenty-one I should find myself the owner of two thousand hectares of mature timber already yielding a great number of pit-props. My mother managed, also, to save some part of her modest income. Even during my father's lifetime, the two of them had "bled themselves white" so as to be able to buy Calèse (forty thousand francs they paid for those vineyards which now I wouldn't part with for a million!). We lived in the Rue Sainte-Catherine, on the third floor of a house belonging to us (it had, together with a number of vacant lots, formed my father's inheritance). Twice each week we received a hamper from the country. My mother went as seldom as possible to the butcher. The only ambition I had at that time was to enter the École Normale. There was a battle royal on Thursdays and Sundays before I could be induced to take a little exercise in the fresh air. I was not in the least like those boys who are always head of the class without any apparent effort. I was a "swot," and proud of it: just a common or garden plodder. I cannot remember ever having taken the least pleasure, while at school, in studying Virgil or Racine. They were "set books" for me, and nothing more. I segregated from among the achievements of the human spirit such subjects as formed part of the curriculum—no others seemed to me to have the slightest importance—and wrote just the sort of essays that one had to write in order to satisfy the examiners: in other words, precisely what had already been written by generations of candidates. That was the kind of little idiot I was, and probably would have continued to be, but for an attack of blood-spitting which terrified my mother and, two months before the École Normale entrance examination, compelled me to abandon all hope of my chosen career.

That was the price I had to pay for an overworked childhood and an unhealthy adolescence. A growing youth cannot, with impunity, sit crouched over a table far into the night, and despise all forms of physical exercise. Am I boring you? I am terrified of boring you. You mustn't skip a line. You must take my word for it that I am confining myself strictly to the essentials of my story. The drama of our two lives, yours and mine, was conditioned by things which happened to me as a young man, things you never knew or, having known, promptly forgot.

At any rate, these first few pages will have shown you that I have no intention of letting myself off easily—and that must be not a little satisfying to your hatred. . . . Please don't protest. . . . If you have begun to think about me now, it is solely in the hope of finding nourishment for your hostility.

I don't want to be unjust in my attitude to the undersized and sickly creature whom I left, just now, poring over his lexicons. When I read other men's recollections of childhood, and take notice of the paradise which seems to fascinate their backward gaze, I cannot help feeling a sharp spasm of pain. "How about myself?" I ask; "why this sense of a waste-land ever since my earliest years? Maybe I have forgotten what these others remember: maybe I, too, trailed clouds of glory. . . ." But, alas, I can recall nothing but desperate struggles, nothing but the embittered rivalry in which I was involved with one chap called Hennoch and another called Rodrigue. I instinctively repulsed all friendly advances. There were some, I remember, on whom the prestige of my successes exerted a species of attraction, so that they were fascinated by my very churlishness. I did not suffer affection gladly: I had a horror of "sentiment."

Were I a professional writer, I could not compose a single "touching" passage from the record of my school years. . . . But wait, I *do* recollect one incident, trivial though it may appear. I recalled very little about my father, but there were moments at which I felt convinced that he was not really dead at all, but only that, as the result of a combination of circumstances, he had somehow vanished. On such occasions I would run all the way along the Rue Sainte-Catherine on my way home from school, keeping to the middle of the road, and dodging the traffic, because I was afraid that the crowded pavement would slow me down. I would take the stairs four at a time—only to find my mother darning by the window, and the photograph of my father hanging in its usual place to the right of my bed. Then, scarcely responding to my mother's kiss, I would settle down to my books.

After the blood-spitting incident which changed the whole pattern of my future, I spent several melancholy months in a cottage at Arcachon. The ruin of my health had put a full-stop to any hope of a university career. My poor mother got on my nerves. She seemed to take no account of my changed circumstances, and to be wholly unconcerned about what was to happen to me. Each day, she lived for "thermometer-time." All her sorrow, all her joy, seemed to hang upon the record of my weekly weighings. When, later, it was my fate to lead the life of an invalid, without anybody showing the least interest in the state of my health, I realized that I was suffering the just punishment for my hardness of heart, for the unyielding resentment of the spoiled child which I had shown in those earlier years.

With the first of the fine weather I began, as my mother put it, to "look up." Indeed, I was like somebody reborn. I broadened out and grew stronger. My body had suffered cruelly from the discipline I had imposed upon it, but now, in the dry air of the forest, with its furze and arbutus, which surrounded Arcachon in the days when it was no more than a village, it began to put forth new blossoms of health.

About this time I learned from my mother that there was no need for me to worry about the future; that we were the possessors of a handsome fortune which was increasing year by year. I could well afford to wait, since, almost certainly, I should be released from military service. All my masters had been struck by my unusual fluency in speaking. My mother was anxious for me to read law, and seemed convinced that, without fatiguing myself unduly, I could easily become a success at the bar, unless, of course, I felt attracted to politics. . . . On and on she talked, pouring out all her plans for me, and I sat there listening, in a mood of sulky hostility, staring out of the window.

I began to run after women. Noticing this new development, my mother adopted an attitude of frightened tolerance. In later years, as a result of living in close contact with your relations, I have learned how seriously sexual irregularities are regarded in religious families. The only thing that worried my mother was the possible ill effect of such indulgences on my health. Once she was assured that I was being reasonably careful she shut her eyes to my nocturnal outings, though always stipulating that I should be home by midnight. Don't be afraid that I am going into the details of my amorous adventures. I know how all that side of life disgusts you, and, anyhow, they were too trivial and too squalid to deserve recording.

But this I will say, that even in those early days I paid a high price for them. I suffered from the fact that I was deficient in charm, that my youthfulness paid such poor dividends. It was not, I think, that I was ill-looking. My features were "regular," and Geneviève, who is the living image of me, was very pretty as a girl. No, my trouble was that I am one of those who, in popular parlance, have never known what it is to be young. There had been an over-plus of gloom, a lack of freshness, about my early years. The very look of me was enough to produce in others a sense of chill, and the more I realized this, the less accommodating did I become. I have never learned how to wear my clothes, how to choose a tie, or tie it when chosen. I have never in all my life known what it is to be unself-conscious, or to laugh or play the fool. I cannot imagine myself forming one of a party on the "spree." I am by nature one of Nature's wet blankets. At the same time, I am cursed with an excess of sensitiveness, and I was never able to stand being laughed at, no matter how good-humoured the laughter might be. On the other hand, whenever I made a joke at other people's expense, I always, without meaning to, struck so savagely that my victims never forgave me. I invariably chose to make fun of the one thing, some physical infirmity, for instance, about which I ought to have kept silent. Because of my shyness, and because of my pride, I adopted to women that superior attitude of the hectoring schoolmaster which, of all things, they most resent. I never noticed what they were wearing. The more conscious I was of their dislike, the more intolerable did I become. My youth was a prolonged condition of suicide. I was deliberately uncouth simply because I was afraid of being unconsciously so.

Rightly or wrongly I blamed my mother for this temperament of mine. I had got the idea that I was paying for the fact that, ever since my childhood, I had been cosseted, supervised and looked after far too much. I was abominably brutal to her at this time. She doted on me, as I have said, to a ridiculous extent. I could not forgive her for lavishing on me the affection which I was fated to have from nobody else. You must forgive me for harping on this subject. Only the thought of what she gave makes it possible for me to endure that failure to give which has always marked your attitude to me. It is right and proper that I should pay the price of my misdeeds. She has been dead now, poor woman, for many years, and the memory of her lives only in the heart of an old and worn-out man. How terribly she would have suffered could she have foreseen how the future was to avenge her!

Yes, I was a brute. In the little dining-room at the cottage, under the hanging lamp at meal-times, I would answer her timid questions with the barest monosyllables, or would fly into sullen rages on the slightest excuse, and often on no excuse at all.

She made no attempt to understand, never tried to discover the reasons for my outbursts of temper, but submitted to them as to the whim of some angry God. It was because I had been ill, she said: I must learn to relax. And then she would go on to explain that she was too ignorant ever to hope to be able to understand me. "I realize that an old woman is no fit companion for a boy of your age. . . ." In the past she had been careful, not to say miserly, about money, but now she gave me far more than I asked for, encouraged me to spend lavishly, and used to bring me back from Bordeaux the most ridiculous ties which I obstinately refused to wear.

We made friends with some neighbours, to whose daughter I proceeded to lay siege—though I did not care two pins about her. She had been ill, and was spending a winter of convalescence at Arcachon. My mother was terribly worried. She was afraid I might catch something from her, or compromise her by my attentions and be jockeyed into an engagement. I realize now that I went on with my courtship (which, as it happened, was entirely without effect) simply and solely with the intention of hurting her.

We returned to Bordeaux after a year's absence. We had moved. My mother had bought a house on one of the boulevards, but had said nothing to me about it, because she wanted to spring it upon me as a surprise. I was staggered when the front-door was opened by a man-servant. The whole of the first floor was reserved for my especial use. Everything looked brand new. I was secretly dazzled by a luxury which, looking back, I now see must have been pretty awful. But I kept my pleasure to myself, and, such was my cruelty, spoke to her only in disparagement of her efforts, and nagged at her about the expense.

It was then that she gave me a triumphant account of her stewardship—though there was absolutely no need for her to do so, since most of the money came from her side of the family. An income of fifty thousand francs, to say nothing of what the timber brought in, constituted at that time, and especially in the provinces, a very "tidy" fortune. Any other young man would have used it to make a career for himself, and to buy his right of entry into the highest ranks of local society. In my case, it was not ambition that was lacking, but the dislike which I felt for my companions in Law School and concealed with difficulty.

Most of them were the sons of leading families in the city, and had been educated by the Jesuits. As a mere Secondary-School product, and the grandson of a shepherd, I could not forgive them for the hateful sense of envy which their manners roused in me, though I regarded them as my intellectual inferiors. Envy of those whom one despises is a degrading passion and may well poison a whole life.

But I did envy them, and I did despise them, while their contempt of me (probably the product of my imagination) served to exacerbate my resentment. To a youth of my temperament it never even occurred to try to win their friendship. In fact, I did all I could to make common cause with their adversaries. That hatred of religion which, for so long, has been my dominant passion, which has caused you so much suffering and has set a wall of enmity between us, started in Law School, in 1879 and 1880, when Article 7 was voted by the Chamber. It was the year which saw the famous Decrees and the expulsion of the Jesuits.

Until that time I had been indifferent to such matters. My mother never talked to me about religion, except to say—"I am quite easy in my mind: if people like ourselves are not saved, then nobody will be." She had me baptized. My first Communion, which I took while at school, left on me the impression merely of a boring formality, and my memory of it is extremely vague. In any case it was unique. I never took Communion again. My ignorance in all matters touching religion was profound. When, as a child, I used to pass priests in the street, I always thought of them as of people wearing a disguise, as a species of maskers. I never grappled with problems of faith, and when, later, I came up against them, I approached them only from the political angle.

I founded a study-circle which used to meet at the Café Voltaire. Its value to me was that of a training-ground in public speaking. The boy who was so shy in his personal dealings with others became a totally different person in open debate. I had a number of followers, and thoroughly enjoyed the feeling that I was their leader, but this did not prevent me from despising them, just as I despised the middle-class youths among my fellow students. I resented the simple-minded way in which they exhibited their petty motives, because it forced me to realize that my own motives were precisely similar. They were the sons of minor Civil Servants, former scholarship boys, intelligent, ambitious, but embittered. There was no affection in the flattery they offered me. I asked them to dinner once or twice, and those evenings were for them red-letter occasions, much talked about. But their manners disgusted me, and a time came when I could no longer resist the temptation to make fun of them. They were mortally offended, and never forgot.

Nevertheless, my hatred of religion, and of all that had to do with it, was perfectly sincere. My social conscience was beginning to give me trouble. I made my mother pull down the wattle-and-daub cottages in which our farm-hands lived on an insufficient diet of thin wine and black bread. For the first time in her life she tried to stand up to me: "You'll get no thanks for it. . . ."

I did not press the point. I knew only too well that my adversaries and I had the same ruling passion—land and money—and I hated having to admit it. There are, in all societies, the "haves" and the "have-nots," and I realized that I should always belong to the "haves." My fortune was as large as, if not larger than, that of the solemn asses who, I thought, averted their eyes when they saw me, but would be only too glad to take my hand if I should offer it. There was no lack of those, both of the Right and of the Left, who were delighted at a chance of throwing my two thousand hectares of timber and vineyard in my teeth on the public platform.

You must forgive me for dwelling on this subject. It is essential that you should have a thorough grasp of these details if you are to understand what our meeting meant to the sort of disgruntled creature I had become, and what wonderful hopes I built on our mutual love. That I, the son of peasants, whose mother had gone about with her head tied up in a handkerchief, should actually marry into the Fondaudège family, was something at which the imagination boggled. It was beyond my power to conceive.

III

I BROKE off in my writing because the light was getting bad, and because I could hear voices below. Not that any of you were making much noise. Far from it, you were being particularly careful to keep your voices down, and that was what worried me. Formerly, I could always overhear your conversations from this room, but now you have grown suspicious, and have taken to whispering. You told me the other day that I was getting "hard of hearing," but that is not true. I can catch the sound of trains rumbling over the viaduct perfectly well. No, I certainly am not deaf. The truth of the matter is that you are all of you talking in low voices. You want to make quite certain that I shall not know what you are talking about. What is it that you want to keep from me? Business worries? There they all are, hanging round you, on the look-out for what they can pick up—our son-in-law in the rum trade, and our grandson-in-law who does nothing, and our son, Hubert, the stockbroker . . . the chap who pays 20 per cent. and has everybody's money to play with!

Don't rely on me: I'm not shelling out! "It would be so easy" —you'll murmur to me to-night—"to fell some of the pines." Yoy will remind me that Hubert's two girls have been living with their parents-in-law since their marriage, because they can't afford to furnish homes of their own. "We've got masses of stuff just rotting away in the loft: it wouldn't cost us anything to lend them some of it. . . ." That's the suggestion you'll be making to me in an hour or so. "They resent our attitude. They never come to see us. I'm being cheated out of my own grandchildren. . . ." That's what you've all been whispering about so busily.

I've been reading over the stuff I wrote yesterday evening. I must have been suffering from a sort of delirium. How could I so let my feelings get the better of me? I started this as a letter, but it's a letter no longer. It has become a diary, now and then broken off, now and then resumed. . . . Shall I tear it up and begin all over again? No, I can't do that: time is pressing. What I have written I have written. After all, didn't I want to make a clean breast to you of everything?—didn't I want to force you to look into the bottom of my mind? For thirty years I have been nothing to you but a machine for dealing out thousand-franc notes, a machine that has been running badly, a machine that you've got to patch up until the happy day when you'll be able to break it open, empty it, and plunge your hands into the treasure it contains.

There, I'm letting my temper run away with me again. I'm back at the point where I left off. I must trace this evil mood of mine to its source, must recall that fatal night. . . . But first of all, I would have you cast your mind back to the occasion of our first meeting.

In August, 1883, I was staying with my mother at Luchon. At that time the Hotel Sacarron was crammed with heavily upholstered furniture, cushions, and stuffed chamoix. After all these years it is the limes of the Allées d'Ettigny that I smell when the season comes round for the limes to flower. The patter of mules, the tinkling of bells, the crack of whips, used to wake me in the mornings. The water of the mountain torrents gurgled in the streets. The air was full of voices calling *croissants* and milk loaves. Guides rode by on horseback. I used to watch the parties of climbers setting out.

The whole of the first floor was occupied by the Fondaudège family. They had King Leopold's suite. "They must be making the money fly!" said my mother. But that didn't prevent them from being always in arrears when it came to settling their business debts (they had taken a lease of a big plot of land which we owned in the docks, for purposes connected with their shipping interests.)

My mother and I always dined at the *table d'hôte*, but you and your family had meals served to you separately. I can still remember that round table in the window, and your fat grandmother who concealed her baldness under an arrangement of black lace with quivering jet ornaments. I felt convinced that she was smiling at me, but it was the way her tiny eyes were set in her face, and her great slit of a mouth, which produced that impression. A nun waited on her, a woman with a puffy, bilious face swathed in starched linen. How beautiful your mother was! She wore nothing but black, being in perpetual mourning for the two children she had lost. It was she, not you, who was the first object of my furtive admiration. The nakedness of her throat, her arms and her hands, set my heart beating. She wore no jewellery. I played with the idea of stalking her à la Stendhal, and gave myself until the evening to murmur a word to her, or to slip a note into her hand. You I scarcely noticed. I had an idea that young girls did not interest me. Besides, you had that particular arrogance which takes the form of never looking at other people, and is tantamount to denying their existence.

One day, on my way back from the Casino, I came on my mother in conversation with Madame Fondaudège. The latter's manner was obsequious, and just a little too friendly. She gave me the impression of somebody who knows that it is useless to try to lower herself to the level of her companion. Mother, on the other hand, was speaking in a loud voice. She was dealing with a tenant, and, in her eyes, a Fondaudège was no more than a debtor in arrears. A countrywoman by nature, and an owner of land, she had a profound distrust of big business and of the kind of fortunes it produced, none of them built on a foundation of solid property. I broke in on the discussion just as she was saying: "Of course I have complete confidence in Monsieur Fondaudège's signature: all the same——"

For the first time in my life I intervened in a business argument. Madame Fondaudège got the extension she wanted. I have often thought, since then, that my mother's peasant shrewdness did not mislead her. Your family has cost me a pretty penny, and if I had just sat back and let myself be sucked dry, your son, your daughter and your grandson-in-law would very soon have made ducks and drakes of my fortune and swallowed it up in their business speculations. Business indeed!—what has it ever amounted to?—a ground-floor office, a telephone and a typist! . . . Behind that setting the money has been drained away by the bucketful. . . . But I anticipate: we are still in 1883 at Bagnères-de-Luchon.

That powerful family of yours was now all smiles. Your grandmother went on talking the whole time because she was deaf. No sooner did I have an opportunity of chatting with your mother after dinner than I found that she bored me and completely upset all my preconceived romantic ideas. You will, I am sure, forgive me if I point out that her conversation was tedious in the extreme. So limited was the world in which she lived, and so jejune was her vocabulary that, after the first few minutes, I had had enough and was at my wits' end to keep the talk going at all.

My attention, thus diverted from the mother, became fixed upon the daughter. I failed, at first, to notice the suspicious absence of all obstacles to our intimacy. But then, why should it have occurred to me that your family might be congratulating themselves on having made a good "catch"? I remember one drive, in particular, up the Valley of the Lys. Your grandmother and her nun were in the back of the victoria: you and I occupied the little let-down seats facing them. God knows there were carriages and to spare in Luchon! Only the Fondaudèges would have dreamed of bringing their own!

The horses proceeded at a walking pace, moving in a cloud of flies. The good sister's face was shiny, and her eyes half shut. Your grandmother sat flapping a fan which she had bought in the Allées d'Ettigny. It was decorated with a picture of a matador giving the *coup de grâce* to a black bull. You had long gloves, in spite of the heat. Everything you wore was white, down to your high-laced boots. Ever since the death of your two brothers, you said, you had had "a devotion to white." I did not know what "having a devotion to white" meant. I have learned since what a point your family made of these rather exotic "devotions." In my then state of mind I thought it all rather poetical. How can I possibly make you understand the emotion that you roused in me? I had become suddenly aware that I was no longer unpleasing, had ceased to repel, was not odious any more. One of the most important moments of my life was when you said: "How extraordinary that a man should have such long lashes!"

I was careful to keep my advanced ideas dark. I remember how, in the course of that drive, we got out in order to lighten the carriage on a hill, how your grandmother and her nun told their beads, and how the old coachman, long trained in the way he should go, made his responses to their *Ave Marias*. You looked at me with a smile, but I remained solemn. It cost me nothing to accompany you to eleven o'clock Mass on Sundays. There was, for me, no metaphysical idea attached to the ceremony. It was merely the religious exercise of a class in which I was proud to find myself numbered, a species of ancestor-worship adapted to the use of the bourgeoisie, a hotch-potch of rites with nothing but a social significance. Occasionally you would give me a sidelong glance, and the memory of those Masses remains associated in my mind with the staggering discovery which I made at that time, that I was capable of arousing interest, pleasure, and emotion in another. The love which I felt was all mixed up with the love which I inspired—or thought I inspired. There was nothing real about my own feelings. What counted for me was my belief in the love which *you* felt. I caught my reflexion in the mirror of somebody else's personality, and in the image thus presented there was nothing repulsive. In that blissful state of relaxation I blossomed and flowered. I remember how I thawed in the warmth of your gaze, how emotion gushed from the opened freshets of my being. The most ordinary expressions of affection—the pressure of a hand, a flower laid between the pages of a book—were wholly new to me, and I succumbed to their enchantment.

The only person who did not benefit from this change in me was my mother. I felt that she was hostile to the dream (the lunatic dream, I thought) which was forming in my mind. I resented the fact that she was not dazzled. "Can't you see," she kept on saying, "that these people are trying to land you?" It never occurred to her that by talking like that she might well destroy the immense happiness I was feeling just because, for the first time, I believed that I had found favour in a young woman's eyes. There was at least one woman in the world, I told myself, who found me attractive, who might actually entertain the idea of marrying me. For that was what I believed, in spite of my mother's scepticism. You were too great and powerful as a family (so ran my silent argument) to find any advantage in a marriage with such as me. Nevertheless, I regarded my mother almost with hatred for throwing even a shadow of doubt on the reality of my bliss.

She went her own way, and set about finding out what she could. The sources of her intelligence were the leading Banks. It was a great day for me when she had to admit that the House of Fondaudège, in spite of occasional difficulties, still enjoyed a high reputation. "Their profits are fantastic, but they are living at too high a rate," she said. "Everything goes on horses and liveried servants. They are more intent on cutting a dash than on putting money by."

This verdict of the Banks set the seal upon my happiness. The disinterestedness of your family was proved. Your people were smiling on my suit because they liked me. It seemed to me, suddenly, the most natural thing in the world that I should be generally liked. I was allowed to walk alone with you, of an evening, in the Casino gardens. How strange it is that when life is just beginning for us, and when a little happiness comes our way, no warning voice is heard. "However long your life, you will never know any bliss comparable to these few hours. Drink them to the dregs, because Fate holds nothing more in store for you. This first gushing of cool water is also the last. Quench your thirst once and for all, for you will never again have an opportunity to drink." If only someone had said that!

For I was convinced, on the contrary, that a long life of passionate happiness was opening out before me. I set too little store on the evenings which we spent together, motionless, under the sleeping trees.

Signs there were, however, though I failed to interpret them aright. Do you remember one night in particular, when we were sitting on a bench by the winding path that climbs the hill behind the Hot Baths? All of a sudden you started to sob. The fragrance of your wet cheeks comes back to me still, as of an unknown sorrow. I thought your tears were those of happy love. I was too young to know the meaning of that choking misery. True, you hid it from me. "It's nothing," you said: "it's just being here with you."

You were not lying to me, liar though you are. It was, indeed, because I was with you that you cried, with me; and not with someone else, with that other whose name, at long last, you told me in this very room where I sit writing now, an old man near his death, surrounded by a battery of eager eyes strained for the coming kill.

There, on that bench by the winding path at Superbagnères, we sat. My face was pressed against your neck, your shoulder, and in my nostrils was the scent of a very young girl in tears. It was mingled with the scent of wet leaves and of mint in the warm, moist Pyrenean night. The branches of the lime-trees round the bandstand on the Place des Thermes below us caught the glint of lamps. An old Englishman from the hotel was catching the moths that fluttered round them in a long-handled net. "Lend me your handkerchief," you said. I wiped away your tears, and treasured the handkerchief against my heart.

I need say no more than that I had become a different person. There was a radiance in my face—I knew it from the way the women looked at me. Those evening tears brought no suspicion in their train.

Besides, for one night such as that there were many when you were all happiness, when you leaned on me and clung to my arm. I walked too quickly for you, and your efforts to keep up with me made you out of breath.

I was, as a lover, very self-controlled. You appealed to some part of me that was untouched, unspoiled. Never once was I tempted to abuse the confidence which your parents placed in me. I did not so much as dream that their attitude might be the result of cold calculation.

I was a changed being, so completely changed that one day—it's only now, after forty years, that I can pluck up sufficient courage to make this confession. It won't, I think, when you read this letter, give you much cause to feel triumphant. Here it is. One day, when we were driving through the Lys Valley, we got out of the victoria. The streams were gurgling. I was rubbing a leaf of fennel between my fingers. The lower slopes of the mountains were growing dark, but the light was still secure upon their peaks. . . . An intense feeling suddenly came over me, an almost physical certainty that another world *did* exist, a reality of which we know only the shadow.

That feeling lasted for a moment only. In the course of a long and miserable life I have had comparable experiences, but only at wide intervals. The very strangeness of what happened to me then gave it an enhanced value in my eyes. That is why, in our terrible religious squabbles of a later date, I had to keep the memory of it from my mind. I owe it to you to make this admission. But the time has not yet come for me to embark upon that subject.

There is no point in my recalling our engagement. The whole thing was settled one evening. It happened without my meaning it to. I rather think that you interpreted something I said in a sense different from the one I intended. I found myself bound to you, and was too staggered to protest. What is the use of going over all that old ground again? There was, however, one horrible incident which I still cannot get out of my mind.

There and then, on the spot, you made a condition. In what you called the "interests of harmony" you flatly refused to consider the idea of my mother living with us, or even of having her under the same roof. You and your parents had quite made up your minds. You wouldn't even discuss the matter.

How vividly, after all these years, I remember that stifling hotel room with its open window giving on to the Allées d'Ettigny! Through the lowered venetian blind a golden powdering of dust drifted in on us. In our ears was the cracking of whips, the sound of a Tyrolean tune. My mother had a headache and was lying on the sofa, dressed in a skirt and a petticoat-bodice (she had never in her life possessed a dressing-gown, a peignoir or a wrap). She would, she said, give up the ground-floor suite to us and make do with one room on the third floor. I snatched at this opportunity, and took the plunge.

"Isa thinks that it would be very much better . . ."—and all the time I was talking I kept glancing furtively at her old face, and looking away again. She was crumpling the trimming of her bodice between her gnarled fingers. If only she had put up a fight I could have dealt with the situation, but her silence made anger impossible.

She pretended not to be hurt, or even surprised. When at last she did speak she chose her words carefully, so as to lead me to suppose that she had always known our separation to be inevitable.

"I shall spend most of the year at Aurigne," she said: "it's in better condition than the other farms, and you can have Calèse. I'll have a little garden-room run up at Aurigne. Three rooms will be quite enough for me. It won't cost much, but it's a nuisance, all the same, to incur even a small expense when I may be dead by next year. But you'll find it come in useful, later, for the duck-shooting. It'll be pleasant living there in October. I know you don't care much about shooting, but you may have children who will."

No ingratitude of mine could ever exhaust the treasures of her love. Driven from one position, it reformed its ranks elsewhere. It took what I left, and made do. But that same evening you said:

"Is there anything wrong with your mother?"

Next day she looked just as usual. Your father arrived from Bordeaux with his eldest daughter and his son-in-law. Somebody must have told them what was going on. They looked me up and down. I could almost hear them comparing notes: "D'you think he'll do? That old mother of his is really the last straw. . . ." I shall never forget my surprise when I saw your sister, Marie-Thérèse—the one you called Marinette. She was older than you by a year, but looked younger, with her slim body, her long neck, the great coil of hair that looked too heavy for her, and those childlike eyes. The old man to whom your father had sold her, Baron Philipot, gave me the horrors. But since his death I have often thought that that sexagenarian was one of the unhappiest men I have ever come across. What tortures the poor fool must have suffered in his efforts to make his young wife forget that he was old! He was so tightly buckled into his stays that he could scarcely breathe. His high, wide, starched collar scarified his jowl and his dewlaps. The refulgence of his dyed moustache and whiskers merely accentuated the purple ruin of his face. He scarcely listened when anyone spoke to him, was always looking round for a mirror, and, when he found one, how we laughed (do you remember?) at the way the old idiot mopped and mowed at his reflexion, and could never keep his eyes off himself! He was incapable of smiling, because of his false teeth. By an exercise of will-power—which never failed—he kept his mouth perpetually shut. We used to notice, too, the peculiar way in which he put on his hat so as not to disarrange the extraordinary lock of hair which started from the nape of his neck and spread out over his skull like the delta of a half-dried-up river.

Your father, who was his contemporary, was still attractive to women, in spite of his white beard, his baldness and his paunch. Even in business matters he laid himself out to exert his charm. My mother was the only person who stood out against him. Maybe the blow I had just dealt her had had a hardening effect. She argued every clause of the marriage contract as though it had been a deed of sale or a lease. I pretended to be indignant at her demands—though I was secretly overjoyed to think that my interests were in such good hands. If, to-day, my fortune is entirely separate from yours, if you have so little hold on me, I owe it all to my mother who insisted on the most rigorous form of settlement, and behaved as though I were a daughter who had made up her mind to marry a debauchee.

As soon as it became clear that the Fondaudège family was not going to use these demands as an excuse for breaking off the engagement, I was able to sleep calmly in my bed. They put up with me—or so I thought—because you had set your heart on having me as a husband.

Mamma would not hear of an "allowance," but insisted that

your dowry should be paid down in cash. "They keep on quoting Baron Philipot as a precedent," she said: "apparently, he took the eldest without a sou . . . and so I should think! They must have got a pretty return from handing over the poor child to that nasty old man! But with us, the shoe's on the other foot. They thought I should be dazzled at the prospect of marrying my son into their precious family. That shows how little they know me!"

We two, the "turtle-doves," made a great show of not being interested in the discussion. I imagine that you felt no less confidence in the genius of your father than I did in that of my mother. As a matter of fact, I suspect that neither of us quite realized what a store we both of us set by money.

No, that's unfair. You've never been fond of money except for the children's sake. No doubt you'd gladly have murdered me if, by doing so, you could have made them richer. But, then, you'd have gladly given them the bread out of your own mouth.

I, on the other hand, adore money, and I don't mind admitting it. It gives me a sense of security. So long as I remain in control of my fortune, you have no weapon against me. "At our age one needs so little"—that is your constant refrain; but how wrong you are! An old man lives only by virtue of what he possesses. As soon as he's got nothing, out he goes on the scrap-heap. For us the only choice is between the alms-house, the workhouse and a private fortune. One is always hearing of peasants who let their old parents starve to death after they have stripped them of everything. The same holds good, as I know from experience, though with rather more form and ceremony, of the middle-classes. Yes, I *am* afraid of being poor. I have the feeling that I can never pile up enough gold. You want it because it attracts you. I want it because it is my only protection.

The hour of the Angelus has gone by, and I did not hear the bell. . . . But, of course, it wouldn't have been rung to-day because it's Good Friday. The men of the family are arriving to-night by car. I shall come down to dinner. I want to see the whole gang. I feel much stronger when they're all ranged against me than I do when they tackle me separately. And there's another reason. I like making a point of eating my cutlet on this day of penitence—not out of bravado, but just to show you that I have kept my will-power intact, that I am not prepared to yield on a single point.

All the positions which I have occupied for the last forty-five years, and from which you have failed to dislodge me, would fall one by one if I made the least concession. With the rest of the family fasting on beans and salt fish, my Good Friday cutlet will serve as a sign that you don't stand a chance of skinning me so long as there is breath in my body.

IV

YOU see, I wasn't wrong. My presence among you yesterday evening completely upset your plans. Only the children, sitting apart at their own table, were happy, because on Good Friday they have chocolate and bread-and-butter for supper. I must say I find it difficult to tell who's who among them. Janine, who's my granddaughter, has a child of her own old enough to walk. . . . I let everyone see that there was nothing wrong with my appetite. So that the children shouldn't get any false ideas about my cutlet, you had told them that the state of my health and my great age made it necessary. . . . What really did terrify me was Hubert's optimism. He said he felt confident that the market would show an upward trend soon—but with the air of a man for whom that hypothetical trend was a matter of life and death. I can never get over the fact that he's my son—but he is. Yes, this man of forty's my son. My reason admits it, but not my imagination. For some curious reason I can't face it. And suppose things do go wrong for him? After all, a stockbroker who offers such high dividends plays high and takes big risks. . . . One of these days I shall be told that the family honour is in jeopardy. . . . The family honour, indeed! That's an idol before which I will *not* sacrifice. The sooner I make up my mind on the point, the better. I've got to stand my ground and not allow myself to get sentimental —more especially as there is always that old Fondaudège uncle in the background who'll play up even if I don't. . . . But I'm digressing, going off on a false scent, or, rather, I'm shirking the recollection of that night when, though you did not realize it at the time, you destroyed all our hopes of happiness.

It's odd to think that you've probably forgotten all about it. A few hours in the warm dusk of this room decided our destinies. Every word you spoke increased the distance between us, and yet, you noticed nothing. Your memory, which is a junk-shop of a thousand trivialities, has retained not one single iota of that disaster. You make a great to-do about believing in the life everlasting, but you didn't seem to realize that what you were gambling with at that moment, what you were endangering, was my immortal soul. The birth of love in my heart had made me sensitive to the climate of faith and adoration which was the ambiance in which you lived. I loved you, and I loved the spiritual elements in your being. When you knelt down in your long, schoolgirl's night-gown, I felt deeply moved.

We occupied this room where I now sit writing. Why did we come to Calèse, to my mother's, when we got back from the honeymoon? (I had refused her offer of the place. It was her creation, and she loved it.) When, later, I sought out food for my rancour, I remembered a number of circumstances which had, at first, escaped me, or from which I had deliberately averted my gaze. In the first place, on the ground that an uncle once removed had just died, your family had insisted on keeping the wedding ceremony as quiet as possible. It was as plain as houses that they felt thoroughly ashamed of the connexion. Baron Philipot had put it about that his young sister-in-law had fallen madly in love with a young man at Bagnères-de-Luchon, a charming enough fellow, with a future before him and plenty of money, but of doubtful birth. "Fact is," he said, "he doesn't belong." To hear him speak you'd have thought I was somebody's bastard. On the whole, however, he thought my lack of family a good thing. At least there was no need to blush for my relations. All things considered, my old mother was quite presentable, and seemed to know her place. According to him you were a spoiled child who could twist her parents round her little finger, and my fortune had seemed big enough to persuade the Fondaudège clan to consent to the marriage while shutting their eyes to its many disadvantages.

When this tittle-tattle reached my ears it told me nothing, really, that I did not know already. I was so happy that I refused to attach any importance to it. Truth to tell, the almost secret way in which the wedding was carried through suited me very well—for how could I have possibly found groomsmen in the down-at-heels circle of which I was the centre? Pride kept me from making advances to those who had so recently been my enemies, though my brilliant marriage would have made reconciliation easy. I have already, in the course of this confession, shown myself in such ugly colours, that I may as well go further and make no effort to conceal this trait in me which may be described as independence of mind or inflexibility. I refuse to bow the knee to anybody, and I remain true to my ideas. In connexion with this latter point, I may as well say that my marriage had given me a few twinges of conscience. I had promised your parents that I would do nothing which might alienate you from the practice of your religion, but I had in no way compromised my own freedom of action, except in so far as I had undertaken not to become a Freemason. As a matter of fact, you none of you thought of making any further demand on me. In those days the general view was that religion was the wife's affair. In your world, the husband—to use the accepted formula, "accompanied his wife to Mass." I had already, at Luchon, given you ample proof that I wasn't likely to kick at that.

When we returned from Venice in September '85, your parents made excuses for not receiving us in their chateau of Cenon, where, owing to the presence of their friends, and Philipot's, there was no room available. We found it convenient, therefore, to stay for a while with my mother. The memory of the brutal way in which we had treated her did not embarrass us in the least. We were perfectly prepared to live with her for as long as it suited us.

She was careful to give no outward sign of triumph. The house was ours, she said, and we were free to invite whom we liked: she would make herself scarce, and nobody need see her. "I know how to disappear," she added: "I spend almost all my time out of doors." This was true, for she gave much of her attention to the vines, the cellar, the chickens, and the laundry. After meals she went for a while to her own room, and always apologized when she found us in the drawing-room when she came down. She regularly knocked before coming in. I had to explain to her that she mustn't do that, that it wasn't "the thing." She even suggested that you should take over the housekeeping, but you did, at least, spare her that mortification. But that was only because you had no wish to saddle yourself with her duties. How terribly condescending you were to her, and what a humble gratitude she showed!

You did not come between her and me as much as she had feared you would. Actually, I was a great deal nicer to her than I had been before our marriage. Our mad fits of laughter were a never-ending cause of surprise to her. She could scarcely believe that the happy young husband whom she saw before her was the same person as the repressed, unyielding son she had formerly known. She explained the change by the fact that she hadn't known how to handle me. I had always been too far "above" her. You were repairing the damage that she had done.

I remember her admiration when she saw you daubing away at screens and tambourines, and when you sang or played—always breaking down in the same places—one of Mendelssohn's "Songs Without Words" on the piano.

Young women friends sometimes came to see you. "You're going to meet my mother-in-law," you would tell them: "one of the genuine old ladies from the country. You don't come across many of them nowadays." You decided that she had what you called a "style of her own." She had got into the habit of speaking patois to the servants, and that, you thought, was very "smart." You even went so far as to show your visitors a daguerreotype of her at the age of fifteen, in which she appeared with her head tied up in a handkerchief. You were fond of quoting a saying about old peasant families having "more true distinction than many of noble rank. . . ." How very conventional you were in those days! It was motherhood that restored you to your natural self.

I keep shying away from the story of what happened that night. It was so hot that we had left the blinds up, in spite of your terror of bats. When the branches of a lime tree brushed against the house we knew precisely what it was, though the sound was exactly like that of someone breathing at the far end of the room. Sometimes the wind in the leaves was like the noise of rain. The waning moon lit up the floor and the pale phantoms of your scattered clothes. We no longer heard the murmurs of the meadow grass, so much had they become part of the general silence.

"We really must go to sleep," you said . . . but all the time a shadow roamed about our inert and weary bodies. Not alone did we struggle up from the depths: the unknown Rodolphe came with us. Each time I took you in my arms I woke the memory of him in your heart.

When I loosed you from my embrace, we felt his presence. I did not want to suffer: I was afraid of suffering. The instinct of self-preservation applies to happiness as to other forms of life. I knew I must not ask you any questions. I let his name burst like a bubble on the surface of our life. Beneath the waters there slept a principle of corruption, a putrid secret, and I did nothing to stir it from the mud. But you, wretched woman, felt the need to liberate in words the cheated passion that still hungered for satisfaction. One question of mine sufficed to bring it into the open. "Who, precisely, was this fellow Rodolphe?" "I'm afraid there's a lot I ought to have told you—oh, nothing really serious, don't worry."

You spoke hurriedly, and in a low voice. Your head no longer lay against my shoulder. Already the tiny space that separated our stretched bodies had become unbridgeable.

He was the son of some Austrian woman and of a big industrialist from the north. . . . You had met him at Aix when you had been there with your grandmother the year before we had got to know one another at Luchon. He had just left Cambridge. You made no attempt to describe him, but I knew that he possessed all the graces which I felt myself to lack. The moonlight on the sheets illuminated my coarse peasant hands with their spatulate fingers. You had done nothing "wrong," though he was, you said, less respectful than I had been. My recollection of what you confessed is vague: not that it mattered. *That* wasn't what worried me. If you had been genuinely in love with him I could have forgiven one of those short, sharp surrenders in which the innocence of childhood melts into nothingness. But my mind was already full of questions. "How could she have fallen in love with me scarcely twelve months after so great a passion?" I felt frozen by terror. "It was all a sham," I told myself: "she lied to me. That liberating influence was all a make-believe. How could I have been such a fool as to fancy that a young girl could love me—me whom nobody could love?"

The stars of the night's end were twinkling. A blackbird woke. The breeze which we could hear among the leaves, even before we felt it on our bodies, filled the curtains and brought refreshment to my eyes as in the days when I was happy. Only ten minutes before, that happiness had been real to me, and now I was thinking about the "time when I was happy." I asked another question:

"Was it that he didn't want you?" You felt the sting of that. I can still hear the special voice you put on when your vanity was touched. On the contrary, you said, he had been madly in love, and very proud at the thought of marrying a Fondaudège. The trouble was that it had come to the ears of his parents that you had lost two brothers from consumption before they were grown up. In view of the fact that he, too, suffered from delicate health, they wouldn't hear of the match.

I asked my questions very calmly. No words of mine could possibly have given you any idea of what it was you were so busily pulling to bits.

"Actually, darling," you said, "it was quite providential for us, the way things turned out. You know how proud my parents are—rather absurdly so, I must admit. It was their obsession about this marriage which never came off that made our happiness—mine and yours—possible. You must have noticed the importance that people in my little world attach to health where marriage is concerned. Mamma got it firmly fixed in her head that the whole town knew what had happened, and that no one would ever want to marry me. She was quite convinced that I should die an old maid. I can't tell you the life she led me—oh, for months and months—as though I hadn't enough troubles of my own! . . . In the end she persuaded us, both Papa and me, that I was out of the marriage market for good!"

I carefully refrained from saying anything that might have made you suspicious. You repeated what you had said before, that the whole thing had been providential.

"I fell in love with you from the moment we met. We had said many, many prayers at Lourdes before going to Luchon, and as soon as I set eyes on you I knew that they had been answered."

You were far from guessing how those words grated on my nerves. Those who oppose you in religion have, really, a very much nobler idea of it than you realize, or than they realize themselves. Why, otherwise, should they be so affronted at the way in which you debase it? Can you honestly think it right and proper to ask for tangible rewards from the God whom you call your Father? . . . But that's beside the point, which was, quite simply, that you'd all pounced hungrily on the first snail that popped its head out of its shell. After hearing what you had said I could have no doubt of that.

How monstrous a thing our marriage was I realized only at that moment. Before it could take place at all your mother had had to have a brain-storm and infect both you and your father with her own temporary lunacy. . . . You told me that the Philipots had gone so far as to threaten to disown you should you marry me. Actually, at Luchon, while we were all laughing at the old fool, he was doing all he could to persuade your family to break it all off.

"But I stuck to you, darling, and he got nothing for his pains."

Again and again you told me that you had no regrets. I let you talk, and saved my breath. You could never, you assured me, have been happy with the precious Rodolphe. He was too good-looking. Love, for him, meant not giving but taking. The first woman who tried could have got him away from you.

You were blissfully unaware that your voice changed whenever you mentioned him—lost some of its sharpness and became tremulous, with a sort of a cooing sound in it, as though old sighs, treasured within your breast, found freedom when his name was spoken.

He could never have made you happy because he was handsome, charming and beloved! The logical deduction from that was that I could be the joy of your life because I was nothing much to look at and put people off with my surly manners! I gathered from your description that he had the intolerable arrogance of all young Frenchmen who have been to Cambridge and learned to ape the English. . . . Would you really rather have had a husband who couldn't choose a suit or tie a tie, who hated games and was incapable of the sophisticated frivolity which consists in avoiding all serious subjects, in shying away from emotional entanglements or any show of feeling, and living with care-free elegance? You had accepted the inferior me (so I was to believe) merely because I happened to have swum into your ken just when your mother, afflicted by her change of life, had convinced herself that you would never find a husband, because you would not, or could not, remain unmarried a moment longer, and because I happened to have enough money to provide an excuse in the eyes of the world. . . .

I did my best to control my breathing. I clenched my fists, I bit my lips. Many times since then I have felt such a loathing of myself that I have turned with revulsion from the very thought of my body and of my feelings, and always, in such moments, my thoughts have gone back to the young man of 1885, the husband of twenty-three, sitting with his arms tightly crossed in a frenzied attempt to stifle his young love.

I shivered. You noticed it and broke off in the middle of what you were saying:

"Are you cold, Louis?"

"It was nothing," I said: "just a touch of goose-flesh."

"You're not going to tell me you're jealous?—that would really be too ridiculous!"

I swore to you that I did not feel the least twinge of jealousy—and it was true. How could I possibly have made you understand that my personal drama was something far beyond mere jealousy?

You were worried by my silence, but you had not the least idea how deeply I had been wounded. Your hand felt for mine in the darkness; you stroked my face. Your fingers felt no trace of tears, but perhaps the rigidity of my clenched jaws struck you as strange. You took fright. In your effort to light a candle you were lying half across me. The match wouldn't strike. I lay there half stifled under the weight of your hateful body.

"What's the matter with you? Don't lie there saying nothing! You're frightening me!"

I pretended to be surprised. I assured you that there was nothing to be frightened about.

"How silly of you, darling, to give me such a shock! . . . I'm going to put out the light and try to get some sleep."

You said no more. I watched the new day come, the day which would mark the beginning of a new life for me. The swallows were twittering under the eaves. A man crossed the yard, dragging his clogs. All I heard then I can hear still, after forty-five years—cocks crowing, bells ringing, a goods-train on the viaduct. All I smelled then I can smell still—the scent that I love above all scents, of ashes carried by the wind from heath-fires by the sea.

Suddenly I started up:

"Isa, that night you cried when we were sitting on a bench by the winding path at Superbagnères—was it because of him?"

You didn't say anything. I gripped your arm, but you shook yourself free with a sort of animal snarl, and rolled over on your side. Your long hair was all about you as you slept. You lay curled up like some wild young creature of the woods, the blankets piled higgledy-piggledy on your body because of the dawn chill. What should I have gained by rousing you from your child-like slumbers? I knew already what I needed to know without hearing it from your lips.

I got up quietly and padded across on bare feet to the wardrobe mirror. I stared at myself as though I had been a stranger, or, rather, as though I had suddenly become myself again—the man whom nobody loved, on whose account no one in the world had ever had a moment's suffering. I was filled with self-pity, thinking of my youth. I passed a great peasant hand across my unshaven cheeks which were already showing dark beneath a harsh growth of beard with red lights in it.

I dressed in silence and went down to the garden. Mamma

was in the rose-walk. She always got up before the servants so as to air the house.

She spoke to me:

"Enjoying the cool of the day?"

Then, pointing to the mists on the low land:

"It's going to be a scorcher. I must have every shutter closed by eight."

I kissed her with more show of affection than usual. She murmured, very low . . . "Dear boy. . . ." My heart (do you find it odd that I should speak of my heart?) felt ready to burst. A few hesitating words came to my lips . . . but how should I begin what I had to say? . . . would she understand? . . . Invariably I yield to the temptation of silence.

I walked down to the terrace. The young fruit-trees were showing shadowy above the vines. The shoulder of the hill was thrusting the mist aside, breaking it into wisps and shreds. A belfry emerged from the thin fog, then the church to which it belonged, like a living body. It has always been your fixed opinion that churches, and all they stand for, leave me cold . . . let me tell you, then, what I felt at that moment. I felt that a man whose heart is broken as mine had been broken may be impelled to seek the reason for, the meaning of, his undoing: that, possibly, what has happened to him may conceal some significant secret, that what happens—especially in the world of the feelings—may, perhaps, carry a message the meaning of which he must interpret. . . . So, you see, there have been moments in my life when I have been capable of glimpsing things which might, perhaps, have drawn us together. . . .

But on that particular morning my emotion lasted for only a few moments. I still have a picture of myself going back towards the house. It was not yet eight o'clock, and already the sun was hot. You were leaning from your window, holding your hair in one hand, while, with the other, you brushed it. You did not see me. I stood still for a few seconds, looking up at you. I had been caught by a sudden spasm of hatred. After all these years, I can still taste its bitterness.

I ran to my desk and opened the drawer which I kept always locked. From it I took a little crumpled handkerchief, the same that you had used to wipe away your tears one evening at Superbagnères. I, poor fool, had pressed it to my heart. I took it now; I tied a stone to it as I might have done to a puppy I meant to drown, and threw it into the pond, which local country-people call the "gutter."

V

THEN began that era of the Great Silence which has scarcely been broken for forty years. There was no outward sign of collapse. All went on as in the days of my happiness. We remained united in the flesh, but no ghost of Rodolphe was now born of our embrace, nor did you ever mention the dreadful name. At your bidding he had come, had prowled about our bed, had accomplished his work of destruction. All he could do now was to remain silent and await the long sequence of events, the delayed working of cause and effect.

You may, perhaps, have felt that you had done wrong to speak at all. It was not that you expected anything very serious to occur as a result of your admission. Still, it might have been wiser to keep his name out of our talk. I don't know whether you noticed that we no longer indulged in nightly chats. Those interminable discussions of ours were now a thing of the past. Whatever we said to one another we said only after due and careful thought. We were, each of us, on the defensive.

I used to start awake in the middle of the night. It was pain that woke me. I was fastened to you like a fox to the trap. Sometimes I tried to imagine what might have been said between us had I shaken you roughly, had I thrown you out of bed. "You're wrong"—you might have cried: "I didn't lie, and for the very good reason that I was in love with you."—"Yes, at second best, because it's always easy to consent to the physical act—which means nothing—in order to make your partner believe that you love him. I was no monster: any young girl who had truly loved me could have done with me what she would. . . ." Sometimes I groaned in the darkness, but you never woke.

Your first pregnancy made all attempts at explanation useless. Little by little it changed the nature of our relationship. It began before the time of the grape-harvest. We went back to town. You had a miscarriage, as a result of which you were in bed for several weeks. By the following spring you were again with child. I had to take great care of you. Then began that long series of pregnancies, mishaps, and childbed, which gave me more pretexts than I needed for keeping away from you. I plunged into a secret life of debauchery—very secret, for I was beginning to appear more and more frequently in Court—was "feeling my feet," as Mamma said—and had to be careful about my reputation. I had my special times, my regular habits. The man who would live an irregular life in the country has to develop the cunning of the hunted hare. Don't be afraid, Isa, I shall spare you all details of what, I know, fills you with horror. You may rest assured that I shall paint no picture here of the Hell into which I descended almost every day. It was you, once, who had fished me out: it was you, now, who threw me back again.

Even had I been less prudent, you wouldn't have twigged a thing. After the birth of Hubert, you came out in your true colours. You were a mother, and nothing but a mother. You no longer paid the slightest attention to me. You didn't even notice my existence. It is quite literally true that you had eyes only for your young. In sowing the necessary seed, I had done all you wanted of me.

So long as the children were in the grub stage, and did not interest me, there was no cause for quarrel between us. We never met except to perform those ritual acts which the body carries through as a matter of habit, and in which the man and the woman are, each, a thousand miles removed from their own flesh.

You began to take notice of me only when I, in my turn, started to prowl around our young family. You began to hate me only when I claimed my rights in them. It was not paternal instinct that dictated my attitude. I can bring myself now to make that admission, and you ought to be very grateful to me for doing so. I very soon became jealous of the passion that had waked in you. I tried to entice the children away for the sole purpose of punishing you. I deceived myself with any number of high-sounding reasons—duty, for instance, and my refusal to let a bigoted woman stunt young minds. But those were just excuses!

Shall I ever come to the end of my story? I began it for you, and already I feel it to be in the highest degree unlikely that you will be able to bear with it much longer. It is, fundamentally, for myself that I am writing. True to my character of an old barrister, I want to get my brief sorted out, to docket and arrange the various exhibits in that lost cause—my life. . . . Oh, those bells!—of course, to-morrow's Easter. I shall join you all downstairs in honour of the sacred feast—as I promised I would. "The children are always complaining that they never see you" —that's what you said to me this morning. Geneviève was standing beside you, close to my bed. She had something she wanted to ask me. I had heard you whispering together in the passage: "It'll be much better if you speak first . . ."—you said to her . . . I suppose it's something to do with her son-in-law, that blackguard, Phili. How cleverly I kept her from bringing him into the conversation, or mentioning what it was that she was after! She left the room without having managed even to broach the subject. I know perfectly well what it's all about. I overheard your conversation the other evening. The drawing-room window is just below mine, and, when it's open, I only have to lean forward a little. She wants me to advance Phili the capital he needs to buy a quarter share in a Broker's firm. . . . It'd be as good an investment as any other. . . . Oh yes, I know all about that. . . . As though I hadn't seen the storm blowing up, as though I didn't know it was time now to tuck one's money away in a safe place! . . . If only they knew how much I made last month by anticipating the slump!

They've all gone to Vespers. Easter has emptied the house and the fields. I sit here alone, an old Faust separated from the world's joy by the wall of my abominable old age. They've no idea what old age means. During luncheon, they were all ears for what I was saying about business and the Stock Market. I was talking deliberately at Hubert, so that he might get out while there is still time. How worried he looked. . . . Not a born bluffer, our Hubert! He polished off his food. You had piled his plate with the obstinacy of an unhappy mother who sees that her son is devoured by anxiety, and forces him to eat, as though that were so much to the good, were something gained. And his only thanks was to snap your head off. It was me and Mamma over again.

How careful young Phili was to keep my glass filled! What a show of interest his wife, Janine, exhibited in my well-being! "Grandpapa, you *oughtn't* to smoke, really you oughtn't: even one cigarette's too much. Are you *sure* they haven't made a mistake? Is this coffee really free of caffeine?" She's a poor hand at deception, poor dear: her voice gives her away. She's just like you in the early days of our marriage, when you used to put on an act. But that all went by the board when your first child was born, and you became yourself again. Until the day of her death, Janine will be a woman "in the know," repeating everything she hears, provided she thinks it gives her an air of distinction, trotting out second-hand views about this, that and the other, and not understanding a word. How Phili, who's nothing if not natural, an unashamed scavenger, can bear to live with such a little half-wit, beats me. But, no, I'm wrong: one thing about her is perfectly genuine, and that's her passion for him. The reason she's so transparent is that nothing matters for her, nothing really exists for her, but her love.

After luncheon we all sat out on the steps. Janine and Phili kept their eyes fixed on Geneviève, like a couple of dogs begging for crumbs, while she looked at no one but you. You said "no" with an almost imperceptible shake of the head, at which Geneviève got up and turned to me:

"How about taking a turn with me, Papa?" You're all so frightened of me! I took pity on her. I had made up my mind not to budge, but, all the same, I got up and took her arm. We walked round the meadow. The family watched us from the steps.

She lost no time in coming to the point. "I wanted to have a word with you about Phili."

She was trembling. It's horrible to know that one's children are frightened of one. But at sixty-eight a man's not free to decide whether he shall seem unapproachable or not. By that age the general cast of our features is set, and the heart, when it finds that it can no longer give expression to its feelings, grows discouraged. . . . Geneviève had decided what she wanted to say, and out it all came in a rush. . . . It had to do, as I had expected, with Phili's buying a share in a Broker's firm. She stressed the one point of all others best calculated to antagonize me—the fact that Phili's having nothing to do was a constant threat to Janine's married happiness. He was beginning to stray from the domestic hearth. I told her that a share in a Broker's firm would merely serve to supply a man like her son-in-law with convenient alibis. She stood up for him. Phili was universally popular. Why should I be harder on him than Janine was? . . . I protested that I neither judged nor condemned him, that I took not the slightest interest in his love-life.

"Why should I bother about him? He certainly doesn't bother about me."

"He admires you enormously."

This impudent lie gave me the chance to trot out what I was keeping up my sleeve.

"That's as may be, my dear, but it doesn't prevent your precious Phili from referring to me as the 'old crocodile.' It's no good denying it. Many's the time I've heard him say it behind my back . . . and I've no wish to deny the imputation: crocodile I am, and crocodile I shall remain. There's nothing to hope for from an old crocodile—except his death. And even when he's dead"—I was foolish enough to add—"even when he's dead, he can still be up to his old tricks." (I'm sorry I said that: it only roused her suspicions.)

She was knocked of a heap. She tried to explain it all away (as though I care two hoots what Phili calls me!). What I detest about him is his youth. How can she have the faintest idea what a hated and despised old man feels at the sight of a young creature in the pride of life, who has had showered upon him, from youth up, those very things which I have tasted only once in half a century? I loathe and detest all young men, and Phili more than most. Like a cat slipping silently through the window, he has padded into my house, attracted by the smell of what was inside. My granddaughter may not have had much in the way of a dowry—but, oh! her "expectations"—only over our dead bodies do young gentlemen get within touching distance of our children's "expectations"!

Then as Geneviève started snuffling and dabbing at her eyes, I adopted a tone of sweet reasonableness.

"After all, my dear, you've got a perfectly good husband in the rum trade. Surely dear Alfred can find some sort of a job for his son-in-law? Why should I be more generous than you are yourselves?"

Then she started to talk about poor Alfred. What a change! What contempt! what disgust! According to her he's a mean-spirited coward who is drawing in his horns more every day. Once upon a time his business was a large and prosperous affair, but now there isn't a living in it for more than one person.

I congratulated her on having such a husband. When a storm's brewing one's got to shorten sail. The future, I said, belongs to men like Alfred who can take a limited view. In these days, the only hope of making a success of business is to keep going in a small way. She thought I was laughing at her. But I was voicing my profound belief—as is shown by the fact that I keep my own money under lock and key and won't even take chances with the Savings-Bank.

We walked back to the house. Geneviève didn't dare to say another word. I was no longer leaning on her arm. The members of the family, seated in a circle, watched us coming, and, no doubt, were already busy interpreting the unfavourable omens. It was obvious that our return had interrupted an argument between Hubert's little lot and Geneviève's. What an unholy squabble there would be over my pile if ever I agreed to relax my grip! Phili was the only one on his feet. The wind was blowing in his rebellious hair. He was wearing an open-necked shirt with short sleeves. I have a horror of these modern young men who look like athletic girls! His baby cheeks flushed scarlet when, in reply to Janine's stupid question—"Well, have you had a nice chat?"—I replied, very quietly, "We have been talking about an old crocodile. . . ."

Let me repeat, it's not because of that piece of ill-conditioned rudeness that I hate him. They've no idea what old age means. You can't imagine the torment of having had nothing out of life, of having nothing to look forward to but death, of feeling that there is no other world beyond this one, that the puzzle will never be explained, the key never given to us. . . . You haven't suffered what I have suffered. You never will suffer what I am suffering now. It is not for your death that the children are impatient. They are fond of you in their own way, they love you. . . . From the very first they took sides with you against me. I had a very warm feeling for them. I can remember Geneviève—this fat, forty-year-old woman who, a moment or two back, was trying to wheedle four hundred thousand-franc notes out of me for her scamp of a son-in-law, as a little girl perched on my knee. As soon as you saw me paying any attention to her, you called her away. . . . But if I go on mixing present and past like this, I shall never get to the end of my confession. I really must try to put a little order into my thoughts. . . .

VI

I DON'T think that I began to hate you from the first year after that disastrous night. My hatred grew, by slow degrees, as I came to realize how completely indifferent you were to me, how nothing really existed for you outside the circle of your puling, screaming, greedy little scraps of humanity. You did not even notice how, though I was not yet thirty, I had become an overworked Chancery barrister with a big reputation at the most important Bar in all France after that of Paris. It was the Villenave case (1893) which gave me the chance to prove myself a great Criminal lawyer as well (it is exceedingly rare to excel in both branches). You were the only person who remained deaf to the universal applause of my gifts as a pleader. That was the year, too, in which our misunderstandings turned to open warfare.

The notorious Villenave case set the seal on my reputation. It also gave a further twist to the vice which was crushing out my life. Perhaps up till then I had still retained a tiny shred of hope, but I saw now, beyond all power to doubt, that, so far as you were concerned, I had ceased to exist.

I wonder whether you remember the story of that Villenave couple? They had been married for twenty years, and were still so devoted to one another that they had become almost a legend. People talked of being as "loving as the Villenaves." They lived with an only son of fifteen in their chateau at Ornon, just outside the city, seeing very few people, and utterly self-sufficient. "It's the sort of thing one reads about in books," said your mother, using one of those ready-made phrases the secret of which her granddaughter Geneviève has inherited. I don't mind betting that you have forgotten everything to do with their story. If I tell it over again now, you'll just laugh at me as you always did when I described my triumphs of cross-examination at the dinner table. . . . Well, that can't be helped.

One morning, their servant, who was doing the downstairs rooms, heard a pistol-shot on the first floor, followed by a cry of pain. He rushed upstairs. The door of his master's bedroom was locked. He could hear low voices, the sound of things being moved about, and agitated steps in the bathroom. He kept on rattling the handle, and, in a moment or two, the door was opened. Villenave was lying on the bed in his night-shirt, covered in blood. Madame de Villenave, her hair disordered, and wearing a dressing-gown, was standing at the foot of the bed with a revolver in her hand. She said: "I have wounded Monsieur de Villenave. Get a doctor, a surgeon and the Police Inspector—hurry! I will stay here." They could get nothing more out of her than that single statement—"I have wounded my husband"—and this was confirmed by Monsieur de Villenave as soon as he was able to speak. He refused to give any further information.

The accused would do nothing about appointing Counsel to represent her at the trial. I was entrusted—as the son-in-law of a friend of theirs—with her defence. She maintained an attitude of unshakable obstinacy. Though I went every day to see her in prison, I could get nothing out of her. The city was filled with the most ridiculous rumours. Personally, I was convinced of her innocence from the very first. She was accusing herself, and the husband who loved her remained completely acquiescent. What an unerring nose do the unloved have for the scent of passion in others! This woman was entirely possessed by conjugal love. She had not fired at her husband. Might it be that she had tried to fling herself between him and a rejected lover? There had been no visitor to the house since the previous evening . . . there was no intimate friend who came regularly to see them . . . well, it's all ancient history now, and I won't go into details.

Up to the morning of the day of the trial I had decided to

adopt a purely negative attitude, and merely to argue that Madame de Villenave could not have committed the crime which she was as good as confessing. But, at the very last moment, the evidence of her son Yves, or, rather (for in itself that evidence was quite unimportant and shed no light on the mystery), the beseeching and commanding look which his mother kept steadily fixed on him all the time he was in the witness box, as well as the obvious relief which she showed when he left it, told me the truth. I denounced the son. I described him as a morbid adolescent who had been driven to a jealous frenzy by the love lavished upon his father. I flung myself with a sort of passionate logic into a spur-of-the-moment argument which has since become famous, and in which Professor F——, on his own admission, found the essential germ of his theory. It has shed new light not only on the psychology of adolescence, but on the treatment of its neuroses.

If I stir these old memories, it is not, my dear Isa, because I have the slightest hope of rousing in you, after forty years, the admiration which you did not feel at the moment of my triumph when my picture was appearing in the newspapers of two hemispheres. Your complete indifference in this supremely important moment of my career revealed to me the extent of my solitude and abandonment. But there was more to it than that. For weeks on end I had had before my eyes, between the four walls of a cell, a woman who was sacrificing herself with the sole purpose of saving, not so much *her* child, as her husband's, the heir to his name. It was he, the victim, who had implored her to take the blame. So great was her love that she had been willing to let the world believe that she was a criminal, that she had tried to murder the man whom she adored to the exclusion of everybody and everything in the world. Conjugal, not maternal, love had been the mainspring of her action (as was proved by the sequel, for she separated from her son, and has always found some excuse or other for living away from him ever since).

I, too, might have been loved as Villenave was loved. Of him, too, I saw a good deal at the time of the trial. What had he got that I hadn't? True, he was well-born and averagely good-looking, but I don't think he was very intelligent. His hostile attitude to me after the trial proved that. I, on the other hand, was in my own way something of a genius. If, at that moment, I had been blessed with a wife who loved me, to what heights might I not have risen? Nobody can go on indefinitely believing in himself unless he gets some help from outside. There must be some other person to give him assurance of his abilities, someone to crown him when the day of recognition comes. When, as a schoolboy, I used to walk back from the dais on Prize Day, with my arms full of books, it was always my mother's eyes that I tried to catch in the crowd, and it was she who, to the sound of a military band, really placed the laurel-wreath upon my freshly cropped head.

At the time of the Villenave case she was beginning to fail, though I realized it only by degrees. The extent to which she was entirely wrapped up in a little black dog, which barked furiously every time I approached her, gave me my first inkling of her declining powers. Whenever I went to see her she would talk about nothing else. She no longer listened to anything I said.

In any case, her feeling for me could never have been a substitute for the love which might have saved me at this turning-point of my life. Her ruling vice was the love of money, and this I have inherited. The passion is in my blood. She would have done everything she could to keep me in a profession which, to use her own words, brought in "big money." At that time, the idea of writing attracted me. Many newspapers, and all the important Reviews, approached me with offers. In addition, the Left-wing parties wanted me to stand at the next election for the constituency of La Bastide (the man who finally accepted, in my place, got in without the slightest difficulty), but I refused to listen to the call of my ambitions because I didn't want to give up the chance of earning "big money."

In that, I was falling in with your wishes, too. You had made it quite clear to me that you would never leave the provinces. A genuinely loving wife would have taken pleasure in my fame, would have taught me that the art of living consists in abandoning a base passion for one more noble. Those idiot journalists who make a great show of indignation when some man of law takes advantage of his position as a Deputy or a Minister to enjoy a few trivial pickings would be better employed in expressing admiration of those who have succeeded in establishing an intelligent hierarchy among their passions, and have preferred glory in the field of politics to big profits in business. If you had had any real love for me you could have saved me from my ingrained habit of never setting anything above immediate gain, of being incapable of giving up the mediocre and squalid temptation of big fees for the shadow of power. After all, there is no shadow without a reality that projects it. The very shadow itself is a reality. As things turned out, there was nothing for me to do but go on making "big money," just like the grocer at the corner.

That's all I have left—the money I earned in the course of those terrible years, the money you're mad enough to want me to give away. The very idea that you might enjoy it after my death is intolerable to me. I told you, at the beginning of this screed, that I had, at one time, taken steps to see that you should be left with nothing, at the same time giving you reason to believe that I had now abandoned this particular plan of revenge. But I had not then taken into account the tidal movement of my hatred. Sometimes it ebbs, and I grow soft . . . sometimes it flows, and then the muddy waters engulf me.

After what happened to-day, after this Easter incident, this concerted attack undertaken with the object of stripping me bare in the interests of dear Phili, I feel differently. I have had a view of the family pack sitting back on its hunkers round the door, and spying on my movements. I am obsessed by the idea of so dividing up my property that you'll all be at one another's throat. Oh yes, you'll fight like dogs over the land and over the securities. Don't bother—you're going to get the land all right, but the securities no longer exist. The ones I mentioned on the first page of this letter I sold last week at the top of the market. Since then, they've been falling every day. Ships have a way of foundering as soon as I abandon them. I'm never wrong. My millions of liquid capital you shall have—but only if I decide in your favour. There are days when I make up my mind not to leave you a penny of it.

I can hear the whole lot of you whispering your way upstairs. You stop: you talk freely without fear of waking me (the accepted view is that I am deaf). I can see the light of your candles underneath the door. I recognize Phili's falsetto (anybody would think his voice is still breaking), and catch a sudden burst of stifled laughter, the sound of young women clucking. You're calling them to order: you're just going to say—"He isn't asleep, I know he isn't." . . . You creep up to my door; you listen; you look through the key-hole. The lamp gives me away. You've returned to the pack. I think you must be whispering—"He's still awake; he's listening to you. . . ."

They tip-toe away: the stairs creak: door after door closes. On this Easter night the house is full of couples. I might be the living trunk from which these young shoots have sprung. Most fathers are beloved: but you were my enemy, and my children have gone over to the enemy.

It is to this war between us that I must turn now. I feel too weak to go on writing, yet hate the thought of going to bed, even of lying down in the rare moments when the state of my heart permits it. At my age, sleep attracts the attention to death. One mustn't look as though one were dead. I have a feeling that so long as I am on my feet death can't come near me. What is it that I dread about death?—physical pain? the awful struggle at the end?—no, not that, but the feeling that to die is to become nothing, that our state in the grave can be expressed only by the symbol ——

VII

SO long as our three little ones remained in the limbo of infancy, the enmity between us was still disguised. But there was a heavy atmosphere about our home. Your indifference to me, your complete detachment from everything that had to do with me, kept you from feeling any discomfort on that account, or even from noticing it. Besides, I was never there. I lunched alone at eleven, so as to get to the Courts by midday. Work took up most of my time and—well, you can guess what I did with such brief snatches of leisure as I might have been able to give my family. Why did I turn to this hideous, bare skeleton of debauchery? It was stripped of everything that usually provides some excuse even for animal passion. It had been reduced to pure horror, without a hint of feeling to justify it, without the least pretence of sentiment. I might so easily have had the kind of adventures that the world approves. A lawyer of my age could scarcely avoid certain temptations. There were many young women ready and eager to get under the skin of the public figure, and rouse the man. . . . But I had lost faith in the creatures, or, rather, in my power to attract any of them. I at once detected the self-interest which animated those who were "ready and willing," those of whose charms I was conscious. The fixed idea that what they were looking for was a certain security of tenure chilled my ardour. Why should I mind admitting that, in addition to the tragic certainty of feeling myself to be somebody whom no one would ever love, I was a victim to the suspicion which afflicts most rich men, and makes them feel that they are being deceived and exploited? I had put you on a fixed allowance, and you knew me too well to expect a penny more than the agreed sum. It was calculated on a generous basis, and you never exceeded it. I felt no threat of danger from that quarter. But with other women it was quite a different kettle of fish! I was one of those fools who believe that there are only two classes of women—those who indulge in love for its own sake, and those debased creatures who are out only for what they can get. In fact, most women oscillate between the two. They want to give free rein to their amorous tendencies, and they want to be "kept," protected and spoiled. At sixty-eight I look back with a lucidity which, at times, makes me want to howl, at all that I rejected in those days, not from any sense of virtue, but because I was mistrustful and cowardly. The few "affairs" which I did begin soon ended, either because my naturally suspicious nature misinterpreted even the most innocent of requests, or because I made myself odious by reason of those manias of mine which you know only too well—endless quarrels with waiters or cab-drivers on the subject of tips. I like to know in advance precisely what I've got to pay. I like to work to a tariff. It's not easy to confess this. What I found attractive in mercenary love was, probably, that it had a fixed price. But in a man of my sort what possible connexion could there be between mere self-indulgence and the cravings of the heart? I had ceased to believe that the cravings of the heart could ever be satisfied, and I took good care to stifle them as soon as they showed their heads. I was a past master in the art of destroying all sentiment at the precise moment when the will begins to play a decisive part in matters of love, when a man can still stand on the sidelines of passion and is free to surrender or to hold back while there is still time. I chose the simplest satisfactions—those that may be had for an agreed outlay. I hate being "done," but what I owe I pay. You're always girding at me for being "close," but that doesn't prevent me from having a horror of debts. I pay cash for everything. My tradesmen know this and bless me. I can't bear the thought that I owe any man a penny. Love, I thought, was something in which one was perpetually giving . . . and I found it disgusting.

Perhaps I'm making too much of all this, and fouling my own nest. I have loved, and even perhaps been loved. It was in 1909, when my youth was already on the wane. Why should I pass over that particular adventure in silence? You knew all about it. You made no bones about recalling it when you wanted to drive me into a corner.

She was a young schoolteacher, who had been charged with infanticide, and I saved her. She gave herself to me at first out of sheer gratitude, but later . . . yes, for one year I knew what real love was. What ruined everything was my inability to keep my demands in check. Not content with letting her live in mean circumstances which were only just one degree above actual poverty, I had to have her constantly at my beck and call. I never let her see anybody. She always had to be there when I wanted her during my brief periods of leisure, and not there when I didn't. She was my property. My passion for possession, and for using and abusing what I possess, extends to human beings. I ought to have been a slave-owner. For this one and only time I thought I had found a victim really made to the measure of my demands. I kept a close watch even on the expression of her face. . . . But I'm forgetting my promise not to tell you about this side of my life. The long and the short of it is that she ran away to Paris. She couldn't stand it any longer.

"It's not only us you can't get on with. Everyone's afraid of you, and keeps out of your way. You must know that, Louis!" If you've said that once, you've said it a hundred times, and it's perfectly true. At the Law Courts I was always a lone wolf. I was elected to the Bar Council—but only at the last possible moment. They'd chosen too many fools in my stead for me ever to be ambitious of the Presidency. I'm not sure, as a matter of fact, that I ever really wanted it. It would have meant being a representative, entertaining. Honours like that cost a deal of money, and the game's not worth the candle. You wanted it for the sake of the children. You've never wanted anything for me. "Do it for the sake of the children."

During the year immediately following our marriage, your father had his first stroke, and the chateau of Cenon was closed to us. You very quickly adopted Calèse. The only thing of mine you've ever really made your own is my land. You took root in my soil, but our roots never met. Your children spent all their holidays in this house and garden. Our little Marie died here. But, so far from her death giving you a horror of the place, you have invested the room in which she lived her last days with a sort of sacred character. . . . It was here that you hatched your brood, that you tended the sick, watched by the cradles, and sent an endless succession of nurses and governesses packing. It was on lines strung to the apple trees that Marie's tiny dresses were hung out to dry, and a long sequence of innocent garments. It was in this drawing-room that the Abbé Ardouin used to group the children round the piano and make them sing choruses which, so as to avoid my anger, were not always sacred in character.

Smoking in front of the house on summer evenings, I used to hear their pure young voices. I can still recollect that air of Lulli's, "*Ah! que ces bois, ces rochers, ces fontaines. . . .*" There was about it all a sense of quiet happiness from which I felt myself excluded. It was a zone of dreamlike innocence which I was forbidden to enter. It was a quiet sea of love which died into nothingness a few feet from the rock of my presence.

When I entered the drawing-room, the voices fell silent. Geneviève took herself off with a book. Marie was the only one who wasn't frightened of me. I called to her and she came. I snatched her up in my arms, and she nestled there happily enough. I could feel her little bird's heart beating. I let her go, and at once she fluttered away into the garden. . . . Marie!

Very early on the children began to show surprise at my

absence from Mass, and at my Friday cutlet. But the struggle that you and I were waging very rarely flared up when they were present, and if it did, I was usually beaten. After each one of my defeats, the war went underground again. Calèse was the battlefield, for when we were in Bordeaux, I was scarcely ever at home. But the legal vacation coincided with the school holidays, and August and September found us all together here.

I remember one occasion when we had a head-on clash (it had to do with some joke I had made in Geneviève's hearing, when she was reciting her Scripture lesson). I asserted my right to defend my children's minds, you, yours to protect their souls. I had been routed once already when I agreed that Hubert should be entrusted to the Jesuit Fathers, and the younger children to the Ladies of the Sacred Heart. I had yielded to the prestige which the traditions of the Fondaudège family always enjoyed in my eyes. But I was hungry for revenge, and, on that particular occasion, what mattered to me was that I had hit on the one subject capable of making you really wild. When *that* was under discussion you had to abandon your attitude of indifference and listen to what I was saying, no matter how much you might hate it. At last I had found a way of bringing you to battle. Formerly my irreligion had been no more than a mould into which I ran the various humiliations which, as the son of a peasant father who had made money, I had had to endure from my superior middle-class companions. But now I filled it with all the frustrations I had met with in love, and an almost limitless extent of rancorous resentment.

The dispute started again during luncheon (I had asked what possible satisfaction it could give the Eternal Being to see you eating salmon-trout instead of boiled beef). You left the table. I remember the expression on the children's faces. I followed you to your room. Your eyes were dry: you spoke quite calmly. I realized then that you hadn't been so wholly unaware of the life I had been leading as I had supposed. You had come across certain letters which contained quite enough evidence to get you a separation. "I have stayed with you for the sake of the children," you said. "But if your presence here is going to endanger their spiritual well-being, I shall not hesitate for a moment."

No, you certainly would not have hesitated to leave both me and my money. Ruled though you might be by self-interest, you would have consented to any sacrifice that might have been necessary to keep the teachings of the Church—that agglomeration of habits, formulæ and general nonsense—unsullied in those little brains.

I did not keep the letter of abuse you sent me after Marie's death. You were too strong for me. Any legal proceedings between us would seriously have imperilled my own position. In those days, and in provincial circles, such things were not taken lightly. There was already a rumour going about to the effect that I was a Freemason. My opinions had made me more or less of an outcast from local society. But for the prestige enjoyed by your family, they might have done me a lot of harm. Worst of all, had there been a legal separation, I should have had to surrender the Suez Canal shares which formed part of your dowry. I had come to regard them as my own property. I couldn't face the thought of having to give them up—(to say nothing of the allowance your father made us).

I ate humble pie and agreed to all the conditions you laid down. But I made up my mind to devote my leisure to the task of winning over the children. I came to that decision at the beginning of August, 1896. Those sad and blazing summers of long ago have become confused in my mind, and my memories of that time cover a period of, roughly, five years (1895-1900).

I thought it would not be difficult to renew my hold over the children. I reckoned on my authority as their father, and on my intelligence. It would be a mere nothing, I thought, to work on a boy of ten and two little girls. I remember the surprise and uneasiness which they showed when I suggested one day that they should go for a long walk with Papa. You were sitting in the courtyard, under the silver lime. They looked at you enquiringly. "There's no need for you to ask my permission, my pets!"

We started off. How does one talk to children? Accustomed though I am to standing up to the Public Prosecutor, to Defending Counsel when I'm appearing for the defendant in a Civil suit, to a whole courtful of hostile lawyers, and though Assize Judges go in fear of me, I confess that children get me down—children, and members of the lower orders, even peasants, though I am a peasant's son myself. In their presence I become unsure of myself and tongue-tied.

They were very nice to me, but obviously on their guard. You had long ago thrown a holding-force into those three hearts! You controlled all the approaches. Not one step could I take without your permission. You had made no attempt to undermine my authority—oh, you were far too scrupulous for that! but you had let them see pretty clearly that a lot of praying would have to be done for poor Papa. No matter how erring I might be, I occupied a perfectly definite place in their scheme of things—I was the "poor Papa," the object of their prayers, the misguided pagan ripe for conversion—and anything I might say or hint on the subject of religion merely confirmed the rather crude idea they had of me.

They lived in a world of marvels. Its landmarks were the feast-days of the year, each of them celebrated with solemn piety. *You* could get them to do anything you wanted just by talking about the First Communion which they had either made recently or were about to make. When, in the evening, they sang on the front steps at Calèse, it was not always the airs of Lulli—which were included for my especial delectation: there were psalms, too. From far away I could see the vague blur made by your little group, and, when there was a moon, could make out the three little lifted faces. The sound of my footsteps on the gravel interrupted their singing.

On Sundays I was awakened by the bustle you all made in getting off to Mass. You were always afraid of being late. The horses pawed the ground: the cook hadn't turned up and had to be called. One of the children had forgotten a prayer-book. A shrill voice cried: "Which Sunday after Pentecost is it?"

When they got back and came in to give me a kiss they always found me still in bed. Little Marie, who must have recited all the prayers she knew with a special "Intention" for me, stared solemnly into my face, doubtless hoping to discover some slight improvement in my spiritual state.

She was the only one of them who did not irritate me. The two elder were already smugly ensconced in the beliefs to which you clung with so sure a feeling for that middle-class comfort which, at a later date, was to make them turn their backs on all the heroic virtues and sublime lunacies of the Christian faith. In her, on the contrary, there was a touching ardour, a genuine feeling of compassion for the farm labourers and the poor. People said of her: "She'd give everything she has: money just trickles through her fingers. It's all very charming, of course, but that sort of generosity needs careful watching. . . ." They said, too: "No one can resist her, not even her father." She used to climb on my knee of an evening of her own accord. Once she fell asleep with her head on my shoulder. Her curls tickled my cheek. I was suffering agonies, because I had to keep so still, and I wanted to smoke. But I sat there like a graven image, and, when the nurse came to fetch her at nine o'clock, I carried her all the way up to her room. You all stared at me in amazement, as though I had been the wild beast in the legend who licked the feet of the child martyrs. Shortly after that—it was on the morning of the 14th of August, she said to me—you know how children do:

"Promise—there's something I want to ask you, but you must promise first to do what I say. . . ."

She reminded me that you were going to sing at the eleven o'clock Mass next day, and that it would be nice of me to go and listen.

"You've promised! you've promised!" she kept on saying as she kissed me: "you've given your word!"

She took my kiss for a promise. The whole house was told about it. I felt that I was under observation. The "master" was going to Mass next day—fancy that! he who never, as a rule, put his foot inside a church! It was an event of immense significance.

I sat down to dinner that evening in a mood of irritability which I could not long conceal. Hubert asked you something—I forget what—about Dreyfus. I remember protesting furiously against your reply, and leaving the room. I did not come back, but packed my bag, took the 6 a.m. train on the 15th, and spent a hideous day in Bordeaux where the heat was stifling and everybody seemed to have gone away.

It seems odd to me now that you should ever have seen me again at Calèse after that. How came it that I always spent the school holidays with the family instead of in travelling? No doubt I could concoct all sorts of admirable explanations, but the real truth was my dislike of incurring a double expense. The idea that anyone could set off on a trip and spend a lot of money without first emptying the larder and locking up the house, never occurred to me. All the pleasure of going away would have been ruined for me by the knowledge that the household expenses were piling up all the time. So, I just crawled back to the family swill-pail. There was food waiting for me at Calèse, so why should I feed elsewhere? My mother had bequeathed to me her mania for "economy," and I had made a virtue of it.

Back I came, then, but with such resentment in my heart that not even Marie could soften me. I began to use tactics of a different kind against you. Instead of delivering a frontal attack on your beliefs, I did all I could, no matter how trivial the circumstances, to show how ill your practice squared with your faith. You must admit, my poor Isa, that, good Christian though you were, I had an easy enough task! You had forgotten, if, indeed, you had ever known, that charity is synonymous with love. You gave its name to what you regarded as your duties to the poor. These you scrupulously observed, always with a weather eye open on your eternal salvation! I realize that a profound change has come over you in recent years. To-day you visit cancer cases in hospital—I know all about that: but, at the time I am speaking of, once you had helped the poor—*your* poor—you felt all the freer to demand from those who were dependent on you what you regarded as your due. You made no compromise with the duty of the housewife, which is to get the largest possible amount of work in return for the lowest possible wages. The wretched old crone who came every morning to our front door with her cart could never sell you so much as a lettuce without your whittling down her meagre profit to the last farthing. If she had been a beggar, you would have given freely of your "charity."

When your frightened servants ventured to ask you for a "rise," you were at first amazed, and then so furiously indignant that you always ended by getting your way. You had a sort of genius for being able to demonstrate that they really had all they could reasonably want. You managed to pile up the total of their advantages: "You have a roof over your heads, a cask of wine, and half of a pig which you fatten on *my* potatoes, to say nothing of a garden in which you can grow vegetables." The poor devils never realized, till you told them, how well off they were! Your maid, you said, could save every penny of the forty francs you paid her every month! "She gets all my old clothes and underlinen and shoes. What can she find to spend her money *on*? If I gave her more, she'd only hand it over to her family!"

I admit, of course, that you looked after them devotedly when they were ill. You never left them to their own resources. I am well aware that you were, for the most part, always respected, and sometimes loved, by your staff. It is the foible of domestics to despise weak mistresses. In all such matters you were a true representative of the ideas of your class and period. But you could never bring yourself to admit that the Gospel condemned them. "*I* always thought"—I would say—"that Christ laid it down . . ." Remarks of that kind invariably brought you up short. You didn't know what to answer, and you were furious because of the children. You unfailingly finished up by falling into the trap. "We're not meant to take those things literally . . .," you would stammer, and that gave me just the chance I needed to triumph over you. I would floor you with examples, all going to show that sanctity consists, precisely, in taking the Gospels literally. If you were foolish enough to reply that you were not a saint, I would quote the precept: "Be ye perfect, even as your Father in heaven is perfect."

You must admit, my poor Isa, that I did what I could in my own way, and that if, now, you visit cancer cases, it is to me in part that they owe your devotion! In the old days, your love of your children obsessed you to the exclusion of every other consideration. All your reserves of kindness and self-sacrifice were used up on them. They filled your vision: you couldn't *see* anybody else. It wasn't only from me that they had alienated you, but from the whole of the rest of the world. The only thing you could speak about to God was their health and their future. That's where I got my chance. I would ask whether, as a Christian, you ought not rather to demand for them every kind of cross—poverty, sickness. You would cut me short: "I'm not going to answer you: you're talking about what you don't understand. . . ." Unfortunately for you, we had as a tutor a young seminarist of twenty-three, the Abbé Ardouin. I was merciless in my appeals to him for support, and caused him much embarrassment, since I never asked his opinion except when I knew that I was in the right. He was incapable of saying anything but what he really thought. As the Dreyfus case developed, I found innumerable opportunities for setting him at odds with you. "So you're in favour"—you would say—"of undermining our whole military system for a . . ." The mere word "Jew" released the full spate of my pretended indignation, and I would keep on until I had forced the Abbé to admit that no true Christian ought to connive at the condemnation of an innocent man, even though the safety of the country might be at stake.

But I made no attempt to convince you and the children, whose whole knowledge of the "affair" was derived from caricatures which appeared in the "right-thinking" newspapers. You closed your ranks against me, and presented an impenetrable front. Even when I seemed to be in the right, you suspected me of trickery. Things got to such a pitch that you deliberately said nothing when I was within earshot. I had only to come near—and it's just the same now—for all discussion to stop. But there were times when I hid in the shrubbery without your knowing I was there, and then I would put in my oar before you had time to retreat. You couldn't avoid the issue then.

Talking of the Abbé Ardouin to your friends, you would say: "The man's a perfect saint. He's no more capable of thinking evil than a child. My husband plays with him like a cat with a mouse. That's the only reason he puts up with him. As a rule, he hates the very sight of a cassock. . . ."

The only reason I'd agreed to having a priest for tutor was, as a matter of fact, that no layman would have agreed to work all through the holidays for a hundred and fifty francs. At first I treated the tall, black-haired, shy young man with the weak eyes, as completely insignificant. I took no more notice of him than I did of the furniture. He saw to it that the children did their work, took them out for walks, ate very little, and never uttered a word. As soon as dinner was finished, he went up to his room. Sometimes, when there was nobody about, he played the piano. I know nothing of music, but he was, as you said, "a nice person to have about the place."

One incident there was which I am sure you have not forgotten. What you have never known is that it established between the Abbé Ardouin and me a secret current of sympathy. One day the children told me that the Curé had called. I at once took refuge in the vineyard, as I always did on such occasions. But you sent Hubert to fetch me back. The Curé had something urgent to say to me. With much grumbling I returned to the house, because I was really rather frightened of the little old man. He had come, he said, to unburden his conscience. It was he who had recommended the Abbé Ardouin as a thoroughly reliable young seminarist who had been prevented, by ill health, from taking Orders at the normal time. He had just learned, in the course of a retreat, that this postponement had actually been a disciplinary measure. The Abbé was, to be sure, very pious, but he was mad about music, and had been tempted by one of his co-seminarists to slip out one night and go to a charity concert at the Grand Theatre. They were in lay dress, but were recognized and denounced. What made matters worse was that one of the performers was Madame Georgette Lebrun, and she had sung excerpts from *Thais*. At sight of her bare feet and Greek tunic, held up under the arms by a silver girdle ("and that was all: not so much as a hint of a shoulder-strap"), there had been an "Oh!" of indignation. In the Union Club Box an old gentleman had exclaimed: "This is really going a bit *too* far . . . where does she think she is?" Such was the spectacle to which the Abbé Ardouin had been exposed. One of the delinquents had suffered immediate expulsion: the other—the

Abbé—had been pardoned. He was a prize student. But his Superiors had postponed his ordination for two years.

We were all of us unanimous in declaring that he enjoyed our full confidence. From then on, however, the Curé showed the greatest coldness to the young man who, he said, had deceived him. No doubt you remember the incident. What you have never known is that, on the same evening, while I was smoking on the terrace, I saw coming towards me in the moonlight the emaciated figure of the guilty man. He addressed me with considerable embarrassment, and asked to be forgiven for having introduced himself into my family without first explaining that there was a slur upon his character. When I told him that the escapade which had caused all the trouble made me like him the more, he suddenly adopted an intransigent attitude, and proceeded to argue against himself. I couldn't, he said, realize the heinousness of his offence. It was not merely that he had broken his vow of obedience: he had sinned against his vocation and against the moral code. He had been a cause of scandal. The whole of the rest of his life would not be long enough to enable him to make proper reparation for his misdeed. . . . I can still see that tall, bowed back, and his shadow in the moonlight, cut in two by the parapet of the terrace.

Prejudiced though I might be against men of his cloth, I could not, witnessing his shame and sorrow, suspect him of the faintest tinge of hypocrisy. He excused his silence to us on the ground of his need. But for the job we had offered him, he would have had to live for two months at the cost of his mother, a poor widow of Libourne, who went out charing. When I replied that, so far as I could see, there had been no obligation upon him to mention something that had to do merely with seminary discipline, he took my hand and uttered the following extraordinary words. It was the first time that anything of the sort had been said to me, and I don't mind confessing that I felt knocked sideways.

"You are" he said, "a very good man." You know that laugh of mine which, even in our first years together, got on your nerves, that sort of private chortle which has the effect of killing any gaiety within the radius of my presence?—well, it racked me that evening as I looked at the shocked and gawky seminarist in front of me. After a while I was able to get out:

"You can't know, Monsieur l'Abbé, how comic that sounds. Ask those who know me whether I am good! Question my family, my professional colleagues! Why, malevolence is my leading characteristic!"

He replied, rather shyly, that those who are truly malevolent don't talk about it.

"I defy you," said I, "to find what you would call a single good action in the whole course of my life."

Then, intending a reference to my calling, he quoted the words of Christ: "I was in prison, and ye visited Me. . . ."

"That's how I make my living, Monsieur l'Abbé. I act from purely self-interested motives. There was a time when I even bribed the gaolers to mention my name, at suitable moments, to those awaiting trial . . . not much goodness there, eh?"

I have forgotten what he said to that. We strolled together under the lime-trees. How surprised you'd have been if I had told you that the presence of that frocked priest somehow brought me peace of mind. But it did.

It was my habit to get up before sunrise and go down into the garden to breathe the morning coolness. On those occasions I used to watch the Abbé setting off for Mass. He walked quickly, and was so much absorbed in his own thoughts that he sometimes passed quite close to me without so much as being aware of my presence. Those were the days when I was lashing you with my mockeries, and doing everything I could to prove that your actions were at odds with your principles. . . . Nevertheless, my conscience was not altogether confortable. Each time I caught you out in some meanness, some lack of charity, I pretended that there was not a trace of Christ's spirit among the lot of you, But I knew perfectly well, all the time, that beneath my roof. and unsuspected by the other inmates, there dwelt a man who lived in strict obedience to its promptings.

VIII

THERE was one occasion, however, when you really did fill me with genuine and unfeigned horror. At some time in '96 or '97—you will remember the exact date—our brother-in-law the Baron Philipot died. Your sister, Marinette, woke one morning and said something to him. He did not answer. She opened the shutters and saw the old man's upturned eyes and sagging jaw. It took her quite a little while to realize that she had been sleeping for a considerable time beside a corpse.

I don't think any of you fully realized the beastliness of that old wretch's will. He left his wife an enormous fortune, on one condition—that she should never marry again. If she did so, the bulk of the money was to go to his nephews.

"We shall have to take great care of her," your mother kept on saying. "Fortunately, we are a very united family. The poor darling mustn't be left alone for a moment."

At that time Marinette was about thirty, though she looked, as you will remember, little more than a girl. She had let herself be married off to an old man without a word of protest, and had put up with him very patiently. It never occurred to you that she might find some difficulty in shouldering the responsibilities of perpetual widowhood. You entirely discounted the shock of her release, the effect upon her of emerging suddenly from a dark tunnel into the full light of day.

Don't be afraid, Isa, that I am going to abuse the advantage which that situation offered me. It was only natural that you should want all those millions to stay in the family, that you should hope our children would ultimately enjoy them. It was wrong, you thought, that Marinette should get no reward for ten years of slavery to an old man's whim. You behaved as all good parents would have behaved in the circumstances. Celibacy seemed to you to be a perfectly natural condition. I don't suppose you remembered the time when you had been a young wife. That chapter had been long since closed. You were a mother. The other implications of marriage had ceased to exist for you and for your parents. Imagination has never been an outstanding characteristic of your family. In this matter of sexual relationships, your attitude was neither that of brute beasts nor of ordinary human beings.

It was agreed that Marinette should spend the first summer of her widowhood at Calèse. She accepted the suggestion gladly, not that there was much intimacy between you, but she was fond of our children and especially of Marie. I scarcely knew her. What at first struck me about her was her gracefulness. She was a year older than you, but seemed very much your junior.

Recurrent pregnancies had given you a heavy look, whereas she, apparently, had emerged intact from the old man's bed. Her face was the face of a child. She wore her hair high, in the fashion of the day, with a fluff of darkish fair strands in the nape of the neck (people to-day have forgotten that outmoded marvel—a tousled nape!). Her eyes were rather too round, and gave her the appearance of perpetual surprise. I used to encircle her "wasp-waist," jokingly, with my two hands. But the prominence of her breast and hips would, to-day, have seemed almost monstrous. Women at that time looked like hot-house flowers. Her gaiety surprised me. The children thought her great fun, for she organized games of hide-and-seek in the loft, and played with them at Tableaux Vivants in the evenings. "She's a little too feather-headed," you used to say, "and doesn't seem to realize her position."

You found it already a strain on your patience to see her going about all week in white dresses; and when she attended Mass without a veil, and refused to wear so much as a border of crape, you considered her behaviour definitely shocking. The heat, according to you, was not an adequate excuse.

She had shared only one amusement with her husband—riding. Baron Philipot had been a champion horseman, and until the last day of his life had rarely missed his morning canter. She had had her mare sent to Calèse, and, since there was nobody to accompany her, had taken to going out alone. This you thought doubly scandalous. It was unseemly for a three-months-old widow to take any kind of exercise, but that she should go riding without somebody in attendance passed all bounds.

"I shall let her know what the family thinks of such behaviour," you said more than once. And so you did, but she continued to have her own way. At last, tired of squabbling, she asked me to act as her escort, and promised to find me a very quiet mount (she, of course, paying for everything).

We used to start off at dawn, because of the flies, and because we had to walk the horses for two kilometres before reaching the nearest stretch of pine-wood. We used to mount at the front steps. Marinette would stick her tongue out at the closed shutters of your room, pin a dew-drenched rose to her habit, and say, as she did so, "*Quite* unsuitable for a widow!" The church bell would be ringing with short sharp strokes for early Mass, and the Abbé Ardouin would give us a shy greeting before vanishing into the mist which hung above the vines.

We spent the time until we reached the woods in chatting. I realized that I enjoyed a certain degree of prestige in my sister-in-law's eyes, not so much because of my position at the Bar, but because of the subversive ideas which I preached in the bosom of the family. Your principles were too much like those of her late husband. A woman always thinks of ideas, whether about religion or anything else, in terms of a *person*. For her they take tangible form, and the form may be either hated or adored. It would not have been difficult for me to take advantage of rebellious youth; but though I found it easy enough to act as her echo so long as it was all of *you* she inveighed against, I found it impossible to approve the contemptuous way in which she spoke of the millions she would lose in the event of her marrying again. I had every reason in the world to agree with her, and to take a high line of romantic nobility, but I could not pretend, even half-heartedly, to agree with her when she spoke of the loss of such a fortune as something not worth worrying about. If I am to be perfectly frank, I think I ought to admit that the idea of her dying, and of the money coming to us, was not wholly absent from my mind (and when I say "us," I don't mean the children—to whom I scarcely gave a thought—but, primarily, to myself).

Try as I might to school myself to use the words she would have liked to hear, it was no good. What I actually said, was: "My dear Marinette, you can't be serious! Think of it, seven million! It is impossible to be indifferent to seven million! No man in the world is worth the sacrifice of even a fraction of such a sum!—and, when she maintained that happiness was more important than money, I told her that nobody could give up such a fortune and be happy.

"It's all very well for you to say you hate them!" she exclaimed: "you're really one of them, you know!"

Then she set off at a gallop, with me following. Her verdict had been passed on me: all hope was lost. What a price I was paying for my lunatic love of money! I might have found in Marinette a younger sister, a mistress. . . . You'd like me, wouldn't you, to sacrifice to you that to which I've sacrificed everything else? Oh no, my money's cost me far too dear for me to give up a single penny of it until I've breathed my last!

But you never give up, do you? I can't help wondering whether Hubert's wife, who forced her presence on me last Sunday, was really acting as your delegate, or whether she came of her own accord. Poor Olympe! (why on earth did Phili nickname her Olympe?—we've all forgotten what her real name is) . . . on the whole, I'm inclined to believe that she said nothing to you about her coming to see me. You've never made her one of yourselves, you don't regard her as belonging to the family. She is completely indifferent to everything outside the boundaries of her narrow world. She knows nothing of the laws of the "tribe," and has no idea that I am "the enemy." That's not because she is either benevolent or sympathetic, but simply because she never thinks about other people, and doesn't even bother to hate them.

"He's always very nice to me," she says, whenever my name is mentioned in her hearing. She is entirely unaware of my bitterness, and because, simply from a spirit of contradiction, I take up the cudgels in her favour against the lot of you, is convinced that I find her attractive.

Reading between the lines of her confused outpourings, I gather that Hubert has "got out" in time, but that he has had to call on the whole of his private fortune, as well as on his wife's dowry, to save the business. "He says he's bound to get his money back, but that he must have an advance . . . he calls it a mortgage on his expectations. . . ."

When she said that, I nodded my head. I agreed with everything, and pretended not to have the remotest idea what it was she wanted. I can play the innocent very successfully at such times!

If only poor Olympe knew what I sacrificed to money in the days when I was still relatively young!

On those mornings of my thirty-fifth year, we used to jog back, your sister and I, letting the horses take their own pace, along the road which was already feeling the heat of the sun, between the sprayed vines. She sat there in the saddle mocking at me while I talked about the millions that she mustn't, on any account, lose. Each time that I managed to free myself from the obsession of that menaced fortune, she would laugh at me with a sort of contemptuous kindness. I tried to defend myself, but only succeeded in getting into deeper water.

"It's in your own interest, Marinette, that I'm talking like this. You don't really think, do you, that I'm the sort of man to let himself be hag-ridden by the problem of his children's future? I know that Isa doesn't want the money to slip between their fingers, but I . . ."

Then she would laugh, and say between partly clenched teeth:

"You're quite horrid enough as it it is. . . ."

I protested that I was thinking only of her happiness. She shook her head with an air of disgust. What really made her envious, though she never admitted it, was not so much marriage as motherhood.

Oh, she despised me all right! But when, after luncheon, in spite of the heat, I left the dark, cool house where the members of the family were dozing, sprawled on the leather sofas and in the wicker chairs, when I threw back the shutters of the French windows, and slipped out into the blazing blue, I didn't have to look back. I knew perfectly well that she would follow. I could hear her footsteps on the gravel. She walked with difficulty, catching her high heels in the baked earth. We stood together with our elbows on the parapet of the terrace. She played a sort of game with herself, which consisted in seeing how long she could keep her bare arm on the hot stone.

The plain beneath gave itself to the sun in a silence as deep as when it sleeps under the moon. The Landes ringed the horizon in an immense black semicircle on which the metallic sky pressed like a weight. Not a man, not an animal, would stir out of doors till four o'clock. The flies buzzed, but made no effort to move away. They were no less motionless than the pillar of smoke rising from the plain straight and still in the airless heat.

I knew that the woman at my side could never love me, that

everything about me was odious to her. But we were the only two living things in that lost land, imprisoned in its summer torpor. She was young and tormented, spied upon by her family, and she turned to me as unconsciously as the heliotrope turns to the sun. And yet, had I betrayed by a single word the emotions of my heart, she would have given me only mockery in return. I was perfectly well aware that she would have repulsed with disgust any advances on my part, however timid. There we stood together, on the edge of that immense vat in which the future harvest of the grapes was fermenting under the blue-tinted leaves, drowsing in the sun.

And what did you think, Isa, about those morning rides and close confabulations while the rest of the world was sunk in siesta? I know what you thought, because on one occasion I overheard you. Through the closed shutters of the drawing-room I heard you say to your mother, who was staying with us at Calèse (no doubt she had come to reinforce the watch that was being kept on Marinette):

"He's a bad influence on her, but only because of his ideas. Apart from them he serves as a distraction. I can see no harm in their going about together."

"Yes, he *is* a distraction for her, and that's all that really matters," your mother replied.

You were delighted to think that I was a distraction for Marinette. "But after the holidays," you said more than once, "we shall have to find some other way of keeping her amused." You may have despised me, Isa, but your contempt was nothing to mine when I heard you talk like that. I suppose it never occurred to you that there might be any danger. Women have a way of not remembering what they have ceased to feel.

Nothing, to be sure, could possibly happen during those after-luncheon intimacies poised above the plain. Empty though the world was, we were standing, as it were, bang in the middle of a stage. Had there been but one peasant who had not surrendered to siesta, he would have been bound to see us there, a man and a woman motionless as two trees, gazing down at the incandescent earth, and so close together that neither could have made the slightest movement without touching the other.

But our nightly strolls were no less innocent. I remember one August evening in particular. Dinner had been made stormy by a discussion of the Dreyfus case. Marinette, who, with me, represented the party for revision, had by now surpassed me in the art of bringing the Abbé Ardouin into the open and forcing him into taking sides. You had mentioned with enthusiasm some article of Drumont's, and Marinette, as though butter wouldn't melt in her mouth, had said:

"Do tell me, Monsieur l'Abbé, is it permissible for us to hate the Jews?"

That evening, much to our delight, he did not take refuge in easy evasions. He spoke of the greatness of the Chosen People, of the part they had played as witnesses to the truth, of their conversion, which had been foretold and would herald the end of the world. And when Hubert protested that we needs must hate our Lord's butchers, the Abbé replied that each of us had the right to hate one of Christ's butchers, and one only—himself, but no one else.

Thoroughly put out, you retorted that the only result of such highfalutin theories would be the surrender of France into the hands of her enemies. Fortunately for the Abbé, you then turned the conversation on to Jeanne d'Arc—and she made all well again. One of the children, out on the steps, exclaimed:

"How lovely the moon is to-night!" I went out. I knew that Marinette would come too. I heard her say in a low voice, "Wait for me." . . . She was wearing a "boa" round her neck.

The moon was rising full in the east. She expressed admiration of the long shadows cast by the elms on the grass. The farm-workers' cottages stood blind-eyed in the white radiance. A few dogs were barking. She asked me whether it was the moon that made the trees so motionless. She said that on such a night the whole of creation was but a torment to the lonely. "An empty stage!" she said. Everywhere, at this very moment, lips were pressed to lips, shoulders touched, heart responded to heart. I could distinctly see a tear quivering on her lashes. In the world's stillness her breathing was the only sign of life. . . . It was eager, it was hesitant. . . . You died in 1900, Marinette. What remains of you now? What remains of the body that was buried thirty years ago? I can remember the smell of it in the darkness. Perhaps, only if we have conquered the body can we believe in the body's resurrection. The punishment of those who have abused it is that they cannot even imagine that it will rise again.

I took her hand, as I might have taken the hand of an unhappy child, and, like a child she leaned her head upon my shoulder. I received the gift of it merely because I happened to be there. The earth receives the fallen peach. Most human beings come together not as the result of any deliberate choice, but like trees which have grown side by side, their branches interlacing in the simple process of their growth.

But what made me infamous at that moment was that I thought of *you*: thought how I might be revenged on you, how I might make use of Marinette to cause you suffering. It may have been for a fleeting second only, but it is true, nevertheless, that the idea of such a crime did enter my head. We took a few uncertain steps outside the zone of moonlight towards a clump of syringas and pomegranate trees. But Fate intervened. At that precise moment I heard steps in the lime walk—the walk which the Abbé Ardouin used every morning on his way to Mass. It was almost certainly he. . . . I thought of what he had said to me one evening—"You are a very good man." If only he could have read my heart at that moment! Perhaps the shame that overcame me at the thought was my salvation.

I led Marinette back into the light, and made her sit down. I dried her eyes with my handkerchief, and spoke to her as I might have spoken to Marie if she had fallen and I had picked her up under the limes. I pretended that I had not noticed the hint of an emotional disturbance in her tears, and in the soft yielding of her body.

IX

NEXT morning she did not ride. I went into Bordeaux (I spent two days of each week there, even in vacation time, so as not to interrupt my consultations).

The Southern Express was standing in the station just as I was getting into the train to go back to Calèse, and great was my astonishment to see, through the window of a coach labelled *Biarritz*, Marinette in a grey tailor-made suit and without a veil. I remembered that a friend of hers had been pressing her for some time to join her at Saint-Jean-de-Luz. She was reading an illustrated paper and did not see the signs I made. That evening, when I mentioned the incident to you, you paid little attention to what you thought was a brief indulgence in liberty. You told me that, shortly after I had left, Marinette had received a telegram from her friend. You seemed surprised that I did not know this. Perhaps you had suspected us of having arranged to meet secretly in Bordeaux.

Besides, you had other things to think of. Little Marie had been sent to bed with a temperature. She had been suffering for some days from diarrhœa, and you were uneasy. I will do you the justice to say that whenever any of the children were ill, nothing else mattered to you.

I want to pass quickly over what followed. After more than thirty years it is only with an immense effort that I can bring my mind to dwell on it.

I know the substance of your charge against me. You had the effrontery to tell me to my face that I was against having a second opinion. I have no doubt that if we had called in Professor Arnozan he would have diagnosed what we took to be influenza as typhus. But cast your mind back. Once, but only once, you did say, "Mightn't it be as well to have Arnozan?" My reply to that was: "Dr. Aubrou tells me that he's been attending more than twenty cases of this type of influenza in the village. . . ." You didn't insist. You pretend now that you raised the point again next day, that you begged me to send a telegram to Arnozan. Had you done so I should have remembered it. The fact is, I've chewed old memories over and over through so many days and nights, that I'm no longer sure what actually did happen. I know I've always been a miser about money, but not to the extent of trying to save expense where Marie's health was concerned. So it can't have been that, apart from the fact that Arnozan worked for the love of God and humanity. If I didn't call him in, the reason is that we were still convinced that it was simply a case of influenza which had "gone to the bowels." That ass Aubrou made Marie eat so as to keep up her strength. It was he who killed her, not I. You were entirely of my opinion, and if you say now that you urged me to call in Arnozan, you are lying. I was not responsible for Marie's death. That you should ever have accused me of such a thing is horrible. All the same, you *believe* I was: you've always believed it.

Oh, that relentless summer! the frenzy of the heat, the ferocious scraping of the grasshoppers. It was impossible to get any ice. All through those endless afternoons I sat wiping the sweat from her tiny face, which seemed to be a target for every fly within reach. Arnozan came at last, but too late. He changed the treatment, but by that time all hope of saving her was gone. It was probably only because of her delirium that she kept on saying—"for Papa!—for Papa!" . . . Do you remember the sound of her voice when she suddenly cried out, "Please, God, I am only a child . . .," and how she stopped, and went on, "No, I can stand it, I can . . ."? The Abbé gave her some water from

Lourdes to drink. Our heads, yours and mine, came together above her exhausted body: our hands touched. When it was all over, you thought me callous.

Do you really want to know what was going on in my mind? I was thinking how strange it seemed that you, a Christian, should set such store by the *corpse*. You wouldn't leave it. We tried to get you to eat: we kept on telling you that you would need all your strength. But only by using force could we make you leave the room. You sat beside the bed, touching her cold forehead and her cheeks in a sort of fumbling way. Her hair, which still had life in it, you kissed, and now and again you slipped to your knees, not to pray, but so that you could press your face against the cold and rigid hands.

The Abbé Ardouin raised you up, and spoke of how we must make ourselves like little children if we are to enter the Kingdom of the Father. "She lives, she sees you, she is waiting for you." But you shook your head. The words did not even penetrate to your brain. Your faith was useless to you. You had thoughts for nothing but that flesh of your flesh, which was going to be laid in the earth and would soon know corruption. It was I, the unbeliever, who realized, as I looked at what was left of Marie, the full meaning of the word "remains." I was overwhelmed by a sense of departure, of absence. She was no longer there. *That* was not her: "Is it Marie that ye seek . . .?—she is no longer here. . . ."

Later, you accused me of being quick to forget. Only *I* know what broke in me when I kissed her for the last time as she lay in her coffin. But what lay there was not really her. You held it against me that I did not accompany you to the cemetery, when you visited it almost every other day. "He never sets foot inside the place"—that was your constant complaint. "And yet," you would say, "she was the only person he seemed to have any feeling for. . . . The truth of the matter is—he's quite heartless. . . ."

Marinette came back for the funeral, but left again three days later. You were blinded by your grief and never saw the threat that was gathering in that direction. You even seemed relieved when your sister went away. Two months afterwards, we heard of her engagement to a literary gent, a journalist whom she had met in Biarritz. It was too late, then, to put a spoke in her wheel. You showed yourself to be utterly unforgiving. It was as though some long-repressed hatred of Marinette had suddenly burst free. You didn't, you said, want to know the "creature"—who, as a matter of fact, was quite an ordinary sort of chap, pretty much like any other. His only crime was that he had deprived our children of a fortune. Not that he derived any benefit from it himself, since most of it went to Philipot's nephews.

But reason was never your strong suit. You were quite unscrupulous. I have never known anybody who could be so serenely unjust. God knows what peccadilloes you may have confessed in the secrecy of your heart—but there was certainly not one of the Beatitudes which you did not deny by the actions of your life. You thought nothing of accumulating false reasons against those you hated. You had never seen your sister's husband, and knew nothing whatever about him, but that did not prevent you from saying: "She fell a victim to some sort of adventurer she met at Biarritz, a regular lounge-lizard type. . . ."

When the poor girl died in child-bed (I don't want to judge you as harshly as you judged me in the matter of Marie), it wasn't only that you showed next to no regret. Events had proved you right. It had been bound to end like that. She had dug her own grave, and you had nothing with which to reproach yourself. You had done your duty. The wretched woman had known perfectly well that her family would always take her back if she made the slightest sign. You, at least, had had nothing to do with the business—that must have been a comforting thought! You had been firm—but at what a cost! "There are times when one has got to learn to trample on one's feelings!"

I don't want to be too hard on you. I realize that you behaved well to little Luc, Marinette's son, when there was no one to bother about him after your mother's death. You made yourself responsible for him during the holidays, and went to see him once each winter in the school just outside Bayonne where he had been placed. "You did your duty"—such were your words —"even if his father didn't do *his*."

I have never told you how I came to meet Luc's father. It was in Bordeaux, in the September of 1914. I was trying to find a safe-deposit at a Bank. The fugitives from Paris had taken them all. At long last, the manager of the Crédit Lyonnais notified me that one of his clients was returning to the capital and might, perhaps, consent to let me have his. When he told me his name I realized that it was Luc's father. He was very far from being the monster you thought him. I tried in vain to recognize, in this man of thirty-eight, lean, hollow-cheeked and worried to death by the constant threat of medical boards, the being whom, fourteen years earlier, I had seen at Marinette's funeral. I had a business talk with him. He expressed himself with the utmost frankness. He was living with a woman, but didn't want Luc to have anything to do with her. It was out of consideration for the boy that he had handed him over to the tender mercies of his grandmother. My poor Isa, if only you and the children had known what I offered him at that meeting! I can tell you now. My suggestion was that he should keep the safe-deposit in his own name, giving me power of attorney. I, for my part, was to leave all my liquid assets there, with a document stating that they were Luc's property. So long as I lived he would have been powerless to touch them, but, after my death, could have taken possession without your knowing a thing. . . .

Obviously, I should have been putting myself and my fortune into his hands. How I must have hated you at that moment! But the man wouldn't play. He was too frightened. He spoke of his "honour."

How came it that I could have entertained such a mad idea? At the time I am speaking of our children must have been within measurable distance of their thirties. They were married, were definitely on your side, were opposed to me on every conceivable issue. You were working in secret. I was the enemy. God knows you were not on particularly good terms with any of them, and especially not with Geneviève. Your grievance against her was that she left you out of everything, that she never asked your advice. But against me you maintained a common front. Nevertheless, everything between us was conducted in a muted key, except on solemn occasions. For instance, there were terrible battles over the children's marriages. I set my face against giving anything in the nature of a dowry, and insisted on an allowance in each case. I refused to render an account of my financial position to either of the families concerned, and stuck to my point. I had all the cards in my hand. Hatred was my strong suit, hatred and love—the love that I felt for young Luc. And the families put up with me, because they felt so sure that my fortune was immense.

My silence worried you. You wanted to know. Sometimes, Geneviève tried to get on the soft side of me. I could hear the poor ungainly creature clumping along in her clogs a mile off! I often said to her, "You'll bless me when I'm dead," just for the pleasure of seeing the greedy glint in her eyes. She passed on those wonderful words of mine to you. The whole family was in a state of trance. And all the time I was trying to find some way of leaving you nothing beyond what could not be concealed. I thought only of young Luc. I even played with the idea of mortgaging the land. . . .

But on one occasion I did let myself be taken in by your play-acting. It was the year after Marie's death. I was ill. Some of my symptoms were not unlike those of the disease which had carried off our little daughter. I hate being fussed over. I have a horror of doctors and drugs. You nagged me until I agreed to stay in bed and see Arnozan.

You nursed me devotedly—that goes without saying—but also with a certain uneasiness. Sometimes, when you asked me how I was feeling, I thought I heard a note of anxiety in your voice. When you felt my forehead, you did it much in the same way as you would have done if I had been your child. You wanted to sleep in my room. If I was restless in the night you got up and fetched me a drink. "She is really fond of me," I used to say to myself: "who *would* have thought it!—I suppose it's because of what I make!" But there I was wrong. You don't love money for its own sake. It's more likely that what was worrying you was the thought that my death would leave the children poorer. But it wasn't that either.

When Arnozan had finished examining me, you had a conversation with him out on the steps, and you raised your voice once or twice as you so often do. It's a habit that's always giving you away. "I want you to let it be known, doctor, that Marie died of typhoid. People are saying it was consumption because of what happened to my poor brothers. There's so much ill-nature in the world. Once an idea gets about, it has a way of persisting. I'm so terribly afraid of the harm that sort of talk might do to Hubert and Geneviève. If my husband had been seriously ill it might have given substance to that sort of gossip. For some days I felt very anxious about him—thinking of the children. One of his lungs, you know, was affected before his marriage. That's a matter of general knowledge. People do so love that sort of thing. Even if he had died of some infectious disease, they wouldn't have believed it any more than they did in the case of Marie. And my poor darlings would have been the ones to suffer. It used to make me wild to see how little care he took of himself! He wouldn't even stay in bed—as though he had only himself to think of! But he never worries about anybody else, not even the children! . . . Men like you, doctor, find it difficult to believe that people like him exist. You're just like the Abbé Ardouin—who never thinks evil of anybody. . . ."

I lay there in bed, laughing to myself, and when you came back you asked me what I was laughing at. "Oh, nothing," I said. It was a kind of private language of our own. "What are you laughing at?" one of us would say.—"Oh, nothing." "What are you thinking about?"—"Oh, nothing."

X

I TAKE up this narrative again after an attack which has kept me in your power for close on a month. When illness weakens me, the family circle closes about my bed. The whole lot of you are there, watching me.

On Sunday Phili came to keep me company. It was hot: I answered him in monosyllables. I lost the thread of my ideas . . . for how long I can't say. The sound of his voice woke me. I saw him there in the half-light with his ears pricked. His eyes were glittering like a wolf-cub's. He was wearing a gold chain just above his wrist-watch. His shirt was open, and his chest looked like a child's. I dozed off again. The creaking of his shoes roused me, and I lay watching him through half-closed eyes. He was feeling my jacket, just where the inside pocket is in which I keep my note-case. My heart was thumping, but I forced myself to lie still. Perhaps his suspicions were aroused: anyhow, he went back to his chair.

I pretended that I had just woken up, and asked him whether I had been asleep for long.

"Only a few minutes, Grandpapa." I felt that terror which visits old men when they know that young eyes are watching them. Am I going mad? I got the idea that he was quite capable of killing me. Hubert once said that Phili would stick at nothing.

I want you to know, Isa, how wretched I have been. By the time you read these pages it will be too late for you to show me pity, but I like to think that you may feel a little. I do not believe in the everlasting hell-fire of your creed, but I do know what it is to be damned in this life, and outcast. I realize only too clearly that whatever road I choose I am bound to lose my way. All through my life I have chosen wrongly. I have never learned how to live—not in the sense that those of this world understand living. Of the art of life I have, quite literally, known nothing. I am in torment, Isa. The south wind is burning up the air. I am thirsty, and have nothing with which to assuage my thirst but a luke-warm tap. I am the owner of millions, but am without so much as a glass of cold water to my name.

Phili's presence terrifies me. I think I put up with it only because he reminds me of somebody else, of that young Luc, our nephew, who would now be a man of over thirty. I have never denied your virtues, but he gave you no opportunity to show them. You never liked him. There was nothing "Fondaudège" about Marinette's boy. He had jet-black eyes. His hair grew low over his forehead and swept back from his temples in what Hubert used to call a couple of "love locks." In that school at Bayonne where he was a boarder his reputation for work was bad. But that, you said, was no concern of yours. You had quite enough to do looking after him in the holidays. He took no interest in books. Though this countryside is poor in game, he managed to find something to kill every day, contriving to "get" the one and only hare that lurked, each year, in the trenched earth of the vineyard. I can see him still, holding the dead beast by the ears, its muzzle smeared with blood, and waving triumphantly to us as he tramped back between the growing grape-shoots. I used to hear him starting out at dawn. I would open my window, and his clear young voice would call up to me through the mist: "Just off to take a look at my night-lines."

He invariably looked me straight in the face. There was nothing shifty about his eyes. He wasn't frightened of me: the idea of being frightened of me never entered his head. If I happened to come home unexpectedly after a few days' absence, and caught the smell of cigar smoke in the house, or found the carpet up in the drawing-room with all the signs of a hastily interrupted party (I had only to turn my back for Geneviève and Hubert to provoke an "invasion"—in spite of my strict injunctions to the contrary—and you always aided and abetted their disobedience, because, you said, "one must return hospitality"), it was invariably Luc they sent to make their peace with me. The terror I inspired just made him laugh. "I went into the drawing-room while they were dancing, and called out, 'Here's Uncle, he's come by the short cut!'—and, by Jove, you should have seen them hop it! Aunt Isa and Geneviève spirited the sandwiches away into the pantry! What a hullabaloo!"

That boy was the only person in the world I couldn't scare. Sometimes, when he set off on a day's fishing, I used to go down to the river with him. Usually, he could never keep still, was for ever dashing about here, there and everywhere, but on those occasions he was capable of standing perfectly motionless for hours on end, all eyes. It was exactly as though he had been turned into a tree: the slow, noiseless movements of his arm was like that of a swaying branch. Geneviève was perfectly right when she said that he would never be "literary." He couldn't be bothered to go out on the terrace at night to look at the moon. He was entirely without a feeling for nature, because he *was* nature, was wholly absorbed into it, was one of its forces, a living spring among its many springs.

I used to think of all the drama his young life had known—a dead mother, a father who was never mentioned in our presence, a lonely life in a remote school. Much less than all that would have sufficed to fill *me* with bitterness and hate. Everybody loved him, and that seemed strange to me, whom everybody loathed. Yes, everybody loved him—even I. He had a smile for all, including me—but not more for me than for the others.

His nature was purely instinctive, and what struck me more and more, as he grew older, was his purity, his unawareness of evil, his utter disregard of it. I don't mean to imply that our children weren't "good." Hubert, as you always said, was a model youth. In that respect, I must admit, your early training had borne fruit. I wonder whether, if Luc had lived into manhood, he would have remained so utterly untroubled. I never got the impression that, with him, purity was something he had been taught, something of which he was conscious. It had the limpid quality of water running over a stony bed. It glittered on him like the dew on grass. I dwell on this, because it had a profound effect on me. Your parade of high principles, your hints, your expression of distaste, your pursed lips—these things never made me so truly aware of evil as did that boy, though I was not conscious of it at the time, nor for many years afterwards. If, as you hold, humanity carries in its flesh the stigma of original sin, then, all I can say is that no living eye can ever have seen the mark in Luc. He had come from the hand of the potter uncracked and lovely. I felt myself, in comparison with him, deformed.

Is it accurate to say that I loved him like my own son? No, because what I loved in him was that complete absence of all trace of myself. I know only too well what of myself I have bequeathed to Hubert and Geneviève—sharpness of temper, the exorbitant value which they attach to material things, and a certain violence of contempt (in Geneviève's treatment of her husband, Alfred, there is a relentless quality which I recognize only too well). I could always feel quite sure that I should never bump up against myself in Luc.

During the rest of the year I scarcely thought of him. He spent Christmas and Easter with his father, and returned to us only with the coming of the summer holidays. In October he migrated with the other birds.

Was he religious minded? You used to say: "Even in a young animal like Luc one can see the influence of the good Fathers. He never misses taking Communion on Sundays. . . . I know, of course, that he hurries through his act of contrition, but, after all, no more is asked of any of us than we can give."

He never spoke to me about religion, even indirectly. His talk was always of the concrete. Sometimes when he pulled from his pocket a knife, a float, or a whistle for luring larks, his little rosary of black beads would fall to the ground. When that happened, he would hurriedly pick it up. But perhaps on Sunday mornings he did seem a little less scatter-brained than on other days, less evanescent, less imponderable, and as though charged with some unfamiliar current.

The links that bound me to Luc were many, but one of them may cause you some surprise. At times, on those Sunday mornings, I thought I could detect in the young fawn whose leapings were, for the moment, stilled, the brother of the little girl who had fallen asleep twelve years earlier—of our Marie. And yet, how different they were! She, you will remember, could never bear to see an insect crushed, and loved to line a hollow tree with moss, and set in it a statue to the Virgin. All the same, in Marinette's son, in the boy whom you used to call "a little animal," I seemed to see Marie again: or, rather, what I felt was that the same fresh spring, which had bubbled up in her and then gone underground again, was once more gushing at my feet.

When the war broke out Luc was not quite fifteen. Hubert was mobilized into the auxiliary forces. The medical boards to which he submitted with philosophic resignation, filled you with anxiety. For years his narrow chest had been a nightmare to you, but now your hopes were centred on it. When the deadliness of office work, and occasional jeers, made him eager to volunteer for active service (he really did try), you began to speak openly of what, for so long, you had been careful never to mention. "With your heredity . . ."—that was how you put it.

My poor Isa, don't be afraid. I'm not going to throw stones at you. You have never taken the slightest interest in me, have never really noticed me at all, and in those days you did so less even than usual. You had no idea of the mounting terror in me as winter followed winter. Luc's father was called up in one of the Ministries, and we had the boy with us, not only in the summer holidays, but at Christmas and Easter as well. The war filled him with enthusiasm. The only thing he was afraid of was that it might be over before he was eighteen. Formerly, he had never opened a book, but now he took to poring over maps and military manuals. He embarked methodically on a course of physical exercises. At sixteen he was already a full-grown man—and a tough one at that. He had no feelings to spare for the wounded and the dead. I gave him to read the grimmest accounts I could find of life in the trenches, but the picture he derived from them was of some terrible and magnificent form of sport in which all were not privileged to take a part. He would have to hurry up! How fearful he was of being too late! His idiot of a father had already given him written permission to offer himself as a volunteer, and this he carried in his pocket always. As the fatal day in January '18 approached, I followed with frightened concentration old Clemenceau's career, always on the watch for something to happen. I felt as must have felt those parents of men held prisoner, who used to watch for Robespierre's fall, hoping against hope that the tyrant would be laid low before their loved ones came to trial.

When Luc was under instruction in the training-camp at Souges, you used to send him knitted mufflers and all sorts of little comforts, but you used to say things, my poor Isa, which made me feel like murder—for instance: "Of course it would be terrible if anything happened to the poor boy—but, at least, he wouldn't leave anyone behind him." . . . I know you didn't mean any harm. . . .

A day came when I realized that it was no longer any good hoping that the war might be over before Luc was called up. When the front was broken on the Chemin des Dames, he came to say good-bye, a full fortnight earlier than he had expected. Well, it couldn't be helped. . . . And now I must pluck up courage to tell you of an incident so horrible that it still wakes me at night and makes me cry aloud. On the day to which I have referred, I went into the study to fetch a leather belt which I had got the local saddler to make to my own specification. Then, I climbed on a stool and tried to pull towards me a plaster cast of the head of Demosthenes which stood on top of the book-shelves. But I could not move it. It was full of gold coins which I had hidden there since the war began. I plunged my hand into all that gold which represented for me what I most valued in the world, and began to stuff the leather belt with money. When I got down from the stool, the swollen snake, gorged with metal, was hanging round my neck and weighing me down.

Shyly I held it out to Luc. At first he did not grasp what it was that I was offering him.

"What on earth do you expect me to do with that, Uncle?"

"It may come in useful in billets, or if you're taken prisoner . . . or in other ways. With money you can do anything."

"Oh!" said he, with a laugh. "I've got quite enough to carry as it is. . . . You didn't really think, did you, that I'd load myself up with all that money? The first time I went into the line, I'd have had to bury it in the woods!"

"But, my dear boy, at the beginning of the war, everyone who had any gold took it with him."

"That's because they didn't know what they were in for, Uncle."

He was standing in the middle of the room. He had thrown the money-belt on the sofa. Strong though he was, he looked terribly frail in his ill-fitting uniform. The collar was far too big for him, and his neck looked like a drummer-boy's. His cropped hair had taken all character from his face. He had been made ready for death, decked for the sacrifice. He was just another item in the mass, without identity, anonymous, as good as vanished. For a moment he stared at the belt, then he raised his eyes to mine with an expression of mockery and contempt. All the same, he gave me a hug. We went down with him to the front-door. He turned his head and shouted back: "Much better take all that to the Banque de France." By that time I could no longer see anything, but I heard you say, with a laugh:

"Don't be too sure of that! it's asking a lot of him!"

Somebody shut the door. I stood in the hall quite motionless. You said:

"You knew perfectly well, didn't you, that he wouldn't accept the money? It was a perfectly safe gesture on your part."

I remembered that the belt was still on the sofa. One of the servants might quite easily have found it there: one could never be sure. I hurried upstairs, looped it round my neck again, and emptied the contents back into the head of Demosthenes.

I scarcely noticed my mother's death, which took place a few days later. Her mind had been wandering for years, and she no longer lived with us. It is only now that I think of her every day, remember her as the mother of my childhood and young manhood. The picture of her in those last years has faded from my mind. Though I hate cemeteries, I still go, at times, to visit her grave. I used to take flowers, but I have given up doing that, because I noticed that they were always stolen. The poor sneak the roses of the rich for the benefit of their own dead. I ought to have a railing put up, but everything's so expensive nowadays.

Luc has no grave. He just disappeared, was one of the "missing." I keep in my note-case the only card he had time to send me. It was one of the printed Field-Service affairs: "All well: have received your parcel. Love." The word love was in his own handwriting. That message at least I did get from my poor child.

XI

TO-NIGHT I woke, fighting for breath. I felt a compulsion to get up. I dragged myself to my chair, and sat, reading over, to the accompaniment of a howling wind, the last few pages I had written. I was appalled by the light they shed on my deepest self. Before settling down to go on with them, I leaned for a while at the window. The gale had dropped. Calèse was wrapped in sleep. There was not so much as a breeze, and the sky was full of stars. Suddenly, about three o'clock, there was another squall. The sky rumbled, and heavy, icy drops began to fall. They rattled on the tiles so loudly that I feared they might be hail. I thought that my heart had stopped beating.

The grapes have barely "set." Next year's harvest covers all the slopes. But it seems that it may be with it as it is with those young animals which the hunter tethers and then leaves in darkness to attract the prowling beasts of prey. Clouds, heavy with thunder, are snuffling round the proffered vines.

But what do I care now about the grape-harvest? I have nothing left to harvest in this world. The only thing left for me to do is to get to know myself a little better. Pay attention, Isa. After my death, among my papers, you will find a statement of my last wishes. They date from the months immediately following Marie's death, those months during which I was ill, and you were worried on account of the children. You will find, too, my profession of faith. It runs something like this: "Should I agree, at the moment of my death, to accept the ministrations of a priest, I herewith, while my mind remains clear, protest against the advantage that will have been taken of my weakening powers—physical as well as mental—to extort from me what my reason rejects." I owe you that confession. It is, on the contrary, when I study myself, as I have been doing for the past two months, with a closeness of attention which is stronger than my feeling of disgust, and when I feel my mind to be at its clearest, that the temptations of Christianity most torment me. It is then that I feel it impossible to deny that a way does exist in me which might lead me to your God. If I could reach the point of feeling satisfied with myself, I could fight this sense of pressure with more hope of success. If I could despise myself unreservedly, then the issue would be settled once and for all. But when a man is as hard as I am, when his heart, as in my case, has become dead wood, when he can inspire only hatred, and create about himself nothing but a waste land, then he has no defence against the onrush of hope. . . . I wonder if you really understand what I am getting at, Isa? Perhaps it is not for you, not for the army of the just, that your God came into the world, if come He did, but for us. You have never known me, have never realized the kind of man I am. Do I seem less horrible to you, now that you have read these pages? You must surely see by this time that there does exist in me a secret string which Marie could touch merely by snuggling into my arms, or little Luc, when, returning from Mass on Sundays, he would sit down on the bench in front of the house and stare at the distant plain.

Don't please think that I am painting too pretty a picture of myself. I know my heart—it is a knot of vipers. They have almost squeezed the life out of it. They have beslavered it with their poison, but, underneath their squirming, it still beats. Impossible now to loosen the knot. I can fight free only by cutting it with a knife, by slashing it with a sword: *I am come to bring not peace but a sword.*

It may well be that to-morrow I shall deny what I here confess, just as, to-night, I have denied those final wishes which I confided to paper thirty years ago. I have seemed to hate, with a hatred for which I may yet make atonement, all that you profess: and I shall still go on hating those who call themselves Christians.

But is it not because so many of them degrade hope and distort a Countenance, *that* Countenance, *that* Face? You will say that a man, heavy as I am with abominations, has no right to sit on them in judgment. But isn't there, Isa, in my very vileness something (I don't know what) which, more than all their virtues, resembles the Sign of your adoration? What I am writing here must seem to you nothing but an absurd blasphemy. But you must prove it to me. Why do you not speak to me? Why have you never spoken to me? Perhaps, who knows? some word of yours might rend my heart. I feel to-night that even now it is not too late for us to start again. Suppose I don't wait until I am dead to let you see these pages? Suppose I beg you, in the name of your God, to persevere with them to the end? Suppose I wait until you have reached the last word? Suppose I saw you come into my room with tear-stained face and open arms? Suppose I asked your pardon? Suppose we knelt down, side by side, and prayed?

It seems as though the storm is over. The dawn stars are twinkling in the sky. I thought the rain had started again, but it was only the dripping of the trees. If I lie down again I shall have to fight for breath. I can't write any more. Now and again I drop my pen, and let my head fall against the hard back of the chair.

A hiss like that of a wild beast, then a deafening din and a great glare filling all the sky. In the panic silence that followed, I heard the sound of fireworks on the hills, set off by the vine-growers to scatter the clouds or resolve the hail to water. Rockets were leaping into the air from the darkness where shrouded Barsac and Sauterne were waiting in terror for the coming of the scourge. The bell of St. Vincent's, which keeps the hail away, has been ringing with might and main. The sound of it is like that of someone singing in the night because he is afraid. Suddenly, from the roof there came that noise as of a handful of flung pebbles . . . hailstones! Time was when I should have rushed to the window. I could hear the sound of shutters flung back, and your voice crying down to a man who was hurrying across the yard: "Is it serious?" . . . " 'Tis all mixed with rain," he replied; "and that be lucky: but 'tis coming down proper hard." A frightened child has just run barefoot down the passage. I find myself, from force of habit, reckoning: "A hundred thousand francs gone west . . ."—but I have not stirred. Nothing, in the old days, could have kept me from rushing downstairs—one night they found me out among the vines, wearing my slippers, holding a candle, and bare-headed under the hail. Some profound peasant instinct had driven me out as though to fling myself upon the ground and cover the beaten vines with my body. But to-night I have become a stranger to all that was once best in me. Those restricting bonds have, at last, been loosened, by what or by whom I do not know. The cables have been cut, Isa, and I am adrift. What power is leading me on? Is it blind—or is it love? Perhaps it may be love. . . .

PART TWO

XII

PARIS, RUE BRÉA.

WHAT induced me to pack this note-book? What has this long-drawn-out confession to do with me now? I have broken with my family for ever. She for whom I laid myself bare in these pages can exist for me no longer. Why, then, resume the task? The answer to that question is, I suppose, that, though I did not know it at the time, the setting down of all my thoughts on paper brought me comfort and release. What a revelation of my state of mind those last lines contain, written on the night of the hailstorm! I must have been within measurable distance of madness. . . . No, no, I won't even mention that word: I mustn't, because they are quite capable of quoting any mention of it against me, should these pages ever fall into their hands. They are no longer addressed to anybody in particular, and, when I feel myself getting worse I shall have to destroy them, unless, of course, I decide to leave them to the unknown son in search of whom I have come here to Paris. I longed to reveal the fact of his existence to Isa in that passage which deals with my love affair of 1909. I was actually on the point of confessing that when my mistress ran away it was because she was with child and had made up her mind to find a hiding-place in Paris.

I thought I was being very generous because I allowed mother and child six thousand francs a year before the war. It never occurred to me to increase the sum. If the two people I have found here are ground down and enslaved by sordid toil, the fault is mine. On the pretext that they live in this district, I am staying at a *pension* in the Rue Bréa. There is scarcely room, between the wardrobe and the bed, for me to write: and, oh! the din! In my days Montparnasse was quiet. Now it appears to be inhabited exclusively by lunatics who never go to bed! The family made considerably less noise on the front steps at Calèse that night when I saw with my own eyes and heard with my own ears . . . but what's the point of reviving that memory? . . . I suppose that by giving it shape and form I shall free my mind of an obsession, at least for a while. . . . After all, why should I destroy these pages? My son and heir is entitled to all the information about myself that I can give him, and this confession will, to some extent, fill out the gap which I have set between us ever since he was born.

We have had two meetings, and I can now, alas, make up my mind about him. He is not the kind of man to take the slightest interest in what I have written. How can a miserable junior clerk, a numskull who spends all his spare time betting on horses, hope to understand?

All that night in the train, between Bordeaux and Paris, I spent the time imagining his reproaches and formulating my defence. What a hold the tawdry conventions of novelists and playwrights have over one! I felt so sure of finding myself confronted by the bastard of fiction, all bitterness and noble sentiments! I endowed him, turn and turn about, with Luc's nobility and Phili's looks. I was ready for anything—except only that he would turn out to be the living image of myself! Are any fathers really pleased to be told that their sons are "just like" them?

I realized the full extent of my self-loathing when I was brought face to face with this pale image of myself. In Luc I had loved a son who was utterly unlike me. In Robert's case, there is only one difference between us—he has shown himself to be quite incapable of passing even the simplest examination. He has tried again and again, but always with the same result, failure. His mother, who has worked herself to the bone, despises him for this lack of success. She can't help constantly referring to it. He hangs his head. He hates the idea of so much money being thrown down the drain. In that respect he is indeed my son! But the fortune I am bringing him is beyond the power of his miserable comprehension to grasp. It means nothing to him: he doesn't really believe in it. The truth of the matter is, both he and his mother are thoroughly frightened—"It's not legal . . . we might be caught."

This pale, flabby woman with the faded hair, this caricature of the girl I loved, just sat and stared at me when I went to see her (she still has beautiful eyes). "If I'd passed you in the street," she said, "I'd never have recognized you!" Should I have recognized her? I had steeled myself against possible reproaches, against her wish to be revenged for what had happened, against everything, in fact, except this dreary indifference. Embittered, worn down by eight hours a day at the typewriter, she lives in a constant dread of scandal. Years ago she ran foul of the Law, and since then has had a morbid terror of it. I explained my whole scheme to them. The idea is that Robert should rent a safe-deposit in his own name, and that I should at once transfer to it such of my fortune as can be moved. He would give me power of attorney to have access to it, and take a solemn oath not to touch a penny of it till I am dead. Naturally, I should insist on his giving me a signed statement to the effect that everything in the safe-deposit belongs to me. I am not going to put myself in the hands of a complete stranger. But both mother and son have raised an objection. At my death, they say, the paper will be found. The fools don't trust me!

I have tried to make them realize that we should be perfectly safe in the hands of a country lawyer, some fellow like Bourru, who owes everything to me, and with whom I have done business for forty years. He is keeping, locked away, an envelope on which I have written: "Please burn on the day of my death," and I am quite sure he will burn it, with all its contents. Into that envelope I should put Robert's signed statement. I am the more certain that Bourru will burn the packet because there are in it certain documents which it is very much to his interest to see out of the way. But Robert and his mother are afraid that, once I am dead, Bourru won't burn anything, and will start blackmailing them. The same idea, I confess, had occurred to me, and, to guard against it, I am prepared to put evidence into their hands which would be sufficient to send him to penal servitude. I should make it a condition that the paper must be burned in their presence, and that then, and then only, they give back to him the weapon with which I shall have provided them. What more can they want?

But they can't grasp it. They're too pigheaded. One is a fool, the other an imbecile. I am offering them millions, and instead of going down on their knees in gratitude—as I fully expected they would—they go on arguing and splitting hairs! . . . Even supposing the thing is a bit risky, surely the game is worth the candle? But no, they won't sign. "In the first place, the Income Tax authorities might make difficulties."

The fact that I didn't slam the door in their faces proves how bitterly I hate the rest of my family. Incidentally, they're frightened of the family, too. "They'd smell a rat, they'd bring an action against us. . . ." They've already got it firmly fixed in their heads that my relations have warned the police, and that I'm being watched. They won't see me except after dark, and in odd, out-of-the-way places. Do they expect a man in my state of health to sit up half the night and spend my life in taxis? I've no reason to suppose that anybody at home is suspicious. This isn't the first time I've taken a trip alone. They can't know that I was present, though invisible, at the council of war they held the other night at Calèse. In any case, they won't have got on my trail yet. This time, nothing's going to keep me from reaching my goal. The day Robert consents to play ball I can sleep in peace. He's too great a coward to be careless.

It's the thirteenth of July to-night, and there's a band playing in the open air. Couples are dancing at the end of the Rue Bréa. Oh, for the peace and quiet of Calèse! I remember my last night there. In spite of doctor's orders I had taken a tablet of veronal, and had fallen into a deep sleep. I awoke with a start and looked at my watch. It was one o'clock in the morning. I could hear several voices, and that frightened me. I had left the window open. There was no one in the courtyard nor in the drawing-room. I went into my dressing-room which looks north and is on the same side of the house as the steps. It was there that the family, contrary to habit, was making a night of it. At that late hour they had no reason to believe they would be overheard. The only windows on that side of the house are those of the various dressing-rooms and of the corridor.

The night was still and warm. Every now and then there was a pause in the conversation, and I could hear Isa's rather wheezy breathing, and the sound of a match being struck. There was not enough breeze to rustle the leaves on the dark elms. I didn't dare lean out, but I could recognize my enemies by their voices and their laughter. They were not arguing. Isa or Geneviève would say something, and then there would be a prolonged silence. But all of a sudden, Hubert spoke. At once Phili flared up, and then they all started talking at once.

"Are you quite sure, Mamma, that the papers in his study safe are really of no value? Misers are always careless. Don't you remember all the money he wanted to give young Luc . . . where's he hidden that?"

"He realizes that I know the combination: it's 'Marie.' He never opens the safe except when he wants to look at an Insurance Policy or a Tax Return."

"But, Mamma, there might be some record of how much this money amounts to. . . ."

"There's nothing in the safe but papers relating to his house property; I'm sure of that."

"Don't you think all that's terribly significant?—I mean, doesn't it show that he's taken every possible precaution?"

There was a yawn from Phili: "What an old crocodile!" he muttered; "just my luck to hit on a crocodile like that!"

"If you want my opinion," said Geneviève, "you won't find anything in his safe-deposit at the Crédit Lyonnais either. What do you think, Janine?"

"But there are times, Mamma, when it really does look as though he's got a sort of feeling for you. Wasn't he ever nice to you when you were children? If not, that must have been because you didn't know how to get round him, because you weren't clever. You ought to have tried to appeal to his better nature and win him over. I'm sure I could have succeeded if he hadn't had such a horror of Phili."

Hubert broke in with a bitter comment: "There's no doubt your husband's insolence has cost us pretty dear."

I caught the sound of Phili's laugh, and leaned forward a little. The flame of a cigarette lighter lit up for a moment his cupped hands, his flabby chin and thick lips.

"It didn't need me to set him against you!"

"That's not true: he hated us much less in the old days."

"Don't forget what Grandmamma told us, about how he behaved when the little girl died," went on Phili: "how he didn't seem to care, and never set foot in the cemetery."

"That's going a bit too far, Phili: if ever he cared for anyone in the world it was for Marie."

But for this protest of Isa's, made in a faint and trembling voice, I could not have controlled myself. I sat down on a low chair and leaned forward, resting my head against the window-sill. Geneviève was speaking:

"If Marie had lived, nothing of all this would have happened. He would have been bound to watch over her interests."

"Oh, come! he'd have got his knife into her, as he has into

everybody else! He's a monster, and doesn't know what human feelings mean!"

Once again Isa protested:

"You mustn't talk about my husband like that, Phili, in front of me and his children! You do owe him *some* respect."

"Respect?"

I thought I heard him mutter something like—"If you think it's fun for me to have got mixed up with a family like this! . . ."

His mother-in-law broke in dryly:

"Nobody forced you!"

"Every kind of glittering expectation was dangled before my eyes. . . . Oh, now Janine's blubbering . . . what have I said that's so extraordinary?"

The sound of his voice faded away in a sort of exasperated grumble. I could hear nothing but the noise Janine made in blowing her nose. A voice which I could not identify murmured: "How bright the stars are!" St. Vincent's clock struck two.

"Time for bed, children."

Hubert protested that they couldn't separate before something had been decided. It was high time to act. Phili agreed. He didn't think I could last much longer, and once I was dead it would be too late. It was a pretty sure thing that I had taken steps.

"Children, children, what do you expect me to do? I've tried my best, and there's nothing more to be done."

"Oh yes there is," said Hubert; "you could . . ." What was he whispering? Just what I most wanted to know I couldn't hear. I gathered from the tone of Isa's voice that she was shocked, scandalized.

"No, I couldn't possibly agree to that. . . ."

"It's not a question of personal feelings, Mamma, but of saving our inheritance."

There were more vague murmurings, cut short by Isa:

"But that would be a terrible thing to do!"

"But, don't you see, you're playing his game, Grandmamma? He can't disinherit us unless you agree, and this is a case of silence giving consent. . . ."

"Janine, my dear, how can you!"

Poor Isa! She had spent endless nights sitting up with this squalling little brat, and had even taken her into her own room because her parents wanted to sleep, and no nurse would put up with her. . . . There was an edge to Janine's voice which I wouldn't have let pass for a moment. She went on:

"I don't like saying things like this to you, Grand'ma, but it's my duty. . . ."

Her duty! that was the name she gave to the urgencies of her body, to the terror she felt at the idea of being abandoned by the scoundrel whose idiotic laugh now floated up to me.

Geneviève backed up her daughter. It was quite true, she said: weakness might so easily turn to complicity.

Isa sighed:

"Perhaps the best thing would be to write him a letter . . ."

"Oh, for Heaven's sake, no letters!" Hubert protested. "Letters are always our undoing! I do hope, Mamma, that you haven't already written to him?"

She admitted that she had, just once or twice—"but nothing threatening or abusive." She was obviously embarrassed. I laughed to myself. Oh yes, there had been letters all right, and I was taking good care of them. Two contained passages of pretty serious abuse, but the third was couched in almost affectionate terms, quite affectionate enough, anyhow, to make it certain that she would lose any suit for separation which those idiotic children might persuade her to bring.

The feeling of uneasiness was now general. It was just as when a dog starts growling, and the rest of the pack follow suit.

"Oh, don't say that you've written him any letters that might be dangerous to us, Grand'ma."

"I don't *think* I have, though I'm afraid there was one . . . I know that Bourru, the lawyer over at St. Vincent . . . I think my husband's got some hold over him (anyhow, he's a nasty creature, and a hypocrite to boot) . . . did say that it was most unwise of me to have written. . . ."

"What was it you wrote? Nothing abusive, I do hope?"

"There was one in which I reproached him a little too violently after Marie's death, and another in 1909 referring to a liaison of his which was rather more than usually persistent. . . ."

Hubert groaned out something about it's being "very serious, extremely serious," but she tried to reassure him by adding that she had made everything all right since by expressing her regrets and admitting that she had been wrong. . . .

"That just about puts the lid on it! . . . so he knows he can't be dragged into court now! . . ."

"But, after all, why should you think he means to treat you all so badly?"

"You'd realize soon enough if you weren't completely blind. The dark mystery of his financial operations: the hints he drops: that remark he made to Bourru, in front of witnesses, when he said: 'They'll look pretty silly when the old man dies. . . .' "

They went on talking as though Isa had not been present. She struggled out of her armchair with a groan. She oughtn't, she said, to stay out after dark, with her rheumatism. The children did not so much as answer her. I heard the inattentive "good-nights" they gave her without bothering to interrupt what they were saying. It was she who had to move round the circle distributing good-night kisses. They none of them budged. I thought it safer to lie down again in bed. I heard the sound of her heavy steps on the staircase. She came right up to my door. I could clearly catch the noise of her uneasy breathing. She put her candle down and opened the door. She came across and stood close to my bed, leaning over me, with the object, no doubt, of making quite sure that I was asleep. What a long time it seemed!

I was afraid of giving myself away. Her breath was coming in little gasps. At last she went out and closed the door. As soon as I heard her bolt her own, I went back to my listening-post in the dressing-room.

The children were still there, but now they were talking in whispers. Much of what they said escaped me.

"Don't forget," observed Janine, "that he came of a different social class. . . . Phili, darling, you're coughing, *do* put on your overcoat."

"Actually, it's not his wife he most hates" (Geneviève now), "but us. What a fantastic situation—if you read of it in a novel you wouldn't believe it! It's not for us to judge our mother," she wound up, "but I do think she's been a bit too forgiving. . . ."

"Damn it all!" (Phili). "She can always get her marriage settlement back. Old man Fondaudège's Canal shares must have gone up a good deal since '84!"

"B-but they've been . . . sold."

I recognized the hesitant tones, the hemming and the hawing, as coming from Geneviève's husband. Until that moment the wretched Alfred had not opened his lips. His wife cut him short. She spoke in the sharp, shrill voice which she keeps for him:

"You must be mad! The Suez Canal shares sold?"

Alfred explained how, in the May of that year, he had gone into his mother-in-law's room and found her signing some documents. She had said: "I'm told that now's the moment to sell. They're standing very high, and will almost certainly drop."

"And you mean to say you never told us?" exclaimed Geneviève. "Really, I believe you must be half-witted! He actually made her sell the Suez?—is *that* what you're trying to explain? You just casually mention it as though it were the most natural thing in the world!"

"But, Geneviève, I thought your mother would tell you what she'd done. In any case, by the terms of her settlement, she remains mistress of her own property."

"That's all very well, but it's more than likely that he pocketed the profits of the sale! What's your opinion, Hubert? To think he never breathed a word—and that's the man I'm tied to for the rest of my life!"

At this point Janine told them to speak lower, so as not to wake her little girl. For the next few moments I heard scarcely a word. Then, once again, Hubert's voice rose above the general buzz.

"I've been thinking about what you were saying just now.... But, you know, we should never get her to agree, and even if we did manage to convince her, it would be a long, slow business...."

"She might prefer it to a separation. Separation, you see, is bound to lead, sooner or later, to divorce, and that would involve a case of conscience.... Of course, what Phili proposes does sound a bit shocking at first, but after all, *we're* not going to have to say the word: it won't be for *us* to make the final decision. All we've got to do is to get the thing started. Nothing will happen unless the competent authorities think it necessary...."

"Well, as I said before," remarked Olympe, "you'll all of you be going to a lot of trouble for nothing...."

Hubert's wife must have been thoroughly outraged to raise her voice as she did. She maintained that I was a perfectly sensible man, a man of sound judgment. "I don't mind admitting," she said, "that we quite often agree about things, and that if you weren't for ever butting in, I could do anything I liked with him...."

Phili must have made some pretty insolent reply, though I couldn't hear what it was. They all laughed, as they always do when Olympe joins in. I caught a few disjointed phrases.

"He hasn't conducted a case for five years . . . hasn't been up to it."

"Wasn't that because of his heart?"

"His heart's bad *now*, but when he gave up practising there was nothing particularly wrong with him. The real trouble was he was always getting at odds with his colleagues. There were quite often scenes when he was conducting a conference —I've got first-hand evidence of that. . . ."

I strained my ears, but it was no good. Phili and Hubert had drawn their chairs together. All that reached me was an indistinct murmur. Then, suddenly, there was another outburst from Olympe:

"He's the only one of the whole lot of you I can talk to about books, or discuss general ideas with, and you want . . ."

Phili said something in reply. I caught the word "looney." One of Hubert's sons-in-law, who scarcely ever says anything at all, gave a sort of a splutter:

"You might be at least decently polite to my mother-in-law. . . ."

Phili protested that he was only joking. Weren't they both of them playing the part of victims in this business? Hubert's son-in-law asserted, in a trembling voice, that he didn't look on himself as a victim, and that he'd married his wife for love, at which there was a chorus of "Same here!—Same here!—Same here!" Geneviève mockingly remarked to her husband:

"You'll be saying next, I suppose, that *you* married me without knowing how much my father was worth?—But *I* happen to remember that on the night we became engaged you whispered: 'What's the odds? It doesn't matter if he won't talk about it, we *know* it's enormous. . . .' "

There was a general burst of laughter, followed by a babble of voices. Once again it was Hubert who dominated the meeting. For a moment or two nobody interrupted him. It was only his final remark that I heard:

"The one thing that really matters in all this affair is justice and morality. We are defending our inheritance, the sacred rights of the family. . . ."

In the deep hush that comes before the dawn, I could hear more clearly:

"Have him watched? he's too well in with the police! I've proof of that—they'd put him wise . . ." (then, a few moments later) ". . . everyone knows he's as hard as nails and as greedy as you make 'em. I've even heard it whispered that he hasn't been all he should be in business . . . though, of course, no one's ever doubted his good sense and his judgment. . . ."

"Well, there's no denying that his feelings for us are inhuman, monstrous and unnatural. . . ."

"But do you really think, Janine, my dear," said Alfred to his daughter, "that *that* would be sufficient to get him certified? . . ."

It had been beginning to dawn on me, and now I knew! I felt perfectly calm: certainty had brought a sense of peace. It was they who were the monsters, I who was the victim. The fact that Isa had been absent gave me pleasure. So long as she had been with them, she had, to some extent, protested. In her presence they had not dared to mention the plan which I had just overheard. Not that it terrified me. Poor fools!—as though I were the kind of man to let himself be put under restraint or shut away! Long before they so much as raised a finger, I could put Hubert in a hopeless position. He had no idea what a hold I had over him. As to Phili—there was a whole dossier about *him*. . . . I have never really seriously intended to make use of it . . . and I shan't have to. It'll be quite enough if I show my teeth.

For the first time in my life I felt the satisfaction of being outdone in malevolence. I did not in the least want to be revenged on them, or, rather, the only vengeance I envisaged was to snatch from their grasp the inheritance over which they were hanging in a fever of impatience, and sweating with anxiety.

"A shooting star!" cried Phili: "I had no time to make a wish."

"One never does have time," said Janine. Her husband, with that childish gaiety which he has never lost, said:

"Whenever you see one you should cry 'millions'!"

"What an ass you are, Phili!"

They all got up. The garden chairs scraped on the gravel. I heard them shoot the bolts of the front door, and the smothered laughter of Janine in the passage. One after the other the bedroom doors were shut. I had decided what to do. I had had no attack now for two months. There was nothing to keep me from going to Paris. As a rule, when I started on a trip I said nothing about it. But I did not want them to think I was running away. I spent the time until morning in going over the plans I had already made, dotting the i's and crossing the t's.

XIII

WHEN I got up at midday, I had no feeling of fatigue. I put a call through to Bourru and he arrived after luncheon. For nearly three quarters of an hour we walked up and down under the limes. Isa, Geneviève and Janine were watching us from a distance, and I thoroughly enjoyed the thought of how anxious they must be. What a pity that the men were all in Bordeaux! "Bourru," they were fond of saying, "is his evil influence"—that wretched, petty attorney who was more wholly in my power than any slave could have been! It was a sight for sore eyes to see the poor devil twisting and turning in his terror lest I might leave my heir some weapon which could be turned against him. "But," I told him, "don't you see, once you've burned the signed receipt, we'll hand everything over. . . ."

When he left, he made a profound bow to the ladies, who scarcely acknowledged it, and rode off on his squalid bicycle. I joined the three females and explained that I was leaving that evening for Paris. When Isa protested that I was much too ill to travel alone, I said:

"I've got to see about my investments. You may not believe it, but it's of you I'm thinking."

They looked at me uneasily. The note of irony in my voice gave me away. Janine, with a glance at her mother, plucked up courage to say:

"Grand'ma or Uncle Hubert could easily go instead. . . ."

"There's something in that, my dear . . . but, you see, I've always been in the habit of seeing to these things myself. I know it's very wrong of me, but I don't trust anybody."

"Not even your own children? Oh, Grand'pa!"

She stressed the word "Grand'pa" in a rather priggish way.

Her coaxing manner was hard to resist. How exasperating that voice of hers could be—the same voice that I had heard the night before mingled with the others.

I gave vent to a laugh, that dangerous laugh of mine which makes me cough. It plainly terrified them. I shall never forget the look of exhaustion on poor Isa's face. They must have been at her already. Janine would probably return to the charge as soon as I had left them: "Don't let him go, Grand'ma! . . ."

But my wife was in no mood to attack. She was at the end of her tether, completely done up. I had heard her, a few days back, say to Geneviève: "I'd like to go to sleep and never wake up. . . ."

She produced a softening effect on me, just as my poor mother used to do. Worn out though she was, a broken-down old machine, good for nothing, the children were still trying to set her against me. Of course they were fond of her in their own way. They made her see the doctor and keep to a diet. . . .

As soon as her daughter and granddaughter moved away, she came up to me.

"I need some money . . .," she began hurriedly.

"To-day's the tenth: I gave you your month's allowance on the first. . . ."

"I know, but I had to lend some of it to Janine. They're terribly hard up. I can save while we're at Calèse. I'll pay you back out of my August allowance."

I said it was no business of mine, but that I was certainly not going to keep that fellow Phili.

"I've got several bills outstanding, too, with the butcher and baker, for instance, look. . . ."

She took them out of her bag. I felt sorry for her, and offered to write out cheques for them. "In that way I shall know that the money won't go into anyone else's pocket." She agreed. I took out my cheque-book, and noticed that Janine and her mother in the rose-garden were looking at us.

"I don't mind betting," I said, "that they think you're talking to me about something quite different."

Isa trembled. In a low voice she said: "About what?" At that moment I felt a tightening in my chest. I clutched at it with my two hands in a way that she knew only too well. She came close to me:

"Are you in pain?"

I clung to her arm for a moment. There, under the limes, we must have looked like an old married couple ending their lives after long years of happy union. "It's better now," I brought out. She must have thought that this was the moment to speak, a unique opportunity: but she had no strength left. I noticed that she, too, was struggling for breath. Ill though I was, I had put up a fight. She had surrendered, given in. She had nothing with which to fight.

She seemed to be looking for the right words, glancing furtively the while at her daughter and granddaughter, as though to draw courage from their proximity. In the face she turned to me I saw an indescribable weariness. There may have been something of pity in it, there certainly was something of shame. The children must have wounded her to the heart on that memorable night.

"I'm worried at the thought of you going off alone."

I said that should anything happen to me while I was away, it wouldn't be worth having me brought back here.

She begged me not to talk like that. I said: "It would be just a waste of money, Isa. Cemeteries are much of a muchness everywhere."

"I feel the same," she said. "They can bury me anywhere they like, for all I care. There was a time when I wanted to lie near Marie . . . but what is there left of her?"

Once again I realized that, for her, Marie was no more than dust and ashes. I dared not tell her that, for years past, I had felt my child to be alive, that I had, as it were, breathed her in, had been conscious of her as of a fresh breeze blowing through the darkness of my days.

Geneviève and Janine did not get much satisfaction from their spying. Isa seemed to be utterly exhausted. Was it that she realized at last the nothingness of what she had been fighting for all these years? Geneviève and Hubert, goaded by their own children, had set this old woman on to me, Isa Fondaudège, the young, sweet-scented girl of those nights at Bagnères.

For close on half a century we two had been enemies, and now, on this heavy afternoon, the enemies had suddenly become aware of the bond created, in spite of the long-drawn-out struggle, by a shared old age. We might seem to hate one another, but, for all that, we had reached the same point in the road. There was nothing now beyond that promontory on which we stood awaiting death. Nothing, at least, for me. She had her God, or should have had. All the things to which she had clung with such bitter determination (and I, too, had clung with desperation) were fallen away; all the greedy desires which had stood between her and the Eternal Being. Could she see Him now that there was nothing to impede her sight? No, there were still the demands and ambitions of her children. It was *their* greediness that now hung about her neck like a burden. She must begin all over again, and be hard on their account. Worries about money, worries about health, schemes of ambition and of jealousy. There they all were in wait for her, like a schoolboy's exercise on which the master has written—"To be done again."

She turned her head and looked again towards the walk where Geneviève and Janine, armed with pruning clippers, were making a pretence of trimming the roses. From the bench on which I had sat down to recover my breath, I watched my wife move away. She was hanging her head like a child in fear of a scolding. The excessive heat of the sun was sure portent of a storm. She was walking with the gait of those to whom walking is painful.

I could almost hear her groaning, "Oh, my poor legs!" Husbands and wives of long standing never hate one another as much as they think they do.

By this time she had reached the children. Obviously they were blaming her for something. All of a sudden, I saw her coming back towards me red in the face, and out of breath. She sat down beside me with a groan.

"This stormy weather tires me so! My blood-pressure's very high these days. . . . Listen, Louis, there's something I'm worried about. . . . How have you reinvested the money from those Suez Canal shares which were part of my settlement? I know there were some other documents you got me to sign. . . ."

I gave her the figure of the enormous profit I had realized for her by selling just before the market broke, and explained that I had put the proceeds into debentures.

"Your settlement has been breeding, Isa. Even allowing for the depreciation of the franc, you'll be amazed. Everything's in your name at the Westminster Bank, your original settlement, and the profits. . . . It's nothing to do with the children . . . you can be quite easy in your mind. My money is my own, and what that money has produced, but what was yours is yours still. You can reassure those angels of unselfishness over there."

Suddenly she gripped my arm:

"Why do you hate them so, Louis? Why do you hate your own flesh and blood?"

"It's you who hate me, or rather, it's my children. *You* merely ignore me, except when I get on your nerves or frighten you. . . ."

"You might add 'or when I torture you.' Don't you know that I have suffered abominably at times?"

"Oh come! you had eyes for nobody but the children. . . ."

"I had to cling to them. What had I got but them?"—and, in a lower voice, she added: "You know perfectly well that you neglected me, that you were unfaithful to me from the very first year of our marriage."

"My poor Isa, you can't make me believe that my occasional wild oats really meant anything to you . . . as a young wife you may, perhaps, have been a bit hurt in your pride, but . . ."

"You really sound as though you mean what you say. . . . Why, you never even noticed whether I was there or not! . . ."

A feeling of hope set me trembling—which was strange, when you come to think that we were talking of emotions long since dead—of the hope I had entertained, unknown to myself, forty years before, that perhaps I was loved. . . . But no, it was asking too much that I should believe that now. . . .

"You never spoke a word, you never uttered a sound. All you needed was the children."

She hid her face in her two hands. I was more conscious than I had ever been before of their prominent veins and discoloured patches.

"My children! Do you realize that when we took to having separate rooms, I never, for years and years, had one of them to sleep with me, even when they were ill, because I was always half expecting, half hoping, that you would come!"

Her old woman's hands were wet with tears. This was Isa. I alone could see, in that thickened, almost crippled body, the young girl "with a devotion to white" whom I had known on a road in the Valley of the Lys.

"It's disgraceful, it's ridiculous, at my age, to recall such memories . . . ridiculous, especially . . . Please forgive me, Louis."

I stared at the vines and said nothing. I was a prey to sudden doubt. Is it possible that a man can live for nearly half a century noticing one side only of the person who shares his life? Can it be that, from long habit, he picks and chooses from among her gestures and her words, keeping for use only those that feed his grievances and perpetuate his resentments? There is a fatal tendency in all of us to simplify others, to eliminate in them everything that might soften the indictment, give some human lineaments to the caricature which our hatred craves in order to justify itself. . . . Perhaps Isa noticed my uneasiness; I wonder. At any rate, she was a shade too quick about scoring her next point.

"Say you won't go to-night!"

I fancied that I caught the familiar glint in her eye which always tells me when she thinks she's "got" me. I pretended to be surprised, and answered that I saw no reason for putting off my journey. We went back to the house together. Because of my heart we did not climb the slope by the elms, but took the lime walk which leads round to the far side. In spite of everything, I still felt doubtful and uneasy. What if I didn't go? What if I gave Isa what I have written? . . . What . . .

She laid her hand on my shoulder. How many years was it since she had last done that?

The lime walk ends in front of the house, on the north side.

"Cazau never tidies up the garden chairs. . . ."

I gave them an absent-minded glance. The empty chairs were still set in a close circle. Those who had occupied them had felt it necessary to draw them together so that they could keep their voices low. I could see heel-marks on the ground. The butts of Phili's special brand of cigarette were lying all over the place. Only a night or two ago the enemy had camped there, taking council under the stars, discussing in my own home, in front of the trees which my father had planted, the advisability of putting me under restraint, of having me shut away. Once, in the dark hours, in a moment of self-deprecation, I had compared my heart to a knot of vipers. How wrong I had been! The knot of vipers was outside myself! On that night of plotting they had wriggled free of me and twined themselves into a tangle, into a hideous circle at the foot of these steps. Their slime was still visible on the ground.

You shall have that money back, Isa, I thought: the money of yours which I have set to breed, but nothing more, nothing else. I would even find some way of keeping the estate out of their hands. I would sell Calèse and the stretch of heath. Everything that had come to me from my family should go to that unknown son of mine, to the boy whom I was to see in two days' time. Whatever he might turn out to be, at least he had one great advantage—he didn't know you. He had taken no part in your plotting. He had been brought up far from my sight, and could not hate me, or, if he did, the object of his hatred was an abstract being having no connexion with myself.

Angrily I broke free and hurried up the steps, forgetful of my old man's heart. Isa called after me: "Louis!" But I did not even turn my head.

XIV

I COULD not sleep, so I dressed and went out into the street. In order to reach the Boulevard Montparnasse I had to force my way through the dancing couples. In the old days, even a dyed-in-the-wool Republican such as I was avoided the 14th July merrymaking. No respectable citizen would have dreamed of taking part in the festivities of the street. But this evening, in the Rue Bréa, and in front of the Rotonde, the men who were dancing were far from being rowdies. There was nothing vicious about them. For the most part they were well-set-up, bare-headed young fellows. Some of them wore short-sleeved, open-necked shirts. Very few of the girls were tarts. They clung to the wheels of such taxis as broke up the dancing, but gaily and without hostility. A young man who had jostled me by accident cried: "Way for the noble ancient!" I moved between a double row of radiant faces. "Not sleepy, Grand'pa?" a chap with a dark complexion and hair growing low over his forehead flung at me. Luc would have learned to laugh just like that, to dance in the streets, and I, who had never known what it meant to relax and enjoy myself, would have caught the secret from my poor boy. He would have revelled in the scene, would have taken his fill of it, and he wouldn't have wanted for money. . . . Fill? . . . it was with earth his mouth was filled now. . . . So ran my thoughts, while, conscious of the old familiar tightness in my chest, I sat in front of a café with the fun going on all round me.

And then, quite suddenly, in the crowd that swarmed along the pavement, I saw myself. It was Robert in the company of a rather seedy individual. How I hate Robert's long legs, his stocky body, so like my own, and his absence of neck! In him my defects are exaggerated. *My* face is long, but his is like a horse's—the face of a hunchback; and his voice is a hunchback's too.

I called to him. He broke away from his companion and looked about him uneasily.

"Not here," he said; "meet me on the right-hand pavement of the Rue Campagne-Première."

I pointed out that we could not be more effectively concealed than at the heart of this hubbub. He let himself be persuaded, took leave of his friend, and sat down at my table.

He had a sporting paper in his hand. To break the silence I tried to talk about horses. I'd got into the way of it with old Fondaudège, years ago. I told Robert how, when my father-in-law betted, he always took all sorts of considerations into account—not only the animal's pedigree to the third and fourth generation, but the ground-conditions that suited it best and . . . He interrupted me:

"I get my tips at Dermas's" (Dermas is the name of the draper's shop in the Rue des Petits-Champs, where he's fetched up high and dry in a job).

The only thing he cared about was winning. Horses as horses bored him.

"Give me bicycles every time!" he said, and his eyes sparkled.

"Soon it'll be motors," I said.

"That's what you think!"

He moistened his thumb, took out a slip of cigarette-paper and rolled himself a cigarette. Silence once more descended between us. I asked whether the slump had made itself felt in his business. He replied that some of the staff had got the sack, but that he was safe enough. Not once did his talk stray outside the narrow circle of his personal concerns. It was into the lap of this nit-wit that millions were to fall! Suppose I give it all to charity, I thought; or distribute it piecemeal? . . . No, for in either case *they* would have me put away. By Will, then?—impossible to exceed the legally stipulated proportion. Oh, Luc, if only you were alive! . . . True, he wouldn't have accepted it, but I could have found some way of enriching him without his knowledge . . . by settling money, for instance, on the woman he might have loved. . . .

"Look here, sir. . . ."

Robert stroked his chin. His hand was red, the fingers spatulate.

". . . I've been thinking things over. What if that lawyer fellow, Bourru, should happen to die before we had burned the paper? . . ."

"Well, his son would succeed him, and the weapon I've given you against the father could, should the occasion arise, be used against the son."

Robert went on stroking his chin. I made no attempt to say more, so fully occupied was I with the feeling of tightness, with the agonizing constriction, in my chest.

"And again, what if Bourru burns the paper and I hand over what you'd given me to make him act proper? What's to stop him from going to your family and saying, 'I know where the dough is, and I'm ready to sell the secret—so much for giving you the low-down, and a bit extra if you get your hands on it'—making it a condition that his name shan't be mentioned? . . . *He'd* be in the clear. There'd be an enquiry, and it'd come out as I really was your son, and that since your death mother and I had been blowing it. . . . And we should either have to make a correct tax return or keep the whole thing dark."

He was expressing himself with precision. His mind was no longer sluggish. It had been slow in getting started, but now there was no holding it. The dominating instinct in this wretched counter-jumper was peasant caution, peasant mistrust and a horror of taking risks. He wasn't going to leave anything to chance. No doubt he would have preferred a hundred thousand francs in cash to the danger involved in having to conceal so vast a fortune.

I waited until my heart felt easier and the tightness had loosened. Then:

"There's something in what you say," I replied, "and I'll do what you want. You needn't sign anything. I'll trust you. As a matter of fact it would be perfectly easy for me to prove that the money is mine. Not that it really matters, because in six months, or a year at most, I shall be dead."

He made no gesture of protest. The commonplace that anyone else might have uttered was quite beyond him; not that he was more callous than other young men of his age, but simply that he had been badly brought up.

"That might work," he said.

He chewed my suggestion for a few moments, and then continued:

"I'd have to look in now and again at the safe-deposit, even with you alive, just so's the Bank people'd get to know my face. I might go and get some of the money for you when you wanted it."

"If it comes to that, I've got several safe-deposits abroad. If you'd rather, if you believe it would be less risky . . ."

"What, leave Paris! . . . what do *you* think!"

I pointed out that he could go on living in Paris and take an occasional trip when necessary. He asked whether my fortune was in securities or cash.

"I'd rather you gave me some sort of paper, something like you being of sound mind had left everything to me . . . just in case anything leaked out and I was accused of theft—one never knows. Besides, my conscience would be easier. . . ."

He stopped speaking, bought some pea-nuts and started to eat them voraciously, as though he were hungry. Suddenly:

"What's your family done to you?" he asked.

"Take what I offer," I said dryly, "and don't be inquisitive."

A little colour showed in his flabby cheeks. His smile was of the uncomfortable, self-conscious kind which he probably assumed when he was being hauled over the coals by his employer. It revealed the strong, pointed teeth which were the only good feature in his otherwise unpleasing face.

He went on shelling peanuts without saying anything more. There was nothing in his expression to show that he was in the least dazzled. Obviously his imagination was getting to work. I had stumbled on the one person incapable of seeing anything in this marvellous windfall but the very small risks involved. But dazzled was just what I wanted him to be. . . .

"Haven't you got a girl?" I asked him point-blank. "You could marry her and live in solid, respectable comfort."

He made a vague gesture and shook his head with a hang-dog expression. I pressed my point.

"You could marry anybody you like. If there's any girl who seems out of your reach . . ."

He pricked up his ears at that, and, for the first time, I saw a glimmer of excitement in his eyes.

"I could marry Mademoiselle Brugère!"

"And who is Mademoiselle Brugère?"

"I was only joking. She's one of the heads at Dermas's. Proper stuck up—won't so much as look at me; doesn't even know I exist. I say, that's an idea!"

I assured him that with a twentieth part of my fortune he could marry any "head" in Paris.

"Mademoiselle Brugère!" he said again. Then, with a shrug, "No, that's too much to expect!"

My chest was hurting. I signed to the waiter. It was then that Robert did a most surprising thing.

"No, look here, it's the least I can do. . . ."

I put my money back in my pocket with a feeling of satisfaction. We got up. The musicians were packing their instruments. The festoons of electric lights had been extinguished. There was no longer any reason why Robert should be afraid of being seen with me.

"I'll walk back with you," he said. I asked him to go slowly because of my heart. I was surprised that he did nothing to hasten the execution of our plans. I told him that if I died in the night he would lose a fortune. He showed complete indifference. All I had done was to throw him out of his stride. He was about my own height. Would he ever manage to look like a gentleman? This son and heir of mine was a poor creature! I tried to give an intimate turn to the conversation. I told him that I was filled with remorse to think that I had left him and his mother to their own resources. This seemed to surprise him. He thought it "very handsome" of me to have made them an allowance. "There's lots as wouldn't have done that." Then he said something quite horrible: "After all, you weren't the first. . . ." Obviously, he had no illusions about his mother!

When we reached my door he said:

"I've got an idea . . . what about my taking a job which would keep me hanging round the Stock Exchange? That'd explain my good luck, wouldn't it?"

"You watch your step," I said; "you'd very soon lose everything."

He stared at the pavement in a preoccupied manner. "I was thinking about the Income Tax people. . . . What if the collector started making enquiries?"

"But this is a cash transaction, an anonymous fortune tucked away in a safe-deposit which no one but you in all the world would have the right to open. . . ."

"Oh, I know all about that, still . . ."

I was out of all patience, and slammed the door in his face.

XV

CALÈSE.

A FLY is buzzing against the window. I can see the slope of the hill. It looks numbed and lifeless. The wind is moaning and driving a mass of sagging cloud before it. Its shadow lies across the plain. This deathlike stillness means that everything is waiting for the first rumble of the thunder. On just such a day of summer, thirty years ago, Marie said: "The vines are frightened. . . ." I have reopened this note-book. Yes, no doubt of it, the handwriting is mine. I examine the letters closely. I can see under each line the mark made by the nail of my little finger. I will tell the story to the end. I know now for whom it is intended. This confession had to be set down in black and white, but many pages of it I shall have to suppress, because the reading of them would be more than they could bear. Even I can't look through them without a pause. Every now and again I break off and hide my face in my hands. Here is the portrait of a man, of a man among other men. This is I. You may spew me forth, but that doesn't alter the fact that I exist.

On that night of the 13th/14th July, after leaving Robert, I was barely strong enough to undress myself and lie down on my bed. It was as though a huge weight were crushing the life out of my body. All the same, I did not die. The window was open . . . had my room been on the fifth floor . . . but it was on the first, and if I had jumped I should probably not have been killed. It was that probability alone which kept me from trying. . . . I could scarcely stretch out my hand for the pills which usually bring me relief.

At dawn someone did at last answer my bell. A local doctor

came along and gave me an injection, as a result of which I was able to breathe normally again. He told me that I was to make no movement of any kind. As the result of extreme pain one becomes as submissive as a young child. There was not the slightest danger of my budging. I was no longer distressed by the ugliness, by the disgusting smell, of the room and the furniture, or by the noise of that stormy 14th July. Nothing distressed me now because I was no longer in pain. To be free from pain was all I asked. Robert came to see me in the evening, but did not repeat the visit. His mother sat with me for two hours on her way home from the office, did me a few small services, and brought me my mail from the *poste restante* (no letter from the family).

I made no complaint, and was very docile. I drank everything the doctor had prescribed. When I spoke of my plan, she changed the subject. "There's no hurry," she kept on saying. I sighed. "But there is," I said; "and the proof of that is here"—pointing to my chest.

"My mother's attacks were worse than yours, and she lived to be almost eighty. . . ."

One morning I felt better than I had done for a long while. I was very hungry. The food in my *pension* was uneatable. I was seized by a sudden desire to lunch at a little restaurant on the Boulevard Saint-Germain where I knew the cooking was good. The size of the bill there caused me less astonishment and anger than in most of the squalid eating places I usually frequented in my terror of spending too much money.

The taxi put me down at the corner of the Rue de Rennes. I took a few steps to test my strength. All was well. It was barely noon. I decided to have a bottle of Vichy at the *Deux Magots.* I found a seat inside, on the settee that runs along the wall, and gazed absent-mindedly out of the window at the Boulevard.

My heart gave a little jump. Just outside, separated from me by no more than the thickness of the glass, I saw a familiar vision of narrow shoulders, bald patch, grizzled nape and undistinguished, projecting ears. . . . It was Hubert, peering so near-sightedly at a paper that it was almost touching his nose. Obviously, he had not seen me come in. The beating of my sick heart quietened down. A horrible joy possessed me. I was spying on him, and he did not know that I was there!

It was difficult to imagine Hubert anywhere but in one of the fashionable cafés of the Grands Boulevards. What was he doing in this part of the town? His presence there was certainly not accidental. I had only to wait, having paid for my Vichy, so as to be free to get up and go out should it be necessary.

It was clear that he was waiting for somebody. He looked at his watch. I thought I knew who it was who would worm his way to him between the tables, and was almost disappointed when I saw Geneviève's husband get out of a taxi. Alfred was wearing a straw hat cocked over one ear. When he was away from his wife, this fat little man in his forties reverted to type. His provincial dandyism was instriking contrast to Hubert's dark clothes. Hubert, said Isa, always dressed "like a Fondaudège."

Alfred took off his hat and mopped his shining forehead. He ordered an aperitif and swallowed it at a gulp. His brother-in-law was already on his feet, consulting his watch. I made ready to follow them. No doubt they would take a taxi. I would do the same and try to follow them, by no means an easy thing to do. But even to have got wind of their presence was something gained. I waited until they were on the kerb before leaving my retreat. They did not, however, hail a cab, but crossed the Square, and made towards Saint-Germain-des-Prés, talking all the while. I was surprised and gratified to see them enter the church. A detective who watches a thief walking straight into a trap could not have had a more delicious emotion than the one that made me catch my breath. I took my time. They might have looked behind them, and, though my son is near-sighted, my son-in-law has extremely good eyes. In spite of my impatience, I waited for two good minutes on the pavement. Only then did I enter the porch in their wake.

It was a little after noon. I moved carefully up the almost empty nave, but soon realized that the objects of my search were not there. It occurred to me for a moment that they might have seen me, that they had come into the church in order to throw me off the scent, and had left it again by one of the doors in the side-aisles. I retraced my steps and went into one of the transepts—the one on the right, being careful to conceal myself behind the enormous pillars. Suddenly, in the darkest part of the apse, I saw them against the light. They were sitting on two chairs, and between them was a third person, a person with humble, drooping shoulders, whose presence there in no way surprised me. It was the same individual whom, a while back, I had expected to see gliding towards my legitimate son between the tables. It was my other son, that miserable worm, Robert.

I had foreseen this treachery, but from weariness or laziness had not given it much thought. From the moment of our first meeting I had realized that this lily-livered creature had no stomach for the fight, and that his mother, haunted by memories of the Law, would advise him to come to terms with the family and sell his secret for what he could get. I looked at the back of his idiotic head. He was firmly wedged between the two solid citizens, one of whom, Alfred, was what is commonly called a "good sort" (though with a keen eye to his own interests, even if he was inclined to take the short view—and, as a matter of fact, he found the short view pretty remunerative), while the other, my charming Hubert, was as sharp as you make 'em, and had just that air of arrogant authority (his legacy from me) against which Robert would be powerless. I looked at them from my pillar, much as one might look at a spider busy with a fly, when one has made up one's mind to kill both fly and spider. Robert's head drooped more and more. He had probably begun by saying "Fifty-fifty," secure in the belief that he held all the cards. But merely by making himself known to them, the poor fool had put himself in their hands, and couldn't do anything but throw up the sponge. Watching the unequal battle, which I alone knew to be vain and futile, I felt like a god preparing to crush these miserable insects with my powerful hand, to stamp these twined snakes into the ground. I laughed.

Only ten minutes were necessary to reduce Robert to silence. Hubert was displaying a fine eloquence, and was, no doubt, issuing his orders. The victim was expressing his agreement with brief movements of the head, while his servile back grew rounder and rounder. Alfred, lolling as though in an armchair, with his right foot resting on his left knee, had tilted his seat and thrown his head backwards, so that I got an upside-down view of his flabby, bilious, black-bearded face.

At last they got up. I followed them, still taking great care not to be seen. They were walking slowly. Robert was between them with hanging head, and I half expected to see handcuffs on his wrists. His great red hands were kneading a soft felt hat of dirty grey. I had thought that nothing in the world would ever surprise me again, but I was wrong. Alfred and Robert made straight for the door, but Hubert dipped his fingers in the Holy Water stoup, turned towards the High Altar, and made a flamboyant sign of the cross.

I was in no hurry now. I could afford to be calm. There was no point in following them. I knew that that evening, or the next day, Robert would at last urge me to carry out my plans. What should be my attitude? I had plenty of time in which to think about that. I was beginning to feel tired, and sat down. What was uppermost in my mind at the moment, dominating everything else, was a feeling of irritation at Hubert's pious gesture. A young girl in the row in front of me, decently dressed and with no particular claim to looks, put a cardboard hat-box on the ground beside her, and knelt. I had a side-view of her. Her head was slightly bent, and her eyes were fixed on the same distant little door which Hubert, his family duty done, had just so gravely saluted. She was smiling faintly, and was quite motionless. Two seminarists came in next. One of them, tall and very thin, reminded me of the Abbé Ardouin; the other was short, and had a chubby face. They made their genuflexion side by side, and, like the girl, seemed stricken into immobility. I looked at what they were looking at, and tried to see what they were seeing. But there's nothing here, I said to myself, but silence, coolness and the smell of old, sunless stones. Once again the face of the little work-girl held my attention. Her eyes were shut now. Their lids, with their long lashes, reminded me of Marie's as I had seen them on her death-bed. I could feel, almost within reach of my hand, and at the same time infinitely distant, the presence of an unknown world of goodness. Isa had often said to me: "You never see anything but evil—you find it everywhere. . . ." That was true . . . and yet, it was not true at all.

XVI

I HAD my luncheon. My mind felt relaxed and almost gay. I had not felt so well for a long time. It was as though Robert's treachery, far from upsetting my plans, had given them a helping hand. A man of my age, I thought, who has been living under sentence of death for years, does not seek elaborate reasons for his changes of mood. They are organic. The myth of Prometheus means that all the sorrows of the world have their seat in the liver. But it needs a brave man to face so humble a truth. I was conscious of no physical discomfort. I digested my underdone steak without the slightest difficulty. I was glad it was so large because that meant I shouldn't have to spend money on another course. I would just have some cheese, which is both nourishing and cheap.

How should I behave to Robert? I must train my guns now on a new target. But I could not concentrate my mind. Besides, why burden myself with a plan? I should be better advised to trust to the inspiration of the moment. I dared not admit to myself that I was thoroughly looking forward to the fun of playing, like a cat, with this dim little field-mouse. Robert wasn't within miles of suspecting that I had smelt a rat. . . . Am I cruel? Yes, I suppose I am, but no more so than anybody else, than all the other men in the world, than women, than children, than all except those (I thought of the little work-girl whom I had seen in Saint-Germain-des-Prés) who are in the service of the Lamb.

I took a taxi back to the Rue Bréa, and lay down on my bed. The students who formed the main clientele of the house were away on holiday. I rested in peace and quiet. The fact that the top half of the door was glazed, though a grubby half-curtain concealed the panes, removed all sense of privacy. Several small pieces of wooden moulding belonging to the "Renaissance" style bedstead had come unstuck, and lay, carefully gathered together, in a gilded bronze "tidy" which stood on the mantelpiece. The wall-paper, designed to imitate watered silk, was disfigured by a number of spreading damp-stains. Even with the windows open, the room was filled with a smell from the pretentious, red-marble-topped commode. A cloth, with a mustard-coloured ground, covered the table. I found the general effect pleasing. It seemed to sum up the whole of human ugliness and ostentation.

I was awakened by the rustling of a skirt. Robert's mother was sitting by my bed. The first thing I noticed about her was her smile. Her obsequious attitude would have sufficed to put me on my guard, even if I had known nothing, and to warn me that I had been betrayed. There is a particular species of kindliness which always goes with treachery. I returned the smile, and told her that I was feeling better. Twenty years before her nose had not been so big. In those days, too, her large mouth had been adorned by a handsome set of teeth which Robert had inherited. But to-day her smile revealed a "plate." She must have been walking fast, and the sour smell of her body battled successfully with the emanations from the marble-topped commode. I begged her to open the window wider. She did so, and then came back, still smiling. Now that I was feeling well, she said, Robert was entirely at my disposal for the "business in hand." To-morrow, Saturday, he would be free from midday on. I reminded her that the Banks are closed on Saturday afternoons. In that case, she decided, he had better ask for some time off on Monday morning. There wouldn't be any difficulty about his getting it. Besides, there was no longer any need for him to keep on the right side of his employers. She seemed surprised when I insisted that Robert should stick to his present job for a few weeks longer. When she took leave of me, she said that she would come again with her son next day to see me. I begged her to let him pay his visit unaccompanied. I wanted, I said, to have a little talk with him, so that I might get to know him better. . . . The poor fool made no attempt to disguise her anxiety. She was pretty obviously afraid that her son would give himself away. But when I adopt a certain tone of voice, no one thinks of questioning my decision. I had no doubt that it was she who had urged Robert to come to terms with my family. I knew that frightened, uncomfortable young man too well by this time not to realize that he must be feeling very uneasy in the part he had agreed to play.

When the poor fool entered the room next morning, I saw at once that I had underrated the effect of the situation on him. It was obvious, from the appearance of his eyes, that he had not slept, and he seemed quite unable to look me in the face. I made him sit down and told him that I thought him looking far from well. I was affectionate, almost tender, in my manner. I described, with the eloquence of a practised lawyer, the perspectives of happiness now opening before him. I drew a picture of the house and park I was going to buy, in his name, at Saint-Germain. It was to be furnished throughout in "period" style. There would be a pond well stocked with fish, a garage for four cars, as well as many other "features" which I improvised as I went along. When I spoke about a car, and suggested one of the biggest American makes, he was like a man in mortal agony. Obviously, he had promised not to accept a penny of my money during my lifetime.

"All your troubles are over," I said. "There is nothing for you to do now but to sign the deed of purchase. I have already arranged to hand over to you on Monday a sufficient number of securities to bring you in an income of a hundred thousand francs a year. That will keep you going. But the bulk of my liquid capital is in Amsterdam. We must go there together the week after next so as to get everything straightened out. . . . Is there anything wrong, Robert?"

"I . . . I . . . won't touch a penny during your lifetime," he stammered. ". . . I shouldn't like to . . . I don't want to deprive you of anything. Please don't insist. . . . It'd only make me feel awful!"

He was leaning against the wardrobe, his left elbow supported in his right hand, and biting his nails. I gave him the look that opposing counsel have learned to dread. In just such a way had I been used to fix my victim in the box, keeping my eyes riveted on him until he collapsed into the arms of the attendant police officer.

Actually, I forgave him. I felt that a burden had been lifted from my shoulders. How frightful to have had to end my days in the company of such a worm! I didn't hate him—merely, as it were, dropped him in the ash-can. All the same, I could not resist the temptation to have a little more fun with him.

"I must say, Robert, your feelings do you credit. How charming of you to want to wait until I am dead! But I am not going to accept such a sacrifice. Everything shall be yours on Monday. By the end of next week a large part of my fortune will be in your name. No," I went on dryly (he had begun to protest), "not another word. I have made my offer and it's up to you to take it or leave it."

He still refused to meet my eyes. He needed, he said, a few days in which to think things over—by which, of course, the poor idiot meant to write to Bordeaux for orders.

"Your attitude surprises me, Robert. It really is very odd."

I thought I was looking at him more kindly, but my expression is apt to be a good deal fiercer than the feelings which inspire it. In a perfectly expressionless voice, Robert muttered:

"Why are you staring at me like that?"

I could not help imitating him. "Why am I staring at you

like this? I might equally well ask why you can't look me in the face."

Those who are accustomed to being loved instinctively make all the gestures, and say all the things, most likely to win over their interlocutors. I, on the other hand, have grown so used to being hated and to frightening people, that my eyes, my brows, my voice and my laugh automatically become the servants of this detestable gift of mine, so that they deliver their message even before I mean them to. The poor lad was twisting and turning under a gaze which I had thought to make sympathetic: but the more I laughed, the more ominous did my gaiety seem to him.

Much in the manner of a slaughterman giving the *coup de grâce* to an animal, I fired a point-blank question at him:

"How much did they offer you?"

I had used the second person singular, and the effect of this, whether I liked it or not, was to give to my words a tone not so much of friendliness as of contempt.

"Who d'you mean?" he stammered.

He was clearly prey to an almost superstitious terror.

"The two gentlemen," I said; "the fat one and the thin one . . . yes, the thin one and the fat one."

I wanted to get the whole thing over and done with. The idea of prolonging the scene gave me the horrors (as when one can't bring oneself to crush a centipede under one's boot). "Come, don't take it so hard," I said; "I've forgiven you."

"*I* didn't want to do it . . . it was . . ." I put my hand over his mouth. I couldn't have borne to hear him accuse his mother.

"Ssh! no names! . . . how much *did* they offer you?—a million?—five hundred thousand?—less than that? Oh, surely not!—three hundred?—two hundred?"

"Not any sum down at all, but a regular allowance. That was what tempted us: it gives us a greater feeling of security. Twelve thousand francs a year."

"Starting from to-day?"

"No, from when they come into their inheritance. . . . They hadn't foreseen that you'd want to put everything in my name now, at once. . . . But is it too late? . . . Of course, they might sue us . . . unless we could keep the whole thing on the q.t. . . . Oh, what a fool I've been! I deserve everything that's coming to me!"

He sat on the bed, shedding squalid tears. One of his hands hung down, red and enormous.

"After all, I *am* your son," he whined; "don't let me down."

With a clumsy movement he tried to put his arm round my neck. I freed myself—but not roughly. I went over to the window, and, without turning round, said:

"From the first of August you will receive a monthly sum of fifteen hundred francs. I shall take immediate steps to see that this amount is paid to you for life. Should you predecease your mother, it will revert to her. My family must never know that I got wind of the little plot hatched in Saint-Germain-des-Prés" (the name of the church made him jump), "and I need scarcely point out that the least indiscretion on your part will mean that you lose everything. All I ask in return is that you shall keep me informed of anything they may be planning against me."

He knew now that nothing escaped me, and realized precisely what any future treachery would cost him. I made it quite plain that I wished never to see him or his mother again. They must write to me, *poste restante*, at the usual office.

"When are your accomplices of Saint-Germain-des-Prés leaving Paris?"

He assured me that they had taken the late train on the previous night. He made a great show of gratitude and of promises for the future, but I cut him short. He was, no doubt, flabbergasted by what had happened. A fantastic God, moving in a mysterious way, whom he had betrayed, had seized him, let him go, and picked him out of the abyss into which he had fallen. . . . He shut his eyes and went limp. Squirming like a mongrel cur, his ears flattened to his head, he cringingly took the bone I had flung to him, and made off.

Just as he was going out of the door, a thought occurred to him. How, he asked, would he receive this allowance? Through what channel?

"You will receive it," I said dryly. "I always keep my promises. The rest does not concern you."

With his hand on the latch, he still hesitated.

"I'd rather have it in the form of a Life Insurance Policy, or something like that, taken out with a good, reliable firm. . . . I should feel easier in my mind . . . I wouldn't have to worry . . ."

With sudden violence I wrenched open the door which he was holding ajar and pushed him into the passage.

XVII

I LEANED against the mantelpiece and mechanically counted the scraps of varnished wood in the "tidy."

For years I had dreamed of this unknown son of mine. Never, in the whole course of my wretched existence, had I lost the feeling that he was there. In some spot of the earth there lived a child born of my body whom I might one day find again, who might, perhaps, at some distant date, bring me comfort. That he was of humble condition served to tighten the bonds between us. I had liked to think that he resembled my legitimate son in nothing. I had endowed him in my mind with simplicity and strength of affection, two qualities which are by no means rare among the common people. And now, after all these years, I had played my last card. There was nothing to be hoped from him, nor from any living person. There was nothing left for me to do but curl up and turn my face to the wall. For forty years I had cheated myself into believing that I could accept the fact of hatred—both of the hatred I inspired and the hatred that I felt. But, like other human beings, I had cherished a hope and assuaged my hunger as best I could, waiting until I should be driven back on my last reserves. That moment had come, and it was all over.

I could not even look forward to the horrible pleasure of scheming how best to disinherit those who had wished me ill. Robert had put them on the scent, and, sooner or later, they would discover my hoards, even the ones that did not stand in my own name. Think of some other way? . . . Oh, if only I could go on living, could have time enough in which to spend everything and *then* die . . . leaving behind me not even enough to pay for a pauper's funeral! But all my life long I had saved. For years I had satisfied my lust for "putting by." How, at my age, could I learn to be a spendthrift? Besides, thought I, the children have got their eyes on me. Anything of that sort I might do would merely put a dangerous weapon into their hands. . . . I should have to ruin myself secretly, by driblets. . . .

But alas! I shouldn't know how! I was quite incapable of losing my money. If only it were possible to stuff my grave with it, to return, earth to earth and dust to dust, clasping in my arms my gold, my notes, my shares! If only I could give the lie to those who preach that, when we die, we must leave the goods of this world behind us!

There was, of course, "Charity." Good works are trap-doors opening into depths which can swallow everything. Why not send anonymous gifts to the Relief Committee, to the Little Sisters of the Poor? Why not, at this fag-end of my life, begin to think of others, of those who were not my enemies? But the horror of growing old consists in this, that one's age is the sum total of one's life, and not one figure of it can we change. It has taken me sixty years—I thought—to "create" this old man now dying of hatred. I am what I am. I should have to become somebody else. . . . Oh God! . . . Oh God . . . if only You existed! . . .

It grew dark, and a maid came in to turn down my bed. But she did not close the shutters. I lay down in the half-light. I dozed, in spite of the noise in the street and the glare of the lamps. Every now and again I returned to full consciousness for a brief moment, as one does on a journey when the train comes to a stop. Then, once more, I dropped off. Though I did not feel any worse, I got the idea that I had only to stay as I was and wait patiently until my sleep should become eternal. I still had to make arrangements for the promised allowance to be paid regularly to Robert. I wanted, too, to look in at the *poste restante*, since there was nobody now to do that for me. For the last three days I had not read my mail. One of the most ineradicable of human beliefs is that *some* day a mysterious letter will turn up. What better proof could there be that hope springs eternal in the human breast? We are none of us without it.

It was this preoccupation with the idea of letters that got me out of bed next day, about noon, and sent me off to the post office. It was raining. I was without an umbrella, and kept close to the walls. My appearance aroused curiosity. People began to look round at me. What's so odd about me?—d'you take me for a lunatic? . . . If you do, you mustn't let on—my children might take advantage of a thing like that! Don't stare at me so! I'm just like everybody else—except that my children hate me and that I ought to take steps to protect myself from them. But that doesn't mean I'm mad. There are times when I am under the influence of all the drugs that an angina patient has to take. Yes, I *do* talk to myself, but that's because I am always *by* myself. Conversation is a necessity of all human creatures. What is there so extraordinary in the words and gestures of a lonely old man?

The packet I was given contained some printed matter, some letters from the Bank, and three telegrams. They probably had to do with Stock Exchange transactions which it had been impossible to put through. I delayed opening them until I should be seated in a cheap eating-house. . . . Several builder's labourers, looking like pierrots of varying ages, were seated at a long table eating their not very generous portions, drinking their litres, and scarcely speaking a word. They had been working in the rain all morning. At half-past one they would start again. It was the end of July. The stations were full of holiday-makers. . . . Would they have understood anything of the torment seething in my mind?—Of course they would: how could an old lawyer doubt it? My first case had had to do with children who had gone to law in some quarrel about looking after their father. The wretched man went to one or other of them every three months, only to be received with curses. The one point on which he had found himself in agreement with his sons was in calling loudly on death to bring them all release. Many was the form in which I had witnessed this drama of the old father obstinately refusing, year after year, to hand over the money-bags, and then, finally, letting himself be wheedled out of his rights, only to die of overwork and hunger at the hands of his children. Oh yes, the emaciated labourer with the gnarled hands, seated only a few feet from me, and slowly mumbling his bread between toothless gums, would surely know all about that.

No one, in these days, shows any surprise at the sight of a well-dressed old man in a cheap eating-house. I cut up a piece of pallid rabbit and amused myself by watching the raindrops running together on the window-pane. I spelled out the name of the proprietor upside down. In feeling for my handkerchief, I came on the packet of letters. I put on my spectacles and opened one of the telegrams at random. "Mother's funeral to-morrow 23 July nine St. Louis church." It was dated that morning. The other two, sent off the evening before, must have followed one another at a few hours' interval. One of them said: "Mother desperately ill return." The other: "Mother dead. . . ." All three were signed "Hubert."

I crumpled up the telegrams and went on eating, my mind preoccupied with the thought that, somehow, I should have to muster up sufficient strength to take the night train. For several minutes I was concerned with nothing else. Then another feeling began to emerge—a feeling of amazement that I should have survived Isa. It had long been an understood thing that I was under sentence of death. Neither I, nor anybody else, had doubted for a moment that I should be the first to go. Plans, intrigues, plots—all had been centred on the days immediately following my death, which could not now be long delayed. I had been as certain of that as any member of my family, had always seen my wife in the character of a widow, encumbered by crape when she went to open my safe. No astronomical disaster could have caused me more surprise—or uneasiness—than this death. Automatically, the business-man side of me began to take stock of the situation, began to wonder how it could be used to advantage against my enemies. Such were my feelings until the train actually started.

It was only then that my imagination began to take a hand. For the first time I conjured up a vision of Isa as she must have looked in her bed on the previous day, and on the day before that. I saw the whole scene—her room at Calèse (I did not know then that she had died in Bordeaux). "Putting her into her coffin," I murmured to myself, and yielded to a cowardly feeling of relief. What would have been my attitude had I been there? How should I have behaved under the watchful and hostile eyes of my children? That problem no longer arose. Furthermore, the fact that I should have to go straight to bed as soon as I arrived would settle every difficulty of that kind. There could be no question of my being at the funeral. Only a moment ago I had made an effort to go to the lavatory, and had had to give it up. This evidence of my weakness did not frighten me. Now that Isa was gone, I no longer lived in hourly expectation of my end. My turn had gone by. But I *was* afraid of having an attack, the more so since I was alone in the carriage. I should be met at the station (I had sent a telegram) no doubt by Hubert.

But it was not Hubert who was waiting for me. What a relief it was to see Alfred standing there with his fat face showing all the marks of a sleepless night! The sight of me seemed to frighten him. I could not manage to get into the car unaided, and had to take his arm. We drove in the gloom of a rainy Bordeaux morning through a district given over to slaughter-houses and schools. There was no need for me to talk. Alfred went into the smallest details. He described the exact spot in the Public Gardens where Isa had collapsed (in front of a clump of palms just before one gets to the green-houses), the chemist's shop into which she had been taken, the difficulty they had had in getting her heavy body upstairs to her room on the first floor, the blood-letting, the tapping. . . . She had been fully conscious all night, though she was suffering from cerebral hæmorrhage. She had kept on asking for me by means of signs, and had fallen asleep just as the priest arrived with the consecrated oils. . . . "But she had taken Communion the day before. . . ."

Alfred wanted to drop me at the front door (which was already draped in black) and hurry home, explaining that he had barely time in which to get dressed for the ceremony. But he had to resign himself to the necessity of helping me out of the car. He gave me his arm up the first few steps. I did not recognize the hall. In the dim interior great stands of candles were burning round a massed bank of flowers. I blinked my eyes. I felt lost, as one sometimes does in dreams. There were two motionless nuns. They must have been provided by the undertaker along with the other fittings. Behind this hotch-potch of fabrics, flowers and lights, the familiar staircase, with its shabby carpet, climbed into the region of everyday life.

Hubert came down. He was in evening dress, and looked very correct. He held out his hand to me and said something, but his voice seemed to come from very far away. I tried to answer, but failed to make a sound. His face drew closer and became enormous. Then I lost consciousness. I learned later that my fainting fit lasted for a bare three minutes. I came to myself in what had once been my waiting-room in the days when I was still practising at the Bar. There was the sharp prick of smelling-salts in my nose. I recognized Geneviève's voice: "He's coming round." I opened my eyes. They were all there, bending over me. Their faces seemed different—red, puffy, and some of them with a greenish tinge. Janine, more robust than her mother, had the appearance of being her contemporary rather than her child. Hubert's face, in particular, showed the effects of tears. He had the same ugly, pitiful look as when, a child, he had been taken by Isa on her lap, and she had said, "The poor little mite's really unhappy. . . ." Only Phili appeared to be completely unchanged. Wearing the dress-suit which he had dragged through all the night-haunts of Paris and Berlin, he looked at me with the customary expression of bored indifference on his handsome face. He might have been just off to a party, or, rather, just back from one, drunk and slovenly, for he had not yet tied his tie. Behind him I could make out a number of anonymous veiled women, who must have been Olympe and her daughters. Other shirt-fronts gleamed in the half-light.

Geneviève held a glass to my lips, and I gulped down some of its contents. I told her that I was feeling better. In a gentle, kindly voice she asked whether I would like to go to bed at once. I said the first thing that came into my mind:

"I should so much have liked to go with her to the end, not having been here to say good-bye."

I repeated the phrase, like an actor seeking the correct inflexion—"not having been here to say good-bye . . ."—and the flat words, serving no purpose beyond that of saving appearances. They had come to me only because they belonged to the part I was playing in the funeral ceremony, and suddenly awoke in me, with a sudden jerk, the very feeling of which they were the expression. It was as though I had told myself something which, till then, I had not realized. I should never again see my wife. There could never, now, be an explanation between us. She would never read these pages. Things would remain for all eternity in exactly the same state in which they had been when I left Calèse. We could not start afresh, wipe the slate clean, and try again. She had died without knowing me, without understanding that there was more in me than the monster, the tormentor, she thought me to be, that behind the mask there did exist a totally different man. Even if I had arrived at the last moment, even though no word had passed between us, she would have seen the tears which were now running down my face, and would have died in the knowledge of my despair.

Only my children, speechless with astonishment, were witnesses of the scene. Probably, in the whole course of their lives, they had never seen me cry. The old surly, terrifying face, the Medusa's head at which they had none of them been able to look, had undergone a metamorphosis, had become simply that of a human being.

I heard a voice (it was probably Janine's):

"If only you hadn't gone away! Why did you?" Yes, why, indeed, had I gone? But I *could* have got back in time had the telegrams not been addressed to the *poste restante*, but delivered to me at the Rue Bréa. Hubert was foolish enough to add:

"Going away like that, without leaving an address . . . how could we possibly guess?"

A thought, till then vague in my mind, became, on a sudden, crystal-clear. Pressing with my two hands on the arms of the chair, I struggled to my feet, trembling with anger, and shouted in his face the one word—"Liar!"

He was taken aback. "Papa!" he stammered, "you must be mad!"

But I went on: "Yes, you're liars, the whole lot of you. You knew my address perfectly well. I dare you to tell me to my face that you didn't!"

He protested feebly: "But how could we have known it?"

"You were in touch with somebody very close to me . . . you can't deny that, you know you can't!"

The whole family stared at me in a sort of petrified silence. Hubert shook his head like a child caught out in an untruth.

"You didn't give him much for his treachery: you weren't exactly generous. Twelve thousand francs a year in return for a fortune isn't much!"

I laughed and laughed until I was caught in a fit of coughing.

They could none of them find anything to say. Phili muttered in a low voice: "Dirty trick. . . ."

I went on with what I had been saying, though I lowered my voice in deference to a gesture of appeal from Hubert, who was striving in vain to get a word in:

"You were the cause of my not coming back. You were being kept informed of my every movement; but I mustn't be allowed to know that. If you had sent me a telegram addressed to the Rue Bréa, I should realize at once that I had been betrayed. Nothing in the world would have induced you to take such a step, not even the prayers of your dying mother. No doubt you felt sorry, but you were cold and calculating. . . ."

All this I said to them, and other things still more horrible. Hubert begged his sister to intervene. "Make him stop! Make him stop! Somebody will hear him!" he said in a choking voice. Geneviève put her arm round my shoulders and made me sit down again.

"Not now, Father; not now. We'll talk about all that later when we're not so upset. I beg you, in the name of her who is still with us . . ."

Hubert's face was livid. He put a finger to his lips. The chief undertaker's man came in with a list of the pall-bearers. I took a few steps. I did not want any of their supporting arms. I stumbled, and they drew aside to let me pass. I was able to cross the threshold of the mortuary chapel, and squat down on a *prie-Dieu*.

Hubert and Geneviève followed me. Each taking an arm, they led me away, and I made no effort to resist. They got me upstairs with considerable difficulty. One of the nuns agreed to keep an eye on me during the ceremony. Hubert, before leaving, with a great show of ignoring what had just passed between us, asked me whether he had done right in arranging for the President of the Bar Council to be one of the pall-bearers. I turned away to the streaming window and said nothing.

Already there was a sound of many feet. The whole town

would come to sign the visitors' book. On the Fondaudège side there were innumerable connexions, and on mine, the Bar, the Bank, and the world of business. . . . I was conscious of a lightness of heart. I felt like a man who has just been acquitted of a crime, whose innocence has been declared to the world. I had convicted my children of lying, and they had made no attempt to deny their responsibility. While the whole house was echoing to the sound of feet—as though some strange ball without music was in progress—I forced myself to concentrate my thoughts upon their guilt. It was they alone who had prevented me from hearing Isa's last farewell. I stuck spurs deep into my ancient hatred, but, like a foundered horse, it would not respond. Perhaps the reason lay in my physical prostration, or in my satisfaction at the knowledge that I had had the last word. I cannot be sure.

I could no longer hear the sing-song of the priest's voice. The sounds of the funeral died away, and a silence as deep as that of Calèse filled the huge house. Isa had emptied it of its inhabitants. Behind her corpse she trailed the paraphernalia of her home. No one was left within its walls but I and the nun, who was finishing, at my bedside, the telling of her beads which she had begun beside the bier.

The silence made me sensitive once more to the fact of eternal separation, to that departure from which there is no return. Again I felt a tightness round my heart because now it was too late, and all was over between us. Propped up against the pillows of my bed, that I might breathe the more easily, I looked round at the Louis XIII funiture which we had chosen in Bardie's shop at the time of our engagement. It had been hers until she inherited her mother's. This bed it was, this melancholy bed, which had been the silent witness of our bitter wordlessness.

Hubert and Geneviève came in alone. The others had stayed outside in the passage. I realized that they could not get used to the sight of my tears. They stood beside my pillow, the brother, a bizarre figure dressed for the evening at midday, the sister, a mound of black picked out by a white handkerchief, and her veil thrown back to reveal a round and puffy face. Grief had unmasked us all, and we did not recognize one another.

They were worried about my health. Geneviève said:

"Almost everybody was at the cemetery: she was much beloved."

I asked them about the day before her stroke.

"She wasn't feeling well. She may, I think, have had a presentiment, because the day before she was due to go to Bordeaux, she spent hours in her bedroom, burning piles of letters. We thought the chimney must be on fire."

I broke in. A sudden idea had occurred to me. . . . Why hadn't I thought of it before?

"Geneviève, do you think my going away had anything to do with it?"

She answered with a satisfied air that, no doubt, "it had been a blow."

"But you didn't tell her, didn't keep her informed of what you had discovered?"

She shot a questioning glance at her brother: ought she to seem to understand? I must have presented an odd appearance at that moment, for, certainly, they seemed very much afraid. While Geneviève helped to prop me up in bed, Hubert hurriedly replied that his mother had been taken ill more than ten days after my departure, and that they had decided, throughout that period, not to include her in their melancholy discussions. Was he speaking the truth? In tremulous tones, he added:

"If we had yielded to the temptation of mentioning to her the uneasiness we were feeling, then, indeed, the prime responsibility would be ours."

He half-turned away, and I could see his shoulders moving convulsively. Somebody pushed the door open, and asked whether they were *ever* going to have something to eat. I heard Phili's voice: "Well, I can't help it, can I, if I'm starving?". . . Geneviève asked me through her tears what I would like for luncheon. Hubert said that he would come back after the meal, and that we must have everything out, once and for all, if I felt strong enough to listen. I nodded my agreement.

When they had left the room, the good sister helped me to get up. I was able to take a bath, dress myself, and drink a cup of beef-tea. If there was to be a discussion I did not want to play the part of a sick man to be dealt with gently and protected.

On their return I was a very different person from the old gentleman who had aroused their compassion. I had taken the necessary drugs, and was sitting upright. I felt less congested, as I always do when I leave my bed.

Hubert had changed into a day suit, but Geneviève was swathed in an old dressing-gown belonging to her mother. "I've nothing black to wear," she said. They sat down facing me. After a few conversational phrases:

"I've thought a good deal about this," Hubert began.

He had carefully prepared his speech, and addressed me as though I had been a meeting of shareholders. He weighed each word, and seemed anxious to avoid any show of anger.

"While I was sitting by Mamma, I scrupulously examined my conscience. I made a great effort to alter my point of view and to put myself in your place. We had regarded you as a father whose fixed idea was to disinherit his children, and that, to my mind, makes our behaviour legitimate, or, at least, excusable. But we have given you a certain advantage over us by the violence with which we fought our cause, and by . . ."

He seemed to be looking for the right word. I murmured, very quietly, "and by your cowardly plots."

His cheeks showed a patch of colour. Geneviève at once reacted:

"Why 'cowardly'? You're in a much stronger position than we are. . . ."

"Oh, come! . . . a very sick old man against a pack of healthy young animals!"

"In a family like ours," said Hubert, "a very sick old man is distinctly privileged. He never leaves his room: he can be constantly on the watch: he has nothing to do but observe the habits of his children and take advantage of them. He can make his plans undisturbed, and arrange his moves at leisure. He knows all there is to be known about those round him, while they know nothing whatever about him. He has reconnoitred the best vantage-points for listening . . ." (here I could not help smiling, and they smiled too). "Yes," Hubert went on, "the members of a family are always lacking in prudence. They argue, they raise their voices. In a very short while everyone is shouting without realizing it. They rely too much on the thickness of the walls in an old house, oblivious of the fact that the floors are flimsy, and that there are always open windows to be reckoned with. . . ."

These allusions had the effect of, to some extent, diminishing the tension between us. It was Hubert who first brought the conversation back to its serious level.

"I see now that we must have seemed blameworthy. It would be easy enough for me to plead legitimate self-defence, but I want to avoid anything that might embitter this discussion. It is no part of my intention to name the aggressor in this wretched quarrel. I am even prepared to plead guilty. But you must realize . . ."

He had got up, and was wiping the lenses of his spectacles. The eyes blinked in his worn and harassed face.

". . . You must realize that I was fighting for the honour, for the very existence, of my children. It is impossible for you to imagine the situation in which we find ourselves. You belong to a different century. You have lived your life in a fabulous period when a careful man could plan his future on a basis of safe investments. Oh, I know that you are fully aware of what is happening in the world, that you saw the storm coming before anybody else did, that you realized in time . . . but that was because you had retired from active business, because you were, if I may say so, an onlooker. You could judge the situation quite coolly; you dominated it, you were not, as I am, up to the ears in it. . . . The awakening has been too sudden. . . . It's been impossible, as yet, to look round. . . . This is the first moment that all the branches of the tree have given way at the same moment. There is nothing left to cling to, nothing on which one can get a hold. . . ."

There was something of desperation in the way he repeated those words—"nothing, nothing at all. . . ." How deeply *was* he committed?—on the edge of what abyss was he struggling? Afraid that he might have given himself away, he checked his flow of eloquence, fell back on the usual commonplaces—the drive for industrial re-equipment in the post-war period, over-production, the fall in purchasing power. What he said did not matter: it was this desperation of his that held my attention. It was borne in on me at that moment that my hatred was dead, and dead, too, my desire for reprisals. Perhaps they had been dead for a long time. I had been piling coals on my anger, had been tearing myself to pieces. But what was the use of refusing to look facts in the face? My feelings, as I sat there in my son's presence, were confused, but my dominant emotion was one of curiosity. How strange it all seemed—the wretched man's obvious agitation and terror, the horrors which it needed only a word from me to dissipate! I thought of the fortune which, so it seemed, had been my life's obsession. I had tried so hard to give it away or lose it. I had not been free even to dispose of it as I had wished, and now I felt, suddenly, wholly detached. It no longer interested me, was no longer any concern of mine. Hubert had left off speaking, and was watching me from behind his spectacles. What was I scheming?—what new blow preparing? There was already a sort of fixed grin on his face. He drew himself up and raised his arm like a child preparing to ward off attack. He began again to speak, and now his voice was timid:

"All I ask is that you should set me on my feet. Taking into consideration what will be coming to me from Mamma, I shan't now need more than . . ." (he hesitated a moment before naming the figure) . . . "more than a million. Once I've wiped the slate clean, I shall be able to manage. Do what you like with the rest. . . . I undertake to bow to your wishes. . . ."

He swallowed, and continued to observe me furtively. I was careful to keep my face a blank.

"And what about you, my dear?" I asked, turning to Geneviève. "You're right as rain, aren't you?—married to a clever husband. . . ."

It always irritated her to hear her husband praised. She protested that the business was on its last legs. Alfred had bought no rum, now, for two years. At least that meant that he had made no bad deals, which was a comfort. They'd got enough to live on, certainly, but Phili was threatening to desert his wife and child, and was waiting only until he knew for certain that all hope of getting some of the family fortune was gone. "Good riddance!" I muttered, but she took me up sharply.

"Oh, we all know he's a rotter—Janine no less than the rest of us—but if he leaves her she'll die. I mean it—she'll die. That's something you can't understand, Father: you're not made that way. Janine knows a great deal more about Phili than all the rest of us put together. She has often told me that he is far worse than we could possibly imagine. But that doesn't alter the fact that she would die if he left her. I know it must sound nonsense to you. Things like that are beyond your comprehension. But surely a man as intelligent as you can understand a thing even if you don't feel it?"

"You're tiring Papa, Geneviève. . . ." It had occurred to

Hubert that his clumsy sister might have "put her foot in it," that I might be hurt in my pride by what she had said. He could see from my face that I was suffering, but he could not know why, could not know that Geneviève had opened an old wound and was jabbing at it.

"Lucky Phili!" I sighed.

I could read amazement in the glance that passed between my two children. They had always, quite honestly, believed me to be half-mad. Perhaps if they had had me locked up, they would have done so with an easy conscience.

"A blackguard!" muttered Hubert; "and he's got a hold over us!"

"His father-in-law looks on him with a rather kindlier eye," I said. "Alfred is always saying that he's a queer fish, but not really bad at heart."

Geneviève flared up:

"That's because he's got a hold over Alfred, too! The son-in-law has corrupted the father-in-law—everyone knows that! They're constantly being seen together consorting with women. . . . The shame of that was one of the things that made Mother's life a misery. . . ."

She dabbed at her eyes. It was clear that Hubert thought I was trying to distract their attention from what really mattered.

"That's not the point, Geneviève," he said with a show of irritation. "To hear you talk one would imagine that you and your children are the only people in the world."

She turned on him in a fury. Of the two of them, which was the most selfish?—that's what *she* would like to know!

"It's only natural," she went on, "to put one's own children first. I have always done everything for Janine, and I'm proud to admit it, just as Mamma did everything for us. I'd go through fire . . ."

Her brother broke in on her. I recognized myself in the

sharpness of his tone. "And see that others went through it, too!" he said.

What fun I should once have got from their quarrel! I should have hailed with delight these preliminary signs of a battle to the death over the few leavings of my fortune which I could not keep from them. But the only feeling of which I was conscious now was one of faint disgust and boredom. . . . If only the whole wretched business could be settled once and for all! If only they would leave me to die in peace!

"It's odd, my children," I said to them, "that I should end by doing what I've always considered as the height of folly. . . ."

Their snarlings were all forgotten in an instant! They turned on me a hard, suspicious look. They were waiting, their guard was up.

"I've always thought of myself in terms of the old farmer robbed of his livelihood, and left by his children to die of hunger. If he took too long over his dying, well then, a few eiderdowns piled conveniently on his face would hasten the processes of nature. . . .

"Father, *please* . . ."

The look of horror with which they protested was not assumed. Hastily I changed my tone.

"You're going to be busy, Hubert. Sharing out the pickings won't be easy. I've got my money stowed away in a great number of places—here, in Paris, abroad. Then there's the real estate, my various houses. . . ."

At each word their eyes grew rounder. They couldn't believe their ears. I saw Hubert's thin hands open and shut.

"I want everything to be settled before my death, at the same time as you wind up your mother's estate. I shall retain Calèse for my own use, both the house and the park (the cost of upkeep and repairs to fall on you). I don't want to hear another word about the vines. A monthly income—the amount of which remains to be settled—will be paid me by my lawyer. . . . Just hand me my wallet . . . yes, it's in the left-hand pocket of my coat."

Hubert gave it to me with a trembling hand. I took out an envelope.

"This will give you some idea of the total amount of my fortune . . . you had better take it to Arcam, the barrister. . . . No, on second thoughts, it would be better to ring him up and ask him to come round. I'll give it him myself, and confirm my dispositions in your presence."

Hubert took the envelope, and said with an air of acute anxiety:

"You're not laughing at us, are you?"

"Ring up the lawyer: you'll soon see whether I'm laughing. . . ."

"No," he said; "not to-day, it would be scarcely decent. . . . We ought to wait a week."

He passed one hand over his eyes. Clearly, he was feeling ashamed, was forcing himself to think of his mother. He turned the envelope over and over in his fingers.

"All right then, open it," I said; "open it and read what's inside. You have my authority to do so."

He went quickly across to the window and broke the seal. He fell on the letter like a starving man on food. Geneviève could restrain herself no longer, but got up, joined him, and peered greedily over his shoulder.

I looked at the brother and sister. There was nothing in the sight to cause me horror. A man of business threatened with ruin: a father and a mother who had suddenly come into the millions which they had thought lost to them for ever. No, they caused me no sense of horror. But my own indifference astonished me. I was like a patient who comes round from an operation and says that he has felt nothing. I had torn out of myself something which I had always thought was deeply rooted in my being—

and I felt nothing but relief, nothing but a sort of physical lightness! I was breathing more easily. What, after all, had I been doing for years but trying to get rid of this fortune, trying to load it on to somebody who was not a member of my family? But always I had been deceived in the object of my wishes. We do not know what we desire: we do not love those whom we think we love.

I heard Hubert say to his sister: "It's enormous, simply enormous—a vast fortune!" They exchanged a few words in low voices. Geneviève declared that they could not accept such a sacrifice, that they had no wish to strip me naked.

The words "sacrifice" and "strip" sounded strange in my ears. Hubert was insistent.

"You have been influenced by the emotion of the moment. You think you are more ill than you are. You're not seventy. People with your ailment live to a great old age. After a while you will regret what you have done. I will relieve you of all business worries, if you like, but you must enjoy in peace what belongs to you. We want only what is just. We have never asked for anything but justice. . . ."

I was overcome by a sense of weariness. They saw my eyes close. I told them that my mind was made up, that I would say no more on the subject except in the presence of a lawyer. They were already at the door. Without turning my head, I called them back.

"I forgot to tell you that a monthly allowance of fifteen hundred francs is to be paid to my son Robert. I have promised him that. Remind me of it when we draw up the agreement."

Hubert blushed. This particular arrow had taken him by surprise. But Geneviève read no malice into what I had said. Round-eyed, she made a rapid calculation:

"Eighteen thousand francs a year," she said. "Don't you think that's rather a lot?"

XVIII

THE grass looks lighter than the sky. A thin vapour is rising from the soaked earth. The ruts, brimming with rain, reflect a muddy blue. I feel as interested in everything as I used to do when Calèse still belonged to me. Now, I am possessed of nothing, yet do not feel my poverty. The sound, at night, of rain upon the rotting vines makes me no less sad than when I was the owner of the threatened crop. What I thought of as love of my land was no more than the physical instinct of the peasant; for I come of a long peasant line and was born of those who, through the centuries, had scanned the sky with anxious looks. The money to be paid to me each month will accumulate at the lawyer's. I have never wanted for anything. All my life long I have been the prisoner of a passion which never really possessed me. Like a dog barking at the moon, I was held in thrall by a reflection. Fancy waking up at sixty-eight! Fancy being reborn at the very moment of my death! If only I may be granted just a few more years, a few months, a few weeks. . . .

The nurse has gone. I am feeling much better. Amélie and Ernest, who served Isa, are to stay on with me. They know how to give injections. Everything lies ready to my hand, the little bottles of morphine and of nitrite. The children are so busy that they scarcely ever leave town. They turn up here only when they want to know something about a valuation. . . . They get along without too much quarrelling. They are so terrified of being "done down" that they have agreed, rather foolishly, to divide up all the complete sets of damask linen and glassware. They would cut a piece of tapestry in two rather than let any one of them have the benefit of it. They would prefer to see everything spoiled than get unequal shares. It is what they call having a "passion for justice." They have spent their lives giving high-sounding names to sordid instincts. . . . No, I ought to scratch that sentence out. For all I know, they may be prisoners, as I was, of a passion that does not really go deep.

What do they think of me? That I have been beaten, presumably, that I have been forced to surrender. They've "got me." All the same, each time they visit me they show respect and gratitude. But that doesn't prevent them from being in a constant state of amazement at my attitude. Hubert, in particular, keeps a watchful eye on me. He is suspicious. He is not quite sure that I have been disarmed. You can be quite easy in your mind, my poor boy. I was never really an object of terror even when I returned as a convalescent to Calèse, and now . . .

The elms along the roads and the poplars in the meadows stand massed together. Between their dark-hued trunks the mist accumulates, and the smoke of bonfires, and the breath of the huge earth when it has drunk deep. For we have waked to find the autumn all about us. The grapes still glittering from the recent storm will never recover what this rainy August stole. But for us, perhaps, it is never too late. I must never stop telling myself that it is never too late.

It was from no feeling of devotion that I went into Isa's room the day after I got back. What led me there was idleness, that complete lack of occupation which seizes me in the country. I never know whether I most enjoy or dislike it. I was tempted to push the half-open door, the first door on the left at the top of the stairs. The window was flung back; the wardrobe and the chest of drawers were empty. The servants had swept the place clean, and the sun, even in the farthest corners, had eaten up the last impalpable remains of a completed destiny. The September afternoon was buzzing with sleepy flies. The thick round tops of the lime trees looked like bruised fruit. The blue, deep at the zenith, showed pale behind the dozing hills. A burst of laughter came up to me from some girl I could not see. Sun-bonnets were moving among the vines. The grape-harvest had begun.

But the wonder of life had withdrawn from Isa's room. A pair of gloves and an umbrella lying on the floor of the wardrobe looked dead. I gazed at the old stone mantelpiece on the spandrel of which were carved a spade, a sickle and a blade of corn. These old-fashioned hearths, in which whole trunks can burn, are masked in summer by large screens of painted canvas. This particular one had a picture of two oxen ploughing. One day, when I was very young, I had slashed it with a pen-knife in a fit of temper. It was only leaning against the fireplace. I tried to adjust it properly, but it fell, revealing the black square of the grate, filled with ashes. Then I remembered what the children had told me about Isa's last day at Calèse: "She was burning papers: we thought there was a fire.". . . I realized how strongly she must have felt the approach of death. It is impossible, at one and the same time, to think of one's own death and that of another person. Obsessed by the certainty of my approaching end, I had, quite naturally, not felt worried by Isa's blood-pressure. "It's nothing—just old age," our idiotic children had gone on saying. But she, when she had kindled this great fire, had known that her hour was at hand. She had wanted to disappear utterly, and so had set about effacing every tiny trace of herself. I stared into the hearth, at the scraps of grey fluff which the wind was gently fluttering. The tongs she had used were still in their place, between the chimney and the wall. I took them, and started to rummage in the heap of dust, that last remains of an utter nothingness.

I searched as though the secret of my life lay hidden there, the secret of our two lives. The farther I probed with the poker, the thicker lay the ashes. I brought out a few scraps of paper which the thickness of the bundles must have saved from the flames. But all I could recover were a few words, a few broken phrases, which conveyed no meaning. All were in the same handwriting. I could not recognize it. My hands were trembling: I worked feverishly. On one tiny fragment, smeared with soot, I could make out the word PAX. Beneath it was a small cross, a date, 23 February, 1913, and the words "*my dear daughter. . . .*" I set myself to assemble the letters written on the margin of some other pieces of charred paper, but all I could get was this: "*You are not responsible for the hatred which this rouses in you. Only if you yielded to it would you be to blame. Far from that being so, you try . . .*" As the result of much effort, I succeeded in reading a little more: "*. . . judge the dead rashly . . . the affection which he feels for Luc does not prove*". . . Soot hid all of the rest, except one single phrase: "*Forgive, not knowing what it is that you have to forgive. . . . Offer for him your . . .*"

There would be time enough later for me to think of what I had read. My only concern at the moment was to find more. I searched every nook and cranny of the hearth, crouching so awkwardly, that I found it difficult to breathe. The discovery of a note-book bound in American cloth set my heart beating. It looked intact, but, on examining it, I found that none of the pages had escaped the fire. The only words I could decipher were on the inside of the cover, in Isa's hand: FLOWERS OF THE SPIRIT, and, underneath, "*My name is not the name of Him who damns: I am called Jesus*" (Christ to Saint François de Sales).

There were several more quotations, but all of them illegible. I spent some time longer bending over the burned-out ashes, but in vain. I could find nothing more. I scrambled to my feet and looked at my black hands. In the mirror I could see my smeared forehead. Suddenly, as in the days of my youth, I was seized with a longing to go for a walk. Forgetful of my heart, I hurried downstairs, far too fast.

For the first time for weeks I made my way to the vines. Half stripped of their fruit, they were slipping back into their winter sleep. The landscape was light and limpid. It seemed to have become distended, like those blue-tinted bubbles which Marie used to blow from the end of a hollow straw. Already the ruts and the deep hoof-marks of oxen were hardening under the influence of sun and wind. I walked on, carrying within me the picture of an unknown Isa, of a woman racked by powerful passions which only God could master. The busy housewife had, all the while, been a wildly jealous sister. Luc had been to her an object of loathing. . . . How could a grown woman have brought herself to hate a little boy? . . . Was it the thought of her own children that had been at the bottom of that bitter resentment, the knowledge that I loved Luc so much more deeply than I ever loved them? But Marinette, too, she had detested. . . . It was *I* who had caused her all that suffering. Yes, it was true, I had had it in my power to torture her! What a mad dance it had been! Marinette was dead, Luc, too, and now Isa: and here I was, an old man, still on his feet, it was true, but standing at the very edge of that same grave which had swallowed the rest of them, and filled with a wild delight because at last I knew that I had not been an object of indifference to her, but had raised a storm to beat about her heart.

It was laughable. I actually laughed aloud, panting a little, leaning against one of the vine stakes, and looking at the pale sea of mist in which villages and village churches and poplar-lined roads lay drowned. The setting sun pierced through with difficulty to light that buried world. I could feel, I could see, I could touch my guilt. It was not only that my heart had become a nest of vipers, that it had been filled with hatred for my children, with a lust for vengeance and a grasping love of money. What was worse than that was that I had refused to look beyond the tangle of vile snakes. I had treasured their knotted hideousness as though it had been the central reality of my being—as though the beating of the life-blood in my veins had been the pulse of all those swarming reptiles. Not content with knowing, through half a century, only of myself what was not truly me at all, I had carried the same ignorance into my dealing with others. The expression of squalid greed on the faces of my children had held me fascinated. Confronted by Robert, I had been able to see only his stupidity, because it was all I had wanted to see. I had never once realized that the superficial appearance of others was something I must break through, a barrier that I must cross, if I was ever to make contact with the real man, the real woman beyond and behind it. That was the discovery I ought to have made when I was thirty or forty. . . .

But now I am an old man. The movement of my heart is too sluggish. I am watching the last autumn of my life as it puts the vines to sleep and stupefies them with its fumes and sunlight. Those whom I *should* have loved are dead, and dead, too, those whom I *could* have loved. I have neither the time now, nor the strength, to embark upon a voyage of exploration with the object of finding the reality of others. Everything in me, even my voice, even my gestures, belongs to the monster whom I reared against the world, the monster to whom I gave my name.

Were those, in strict accuracy, the thoughts on which I brooded as I stood leaning against a vine-stake at the far end of one of the planted rows, with my face turned towards the gleaming hill-slopes of Yquem under the setting sun? One incident there was—and I must mention it here—which doubtless made them clearer in my mind. But it did not create them. They were there already on that evening, as I walked back to the house, my heart filled with the peace that lay upon the earth. The shadows were lengthening. The whole earth was wide open, awaiting the bounty of nature. In the distance the half-glimpsed hills were like bowed shoulders patiently hoping for the darkness and the mist to cover them so that they might stretch themselves, perhaps, lie down and fall into a human sleep.

I had expected to find Geneviève and Hubert at the house. They had promised to dine with me. For the first time in my life I was looking forward to their company, was thinking of it in a mood of pleasurable anticipation. I was impatient to show them my change of heart. Not one minute must I lose in getting to know them, in getting them to know me. Would there be time, before I died, to put my new discovery to the test? I longed to drive post-haste to the goal of my children's affection, to break through every obstacle that stood between them and me. At last I had cut through the knot of vipers. So quickly would I win their love that when the moment came for them to close my eyes, they would do so with tears.

They had not yet arrived. I sat on the bench close to the road, listening to the passing cars. The more they delayed, the more did I long for them to come. Several times I had a return of my old anger. What did they care about keeping me waiting! It didn't matter to them if I suffered on their account! They were doing it on purpose! . . . But I took a hold on myself. There might be reasons for their lateness of which I knew nothing, and it was unlikely that they would be those on which I habitually fed my resentment. The gong sounded for dinner. I went to the kitchen to tell Amélie that we must wait a little longer. Only on very rare occasions did I venture into her world of black rafters and pendent hams. I sat down in a wicker chair close to the fire. Amélie, her husband, and Cazau, the bailiff, were there. I had heard their loud laughter while I was still some way off. As I entered the room they all fell silent. An atmosphere of respect and terror enveloped me. I never talk to servants. It is not that I am a difficult or unreasonable master, but simply that, for me, they don't exist. I don't see them. But this evening I found their presence comforting. Because my children had not turned up, I should have liked to eat my dinner on the corner of the table which the cook used for chopping up the joints.

Cazau had made his escape. Ernest was putting on a white

jacket, preparatory to serving at table. I tried to find something to say, but all in vain. I knew absolutely nothing about these two human beings who had been our devoted attendants for the past twenty years. At last, I remembered that, in the old days, their married daughter from Sauveterre de Guyenne had been in the habit of coming to see them, and that Isa had always refused to pay her for the rabbit she brought, on the ground that she had so many meals in our house. Without turning my head, I rather hurriedly asked:

"And how is your daughter, Amélie? Still living at Sauveterre?"

She bent her sun-tanned face to mine and stared.

"Surely, sir, you know that she is dead? . . . It'll be ten years on the twenty-ninth, Michaelmas Day . . . have you forgotten, sir?"

Her husband said nothing, but his eyes looked hard. He thought I had been only pretending to forget. I stammered out: "Oh, I'm so sorry! . . . this old head of mine . . ."—but, as always when I am embarrassed or nervous, I giggled. I just could not help it. Then the man announced in his usual voice that dinner was ready.

I got up at once, went into the ill-lit dining-room, and sat down opposite the ghost of Isa. There, next to her, was where Geneviève had always sat, and then, in order, the Abbé Ardouin, Hubert. . . . My eyes wandered to Marie's high-chair, standing between the sideboard and the window. It had descended, first to Janine, then to Janine's daughter. I went through the pretence of swallowing a few mouthfuls. . . . The expression on the face of the man who was serving me was horrible.

A fire of vine-shoots had been lit in the drawing-room. Here, each generation as it ebbed had left its shells—its albums, caskets, daguerreotypes and patent lamps. The small tables were covered with knick-knacks from which all life had drained away. The heavy tread of a horse in the night, the sound of the wine-press which is built on to the house, tore at my heart-strings. "Oh, my children, why didn't you come?" The words were the formulation of my wretchedness. Had the servants been listening outside the door, they would have thought there was a stranger in the room with me, for neither voice nor words would they have connected with the miserable old man, who, as they believed, had deliberately pretended not to know that their daughter was dead.

All of them, wife, children, masters and servants, were in league against my soul. I must play my hateful part at their dictation. I was painfully caught in the rigidity of the expected attitude. I had modelled myself on the image projected by their hatred. What madness, at sixty-eight, to hope to swim against the stream, to impose on them a new vision of the person I really am and have always been! We see only what we are accustomed to see. You, too, my poor children, I do not truly see. Were I younger, the lines would be less deeply graven, the habits less unalterably rooted. But I doubt whether, even in my youth, I could have broken the spell. Some especial strength was needed, I said to myself. Yes, but what strength? The aid of some *person*, of someone in whom we might all have been reunited, of someone who would, in the eyes of my family, have guaranteed the victory which I had won over myself, of someone who would stand my witness, who might relieve me of my hideous burden, and bear it on his own shoulders. . . .

Even the genuinely good cannot, unaided, learn to love. To penetrate beyond the absurdities, the vices, and, above all, the stupidities of human creatures, one must possess the secret of a love which the world has now forgotten. Until that secret shall have been rediscovered, all betterment in conditions of life will be in vain. I used to think that it was selfishness which kept me uninterested in questions of sociology and economics, and to some extent that was true, for I have been a monster of solitude and indifference. Still, I had a feeling, an obscure certainty, that it was no use merely to revolutionize the face of the world, that what was needed was the power to reach the world through the medium of the heart. Him whom I seek can alone achieve that victory, and he must needs be the heart of all hearts, the burning centre of all love. The desire I felt may well have been a prayer. On that night I was within an ace of falling on my knees with my arms on the back of a chair, as Isa used to do, long summers ago, with the three children pressing round her. In those days I would come back from the terrace towards the lighted window. I would muffle my footsteps and, invisible in the darkness of the garden, look on the group at prayer within. "*Prostrate at Thy feet, O God*"—Isa would say—"*I thank Thee that Thou hast given me a heart to know and love Thee. . . .*"

I remained standing in the middle of the room, swaying on my feet as though I had received a blow. I thought of my life and saw what it had been. No one could swim against such a current of mud. I had been a man so horrible that he could have no friend. But wasn't that, I asked myself, because I had always been incapable of wearing a disguise? If all men went through life with unmasked faces, as I had done for half a century, one might be surprised to find how little difference there was between them. But, in fact, no one lives with his face uncovered, no one. Most men ape greatness or nobility. Though they do not know it, they conform to certain fixed types, literary or other. This the saints know, and they hate and despise themselves because they see themselves with unclouded eyes. I should not have been so universally condemned had I not been so defenceless, so open and so naked.

Such were the thoughts which haunted me that evening, as I wandered about the darkened room, stumbling against those heavy pieces of furniture in mahogany and rosewood, poor wrecks buried in the sands of a family's past, on which so many bodies, now turned to dust, had at one time leaned and lain.

Children's boots had soiled the sofa where they had snuggled with a volume of *Le Monde Illustré* of 1870. The dark stains on its covering were as they had always been. The wind was moaning round the house, stirring the dead leaves of the limes. In one of the rooms the shutters had been forgotten and left open.

XIX

NEXT day I waited impatiently for the coming of the postman. I paced up and down the garden as Isa used to do when the children were late and she felt anxious. Had they quarrelled? Was one of them ill? I fretted myself "into a fever," and became as clever as Isa had ever been in the art of formulating and encouraging fixed ideas. I walked among the vines with the absent-minded and remote look of those who brood upon a trouble. But I remember, too, that I noticed this change in myself and derived no little pleasure from the realization that I was ill at ease. The mist was a sounding-board. I could hear the plain, though I could not see it. Wagtails and thrushes were making merry in the furrows where the grapes were not yet rotting. Luc, as a child, when the holidays were ending, had loved these sober-footed mornings. . . .

A line from Hubert, dated Paris, did little to reassure me. He had been obliged, he said, to leave in a hurry. Something serious had happened. He would tell me about it on his return, which would be, he hoped, in two days' time. My mind immediately went to difficulties of a financial nature. Had he, perhaps, been doing something illegal?

By the afternoon I could stand the suspense no longer. I had myself driven to the station, where I took a ticket to Bordeaux, though I had promised not to do any more travelling alone. Geneviève was now living in our old house. I ran into her in the hall, just as she was saying good-bye to someone I did not know, but who looked like a doctor.

"Hasn't Hubert told you?"

She took me into the waiting-room where I had fainted on the day of the funeral. I breathed more freely when I knew what the trouble was. Phili had run away. I had feared something much worse. But he had gone in company with a woman who had "a hold on him," and after a terrible scene which had left Janine without a vestige of hope. The poor child was in a state of complete prostration from which it seemed impossible to rouse her, and the doctor was worried. Alfred and Hubert had pursued the fugitive to Paris. Judging from a telegram which had just arrived, their efforts had been fruitless.

"When I think of the allowance we made them . . . Of course we were wise to possible risks and had not given them control of any capital. Still, the income was by no means inconsiderable. Janine was always terribly weak with him. He could get anything he wanted out of her, and was constantly threatening to abandon her, because he felt convinced that you were not going to leave us anything. It's so extraordinary to me that he should have chosen just the very moment when you'd handed over the whole of your fortune to run away—how do you explain it?"

She came to a dead stop, her eyebrows raised, her eyes dilated. Then she leaned against the radiator, rubbing her hands together.

"This woman," I said, "is, I suppose, rich?"

"Far from it—she's a teacher of singing. You know her quite well: it's Madame Vélard. She's by no means young, and she's knocked about a bit. It's all she can do to make a living. How do you explain it?" she said again.

She did not wait for my answer, but went on talking. At that moment Janine came into the room. She was wearing a dressing-gown, and put up her face for me to kiss. She was no thinner, but despair had wiped the heavy, unattractive face clean of all that, at one time, I had hated in it. The poor creature, formerly so daubed and mannered, had become frighteningly simple and bare. The crude light of a hanging lamp beat down on her, but she stood there unblinking. All she said was, "I suppose you know," and collapsed on to the sofa.

I don't think she even heard what her mother was saying, the interminable catalogue of grievances which Geneviève must have been pouring out over and over again since Phili left.

"When I think . . ."

Every sentence began with that "When I think . . ."—a surprising statement from one who thought so little. They had, she said, consented to the marriage, although, at twenty-two, Phili had already run through a considerable fortune which had come to him while he was still very young (in view of the fact that he was an orphan and had no near relations, it had seemed best to give him full control of his money). The family had shut their eyes to the very unsavoury life he had been leading . . . and this was all the thanks they got! . . .

I tried in vain to control my mounting irritation. My old perversity stirred in its sleep. As though Geneviève herself, Alfred, Isa, and all their friends, had not been continually at Phili, holding out a thousand dazzling prospects!

"What I find quite extraordinary," I said, "is that you seem really to believe what you're saying. And yet, you must know that you were all of you running after him. . . ."

"I won't have you stick up for him, Father! . . ."

I protested that it was not a question of sticking up for him. But we had been wrong to paint Phili blacker than he was. No doubt he had been made to see too clearly that, once the fortune was assured, he would have to swallow every kind of insult, that they were banking on his becoming resigned to having his wings clipped. The trouble was that human beings are never so base as we believe them to be.

"When I think that you can stand there and defend a wretched creature who has abandoned his young wife and his little girl . . ."

"Geneviève!" I cried in exasperation. "You don't begin to understand what I am saying. Do at least make an effort. I quite agree that it is a shocking thing for a man to abandon his wife and child, but the culprit might have yielded to ignoble motives instead of to higher ones. . . ."

"So you think it noble," said Geneviève, with mulish obstinacy, "to abandon a wife of twenty-two and a young child. . . ."

That was the limit of her vision. She simply had no idea of what I was talking about.

"Oh, don't be such a fool . . . unless it is that you are deliberately pretending not to understand. My point is that I find Phili a good deal less despicable now that . . ."

Geneviève cut me short, saying that I might at least wait until Janine had left the room before insulting her with this defence of her husband. But the girl who, until now, had not opened her lips, suddenly said, in a voice which I had difficulty in recognizing:

"What's the use of denying it, Mamma? We treated Phili like mud. Don't pretend you've forgotten. When all this business of sharing out Grand'pa's money began, we thought we'd got him where we wanted him. He was just like a dog I was dragging about on a lead. I had resigned myself to the fact that he didn't love me. That didn't hurt any more. I had got him: he was mine: he belonged to me. I held the purse strings and I could make him pay through the nose. That was your expression, Mamma. Don't you remember how you said to me: "Now you can make him pay through the nose . . ."? We thought that money was the only thing he cared about. He may have thought so, too, but his anger and his sense of humiliation were too much for him. Because, you see, he doesn't love this woman who's stolen him away. He told me so himself, before he left, and he flung so many horrible things in my face that I am sure he was speaking the truth. The point is that she doesn't despise him, and doesn't make him feel like a worm. She gave herself to him: she didn't snatch him. I was just handed to him on a plate!"

She repeated the last words as though she were flagellating herself. Her mother shrugged, but was pleased to see her tears. . . . "She'll feel better after this." Then she went on: "Don't worry, darling, he'll come back. Hunger drives the wolf out of the woods. . . . When he's been roughing it for a bit . . ."

I felt sure that talk like that would only disgust Janine. I got up and took my hat. The idea of spending the rest of the evening with my daughter was more than I could stand. I told her that I had hired a car and was going back to Calèse. Suddenly Janine said:

"Take me with you, Grand'pa. . . ."

Her mother asked her whether she had gone mad. She must stay where she was. The lawyers needed her presence. Besides, she would be "miserable" at Calèse.

She followed me out on to the landing, and attacked me violently for having humoured Janine.

"You must admit that if she gets rid of that creature it'll be a case of good riddance. One can always get an annulment, and with all that money Janine might make a splendid marriage. But she's got to be quit of him first. . . . You always detested Phili, and now you must needs go singing his praises to her. . . . Whatever happens, she mustn't go to Calèse . . . a nice state she'd come back in! Sooner or later, if she stays here, we shall manage to take her mind off her troubles . . . she'll forget. . . ."

Unless she dies, I thought, or drags on a miserable existence with a pain that never lessens, that no lapse of time will ever change. It may be that Janine belongs to that peculiar race of human beings which an old lawyer is best fitted to understand. She may well be one of those women in whom hope is a disease, who can never be cured of hoping, and, at the end of twenty years, still watches the door with the eyes of a faithful dog. I went back into the room where Janine was still seated, and said to her:

"When you're ready, my child. . . . You are always a welcome visitor."

She gave no sign that she had taken my meaning. Geneviève had followed me in, and now said, suspiciously: "What was that you were saying to her?" I learned later that she had accused me of having "changed Janine's mind" during the few seconds I was alone with her, of having "filled her head with all sorts of ideas." I went down the stairs, remembering only that the girl had said "Take me with you. . . ." She had asked me to take her. Instinctively, I had, when talking of Phili, said just what she needed to hear. Maybe I was the first person who had not wounded her susceptibilities.

I walked through Bordeaux. It was the first day of the new term, and the streets were all a-glitter. The mist had left a dampness on the pavements of the Cours de l'Intendance, and they shone. The voices of the noonday crowd drowned the rattle of the trams. I was no longer aware of the smells of my childhood. I might have found them again in the melancholy surroundings of the Rue Dufour-Dubergier, of the Rue de la Grosse Cloche. There, perhaps, I might have come, at some dark street corner, on an old woman hugging a steaming pot of those boiled chestnuts which smell of aniseed. I did not feel sad. Someone had listened to me and had understood. The two of us had come together, and that, in itself, spelled victory. But with Geneviève I had failed. When I am faced by a certain type of idiocy I can do nothing. One can touch a living soul through a curtain of vice and crime no matter how dense and dark: but vulgarity is an insurmountable barrier. Well, it couldn't be helped. I would follow my own line. Impossible to shatter the stones of all these graves. It would mean happiness for me if I could reach to the heart of one single being before I died.

I slept at an hotel and did not return to Calèse until the following morning. A few days later Alfred came to see me, and from him I learned that my visit had had disastrous results. Janine had written Phili a crazy letter in which she said that she had been to blame for everything, and had asked him to forgive her. "Women are all the same. . . ." I knew what the fat idiot was thinking, though he did not dare to put it into words: "She's her grandmother all over again."

He made it quite clear that a suit for separation would now stand no chance of success, and that Geneviève held me responsible. I had worked on Janine. I asked my son-in-law with a smile what possible motives I could have had for doing a thing like that. He didn't, he said, share his wife's point of view, but explained that, according to her, I had acted from malice, from a desire to revenge myself, perhaps even from a sheer love of mischief.

The children did not come to see me again. Two weeks later, Geneviève wrote me a letter in which she explained that they had had to send Janine to a nursing-home. There was no question, of course, of insanity. They had great hopes that, if she were left to herself, she would get better.

I, too, was left to myself. I felt perfectly well. Never had I had so long a respite from my heart. For the whole of that fortnight, and well beyond it, the autumn sunshine lay upon the earth, as though reluctant to depart. Not a leaf had fallen yet, and the roses bloomed again. This new estrangement from my children should have made me suffer. Hubert put in an appearance only when there was business to discuss. He was dry and formal, perfectly polite, but on his guard. The influence which, my children insisted, I had brought to bear on Janine had lost me all the ground that I had gained. In their eyes I was once more the enemy, a treacherous old man, capable of anything. The only one of them all who might have understood me was shut away, and cut off from all communication with the living. But I was conscious only of a deep sense of peace. Stripped of everything, isolated, and with a terrible death hanging over my head, I remained calm, watchful, and mentally alert. The thought of my melancholy existence did not depress me, nor did I feel the burden of my empty years. . . . It was as though I were not a sick old man, as though I still had a lifetime before me, as though the peace of which I was possessed was Somebody.

XX

IT is a month now since Janine ran away from the nursing-home and came here. She is not yet cured. She believes that she has been the victim of a plot, and says that she was shut away because she refused to attack Phili and ask him for a separation and an annulment. The others imagine that it is I alone who have put these ideas into her head, and have set her against them, whereas, if the truth be told, I have been fighting tooth and nail, all through the interminable days at Calèse, against her illusions and her fancies.

Outside, the rain has been rotting the leaves and making them indistinguishable from the mud. Heavy clogs crunch the gravel of the courtyard. A man passes, his head enveloped in a sack. So stripped has the garden become, that there is nothing left to disguise the few poor concessions made to pleasure—mere skeletons of hedgerows, sparse shrubberies shivering under the eternal rain. So penetrating is the dampness of the rooms that, when night comes, we lack the courage to move far from the drawing-room fire. Midnight sounds, but we cannot bring ourselves to go to bed. The embers, patiently piled, collapse in ashes, and I have to renew the old wearisome effort to convince the poor girl that her parents, her brother and her uncle have no malevolent designs on her. I do my best to keep her mind from dwelling on the nursing-home. The conversation always, in the end, comes back to Phili: "You've no idea what he was really like, the kind of man he was at bottom. . . ." I can never feel sure whether these phrases are a prelude to a list of grievances, or to a lyrical outburst. Only the tone in which they are spoken gives me a clue, makes it possible for me to know whether she is about to sing his praises or bespatter him with mud. In either case, the facts which she produces seem to me to be equally insignificant. The poor creature is entirely without imagination, but love has given her an extraordinary power of distortion and amplification. I know her Phili only too well. He is one of those completely negative human beings whom youth, for one fleeting moment, manages to invest with glamour. To this spoiled child, born with a silver spoon in his mouth, she attributes subtleties of feeling, capabilities of villainy and premeditated treacheries—though, as a matter of fact, he is nothing but a mass of automatic reflexes.

What she won't understand is that what he really needs is to feel that he is strong. It was no use trying to bully him. Dogs of his type don't respond to that kind of treatment. They merely slink away and pick up what they can find lying to hand.

She hasn't got the remotest idea of what he is really like. All she knows is that she longs to have him with her. All she feels is a hunger for the endearments which he withholds, and bitter jealousy and horror at the thought that she has lost him. Without eyes to see, a nose to smell, nerves to feel, she runs after him in a demented way, without having the faintest idea of what it is she is pursuing. . . . Are fathers ever really blind? Janine is my granddaughter, but were she my daughter I should still see her for what she is—one of those women who are incapable of receiving anything from another person. With her regular features, her thick, heavy body, and her foolish voice, she is marked with the sign of those who never catch the eye or fill the mind. Nevertheless, when I sit talking to her at night, I find a sort of beauty in her, a beauty not her own but borrowed from despair. Surely there must be a man somewhere whom this display of heat and flame might attract? At present she is burning away unhappily in a waste land beneath a darkened sky, with nobody to see her but an old crock.

Though I have come to pity her in the course of our long vigils, I never tire of making comparison between Phili, who is as like a million others as one white butterfly is like all other white butterflies, and this frenzy of passion which he alone can rouse in his wife, so that nothing else in the whole world, visible or invisible, exists for her. Janine can, quite literally, see nothing but this slightly shop-soiled male who prefers drink to most other forms of self-indulgence, and looks on love as a labour, a duty and a bore. . . . What a tragedy it is!

Sometimes her daughter slips into the room, but she scarcely looks at her, just kisses her curly head in a mechanical sort of way. Not that the child is wholly without influence on her. It was because of her that Janine screwed herself to the point of abandoning her pursuit of Phili (she is quite capable of hounding him, goading him, and making scenes in public). *I* couldn't have stopped her. It is for the child's sake that she has stayed on here. But motherhood has brought her no consolation. It was in my arms, on my knees, that the little girl sought refuge one night as we sat waiting for dinner to be announced. There was a bird-like, nest-like fragrance in her hair which brought back memories of Marie. I closed my eyes and pressed my lips to her head. I restrained myself from hugging her too tightly, while, in my heart, I called upon my long-dead child. It was Luc, too, whom I felt I was embracing. When she was hot from play she had the same salty taste that I used to find in his cheeks when, tired out from running, he fell asleep at table. On those occasions he could not even wait for the dessert, but would go round the company holding up his drowsy face for good-night kisses. . . .

So it was that I dreamed, while Janine moved about the room, pacing, pacing, within the prison of her love.

I remember another evening when she asked: "What can I do to get rid of this pain? . . . do you think it will ever go away?" There was a frost. I watched her open the window and push back the shutters. She bathed her face, her breast, in the frozen radiance of the moon. I led her back to the fire, and, though I am inexpert in the gestures of love, sat awkwardly beside her with my arm about her shoulders. Was there nothing, I asked, that could bring her comfort? "You have your faith." "Faith?" she said vaguely, as though she had not understood. "Yes," I went on, "God. . . ." She raised her ravaged face, and her eyes were full of suspicion. At last she said that she "couldn't see the connexion," but I was insistent, and she continued:

"I'm religious, if that is what you mean. I go to church. Why do you ask me a question like that? Are you laughing at me?"

"Are you quite certain," I went on, "that Phili is really worth all this pain and torment?"

She looked at me with the same morose, irritated expression hat I am used to seeing on Geneviève's face when she doesn't understand what has been said to her, doesn't know what answer to make, and fears a trap. Finally, she plucked up courage to say that the two things "had nothing to do with one another" . . . that she didn't like mixing up religion with matters of this kind, that she was a practising Christian and regularly performed her religious duties, but that she had a horror of morbidity. She might have been saying that she always paid her taxes. It is precisely the attitude that, all my life, I have loathed and detested, the caricature and mean interpretation of the Christian life which I had deliberately chosen to regard as the essence of the religious mind, in order that I might feel free to hate it. One must have the courage to look what one hates full in the face. . . . But had I not already been guilty of self-deception, I asked myself, when, on the terrace at Calèse, the Abbé Ardouin had said: "You are a very good man"? Later, I had shut my ears so as not to hear Marie's words as she lay dying. Nevertheless, at her bedside the secret of death and of life had been revealed to me. . . . A little girl had been dying for me . . . that was something that I had tried to forget. With untiring assiduity I have always tried to find some way of losing the key which a mysterious hand has invariably given to me at the great turning-points of my life (the expression of Luc's face after Mass on

Sunday mornings when the grasshoppers were beginning to scrape, and again this spring, on the night of the hailstorm . . .).

So ran my thoughts that evening. I remember getting up and pushing back my chair so violently that Janine gave a start. The silence of Calèse at that late hour, a thick, an almost solid silence, numbed and muted her grief. She let the fire die down, and, as the room grew colder, moved her chair closer to the hearth until her feet were almost touching the embers. The dying flames seemed to exert a kind of attraction on her hands and face. The lamp on the chimney-piece shone down on her heavy, crouching figure, while I wandered about among the mahogany and rosewood in the encumbered dark. Impotently I prowled around that lump of humanity, that bruised and beaten body. "My child . . .," I began, but could find no words for what I wanted to say. . . . Something, as I sit to-night writing these lines, is stifling me, something is making my heart feel as though it would burst—it is the Love whose name at last I know, whose ador . . .

* * * * *

Calèse, 10th December, 193 . . .

My dear Geneviève:

The drawers here are positively bursting with papers, but I hope, by the end of this week, to have got them into some sort of order. My immediate duty, however, is to send on to you at once the strangest of strange documents. You know that our father died at his desk, and that Amèlie found him on the morning of the 24th November with his face fallen forward on an open note-book. It is this book which is now on its way to you by registered post.

I am afraid that you will be as pained as I was when you read it. . . . Fortunately, the writing is so bad that the servants will make nothing of it. At first, from motives of delicacy, I decided to keep it from you, thereby saving you a good deal of distress, for it contains passages in which father speaks of you in a way that cannot but wound your susceptibilities. But then I wondered whether I had any right to keep to myself something which is yours as much as mine. You know how scrupulous I am in all that pertains to our parents, and I feel sure that you will understand what prompted me to change my mind. None of us, if it comes to that, shows up very well in these embittered pages. They tell us, alas! nothing that we have not long known. The contempt with which father treated me poisoned my early years. For a considerable period of my life I had no confidence in myself. I quailed beneath that pitiless eye, and it was a long time before I even began to realize my true worth.

I have forgiven him, however, and perhaps I ought to add that what now urges me to bring this document to your notice is, for the most part, a sense of filial duty. Judge him how we may, there can be no doubt that our father emerges from these pages—in spite of the horrible things he says—I won't say as more noble, but certainly as more human (I am thinking, in particular, of his love for our sister Marie, and for young Luc—of which there is much moving evidence). I am in a far better position now to understand the grief which he displayed when our mother died, grief which, at the time, came to us as a staggering surprise. You thought it, I remember, to some extent put on. Should what is there written do no more than throw a light on the feelings which lay so deeply buried beneath the surface of his relentless pride, your reading of his confession will amply compensate for the pain it must otherwise, my dear Geneviève, cause you.

I am grateful for it—as I think you too will be—if only because it serves to ease our conscience. I am by nature a worrier. No matter how many reasons I may have for feeling that I am in the right, a very little will start me on a long process of self-examination. For one who has developed moral sensibility, as I have done, to a high degree, life can never be easy. Pursued by a father's hatred, I have never had recourse to even the most legitimate methods of defence, without being oppressed by feelings of anxiety—I would even say, of remorse. Had it not been that I was the head of the family, and, as such, responsible for the honour of our name and the well-being of our children, I should often have been tempted to give up the struggle rather than suffer those torments and strugglings of the spirit of which you have, more than once, been a witness.

I thank God who, in His mercy, has seen fit to justify me through these, our father's, written words. In the first place they provide confirmation of what we had long suspected about his various schemes for depriving us of our birthright. It is not without a sense of shame that I read about the ways in which he hoped to establish a hold over both Bourru the lawyer and that young chap Robert. Over these disgraceful incidents it is well that we should cast the mantle of Noah. Still, the fact remains that it was my bounden duty to frustrate, at any cost, his many abominable machinations. This I did, and with a success of which I see no reason to be ashamed. Of one thing, my dear sister, you may rest assured, that you owe your fortune to *me*. In what he has written, the wretched man tried hard to convince himself that the hatred which he felt for us died a sudden death. He takes pride in announcing that all concern for worldly goods left him in a flash. I must confess that when I read that I found it very difficult not to laugh. But it is worth noticing the precise moment of this unexpected change of front. It occurred just when his schemes had gone awry, when his natural son had agreed, for a price, to tell us what he knew of them. It was not easy for him to get rid of so huge a fortune. Plans which it had taken him years to perfect could not be rearranged in a few days. The truth of the matter is that the poor man felt his end to be near, and had neither the time nor the means to disinherit us except in the manner which he had decided to adopt, and which we providentially discovered.

As a lawyer he was unwilling to lose his case in the court either of his own or of our judgment. Consequently, he was cunning enough—though half-unconsciously, I admit—to transform actual defeat into moral victory. He persuaded himself that he was no longer interested, that he had become detached from the things of this world. . . . What else could he have done? I, certainly, am not prepared to have dust thrown in my eyes, and I feel pretty sure that you have enough good sense to agree. We need not, I think, go out of our way to admire or to be grateful.

There is another point of which this narrative lifts a weight from my conscience. It is something about which I have long indulged in heart-searchings, though I have never succeeded, I must admit, in altogether ridding myself of a pricking sense of guilt. I refer to the efforts we made—though they came to nothing—to get the view of a specialist on the subject of father's mental condition. I ought, I think, to make it clear that much of my uneasiness on this score sprang from the attitude taken by my wife. I never, as you know, attach very much importance to her opinion. No one could well be less capable than she of holding balanced views on any subject. But in this matter of the specialist she gave me no rest, night or day, and was for ever dinning into my ears arguments, some of which, I now admit, did go home and did make me feel uncomfortable. She succeeded at last in convincing me that father, who had been a great Chancery barrister, a shrewd man of business, and a profound student of psychology, must be good-sense incarnate. . . . Nothing is easier than to paint an ugly picture of children who try to get their old father certified so as not to lose their inheritance . . . you see, I am not mincing words . . . and I have, God knows, spent many a sleepless night brooding on the problem.

Well, my dear Geneviève, this note-book, especially in its final pages, provides ample evidence that the poor man was suffering from intermittent delirium. I am prepared to go further, and to say that we should have been fully justified in submitting the case to a psychiatrist. But what is now far more important is that pages containing so much that might prove dangerous to our children must on no account be divulged to any living soul. I may as well say, at once, that I consider it to be your duty to burn what I have sent as soon as you have read it to the end. We *must not* run the risk of it falling under the eyes of a stranger. You cannot but realize, my dear Geneviève, that though *we* have always maintained the strictest secrecy about our family affairs, that though *I* have always taken steps to see that nothing should leak out concerning the uneasiness we have all felt about the mental state of him who, when all's said and done, was the head of the clan, others, not strictly members of it, have been far from showing the same discretion, or even common prudence. Your wretched son-in-law, especially, has been guilty of spreading the most dangerous stories. We are paying a high price for them now, and I am sure that I am not telling you anything that you don't know already when I say it is common talk in Bordeaux that there is a close connexion between Janine's neurasthenia and the eccentricities popularly attributed to your father as a result of Phili's gossiping.

Tear the thing up, then, and don't talk of it to a soul. I would go further, and say—let there be no mention of it even among ourselves. I don't mind admitting that this extreme caution may, in some ways, be a matter for regret. There are in our father's narrative certain psychological observations, certain impressions of nature, which show that his oratorical training had left him with a real gift for writing. That is but one reason the more for destroying it. A nice thing it would be, wouldn't it, if, at some later date, one of the children should think of publishing it?

But there can be no reason why you and I should not call things by their proper names. Now that we have read this record through, we can have few illusions about father's semi-insanity. I can see now what your daughter meant (at the time I took it for a sick woman's whim) when she said: "Grand'pa is the only truly religious person I have ever met." The poor child had let herself be taken in by his vague aspirations and hypochondriacal fancies. All through his life he had been the enemy of his family, hated by everybody, and without a single friend. He had been unfortunate in love, as you will see (there are some very comic details in this connexion!), and so jealous of his wife that he could never forgive her for having indulged in a harmless flirtation when she was a girl. Is it conceivable that, towards the end of his life, he should have felt a desire for the consolations of prayer? I don't think so. What emerges from these pages with dazzling clarity is a state of well-defined mental instability, taking the form of persecution mania and religious hallucination. Is there no trace, you will ask, of genuine Christianity? None at all. Anyone as deeply informed as I am about such matters knows only too well the real value of such outbursts. Not to put too fine a point on it, bogus mysticism of this kind makes me feel physically sick.

But you, being a woman, may feel differently. Should you be inclined, then, to take his religiosity at its face value, all I can say is this: remember that father, with his extraordinary gift for hatred, never loved anything unless it provided him with a *weapon against somebody*. This religious exhibitionism of his amounts only to a criticism, direct or oblique, of the principles in which our mother brought us up from childhood. If he indulged in a murky mysticism, it was only that he might use it as a stick to beat that rational and moderate faith which has always held a place of honour in our family. Truth is poise . . . but I will not plunge deeper into those regions of abstract thought where you would have difficulty in following me. I have said enough. Read the document for yourself. I am impatient to know what you make of it.

I have little space left in which to reply to the important matters on which you have asked my opinion. My dear Geneviève, we are living in days of crisis, and the problems with which we are faced are agonizing. If we keep these piles of bank-notes tucked away in a safe, we shall have to live on capital —and that is always a misfortune. If, on the contrary, we instruct our broker to buy shares, the dividends we may get will be small consolation for the continual fall in the capital value of our investments. Since whatever we do we are bound to lose, the wiser course will be to keep our Bank of France notes. The franc is worth only four sous, but it is backed by an immense gold reserve. On this point father was clear-sighted, and we ought to follow his example. There is one temptation, my dear Geneviève, against which you must fight tooth and nail—the temptation to invest at any price. It is deeply rooted in the French temperament. We shall, of course, have to watch every penny we spend. Should you ever want any advice, you know that I am only too ready to give it. Times are bad, but profitable opportunities may occasionally present themselves. I am, at the moment, keeping a very close eye on a Cinema concern and a new liqueur. Those are the type of investment which the crisis will not touch. In my opinion, it is things of that kind that we ought to watch. We must be bold, but, at the same time, prudent.

I am delighted to know that you have better news of Janine. I don't think that her excessive religious devotion which makes you uneasy need be considered as a serious danger. The important thing is that she should stop thinking about Phili. Her natural sense of proportion will reassert itself. She belongs to a race which has always known how not to misuse the *really good things*.

Until Tuesday, my dear Geneviève, HUBERT.

Janine to Hubert

My dear Uncle:

I am writing to ask whether you will act as judge between Mamma and me. She won't let me read Grand'pa's Journal, because she says it would damage the devotion I have to his memory. But if she's so keen that it shouldn't be damaged, why does she keep on saying: "You've no idea what awful things he says about you. He doesn't even spare your looks . . ."? I am even more surprised that she should be so eager for me to see the very harsh letter in which you expressed your views about the Journal. . . .

Now, for the sake of peace and quiet, she says she'll let me have it if you think I may, and that she leaves the decision entirely to you. I am making this appeal, therefore, to your sense of justice.

Let me dispose at once of the first objection. It concerns me, and me alone. No matter how hard Grand'pa may be on me, he can't be harder than I am on myself, and I am quite sure that the sharp edge of his criticism spares the unhappy girl who spent one whole autumn with him in the house at Calèse, up to the time of his death.

Forgive me, Uncle, if I contradict you on one essential point. I am the only witness in a position to pronounce on the state of Grand'pa's feelings during those last weeks of his life. You denounce what you call his vague and morbid religiosity. But let me tell you this: he had three interviews (one at the end of October and two in November) with the Curé of Calèse, whose evidence, for some reason that I can't fathom, you refuse to accept. According to Mother, the Journal, in which he set down the most trivial incidents of his life, says nothing about those interviews, which wouldn't be the case if they had really been the occasion of a change in himself. . . . But she says, too, that it breaks off in the middle of a word. I have no doubt at all that death surprised your father at the very moment when he was about to make his declaration of faith. It's no use your saying that if he had received absolution he would have taken Communion. I can only repeat what he told me the day before he died, that he was weighed down by a sense of unworthiness. The poor man had made up his mind to wait until Christmas. What reason have you for not believing me? Why treat me as though I were the victim of an hallucination? His voice is fresh in my memory. I can hear it now as it was when he spoke to me on the Wednesday, which was the day before his death, in the drawing-room at Calèse. He said how eagerly he was looking forward to Christmas. It sounded as though he was in a condition of great mental suffering. Maybe the shadow of death was already upon him.

Don't be afraid, Uncle. I am not trying to make him out a saint. I agree with you that he was a terrible, even at times a dreadful, man. That doesn't alter the fact that a great light shone upon him during those last days of his life, and that it was he, and he alone, who, at that moment, took my face between his hands, and entirely changed my way of looking at things. . . .

Doesn't it occur to you that your father might have been quite a different man if only *we* had been different? Don't accuse me of throwing stones at you. I know your good qualities, and I know that Grand'pa was cruelly unjust both to you and to Mother. The real misfortune for all of us was that he took us for exemplary Christians. . . . Don't protest. Since he died I have seen much of people who, in spite of all their faults and weaknesses, live according to their faith and move about their daily tasks in the fullness of Grace. If Grand'pa had lived among them, mightn't he have discovered years ago the harbour which he reached at last only on the very threshold of death?

Let me say again that it is not my intention to abuse my family in the interest of its implacable head. I don't forget (far from it) that poor Grand'ma's example might, in itself, have been enough to open his eyes, had he not preferred to glut his feelings of resentment. But I do want you to know why, in the last resort, I feel that he was right in his attitude towards us. Where our treasure was, there were our hearts also. We thought of nothing but the threat to our inheritance. No doubt there was ample excuse for us. You were a business-man, I was a poor weak woman. But that doesn't alter the fact that, with the single exception of Grand'ma, we never let our principles interfere with our lives. Our thoughts, our desires, our actions, struck no root in the faith to which we paid lip-service. All our strength was employed in keeping our eyes fixed on material things, while Grand'pa . . . I wonder whether you will understand what I mean when I say that where his treasure was, there his heart was *not*? I am quite sure that on this point the document which you won't let me read contains conclusive evidence.

I do hope, Uncle, that you will see what I mean, and I await your reply with confidence.

JANINE.

THE FRONTENAC MYSTERY

Comme un fruit suspendu dans l'ombre du feuillage,
Mon destin s'est formé dans l'épaisseur des bois.
J'ai grandi, recouvert d'un chaleur sauvage,
Et le vent qui rompait le tissu de l'ombrage
Me découvrit le ciel pour la première fois.
Les faveurs de nos dieux m'ont touché dès l'enfance;
Mes plus jeunes regards ont aimé les forêts,
Et mes plus jeunes pas ont suivi le silence
Qui m'entrainait bien loin dans l'ombre et les secrets.

MAURICE DE GUÉRIN

PART ONE

I

XAVIER FRONTENAC glanced shyly at his sister-in-law. She was sitting very upright on the chair which she had drawn to the fire. She made no use of its back, and she was knitting. He could see that she was annoyed, and tried to remember what he had said at dinner. His remarks, in retrospect, seemed to him to have been completely innocent of offence.

His eyes were focused on the great bed with its twisted columns, in which eight years before, his brother, Michel Frontenac, had died with such agonizing slowness. In imagination he could still see the head thrown back, the massive neck, the unshaven stubble, and the cloud of June flies which he had been unable to keep from settling on the sweat-covered face. Nowadays, they might have tried trepanning. Michel might have been saved, might be with them now. . . . Xavier could not take his eyes from the bed, from the walls, though it was not in this room that his brother had died. A week after the funeral Blanche Frontenac, and her five children, had left their home in the rue Vital-Carles, and taken refuge on the third floor of the house in the rue de Cursol, where her mother, Madame Arnaud-Miqueu lived. But the old blue curtains, with their patterning of yellow flowers, still hung before the windows and around the bed. The chest-of-drawers and the wardrobe still faced one another as in the old room. On the mantelpiece the bronze statuette of Faith still stood – a woman in a high-necked, long-sleeved dress. Only the lamp was different. Madame Frontenac had bought one of an improved design, much admired by all the members of the family: an alabaster column topped by a glass container in which a broad wick, like a tape-worm, lay soaking. The flame sprouted a cluster of incandescent petals. The shade was a jumble of cream-coloured lace, adorned with bunches of artificial violets.

This marvel served as a lure for the children. They were always hungry for reading. In honour of Uncle Xavier, they were allowed to stay up until half-past nine. The two eldest, Jean-Louis and José, had wasted not a moment before getting down to their books – the two first volumes of Alexandre de Lamothe's *Camisards*. Lying at full length on the floor, with their fingers stuffed in their ears, they were deep in the story, and lost to all else. Xavier Frontenac could see nothing but their round, cropped heads, their projecting ears, their big knees, all scratched and scarred, their grubby legs, and their nailed boots with the laces tied in knots.

Yves, the youngest, whom no one would have thought was ten years old, was not reading. He sat perched on a stool at his mother's side, rubbing his face against her knees, as though trying, instinctively, to get back into the body from which he had emerged. He was thinking that between tomorrow's blackboard, between Monsieur Roche's German lesson, and going to bed, a whole blessed night would intervene. 'I may die – I may fall ill' . . . He had deliberately forced himself to over-eat of every dish.

Behind the bed, the two little girls, Danièle and Marie, sat learning their catechism. Their uncontrollable and stifled laughter could be plainly heard. Even at home the atmosphere of the Sacred Heart isolated them. They could think of nothing but their mistresses and their school-friends, and, quite often, lay talking in their twin beds until as late as eleven o'clock.

Xavier Frontenac looked at the bullet-heads gathered at his feet, at Michel's children, at the last of the Frontenacs. Lawyer and man of business though he was, he felt his throat contract.

His heart beat quicker. This cluster of flesh and blood was his brother's legacy. Being, as he was, indifferent to anything of a religious nature, he would have hated to think that there was even the hint of a mystery in his feelings. The particular characteristics of his nephews meant nothing to him. Jean-Louis was a schoolboy brimming over with life and intelligence; but, had he been no more than a brainless young animal, his uncle would not have loved him less. What gave them value in his eyes had nothing to do with individual qualities.

"Half-past nine," exclaimed Blanche Frontenac; "time for bed – and don't forget to say your prayers."

On the evenings when Uncle Xavier was present, prayers were not said in common.

"Don't take your books upstairs with you."

"How far have you got?" – asked Jean-Louis of his brother.

"I'm just at the bit where Jean Cavalier . . ."

The little girls presented their damp foreheads to their uncle. Yves hung back.

"You *will* come and tuck me up, mamma, won't you?"

"Not if you set such store by it."

The sickliest of her boys looked back at her from the door with an imploring expression. His socks were barely visible above his shoes. His thin little face was all ears. His left lid drooped and almost completely hid the eye.

When the children had gone, Xavier Frontenac continued to observe his sister-in-law. She was still on the defensive. In what way had he wounded her? He had spoken of women who had a strong sense of duty, women of whom she was typical. He did not realize that the widow found praise of that sort peculiarly exasperating. The poor man was for ever, with a sort of heavy insistence, extolling the splendours of sacrifice, declaring that there was nothing lovelier in the world than the faithful devotion of a woman to her dead husband, than her absorption in her children. It was only in terms of the young Frontenacs that she existed for him at all. It never occurred to him that she might be a young and lonely woman, still capable of sadness and despair. He was not interested in her personal destiny. So long as she did not re-marry, so long as she gave herself to the bringing up of Michel's children, he cared little what might happen to her. That was what Blanche could never forgive. Not that she felt any regrets. On the very threshold of her widowhood she had taken stock of her sacrifice and accepted it. Nothing could have made her go back on her decision. But she was a very religious woman, somewhat scrupulous and arid in her piety, and it would never have occurred to her that without God she could have found the strength to live as she had determined to do, for she was young and ardent, and her heart was hungry. If, on this particular evening, Xavier had had eyes to see he might well have felt a moment's pity – seeing the litter of books on the floor, and all the jumble of the abandoned nest – for this tragic mother with the black eyes, and the sick, lined face, in whom the traces of a former beauty still warred with wrinkles and approaching age. Her greying, rather untidy hair gave her the neglected look of a woman who has nothing to look forward to. The black bodice, buttoned down the front, drew attention to her thin shoulders and sagging breast. Everything about her told of fatigue, of that exhaustion felt by a mother whose children are eating her alive. What she wanted was not to be admired and pitied, but to be understood. Her brother-in-law's blind indifference so angered her that she became violent and unjust. As soon as he was not with her, she was overcome with remorse, and beat her breast: but her good resolutions were not proof against the presence of that inexpressive face, of that little man with the blind eyes, for whom she scarcely existed at all, who would gladly have wiped her altogether from his mind.

There was the sound of a small voice. Yves was calling. He could not control his terror, yet dreaded lest he might be heard.

"Oh, that child!"

Blanche Frontenac got up, but went first to the two older boys. They were already fast asleep, with scapulars clutched in their grubby hands. She tucked them in, and, with her thumb, traced a cross upon their foreheads. Then she went into the girls' room. A light was showing under the door. As soon as they heard their mother they extinguished it. Madame Frontenac re-lit the candle. On the table between the two beds some sections of an orange were lying on a doll's plate. Another plate contained nibbled chocolate and a few crumbs of biscuit. The little imps were hiding under the sheets, and Blanche could see no more of them than plaits of hair tied with faded ribbon.

"No dessert . . . and I shall make a note in your conduct book that you have been disobedient."

She removed the remains of the "midnight feast". But, as she closed the door, she heard a little splutter of laughter behind her. In the room next door, Yves was lying wide awake. He alone was allowed to have a night-light. His shadow showed upon the wall, the head looking enormous, the neck no bigger than a flower's stalk. He was sitting up in bed, and crying. He buried his face in his mother's dress, so as not to hear her reproaches. She had meant to scold him, but could hear the wild beating of his heart, could feel against her body the pressure of his skinny ribs and shoulder-blades. At such times, made aware of the almost endless possibilities of suffering in the small creature before her, she was conscious of something very like terror, and fell to comforting him.

"My little silly . . . my little donkey. How many times have I told you that you are not alone? Jesus lives in the hearts of little children. When you are frightened, you should call on him, and he will comfort you."

"No, he won't, because I have committed terrible sins. . . . It's different with you, mummy: when you're there, I know that you are there . . . I can touch you and feel you. . . . Oh, do stay a little longer!"

She told him that he must go to sleep, that Uncle Xavier was waiting for her. She assured him that he was in a state of grace. There was nothing about her little boy, she said, that she did not know. He grew calmer. From time to time, but at long intervals, a sob shook him.

Madame Frontenac tip-toed from the room.

II

AS she entered the room, Xavier Frontenac gave a start.

"I think I must have dropped off . . . I find these tours of inspection round the family estates rather tiring."

"Well, you have no one to blame but yourself" – there was a note of bitterness in Blanche's voice: "why on earth must you choose to live in Angoulême, so far from all of us? You could quite easily have sold your practice after Michel died. It would have been the most natural thing in the world for you to have made your home in Bordeaux, and taken his place in the business. . . . I know, of course, that we hold the majority of the shares, but the man who really runs it is Dussol,

Michel's partner. Not that I have anything against him: he's a thoroughly decent man: still, the fact remains that because of you, my boys will find it increasingly difficult to fit into the family concern."

She realized, even while she was speaking, how unfair it was of her to blame her brother-in-law. His failure to defend himself amazed her. Not one word of protest did he utter, but sat with hanging head as though she had laid her finger on some hidden wound. It would have been so easy for him to have made a case for himself, to have reminded her how, after old Frontenac's death, which had followed hard on the heels of Michel's, he had renounced all his own holdings in the property, and made them over to the children. Blanche, at first, had thought that he had done so in order to free himself from the tiresome necessity of keeping a watchful eye on the estates. But so far was this from being the case, that he had offered to "run" the vineyards, in which he had ceased to have any lot or part, solely in the interests of his nephews. Every other Friday, no matter what the state of the weather, he left Angoulême round about three o'clock, caught a train at Bordeaux which landed him at Langon, where either the victoria or the brougham, according as the day was hot or cold, was waiting for him at the station. About two kilometres from the little town, just before reaching Preignac, on the main road, the carriage turned in at a gate, and Xavier caught the bitter and familiar smell of ancient box.

Two wings, built by their great-grandfather, completely ruined the façade of the eighteenth-century monastery which had been the home of so many generations of Frontenacs. He climbed the curved entrance-steps, and at once his nose was assailed by the peculiar odour which winter damp imparts to old hangings. Though his parents had survived their eldest son for only a short while, the house had remained open. The gardener was still living in one of the cottages on the estate. A coachman, a cook, and a housemaid had stayed on to look after Félicia, old Frontenac's youngest sister, who had been "backward" from birth (it was said that the doctor had been too vigorous in his manipulation of the forceps).

Xavier's first concern, on these occasions, was to look for his aunt. In fine weather, he would find her dawdling under the glass canopy over the porch; in winter, drowsing by the kitchen fire. He showed no fear of the permanently upturned eyes, of which only the veined whites were visible, of the twisted mouth, of the strange fluff of youthful beard around her chin. He kissed the old lady on the forehead with tender respect, for the name of this monstrous apparition was Félicia Frontenac. She was a member of the family, his father's sister, the sole remaining representative of her generation. When the gong sounded for dinner, he approached the poor, mindless creature, gave her his arm, led her into the dining-room, sat her down opposite him, and fastened a napkin round her neck. It was doubtful whether he even noticed the food dribbling from the horrible mouth, or heard her eructations. The meal over, he led her out with the same ceremony, and handed her over to the care of old Jeannette.

Left to himself, he made his way to the immense room in the wing which looked out on to the river and the slope of the hill, the room which, for so many years, he and Michel had shared. In winter-time a fire was kept burning there all day long. In fine weather, the windows were left open, and he could look out at the vineyards and the pastures. A nightingale ceased its song in the catalpa tree where nightingales had always been. . . . Michel, as a young man, used to get up in order to listen to them. In imagination, Xavier could see the white, lanky figure leaning out over the garden. Half asleep, he would call out to him: "Come back to bed, Michel: it's silly to run the risk of catching a cold!" For a bare handful of days and nights the flowering vines would smell of mignonette. . . .

He opened a volume of Balzac, in an attempt to rid himself of ghosts. But the book slipped from his hands. He thought of Michel, and tears came into his eyes.

Always, at eight o'clock next morning, the carriage was waiting, and he spent the day visiting his nephews' land. From Cernès in the marsh, where the grape crop gives a heavy wine, he went to Respide, on the outskirts of Saint-Croix-aux-Monts, where the vines are as good as in Sauterne: then, over towards Couamères, on the Casteljaloux road, where cattle were raised, but always at a dead loss.

Everywhere he went he had to make enquiries, study account books, smell out the tricks and cunning of peasants who would have got the better of him but for the anonymous letters which he found each week in his post. Finally, having done his duty by the children, he returned to the house so worn out that, after a hurried meal, he went straight to bed. He thought that he was sleepy, but sleep would not come. The dying fire woke him with its flicker of low flames on the ceiling and the mahogany chairs – or, in springtime, the nightingale to which the ghost of Michel still listened.

Next morning, being Sunday, Xavier got up late, put on a starched shirt, a pair of striped trousers, a short jacket, made of cloth or alpaca, narrow, pointed button-boots, a bowler or a straw hat, and made his way to the cemetery. The custodian, seeing him approach, made him a sign of welcome. Xavier did his best, with endless tips, to win the man's favour in the interests of the dead. That was the most he could do for them. Sometimes his pointed boots stuck in the mud, sometimes they were covered in dust from the cinder paths. The sanctified earth was a maze of mole-runs. He, a living Frontenac, stood uncovered in the presence of all the Frontenacs who had to dust returned. There was nothing he could say, nothing he could do. Like most of his contemporaries, obscure and eminent alike, he was walled up in his materialism, his determinism, prisoner of a universe that was infinitely more limited than Aristotle's had ever been. He stood, holding his bowler in his left hand while, with his right, just to keep himself in countenance in this city of the dead, he plucked a few overblown roses.

In the afternoon, the five o'clock express took him back to Bordeaux. After buying some cakes and some sweets, he rang his sister-in-law's doorbell. There was a sound of scampering footsteps in the passage. The children cried: "It's Uncle Xavier!" Small hands scrabbled competitively at the latch. Nephews and nieces flung themselves between his legs, eager for parcels.

"I'm sorry, Xavier" – Blanche Frontenac was saying (her second thoughts were always kindly): "you must forgive me – I'm not always mistress of my nerves. . . . You are a model uncle. Of that I need no reminder. . . ."

As always, he seemed not to hear, or, rather, to attach no importance to, what she was saying. With his hands tucked under his coat-tails, he paced the room. With a round and anxious eye he murmured that it was "no good doing things by halves. . . ." Once again the certainty was borne in on Blanche that she had deeply wounded him. She did what she could to reassure him. There was no reason at all, she said, why he should live in Bordeaux if he preferred to stay on in Angoulême, or concern himself with the sale of timber, if he had a liking for the law. She added:

"I know that your practice is small, and does not really take up all your time . . ."

Again, a look of fear came into his eyes, as though he were

terrified lest she might read his secrets. She invariably tried hard to win him over, though the most he ever gave her was a feigned attention. She would have been overjoyed had he confided in her: but there was a wall between them. To her he never spoke of the past, nor, especially, of Michel. He had his memories, but they belonged to him alone. They could be shared with nobody. He honoured her as the mother and protector of the last of the Frontenacs, but regarded her as a member, only, of the Arnaud-Miqueu family, as a woman of great gifts, but, for all that, an outsider. Disappointed, and a prey once more to irritation, she held her peace. Why wouldn't he go to bed? He sat, resting his elbow on his skinny legs, poking the fire as though there were nobody else in the room.

"By the by," he said suddenly: "Jeannette asked me for some patterns of material. It seems that Aunt Félicia needs a new spring dress."

"Ah " – said Blanche – "Aunt Félicia!" Then, prompted by some devil –

"It's high time," she added, "that you and I had a serious talk about Aunt Félicia."

She had won his attention at last. The globular eyes came to rest on her face. What hare was she going to start now? She was so touchy, always so ready to take the offensive, that one could never be sure.

"You must admit that it is scarcely reasonable to pay the wages of three servants and a gardener just to look after a poor, half-witted creature who would be far better tended, and, which is perhaps more important, far more efficiently supervised, in a Home. . . ."

"A Home? . . . Aunt Félicia in a Home?"

She had certainly succeeded in breaking down his reserve! His mottled cheeks, from being red grew purple.

"So long as I live" – he exclaimed in a high-pitched voice –

"Aunt Félicia will never be asked to leave our family house. My father's wishes will be carried out to the letter. He was never separated from his sister. . . ."

"Oh, come now! He used to leave Preignac every Monday morning, give the whole week to business, and not get back from Bordeaux until Saturday evening. It was your poor mother, unaided, who had to cope with Aunt Félicia!"

"And she was only too pleased to do so! . . . You know nothing about our family attitude in such matters. . . . It would never have occurred to her even to wonder . . . Félicia was her husband's sister. . . ."

"That's what *you* think . . . but the poor dear used to pour herself out to me, used to tell me of the long years of solitude when she had had to live in unrelieved intimacy with an idiot. . . ."

Xavier burst out in a fury:

"I refuse to believe that she ever complained; least of all, that she complained to you. . . ."

"You forget that my mother-in-law regarded me as one of the family. She was fond of me. In her eyes I was never a stranger."

"Would you mind leaving my parents out of this?" – he broke in acidly. "Where family duty is in question, the Frontenacs have never considered money. If you find it too much of a burden to defray half the expenses of the Preignac house, I am prepared to shoulder the whole cost myself. You seem to forget, too, that Aunt Félicia had certain rights under our grandfather's will, rights of which my parents took no account when the estate came to be broken up among the heirs. My poor father never bothered his head about the law. . . ."

Blanche, stung to the quick, made no further attempt to hold back what she had been keeping in reserve ever since the argument started:

"I may not be a Frontenac, but I consider it to be my children's duty to contribute to their great-aunt's maintenance, and even to assure the continuance of a ridiculously expensive style of living which she is in no condition to enjoy. Since that is your whim, I bow to it. But what I will not have" – she went on, raising her voice – "is that they should be made the victims of that whim, and that because of you their future happiness should be endangered. . . ."

She broke off. The silence that followed was a carefully calculated effect. He could not, for the life of him, see what she was getting at.

"Aren't you ever afraid of what people may say about her? Has it never occurred to you that she may be regarded as a congenital lunatic?"

"Really! – everyone knows that the poor woman's head was crushed by the doctor's forceps."

"Everyone at Preignac, between 1840 and 1860, knew it: but if you think that the present generation have such long memories, you are very much mistaken . . . No, my dear Xavier: it is time you plucked up courage to look your responsibilities in the face. You insist that Aunt Félicia shall continue to live in the home of her fathers – though, in fact, she makes use of little more than the kitchen – and shall be looked after by three servants who are free to do exactly as they like. For all we know, they may make her life a misery. . . . But it is your brother's children who will suffer for all this when they reach the marrying age. They may well find that all doors are closed to them. . . ."

Blanche's victory was complete – so complete, that she began to feel afraid. Xavier Frontenac had the look of a man who has been utterly crushed. But there was nothing factitious about her anxiety. The idea that Aunt Félicia might be a source of great embarrassment to the children, was of no recent birth.

The threat, however, was not immediate, and she had, perhaps, exaggerated. . . .

Xavier was too honest not to admit defeat:

"I fear that that had never occurred to me. My poor Blanche, where the children are concerned I am terribly thoughtless."

He began to pace up and down the room. His knees were slightly bent, and he dragged his feet. Blanche's anger had evaporated no less quickly than it had formed. Her triumph was already making her feel guilty. There was still time, she protested: everything could be put right. No one in Bordeaux even knew of Aunt Félicia's existence. She wouldn't live for ever, and would soon be forgotten. Seeing that Xavier was still gloomy, she added:

"A great many people think that she had a fall when she was a child. That, in fact, is the general view. . . . I don't believe she has been regarded as an actual lunatic. But, later on, she might be. . . . Our duty is to avert a possible danger. . . . You mustn't let yourself get into a state about it, my poor dear. You know how prone I am to be carried away, how I always exaggerate. . . . I'm made like that."

His breath was coming in little gasping intakes. Both his father and his mother had died, she remembered, of heart trouble. ('I might be the death of him.') He had sat down again by the fire, all hunched in his chair. In an effort to control her thoughts she closed her eyes. Their long, dark lashes softened the hard lines of the embittered face. He did not guess that the woman beside him was humbling herself, was suffering agonies because of her inability to discipline her feelings. The confused muttering of a child, caught in a dream, broke the silence of the room. It was time, said Xavier, to go to bed: he would think over what they had been talking about. She assured him that they had plenty of time, that no decision need be taken immediately.

"I cannot agree with you there: we must act quickly. After all, what is at stake is the children's future."

"You let yourself worry too much," she said briskly: "I know I am always blaming and criticizing you, but, for all that, I do realize that there are not many such uncles in the world. . . ."

He made a gesture which might have meant – "you don't know . . ." Most certainly he had got something on his conscience, but what it was she could not imagine.

A few minutes later, kneeling at her evening prayer, she tried in vain to bring her mind to bear upon the familiar words. When Xavier next came she really would make an effort to find out more about him. But it wouldn't be easy, because he so rarely gave himself away to anybody, and never to her. . . . She found it impossible to concentrate. It was high time for her to be in bed and asleep: tomorrow morning she must be up early, otherwise José, her youngest, would never do a scrap of preparation before starting for school. He was as regularly at the bottom of his class as Jean-Louis was at the top. It wasn't that he lacked the intelligence, the quickness, of the other two, but only that he seemed to have a positive genius for letting his mind wander, for not listening to what was being said to him. He was one of those boys on whom words make no impact, in whom absent-mindedness ranks almost as a gift; one of those boys who go mentally flaccid when grown-up persons try to get anything out of them, who sit over their torn school-books and smudged notes in a mood of heavy listlessness. Their minds, nimble enough in other respects, are far away among the tall Whitsun grasses, along the river bank, intent on crayfish. Blanche knew that for three-quarters of an hour she would struggle in vain with this sleepy child of hers, who would be as incapable of concentrating, as empty of thought, and even of life, as an abandoned chrysalis.

Would she, when the children had gone, bother about breakfast? Yes, of course she would: no purpose could be served by starving herself. . . . How, after the way she had behaved this evening to her brother-in-law, could she take Communion? . . . Then there would be the Charity Organization, and, after that, her meeting with the architect to discuss the house in the rue St. Catherine. And, of course, she must find time to visit her poor. She must remember, too, to look in at Potine's to arrange for a parcel of groceries to go to the Rescue Home. I am particularly devoted to this Charity . . . In the evening, after dinner, when the children had gone to bed, she would run downstairs to see her mother. Her sister would be there, with her husband. Perhaps Aunt Adila, too, or the Abbé Mellon, the senior priest of the parish. . . . There are women who know what it is to be loved. . . . Now that she had got all these children no one would ever want to marry her unless for her money. . . . That was not quite true. . . . She had every reason to believe that she was still attractive. . . . There had been incidents – but she mustn't think of them. But hadn't she, perhaps, begun to think of them a little? . . . Above all, none of this scrupulosity. There could be no question of her depriving her children of any part of herself, however small. . . . There was nothing meritorious in that decision, it was just the way she was made. . . . She was so sure that they would pay in their flesh for any evil action of hers . . . and yet, that was a baseless fear, as she very well knew. She was condemned for ever to sacrifice herself for her children. The knowledge of that had been a cause of much suffering. . . . A woman with nothing to look forward to . . . I am a woman with nothing to look forward to . . . She pressed her hands to her eyes, and drew her fingers down her face . . . must really make an appointment with the dentist . . .

A voice called to her. Yves again! She tip-toed to his room.

He was asleep, but restless. He had thrown off his blankets. One brown, emaciated leg was hanging over the side of the bed. She covered him up and tucked him in. He turned his face to the wall, muttering uneasily. She touched his forehead and his neck, thinking that he might be feverish.

III

UNCLE XAVIER turned up regularly, every other Sunday. But his sister-in-law came no nearer to discovering his secret. His reappearances were, for the children, no less to be counted upon than the monthly whole holiday, than the weekly Communion, than the recurrent "Essay", and the reading over of Friday's notes. He was a fixed star in the sky of childhood, his movements so adjusted to a clockwork precision, that nothing unusual, it seemed, could possibly interrupt their sequence. Blanche might have been tempted to believe that she was dreaming, had it not been that his silences, his air of absorption, his restlessness, his unseeing stare, and the puckered expression on his round face (as though some fixed idea were working in his mind) reminded her of the time when she, too, had been going through a crisis of scruple. This deeply religious woman could detect in the brother-in-law to whom religion meant nothing, the symptoms of that same ailment of which Father de Nole had cured her. She knew that trouble all too well, and would, if she could, have reassured him. But he gave her no chance of coming to grips. Still, she had, blessedly and all unexpectedly, reached a point at which she could, at least, be sure that she no longer irritated him. Far less than formerly did they get on one another's nerves. Did he realize the extent of her efforts? She, who once had been so jealous of her authority, now asked his advice on everything that had to do with the children. Did he think it would be a good thing to buy a saddle-horse for Jean-Louis, who was the best rider in the school. Ought she to make Yves take riding-lessons, in spite of his fear of horses? Would it be advisable to let José become a boarder?

Fires were no longer necessary, nor even lamps. The only place in the whole house which remained dark was the corridor, up and down which, for a few minutes before dinner, Blanche would walk, saying her Rosary, with Yves at her heels, holding up her dress with two hands, lost in a dream of magnificence which he would share with no one. The air was filled with the chirruping of swifts. The noise of the trams in the Cours d'Alsace made it impossible to hear oneself speak. The ships' sirens seemed to bring the harbour to their very door. The heat, said Blanche, would melt the children's brains. They invented idiotic games, such as staying in the dining-room when dinner was over, with their napkins on their heads, then hiding away in some obscure corner and rubbing noses – which they called playing at "Communities".

One Saturday in June, when Blanche had long given up thinking about Uncle Xavier's secret, the key to it was suddenly put into her hand. Light shone suddenly from the most unexpected of quarters. The children had retired to bed, and she had gone down, as usual, to see her mother. After passing through the dining-room where the table had not yet been cleared, and a strong scent of strawberries hung on the air, she had opened the door of the small drawing-room. Madame Arnaud-Miqueu was sitting in a leather armchair which she completely filled. She called to her daughter, and kissed her with the almost ravenous intensity which was habitual with her. Blanche could see on the balcony her brother-in-law Caussade, her sister, and the huge bulk of Aunt Adila, Madame Arnaud-Miqueu's sister-in-law. They were laughing and talking at the tops of their voices, and would have been audible to all the neighbours, had it not been that everyone within hearing distance was being equally clamorous. Down in the street some boys were singing:

> "*Et l'enfant disait au soldat:*
> *Sentinelle, ne tirez pas*
> *C'est un oiseau qui vient de France!*"

Aunt Adila caught sight of her:

"This is no place for you, Blanche, my dear!"

Caussade shouted above the din of the trams:

"I was hoping you'd come. . . . I've got a piece of news for you, a real gem. . . . Keep a tight hold on yourself, you'll never guess!"

"Come on, Alfred, out with it!" – broke in his wife: " she's given it up as a bad job."

"The fact is, my dear, I happened to be appearing yesterday in a case at Angoulême, and it came to my knowledge that your Monsieur Xavier Frontenac is quite openly and blatantly keeping a woman . . . what d'you say to that?"

His wife interrupted him: if he wasn't careful, he'd frighten Blanche, and get her all worked up!

"It's nothing to worry about. No fear of his ruining his nephews. From what I can hear, the poor creature of his choice is scarcely living in what might be called guilty luxury."

Blanche cut him short with the driest of dry comments. She was quite easy on that score, she said, and, in any case, Xavier Frontenac's private life was none of her business – or of theirs.

"See, she's gone all hoity-toity: I told you she would."

"She bullies him like anything herself, but as soon as anybody else says a word, she's up in arms!"

Blanche protested that there was no question of her being what they called "up in arms". Since Xavier, unfortunately for himself, was completely devoid of religious feelings, she couldn't see what there was to stop him from behaving just exactly as he liked.

The voices became less strident. Alfred Caussade, in order to calm his sister-in-law's fears, explained that Xavier Frontenac was an almost legendary figure in Angoulême, where the meanness with which he treated his lady-friend had made him a positive laughing-stock. There was no need for Blanche to lose a moment's sleep. The poor woman earned her living by doing odd jobs of sewing, and he wouldn't hear of her giving up her work. He had furnished a room for her on the cheap, and paid her rent. That was the full extent of his generosity. The thing was a public scandal . . . at which point, Alfred stopped, considerably abashed. Blanche, who was quite unperturbed by dramatic situations, had folded up her work and risen from her chair. She kissed Madame Arnaud-Miqueu, and left the room without addressing a word to her embarrassed relatives. The spirit of the Frontenacs had taken complete possession of her, so that she shook like a Pythian priestess. When she got upstairs, her hand was trembling so violently, that she could scarcely put the key in the lock.

She had come back a good two hours earlier than usual, and it was still daylight. She found the three boys squatting at the window in their nightgowns. They were spitting on the sill and rubbing away at the moist patch with an apricot stone. The object of this proceeding was to wear down the two sides of the stone until it was thin enough to pierce, after which the kernel could be extracted with a needle. If they went on long enough their labours would be rewarded with a whistle, though it never functioned as such, and was always, eventually, eaten. They were amazed at the mildness of their mother's scolding, and scampered away like rabbits. Blanche Frontenac's mind was entirely occupied with the thought of Xavier. She would be seeing him on the next evening, which was one of his regular Sundays. She conjured up a picture of him as he must be at this moment, alone in the huge dead house at Preignac.

On that same evening, Xavier Frontenac had spent a short while sitting under the glass awning. But the heat in the vineyards had been intense, and he was afraid of catching a chill. He wandered about for a moment or two in the hall, and then decided to go upstairs. Far more than the rainy nights of winter, when the fire kept him company and tempted him to read, did he dread these June twilights, "Michel's evenings". In the old days he had laughed at Michel because of his mania for quoting Hugo in and out of season. But now, some of those quotations, rich with the modulations of that loved voice, came back into his mind. He must remember them, so as to hear again his brother's monotonous and muted tones. And so it was that this evening, close to the open window, with the river invisible beyond, Xavier recited to himself, with varying intonation, as though seeking some particular note, some special harmony:

Nature au front serein, comme vous oubliez!

The meadows were strident. As always, the darkness was loud with the croaking of frogs, with laughter, and with the barking of dogs. Leaning from the window, the lawyer from Angoulême spoke aloud, as though each word were being whispered in his ear:

A peine un char lointain glisse dans l'ombre, écoute. . . . Tout dort et se repose et l'arbre de la route. . . . Secoue au vent du soir le poussière du jour. . . .

He turned his back on the window, lit a cheap cigarette, and, as his habit was, began to shuffle up and down the room, with the bottom of his trouser-leg caught between ankle and slipper. He was, he kept saying to himself, betraying Michel in the persons of his children. He chewed at the cud of an old remorse. When he had taken his Law Finals in Bordeaux, he had already been acquainted with this woman. Even in those days she had been shop-soiled, and there had been little in age between them. Why she had had such influence over him he did not seek to discover. In order to answer that question he would have had to probe the mystery of his shyness and his phobias, of his ineffectiveness and of his morbid anxieties. She was a kindly creature with a strong maternal instinct, and she did not laugh at him. In that, perhaps, lay the secret of her power.

Even while Michel was still living, Xavier had accepted the irregular relationship with anything but a light heart. Strictness in morals was traditional in the Frontenac family, and the product not so much of religion as of a republican and peasant past. Neither Xavier's grandfather nor his father could endure dirty talk, and the highly reprehensible domesticities of Uncle Péloueyre, Madame Frontenac's elderly bachelor brother, whose family had inherited the estate of Bourideys, in Les Landes, had always been regarded as a crying scandal. Gossip had it that he used to receive his paramour at Bourideys, in the very house where his parents had died, and that she used to have the effrontery to let herself be seen on the front-door step, at eleven o'clock in the morning, wearing a pink wrap, with nothing on her feet, and her hair hanging down her back. It was in her room in Bordeaux that Uncle Péloueyre had died on the very same day that he had gone into town to make a will in her favour. It gave Xavier the horrors to think that he was following in the old man's footsteps, that he was continuing, without meaning to, the same tradition of dissipation. . . . He only hoped that the family would never know anything about it, would never discover his shameful secret! Fear that they might do so had been behind his decision to buy a practice at some little distance from Bordeaux. He had hoped that the silence of Angoulême might close about his private life.

When Michel died, the family had left him no time to brood over his sorrow. His parents, who were still living, and Blanche, had forced him from his condition of dazed misery. They made it quite clear to him what the family had decided. It "went without saying" that he would sell his practice, leave Angoulême, and take Michel's place in the business. Xavier protested in vain that he knew nothing whatever about timber. They assured him that Arthur Dussol, his dead brother's partner, would be there to help him. All the same, he put up a desperate struggle. The idea of giving up Joséfa was more than he could bear, and if they settled down together in Bordeaux, the secret would be public property in next to no time. He would be sure to run into Blanche and the children when he was out walking with her on his arm. . . . The very thought of such an appalling contretemps made him turn pale. Now that he had become his nephews' guardian it was more than ever important that the scandal of his private life should be concealed. After all, with Dussol in charge of the business there was little likelihood of the children suffering financially, for most of the shares were in Frontenac hands. All that mattered to Xavier was that his manner of life should not be made known. He stuck to his point. For the first time in his life he set himself up against his father, who was already at death's door.

But even after the business difficulties were settled, Xavier had found it impossible to recover his peace of mind. He could not quietly resign himself to his grief. Remorse still gnawed at him – the same remorse as now set him pacing this childhood's room, between his own bed and the one on which he could still, in imagination, see Michel lying. The family property must come to Michel's children: to keep even a penny of it from them would be tantamount to theft, but it so happened that he had promised Joséfa to deposit in her name on each successive first of January, for the next ten years, the sum of ten thousand francs. It was an understood thing that this should be the sum total of his responsibility, except that, during his life-time, he should continue to pay her rent, and allow her a monthly sum of three hundred francs. By skimping himself (his avarice was a standing joke in Angoulême) he managed to save twenty-five thousand francs a year, but of this only fifteen thousand went to his nephews. He was regularly stealing – so he put it to himself – ten thousand francs each year from them, to say nothing of what he was paying currently to Joséfa. It was true, no doubt, that he had surrendered all claims to profits from the estate, and that, after all, everyone is free to do what he likes with his income: all the same, there did exist a secret law, an obscure law, a Frontenac law, the overriding claims of which he admitted without so much as questioning its justice. He was an old bachelor, and he held what money he had as a sacred trust for the children of Michel, whose physical legacy was apparent in Jean-Louis's black eyes, the tiny birthmark close to Danièle's left ear, and Yves's drooping eyelid.

There were times when he could lull his feelings of remorse into unconsciousness, weeks together when he did not even think of it. But the need to conceal the manner of his life was something that never left him. His one hope was that he would die without the family ever suspecting him of concubinage. On this particular evening he was entirely without suspicion that Blanche was lying wide-eyed in the great pillared bed in which his brother had died, walled in by the airless Bordeaux darkness, thinking about him, and forcing herself to face the strangest of strange duties. Even at the risk of impoverishing her children, she must do all in her power to persuade her brother-in-law to get married. It wasn't enough merely not to dissuade him from regularizing the position. She must actively urge him to do what was right and proper. It was her duty to make this decision, whether or no it was heroic on her part to do so. . . . The very next day, she would force him into the open, would compel him to discuss this burning question, would open her offensive.

But he was far from being responsive to her suggestion. During dinner, Blanche took advantage of some casual remark let drop by Jean-Louis, to say something to the effect that there was still plenty of time for Uncle Xavier to settle down and have children of his own.

"I very much hope," she said, "that he has not given up the idea. . . ."

But he chose to treat the whole thing as a joke, into which he entered whole-heartedly, and proceeded with a certain nimbleness of humour which he could show on occasion, to describe the imaginary lady of his choice, much to the children's delight.

When they had gone to bed, and brother and sister-in-law were leaning together at the window, she made a valiant effort:

"You know, Xavier, I was quite serious in what I said at dinner. I should be quite honestly delighted to hear that you had decided to get married, no matter how late in the day."

His response to this was to say that he had no intention of ever getting married, and this he announced so drily that it was impossible for her to continue the discussion. There was nothing in the incident to arouse his suspicions, for the idea of making Joséfa his wife had never entered his mind. It would be no less than sacrilege to give the Frontenac name to a woman from nowhere, who had played fast and loose with her life. To bring such an individual into his parents' house, to introduce her to Michel's wife and Michel's children, was inconceivable. Consequently it never occurred to him that Blanche might have got wind of his secret. Irritated, but by no means worried, he turned from the window, and asked whether she would very much mind if he went to his room.

IV

SLOWLY the stream of childhood flowed, with that calm regularity which seems to leave no room for chance or accident. Every hour of every day was filled to the brim with its appointed tasks and occupations – breakfast, followed by school; the ride home in the bus; the stairs taken four at a time; the smell of dinner; Mamma; *The Mysterious Island*; bed-time. Even illness had its place (Yves's whooping-cough, José's feverish cold, Danièle's scarlatina) in the ordered sequence of events. It was a source more of pleasure than discomfort, stressing a date, setting a landmark for memory – "the year you had that attack of fever"... A succession of summer holidays opened into the pillared aisles of the Bourideys' pine-woods, and the house now purged of Uncle Péloueyre. Were the noisy cicadas the same as had scraped away a year before? From the wine-growing estate at Respide came hampers of peaches and greengages. Nothing changed except that Jean-Louis's and

José's trousers were lengthened. . . . Blanche Frontenac, once so slim, was developing a middle-aged spread, and beginning to worry about her health. She was convinced that she had got a cancer, and, tormented by this fear, worried incessantly about what would become of the children when she was no longer there. It was she, now, who took Yves in her arms, he who, at times, resisted. She had any number of medicines which had to be taken before and after meals, but never, for a moment, would she let anything interfere with her duty of bringing up Danièle and Marie in the way that they should go. The little girls already showed sturdy legs and large, sagging behinds. They were two little brood-mares in the making, and found an outlet for their maternal cravings in ministering to the children of various washerwomen and chars.

Easter, that year, fell so early that the Frontenac children were back at Bourideys by the end of March. Spring was in the air, though as yet the material signs of it were few. The oaks in their dress of last year's leaves seemed still constricted by the hand of death. From beyond the meadows the cuckoo called. Jean-Louis, his small-bore rifle on his shoulder, tramped the woods, fondly thinking he was out after squirrels, though really he was looking for the Spring. Spring prowled through the days of imitation Winter like someone whom one feels quite close but cannot see. Now and again he thought that he could smell it, only to find it gone again. It was cold. For one brief moment the afternoon light touched the trees with a soft finger, so that the pine-bark glowed like scales, its gummy wounds holding the gleam of sunset. Then, suddenly, everything went dull. The West wind drove the heavy clouds so low that they hung about the tree-tops, and drew from the ranks of sombre trunks a prolonged moaning. . . . It was as he approached the meadows watered by the Hure that Jean-Louis came at last upon the Spring caught in the river grasses which were already thick along the banks. It oozed from the sticky and half-opened alder buds. He leaned above the water to watch the living, floating tresses of the weed – the hair of those whose faces must, since the world's creation, have lain buried in the sand which had been worked into ridges by the river's gentle flow. The sun came out again. Jean-Louis leaned his back against an alder trunk, took from his pocket a school edition of the *Discourse on Method*, and for ten minutes paid no more attention to the Spring. Then his attention began to wander. His eyes lighted on the demolished hurdle which he had had put up in August as a jump for his mare "Tempest". He must tell Burthe to mend it. He would ride over tomorrow morning to Léojats . . . he would see Madeleine Cazavieilh. . . . The wind had moved into the east, and came to him rich with village smells – turpentine, warm bread, the smoke of wood-fires cooking humble meals. The mingled scent augured fine weather and filled the boy with happiness. . . . He began to walk through the grasses already drenched with moisture. Primroses were glowing on the sloping bank which closed the meadow to the west. The young man crossed it, skirted a recently cleared patch of heath, and made his way down the hill again towards the oak coppice through which the Hure flowed on its way to the mill. Suddenly he stopped dead, choking back a laugh. A queer little cowled monk was seated on a pine-root. He was holding a school exercise-book in his right hand, and was intoning to himself in a low voice. It was Yves, who had pulled the hood of his cape over his head, and was sitting there, stiff, still and mysterious, quite sure that he was alone, and behaving as though the angels had charge over him. Jean-Louis no longer wanted to laugh, because there is always something faintly terrifying in the sight of someone who believes himself to be unobserved. He felt shocked, as though he had broken in on a forbidden mystery. His first instinct was to move away and leave his younger brother to his incantations. But the love of teasing, all-powerful at that age, set him creeping towards the innocent object of his attention, whose sense of hearing was deadened by his hood. He hid behind an oak, a stone's throw from the root on which Yves sat enthroned, though too far from him to catch the sense of the words which escaped on the West wind. Then, with one bound, he was on top of his victim and, before the younger boy could so much as utter a cry, had snatched the exercise-book from his hand, and was racing at top speed for the park.

We never fully measure the effect of what we do to others. Jean-Louis would have been deeply distressed could he have seen the expression on the face of his younger brother, who stood there on the heath, as though turned to stone. . . . In a sudden access of despair, he flung himself to the ground, and lay with his face buried in the sand, muffling his cries. What, unknown to anyone, he had written, what was his, and his alone, what was a secret between himself and God, had been given now to others to mock and laugh at. . . . He began to run towards the mill. Was he, perhaps, thinking of the weir in which some years before a child had been found drowned? More likely, by far, that he had in mind, as often previously, to run just on and on, and never to go home again. But soon he was out of breath. His progress was slow because of the sand in his shoes, and because a pious child is ever borne up by angels. . . . "For he shall give his angels charge over thee: to keep thee in all thy ways. They shall bear thee in their hands: that thou hurt not thy foot against a stone. . . ." Suddenly a comforting thought came to him. Nobody in the world, not even Jean-Louis, could decipher his secret writing. It was more illegible even than the writing which he used at school. And what *could* be made out would be unintelligible. It was idiotic to work himself into a state. How could others possibly understand a language to which even he sometimes lacked a clue?

The sandy path ended at the bridge leading to the mill. The meadows were hidden by the mist that rose from them. The mill's old heart was still beating in the gathering dusk. A horse's rough head was hanging over the half-door of the stable. The low-built, humble, cottages with their smoking chimneys, the stream, the meadows, all combined to make a little clearing of greenery, of flowing water, and of hidden life, framed within the ancient pine-trees of the parish. Yves had his own ideas about them. At this hour the mystery of the mill must not be disturbed. He retraced his steps. The first bell began to sound for dinner. A shepherd's sharp cry rang through the wood. He found himself caught in a rushing tide of dirty wool, and his nose was assailed by a powerful stench of grease. He could hear the lambs before he saw them. The shepherd did not return his greeting, and his heart felt heavy. By the great oak, which marked the beginning of the long ride, Jean-Louis, holding the exercise-book in his hand, was on the look-out for him. Yves stopped, a prey to uncertainty. Should he be angry? A cuckoo uttered its last call over in the trees towards Hurtinat. The two boys stood motionless, a few paces apart. Jean-Louis was the first to move. He took a step forward:

"Not angry with me?"

Yves could never stand out against a kindly word, nor remain proof when a voice had more in it than usual friendliness. Jean-Louis was frequently rough with him, was over-fond of growling that he "needed a good shaking", and, what most exasperated Yves, of saying – "when you get into the army . . ." but this evening all that he remarked was:

"You aren't, are you?"

There seemed nothing to say. Yves put his arm about his

elder brother's shoulder. The latter freed himself from the embrace, but not unkindly.

"You know," he said, "they're most awfully good."

The other looked up, and asked him what was awfully good.

"What you've written . . . they're more than awfully good," he added with enthusiasm.

Together, they walked down the darkening ride between the pines.

"Are you laughing at me, Jean-Louis? – are you pulling my leg?"

They had not heard the second bell. Madame Frontenac came out on to the steps and cried:

"Children!"

"Look here, Yves, let's take a stroll in the park this evening, just the two of us. I want to talk to you: and – oh yes, bring the book."

In the course of the meal, José – who had bad table-manners, wolfed his food – as his mother never tired of telling him – and had not washed his hands, described his trip with Burthe into the heath-lands. The bailiff was training the boy to recognize the estate boundaries. . . . José's sole ambition was to become the "peasant" of the family, but he despaired of ever being able to pick up the boundary marks. Burthe would count the number of pines in a row, make his way through the furze, dig in the ground, and, lo and behold! a buried stone would come to light which had been set there by shepherd ancestors many centuries before. . . . These hidden evidences of tenure, concealed and overgrown, but always there, moved José to a sense of almost religious awe, which doubtless sprang from some hidden depth of race-memory. Yves, forgetful of his food, and glancing furtively at Jean-Louis, let his mind, too, dwell on these boundary marks of mystery. They came to life in his heart. They lay deep in that secret world brought by his poetry from the dark.

The two boys tried to leave the house without being seen. But their mother caught them. "The air's damp down by the stream. . . . Have you got your capes? . . . Whatever you do, keep on the move, and don't loiter."

The moon had not yet risen. The breath of winter was coming from the icy stream and from the meadows. At first they were at a loss to find the path, but very soon their eyes grew accustomed to the darkness. The upward thrust of the serried pines struck at the stars which hung above them, or seemingly, swam in the puddles of clear sky framed in the black tree-tops. . . . Yves, as he walked, felt that some weight had been lifted from him, that, deep within himself, a stone had been loosed by that elder brother who, from the distance of his seventeen years, was speaking to him in short embarrassed sentences. He didn't, he said, want to make Yves too self-conscious. He was afraid he might trouble the pool from which his inspiration flowed. . . . Yves reassured him, explaining that his poetry was first like hot lava which could not be controlled. Later, when the stuff had cooled, he worked on it, unhesitatingly scrapping adjectives, and removing all the odds and ends of rubbish which had been caught up in the molten mass. The young boy's certainty overcame all Jean-Louis' doubts. How old was Yves? Just turned fifteen . . . would genius outlive childhood?

"Which bits did you like best, Jean-Louis?"

It was an author's question: an author had just been born.

"It's so difficult to choose. I love the passage in which you describe the pines as absolving you from suffering, as bleeding in your stead, and of how you imagine them at night, weeping and growing weaker: the moaning is not theirs, you say, but the voice of the sea caught in their crowded tops. Oh, yes, and then that bit . . ."

"I know," said Yves – "the moon . . ."

They were without knowledge that on a March night in '67 or '68, Michel and Xavier Frontenac had been walking together along this same path. Xavier, too, had said "the moon" . . . and Michel had quoted the line – "*Elle monte, elle jette un long rayon dormant* . . ." Then, as now, the Hure was flowing on its silent way. After thirty years, the water was different, but not the sound of its rippling: and here, beneath the pines, was another love, and yet, the same.

"Mightn't it be a good thing to show them to somebody?" – Jean-Louis asked . . . "it did occur to me that perhaps the Abbé Paquignon" (his Professor of Rhetoric, whom he admired and respected) – "but I'm afraid that even he mightn't understand. He'd say that what you write isn't poetry, and, if it comes to that, it isn't. It's like nothing I've ever read. Criticism might worry you . . . might make you try to correct . . . anyhow, I must think about it."

Yves surrendered to a sense of complete confidence. The fact that Jean-Louis had testified to his productions was enough for him. He relied utterly on his big brother. All of a sudden, he felt ashamed, because they had been talking of nothing but his poems.

"And what about you, Jean-Louis? You aren't going to become a timber-merchant, are you? You won't let them do that to you? . . ."

"My mind's quite made up: the Normale, and a degree in philosophy . . . that's what I've got to do. . . . Isn't that mamma over there on the path?"

She had been afraid that Yves might catch cold, and had come out with a coat for him. When she reached them: "I'm growing heavy on my feet," she said, and leaned on her two sons . . . "are you sure you weren't coughing? Jean-Louis, didn't you hear him cough?"

The sound of their feet on the entrance-steps woke the girls, whose room looked out upon the terrace. The light in the billiard-room was dazzling, and they had to narrow their eyes.

Yves, as he undressed, looked at the moon over the motionless and brooding pines. No nightingale was singing as when his father, at the same age, had leaned from a window above the garden at Preignac. But the owl, perched on a dead branch, had, perhaps, a purer note.

V

NEXT day, Yves was not in the least surprised to find that his elder brother was, once again, his slightly churlish self, and behaved as though there were no secret between them. It was the scene of the previous evening that had seemed strange to him. It is enough for brothers to be aware that they are sprung from the same root, to know that they are twin suckers of the same plant. Such matters are not, as a rule, talked about between them. Of all loves, brotherly love is the least vocal.

On the last day of the holidays, Jean-Louis made Yves go out on "Tempest". As always happened, no sooner did the mare feel the boy's nervous knees against her flanks, than off she started at a gallop. Yves clung shamelessly to the saddle. Jean-Louis cut through the pines, and took up a position in the middle of the ride, with his arms outstretched. The mare pulled up short: Yves described a parabola, and found himself sitting on the sandy earth, while his brother announced that "he'd never be anything but a little sissy".

That was not what had shocked the younger boy. Something there was, however, that had come to him as a disappointment, though he did not like to admit it even to himself. The fact of the matter was that Jean-Louis was still paying frequent visits to the Cazavieilh cousins at Léojats. It was common knowledge to everyone in the family – and in the village, too – that each sandy track led, for Jean-Louis, to Léojats. In years gone by, the Cazavieilhs and the Frontenacs had fallen out over a will. But when Madame Cazavieilh died, they made up their differences though, as Blanche said, "there have never been any very warm feelings between us" . . . Nevertheless, on the first Thursday of each month she had got into the habit of asking Madeleine over. The girl already ranked as one of the seniors at the Sacred Heart, at a time when Danièle and Marie were still very low down in the school.

Madame Frontenac was conscious of two opposed feelings – anxiety on the one hand, pride on the other. She was always slightly uneasy when Burthe reported that "Monsieur Jean-Louis is a frequent visitor. . . ." She feared to see him tied up so young. At the same time, the knowledge that Madeleine would come into her mother's money when she married, was by no means unwelcome. Above all, she hoped that her great strapping son would be saved by a pure and passionate attachment from falling into evil ways.

Yves, for his part, was disappointed when, the day after that unforgettable evening, he learned in a few words exchanged with his brother that the latter had just come back from Léojats. Surely, what he had found in the school exercise-book should have turned his thoughts away from this lesser pleasure? Oughtn't everything, from now on, to seem, by comparison, trivial and colourless? To Yves, this love affair was merely a matter of languorous glances, snatched kisses, and much holding of hands – in fact, of all the romantic rubbish which he held in such contempt. Now that Jean-Louis had penetrated to his secret, had found his way into a world of marvels, what was there for him to seek elsewhere?

No doubt Yves was already aware of the existence of young girls. At High Mass at Bourideys, he admired the female singers, with their long, white necks enhanced by black ribbons, grouped round the harmonium, as on the edge of a shallow bowl, and distending their throats which looked as though they were already chock-full of maize and millet. His heart, too, beat quicker when he saw the Dubuch girl – whose father was the largest landlord of the neighbourhood – ride by on her pony, the dark curls bumping on her skinny shoulders. Compared to this sylph how gross did Madeleine Cazavieilh seem! A great bow of ribbon bloomed on the hair which she wore in a large coil on top of her head (a door-knocker, Yves called it). She almost always sported a bolero, very short under the arms, which accentuated the roundness of her buxom figure, and a skirt which "flared" from a remarkably full waist-line. When Madeleine Cazavieilh crossed her legs it was evident that she had no ankles. . . . What charm could Jean-Louis find in this lumpish young woman in whose placid face not a muscle ever seemed to stir?

If the truth be told, Yves, his mother, and Burthe, would have been not a little surprised could they have been present at those visits: so little of any kind happened. It was as though Jean-Louis had come to see, not Madeleine, but Auguste, Cazavieilh. One great passion only did they have in common, horses, and so long as the old man was with them, conversation never flagged. But in the country there is never any peace and quiet. Some farmer, or some local tradesman, is always sure to want a word with the master. It is impossible to keep the front-door shut as in a town. The two young people dreaded the moment when Monsieur Cazavieilh would leave them alone together. Madeleine's calm exterior deceived all the world – except Jean-Louis. Perhaps what he loved in her more than anything else was a hidden surge of restlessness, invisible to others, which, as soon as they were left alone, broke through her seeming imperturbability.

On the occasion of Jean-Louis's last visit before the end of the Easter holidays, they walked together under the old leafless oaks which stood in front of the freshly plastered house, the walls of which bulged with age. Jean-Louis was talking about what he planned to do after he had left college. Madeleine was listening with close attention, as though his future concerned her no less than him.

"Naturally, I shall write a thesis . . . you can't see me remaining a simple schoolmaster all my life, can you? . . . I want to be a member of a university faculty."

She asked him how many months the thesis would take. He replied eagerly, that it wasn't a question of months, but of years. He spoke to her of the great philosophers. The essentials of their systems, he said, were already present in the theses they had offered. She, indifferent to the names he mentioned, dared not ask the one question which was of interest to her: would he put off marrying until he should have finished this work he spoke of? Was the preparation of a thesis compatible with family life?

"If I could get the job of a Reader at Bordeaux . . . but that is very difficult."

When she interrupted him with the rather foolish suggestion that her father might be able to pull strings, he protested acidly that he did not wish to be "indebted to a Government of Free-Masons and Jews". She bit her lip. As a daughter of a member of the General Council, a moderate Republican, who had no thought in his head but to be "on good terms" with everybody, she had been accustomed since childhood to see her father soliciting for all and sundry. There was not a decoration, not a job as road-surveyor or postman in the parish, which had not been given as the result of his good offices. She blamed herself for thus hurting Jean-Louis's feelings. Should the occasion arise, however, she would see what could be done, though she would be careful not to let him know what was in the wind.

Apart from these exchanges, some of which would seem to imply that their two lives might one day merge, the two young people made no gesture, nor exchanged a word, of tenderness. And yet, years afterwards, when Jean-Louis thought back to those morning visits at Léojats, his memory was of a happiness that had been not of this world. He saw, in the retrospect of imagination, little flurries of sunshine upon the crayfish stream and under the oaks. He followed Madeleine in recollection, and remembered how their legs had pushed aside the dense grasses, thick sown with buttercups and daisies in those old times of Whitsun holiday. They had walked upon the meadows as upon a sea. The winged beetles quivered in the light of the setting sun. No physical endearment could have added to their shared delight, might, indeed, have spoiled it, making a distorted image of their love. Not in words nor attitudes did the two young people give any formal shape to what held them breathless under the oaks of Léojats, to the immense and nameless wonder of their experience.

By what strange jealousy was Yves tormented! It was not caused by anything that Jean-Louis felt for Madeleine. His suffering came from the knowledge that another human creature could snatch his big brother from the life which they had always known, that the power to hold him in enchantment had passed from himself elsewhere. But these stirrings of pride did not prevent him from yielding to the humility of his years.

Jean-Louis in love meant for him Jean-Louis grown up. A youth of seventeen in love with a young girl, has no longer part or parcel in such things as happen in the world of those not yet of man's estate. For Yves, the poems he wrote belonged to the mysterious world of children's stories. Far from thinking of himself as "old for his age", he knew that the dream in which his work was born was that of childhood. Only if one was a child, he thought, could one share in so incomprehensible a game.

But when the day came for going back to Bordeaux, he realized how wrong he had been to lose confidence in his elder brother. . . . This revelation came to him at the moment least expected, and in the most unlikely place. At Langon station the Frontenac family had left the Bazas train, and were seeking, helplessly, for vacant seats in the express. Blanche was running down the platform. The children kept at her heels, dragging with them a basket containing a cat, birds in cages, a frog in a glass jar, several boxes of "souvenirs" – pine-cones, strips of tree-bark sticky with resin, and flints. With terror, the various members of the family were facing "separation". At that moment, the station-master approached Madame Frontenac, raised his hand to the peak of his cap, and told her that he was going to attach an extra second-class coach to the train. As a result of this, the Frontenacs found themselves all together in the same compartment, though bumped and shaken as one always is at the rear end of a line of railway coaches, breathless, but happy, and wondering audibly about the fate of the cat, the frog, and the umbrellas. It was just as they were drawing out of the station at Cadillac, that Jean-Louis asked Yves whether he had a "fair-copy" of his poems. Why, of course they had been copied into a handsome note-book, but Yves had not been able to change his handwriting.

"Let me have them this evening, and I'll see what I can do. I may not be a genius, but my writing is extremely legible. . . . Why? . . . Can't you see, you little silly? But for heaven's sake, don't go getting ideas. . . . Our only chance is to get the professionals to grasp what you're after. We're going to send your poems to the *Mercure de France*. . . ."

Yves, pale to the lips, could only go on repeating that "that would be wonderful", Jean-Louis begged him again not to start counting his eggs before they were laid.

"They must get a whole pile of stuff every day. They probably chuck most of it into the waste-paper-basket unread. The great thing is to get someone to look at your stuff, someone who knows what's what. But you mustn't count on anything: it's one chance in a thousand – rather like throwing a bottle into the sea. Promise me that once the parcel's sent off you won't think any more about it?"

"Why, of course," said Yves: "no one'll ever look at them."

But his eyes were agleam with hope. He began to worry. Where could they find a big enough envelope? How many stamps would they have to put on it? Jean-Louis shrugged his shoulders. They would send the packet by registered post. He would look after all that part of the business.

At Beautiran a lot of people with baskets invaded the carriage. The Frontenacs had to crowd up together. Yves recognized one of his schoolmates, a country boy, a boarder, who was very good at games but with whom he had had nothing to do. They exchanged a brief greeting. Each was carefully studying the other's mother. Yves wondered what he would have thought of that fat, sweating woman if he had been her son.

VI

HAD Jean-Louis been at Yves's side during the sweltering weeks which immediately preceded Prize-Day, he would have put him on his guard against the folly of waiting in daily expectation of an answer. But scarcely had term begun than he took a decision which met with the admiring approval of all the members of the family, with the single exception of his younger brother, to whom it was the cause of profound irritation. Having made up his mind to take his finals in Science as well as in Philosophy, Jean-Louis asked to be allowed to become a temporary boarder, and so waste no time in going to and from school. Yves made a point of addressing him as Mucius Scaevola. He had a horror, he said, of all such manifestations of "nobility". Left to himself he had thoughts for nothing but the fate of his manuscript. Every evening, when the postman came, he asked his mother for the key of the letter-box and rushed downstairs four steps at a time. His hopes were regularly disappointed, but he consoled himself with the thought that perhaps next day . . . He invented rational explanations for having to wait: manuscripts would not, of course, be read as soon as they reached the office, and then, no matter how enthusiastic the reader might be, he would have to bring persuasion to bear on Monsieur Valette, the editor of the *Mercure*. The blossoms on the chestnut trees faded. The last of the flowering lilacs was alive with may-bugs. The Frontenacs received from Respide so many hampers of asparagus that they "didn't know what to do with it all". Yves's hopes, like the water in the river-beds, fell lower with every day that passed. He became embittered. The fact that his nearest and dearest failed to detect a bright nimbus about his head, made him hate them. They, for their part, and without intentional malice, were careful to sit on him. "If anyone squeezed your nose, milk would come out!" Yves was fully convinced that his mother was lost to him. He felt estranged from her by the things she said – pecks administered by the hen to the growing chick who would follow her about. If, he thought, he explained what he was feeling, she wouldn't understand. If he read his poems to her, she would merely treat him as a little silly, or as quite mad. He did not know that the poor woman had a far deeper knowledge of her youngest son than he could imagine. She knew perfectly well that he was different from the others, though in what way, precisely, she could not have said. He was the sole puppy of the litter with a touch of wildness.

It was not the others who despised him, but he himself who held firmly to the conviction that he was insignificant and worthless. His narrow shoulders and weak arms filled him with feelings of disgust. All the same, the ridiculous temptation came to him one evening, when the family was assembled in the drawing-room, to jump on the table and cry – "I am a king! I am a king!"

"It's just a phase . . . you'll see, it will pass" – that was Madame Arnaud-Miqueu's constant refrain, whenever Blanche unburdened herself. Yves never wore hats now, and washed his hands as seldom as possible. Since the *Mercure* remained silent, since Jean-Louis had abandoned him, since no one now would ever know that a remarkable poet had been born in Bordeaux, he would find food for his despair in making himself even more unpleasant to look at than he was; would hide his genius in a gaunt and grubby body.

He was seated one June morning in the school bus, reading over the most recent of his poems, when he noticed that his neighbour kept peering over his shoulder. . . . The boy in question was one of the seniors, a fellow called Binaud, who was in his philosophy year and a rival of Jean-Louis, than whom he seemed considerably older. . . . He had already started to shave, and his smooth, baby cheeks were covered with cuts. Yves pretended to have noticed nothing: but he moved his hand slightly so as not to impede the other's view, and was careful not to turn the page until he felt quite sure that the boy beside him had read to the bottom of the preceding one. Suddenly, the Nosy Parker, without a word of apology, asked him where he had "picked *that* up". Yves remained silent, and he pressed his question.

"Come on, tell me who wrote it?"

"Guess."

"Rimbaud? – no, of course not, you wouldn't know anything about him."

"Who's Rimbaud?"

"I'll tell you all about Rimbaud, if you'll tell me where you copied that poem."

Here, at last, was someone to take the place of Jean-Louis, the traitor. A stranger should be admitted to the secret of his glory and his genius. With flaming cheeks he said:

"I wrote it myself."

"No, really, joking apart?" Obviously, the other did not believe him. As soon as he was convinced that Yves was speaking the truth, he felt ashamed to think that he had been seriously interested in the outpourings of a mere kid. There couldn't be anything in it if *he* was the author. Somewhat lackadaisically, he said:

"You must show me some more of your stuff . . ."

Yves opened his brief-case, but the other checked him with a touch on the arm:

"Not now: I've got too much work to do. But if you happen

to be anywhere near the rue Saint-Genès on a Sunday evening, just ring the bell at 182 . . ."

Yves did not understand that he was being asked merely to leave his note-book there. To read his poems aloud to somebody! – what a dream of delight! Jean-Louis had never asked him to do that! In spite of his shyness, he could pluck up courage to read them to this stranger. The big fellow would listen with respect, and perhaps, as the reading progressed, with amazement.

Binaud was careful not to sit next to Yves again in the bus. But the younger boy found no reason for taking offence at that, because the examinations were approaching, and whenever the candidates had a moment, they buried their noses in their books.

He let two Sundays go by before making up his mind to call. With the dry heat of July, melancholy descended upon Bordeaux. No water trickled along the gutters. The cab-horses all wore straw hats with two holes in them for their ears. The new electric trams carried a cargo of collarless and shirt-sleeved men. The unbuttoned bodices of the women made them look hump-backed. Cyclists sweated at their task, their faces almost touching their handle-bars. Yves turned his head to see Madame Escarraguel's motor-car go by, making a noise like a wagon-load of old iron.

No. 182 rue Saint-Genès was a single-storeyed house of the kind that Yves knew as a "lean-to". He rang the bell. His mind was far away. No boy with the name of Binaud had any place in it. But the tinkling soon roused him. It was too late now to make his escape. He heard a door bang and the sound of a half-whispered confabulation. At last, a woman in a dressing-gown appeared on the threshold. She was thin, with a yellowish complexion. Suspicion gleamed in her eye. Her thick hair, of which she must have been very proud, seemed to have devoured her physical substance. It, alone, was living and luxuriant. The rest of her was wasted. Probably she was being eaten away by some internal tumour. Yves asked whether Jacques Binaud was in. The school cap in his hand must have reassured the woman, for she admitted him into the passage and opened a door in the right-hand wall.

It must once have been the drawing-room of the house, but was now transformed into a dressmaker's workshop. Paper patterns lay all over the table. An uncovered sewing-machine stood in front of the window. Obviously, the woman had been disturbed at her labours. A highly-coloured Salomé in terra-cotta, of Austrian manufacture, stood on the mantelpiece. Yves could hear somebody moving about next door, and the sound of an irritable voice – no doubt, Binaud's. . . . Without meaning to, he had intruded into the home of one of those "modest" state functionaries who are bitterly proud, for ever struggling to "keep up appearances", and careful to see to it that no stranger shall penetrate behind the scenes of their grinding lives. Obviously, Binaud had merely meant him to leave his manuscript, and nothing more . . . as was witnessed by the first words uttered by the youth when at last he appeared, coatless, and with his shirt unbuttoned. He had an enormous neck the back of which was a mass of small boils. So Yves had brought his poems, had he? He really shouldn't have gone to all that trouble.

"With the examinations only a fortnight off, I really haven't a moment, as you may imagine. . . ."

"You said . . . I thought . . ."

"I imagined you'd just drop your note-book in the next Sunday . . . but since you've come, let's have a look at 'em."

"No," said Yves; "no, I don't want to bore you. . . ."

He had only one wish, to get clear of this lean-to, this pervasive smell, this horrible youth. The latter, meanwhile, and no doubt on account of his friend, Jean-Louis, had recovered his temper and was trying to keep his visitor from going. But the boy had already made his way back to the street, and was now striding along in spite of the stuffiness, drunk with despair and resentment. . . . But he was only fifteen, and as soon as he reached the Cours de l'Intendance he went into Lammanon's tea-shop where he found consolation in an ice-cream. But when he left it, he found his sense of vexation waiting for him upon the pavement, a vexation out of all proportion to the visit which had gone so much awry. Every human being has his peculiar form of suffering, the laws of which take shape in earliest youth. So intense, on this particular evening, was Yves's wretchedness, that he felt he would never come to the end of it. He did not then know that he stood on the threshold of a whole sequence of glorious days, of weeks during which he would bask in the bright light of happiness, and that hope was about to bathe him in a radiance as changeless, and, alas, as deceptive, as the sunlight of the summer holidays.

VII

XAVIER FRONTENAC was now enjoying the most peaceful period of his life. His scruples had been set at rest, and since the capital sum promised to Joséfa had all been paid, there was no reason why he should not start putting money aside for his nephews. He was, on the other hand, still haunted by the dread that the family might get wind of her existence. His anxiety grew with the growth of the young Frontenacs, and gave him most trouble when they came within measurable distance of the age at which the risk of their being shocked, and even influenced by his sad example, was greatest. There was, however, comfort in the thought that once they were grown up they could begin to look after their property for themselves. He had made up his mind that, when he thought the right moment had come, he would sell his practice and go to live in Paris. He explained to Joséfa that the capital would provide them with a safe refuge. The earliest motor-cars were already making distances seem shorter, and he couldn't help but feel that Angoulême was very much nearer to Bordeaux than it had been in the old days. In Paris they would be able to go about together, and visit the theatres without risk of being recognized.

He had already taken steps to dispose of his practice. Although he would not actually give it up for another two years, he already had standing in his name a deposit account of considerably larger proportions than he had expected. So great was his satisfaction at this state of affairs that he felt justified in putting into effect a long-standing promise that he and Joséfa should make a circular tour of Switzerland. When he mentioned this she showed so little pleasure that he felt disappointed. The truth of the matter was that the prospect seemed so wonderful to the poor woman, that she could not really believe in it. Had it been merely a question of spending a week at Luchon, as they had done in '96, she could have taken it in . . . but to go to Paris, and on to Switzerland . . . well, she shrugged her shoulders and continued with her sewing. Nevertheless, when she saw Xavier deep in guides and time-tables, busily planning their itinerary, the incredible happiness did seem to be taking form and substance. She could no longer doubt that his mind was made up. One evening he appeared with the tickets actually in his pocket. Until that moment she had mentioned the trip to nobody, but now she decided that she could safely write to her married daughter at Niort. "I really don't know whether I am sleeping or waking. The tickets are safe and sound in the glass-fronted wardrobe. They have been taken in the names of Monsieur and Madame Xavier Frontenac. They are *family* tickets. I can hardly believe that it is true, my dear. The thought of them makes me come over all funny. *Monsieur and Madame Frontenac!* I asked him whether he would enter us like that in the hotel registers, and he replied that he could hardly do otherwise. My question put him in a bad temper – you know what he's like. . . . He said that he'd been three times to Switzerland and seen everything there except the mountains, because they had always been hidden in clouds, and it had rained all the time. I hadn't the courage to tell him that I shouldn't mind, because what'll please me most will be going to all those hotels as Xavier's wife, and only having to ring a bell for breakfast. . . ."

Monsieur and Madame Frontenac . . . These words, seen on the tickets, had not produced any great effect on Xavier, but, then, he had not foreseen that the problem of their identity would present itself afresh each time they arrived at an hotel. . . . Joséfa would have been much wiser not to have sown this new anxiety in his mind. It entirely spoiled his pleasure. What a fool he had been to pile up all this trouble for himself! – fatigue, expense, and the spectacle of Joséfa playing the great lady (to say nothing of the fact that the local papers would probably list them under the heading of "Visitors", as *Monsieur and Madame Frontenac*). But it was too late to start worrying now. The tickets were taken. The wine had been drawn.

On the afternoon of the second of August, the day before they were due to start, at the very moment when, in Angoulême, Joséfa was putting the finishing touches to an evening dress designed to dazzle the hotels of Switzerland, Madame Arnaud-Miqueu, walking along a street in Vichy, had one of those attacks of dizziness which she described by saying that her head felt as though "it was going round". This particular attack was sudden and violent. Her hand slipped from the arm of her Caussade daughter, and her head struck the pavement. She was carried back to the hotel, apparently at her last gasp.

Next morning, at Bourideys, Blanche Frontenac was taking a last turn round the park before shutting herself away in the coolness of the house. It was already so hot that she found breathing difficult, and the cicadas one by one were breaking into a joyful cacophony. She saw Danièle running towards her, waving a telegram.

"Mother seriously ill. . . ."

Late that same afternoon, a telegraph boy knocked at Xavier Frontenac's door in Angoulême. Joséfa, who rarely ventured to visit him in his home, was, on this occasion, helping him with his packing, and had already, without a word to him, stowed away three of her own dresses in the trunk. As soon as she saw the slip of blue paper in Xavier's fingers, she knew they would not go.

"Oh, damnation . . . !"

The tone of Xavier's voice was, in spite of himself, almost cheerful, because, between the lines of Blanche's message – "Starting for Vichy mother seriously ill please come first train Bourideys look after children" – he could read the assurance that he would never have to write in the register of any Swiss hotel, the words – "*Monsieur and Madame Frontenac*", and that he would be fifteen hundred francs to the good. He passed the telegram across to Joséfa. She realized at once that her hopes were at an end. For fifteen years she had grown used to being sacrificed upon the altar of the Frontenac deity. As a mere matter of form, she said: "It's come too late: the tickets are taken: we have already started. Send a wire from the frontier that you are terribly sorry. . . . After all, the children are nearly grown-up" (from hearing them spoken about so often, she knew quite a lot) – "Monsieur Jean-Louis is close on eighteen, and Monsieur José . . ."

He interrupted her in a fury:

"What's come over you? Have you gone mad? Do you really think me capable of not responding when my sister-in-law appeals to me for help? . . . I've always told you that they must come first. . . . Cheer up, my dear, it only means putting off our holiday. We'll go another time. . . . Be sure to put on your cape, it's getting rather fresh."

With a docile gesture she resumed her dark brown cape with the braided frogs. The high, ruff-like collar framed, in the strangest way, her flabby face with that tip-tilted, "cheeky", nose which alone had the power to awaken memories of the past in him. She had a receding chin, and her hat, perched on top of a thick coil of yellow hair, was a tangle of convincing artificial convolvulus. It was easy to see that her hair, when "down", must reach to her waist. The weight of it broke all her combs. "Your hair's always a mass of pins!"

Submissive though she had become, the poor woman, as she fastened her cape, muttered something to the effect that "one of these days you'll find I've had just about as much as I can stand". Xavier told her sharply to repeat what she had just said, and this she did, though with no great air of conviction. Xavier Frontenac, who treated the members of his family with an excessive delicacy, who was almost morbidly scrupulous in his dealings with them, and in his handling of business matters, went out of his way to behave to Joséfa with a brutal lack of consideration.

"Now that you've made your little pile," he said, "you're at perfect liberty to clear out, if you want to. . . . But you're such a ninny that you'll lose every penny of it. . . . You'll be obliged to sell the furniture," he added, "unless – but don't forget that the bills are all in my name, as is the lease of the flat. . . ."

"What! isn't the furniture mine, then? . . ."

He had touched her on her most sensitive spot. She adored the big bed which had been bought at Leveilley's, in Bordeaux, with its gold fluting, and its head-board crowned by a torch and a quiver. Joséfa had long come to see the torch as a horn of plenty sprouting hair, and the quiver as a similar object filled with goose-feathers. . . . These strange symbols neither worried nor surprised her. The night-table, resembling a richly adorned reliquary, was far too beautiful, she always maintained, for what it held. But the pride and joy of her heart was the glass-fronted wardrobe. The ornamental pediment carried a design of the same horns of plenty interlaced by the same ribbons with an added motif of roses, so deeply carved and undercut that, according to Joséfa, one could count their petals. The mirror was set between two columns which were ribbed to half their height, and terminated, at their bottom end, in human torsos. The inside was of lighter wood which "showed up beautifully" the piles of drawers with lace borders "as broad as your hand", of underskirts trimmed with stiffly starched scallops, and of dainty camisoles – all of which were Joséfa's delight, such a passion did she have for "linen".

"What, isn't the furniture mine?"

She began to sob. He put his arms round her:

"Of course it's yours, you great baby."

"Actually," she said, wiping her eyes, "it's silly of me to cry, because I never really thought we should go. I thought there'd be an earthquake. . . ."

"Whereas, all that's happened is that old Madame Arnaud-Miqueu has taken it into her head to peg out."

He was in high good humour, overjoyed at the thought of joining his brother's children in the country.

"Poor Madame Michel will feel terribly lonely. . . ."

Joséfa thought endlessly, and with deep devotion, of the being whom she had grown accustomed to set on the highest of high eminences. There was a short silence, at the end of which Xavier said:

"If her mother dies, she will be very rich. There will no longer be any need for her to touch a penny of the Frontenac fortune."

He walked round the table, rubbing his hands.

"You must take the tickets back to the Agency. I'll drop them a line. They're clients of mine and won't make any difficulties. Keep the money they give you. . . . There's some of your allowance still owing, and it'll just about cover it" – he added gaily.

VIII

ON the day of Blanche's departure for Vichy (she was to take the three o'clock train), the family lunched in complete silence – that is to say, without speaking, for the absence of conversation made the noise of forks and dishes seem louder than it would have been otherwise. The children's appetite rather shocked Blanche. When she came to die, they would go on eating just as they were doing now . . . but, after all, hadn't she caught herself wondering, only a few moments ago, who would have the house in the rue de Cursol? Storm clouds had driven across the sun, and the shutters had had to be opened. The peaches were attracting the wasps. The dog barked, and Danièle said: "It's the postman." Every head was turned to the window, towards the man who had come from the warren, with his open box slung over his shoulder. Even in the most united of families there is always somebody who is waiting for, hoping for, a letter, of which the others know nothing. Madame Frontenac recognized the writing of her mother who might, at this very moment, be on her deathbed, or dead.... She must have written to her on the very morning of the accident. She hesitated to open the letter, finally made up her mind to do so, and burst into tears. The children were staggered at the sight of their mother's grief. She got up and left the room with her two daughters. No one, except Jean-Louis, had paid any attention to a large envelope which the servant had put in front of Yves. *Mercure de France* . . . *Mercure de France*. Yves couldn't bring himself to open it.... Just a bit of printed matter . . . that was all it was . . . printed matter. His eye caught a sentence. It was about him: about his poems. . . . They had got his name wrong: Yves Frontenoux. There was a letter. "Dear Sir, and dear Poet: in view of their unusual beauty, we have decided to print all the poems you have sent us. We should be obliged if you would correct the proofs and send them back by return of post. . . . So high is our opinion of your work, that the idea of remuneration seems to us to be quite out of place. With every expression of admiration, I remain, dear sir and dear poet, yours sincerely, Paul Morisse. PS. I hope that, in the course of the next few months, I may be allowed to see some of your more recent productions. You will, however, understand that I cannot, in any way, commit this firm to any undertaking in the matter."

Three or four drops spattered the earth at long intervals, and then, at last, the rain set in, a quiet, persistent, downpour. Yves, in his deepest being, was conscious of its freshness. Like the leaves, he rejoiced in the rain. It was as though the clouds had burst on him, and on him alone. He passed the envelope across to Jean-Louis, who, after a quick glance, slipped it into his pocket. The younger children came back into the room. Their mother was calmer now, and would be down when it was time for her to start. . . . Grandmamma said in her letter – "the dizziness in my head is worse than ever. . . ." Yves made an effort to break from his happiness. It was round him like a fire: he could not escape the blaze. He forced himself to follow his mother's journey in imagination – three trains as far as Bordeaux, and then the Lyons express. She would change at Gannat. . . . He had no idea how to correct proofs . . . How could he send them back by return? . . . The letter had been forwarded from Bordeaux . . . that meant that a whole day had been lost already.

Blanche appeared, her face concealed by a falling veil. One of the children cried out – "Here's the carriage!" Burthe was having difficulty with the horse because of the flies. As a rule, the children squabbled about who should go with their mother in the victoria to the station, and come back, not on the let-down seats, but on the "springy cushions". But today, Jean-Louis and Yves ceded their right of precedence to José and the youngsters. They waved their hands and cried:

"We shall expect a telegram tomorrow morning."

At last! . . . there was no one now to dispute their sovereignty over house and park. The sun was shining through the rain-drops. The wild weather had turned strangely mild. The wind in the water-logged branches produced an occasional short, sharp shower. The two boys could not sit down because the garden benches were soaked. Consequently, they read the proofs as they sauntered round the park with their heads close together. Yves said that now the poems were printed they seemed shorter. There were very few misprints, and such as there were they corrected by the artless method they would have used in revising a fair-copy in class. When they reached the great oak, Jean-Louis asked suddenly:

"Why haven't you let me see your latest poems?"

"You didn't ask me to."

Jean-Louis explained that he wouldn't have taken any pleasure in them while the examinations were looming. Yves offered to fetch them.

"Wait for me here."

He dashed away, running towards the house, drunk with happiness, his bare head thrown back. Deliberately, he plunged through the high clumps of broom and under the low-hanging branches, so as to feel the moisture on his face. The breeze created by his rapid progress seemed almost cold. Jean-Louis watched him bounding back towards him. This young brother of his, who looked so ill-kempt and squalid when in town, seemed almost to fly now with an angel's grace.

"Let me read them to you, Jean-Louis. I should so love to read them aloud. . . . Wait till I've recovered my breath."

They were standing with their backs to a tree and the younger boy could hear the beating of his fragile, over-driven heart against the ancient, living, trunk which always, when on the eve of departure at the end of the holidays, he would come to embrace. He began to read in an odd sort of sing-song which Jean-Louis at first thought silly, though, after the first few moments, he decided that no other tone would have been so suitable. Did he think these new poems less good than the earlier ones? He hesitated to pronounce: he would have to re-read them. . . . What bitterness, what sorrow, in one so young! Yves, who, just now, had bounded towards him like a fawn, was reading in a hard, harsh voice. And yet, his only feeling was one of profound happiness. He no longer felt anything of the appalling misery which these poems expressed. He was conscious only of the joy it gave him to have caught and fixed that misery in words which he felt to be eternal.

"You must send them to the *Mercure* at the beginning of the

October term" – said Jean-Louis. "There's no point in being in too much of a hurry."

"D'you like them better than the others?"

Jean-Louis hesitated:

"I think they go deeper."

As they approached the house they saw José and the younger children who had just got back from the station. They looked solemn and important. Marie said it had been awful to see mamma crying so when the train started. Yves turned away, afraid lest they might guess at his happiness. Jean-Louis hastened to find an excuse for him. After all, grandmamma wasn't dead yet. The news might have been exaggerated. This wasn't the first time she had received Extreme Unction – it had happened on three separate occasions . . . besides, Uncle Alfred had a weakness for making things out worse than they were.

Yves broke in thoughtlessly:

"He takes his hopes for fact."

"Oh, Yves, how can you!"

The children were shocked. But Yves was off again like a skittish foal, leaping the ditches, clutching to his heart the proofs which he was going to read for the third time in what he called his "house" – a place no better than a pig-sty, which stood in a wilderness of gorse. . . . There he would gnaw his bone to his heart's content.

José watched him running:

"What a nasty brat it is! – always glum when things are going well, and as happy as a dog with two tails when there's any bad news. . . ."

He whistled to Stop, and went off down the hill towards the Hure to set his ground lines, as unperturbed and happy as though his grandmother had not been at death's door. To feel drunk with happiness, his brother had needed but the first gleam of fame. It was enough for José to be a youth of seventeen with the summer holidays all before him, and a sure instinct for where the eels lay on the bed of the Hure.

IX

DINNER, in the absence of mamma, was noisier than usual. Only the girls, educated at the Sacred Heart, and trained to habits of scrupulosity, thought that "it was no time for joking". But even they could not help laughing when Yves and José imitated the singers round the harmonium in church, with their mouths all screwed up: *Rien pour me satisfaire dans ce vaste univers.* Jean-Louis, serious and sensible as ever, went out of his way to find excuses for himself and his brothers. If they laughed, he maintained, it was because of nervous excitement. Really and truly they felt just as sad as everybody else.

After dinner they went out into the dark night to meet Uncle Xavier who was due to arrive by the nine o'clock train. No matter how late they might be, the Bourideys train was always later still. Huge stacks of freshly-cut planks, exuding resin, stood in a circle round the station. The children wound their way between these obstacles, sustaining sundry bangs and knocks, and losing themselves in the tangle of sweet-scented alleys. Their feet sank deep into the carpet of trodden pine-bark. They could not see it in the darkness, but knew that by daylight it had the colour of dried blood. Yves maintained that the planks were no less than the broken limbs of pines. Torn and stripped, these sacred bodies of the martyrs scented the air.

"What a little ass!" growled José: "what's that got to do with it?"

They saw the gleam of the station lamp. A number of women were talking loud, and laughing. Their voices were piercing. There was something animal about them. The children went through the waiting-room and crossed the tracks. In the silence of the woods they could hear the distant sound of the little train, the rhythmic puffing which they knew so well, and often imitated in the winter days in Bordeaux, so as to remind themselves of the holidays. . . . There was a prolonged whistle, a sound of escaping steam, and the majestic toy emerged from the darkness. There was one traveller only in the second-class coach – it could be nobody but Uncle Xavier.

He had not expected to find them so cheerful. They fought over his bag: they clung to his arms: they went through his pockets till they found what sort of sweets he had brought them. He let them lead him like a blind man between the stacks of sawn planks, and breathed in, happy as always when he made this journey, the night smells of the ancient country of the Péloueyres. He knew that at the road which skirted the town, they would exclaim – "Look out for Monsieur Dupart's dog!" When the last house had been passed, an opening would appear in the dark mass of the woods, a white streak which was the sandy path on which the children's feet would make their old familiar sound. Over there, in the distance, was the kitchen lamp, shining like a great star at ground level. . . . He knew that a delicious meal would be waiting for him, which the children, who had already dined, would not let him eat in peace. When he let some word drop about their poor grandmother, he was greeted by a chorus of voices. They must wait for more accurate news. Aunt Caussade always exaggerated so. No sooner had he swallowed the last mouthful than he was dragged off to make the round of the park, in spite of the darkness. This was a rite which he was never allowed to omit.

"Smells good, doesn't it, Uncle Xavier?"

"It smells marshy," he replied quietly: "and I rather think I am going to catch a chill."

"Look at all the stars."

"I'd rather look where I'm walking."

One of the little girls asked him to recite *le méchant faucon et le gentil pigeon*. When they were small, he had amused them with old stories and bits of nonsense, to which they would always listen with undiminished pleasure and unvarying laughter.

"Aren't you ashamed at your age? – you're not children any longer, you know. . . ."

Again and again during the long days of happiness and sunshine, Uncle Xavier would say – "you're not children any longer . . ." but the miracle was precisely that they could still bathe in the waters of childhood even when childhood had long been passed. They were the beneficiaries of a marvellous respite, of a mysterious dispensation.

Next morning it was none other than Jean-Louis who said:

"Uncle Xavier, do make some fire-ships." He protested, for form's sake, but, that done, took a piece of pine-bark, shaped it into a ship with a few strokes of his knife, and set a lighted match upright in the hull. The current set the flame floating down the Hure, and the young Frontenacs felt again, as they had felt in days long ago, as they thought of the adventures lying ahead for this sliver of Bourideys pine-wood. The Hure would carry it as far as the Ciron; the Ciron flowed into the Garonne not far from Preignac . . . and at long last, the ocean would receive this little piece of wood from the park where all the Frontenacs had grown up. Not one of them would admit the possibility that it might get caught on a root, that it might rot into wreckage long before the Hure stream had carried it beyond the little town. It was essential, it was an act of faith, to believe that from this secret streamlet of Les Landes, the fire-ship would pass into the Atlantic Ocean, "with its cargo of Frontenac mystery" – as Yves put it.

These great boys ran along the bank as they had always done, to keep the fire-ship from going aground. The sun, already fierce, filled the cicadas with a drunken joy, and flies were swarming about every scrap of living flesh. Burthe brought a telegram, which the children opened with eager anxiety: "Slight improvement . . ." – How lovely! – they could enjoy themselves now, and laugh with a clear conscience. But in the days that followed there came a moment when Uncle Xavier, peering at the blue form, read out – "Grandmamma desperate . . .", and the children, in consternation, were hard put to it to know what to do with their happiness. Grandmamma Arnaud-Miqueu was dying in a hot bedroom at Vichy. But here, in the park, the long days of sunshine came to a blazing point. In the forest lands, no eye can see the storms gathering. For a long while they lie hidden behind the pine-trees. Only the rising wind betrays their presence. They leap upon the countryside like robbers from an ambush. Sometimes, copper-coloured clouds would swarm up from the south. A sighing in the branches would make the children say it must be raining somewhere.

But even on the days when the news from Vichy was bad, the silence and the brooding did not last for long. Danièle and Marie put their faith in a Novena which they were making for their grandmother in conjunction with the Carmelites of Bordeaux and the Convent of the Misericorde. José would announce that "something told him she would pull through". Uncle Xavier found it necessary to interrupt a Mendelssohn chorus which they were singing, in three parts, seated on the terrace.

> *Tout l'univers est plein de sa magnificence!*
> *Qu'on l'adore, ce Dieu . . .*"

"If only for the sake of the servants," he would say. But Yves protested that music was no bar to sadness and anxiety, and would wait until the glow of their uncle's cigar had vanished in the darkness of the garden path, to start up an aria from Gounod's *Cinq-Mars*, in his funny, breaking voice.

> *Nuit resplendissante et silencieuse*

He addressed himself to the night as he might have done to a person whose fresh, warm touch he could feel, whose breath was upon his face:

> *Dans tes profondeurs, nuit délicieuse*

Jean-Louis and José, seated on a bench at the top of the steps, leaned their heads back and looked at the shooting-stars. The girls cried out that a bat had got into their room.

At midnight, Yves re-lit his candle, having armed himself with the note-book which he used for his poems, and a pencil. Already the town cocks were replying to their brothers in the remote, forgotten farmsteads. Bare-footed, and in his shirt-sleeves, he leaned at his window and watched the sleeping trees. No one but his Guardian Angel would ever know how closely he resembled his father at the same age.

One morning, a telegram bringing the message "No change", was interpreted as being reassuring. The day was glorious. Distant storms had yielded a touch of coolness. The girls took alder twigs to their uncle for him to cut into whistles. But they insisted that no detail of the operation, none of the sacred rites, should be omitted. In order to strip the bark it was not enough that he should tap the wood with the handle of his penknife. He had also to sing a song in patois:

Sabe, sabe caloumet. Te pourterey un pan naouet.
Te pourterey une mitche toute caoute, Sabarin,
Sabaro . . .

The children took up the idiotic and sacrosanct words in chorus. Uncle Xavier broke off in the middle of what he was doing:

"Aren't you ashamed, at your age, to make me play the fool like this?"

But all of them felt obscurely that, as the result of some singular favour shown by the gods, Time had stood still. Power had been given them to leave the train which nothing halts. In the very process of growing up, they could stand in the shallows of childhood, could dawdle while childhood slipped away for ever.

* * *

The news about Madame Arnaud-Miqueu improved. Things were going better than could have been hoped. Very soon now mamma would be back, and with her there they would have to curb their irresponsible foolishness. The special brand of Frontenac laughter would have to cease.

They set off to meet her. She, too, was coming by the nine o'clock train. There was a moon. The light filtered between the stacks of sawn planks. There had been no need to bring a lantern.

On their return from the station, the children watched their mother as she ate. She had changed. She looked thinner. She described how, one night, grandmamma had been so ill that a winding-sheet had been got ready (when guests die in large hotels, their bodies are removed at once, under cover of darkness). She noticed that they were scarcely listening, that there was some sort of understanding between the children and their uncle, made up of private jokes and words with special meanings. She felt as though she were confronted by a world of mystery into which she had not the right of entry. She stopped talking and relapsed into a mood of gloom. She had not against her brother-in-law the same grounds of complaint as once she had had, because now that she was older the nature of her demands on him was different. But the children's special brand of affection for him wounded her. She hated the knowledge that all their gratitude should be for him.

Blanche's return broke the charm. The children were children no longer. Jean-Louis spent all his time over at Léojats, and Yves began to suffer again from pimples. . . . He had slipped back into his moody and mistrustful attitude. The arrival of the *Mercure* with his poems included in the table of contents did nothing to take the scowl from his face. At first he lacked the courage to show them to his mother or to Uncle Xavier, and when, at last, he brought himself to do so, his worst fears were realized. His uncle could make nothing of them, and quoted Boileau: "What is truly conceived must be clearly expressed." His mother could not help having a momentary feeling of pride, but concealed it. She begged Yves not to leave the Review lying about, because it contained a " disgusting contribution" by a "certain Rémy de Gourmont". José, spluttering with laughter, read out the passages which he found most completely "loony". Yves rushed at him in a fury, and got a good licking for his pains. He found consolation in the many letters he began to receive from unknown admirers. From now on, these continued to arrive, though he failed to realize to the full the significance of that fact. The orderly Jean-Louis found genuine delight in filing and indexing these evidences of success.

In the first storm-laden days of September, the Frontenacs began to get on each other's nerves. They lost their tempers. Quarrels flared up for no particular reason. Yves would throw down his napkin and leave the table; Madame Frontenac would go to her room, and when she came down again, after repeated embassies and deputations of remorseful children, her eyes were often swollen and her face puffy.

X

THE storm of which these were the premonitory rumblings, broke on the September Feast of Our Lady. After luncheon, Madame Frontenac, Uncle Xavier, and Jean-Louis were closeted together in the small drawing-room. The double doors were open, and in the billiard-room beyond, Yves was lying down, trying to get some sleep. The flies were plaguing him, and a large imprisoned dragonfly was bumping against the ceiling. In spite of the heat, the two girls were careering round the house on bicycles, each in a different direction, and uttering screams of delight every time they passed one another.

"We must fix the date of the luncheon before Uncle Xavier leaves," Madame Frontenac was saying. "You must make the necessary arrangements with nice Monsieur Dussol, Jean-Louis. You're going to have to spend most of your life with him, you know, and . . ."

Yves was delighted to hear Jean-Louis's vehement protest:

"No, mamma . . . I keep on telling you, but you won't listen. I have no intention of going into the business."

"That is mere childishness on your part. I refuse to pay any attention to it. . . . You know perfectly well that, sooner or later, you will have to make up your mind to take your rightful position in the firm – and the sooner, the better."

"Dussol may be an excellent fellow," put in Uncle Xavier, "and deserving of the fullest confidence. But the fact remains that it is high time – and more than high time – that a Frontenac was in charge."

Yves had half risen, and was straining his ears.

"I'm not interested in the business."

"What, may I ask, are you interested in?"

Jean-Louis hesitated for a second, went very red, and then boldly announced:

"Philosophy."

"Are you completely out of your mind? Philosophy indeed! You'll do exactly as your father did before you, and your grandfather before him. Philosophy is not a profession!"

"As soon as I've got my degree, I intend to start work on my thesis. I shall take my time over it . . . and eventually I shall get a university post. . . ."

"So that's your ideal, is it!" exclaimed Blanche: "to be a state employee – did you hear that, Xavier? – a state employee! – a young man with the finest business in Bordeaux waiting for him to step into!"

It was at this point that Yves entered the room. His hair was tousled, his eyes blazing. He advanced through the cloud of smoke with which Uncle Xavier's everlasting cigarette enveloped faces and furniture.

"How can you compare . . ." – he began in a shrill voice – "how can you compare the trade of a timber-merchant with the vocation of a man who has dedicated his life to the things of the spirit? . . . it's . . . it's indecent!"

The two elders were dumbfounded. They stared at the

young enthusiast standing there before them in his shirt-sleeves, and with his hair falling over his eyes. His uncle told him in a trembling voice to mind his own business. His mother ordered him to leave the room. But, without paying the slightest attention to them, he went on with his tirade. It was only to be expected, he said, that in such a completely unmeaning place as Bordeaux, a merchant of any kind should rank higher than a scholar, that a wholesale wine-dealer should regard himself as of more importance than a man like Professor Pierre Duheim of the Science Faculty, whose name would probably be entirely unknown there, if it wasn't that people thought he might be useful at cramming brainless young fools for their Finals! (Yves would have felt not a little embarrassed if he had been asked to give a concise account of Professor Duheim's labours.)

"Listen to him standing up and speechifying! . . . You're nothing but an unlicked cub, my boy. Why, if anybody squeezed your nose . . ."

Yves completely ignored the interruption. It wasn't, he said, only in this idiotic town that the things of the mind were held in contempt. All over the country teachers and intellectuals were starved and neglected. . . . "In France their name is mud: in Germany, the word professor is equivalent to a title of nobility. . . . But, then, the Germans are a great people! . . ." He continued, his voice getting shriller and shriller, inveighing against all patriotism and all patriots. Jean-Louis tried in vain to stop him. Uncle Xavier, now quite beside himself, was going on and on without producing the slightest effect:

"*I've* nothing to be ashamed of . . . everyone knows which side *I'm* on. . . . From the very beginning I believed in Dreyfus's innocence . . . but I won't let a young cub like this . . ."

It was then that Yves allowed himself to indulge in a reference to the "defeated of '70" – a piece of insolence so crude that it served to steady him. Blanche Frontenac had risen to her feet:

"So now you insult your own uncle! . . . Leave the room at once, and don't let me see you again!"

He crossed the billiard-room and went down the steps. The blazing heat opened before him and closed again behind. He plunged into the stifling airlessness of the park. Clouds of flies hung buzzing close above the ground. Horseflies clung to his shirt. What he was feeling was not so much remorse as humiliation. He was ashamed at having lost his head and struck out blindly. He should have remained calm and stuck to the point at issue. They were right . . . he was just a kid. . . . It had been horrible of him to say that to his uncle, unforgiveable. How could he get back into favour? The odd thing was that both his mother and his uncle had emerged from the quarrel quite undiminished in his eyes. Though he was still too young to put himself in their shoes, and to understand their point of view, he passed no judgment on them. Mamma and Uncle Xavier were still, as they had always been, special and privileged beings. They formed part of his childhood, were elements in a romantic whole from which it was not in their power to isolate themselves. No matter what they might do, no matter what they might say, thought Yves, they remained inseparable from the mysterious climate of his own existence. They might blaspheme against the things of the spirit, but it made no difference. The spirit dwelt in them, and, though they did not know it, shed a radiance about their feet.

Yves turned back. A threat of storm had dulled the sky. But as yet there was no rumbling of thunder. The cicadas had fallen silent, but there was an intense quivering in the air above the meadow grasses. He walked on, shaking his head like a young colt in an effort to free himself from the horse-flies, which made no effort to escape but let themselves be crushed when he slapped at face and neck. . . . "One of the defeated of '70" . . . He had not meant to be offensive. The children made a regular practice of pulling Uncle Xavier's leg about the way in which he and Burthe had enlisted as volunteers, and how they had never so much as clapped eyes on a Prussian. But this time the words had contained something more than a joke.

He went slowly up the steps and came to a halt in the vestibule. The others were still in the small drawing-room. Uncle Xavier was holding forth: " . . . the day before I was due to go back to the regiment I decided to pay one last visit to my brother Michel. I jumped over the wall of the barrack-yard and broke my leg. In hospital I was put in a ward with the smallpox patients. I might have died there. . . . Your poor father, who knew nobody in Limoges, made so many representations that he finally succeeded in getting me out. Poor Michel, he had tried so hard to join the army, but it was no good (it was the year he went down with pleurisy). . . . For months and months he hung on in that appalling town, where he could see me only for one hour each day. . . ."

He stopped suddenly. Yves had appeared on the threshold. He saw his mother's glowering face turned towards him, and Jean-Louis's anxious eyes. Uncle Xavier did not so much as glance at him. He could not think of anything to say. But at heart he was still only a child, and it was the child who came to his rescue. Without a word he flung his arms round his uncle's neck, and kissed him. The tears were pouring down his cheeks. Then he went to his mother and perched himself on her knee, burying his face in her shoulder as he had been accustomed to do when he was very young.

"It's all very well being sorry, but my boy must learn to control himself, and not give way to temper . . ."

Jean-Louis got up and crossed to the window. There were

tears in his eyes. He held out his hand and announced that he had felt a drop of rain. . . . Nothing that had happened could be of the least use to *him*. The rain was closing in on them – a great spider's web, a net imprisoning him in this small and smoke-filled room. He would never escape from it – never.

It had stopped raining. Jean-Louis and Yves were walking along the ride that led to the great oak.

"You're not going to give in, are you, Jean-Louis?"

The other made no answer. His hands were in his pockets, and his eyes were on the ground. He was kicking a pine-cone before him. But his brother would not leave the subject. At last he spoke in a voice which lacked conviction:

"They tell me it's a duty to all of you: that, left to himself, José wouldn't amount to anything in the business. Once I'm in control, he can be taken in. . . . They even seem to believe that the day will come when you, too, will be only too glad to join me. . . . Now, don't go off the deep end. They can't, you see, understand the kind of person you are. Would you believe it, they've even foreseen the possibility that Danièle and Marie might get hooked up with chaps who've got no regular jobs. . . ."

"No one could accuse them of not looking ahead!" – exclaimed Yves (it made him furious to think that they actually believed it possible that he, too, might one day settle down to the family feeding-trough) – "Oh, they don't leave anything to chance! They organize everybody's happiness. They can't understand that one might prefer to be happy in one's own way! . . ."

"To them," said Jean-Louis, "it isn't a question of happiness but of acting for the common good, and in the interests of the family. . . . No, it's not a question of happiness. . . . Have you noticed how they never use the word? . . . Happiness . . . I've never seen mamma without that worried and tormented look on her face. . . . If Papa had lived, I don't think it would have made any difference. . . . No, not happiness but duty . . . a certain form of duty which they never shirk . . . and the awful thing, old man, is that – I understand their point of view!"

They had managed to reach the great oak before the rain started again. They could hear the shower pattering on the leaves. But the living bulk of the tree sheltered them beneath its mass of foliage which was thicker than any growth of feathers. Yves, a shade bombastically, spoke of the only real duty, the duty to what we carry within us, to our work – to a Secret word of God, which must be communicated . . . the Message with which we have been entrusted.

"Why d'you say 'we' – speak for yourself, Yves. I believe that you *are* someone with a message, that you *do* carry a secret within you. . . . But how should our mother and our uncle know it? So far as I am concerned, I have a horrid feeling that they may be right. As a teacher I should do no more than explain what other men have thought . . . though even that is one of the finest things in all the world to do . . . work that's enormously worth while giving one's life to. . . ."

Stop jumped out of a bush and dashed towards them with his tongue hanging out. José could not be far off. Yves addressed the muddy dog as though it had been a human.

"Been down in the marsh, haven't you, old man?"

A moment later, José, too, emerged from the underbrush. With a laugh, he displayed his empty shooting-bag. He'd been flogging the Téchoueyre marshes all morning.

"Not a thing! . . . a few landrail, but all of them out of range . . . I dropped a brace of moorhen, but couldn't retrieve 'em. . . ."

He had not shaved that morning. A young stubble showed dark on his childlike cheeks.

"I'm told there's a wild boar out Biourge way."

By nightfall the rain had stopped. For a long while after dinner, under a late moon, Yves watched Jean-Louis pacing up and down between his mother and his uncle. He saw the three shadowy forms turn into the gravel path. Then, the dark patch made by their figures emerged from the pine-trees into the moonlight. Blanche's vibrant tones dominated the talk, interrupted, from time to time, by Xavier's thinner, sharper, tones. Jean-Louis was silent. Yves had a feeling that his brother was lost, that he had been caught in a trap, that there was no hope of his freeing himself. . . . "They shan't get *me* . . ." But even while he was working himself up into a state of resentment against his family, he knew in some obscure fashion that, of them all, he alone clung desperately to his childhood. The King of the alders should never lure him to his unknown realm . . . unknown? . . . Ah, known only too well! The alders from which came that voice of terrible sweetness, are called by dwellers in a Frontenac country, "vergnes", and droop their loving branches above a stream the name of which is part of their secret knowledge. The King of the alders had stolen no Frontenac children from their cradles. What he had done was to prevent them finding a way of escape from childhood. He wrapped them in the winding-sheets of their dead lives, burying them beneath a weight of lovely memories and rotting leaves.

"I am going to leave you alone with your uncle" – Blanche said to Jean-Louis.

She passed close to Yves without seeing him. But he saw her. The moon shone full on her tortured face. Thinking herself alone, she had slipped her hand beneath her blouse. That gland was worrying her . . . all very well to keep on assuring her that it was nothing. . . . She felt it with her fingers. She must not die before Jean-Louis had taken his place as the head of the family business, as the master of the family fortune, as the younger ones' protector. She prayed for her brood. Her eyes, gazing upwards at the sky, saw Our Lady of Perpetual Succour, whose lamp in the cathedral she maintained, spread her enveloping cloak about the Frontenac young.

"Listen to me, my boy" – Uncle Xavier was saying to Jean-Louis. "I am going to talk to you as I would to a man. I have failed in my duty to all you children. I should have taken the place left vacant in the business after your father's death. . . . It is for you to make up for my shortcomings. . . . No, don't protest . . . You are about to say, aren't you? that I was under no compulsion. But you've got enough of the family feeling to realize that I deserted my post. It is for you to join up the ends of the chain which I broke. There is nothing tedious, I assure you, in running a great business which, perhaps, will provide shelter for your brothers, for your sisters' husbands, and, later, for your children. . . . By degrees we can buy out Dussol. . . . All this doesn't mean that you won't be able to keep abreast of what is going on in the world. . . . Your education will be an asset. . . . I was reading, only the other day, an article in the *Temps* which set out to show that knowledge of Greek and Latin and the Humanities is a fine training for future captains of industry. . . ."

Jean-Louis was not listening. He knew that he was beaten. Inevitably, in the long run, he would have surrendered. He was fully aware of the argument which carried most weight with him. Only just now, his mother had said: "We'll have Dussol, and I see no reason why we shouldn't invite the Cazavieilhs too . . ." A moment later she had added: "Once your military service is over, there'll be nothing to stand in the way of your getting married, if you want to."

It was Uncle Xavier now who was walking beside him in a scented cloud of cigar smoke. But an evening would come when it would be a young and rather stocky woman. . . . He could anticipate his calling-up date, and so be free to marry when he was twenty-one. Two more years, and then, all due formalities accomplished, he would be making the round of the park at Bourideys in the darkness, with Madeleine. All of a sudden the thought of marriage and its delights set him trembling from head to foot. His breath came short and sharp. He could smell the wind which had touched the oaks of Léojats in passing, had swept, in the moonlight, round the white house, and filled with its whispering the cretonne curtains of the room where Madeleine was lying, perhaps unable to sleep.

XI

"IT'S a Fouillaron . . . came from Bordeaux in three hours . . . seventy kilometres . . . not a hint of trouble the whole way. . . ."

Madame Frontenac's guests were crowded round Arthur Dussol, who was still buttoned up to the neck in his grey, dust-proof coat. He took off his goggles, and smiled, screwing up his eyes. Cazavieilh, who was bending over the car, with a mingled expression on his face of respect and mistrust, was trying to think of some question to put to its owner.

"Adjustable transmission-belt, you see," said Dussol.

"I needn't ask whether it's the latest model," remarked Cazavieilh.

"Brand new. No one can say" (and Dussol gave the flicker of a smile) "that I'm ever behind the times."

"True enough: one's only got to take a look at your mobile sawing-plant to see that. . . . What, if I may ask, are the special features of this car?"

"Only a short while ago" – began Dussol, as though lecturing to a class – "the normal form of transmission was by chains. But that's a thing of the past. . . . It's all done now by means of adjustable belts."

"What an A1 notion," said Cazavieilh. "Just two adjustable belts – eh? – is that all?"

"Synchronized, of course – it's the chain-belt system. Think of it this way: two cones working quite independently . . ."

Madeleine Cazavieilh led Jean-Louis away. José, who was passionately interested in this talk of cars, questioned Monsieur Dussol on the subject of gears.

"One can vary the speed as much as one likes by means of a simple lever" (Monsieur Dussol, with his head thrown back, and a look of almost religious gravity, seemed prepared to lift the habitable globe) – "just as in the steam-engine," he added.

Dussol and Cazavieilh sauntered slowly off. Yves followed them with his eyes, fascinated by their air of importance, by the self-satisfaction which seemed to drip from them. Now and again they came to a halt in front of one of the pines, looked it up and down, argued about its probable height, and tried to guess its girth.

"What should you put it at, Cazavieilh? . . ."

Cazavieilh mentioned a figure. Dussol gave a great laugh, so that his stomach, which looked as though it were an extra protuberance fastened on to his body, shook.

"You're a long way out!"

He took a measuring tape from his pocket, put it round the trunk, and said with an air of triumph:

"See? – I wasn't so far off, was I?"

"How much d'you think one could get from a tree this size, in terms of planks?"

Dussol brooded over the pine in meditative silence, while Cazavieilh, also silent, watched him in an attitude of respect, waiting for the verdict. Dussol took out his note-book, and plunged into a series of calculations. At last he gave his opinion.

"I'd never have believed it!" said Cazavieilh. "Wonderful, that's what it is, wonderful!"

"I find my eye comes in very useful at sales!"

Yves went back towards the house. The fine September morning was rich with an unaccustomed fragrance of truffles and sauces. He wandered round to the kitchens. The hired butler was in a bad temper, because they had forgotten to decant one of the wines. Yves went through the dining-room. The Dubuch girl would be between him and José. He re-read the Menu: *liévre à la Villafranca, passage de mûriers*, then left the house again and went into the stable-yard where Dussol, a folding-rule in his hand, was measuring the distance between the wheels of a tilbury.

"What did I tell you? – out of the straight: this tilbury of yours wants a lot doing to it: if you don't believe me, measure it up for yourself."

It was Cazavieilh's turn now to squat down beside Dussol. Yves gazed in amazement at the spectacle of the two enormous rumps. At last the two men scrambled to their feet, scarlet in the face.

"You're absolutely right, 'pon my word you really are extraordinary, Dussol!"

A silent chuckle set Dussol quivering. He was bursting with conceit. His eyes were almost invisible. He had just enough intelligence to calculate the profit to be made out of people and objects.

He and Cazavieilh went back towards the house. Now and again they would both of them come to a full stop, gaze at one another as though engaged in resolving some problem concerned with the eternal verities, and then, start off again. Yves, motionless in the middle of the path, felt himself swept suddenly by an intoxicating, a horrible, craving to draw a gun and let fly at them treacherously, from behind: Bang! – right in the back of the neck! Over they'd roll: bang! – bang! – why wasn't he an Emperor, a negro despot!

"I'm a monster!" – was what he said aloud.

The hired butler appeared at the top of the steps:

"Luncheon is served!"

" . . . With the fingers, of course! . . ."

They began to wolf the crayfish, cracking the shells and sucking out the contents with an air of absorbed attention, as though they were torn between a desire to leave nothing in the dish, and a concern to observe the dictates of good manners.

Yves observed at close range the brown-skinned, fragile arm of the Dubuch girl; a child's arm attached to a shoulder which, for all its roundness, produced somehow the impression that it was immaterial. He lacked the courage to do more than shoot a sidelong glance at her face. The eyes were too large: the wings of the nose were wings indeed. The mouth alone, which was fleshy to excess and lacking in colour, struck a human note in this angelic physiognomy. The general view was that it was a pity she had so little hair, but her method of doing it (with a central parting and two coils over the ears) revealed a type of beauty which the world at large has only gradually come to appreciate – the contour of an exquisitely moulded head, the pure lines of a nape. Yves was reminded of the reproductions of certain Egyptian bas-reliefs in a book on Ancient History which he had used at school. Such pleasure did he find in merely looking at this young girl that he made no attempt to talk to her. At the beginning of the meal he had said that living in the country must give her plenty of time for reading. To this observation she had barely deigned to reply, and was now deep in talk with José about riding and shooting. Yves had been accustomed to seeing his brother dishevelled and badly-dressed – a "real man of the woods", as he had called him, and was surprised to notice that today for the first time, his hair was smarmed down, his sun-tanned cheeks closely shaved, and his teeth a glittering white. But the most remarkable thing of all was that he was talking. José who, in the family circle, never uttered a word, was actually making his neighbour laugh! She was quite obviously infatuated: – "How silly you are! I suppose you think that funny!" José never took his eyes off her. There was a fixed look on his face which Yves was too inexperienced to recognize as the very mark and signal of desire. He remembered, however, what their mother had so often said: " – José's the one who is going to need watching. . . . I shall have my work cut out with him. . . ." He never missed a village fair or fête. Yves thought it stupid of him to find so much pleasure in lucky-dips and merry-go-rounds. But on the most recent of these occasions, he had discovered that his brother had given a miss to the wooden horses, and had spent his time dancing with the farmers' daughters.

All of a sudden, he felt sad. It was ridiculous to suppose that the Dubuch girl, who was seventeen, could really take José seriously. All the same, she was enjoying his jokes. There was an understanding between them which went deeper than words. It had nothing in it of deliberate intention, but was controlled by the pulsing of their blood. It occurred to Yves that he was jealous, and he felt ashamed. The real truth was that he was conscious of being ignored, isolated. He did not say to himself – 'I, too, one of these days, and perhaps quite soon . . .'

At the other end of the table, Jean-Louis and Madeleine Cazavieilh were looking precisely as they were to look on the occasion of their betrothal. . . . Yves, who was drinking all the different wines which accompanied the meal, glanced down the table, along the avenue of faces, to where, at the far end, he could see in a haze that elder brother who had fallen into the pit from which he would never succeed in escaping. Beside him, the lovely female who had served as bait, sat quiet, relaxed and happy, her task accomplished. She was not, really, so stocky a figure as she appeared to Yves. She had given up wearing boleros, and had on a white muslin dress which left her handsome arms, and the pure line of her neck, exposed. Her appearance was at once ripe and virginal. She was waiting. Occasionally, she and Jean-Louis exchanged a few words. Yves wished that he could hear what they were saying. Had he done so, he would have been amazed to find how vapid were their interchanges. 'We' – Jean-Louis was thinking – 'have all our lives before us: time enough in which to get to know one another. . . .' They were discussing the mulberries which had just been put before them, and had been so difficult to get hold of, pigeon-shooting, the setting of decoys which would have to be done soon, because the wood-pigeons which herald the coming of the wilder species, would soon be here. . . . All the space of their two lives in which to explain to Madeleine . . . explain what? It was hidden from Jean-Louis that, as those years sped by, existence, for him, would be beset with many dramas, that he would have children, and lose two of them, that he would make an enormous fortune which, towards the end of his life, would collapse – and that through all the changes and chances husband and wife would continue to talk about the same simple, silly things which had been all-sufficient for mutual happiness in this dawning moment of their love, as they sat through an interminable meal, while the wasps buzzed round the piles of fruit, and the ice-pudding melted into a pinkish cream.

Yves contemplated this trivial happiness of Jean-Louis and Madeleine with feelings that partook at once of envy and con tempt. Not once had the Dubuch girl turned towards him. José, the great eater of the family, quite forgot to give himself a second helping of the different dishes. But, like Yves, he was indulging freely in the wines. A light dew of sweat was beading his forehead. Such was the power of the girl's eyes that, when she let them dwell for a moment on some man in whom she took not the slightest interest, he at once imagined that their glorious radiance had been kindled for him alone. The bewitched José decided in the secrecy of his heart that before the night was much older he would take the young enchantress for a stroll.

"You won't go without paying a visit to my pigeon-farm, now, will you? – promise!"

"What, over at Maryan? You must be cuckoo! It's a good half-hour's walk!"

"We could talk there undisturbed."

"Oh, I've had quite enough of your talking, thank you . . . just a lot of nonsense!"

Suddenly, she turned to Yves: her eyes were shining.

"How terribly long this lunch is."

Yves felt so dazzled that he would have liked to hide his face in his hands. In his bewilderment he tried to find something to say. The sweet biscuits had gone round. He looked at his mother. She was in one of those absent-minded fits which came upon her in company, and had forgotten to move. There was a vague and worried look in her eyes. She had slipped two fingers into the opening of her blouse. While the parish-priest was describing his differences with the Mayor, she was thinking of life at its last gasp, of death, of God's Judgment Seat, and of the breaking-up of family estates.

XII

SATED with good food, the men of the party had gathered under the trees for coffee and liqueurs. Dussol had taken Uncle Xavier aside, and Blanche Frontenac followed them with anxious eyes. She was frightened lest her brother-in-law should let himself be "done". Yves made his way round the house, and then started along the deserted ride which led to the great oak. There was no need for him to go far to be out of reach of their voices, out of smelling distance of their cigars. Wild nature was close at hand. Already, though he had gone but a little way, the trees were unaware that there had been guests to luncheon.

He jumped a ditch. He was slightly drunk (though not as much as he feared he might be, for he had let himself go over the wine). His hide-out, his "hut" was waiting for him. Furze bushes, which the peoples of Les Landes call "jaugues", and bracken, high as a man, surrounded and protected it. It was a place sacred to tears and to the reading of forbidden books, a scene of wild outbursts and of inspiration. There he had flung his challenges to God, there he had prayed and there blasphemed. For some days he had not been near it. Already in the untrodden sand lion-ants had dug their tiny holes. Yves caught an ant, and threw it into one of them. The creature tried to climb out, but the crumbling sides gave way beneath it. From the bottom of its prison it sent up a little shower of sand. Barely had it reached the lip of the chasm than it slid down again. Suddenly it felt itself in the grip of a claw. It fought, but the monster pulled it slowly underground. Appalling fate! All around the crickets were shrilling in the still heat of the lovely day. Dragonflies were hovering, reluctant to settle. The pink and russet heather, filled with bees, was already sweet with honey-scent. Yves could see above the sand only the ant's head and two small, despairing feet. Leaning above this diminutive mystery, the boy of sixteen brooded upon the problem of evil. The grub that had devised this trap and must, to live and turn into a butterfly, inflict on ants a ghastly agony; the insect's terrified clamber from the hole, its failures, and the monster gripping it . . . all this nightmare was part of the Great Plan. Yves took a pine-needle and disinterred the lion-ant, a flabby and now powerless grub. . . . The rescued insect went on its way, as busy and preoccupied as its companions, and seemingly oblivious of what it had endured – doubtless because the ordeal had been natural, had been in accordance with Nature's laws. . . . But Nature had not reckoned with Yves. With his troubled heart and his power to suffer, he lay there in a nest of furze. Had he been the sole human being living and breathing on the surface of the earth, still, it was enough for him to be there to destroy the rule of blind necessity, to break the endless sequence of monsters devouring and devoured. *He* could break the chain. The least movement of love could break it. Into the hideous order of the world love could introduce its adorable power of reversal. *That* was Christ's mystery, and the mystery of those who take Christ as their model. "For that art thou set apart . . . I have chosen thee for the upsetting of all things. . . ." Out loud, the boy said: "It is I who am speaking . . ." (he pressed his two hands to his sweating face), "it is always ourselves speaking to ourselves. . . ." He tried not to think. High above him, to the south, into the blue sky rose a covey of wood-pigeons. He followed them with his eyes until they vanished from sight. "Thou knowest full well that I AM who have chosen thee." Yves, squatting on his heels, took a handful of sand and cast it on the empty air. There was a wild look in his eyes, and again and again he cried aloud: "No! . . . no! . . . no!"

"I have chosen thee, have set thee apart from others, have marked thee with my sign."

Yves clenched his fists. This was pure delirium, he told himself: he was flown with wine. He wanted only to be left alone. He wanted no more than to be a boy of his age, just like every other boy of his age. He would know well enough how to escape from solitude.

"Always will I build it up about thee."

"Am I not free? – yes, I am free!" – he cried.

He stood up, and his shadow moved upon the bracken.

"Thou art free to drag through the world a heart which I have not created for the world – free to seek on earth the food for which thou wast not destined, free to try to assuage a hunger which will never find wherewithal to satisfy itself. In no living creature shall it find satisfaction, and thou wilt turn in vain from one to another."

"I am talking to myself," he said again: "I am just like other men: I am their living image."

There was a singing in his ears. A longing for sleep stretched him upon the sand. He lay with his head on his crooked arm. A bee buzzed about him, then flew away to be lost in the spaces of Heaven. . . . The east wind was heavy with the smell of baking bread and sawn wood. He closed his eyes. Flies clung to his face which had a taste of salt. With a sleepy gesture he drove them from him. . . . The sight of him lying there did not worry the evening crickets. A squirrel clambered down the nearest pine, and, on its way to drink at the stream, passed close to him. An ant, perhaps the very ant that he had rescued, began to crawl up his leg with others at its heels. How long would he have had to stay motionless before they grew bold enough to eat him?

The freshness of the stream awakened him. He made his way out of the tangled undergrowth. There were stains of resin on his coat. He picked the pine-needles from his hair. The meadow-mist was creeping gradually into the woods, and it was like the breath from a living mouth in cold weather. As he turned a corner in the ride, he found himself face to face with his mother. She was telling her Rosary. She had thrown an old violet shawl over her party dress. A lace "fall" – "a lovely thing", as she always called it – adorned her bodice. . . . A long gold chain and a string of small pearls were secured by a brooch which carried two large initials, a B and an F, interlaced.

"Where've you been? . . . They were looking for you . . . it was scarcely polite."

He took his mother's arm and pressed against her.

"I'm frightened of people," he said.

"Frightened of Dussol? frightened of the Cazavieilhs? . . . My dear boy, you must be mad!"

"They're ogres, mamma."

"I must admit," she said dreamily, "that they haven't left much."

"Do you think that anything at all will be left of Jean-Louis in ten years' time? Dussol will swallow him, bit by bit."

"What nonsense you do talk!"

The words were uncompromising, but there was a note of tenderness in the voice that spoke them.

"You must try to understand me, darling. I want to see Jean-Louis settled. His home will be your home. As soon as he has a family life of his own I can depart in peace."

"I won't have you say things like that, mamma!"

"Even after that short little walk I've got to sit down: so, you see there is something in what I say."

She dropped on to the bench which stood under the great oak. Yves saw her slip her hand into her bodice.

"You know it's not malignant. . . . Arnozan has told you that a hundred times."

"So they say . . . but that's not the only thing . . . there are the rheumatic twinges round my heart. I don't think you realize how much suffering I have to put up with. You'd better face the truth, my boy: sooner or later you'll have to. . . ."

Once again he pressed against his mother, and took her broad, worn face between his hands.

"You are here," he said: "you will always be here."

She felt him shiver, and asked whether he felt cold. She covered him with her violet shawl. They snuggled together, both enveloped in the same old woollen wrap.

"You had this shawl when I made my First Communion, mamma . . . it smells just the same."

"Your grandmother brought it back from Salies."

Perhaps for the very last time as a small boy Yves pressed against his mother's living body. At any moment she might disappear. But for centuries and centuries the Hure would flow, and until the end of time the mists would rise from these meadows towards the evening star.

"You who know so much, Yves, tell me – do the spirits in Heaven think of those whom they have left behind on earth? . . . That, at any rate, is what I believe. . . . I can entertain no thought against the Faith . . . but how is it possible to imagine a world in which you, my dear ones, will not be all in all to me?"

Then did Yves assure her that all separate loves would be perfected in the one and only Love, that the heart's affection would be lightened and purified of all that once had muddied it. . . . He was amazed at his own words.

His mother murmured on a sigh:

"Oh, how I pray that none of you will ever be lost!"

They got up, and Yves's mind was full of anxious thoughts, while the old woman, now at peace, leaned on his arm.

"I always tell others that they do not know my darling Yves. Hot-headed you may be, but of all my children you are the one who is nearest to God. . . ."

"No, mamma! – please don't say that! No! no! . . ."

Suddenly he broke from her.

"What's wrong with you? what's the matter?" He walked in front of her, his hands in his pockets, his shoulders hunched. She panted in her effort to keep up with him.

Madame Frontenac was tired out. As soon as dinner was over she went to her room. Since the night was fine, the other members of the family started off for a stroll in the park, but no longer in a compact group. Already, life was loosening the bonds which had held the boys together. . . . Jean-Louis passed Yves at a corner of the path, but neither stopped. The elder wanted to be left alone with his happiness. He was no longer oppressed by a sense of diminution, by a feeling that he had fallen from a high estate. Certain things that Dussol had said about the workers had awakened in him preoccupations which were still at the vague stage. He would do good, in spite of his business associate, would further the coming of a Christian social order. He would not be content with wordy theories, but would do something concrete. Whatever Yves might think, *that* was more important than any amount of speculative philosophy. . . . The smallest act of charity ranks immeasurably higher. . . . Jean-Louis could not live happily on the labour of those who were strangers to happiness. . . . 'I want to help them to build homes that shall be conceived in the image of mine . . .' He saw the gleam of Uncle Xavier's cigar. For a while the two of them walked side by side.

"You're happy, my boy, aren't you? – What did I say?"

Jean-Louis made no attempt to explain to his uncle the nature of the projects which had so filled him with enthusiasm. Nor was it possible for his uncle to put into words his own pleasure at the idea of getting back to Angoulême . . . Joséfa had been disappointed in that matter of the trip, but he would make it all up to her, and at little cost to himself – maybe by doubling her monthly allowance. . . . He would say, "After all, if we'd gone, it would all be over by this time. . . ."

'First of all,' Jean-Louis was thinking, 'before I can even think of anything in the nature of a Mission, there are certain essential reforms to be carried through . . . some form of profit-sharing.' From now on he must shape all his reading to that end.

By the light of the moon they saw José cross the ride from one clump of bushes to another. They could hear the crackle of twigs under his feet. Where was this particular Frontenac off to? – this young fox whom they could have trailed by his scent? . . . In the darkness he was, of all of them, the closest akin to the purely instinctive animal, the young male outcast whose fate it would be never to find the female whom he sought. On he went, treading the dead leaves under foot, tearing his hands on the prickly furze, until at last he reached the Home-Farm which lay just beyond the confines of the park. . . . From somewhere under the pergola a dog growled. The kitchen window stood open. The family was grouped about the table, lit by an oil lamp. José could see in profile the married daughter, the one with a thick neck and a small head. He stood there, munching a leaf of mint, and never taking his eyes from her.

Meanwhile, Yves was making the round of the park for the

third time. Not yet was he conscious of the weariness which soon would fling him, utterly worn out, upon his bed. At dinner he had drunk the wine of feasting to the dregs, and now, feeling wonderfully clear-headed, was casting up the day's balance-sheet, and constructing the framework of that doctrine into the secret freedoms of which Jean-Louis was no longer worthy to be admitted. His state of semi-drunkenness had filled him with a facile sense of genius. He would make no choice. He was under no compulsion to choose. He had been wrong to say "No!" to that urgent voice which might, for all he knew, have been the voice of God. Never would he say "No!" to anybody, and from that refusal to refuse would spring his drama and the tensions out of which his work would grow. All his poetry was to be the expression of a rending struggle – to refuse nothing, never to refuse himself to anything. All imaginative work thrives on pain and passion, drawing from them the sustenance which swells the bud of art. But because the poet is torn and rent, so also is he pardoned. *I know that Thou hast kept for the poet a place in the Legions of the Blest . . .*" The monotonous sound of his voice would have thrilled Uncle Xavier, so like it was to Michel Frontenac's.

Blanche was so tired that she expected to go to sleep as soon as she had blown out her candle. But she could hear the children's footsteps on the gravel. . . . She must remember to send some money to the bailiff at Respide . . . she must find out how her balance stood at the Crédit Lyonnais. . . . October Quarter-Day would soon be coming round. . . . Fortunately, the house-property was still intact. But what did all that matter now! She touched the gland with her fingers. She looked into her heart.

Not one of the Frontenacs on this especial night was visited by the slightest presentiment that for all of them an era was to end with the close of these summer holidays. The long, hot days were already fading into a past to which, as they withdrew, they were carrying, never to be restored, the pure and simple pleasures of a happiness that leaves no stain upon the heart.

Yves, alone, was conscious of a change, but the effect of that knowledge was that, more than all the others, he would build for himself a world of illusion. He saw himself standing on the threshold of a life blazing with inspiration and filled with perilous experience. In fact, though he did not know it, he was about to enter upon a period of squalor. For the next four years his every thought would be dominated by the terrors of examinations. The circles in which he must move would be dim and mediocre. The restlessness of puberty and its petty prurience would set him on a level with his companions and make of him their fellow. The time was fast approaching when his main preoccupation would be how to get his mother to let him have a latchkey, and how to wheedle from her permission to stay out after midnight. He would not be unhappy. At long intervals a whisper from his deeper self would drift to the surface of his life, as from some being shrouded and entombed. At such times he would let his companions go their ways without him. Seated alone at a table in the *Café de Bordeaux*, among the thistles and the shapeless women of the *art nouveau* mosaics, he would start scribbling away on sheets of letter-paper, at top speed, without troubling even to form his writing properly for fear of losing the words which are whispered in the poet's ear once, and once only. Then would come Paris, and the task of developing that other self whom, already, a tiny group of enthusiasts would be already praising to the skies, a group so small, that it would be many years before he awoke to his own importance and took the measure of his victory. A product of the Provinces, an admirer of established reputations, he would, for a long time, fail to realize that his was a reputation of a different kind – that his was a genius born in obscurity, working underground like a mole, and not emerging into the light until much journeying in the unseen depths had been accomplished.

But agony lay in wait for him. How could its horror have been foretold to the Yves Frontenac now leaning at his bedroom window in the mild and moist September darkness? The more his poetry won the hearts of others, the more was he to feel himself impoverished. Strangers would drink of those waters, and only he would know how muddied and befouled had grown the source from which they flowed. That knowledge would lie at the roots of his self-distrust, causing him to shrink from the clamorous enthusiasm of the Paris world. It would set him for a long time at odds with the editor of one of the most influential of the "advanced" Reviews, and, in the long run, would make him hesitate to collect his poems into a volume.

Yves, at his window, murmured an evening prayer to the tangled darkness of tree-thick Bourideys and the wandering moon. He was ready and eager for all that the future might hold, even if it turned out to be suffering. What he was not ready to face was the shame of long outliving his inspiration, of using subterfuge to keep his fame alive. He could not foresee that one day he would find words to express this drama in a Journal which, after a great war, would be published, nor that he would resign himself to making it public after a long age of silence. That terrible record was to prove the crowning feature of his reputation, and to do more for his fame than all his poems. It was to bring enchantment and a pleasing turmoil into the hearts of a despairing generation. And so it was that, on this September night, God, maybe, saw this young boy rapt in reverie before the sleeping pines, as the starting-point of a strange sequence of cause and effect. The youth who thought himself so proud was very far then from realizing how wide an influence he would exert. Not even vaguely did he dream that the destiny of many would be different from what on earth and in Heaven it might have been, had no Yves Frontenac been born.

PART TWO

Que les oiseaux et les sources
sont loins! Ce ne peut être que
la fin du monde, en avançant.
RIMBAUD

XIII

"FIVE thousand francs worth of debt in three months! Who would ever have dreamed of such a thing in our day, Dussol?"

"Ah, but we, Caussade, had a proper respect for money – we knew how our dear parents had strained and slaved to put something by. *We* were brought up to believe in saving. 'Discipline – Work – Economy' – such was my admirable father's motto."

Blanche Frontenac broke in on them.

"It's not you we're discussing, but José."

She was sorry now that she had taken Dussol and her brother-in-law into her confidence. . . . When Jean-Louis discovered what was going on, he had had to mention it to Dussol, because José had been pledging the firm's credit, and Dussol had insisted on calling a family-council. But Madame Frontenac and Jean-Louis had been against saying anything to Uncle Xavier. He had a bad heart, and this blow might make it worse. Why, Blanche wondered, had Alfred Caussade been brought into the business at all? Jean-Louis regretted it as much as she did.

The young man sat facing his mother. Office life had aged him. His hair was already receding, although he was not more than twenty-three.

"The boy really must be a half-wit"—said Alfred Caussade – "I gather that quite a lot of fellows have had this woman for nothing . . . ever seen her, Dussol?"

"Once" – replied Dussol – "and not from choice, I can assure you! Madame Dussol wanted to go to the Apollo, just to see what the place is like, you know, and I didn't feel I had any right to refuse to take her. Naturally, we had a box – we didn't want to be seen. The way that creature Stéphane Paros danced! – not a stitch on her legs! . . ."

Uncle Alfred's eyes gleamed. He leaned closer to the speaker:

"I'm told that sometimes . . ."

The rest of the sentence was inaudible. Dussol took off his pince-nez and threw back his head.

"It's only fair to say," he went on, "that she was wearing some sort of close-fitting garment on the upper part of her body – a very flimsy sort of affair, to be sure, still, it did cover her. . . . She always does, I'm told. . . . You can't suppose that I should have exposed Madame Dussol . . . Still, bare legs are bad enough in all conscience. . . ."

"*And* bare feet . . ." put in Alfred Caussade.

"Oh, feet!" – and Dussol made an indulgent grimace.

"Speaking for myself . . ." – declared Alfred with a sort of embarrassed eagerness – "I find bare feet more disgusting than anything else. . . ."

Blanche interrupted him angrily:

"It's you who are being disgusting, Alfred!"

He protested, tugging at his beard, and smoothing it with his hand:

"My dear Blanche! . . ."

"It's time we reached some kind of decision. What do you advise, Dussol?"

"Send him away, dear lady. The sooner he leaves and the further he goes the better. My own choice would be Winnipeg . . . but I know you won't agree to that. . . . We need somebody in Norway . . . the salary won't be large, but there's nothing like roughing it to teach a young man the value of money. . . . D'you agree, Jean-Louis?"

The latter replied, without looking at his partner, that he

was certainly of the opinion that José ought to be got out of Bordeaux. Blanche looked across at her eldest son:

"Oh, but . . . but . . . we've lost Yves already!"

"You should never, dear lady, have let *him* out of your sight!" exclaimed Dussol. "I only wish you had asked my advice. There was no earthly reason why he should go to Paris. You're not, surely, going to tell me that his work made it necessary? I know pretty well what you think about his so-called work! – in that direction maternal affection has certainly not blinded you – you've got too much sound commonsense! I scarcely think that I am destroying any illusions you may harbour, when I say that his literary future . . . and, mind you, I know what I am talking about, I have taken great pains to keep abreast of his productions, even to the extent of reading some of them aloud to Madame Dussol, though I must admit, she very soon begged for mercy! . . . I know, of course, that you'll tell me he has received a certain amount of encouragement . . . but what sort of encouragement, may I ask? Jean-Louise showed me a letter from a Monsieur Gide, but who *he* is nobody knows. There is an economist of that name, to be sure, but unfortunately, it didn't come from him! . . ."

Though Jean-Louis had long realized that his mother never minded contradicting herself, and that logic was not one of her strong points, he was frankly amazed to hear her now opposing Dussol with the very arguments he had himself used against her only the evening before!

"It would be a great deal better if you didn't talk about what you cannot possibly understand. His poems are not written for people like you – who approve only of what is familiar to them, what they have already come across somewhere else. The new shocks them. Isn't that so, Jean-Louis? Yves tells me that even Racine shocked his contemporaries."

"You're not going to tell me that the glories of Racine can

be mentioned in the same breath as the outpourings of *that* young cub!"

"Let me advise you, my poor friend, to give your mind to timber and to leave poetry alone! Poetry is not your concern – any more than it is mine" – she added, in an effort of appeasement – for he was swelling like a turkey-cock, and his neck was turning bright red.

"Madame Dussol and I are at great pains to keep ourselves up to date. I was one of the earliest patrons of the *Panbiblion* library, and my subscription covers periodicals as well as books – we make it a point to know what is going on in the world of the higher journalism. Only the other day, one of my colleagues at the Chamber of Commerce was saying that what makes Madame Dussol's conversation so delightful is that she has read everything, and has such a truly amazing memory that she can tell you the plot of a novel or a play which she hasn't looked at for years, just as though she has only just been reading it. He went so far as to add – and I thought it very wittily put – "A woman like that is a walking library . . ."

"She is to be envied" – said Blanche: "my own memory is like a sieve; nothing sticks in it."

This piece of self-criticism was intended to disarm Dussol.

"Whew!" she exclaimed with a sigh when the two elderly gentlemen had departed.

She drew her chair to the fire. The radiators were full on, but she had never, since moving to this house, got used to the central heating. For her, not being cold meant seeing a fire and roasting her legs. She was in a mood of self-pity. So now she must lose José! – and next year he wanted to enlist as a volunteer in Morocco. . . . She ought never to have let Yves go from her! What Dussol had said was true – though not for anything in the world would she have admitted as much to him . . . the boy could just as well have done his writing in Bordeaux. She felt convinced that he was merely idling away his time in Paris.

"It was you who put the idea into his head, Jean-Louis. He would never have left us of his own accord."

"That's not fair, mamma! You know that since the girls have been married and you have come to live with them in this house, you think of nothing but their family affairs and their children. All that's perfectly right and proper, but Yves would have felt utterly lost in this nursery atmosphere."

"Lost! . . . didn't I sit up every night with him when he had congestion of the lungs?"

"Yes, and he said he liked being ill because it was only then that he felt you were really close to him. . . ."

"He's an ungrateful young scamp, that's the long and the short of it!"

Jean-Louis made no reply, and she went on:

"Tell me, what do you really think he's doing with himself in Paris?"

"Working away at his book, of course, seeing all he can of other writers, talking of what interests him, making contact with editors and people in the literary world . . . all that sort of thing."

Madame Frontenac shook her head: "all that sort of thing" conveyed nothing to her. What she wanted to know was the kind of life he was living. She was afraid that he had lost all his principles. . . .

"But there is a deep note of mysticism in everything he writes . . ." (Jean-Louis flushed scarlet) . . . "Only the other day Thibaudet wrote that his poetry postulates a metaphysic. . . ."

"That's just a lot of words . . ." she broke in. "What are metaphysics worth, if he doesn't take Easter Communion? . . .

a mystic indeed! . . . a young man who absents himself from the Sacraments! . . . really!"

Jean-Louis said nothing, and she went on:

"When you see him on your trips to Paris, what does he talk about? Does he just tell you of the people he's been meeting – and nothing else? surely, as brother to brother . . ."

"Brothers," said Jean-Louis, "have a certain intuition, a certain understanding, about one another, but only up to a point . . . they don't share their secrets. . . ."

"What exactly do you mean? – you're too complicated for me. . . ."

Leaning forward, with her elbows on her knees, Blanche poked the fire.

"What are we to do about José, mamma?"

"Oh, what it is to have sons! . . . Luckily, you, at least . . ."

She looked at him. Was he really as happy as she liked to think? His shoulders carried a heavy load of responsibility, and he did not always get on with Dussol. She felt compelled to admit that sometimes he did not show himself to be prudent, or even possessed of ordinary common-sense. . . . It is all very well for an employer to have a social conscience, but, as Dussol said, it is only when one comes to balance the books that one realizes how much a social conscience costs. She had had to admit that Dussol had been right when he had opposed Jean-Louis's project of setting up "Factory Councils" in which representatives of Workers and Management should sit down together round a table, and when he had set his face against a system of Arbitration Boards, the working of which Jean-Louis had tried to explain to him, though without success. In the matter of one innovation, however, Dussol had finally yielded, and it was the one which, really, was closest to his young partner's heart. "Let him try it out", Dussol had said.

"No doubt it'll cost a pretty penny, but he's got to sow his wild oats some time!"

Jean-Louis's great idea was to give the workers an interest in the business. With Dussol's permission he called them together and explained the scheme. What he proposed was to issue shares to all his workers in proportion to the length of each man's service. Dussol's common-sense attitude was completely vindicated. The men regarded the whole thing as a huge joke. Before a month was out they had sold all the shares allotted to them. "I told him again and again," said Dussol, "that that was what would happen, and now he's seen for himself. I don't regret the cost. He knows at least the kind of people he's dealing with, and he won't be victimized a second time. The really funny thing is that the men respect me for being as hard as nails. They know they can't get round me. I talk their language, and they like me, whereas he, with all his socialistic notions, strikes them as being proud and aloof. It's always me they come to when they want anything."

"If you'd really rather let José stay on in Bordeaux" – said Jean-Louis – "I can't see any real reason why he shouldn't. This Paros woman has sent me word by her man of business that she has got no designs on him, and has never accepted anything from him but flowers. It was scarcely her fault if José always insisted on footing the bill when they dined together. . . . She believed him to be a rich man. . . . In any case, she is leaving Bordeaux next week. . . . All the same, I think it would do him good to have a change of scene until his time for military service comes round. . . . Some other woman might get her claws into him. . . . But I don't at all agree with Dussol that we ought to keep him short of money. . . ."

Madame Frontenac shrugged her shoulders:

"Of course not. When they were all talking just now about

it being such a good thing for young men to rough it, I didn't say anything, because I didn't want to make a fuss . . . but really, what an idea!"

"Shall I go and fetch him? he's waiting upstairs in his room."

"Yes, and switch on the light."

A ceiling-lamp provided gloomy illumination for the Empire room with its faded wallpaper.

Jean-Louis turned with José.

"This is what we've decided, old chap. . . ."

The culprit remained standing in the shadows with lowered eyes. He looked stockier than his brothers, "low on his feet", but with a great spread of shoulder. He had a dark, swarthy face which showed blue to the cheek-bones. Blanche noted in the young man the same power of withdrawal which had marked the schoolboy when she used to hear him his homework in the melancholy evenings of the years gone by. He had never listened to a word she said. No matter how much she might implore and threaten, he had always managed, in the most extraordinary way, to escape into a world of his own, to absent himself. Just as when, in his boyhood, he had buried himself in delightful dreams of summer holidays at Bourideys; just as, later on, he had had no thoughts but for the life of a trapper, and was quite capable of spending whole winter nights in a "hideout", watching for wild duck – so now, the whole force of his awareness, of his desire, had become centred, at one fell swoop, upon a woman – a perfectly ordinary woman, by no means fresh, who was touring the Provinces with a sort of Frégoli act (*The Dancer of Seville – The Houri – The Nautch-Girl*). A friend had introduced her to him after the performance. There had been a party of them in a night-club. That evening, for the first and only time, he had found favour in the lady's eyes, and had become wildly infatuated. She had filled his world to the exclusion of everyone, and everything, else.

The office, in those days, had seen little of him, but Jean-Louis had taken over his work as well as his own. Finally, his timid but mulish obstinacy had got on the lady's nerves. . . .

And now, here he was, standing between his mother and his brother, with a blank, impenetrable look upon his face.

"These debts of yours are a serious matter . . ." said his mother. "But I don't want you to think that it's the money that chiefly worries me. What matters to me, above all else, is the wild way of life into which you have fallen . . . I have always had confidence in my sons, have always believed that they would eschew base actions . . . and now, you, José . . ."

Had her words shaken him? He sat down on the divan with the light full in his face. He had grown thinner: even his temples looked hollow. In an expressionless voice he asked when he was to leave.

"In January, after the Christmas holidays," she said, and he replied:

"The sooner the better."

He was taking it all very well. Everything, Blanche told herself, would be for the best. All the same, she was far from being easy in her mind, and sought for reassurance. It did not escape her that Jean-Louis, too, was looking at his younger brother. Anyone other than themselves would have taken comfort in the young man's quietness. But both mother and brother knew what they were up against. This particular kind of suffering was something with which they were familiar. They were linked physically with the despair before them, which, being a child's, was despair in its worst form, impossible to interpret, and proof against any obstacle of reason, self-interest, or ambition. . . . The elder brother kept his eyes firmly fixed upon the prodigal. The mother rose to her feet. She went across to José, took his face in her two hands, as though to waken him, as though to rouse him from hypnotic slumber:

"José, look at me."

She spoke in a tone of command, and he, with a child's impatience, shook his head, closed his eyes, and sought to free himself from her clasp. In the hard and secret look of her son's face, Blanche saw what she herself had never known – the agony of love. He'd get over it . . . it wouldn't last long . . . only, he had got to reach the further bank and not drown in mid-stream. This boy of hers had always frightened her. When he was young she had never known, with certainty, how he would react. If only he would say something! if only he would complain! But no, there he sat, with his jaw clenched, presenting to his mother the burned-up face of a child of Les Landes (perhaps, long ago, some woman of the family had been seduced by one of those Catalans who lived by selling smuggled matches). His eyes blazed, but their fire was dark, and revealed nothing. Then Jean-Louis, approaching in his turn, took the other by the shoulders and shook him, though without roughness. Several times he said – "José, old man, José, old boy" . . . and succeeded where his mother had failed. He made his brother cry. The mother's tenderness was so familiar to him that it could no longer produce any reaction: but never, until now, had Jean-Louis shown such tenderness. So unexpected was it that he had, perforce, to yield to his surprise. The tears burst from his eyes, and he clung to his brother as though he had been a drowning man. Instinctively, Madame Frontenac had turned away her face and gone back to the fire. She heard the stammered words; she heard the convulsive sobbing. She leaned above the fire, her hands clasped across her mouth.

The two brothers approached her.

"He's going to be sensible, mamma, he's promised."

She drew her unhappy son into her arms. "Darling, you'll never look like this again, will you?"

Once more, and once only, would that terrible expression show upon his face, and that, towards the end of a fine, warm day in late August, at Mourmelon, in 1915, between two army huts. No one would notice it, not even the friend seeking to dissipate his fears:

"There's going to be a terrific artillery preparation. Everything'll be smashed to pieces, and there'll be nothing left for us to do but walk forward with our hands in our pockets and our rifles slung . . ."

To him José Frontenac would show just such a face, drained of all hope, though then it would no longer waken fear in anybody.

XIV

JEAN-LOUIS hurried home. He lived only a few yards away, in the rue Lafaurie de Montbadon. He was eager to tell Madeleine everything before dinner. Yves had given him a disgust of the little house which they had furnished with such loving care. "You're neither a budding dentist, nor a doctor just starting in practice" – his brother had said. "There's no reason in the world why you should display on the mantelpiece, the walls, and even on special stands, the loathsome presents with which your friends have inundated you." Jean-Louis had protested, though half-heartedly: but now it was with Yves's eyes that he saw the crowded cupids in biscuit-china, the art-bronzes, and the Austrian terra-cottas.

"Baby's feverish," said Madeleine. She was sitting beside the cradle. The country girl, transplanted to the city, had thickened.

With her broad shoulders and powerful neck she looked no longer young. Perhaps she was with child? A blue and swollen vein showed just above her breast.

"How much temperature?"

"99·2. She sicked up her four o'clock bottle."

"Did you put the thermometer up her rectum? 99·2's not fever, especially at night."

"It is. Dr. Chatard said it was."

"He meant the under-arm temperature."

"It *is* fever, I tell you: not much, I know, but still, fever."

He made an impatient gesture and leaned over the cradle which smelt of wet straw mattress and sicked-up milk. He kissed the child, and it started to cry.

"Your beard's pricking her."

"Fresh as a peach," he said.

He began walking up and down the room, hoping that she would ask him about José. But she never put, unprompted, the questions that he wanted. He should have known that by this time: but he was always caught off-guard.

She said:

"You'd better start dinner without me."

"Because of the child?"

"Yes: I want to wait until she's asleep."

He felt thoroughly annoyed. This *would* be the evening when they were to have cheese soufflé, which has got to be eaten the moment it comes out of the oven. Madeleine must have remembered it – she was country-bred to her bones, brought up with an almost religious regard for family meal-times, and a healthy respect for food – because almost before Jean-Louis had spread his napkin, she had joined him. No good, he thought, waiting for her to speak first. It was obvious that she wouldn't ask him what had happened.

"Aren't you at all curious, darling?"

She was half asleep, and the eyes she turned to him were puffy.

"Curious about what?"

"José," he said. "It was quite a business. Dussol and Uncle Xavier didn't dare insist on Winnipeg . . . so it's got to be Norway."

"That won't be much of a punishment. . . . I suppose he can get his duck-shooting as easily there as here, and that's all he really cares about."

"Are you quite sure? . . . I wish you could have seen him . . . he loves her, you know" – and Jean-Louis went very red.

"What, a creature like that?"

"You shouldn't jeer at him" – and then, "I wish you could have seen him," he said again.

Madeleine's smile was knowing and unkind. She shrugged her shoulders, but said no more. She wasn't a Frontenac, he reflected, so what was the use of going on about it? She wouldn't understand. She wasn't a Frontenac. He tried to recollect precisely *how* José had looked, to remember the stammered words. That secret passion . . .

"Danièle very sweetly came to tea with me. She brought the pattern for that brassière – you know, the one I told you about."

The solid, sensible Jean-Louis could not but envy folly carried to such desperate lengths. He felt disgusted with himself, and looked across at his wife, who was rolling her bread into a pellet.

"What did you say?"

"Nothing . . . I didn't speak. What's the use? You don't listen to anything I say. You never answer."

"You said that Danièle had come to tea, didn't you?"

"If you promise not to repeat it, I'll tell you something. I rather think her husband has had enough of this living with your mother. He means to move as soon as he gets a rise."

"But they can't do that! It was partly because of them that mamma bought the house. They don't pay a penny of rent."

"That's the only thing that keeps them there. She's a very exhausting person to live with. . . . You know that well enough, you've told me so yourself a hundred times."

"Have I? Yes, I suppose I may have . . ."

"Besides, she'll still have Marie. *Her* husband's a great deal more patient, and has more of an eye to the main chance. He'll never willingly break up such a comfortable arrangement."

Jean-Louis saw his mother in the rather humiliating position of an old country-woman bandied about between her various children. Madeleine would not let the subject drop.

"I'm very fond of her, and she dotes on me. But I know that I couldn't live with her – I just couldn't."

"She, on the other hand, could quite easily live with you."

There was uneasiness in the look which Madeleine turned on her husband.

"You're not angry, are you? It doesn't make me love her any the less. . . . It's just a question of differences in character. . . ."

He got up, went round the table, and gave his wife a kiss. It was his way of saying that he was sorry for what he had been thinking. Just as they were preparing to leave the room, the servant came in with two letters. On one of the envelopes Jean-Louis recognized Yves's handwriting, and he slipped it into his pocket. He asked Madeleine's permission to open the other.

Dear Sir and Benefactor

I take up my pen to let you know as our youngest is agoing to take her first communion Thursday come two weeks and she knows all her prayers and her father and me when we sees her saying of her prayers at night and morning we feel quite soft and silly but annoyed too along of knowing as a festival costs a lot even when its for the Good God and we owing a tidy lot of money here and there. But as I said to my husband your benefactors not the sort to leave you in the lurch you being one as kept your shares instead of selling them off to buy drink like some did and there wasnt not one of them sober for a month after the shares was given out which it was a black shame and those as understood your kind thought being called scabs and arselickers and other things as respect for good manners wont let me write on paper. But as my husband says when a chaps got a boss like that its up to him to show himself worthy by understanding all the good things as he intends to do for the workers. . . .

Jean-Louis tore the letter up, and passed his hand several times over his nose and mouth.

"Do stop that nervous trick of yours," said Madeleine, and added: "I'm absolutely dropping! Heavens! it's only nine o'clock. You won't stay up too late, will you? . . . and do, please, undress in the other room."

Jean-Louis loved his library. Yves's critical comments carried no weight there. It contained nothing but books: even the mantelpiece was covered with them. He closed the door with care, sat down at his table, and balanced his brother's letter on his outstretched hand. He was delighted to find that it felt heavier than usual. He opened it, taking great pains not to tear the envelope. As a good Frontenac should, Yves began by giving news of Uncle Xavier, with whom he lunched regularly every Thursday. . . . The thought of one of his nephews settling in Paris had given the poor man the fright of his life, and he had done everything he could to dissuade Yves from taking such a step. The Frontenacs had pretended not to know why he was so disapproving of the plan. "He is less worried now" – wrote Yves – "because he has discovered that Paris is large enough to make it extremely unlikely that a nephew will run up against his uncle when the latter is out with a lady. . . . Yes, that is the long and short of it. I saw them together the other day in the street. In fact, I followed them for a bit, at a safe distance. She is big and blowzy and blonde and must have been quite a good looker twenty years ago. Would you believe it, they headed straight for a Duval[1] – and I've no doubt he'd bought himself a cheap cigar. When he takes *me* out we always go to Prunier's, and he invariably offers me a Bock or a Henry Clay with the coffee. But that, of course, is because I'm a Frontenac. . . . D'you know, I've actually been to see Barrès! . . ." He went on to describe this visit at length. The evening before, a friend had passed on to him something the Master had said to the effect that the whole thing was an awful bore because he'd have to be careful not to "disappoint young Frontenac" . . . and that had put Yves in a cold sweat. "I don't think I was quite as nervous as the Great Man, though pretty nearly! We left the house together, and as soon as we were in the street the specialist of the human heart thawed a bit. He said . . . I mustn't forget a single one of his precious words . . . he said . . ."

But it was not what Barrès had said that interested Jean-Louis. He read rapidly through this part of the letter, anxious to get on to where Yves should begin to describe his life in Paris, his work, his hopes, the men and the women among whom he lived. He turned a page, and could not keep back an exclamation of annoyance. Yves had carefully erased every line! The same on the back, the same on the page that followed. Nor had he been content with merely crossing out what he had written. Each word had been completely obliterated under a dense tangle of squiggles. Perhaps, beneath this passionate deletion all the secrets of a younger brother might lie con-

[1] The Paris equivalent of an A.B.C.—TRANSLATOR.

cealed! There must, said Jean-Louis to himself, be some way of getting at the text . . . there would almost certainly be specialists in this sort of investigation . . . but, no, he couldn't possibly hand over one of Yves's letters to a stranger. He remembered that there was a magnifying-glass lying about somewhere on his table (another wedding-present!), and began, with its aid, to peer at each concealed word with as much eager intentness as though the fate of the country hung upon his success. But all the magnifying-glass could do was to show him how Yves had gone about the business of foiling just this sort of attempt. Not only had he linked his words by inserting arbitrary letters between them, he had gone to the trouble of making down-strokes where none should be. . . . After working away for an hour, the elder brother had achieved only the most mediocre results. But, at least, Yves's intense efforts to render these pages unreadable were proof of the importance which he attached to them. Jean-Louis sat with his hands on the table. He could hear in the dark and silent street two men talking at the tops of their voices. From the Cours Balguérie came the clanging of the last tram. He stared with tired eyes at the mysterious letter. . . . If he took the car and drove all night, he could be with his brother before noon next day. . . . But he could set off alone like that only if he had some business excuse, and he had none. He had been to Paris three times in a single fortnight when a few thousand francs had been in question, but now that his brother's very safety might be threatened, no one would understand his behaving in so extraordinary a fashion. But threatened by what?

Had Jean-Louis been able to decipher Yves's suppressed intimacies, he would probably have been very considerably disappointed. Discretion rather than shame had dictated the younger brother's cautionary action. 'Of what possible interest can all this be to him?' – he had thought: 'and in any case he wouldn't understand' . . . This latter judgment implied no contempt. The fact of the matter was that when he was away from the members of his family, he thought of them as all compact of innocent simplicity. The people with whom he knocked about in Paris seemed to him to belong to some strange species between which and his country-bred relatives there could be no possible contact. "You just wouldn't know what they were talking about" – was what he had written (not knowing that before the letter was finished he would have scratched all this part out): "they jabber at such a rate, and make so many allusions to people whose nicknames and sexual peculiarities one is assumed to know backwards. I'm always two or three sentences behind, and laugh five minutes after the rest of them. But, since it's the general view that I'm some sort of a genius, this slowness in the uptake is all part of the picture they've made of me, and goes down on the credit-side. Most of them, as a matter of fact, have never read a word I've written, though they pretend to have a complete knowledge of my work. It's me they like, not my productions. Dear old Jean-Louis, it never occurred to us simple Bordeaux folk that the mere fact of being twenty would strike people like that as nothing short of a miracle! We just didn't realize how rich we were! In our homely circle youth isn't rated nearly so high. *We* regard it as the awkward age, the time of fluff and down, of pimples and boils, of moist hands and general grubbiness. The people hereabouts take a more flattering view. Boils don't last. Twenty-four hours is enough to turn you into a representative of the legendary Young. Sometimes a woman will say that she is mad about your poems, that she longs to hear you read them, and her bosom will rise and fall with such a gust of sighs that you'd think she could play the bellows to any fire. This year all doors have opened to my 'marvellous gift of youth' – even very exclusive doors. But literature is a mere excuse, there as elsewhere. No one really cares two hoots about what I *do*, nor understands it. That's not what they're after. All they care about is 'personalities'. I'm a personality, and so would you be, though you mightn't think it. Fortunately, these ogres and ogresses have no teeth left, and are reduced to devouring you with their eyes. They've no idea where I come from, and it wouldn't so much as occur to them to enquire whether or not I've got a mother. I could hate them for no better reason than that they have never asked me for news of mamma. They haven't the least conception what it means to be a Frontenac – even without the particle. The grandeur of the Frontenac 'mystery' is something they have never known. I might be the son of a convict and come straight from prison – it wouldn't make the slightest difference, except that it might give them an added kick. . . . It's enough for them that I am twenty years old, that I wash my hands and the rest of my body, and that I have what they call a 'position' in the literary world, or enough of one to explain my presence – along with Ambassadors and Members of the Institute – at their sumptuous tables – at which, for all their sumptuousness, the wines are badly served, too cold, and in glasses that are too small. . . . As mamma would say, one's only got time for a gulp and a swallow. . . ."

It was at this point that Yves had broken off and, on second thoughts, obliterated what he had written. Nor had it occurred to him that, by so doing, he ran the risk of adding considerably to his brother's bewilderment. Jean-Louis sat and stared at the hieroglyphics. Taking advantage of the fact that he was alone in the room, he surrendered to his nervous trick, and passed his cupped hand slowly over his nose, moustache and lips. . . .

After slipping Yves's letter into his note-case he looked at his watch. Madeleine must be growing impatient. He allowed himself another ten minutes of solitude and silence, took up a book, opened it, closed it again. Was his proclaimed liking for poetry just a pretence? He never, nowadays, seemed to want to read any. But then, he read less and less of anything. Yves had said: 'You're quite right not to clutter up your memory . . . we'd all be much better off if we could forget all the odds and ends we were fools to let ourselves be crammed with. . . ." But Yves said such a lot of things! . . . Since he'd gone to live in Paris one could never be sure whether he was serious or not – probably he didn't know himself.

Jean-Louis noticed the gleam of the bedside lamp showing from under the door. It was a wordless reproach, which meant: "You've kept me from going to sleep. I'd rather lie here waiting for you than be woken up." All the same, he undressed as quietly as possible, and went into the bedroom.

It was very large, and, despite Yves's habit of poking fun at it, Jean-Louis always felt a slight thrill each time he crossed the threshold. The darkness hid the wedding-presents, blurring the outlines of the bronze ornaments and assorted cupids. The furniture was shadowy and vague. The cradle, attached to the immense bed, looked like the basket of a balloon, hanging suspended, as though the child's breathing had been sufficient to inflate the simple curtains.

Madeleine cut Jean-Louis's excuses short.

"I've not been bored," she said: "I've been thinking."

"What about?"

"José," she said.

His mood softened. Just when he had given up all hope, here she was broaching, unprompted, the subject that was nearest to his heart.

"I've hit on the very person for him . . . now don't say 'no' before you've thought about it seriously. . . . Cécile, Cécile Filhot, I mean. She's rich, she's been brought up in the country and is used to men leaving the house before sunrise on a day's shooting, and going to bed at eight. She knows that that kind of man is never at home. She would make him thoroughly happy. I heard him say once that he admired her, that he liked 'great solid women' – those were his very words."

"Oh, but he'd never agree . . . besides, he's still got his three years of military service to do . . . they'll start in twelve months' time . . . he's set his heart on Morocco or one of the Southern Algerian regiments."

"Perhaps, but don't you see that if he were engaged, that'd be a tie. Perhaps papa could wangle it so's he'd get his discharge after a year, as he did in the case of . . ."

"Madeleine, please! . . ."

She bit her lip. The child uttered a faint whimper. She stretched out her arm, and the cradle began to creak like a mill. Jean-Louis was thinking about José's wish to serve in Morocco (it had come to him after reading one of Psichari's books) . . . ought they to encourage him, or try to put a spoke in his wheel?

Suddenly he said:

"I must say it mightn't be at all a bad idea to get him married."

He was thinking of José, but also of Yves. Only in some such room as this, warm and smelling of milk, with its hangings and its padded furniture, a small bundle of wailing life, and a young and fecund woman, could the Frontenac brothers, chased from the family nest and far dispersed, no longer shielded from life by holiday pine-trees and the protective boundaries of a steamy park, find ultimate refuge. Driven from the Paradise of childhood, exiled from its meadow fastnesses, from its bright alders and the streams that wound among the phallic fern, only in some place of hangings and old chairs and cradles, could they find a spot in which to dig their little burrows. . . .

And yet it was this same Jean-Louis, so eager to circle his brothers with protection, and to keep them from the world, who, under the threat of coming war, was strengthening his muscles with daily bouts of exercise. He was concerned to know whether he could get himself transferred from the auxiliary to the fighting forces. But life went on among the Frontenacs as though there were some bond that knit the love of brother for brother with the love of their mother for them all. Rather it was as though those two and differing loves sprang from the same source. Jean-Louis felt for the younger ones, and even for José whose eyes were set so lovingly on Africa, something of the same unquiet and almost agonized solicitude as moved their mother. Tonight, especially, had he felt it, when José's unspoken clamour of despair, and the silence that descends before the storm, had shaken him, though less, perhaps, than Yves's illegibilities. That other letter, too, that begging-letter from a workman's wife, so similar to others that had reached him, had struck deep into his sensibility, and kept a wound wide open. Not yet could he resign himself to taking men as they are. Their crude flatteries got on his nerves, and, even more, their clumsy feigning of religious feelings. These things made him feel ill. He remembered with peculiar vividness the case of an eighteen-year-old boy who had wanted to be baptized. He had himself undertaken his instruction, working at the task with love, only to find, a few days later, that this "godson" had already been baptized through the good offices of a Protestant organization, and had made off with their funds. He knew; of course, that this had been a single, isolated instance, and that there are plenty of good and sincere persons in the world. But, as luck would have it (or, rather, some lack of psychological awareness in himself, an inability to judge his fellow men) he was always being landed in such scrapes. His natural shyness was looked on as aloof superiority. It frightened off the simple, but not the hypocrites and flatterers.

Lying on his back, he gazed at the ceiling in the dim light of the lamp and felt his powerlessness to change the destiny of others. His two brothers would accomplish the work to which they had been called, and, after much wandering, would reach, infallibly, the place at which they were expected, the place where Someone watched for them. . . .

"Madeleine," he asked suddenly, "do you think that one can ever do anything for other people?"

She turned to him a face half dulled with sleep, and pushed the hair from her eyes.

"What d'you say?"

"I mean, do you believe that if one tried hard enough, one could ever transform another's destiny, however little?"

"Oh, that's all you ever think about, changing other people, moving them about, giving them different ideas from the ones they've got. . . ."

"Perhaps" (he was speaking to himself) "all I succeed in doing is to strengthen their natural tendencies. When I think I'm holding them back, they gather themselves for a forward spring along the path traced out for them. And it is usually in the very opposite direction from that in which I want to see them go . . . ."

She stifled a yawn.

"What's the use, darling?"

When, at the Last Supper, the Saviour spoke his sorrowful and tender words to Judas, they merely seemed to drive him to the door and set him on his destined way more quickly.

"Do you realize what time it is . . . after midnight? . . . You'll never be able to get up in the morning."

He switched off the lamp, and lay in the darkness as though at the bottom of the sea, with the vast weight of the waters pressing him down. His head swam with a sense of solitude and anguish. He remembered suddenly that he had forgotten to say his prayers. Grown man though he was, he did precisely as he would have done when he was ten years old. He got up quietly and knelt down beside the bed, burying his face in the sheets. Not a whisper troubled the silence. Not a sound revealed the presence in the room of a woman and a sleeping child. The atmosphere was heavy with a confusion of smells, for Madeleine, like all country folk, had a horror of the night air. Her husband had had to resign himself to sleeping with closed windows. He began by invoking the Holy Spirit: *Veni, Sancte Spiritus, reple tuorum corda fidelium et tui amoris in eis ignem accende* . . . But even while his lips were shaping the lovely formula, he was conscious only of the peace he knew so well, the peace that, in himself, bubbled up everywhere, like a river at its rising, flooding his being, overcoming all resistance, like waters in spate. From past experience he knew that he must not attempt to think, nor yield to the false humility which finds expression in such words as – "It doesn't mean anything: it is a mere surface emotion. . . ." No, he must say nothing at all, must simply accept. Nothing of his former anguish remained. . . . What madness to believe that the apparent consequence of our efforts is of the slightest importance. . . . What counts is the effort itself, the effort to hold the tiller firm, to get the ship back on to its true course – that especially. . . . The unknown, the unforeseeable, the unimaginable fruits of our actions will one day be revealed in the light, those rejected fruits, piled high upon the ground, that we dare not offer. . . . He made a brief examination of conscience. Yes, tomorrow morning he would be in a fit state to take Communion. . . . He let himself relax. He knew precisely where he was, and was still aware of the room's peculiar atmosphere. One thought, and one thought only, gnawed at him – that at this very moment he was yielding to a movement of pride, was seeking a pleasure. . . .

"But, were it thou, Oh Lord . . ."

The silence of the countryside had welled up over the town. Jean-Louis lay listening to the ticking of his watch. In the darkness, he could just make out Madeleine's humped shoulder. His mind was perfectly clear, yet nothing distracted it from the essential. Certain problems rose up within his field of consciousness, but, once resolved, vanished. For instance, thinking of Madeleine, he saw with blinding clarity, that women carry within themselves a world of feelings richer by far than ours, though they lack the power to interpret and express them, and that this constitutes a seeming inferiority. Similarly, with the "People" . . . Their limited vocabulary . . . Jean-Louis had a feeling that he was moving from infinity towards the earth, that his steps were no longer uncertain, that he had touched solid ground, that he was walking on the sea-shore, that he was moving away from his love. He made the sign of the cross, slid down beneath the sheets, and closed his eyes. The sound of a ship's siren on the river scarcely reached him. The rumble of the early market-carts did not awaken him.

XV

THE driver turned his head, without diminishing his speed, and shouted:

"What about stopping at Bordeaux for lunch?"

The Englishman, squashed between the two women at the back of the car, put a question:

"The *Chapon Fin*, eh?"

The young man at the wheel gave him a black look. Yves Frontenac, who was sitting beside him, expressed his nervousness:

"Geo, do, for Heaven's sake, keep your eye on the road . . . look . . . there's a child!"

What a fool he'd been to start out with this car-load of strangers! Three days earlier, he had been dining in Paris at the house of the American woman whose name he could never remember and would, in any case, have been incapable of pronouncing. . . . He had been more than usually "brilliant" (it was generally agreed that he was not to be relied upon: he could, on occasion, be the gloomiest of guests). "You're in luck's way," Geo had said. He was one of Yves's admirers, and was responsible for his presence there: "Frontenac's on top of his form." The Pommery had created a warm feeling of friendship between these various persons who scarcely knew each other. Their hostess was leaving next morning for Guéthary. A three days' trip, no more. She suggested that they should all go with her. It would be too awful to have to separate. From now on, they had got to stick together. . . . The June night was warm. As luck would have it, none of the men was in evening dress. It was simply a question of getting the car round and starting off. They could have baths when they got there. . . .

At Bordeaux, after lunch, Yves had paid his mother a surprise visit. He found her alone. At sight of her son, whom she was not expecting, she went very pale. He kissed her ashen cheeks. The window of the Empire drawing-room was wide open on the noisy smelly street. He could only spare her, he said, a quarter of an hour, because his friends were in a hurry to press on to Guéthary. They wouldn't be stopping in Bordeaux on the way back. Not that it really mattered, because, in less than three weeks he would be coming down to spend a whole month with his mother (her married children had rented a villa out on the Harbour, and there wouldn't be room for her). She had decided to go to Respide, on the slopes above the Garonne, and there wait for Yves to join her, instead of in the muggy heat of Bourideys. It was an article of faith with the Frontenacs that there was "always a breeze at Respide". She spoke of José. He was at Rabat, and had written to say that he was in no danger. All the same, she felt anxious, and would wake up in the night, worrying.

When the quarter of a hour was over, Yves kissed her again. She followed him out on to the landing. "I do hope they're careful, and don't drive too fast. I don't like to think of you rushing along the roads. Send me a wire this evening. . . ."

He took the stairs four at a time. When he reached the bottom, some instinct made him look up. Blanche Frontenac was leaning over the banisters. He saw the drawn face looking down at him.

"Only three weeks," he shouted.

"Yes, and do be careful."

And now, here he was in Bordeaux again on the way back. He would have liked to pay his mother a second surprise visit. But he could *not*, in the city of his birth, entertain these people at the *Chapon Fin*: they'd think he was trying to give them the slip. . . . Besides, Geo had said that he must be back in Paris that night, without fail. . . . He was feeling mad, because the young Englishman was sitting beside the girl, and he couldn't hear what they were saying. Their heads were close together. He could see them reflected in the windscreen. His remarks to Yves were scarcely encouraging: "I don't mind breaking my neck, so long as they break theirs too. . . ." Yves's reply had been: "Look out, there's a level-crossing coming."

He thought he might be able to get away after lunch. But he must wait for the bill. Geo, who was saying little and drinking a great deal, looked at his watch. "We shall be in Paris by seven. . . ." Until they reached the end of their journey his life would be in abeyance. He would be in torment until they reached Paris where he could get the girl to himself between the four walls of a room, and tell her, once and for all, that she wasn't to see that other chap again, that she had got to choose between them. . . . He was at the wheel of the car before Yves had settled up with the waiter. It would have been perfectly possible for Yves to say – "Give me just fifteen minutes," or even, "You go on without me: I'll come by train" – but it never occurred to him to do so. All he was concerned about was to fight down the inner compulsion which urged him to dash off and give his mother a kiss. 'It would be idiotic,' he told himself, 'to upset all their plans just to see her for five minutes, when in less than three weeks we shall be together again . . . I should barely have time to kiss her. . . .' A time was to come when he would never forgive himself for having grudged the few seconds needed in which to press his lips to a still living face. In some obscure region of himself he knew what the future held – for we are always warned. . . . While the women were in the cloak-room, he heard Geo say:

"Yves, do be a good fellow and sit in the back. I shan't feel so nervy with the Englishman beside me."

Yves replied that he himself would feel less nervy – and they set off. He found himself sandwiched between the two women. One of them said to the other:

"What, d'you mean to tell me that you haven't read *Paludes*? . . . it really is a scream . . . yes, Gide."

"I can't say I found it all that funny. . . . I remember now, I did read it. In what way is it funny?"

"I thought it a scream . . ."

"Yes, so you've said, but what is there so funny about it?"

"You explain what I mean, Frontenac."

"I haven't read it," he replied, as bold as brass.

"Not read *Paludes*?" – exclaimed the first speaker in tones of amazement.

"No, not read *Paludes*."

He was thinking of the staircase down which he had come three days earlier. He had glanced up. His mother had been looking over the banisters. 'I shall see her in a fortnight's time,' he thought. She would never know of his inconsiderateness in passing through Bordeaux without finding time to give her a kiss. At that moment he was more keenly aware of his love for her than he had ever been since the days of his young boyhood, when he had sobbed so bitterly on going back to school because of the thought that he would be separated from her each day until the evening. The two women were talking across him, though of whom he did not know.

"He begged me to get an invitation for him out of Marie-Constance. I told him I didn't know her well enough. He said, couldn't it be managed through Rose de Candale. I explained that I didn't want to run the risk of being snubbed for my pains, whereupon, my dear, believe it or not, he burst into tears. His whole future, his reputation, his very life, he said, was at stake. If he wasn't seen at that ball, he'd just have to fade out. I was foolish enough to observe that it was a very exclusive house. 'Exclusive!' he yelped: 'a house where *you're* invited!' "

"But, darling, it really is rather tragic for him. He's told everyone that he's going. The other day, at Ernesta's, I asked him, just for fun and to see how he'd carry it off, what he was going to be dressed as. 'As a slave-merchant,' he answered. The cheek of the man! – when, three days later, Ernesta and I, by agreement, asked him the same question, he said he wasn't at all sure that he was going, because he didn't find parties of that sort particularly amusing. . . ."

"Don't forget that I saw him cry – it really is too bad!"

"But that wasn't all. He went on to say that from what he could hear, Marie-Constance didn't mind whom she asked these days . . . and now that you've passed on what he said to you, I don't mind telling you, darling, that he quoted you as an instance. . . ."

"He's really rather a dangerous man, you know."

"He can start people gossiping. It doesn't matter how discredited a man may be. If he lunches, and dines, and sups out every day of the week, he's bound to be pretty formidable. He lays his eggs in the most likely spots . . . and then when they hatch out, and the little snakes go squirming all over the tablecloth, people don't know that he began it. . . ."

"Perhaps I'd *better* give Marie-Constance a ring this evening, what d'you think? After all, I *have* taken a thousand-franc box . . ."

"If only you can get him that invitation, he'll do anything in the world you want."

"There's nothing I want from him. . . ."

"All the same, you might ask him. . . ."

"What a little bitch you are, darling . . . you don't think, darling, not seriously? . . ."

"I'm not absolutely certain . . . but, after all, it'd only be a bit of what they call a *quid pro quo* . . ."

"A good deal more *quo* than *quid*. . . ."

"You really are a comic! . . . did you hear that, Frontenac?"

What was it his mother had said to him in the course of those five minutes? "There'll be masses of fruit at Respide. . . ."

A fine interchange of dirt was going on above his head between the painted mouths of the two women. He could have contributed to it without difficulty, but the filth which at any moment now might burst from him would belong only to the surface of his mind, and would have no place in those depths of his consciousness where, at this very moment, he could hear his mother saying: "There'll be masses of fruit this year". He could see her leaning over the banisters, watching him go downstairs, keeping him in sight until the last possible moment. The ghastly pallor of her face . . . "the pallor of heart-disease" – the words formed silently in his mind. . . . They came like a revealing flash. But even before he could catch and hold the omen, it had faded.

"Have it your own way . . . but what a fool the woman is! It's no good bores of her water trying to cling. You know as well as I do, that if she thought she could land somebody else, she wouldn't go about playing the poor, helpless little victim! She ought to be thankful that Alberto's put up with her for two whole years. I know he's taken his fun on the side, but even so it's beyond me how he's been patient with her for so long . . . and you know, don't you, that she's not nearly so rich as she led him to think?"

"But, when she starts talking about dying, it really does make one wonder. . . . Personally, I think there'll be a sticky end to it all. . . ."

"I wouldn't let that worry you. If the worst comes to the worst, she'll manage to wound herself just badly enough to get her husband into thoroughly bad odour. . . . You see if I'm not right! . . . She'll be on our backs for ever and ever, I bet! One can't *not* invite her, and if one thing's more certain than another it's that *she's* always free to accept!"

Yves thought about his mother's scruples in the matter of uncharitableness. . . . "I must remember to include that in my next confession" – she would say, when it happened that she had flared up at Burthe. . . . Jean-Louis's goodness of heart . . . his complete inability to smell out evil. . . . How miserable it made him when Yves laughed at Dussol! . . . The world, *this* world, in concert with which the last of the Frontenacs was howling at the top of his voice. . . . In Yves's eyes Jean-Louis's goodness was a counterbalance to the world's savagery. If he still believed in goodness, it was entirely owing to his mother and Jean-Louis. "I send you forth as lambs in the midst of wolves. . . ." Before him there rose on every side a vision of dark crowds with, in the midst of them, a quivering of veils and white coifs. . . . He, too, had been born to partake of this gentleness. He would go to Respide alone with his mother. Three weeks only stood between him and that time of torrid heat when there would be "masses of fruit". He would be careful not to wound her, would avoid giving her pain. This time he would know how not to get irritable. He made a silent promise that on the very first evening he would suggest that they should say their prayers together. She would not be able to believe her ears. He enjoyed in anticipation the joy that she would feel. He would confide in her . . . would, for instance, tell her what had happened to him in a night-club, on an evening of May. . . . It couldn't be helped, she'd got to know that he frequented such places. He would say: "I had drunk a little champagne . . . I was feeling sleepy, it was late. A woman standing on a table was singing a song. I was only half listening to her. The people round about were joining in the chorus. It was a soldiers' song, and everybody knew it. . . . In the middle of the last verse, the name of Christ occurred, all mixed up with a lot of filthy words. At that moment" (Yves had a vision of his mother listening with that look upon her face of passionate concentration . . . "at that moment I was conscious of a feeling of pain, of almost physical pain, as though the blasphemy had struck straight to my heart." She would get up from her chair, would give him a kiss, would say something like – "You see, darling, how grace . . ." He could imagine the night, the swarm of stars in the August sky, the smell of the late crops coming from the mill which would be invisible in the darkness. . . .

During the days that followed he felt reassured. Nothing had happened. Never had he lived so dissipated an existence. It was the time of year when, before the general exodus of summer, those who live for pleasure cram more and more of it into their mouths: the time when those who love suffer agonies at the thought of inevitable separation, and when those who are loved can at last breathe freely: the time when the burned-up chestnuts of the Paris streets see, at dawn, gathered round stationary cars, men in evening dress, and women shivering in the night air, all drawing out their last farewells, so as to keep, as long as possible, from the necessity of parting.

On one such night it so happened that Yves had not gone out. Perhaps he was feeling lazy, perhaps he was ill, perhaps he was suffering from heart-ache. Whatever the reason, he was alone in his small room, suffering from his solitude, as only at that age can one suffer, when solitude seems of all ills the most intolerable, the one from which at all costs, one must escape. His whole existence was so organized that there should never be an evening unfilled. But on this occasion the machinery had broken down. We manipulate others as though they were pawns: we are careful to see that no square upon the board shall be empty. But they, too, play their secret game, pushing us about as the fancy takes them, brushing us aside, so that we feel ourselves laid by, snuffed, extinguished. The voice which, at the very last moment, says on the telephone – "I'm terribly sorry, but I just can't make it," is always the voice belonging to the one of any given couple who need make no excuses, who can follow the whim of the moment. Had Yves's loneliness, on that particular evening, not been due to the absence of a certain woman, he could have dressed, gone out, and hunted up his friends. If he sat motionless, without a light, it was, no doubt, because he had received a terrible blow and was silently bleeding in the darkness.

The telephone rang, but not with its accustomed sound. The trills were rapid and urgent. He heard a lot of "crackling" – then: "Bordeaux's calling you." He thought at first that it must be his mother, and that she was ill. But before he had had time to feel the possibility as pain, a voice, which was indeed his mother's, came through, very faint, and as though speaking from another world. She belonged to the generation which has never learned how to master the telephone.

"Is that you, Yves: mamma speaking."

"I can hardly hear you."

He gathered that she had had an acute attack of rheumatism, that she was being packed off to Dax, and that her arrival at Respide would be delayed for ten days.

"I hope you can join me at Dax, so that we shan't lose any of our time together."

It was to get that promise from him that she had telephoned. He replied that he would join her as soon as she liked. She could not hear him. He repeated what he had said, grew impatient.

"Yes, mamma, I'll come to Dax."

From very far away the poor old voice kept saying the same thing over and over again. "You'll come to Dax, then?" Suddenly, the line went dead. For a while he did all he could to re-establish the connexion, but without success. He remained where he was, not moving from his chair. He felt miserable.

By next day the whole incident had passed from his mind. He resumed his normal existence, enjoying himself, or, rather, pursuing until dawn, the flittings of a woman who was enjoying *herself*. He did not get home until the small hours, and slept late. One morning, the sound of the door-bell woke him. He thought it must be the postman with a registered letter. He pushed the door ajar, and saw Jean-Louis. He took him into the sitting-room and opened the shutters. A yellow fog lay upon the roof-tops. Without looking at Jean-Louis he asked whether he had come to Paris on business. The answer was more or less what he had expected: their mother was not at all well, and Jean-Louis had looked up Yves with the intention of urging him to make an earlier start for the country. Yves looked at his brother. He was wearing a grey suit and a black tie with white dots. He asked why he hadn't been wired for, or rung up on the telephone.

"I didn't want to frighten you by sending a telegram, and it's always so difficult to explain things on the telephone."

"Maybe – but that's no reason for leaving mamma. I'm amazed that you should come away, even for twenty-four hours. Why *have* you come? . . ."

Jean-Louis looked at him fixedly. Yves, rather pale, asked quietly:

"Is she dead?"

Jean-Louis took his hand: his eyes never left his face.

Yves murmured: "I knew it."

"How could you have known?"

He said again, "I – knew it," while his brother hastily embarked upon the details which Yves had not, as yet, thought to demand.

"It was Monday night, no, Tuesday, that she began complaining for the first time. . . ."

It surprised him, all the time he was speaking, to see how calmly Yves had taken the news. He felt disappointed. He might just as well have spared himself the journey, might have stayed beside his mother's body while it was still there, and not lost one of those last, sad moments. He could not guess that a scruple in Yves's mind was "drawing" his sorrow to a point, like one of those abscesses which a doctor deliberately provokes. . . . Had his mother known that he had passed through Bordeaux without troubling to go to see her? Had the knowledge caused her pain? Was he a monster not to have made the effort? If he had spent a few moments with her on his way back from Guéthary, they would probably have been nothing but a repetition of their meeting on his way there—a few pieces of advice, a few requests that he should be careful, a kiss. She would have followed him out on to the landing, would have leaned over the banisters, would have watched him down the stairs for as long as she could see him. Anyhow, if he hadn't visited her again, he had at least heard her voice on the telephone. He had caught everything she had said, though she, poor woman, had had difficulty in hearing his replies. . . . He asked Jean-Louis whether she had had time to mention him. No, she had been expecting to see her "Parisian" so soon again, that her mind had been preoccupied with José, who was still in Morocco. At length Yves's tears began to flow, and Jean-Louis was conscious of a feeling of relief. His own attitude was one of complete calm. He refused to let himself brood upon his sorrow. He looked round the room in which yesterday's untidiness had not yet been cleared away. The Russian "craze" of the last few years was evidenced by the colours of divan and cushions. But the man who lived here, thought Jean-Louis, had probably taken only a passing pleasure in them. He would have said at a guess that his brother was indifferent to such things. . . . For a few moments Jean-Louis was guilty of disloyalty to his mother who was dead, in the interest of his brother who was alive. He gave his mind entirely to the scene about him, trying to discover signs and traces. . . . There was one photograph, and one only – of Nijinski, in the *Spectre de la Rose*. Jean-Louis stared at his brother standing there with his back to the fireplace. He looked so frail in his blue pyjamas, with his hair all anyhow. His face, now that he was crying, was just as it used to be when he was a little boy. Very quietly, Jean-Louis told him to get dressed. Left to himself, he seemed to be putting a silent question to the walls, to the cigarette ash on the table, to the burn in the carpet.

XVI

ALL that the parish could muster in the way of priests and choir-boys walked ahead of the hearse. Yves, who was with his two brothers and Uncle Xavier, was keenly aware of the ridiculous picture they must make in the garish daylight with their woebegone faces, and how absurd his evening clothes and silk hat must look (José was wearing the uniform of the Colonial Infantry). He observed the expressions of the people standing on the sidewalk, the eager, hungry curiosity in the women's eyes. He did not feel particularly miserable, did not, indeed, feel anything at all. He could hear snatches of what Uncle Alfred and Dussol were saying behind him ("you must follow immediately behind us" – the latter had been told: "after all, you're one of the family.")

"She was a woman with a head on her shoulders," Dussol was saying: "and I know no greater compliment than that. I would even go so far as to say that she was a true business-woman – or, rather, that she would have become one if she had had a husband at her side to train her up."

"In business," Caussade remarked, "women can do a lot of things that we can't."

"D'you remember how she behaved at the time of the Métairie affair, Caussade? – that lawyer chap who did a bunk. He got away with sixty thousand francs of hers. She knocked me up at midnight. She was on her way to see Madame Métairie, and wanted me to go with her. Blanche made her hand over a written acknowledgement of all the money owing. That wasn't an easy job, I can tell you: it needed pluck. . . . The legal proceedings dragged on for ten years, but she got every penny, in the long run, and before any of the other creditors, too. That's what I call a nice piece of work!"

"Yes, but I've often heard her say that if it hadn't been for the children, whose trustee she was, she'd never have had the courage to go on."

"That's very likely, because at times she was scrupulous to excess – it was her only weakness. . . ."

Uncle Alfred, with a sanctimonious air, protested that that had been her most admirable characteristic.

Dussol gave a shrug.

"You must forgive me for smiling! I'm an honest man, as men go, and our firm is generally looked upon as an example of everything that's above board. . . . But you and I know what business is. Blanche would have agreed with me. . . . She loved money, you know, and wasn't ashamed of loving it."

"She preferred land."

"But not for its own sake. In her eyes, land stood for wealth. She thought of it in the same way as she thought of bank-notes, the only difference being that she considered it safer. She often told me that, taking one year with another, and allowing for overheads, she reckoned that her landed property brought her in regularly between four and a half and five per cent."

Yves conjured up a picture of his mother as she had looked, sitting at nightfall on the terrace, among the Bourideys pines. Again, he could see her, in imagination, coming towards him along the path that made the circuit of the park, with her Rosary in her hand. He thought of her, too, at Respide, speaking of God beneath the slumbering hills. He searched his memory for things she had said which bore witness to her love of the land. Jean-Louis had told him how, just before she died, she had pointed through the open window at the June sky and the bird-infested trees, and said: "That's what I really regret."

"I'm told" – said Dussol – "that her last words were about the vines. She pointed to them and said: 'How I regret that I shan't be there to see the wonderful harvest!' . . ."

"That's not what I heard. I was led to suppose that she was referring to the countryside in general, and the beauties of nature. . . ."

"That's what her sons say" (Dussol lowered his voice) "but they, of course, interpreted her words in their own way: you know what they're like. . . . Poor Jean-Louis! . . . I prefer my version. It seems to me far more beautiful. I like to think that what she was mourning was the crop that she would never gather, the fruit of the vineyards which she had been at such pains to renew. . . . Nothing will make me believe differently. I knew her for forty years. Once, when she was complaining of her sons, I told her that she was a hen that had hatched out a brood of ducklings . . . how she laughed!"

"No, Dussol, no: she was proud of them, and rightly so!"

"I don't deny it. But I can't help laughing when Jean-Louis insists that she had a liking for all the stuff that Yves produces. Intelligence was her outstanding quality. She was a very model of the normal, good-sense incarnate, and I know what I'm talking about! At the time when I was having all those difficulties with Jean-Louis over his precious profit-sharing schemes and boring social theories, I felt in my bones that she was on my side. She was worried about what she called his 'day-dreaming'. She begged me not to let it influence my opinion of him. 'Give him time' – she used to say. 'You'll see he's got his head screwed on the right way, really.' "

Yves had forgotten all about his ridiculous clothes and patent-leather shoes. He was no longer studying the faces of the people on the sidewalk. Imprisoned in the procession which stretched from the hearse to Dussol (a single word, caught by chance, was enough to tell him all that the man was saying), he moved, with his eyes upon the ground. 'She loved the poor,' he was thinking. 'When we were small she took us into all the slum rooms when she went visiting. Her heart went out to girls in trouble, if only they repented of their ways. She could never read without crying the memories of childhood that found their way into my poems. . . .'

Dussol's voice was droning on and on: "Dealers had to watch their step with her. I've never known anyone with such an eye for accounts, nor anyone who could cut down percentages as she could."

"Did you ever listen to her talking things over with any of her tenants, Dussol? Somehow she always managed to make them pay for their own repairs."

Yves knew from Jean-Louis that this was not true; that leases had been renewed in the most reckless way imaginable, and quite irrespective of enhanced values. All the same, he could not dismiss from his mind the caricature of his mother, as she appeared to other people, stripped of the Frontenac mystery, which Dussol's words had built up. Death condemns us to be the prey not of worms only but of men. They nibble away at remembered lives until there is nothing left of them. Already, Yves, under the influence of this overheard conversation, found himself no longer seeing the dead woman as he had known her. Her flesh had outlived corruption longer than her reputation. It was essential that he should reconstruct his memory of her, and wipe away these alien stains. Blanche Frontenac must again become for him what she had always been. Only if she did, could he go on living, could he survive her. How endless seemed the walk to the cemetery down the long rue d'Arès, past slum dwellings and brothels, with the Family trailing along in dress clothes and shiny shoes – all this grotesque barbarism of funeral pomp, and the hurried muttering of the sublime Office of the Church by priests who, as the saying goes, were "practised" in it – only, too, too practised! Dussol had kept his voice low, but now he raised it again, and Yves could not resist the temptation to listen.

"No, Caussade, I can't agree with you there. She was an admirable woman, but there, I think, she failed. The bringing up of the young was not her strong point. . . . I am not, myself, without a certain feeling for religion. The parish clergy will always find me ready to listen if they think I can help them in their difficulties. They know that, and the knowledge is of some value to them. But if I had had sons I should have seen to it that, once the First Communion was over, they should have turned to and prepared themselves for the serious business of life. Blanche never really took into account the weight of heredity that lay upon her boys. I don't want to speak evil of poor Michel Frontenac . . ."

Caussade protested that Michel had been a professed anti-clerical all his life, but Dussol went on:

"That's as may be, but it doesn't alter the fact that he was a dreamer, the kind of man who will go to a Board Meeting with a book stuffed away in his pocket. That'll show you the sort of chap he was. Why, I've even seen him bring a volume of poetry into the office when there was a sales conference on! Once, when that happened, I picked it up, but he snatched it from me in a shamefaced sort of way. . . ."

"Shamefaced? – why? – was it what's usually called a 'curious' book?"

"Oh, dear me no! He didn't go in for *that* kind of thing – on second thoughts, though, you mayn't be so far out . . . I remember, now, it was one of Baudelaire's . . . *La Charogne* . . . know it? . . . A sensitive soul was Michel, but no good at all when it came to business, and, mind you, I was pretty well placed to judge. It was a good thing for the firm and for the Frontenac children that I was there. Blanche's religious fervour did go some way to developing certain tendencies in *them*, and, well . . . you've only got to look around to see what the results have been. . . ."

Once more, he lowered his voice. Yves repeated to himself those last few words – 'what the results have been'. Could he truthfully be called a man? Yes, but not what Dussol meant by a man. But what, if it came to that, did Dussol mean by a man? And what could Blanche Frontenac have done to make her sons different from what they had become? After all, Jean-Louis had, as they say, founded a family, and was showing himself to be pretty efficient in the business. His influence was a good deal more considerable than Dussol's, and his reputation as a "socially conscious" employer, had spread far and wide.

José was risking his life in Morocco (no, that wasn't quite true: he hadn't stirred from Rabat): and Yves . . . well, at least they must know that he was always being talked about in the papers. . . . In what way were the Frontenac boys different from other boys? . . . To that question he would have found it difficult to find an answer. . . . All the same, that damned Dussol, teetering along behind him like a moving mountain of flesh, still had the power to reduce him to a state of pure gibber, to humiliate him till it hurt.

Standing on the brink of the open grave, in the little knot of "real friends" ("I made a particular point of going with her to the very end"), Yves, his eyes dim with tears, his ears deaf to everything, did, nevertheless, manage to hear, above the rattle of stones on the coffin, and the heavy breathing of the grave-diggers – who looked, for all the world, like stage murderers, – the self-satisfied, the implacable voice of Dussol:

"She was a thoroughly capable woman."

That day, as a mark of respect for the dead woman, no work was done at Respide or at Bourideys. The oxen stayed in the byre, and thought it must be Sunday. The men went to the inn and sat drinking in an atmosphere of anise. A storm was blowing up, and Burthe feared for the hay. How put about the poor lady would have been if she had known that, because of her, it hadn't been got under cover! The Hure flowed on beneath the alders. Close to the old oak, just where the wall had been knocked down, the moon struck a sparkle in the grass from the sacred medal which Blanche had lost three years before, during the Easter holidays, and which the children had long looked for and never found.

XVII

ALL through the following winter, and the early months of 1913, Yves's mood seemed to be more bitter than ever before. He was beginning to lose his hair; his cheeks were sunken; there was a feverish glitter in his eyes, and the bony structure of his brow had become more than usually prominent. All the same, he felt deeply shocked at the ease with which he had become resigned to his loss. He did not really miss his mother at all. Since, for a long time now, he had been living away from her, nothing was altered in the routine of his days, and he would go for weeks together without once thinking of her. The only difference in him was that he had come to demand more of the people he was fond of. The craving to be loved, which his mother had never failed to satisfy, he now centred on others who, though up till now, they might have filled his thoughts, made him restless, and even occasioned him some little suffering, had never really torn his life up by the roots. He had been accustomed to plunge into his mother's love as he had plunged into the park at Bourideys. It led straight into the pine-forest, and, as a child, he had always known that he could walk on and on, night and day, and that in the end he would reach the sea. Into every love he now wormed his way, moved by a fatal curiosity, seeking to find its limits, yet always obscurely hoping that he would never come on them. Alas! a very few steps brought him there, all the more surely because his mania was turning him into a wearisome and insupportable companion. He was for ever demonstrating to the women of his choice that their fondness for him was only a seeming passion. He belonged to that unhappy race of young men who go on, again and again, saying – "You don't love me!" in the hope of getting an assurance to the contrary. But his words had more power to convince than he realized, so that to her who ventured on a mild protest, he would himself give proofs so unanswerable that he ended by convincing her of the truth – that she did not love him, nor ever had done.

In that spring of 1913, he had reached the point at which his sufferings had become like one of those physical ailments for the end of which the patient eagerly watches, hour by hour, in terror at the thought that he may not be able to endure it a moment longer. Even at parties, if the object of his passion happened to be present, he was quite incapable of hiding his wound, but displayed his suffering for all to see, and left a trail of blood wherever he went.

He was quite convinced that he was the prey to an obsession. He found himself continually harking back to instances of treachery which had existed only in his imagination, so that he could never be quite sure, even when he caught his mistress in the act, that he had not been misled by hallucination. If she gave him her solemn word that it had not been her he had seen in a car beside the young man with whom she had been dancing on the previous evening, he allowed himself to be convinced, even though he felt quite certain that he had recognized her. . . . 'I am going mad,' he said to himself, and chose deliberately to believe that he was indeed mad, in the first place, because it would give him some sort of breathing-space, however short, between bouts of suffering, and because he could see in the face he loved a look of unfeigned alarm. "You *must* believe me," she would insist, moved by a fierce longing to console and reassure him. Against this form of hypnotism he was never proof. "Look me in the eyes: *now* do you believe me?"

It wasn't that she was better than anybody else, but he always failed to realize, until it was too late, that he had the power to awaken a sort of patient tenderness in those who, in other ways, were the source of his torment. It was as though, when they were with him, they all unknowingly became saturated with that maternal love the warmth of which had swaddled him for so many years. In August, the earth, impregnated by the sun, retains its warmth until late into the night. And so it was that the love of his dead mother was still about him, softening the hardest hearts.

It was that, perhaps, which kept him from succumbing to the blows that rained upon him. For there was no other support on which he could lean, and he could expect no help from his family. What remained of the Frontenac mystery came to him now only in the form of scattered fragments from a complete and utter wreck. The first time he went back to Bourideys after his mother's death, he felt as though he were walking in a dream, as though he were moving through a past now suddenly materialized. He brooded over the pines rather than saw them. He remembered the secret flow of waters under the alder trees. The ones he looked at were lopped: the new shoots were already intertwined. But he substituted for them in his mind the moss-grown trunks which once, in earlier holidays, the Hure had mirrored. The smell from the meadows worried him because there was more in it of mint than he remembered. He felt himself as much cluttered by the house and park as by his mother's old umbrellas, and those garden hats they could not give away, and would not jettison (there was one very old one embroidered with swallows). A whole section of the Frontenac mystery had, as it were, been sucked into that spot as into a hole in the ground, a cavern in which the mother of Jean-Louis and José, of Yves, of Danièle and Marie Frontenac, had been laid to rest. When, on occasion, a face looked out from a world now three parts destroyed, the effect on Yves was one of nightmare.

One fine morning, in the summer of 1913, he saw, framed in the doorway of his room, a large woman whom he recognized at once, though he had seen her only once before, and then, casually, in the street. The truth was that Joséfa had, for many years, been a constant joke in the Frontenac family. Could it be that he didn't know who she was? Monsieur Yves must surely have been aware of her existence? The young men of the family must always have realized that their uncle did not live alone? Poor man, he had always been at such pains to keep her existence from them, and the knowledge that that was so made her feel awful! . . . But perhaps it was just as well that things had turned out like this. He had recently had two bad attacks of angina at her place (he must be in a bad way, otherwise she would never have had the courage to call on Yves). The doctor had utterly pooh-poohed the idea of his going home, and now the poor dear was worrying himself sick, night and day, at the idea that he might die without ever seeing his nephews again. But now they knew that there had been a woman in their uncle's life, so what point could there be in trying to keep it secret any longer? . . . Nevertheless he would have to be prepared for the revelation, because he had no idea that his wrong-doing had been discovered. . . . She would tell him that the family had only quite recently tumbled to the truth, and that they had forgiven him. . . . Yves remarked, drily, that it was not for the young Frontenacs to "forgive" a man whom they respected more than anybody else in the world. The large woman, however, stuck to her point.

"You see, Monsieur Yves – and I can say this to you now that you are of an age to know what's what – there has been nothing between us for years . . . after all, we're neither of us exactly young . . . besides, I couldn't dream of allowing the poor man to go a-wearing of himself out, and him in such a condition, too. I never could forgive myself if I thought I'd had a hand in killing him. . . . He's more like my child than anything else, and a very young child too. . . . I am not the kind of person you take me for . . . might very naturally take me for. . . . You can ask the parish clergy, if you like: *they* know all about me!"

She spoke mincingly, as they had always imagined she would. She was wearing a Russian-ballet coat with loose sleeves, secured at the waist by a single button. Her eyes still showed as handsome under the cloche hat which did nothing to conceal the thick, tip-tilted nose, the vulgar mouth, the retreating chin. She looked at "Monsieur Yves" with deep emotion. Though she had never met the Frontenac children, she had been familiar with them from their youth up. She had followed their progress through life, step by step, and had taken an interest in all their childish ailments. Nothing was insignificant to her that occurred in the glorious empyrean of the Frontenacs. Far, far above her, they moved as demi-gods, whose smallest gestures she could, by an extraordinary piece of luck, follow from the deep abyss of her own existence . . . and though in the wonderful world of fantasy in which her day-dreams moved, she had often imagined herself as married to Xavier, and participating in moving scenes of family affection, with Blanche calling her "sister", and the children, "Aunt Joséfa", she had never really thought that anything remotely resembling this meeting could ever occur, or that the day would come when she would find herself face to face with one of the young Frontenacs, and speak with him as with an equal.

Yet so vivid was her feeling of having known Yves always, that now, face to face with this lean and melancholy man whom she was seeing for the first time, she found herself thinking 'how thin he has grown!'

"And how is Monsieur José? – still enjoying himself in Morocco? Your uncle is terribly anxious about him. It seems as things over there are beginning to hum, and the papers don't tell you everything by a long chalk! What a good thing it is that your poor dear mother is not here, for she would be worrying herself to a shadow!"

Yves asked her to sit down, but himself remained standing. He made a valiant effort to struggle to the surface of his emotional preoccupations, to seem at least to be listening and taking an interest. To himself he said: 'Uncle Xavier is very ill: Uncle Xavier is going to die. He is the last of the older generation of Frontenacs. . . .' But he lashed at his feelings to no avail. It was impossible for him to feel anything but the frightful threat hanging over his head, the threat of the summer's end, of the weeks and months of separation, weeks and months that would be heavy with storms, beaten by furious rains, burned by devastating suns. The whole of creation, with its stars in their courses and its mortal scourges would soon be rearing itself between him and the object of his passion. When next he found himself close to her it would be autumn. Till then he must fight his way in solitude through an ocean of flame.

It had been arranged that he should spend his holidays with Jean-Louis, in that home which his mother had so ardently desired should be a refuge for him when she was no more. To this necessity he might have resigned himself if only the pain of parting had been shared. But "she" was to go for a long cruise on a yacht. "She" was living in a fever of "tryings-on", and made no attempt to conceal her excitement. Anticipated pleasure shone in her eyes. Nor, for him, was it a matter of imaginary suspicions, of fears now awakened, now allayed. What he had to face was something far worse – the cruel happiness, more murderous than any treachery, felt by a young woman at the prospect of getting away from him. What made her drunk was killing him. With endless patience she had made pretence of tenderness and loyalty. But now, suddenly, she had torn the mask from her face, though not deliberately nor with joy, because she had no wish to cause him pain.

"It's the best thing that could have happened. You know perfectly well that I am bad for you. . . . By October you'll be completely cured. . . ."

"But there was a time when you said you hoped I never should be cured."

"When did I say that? I don't remember."

"Last January: one Tuesday. We were just leaving Fischer's. We passed the *Gagne-Petit*, and you looked at yourself in the window."

She shook her head. She seemed annoyed. Those words of hers had struck sweet music to his heart. For weeks he had lived on them, repeating them over and over to himself, long after their power to charm had vanished. And now, here she was, denying that she had ever spoken them! . . . It was all his fault. He so enlarged the smallest things she said. He had grown into such a habit of giving them a fixed value, an unalterable significance, and, half the time, they expressed nothing but a moment's mood.

"Are you sure I said that? I may have done, it's just that I don't remember."

It was only yesterday evening that Yves had heard that terrible comment. It had been made here between these very same walls where now there sat a fat, fair woman who was giving evidence of heat, heat so extreme that it was difficult to sit in the same room with her, even with the window open. Joséfa seemed now to be thoroughly settled in. Her eyes were fixed, with absorbed attention, on Yves.

"And Monsieur Jean-Louis? – what a splendid young man he is! – and Madame Jean-Louis, such a distinguished-looking lady. That photograph of them together, taken at Coutenceau's with the baby between them, stands on your uncle's desk. Such a sweet little girl! Anyone would know from her mouth and chin that she's a Frontenac! Often's the time I've said to your uncle, 'She's the very spit and image of a Frontenac!' He loves children, even quite tiny ones. . . . When my daughter, the one as lives at Niort and is married to a very solid fellow in the wholesale (and he has to shoulder all the responsibility along of his boss suffering from the rheumatism in his joints) . . . when my daughter brought her baby to see me, he took her on his knee, and my daughter passed the remark as it was easy to see that he was used to children. . . ."

She broke off, suddenly overcome by shyness. Monsieur Yves wasn't being exactly forthcoming. Most probably he took her for a scheming woman. . . .

"I think you ought to know how things are, Monsieur Yves. . . . He gave me a lump sum down, once and for all, and the furniture. . . . It's all there. I wouldn't like to be thought one as could do the least little thing to hurt the family. . . ."

She spoke of "the family" as though no other family existed in the world. To Yves's consternation two tears, as large as lentils, began to trickle down her face. The Frontenacs, he protested, had never suspected her of the slightest impropriety. On the contrary, they felt deeply grateful for the way in which she had looked after their uncle. In his anxiety to treat her with proper consideration, he ignored the claims of common caution, and overshot the mark. She broke down entirely, and her trickle of tears became a flood.

"I do love him so! . . . I do love him so!" she spluttered, "and all of you as well, though to be sure I always knew as I wasn't good enough even to speak to you, but I've always loved every member of the family, as my daughter at Niort can witness to, she having often reproached me for it and complaining that I'm more interested in the Frontenac children than in my own flesh and blood, which it's true. . . ."

Her face was streaming, and she began feeling about in her bag for a clean handkerchief. At that moment, the telephone rang.

"Hullo . . . Oh, it's you . . . dinner? . . . half a moment while I look at my book. . . ."

Yves held the receiver away from his ear for a moment. Joséfa, who was sniffing and watching him closely, was surprised to see that he did not, in fact, look at his engagement book at all, but stared before him with an expression of blissful happiness.

"Yes, I can manage it with a little juggling. . . . It's sweet of you to spare me one more evening. . . . Where? . . . the *Pré Catalan*? . . . Shall I pick you up? . . . but it would be so easy for me . . . why not? . . . what's that? . . . I'm not making a point of anything . . . it's only that I might be a bit late and don't want you to have to hang about alone at the restaurant. . . . I said, I don't want you to have to hang about . . . what's that? . . . you won't be alone? . . . Who's the other? . . . Geo? . . . No, of course I don't mind. . . . I'm not in the least annoyed . . . what? . . . well, of course it won't be the same thing . . . I said, of course it won't be the same thing. . . . I'm not being difficult. . . ."

Joséfa was devouring him with her eyes. Like an old circus horse roused by the sound of distant music, she snuffed the air and pawed the ground. Yves had hung up the receiver, and the face he turned to her was drawn with pain. She did not realize that he was with difficulty keeping himself from showing her to the door, though it did occur to her that the time had come to make a move. He would write to Jean-Louis, he said, about their uncle. As soon as he heard, he would get into touch with her. An endless fumbling ensued while she tried to find a card with her address. At long last, she went.

Uncle Xavier is very ill; Uncle Xavier is dying – Yves spoke the words over and over to himself. He tried to call up visual images to make him realize their import; Uncle Xavier sitting in a big armchair in the gloomy rue de Cursol house, under the shadow of the great parental bed . . . himself, holding out his cheek to be kissed, and his uncle breaking off his reading with a "run along, my chick" . . . his uncle in a city suit, standing on the bank of the Hure, and carving a piece of pine-bark into the shape of a boat . . . *Sabe, sabe, caloumet, te pourterey un pan naouet* . . . But in vain did he cast his net, in vain draw it in filled with a swarm of wriggling memories. One and all, they slipped free and fell back. Those pictures of the past were scrawled over now with larger and more recent figures – the figures of that hateful woman and her Geo. What business had Geo to come butting in? – and why tonight of all nights? It was their last chance of being together. Must Geo come too? . . . Why had she gone out of her way to pick on him, and not on somebody else . . . why this man, who was his friend, of whom he had grown fond? . . . There had been a calculated note of surprise in her voice. She did not want to seem to be concealing the fact that she and Geo had struck up an intimacy. . . . He, too, must almost certainly be going away somewhere this summer, though where, Yves had not succeeded in finding out. Oh God! – *of course*, he was to be one of the yacht party. Geo and she, for weeks and weeks, on the deck, in the cabins – she and Geo . . .

He flung himself face downwards on the divan, and worried the back of his hand with his teeth. This was more than he could bear: this time he *would* get his own back on that bitch of a woman, would really do something that would hurt her! But how could he manage to throw mud without some of it sticking to himself? . . . He'd find *some* way. . . . He'd put her into a book, so's she'd be bound to be recognized! He would conceal nothing! he would smother her with filth! She should appear in his pages as someone at once grotesque and loathsome.... All her little secret habits, all her physical peculiarities, should be writ large.... But it would take time to get it written... much easier, much quicker just to kill her. He could do that this very evening, now, at once. He'd see to it that she was given time enough to realize what was coming to her, time in which to be afraid – she, who was such a coward! She must see herself dying, mustn't die at once, must realize that she had been disfigured....

Slowly the hatred drained from him. He pressed out the last drop. Then, very gently, and in a low voice, he uttered the name he loved so well. Again and again he murmured it, dwelling on each syllable. It was all of her that he could have. No one in the world could stop him from whispering that name, from crying it aloud. But upstairs were the neighbours, who would hear every sound. At Bourideys he could have taken refuge in his little hide-out. By now the bracken must have grown over the tiny arena where once, on an autumn day, long years ago, the future had been revealed to him. In imagination he could see that small, that scarcely perceptible point on the earth's surface, filled with the drone of wasps in the hot morning sunshine. The pale heather would be sweet with the smell of honey, and a light breeze, perhaps, would be drifting down a mist of pollen from the tall pines. He could see, in its every detail, the path that led back to the house under the branchy shadows of the park – could see the exact spot where once he had met his mother. Over her party dress she had thrown the little violet shawl which had come from Salies. She had put it round his shoulders because she had felt him shiver.

"Mamma!" – he groaned: "Mamma!"

He lay there sobbing. He was the first of all the Frontenac

brothers to call upon their dead mother as though she were living still. Eighteen months later it was to be the turn of José, lying with a hole in his belly, through an interminable September night, between the trenches.

XVIII

AS soon as she got into the street, Joséfa's thoughts went back to her patient. He was quite alone, and at any moment he might have an attack. She regretted the long time she had spent with Yves, and reproached herself bitterly. But so well had she been trained by Xavier that it never so much as occurred to her to take a taxi. She hurried towards the rue de Sèvres, where she could catch the Saint-Sulpice-Auteuil tram. She walked, as she always did, with her stomach well forward, and her nose in the air, muttering to herself, much to the delight of the passers-by, the words "Hé-bé!" in an angry, outraged voice. She was thinking of Yves, and now that the young man was no longer there to fascinate and dazzle her with his physical presence, her thoughts were bitter. How little he had seemed to care when she had told him of his uncle's illness! At the very moment when the poor man was drawing near his end, terrified at the thought that he might not be able to say good-bye to his nephews, the young man had been busy telephoning to some countess or other (Joséfa had caught sight of the cards stuck in the frame of Yves's mirror – *Baron et Baronne de . . . Marquise de . . . The English Ambassador, and Lady . . .*) This evening he would be dining to the sound of music with one of those great ladies . . . terrible hussies they were, too . . . she'd read all about *them* in that serial of Charles

Mérouvel's . . . and *he* knew what he was writing about, none better!

These hostile sentiments covered a deep-seated pain. For the first time Joséfa was realizing the simple-mindedness of the poor old fellow who had sacrificed everything to an empty dream of pulling the wool over his nephews' eyes. He had always been so ashamed of the life he was leading – a remarkably innocent life, really! His career of gilded vice had been such a very mild affair! The two of them, he and she, had gone without, and all for the sake of a pack of young fellows who would never know what he had sacrificed for them, and would have laughed if they had been told. . . . She climbed into the tram-car, and sat wiping her purple face. . . . She still suffered from rushes of blood to the head, though less than last year. Pray heaven, nothing had happened to Xavier! It was really very convenient having a tram-stop just in front of the house.

She climbed the four flights of stairs, puffing and blowing. Xavier was sitting in the dining-room, close to the half-open window. He was panting slightly, and was quite motionless. He said that he was suffering scarcely any pain, and that it was marvellous to be without it. He was perfectly all right so long as he did not move. He felt a bit peckish, but would rather go without food than run the risk of an attack. The Metro bridge was almost level with the window, and almost every minute a train went clanging and banging by. It never occurred either to Xavier or to Joséfa to be worried by the noise. They lived hedged in by the pieces of furniture from Angoulême which were far too big for the tiny rooms. The cupid's torch had been badly chipped during the move, and several of the ornaments on the wardrobe had come unstuck.

She soaked some "fingers" of bread and butter in a soft-boiled egg, and tried to get the old man to eat. She spoke to him as she might have done to a child: "Come along, ducky:

come along, my pet . . ." He did not move so much as a muscle. He was like one of those insects who find in immobility their sole means of defence. Towards evening, in the sudden silence between trains, he heard the swifts crying, as once they had cried in the garden at Preignac.

All of a sudden, he spoke:

"I shan't see the children again."

"Time enough later on to think about that . . . though if it would make your mind any easier, I've only to send them a telegram. . . ."

"That will have to wait until the doctor lets me go home. . . ."

"Why shouldn't they come and see you here? You can always say you've moved, and that I'm your housekeeper."

He seemed to hesitate a moment, then shook his head.

"They would see at once that the furniture isn't mine . . . and even if they didn't find out, they couldn't possibly come to a place like this. Even if they never knew, I couldn't let them come here, for the family's sake."

"You talk as though I'd got the plague!" She was up in arms. Never, while Xavier was in health, had she uttered a word of complaint, but now that he was at death's door, she spoke out. He sat quite still, careful not to make the slightest movement.

"You're a good soul . . . but for the sake of Michel's memory his sons must never . . . It's not a question of you, but of principle. . . . Besides, how wretched it would be, after successfully keeping it dark for so long . . ."

"Oh come now: surely you can't believe that they haven't known about it for ages?"

She regretted her outburst when she saw him move uneasily in his chair, and heard his quickened breathing.

"No, I don't mean that. Of course they don't know a thing. What I meant was that, even if they did, they wouldn't hold it against you."

"Oh, I know they are too good-hearted ever to dream of criticizing me, still . . ."

Joséfa moved away from his chair, and leaned out of the window. . . . Good-hearted, indeed! She thought of Yves as she had seen him that morning, at the telephone, pretending to consult his engagement-book, with an expression on his face that was half bewilderment, half happiness. She imagined him now, at this moment, in what she called his "fish-tails", and his "crush-hat", in one of those grand restaurants where there is a little pink-shaded lamp on each table. Trains packed full of men going home after the day's work, were rattling across the iron bridge. Xavier seemed rather more breathless than he had been during the afternoon. He explained by signs that he did not wish to speak, to be spoken to, or to eat. It was as though he were rolling himself into a ball, aping death in order to escape from death's reality. Night fell, warm and close. The window was left open in spite of the doctor's orders. He had told her to shut it, because, when an angina patient, he said, has one of his attacks, he doesn't know what he is doing. . . . Joséfa thought of the world's misery. . . . She was sitting between the window and the sick man's chair. She felt oppressed by the large pieces of furniture which once had been her pride. This evening, suddenly, she saw them as mean and wretched. . . . No more workmen, now. The trains going towards the Etoile were almost empty. That's where one changes for the Porte Dauphine. Joséfa had often got out there with Xavier, squeezed and elbowed by the melancholy Sunday crowds. . . . Just about now, Yves Frontenac must be driving that way in his saloon car. What it must cost to eat the sort of things one saw on the side-tables of fashionable restaurants – the crayfish, and the peaches in their padded boxes, and those things that looked like over-sized lemons! How much, she would never know. She had always, herself, been confined to a choice between one or other of the cheap table-d'hôtes – 3 fr. 50, all in. . . . She looked towards the West, and thought of Yves Frontenac in the company of a lady and another young man.

Dinner was almost over. She had got up, and was making her way between the tables, saying that she had got to do something about her face. Yves made a sign to the wine-waiter to serve the champagne. He seemed to be quite calm: the tenseness had gone from his manner. All through the meal Geo had been engaged in giving the young woman the information she wanted on the subject of cabin-trunks and dressing-cases (he knew a man who could get them for her at wholesale prices). It was quite clear that they were not going to be of the same party. Everything they said pointed, on the contrary, to the fact that they were going to be away from each other for several months, and were facing the prospect with equanimity.

"They're playing that bit of nonsense that was all the rage two years ago," said Geo.

He started humming with the orchestra – "*Non, tu ne saurais jamais . . .*"

"Geo, you can have no idea what a fool I've been. . . ."

Yves looked at the friendly face of the young man, whose hand, as he raised his glass, was trembling slightly. His eyes were shining.

"I thought you were going away with her, that you were trying to keep me in the dark."

Geo gave a shrug and fingered his tie. It was an habitual gesture with him. Then he opened a black-enamel case, and took a cigarette. His eyes never left Yves's face.

"When I think of you, Yves, with all you've got in there" (and he touched his friend's forehead with a nicotine-stained finger) . . . "of you, and this . . . I don't want to be offensive . . ."

"Oh, don't mind me! I know you think she's a little fool – still, preaching doesn't sit very well on you."

"I," said Geo, "am a nobody."

He leaned his charming, rather worn face, slightly forward, raised it again, and smiled at Yves with an expression of affection and admiring respect.

"Besides, I'm not likely to let myself be caught again, until . . ."

He made a sign to the wine-waiter, emptied his glass, and, with a rather wild look in his eyes, gave an order:

"Two brandies . . . You see all these stylish tarts," he went on, "well, I'd give the whole boiling for . . . guess what?"

He leaned forward, and looked across the table with his magnificent eyes. In a tone that was at once ashamed and passionate, he murmured:

"For the little girl who does the washing-up!"

They burst out laughing. Suddenly, a whole world of sadness clamped down on Yves. He looked across at Geo who, like himself, had become gloomy. Was his friend, he wondered, also conscious of this feeling that everything was a hollow, an unending, mockery? Far, far away, beyond immeasurable distances, he thought that he could hear the drowsy murmur of the pines.

"Uncle Xavier . . ." he muttered.

"What did you say?"

Geo put down his glass and signed to the wine-waiter, with forefinger raised, to bring another brandy.

XIX

ONE morning in October, Joséfa found herself standing in the entrance-hall of the d'Orsay Hotel, surrounded by the Frontenac children (with the single exception of José, who was still in Morocco). Their uncle's condition had seemed to be improving during the summer, but a more than usually violent attack had recently laid him low, and the doctor had little hope that he would recover. Joséfa's telegram had been delivered at Respide, where Yves was superintending the wine-harvest, and already thinking about returning to Paris. He was in no hurry to do so, since "she" would not be back until the end of the month. Besides, he had grown used to being away from her, and, now that he was within sight of the exit from the tunnel, would willingly have dawdled.

Intimidated by the presence of so many Frontenacs, Joséfa had at first taken refuge behind a wall of dignity. But her feelings had been too much for her, and she had found it impossible to maintain her carefully considered attitude. Besides, Jean-Louis had found his way to her heart with his very first words. Her worship of the Frontenacs had at last been rewarded. Here was someone who would not disappoint her. It was to him now, as head of the family, that she addressed herself. . . . The two young women were standing rather rigidly aloof, not, as Joséfa thought, out of haughtiness, but because they had not yet made up their minds what attitude they ought to adopt. (She would never have thought they could be such strapping wenches. They appeared to have monopolized all the family ration of fat). Yves, who was always dead-beat after a night journey, had ensconced himself in an armchair.

"I told him that I would pass myself off to you as his housekeeper. Since he never speaks at all now (it's not because he won't but because he's afraid it might bring on an attack), I can't say for sure whether he agreed or not. There are times when his poor mind seems to wander . . . it's difficult to know what he wants . . . the truth of the matter is that he's thinking all the time about that there pain which may return at any moment . . . something dreadful it is, seemingly . . . like as he had a mountain on his chest. . . . I only hope as you'll never see him when he's bad. . . ."

"It must be terrible for you, madame. . . ."

She spluttered through her tears:

"What a kind heart you have, Monsieur Jean-Louis!"

"But at least, in all his bad times, he has had the support of your love and devotion."

Conventional though the words were, they had on Joséfa the effect of an endearment. She had suddenly become one of the family, and stood there crying quietly, her hand clinging to Jean-Louis's arm. Marie whispered in Danièle's ear:

"It was very wrong of him to spend so much money: we shall never get things straight."

It was agreed that Joséfa should prepare their uncle for their coming. They would turn up about ten, and wait outside the front door.

It was only on the squalid landing, where the Frontenac children stood listening, while the other tenants, put wise by the concierge, leaned inquisitive faces over the banisters: it was only when he was sitting on the dirty stone stair, with his back leaning against the scarred surface of the imitation marble, that Yves at last realized the full horror of what was going on behind that closed door. Every now and then Joséfa opened it just wide enough to give passage to her puffy, tear-stained face, and begged them to wait a little longer. Then, putting a finger to her lips, she shut it again. Uncle Xavier, who once every fortnight had entered the gloomy room in the rue de Cursol in Bordeaux, after making his round of the family estates; Uncle Xavier, who could cut a whistle from an alder-twig, was now lying at death's door in the awful slum where this woman lived, just opposite the railway bridge, and not far from the La Motte-Picquet-Grenelle station. Poor man, bound hand and foot by prejudices and phobias, incapable of going back on any opinion that he had inherited, inalterably, from his parents, so great a respecter of the established order, yet such a stranger to any simple and normal way of life. . . .

The smell that filled the stair-well brought back the very atmosphere of the house in the rue de Cursol, as Yves had known it when term began, and he had returned there from the country. It was a smell made up of fog, and damp pavements, and linoleum. Danièle and Marie were whispering. Jean-Louis was standing motionless with closed eyes, his forehead pressed to the wall. Yves made no attempt to speak to him, realizing that his brother was praying. "It is you, Monsieur Jean-Louis," Joséfa had said, "who will have to speak to him of the Good God. He would jump down my throat if *I* so much as tried!" Yves would have liked to follow his example, but his tongue had lost the feel of those forgotten words. It was a far, far call to the distant days when he, too, had only to close his eyes and clasp his hands. . . . How long the time seemed! He knew by heart all the patterns made by the stains on the stairs where he was squatting.

Once more Joséfa pushed the door ajar, and this time she made a sign to them to enter. She showed them into the dining-room and vanished. The Frontenacs held their breath, and scarcely dared to move, because Jean-Louis's boots creaked. The window must have been shut since the evening before.

The stale smells of food and gas had accumulated between these four red-papered walls. The two colour-prints, one of peaches, the other of raspberries, were identical with just such another pair which had once hung in the dining-room at Preignac.

Only later did they realize that they ought not to have gone in all together. If he had first seen only Jean-Louis, their uncle might have grown used to the idea of their presence. It was madness to have crowded in together.

"Here they are, sir," Joséfa said, doing her best to play her chosen part of housekeeper: " – it's a great happiness for you, sir, isn't it, to have them with you? . . . They've all come, except Monsieur José."

Not a move did he make, but sat in the grip of a reptilian immobility. . . . In that terrible face, only the eyes slid from side to side, shifting from one to another of them, as though some threatened blow were about to fall. His two hands clung to his coat, pressed hard against his panting chest. Suddenly, Joséfa forgot her part:

"You won't speak because you're afraid it might do you a hurt, is that it? All right, ducky, don't you say nothing if you'd rather not. You can see them, can't you? – and it makes you happy. Look as much as you like, but don't speak a word. If you come over queer, just you tell me, my pet. If you're in pain, just make a sign. Want your injection, is that it? I'll go and get it ready."

So she lulled and comforted him in such words as one uses to the very young. But the dying man, still tense, still watchful, retained his haunted look. The four Frontenacs, standing in a tight bunch, rigid with anguish, were unaware that they looked just like members of a jury about to be sworn in. At last, Jean-Louis, breaking from the group, laid his arm about his uncle's shoulder.

"Only José's failed to turn up on parade, you see: but the latest news of him is good."

Xavier Frontenac's lips moved. They all of them leaned above his chair, but could not, at first, make out what he was saying.

"Who told you to come?"

"Madame . . . your housekeeper."

"She . . . is . . . not . . . my . . . housekeeper. Understand that: not . . . my . . . housekeeper. You heard how she spoke to me. . . ."

Yves knelt down close to the skinny legs.

"What does it matter, Uncle Xavier? . . . it's of no importance whatever . . . it doesn't concern us. You are our beloved uncle, our father's brother. . . ."

But the sick man, with averted eyes, pushed him away. "You know now! . . . you know now! . . ." he kept on saying with a wild look in his eyes. "I am like Uncle Péloueyre. He shut himself away at Bourideys, I remember, with that woman of his . . . wouldn't see any of the family. . . . Your father . . . who was a very young man, then . . . was deputed to go and see him. . . . I recall how Michel set off on horseback, with a joint, because his uncle liked our Preignac mutton. . . . Your father described how he stood there, knocking at the door. . . . At last Uncle Péloueyre opened it a crack . . . stared at Michel . . . took the joint . . . shut the door and bolted it. . . . I remember his telling us about it . . . it's an odd story . . . but I'm talking too much . . . a very odd story."

He began to laugh in a sort of suppressed and concentrated fashion. He could not stop though the laughter aggravated his condition. A fit of coughing shook him.

Joséfa came back and gave him his injection. He closed his eyes. A quarter of an hour went by. The noise of the trains set the house shaking. When they had passed, nothing could be heard but his terrible, gasping struggle for breath. Suddenly he stirred in his chair, and opened his eyes.

"Are Marie and Danièle here? They will have been in the house of my mistress. I shall have been the cause of their seeing the woman whom I keep. If Blanche and Michel could have known that, they would have cursed me. I have brought Michel's children into the house of my mistress!"

That was all he said. His nose had a pinched look: his face was blue. Raucous sounds came from him, that terrible noise of gurgling which means the end. . . . Joséfa, her eyes streaming with tears, took him in her arms, while the Frontenacs withdrew in terror towards the door.

"You don't need to feel ashamed with them, ducky . . . they're good, they are, they know about things, they understand. . . . What is it? . . . what do you want, my poor chickabiddy?"

In sudden panic she turned towards the children:

"What is he saying? I can't make out what he's saying!"

They could see only too well what that movement of his arm from left to right meant: it meant "Go away!" God would not let her understand that he was dismissing her, his companion of so many years, his only friend, his servant and his wife.

In the darkness, the noise of the last train smothered her groans. She abandoned herself, without restraint, to her grief, feeling the need to cry aloud. The concierge and the daily woman held her by the arms, and dabbed at her temples with vinegar. The Frontenac children had fallen to their knees.

XX

"AND what surprises have you in store for us, now?" Dussol intended the question to be friendly, though he could not suppress a smile.

Yves, curled up on Jean-Louis's divan, pretended that he had not heard. He was to take the night train to Paris. It was late in the afternoon, two days after Uncle Xavier's funeral at Preignac. Dussol, who had not been able to be present (he was a victim, now, to rheumatism, and for the last year had been able to walk only with the help of two sticks), had come to pay his respects to the family.

"I imagine," he said, "that you've got something on the stocks?"

The light had not been switched on, and he could barely see Yves's face. The young man was still silent.

"What a young slyboots you are! Come, now, out with it! . . . fish or flesh? verse or prose?"

At that, Yves made up his mind:

"I'm writing a collection of 'Characters' . . . taken from nature. . . . No merit, I can assure you . . . I have invented nothing . . . merely reproduced most of the types I have come across in the course of my life."

"What is it going to be called? just *Characters*?"

"No: *Mugs*."

There was a moment's silence. Madeleine turned to Dussol, and, in a choking voice, said: "Do let me give you another cup?" Jean-Louis asked something about an important felling operation near Bourideys, for which the Frontenac-Dussol firm was negotiating.

"It's not your fault, I know," said Dussol: "all the same, it's a nuisance that your uncle's death has delayed the conclusion of the deal. Lacagne's in the field, you know. . . ."

"I'm meeting him the day after tomorrow, early, on the site. . . ."

Jean-Louis spoke absent-mindedly. Most of his attention was being given to Yves, whose forehead and hands alone were visible. He got up and turned on the light. Yves half averted his head, revealing to his brother's eyes a crop of tousled brown hair, a hollow, pallid cheek, and the graceful line of his neck.

"I've half a mind to go back to Paris with Yves," Jean-Louis said on the spur of the moment. "I must see Labat . . ."

"But in that case you wouldn't be back in time for your meeting the day after tomorrow," Dussol protested: "Labat can go hang! D'you realize that there's profit in this Bourideys' felling to the tune of a hundred thousand francs?"

Jean-Louis passed his hand over his nose and mouth. Why this sudden feeling of terror – this idea that he mustn't let Yves out of his sight for a single moment?

As soon as Dussol had left, he went into the bedroom. Madeleine followed him.

"Is it because of Yves?" she asked. She had learned to see into her husband's mind, and he knew it. He felt that she could read him like a book.

"I don't mind admitting that I'm worried about him."

She tried to argue. It was all nonsense, really it was. Yves had been upset by Uncle Xavier's death. A few days in Paris would soon put him right.

"We know the kind of way he lives. . . . He keeps the gloomy moods for his family, with the result that you start worrying. From what Dussol's been able to discover, he is not usually regarded as a wet blanket by his friends. Surely you're not going to risk the loss of a hundred thousand francs, just for something that's probably got no existence except in your imagination?"

Instinctively, she had put her finger on the one argument that was always effective with Jean-Louis. It wasn't only his money that was in question, but the family's. For the rest of the evening, he did his best to keep up a conversation with his brother, who seemed perfectly calm, and answered his questions without even raising his voice. There was nothing to justify Jean-Louis's anxiety. All the same, he very nearly did not get out of the railway carriage in which he had installed Yves, when the porter came along shutting the doors.

As soon as they were through the Lormont tunnels, Yves felt that he could breathe more freely. He was on his way back to "her". Each turn of the wheels helped to shorten the distance between them. They had agreed to meet at eleven o'clock next morning in an underground bar, at the corner of one of the Avenues, close to the Etoile. This time he was expecting the worst, and so was armed against disappointment. No matter what she might say or do, he was about to see her again. So long as he had something to look forward to, some meeting arranged for, he could go on living. But he must make his times of seeing her more frequent than they had been during the year just past. He would say: "I find myself gasping for breath rather sooner than I used to. You mustn't expect me to remain out of water for too long. In you I live, and breathe and have my being." She would smile. She knew that Yves had no particular liking for travellers' tales, and would cut short what she had to tell him about the cruise. 'I will make her understand that human geography is the only geography I find interesting: that it's not the views she's seen that I care about, but the people she's met in the course of these three months. No doubt there'll turn out to have been fewer of them than I think. . . . She says there's nothing more important in her life than me. Nevertheless, she's surrounded by adoring males. . . . Who was it she was going about with last year? . . .' He fumbled about with his feet for the bloodstained tracks which lay across the last twelve months. He scratched at himself like a leper, waking old jealousies, making old scabs bleed again. He was rushing on towards a city which had nothing in common with the Paris in which, only one week ago, Xavier Frontenac had died so horribly.

"Darling, *must* you look at your watch? We've been together for exactly ten minutes, and already you're worrying about the time. You just live for the moment when I shan't be with you!"

"Can't we have a little let-up from complaints and reproaches? . . . Tell me, do you think I'm looking brown?"

He thought it tactful to praise her suit and her fox-fur. She was duly pleased. He let her go on for quite a while about the Balearic Islands. Still, on three separate occasions, he had already made her say that she had met no one of any interest to her – except her former husband, whom she had run into in Marseilles. They had had lunch together, like a couple of old friends. . . . He was becoming more and more wedded to his drugs, and had had to hurry away to get a pipe of opium . . . just couldn't do without it.

"And what about you, Yves, my pet?"

All the time he was speaking she was busy with her face, reddening her lips, dabbing her cheeks with powder. When he told her about Uncle Xavier's death, she asked, without any particular show of interest, whether it would make any "difference" to him.

"He had made over most of his fortune to us in his lifetime."

"Then there's nothing particularly exciting about his death, is there?"

There was no spitefulness in the words. . . . He'd have to

start on a whole string of explanations . . . introduce her into a whole world of memories, a universe of mystery. . . . A woman joined the young man who had been sitting alone at the table opposite. They kissed. There were two or three men sitting at the bar. None of them turned round. Motor-buses were rumbling up the Avenue. The electric lights were on. There was nothing to show that it was morning. She was eating cold potato-chips, one by one.

"I'm hungry," she said.

"Lunch any good to you? . . . when can we make a date? – tomorrow? . . ."

"Let me think . . . tomorrow? . . . four o'clock I've got a fitting . . . six . . . no, not tomorrow . . . how about Thursday?"

"Three days from now?" he said, and his voice sounded indifferent. Three days and three nights out of her life about which he would know nothing, days and nights filled with people who were strangers to him, with incidents which would remain for ever hidden from him. . . . He had believed himself to be prepared for just such a situation, had thought he would feel no surprise. But pain is unforeseeable. For months and months he had grown breathless in pursuit of her. Three months' pause, and here was the old dance beginning all over again. But the circumstances were different now. He was all-in, done up. He wouldn't be able to stick the pace. She realized that he was suffering, and took his hand. He did not withdraw it. She asked him what he was thinking about. He said:

"I was thinking of Respide. The other day, after my uncle's funeral, I went there alone from Preignac. My brother had gone straight back to Bordeaux, with my sisters. I had the house opened up for me. I went into the drawing-room. It was full of damp-rot and smelled of mould and decaying floor-boards. The shutters were closed. . . . I lay down at full length on the chintz sofa in the half-light. I could feel the coldness of the wall against my cheek. I shut my eyes and tried to imagine that I was lying there between my mother and my uncle. . . ."

"Yves, you do say the most abominable things! . . ."

"Never had I so completely succeeded in getting into the very skin of death. The walls were thick, the room like some cavern hidden away at the heart of that remote estate . . . night . . . and all around me, life stretching to infinity. . . . I was at peace . . . peace, darling, think of that! . . . finished with the urgency of love . . . Why are we always taught to dread annihilation? . . . The really awful thing is to believe, against all evidence, in life eternal! To live eternally would be to lose the refuge of nothingness."

He saw that she was furtively glancing at her wrist-watch. She said:

"Yves, I really must rush. . . . We'd better not be seen leaving together. Thursday, then? . . . Shall we say seven o'clock at my place? . . . no, half-past . . . no, better make it a quarter to eight. . . ."

"No," said he, laughing: "it shall be eight o'clock!"

XXI

YVES was still laughing as he walked down the Champs-Elysées. There was nothing forced or bitter about his laughter. The sound was so frank and so free that people turned to look at him. . . . It was only just after noon, and he had climbed the stairs from the d'Orsay station in the early hours of the morning. In that brief space of time he had drained to the dregs the delight of seeing her again to which he had been looking forward for three whole months. And now, here he was, wandering the streets. . . . It really was a "scream", as she was so fond of saying. The gay mood was still with him as he dropped on to a bench at the Rond-Point. He felt as much done up as though he had walked all the way from his native heaths. He was conscious of no pain, but only of a feeling of exhaustion. Never had the object of his love seemed to him so utterly worthless as now, when he had been kicked out of her life and trodden under foot, as now, when he was fouled and finished. Nevertheless, his love was still there. It was like a mill, grinding away – on nothing. He had stopped laughing now. His mind withdrew into itself, concentrating upon this strange torment in a non-existent world. He was living through those moments known to all lovers when, with arms still clasped across their breasts, as though what they have been embracing has not really vanished, they strain to their hearts, quite literally – nothing. On this mild, warm noon of October, seated on a bench at the Rond-Point des Champs-Elysées, the last of the Frontenacs could see no future of any kind waiting for him beyond the Chevaux de Marly. Once past *them*, he could not say, for the life of him, whether he would turn to right or left, or go straight on to the Tuileries and enter the mouse-trap of the Louvre.

All around him cars and people swirled and mingled, breaking into different streams at the meeting-place of the Avenues. He felt as utterly alone as he had done once in that narrow clearing, walled in with furze and bracken, where, in his untamed childhood, he had loved to hide. The unbroken roar of the streets sounded to him like the sweet boisterousness of Nature, and the passers-by seemed stranger in his eyes than the pines of Bourideys, the summits of which had once looked down at a tiny Frontenac snuggling at their feet in a thickness of underbrush. Today, these men and women were like flies above the heather, like hovering dragonflies. Now and again, one of them would settle at his side, rub against his sleeve, then, without even seeing him, take flight again. How muffled, now, and distant had that voice become which once had followed this young Frontenac into his secret hut. But, however muted, he could hear it still. Now he could clearly see – so said the voice – all the obstructed paths which once had been foretold, the passions from which there could be no escape. . . . Better turn back . . . turn in his tracks. . . . But how is it possible to turn in one's tracks when strength is spent? To trudge back all that way? – what a climb! and what was there waiting at the end of it? Yves was a wanderer now upon the earth, freed from all human labour. No work was demanded of him. He had finished his task before the hour struck, had handed in his fair copy, and gone off to play. His only occupation was to note, day by day, the reactions of a mind wholly without employment. He could have done no more, and the world demanded no more of him. Which, among the thousands of tasks that set these human ants swarming about his bench, could have served his purpose? Ah, better far to die of hunger. . . . "Yet, you know well," the voice insisted, "that you were created to carry through an exhausting labour, and to that labour you would have submitted, body and soul, because it would not have turned you from the deep-running life of love. That is the one form of work in all the world which would in no wise have diverted you from love, which, at every moment, would have made love manifest and joined you to all men in charity. . . ." Yves shook his head, and cried: "Oh, dear God, let me be!"

He got up, and walked the short distance to the Metro entrance, close to the Grand Palais. He leaned upon the balustrade. It was the hour when the work-rooms all fill up again, when the Metro sucks in and vomits forth a crowd of ants with human faces. For a long while, Yves, with fascinated gaze, followed this ingurgitation, this spewing out, of human creatures. A day was coming – he felt sure of it, and, from the depths of his despair and weariness, he called upon it – when all men and women would be forced to obey this tidal rhythm, all, without one single exception. What Jean-Louis called the "social question" would be present no longer to the finer spirits among mankind. . . . Yves thought: 'I must live to see that day when the lock-gates will open and close at stated intervals before the human flood. When that time comes, no inherited fortune will make it possible for any Frontenac to stand aloof on pretext of thinking, of indulging in despair, of writing a Journal, of praying, of achieving a personal salvation. The people of the lower depths will have triumphed over all human values. Yes, the human being, as such, will have been destroyed, and with his destruction will have disappeared that torment and that dear delight which we call love. No longer will those lunatics exist who can see infinity within the finite. What joy to think that the time may be close at hand when all the Frontenacs – for want of air that they can breathe – will have vanished from the earth: when no creature will exist who can even imagine what I, at this moment, am feeling, as I lean upon this Metro balustrade – this stale sickness of sentiment, this over-chewed cud of brooding on what *she*, since first I knew her, may have said to make me believe that she still clings to me – as the sick man, from among the many things his doctor may have said, isolates just those which once gave him hope, which now he knows by heart (but no longer have they any power over him, dwell on them though he may . . .)

Beyond the Chevaux de Marly he could see nothing more to do than lay him down and sleep. Death had no meaning for him, poor sad immortal. On that side the road was barred. A Frontenac knows that into nothingness no way leads out, and that a guard has been set at the door of the tomb. In the world he was imagining, the world he saw, and felt must come, no man would be haunted by the temptation of death, because the human race of that future date, weighed down by lives laborious and filled with busyness, will seem alive but be already dead. For to have the choice between life and death, a man must be an individual, different from other men, bearing his own existence in his hands, capable of measuring its scope, of judging it with lucid glance beneath the watchful eye of God.

It amused him to think of these things. . . . He made a promise to himself that he would tell Jean-Louis all he had been thinking as he had hung above the entrance to the Metro. What fun it would be to see his brother's surprised face, as Yves described to him the nature of that revolution to come which would be accomplished in the secret places of the heart, achieving a dissociation in man's nature, so that, in the end, he would be turned into something resembling one of the hymenoptera – a bee, an ant. . . . No centuries-old park would ever again stretch branches over one single and continuing family. The pine-trees on the old estates would not in future watch, year after year, always the same children grow, nor, in the thin, pure faces gazing upwards at their crests, recognize the features of their fathers and their grandfathers before them. . . . It was because he was so tired, thought Yves, that his mind was wandering like this. How wonderful it would be to sleep! The question now for him was not of life or death, but only of sleep. He hailed a taxi, and, as he drove, fingered in his pocket a tiny bottle. He held it close to his eyes. It was pure pleasure to decipher on its label the magic formula: *Allylisopropylacetylurea c̄ phenyldimethylpyrazolone ā ā*, gr 1·6.

All through those same hours, Jean-Louis, seated opposite Madeleine at table, standing, while he hastily swallowed his coffee, at the wheel of his car, in his office, as he sat watching his clerk Janin who was making a report to him, kept on saying to himself – 'Yves is not in danger: I've no reason whatever to be anxious. Yesterday evening in the train he seemed calmer than I have seen him for a long time . . . that's what worries me . . . that calmness . . .' From somewhere in the docks he could hear the puffing of a locomotive. Why should he let this business appointment keep him from going? – he could explain it all to Janin. Here he was in the room with him: a man with plenty of initiative, and passionately anxious to get his chance. Already his bright, observant eyes were trying to make out what Jean-Louis was thinking, to get just one step ahead of him . . . and quite suddenly, Jean-Louis knew with absolute certainty that he would start that night for Paris. By tomorrow he would be there. The knowledge brought back his peace of mind. It was as though the unknown power which, since the previous evening, had had him by the throat, now knew it could relax its grip, because he would obey.

XXII

FROM the bottom of a deep pit Yves could hear, infinitely far away, a bell ringing. The confused idea came to him that it was the telephone. Somebody was calling him from Bordeaux to say that his mother had been taken ill (though he knew she had been dead for more than a year). A short while ago she had been in this very room. She had visited it only once in her life (she had come from Bordeaux to see Yves. She had wanted, she said, to be able to visualize his surroundings when she thought of him). She had never come again – until last night. Yves could see her still, as he had seen her in the armchair by his bed, her hands idle, since she was dead. The dead can neither knit nor speak. . . . But her lips had moved. She had had something urgent to impart, but could not make herself heard. She had come in, as she always used to do at Bourideys, when there was something on her mind, without knocking, just pressing the handle gently down, and pushing the door open with her body, lost in her preoccupation, not noticing that she might, perhaps, be interrupting him in his reading or his writing, in his sleep or in a fit of tears. . . . There she had stood, yet, somebody was telephoning from Bordeaux to tell him she was dead. He gazed at her in anguish, striving to catch upon her lips the *something* she wanted to say, and could not. . . . The ringing went on and on. What should he answer? Then the front door banged, and he heard the voice of the daily woman: "Lucky I've got a key. . . ." Then, the other voice, Jean-Louis's (but he's in Bordeaux) . . . "He looks very peaceful . . . he's sleeping quite quietly . . . no, the bottle's almost full, he can't have taken very much. . . ." Jean-Louis was in Bordeaux, but, at the same time, he was here, in this room. Yves gave him a reassuring smile:

"Hullo, old man . . ."

"What are you doing in Paris? . . ."

"Some business brought me up . . ."

Life flowed in on Yves from every side. Slowly it made its way in as the tide of sleep receded. . . . He remembered now: what cowardice! – three tablets! Jean-Louis was asking him what was wrong. Yves made no attempt to pretend. Pretence was beyond his powers: strength had drained from him like blood from a wound. All the circumstances of the time just past came suddenly to focus. Two days ago he had been in Bordeaux: yesterday morning, in the little bar. Then had followed those hours of madness . . . and now, here was Jean-Louis.

"But how did you manage to get away? . . . I thought this was the day of the big deal? . . ."

Jean-Louis shook his head. "A sick man mustn't worry his head over things like that."

And Yves:

"No, I'm not feverish – just knocked-up, all in. . . ."

Jean-Louis had taken his wrist, and now, with his eye on his watch, was counting the pulse-beats, as mamma used to do in the days of their childhood illnesses. Then, with a gesture – which also recalled their mother – the elder brother pushed the hair back from Yves's forehead, so as to make sure that he really was not feverish – perhaps, too, in order to reveal the younger man's face, to see his features clearly: and also, who knows? in a simple access of tenderness.

"Don't get agitated," said Jean-Louis: "don't talk."

"You'll stay with me, won't you?"

"Yes, I'll stay."

"Sit down: no, not on the bed: bring up the arm-chair."

Neither of them moved. The confused sounds of the autumn morning disturbed them not at all. Now and again, Yves, opening his eyes, saw his brother's serious, honest face marked with the strain and weariness of the night. Jean-Louis, freed from the anxious brooding which had been gnawing at him for the last two days, had yielded at last to the deep sense of peace which flowed over him as he sat beside the bed in which his younger brother lay alive and well. About noon, he ate a hurried meal without leaving the room. The day seemed to be running through his fingers like sand through an hour-glass. Suddenly, the telephone bell started to ring. . . . The sick man showed signs of restlessness. Jean-Louis laid his finger to his lips and slipped into the adjoining dressing-room. Yves had a happy feeling that everything now was out of his hands. It was for others to get him out of the mess. Jean-Louis would arrange everything.

". . . . Bordeaux? . . . that you, Dussol? . . . yes, it's me speaking . . . I can hear you . . . I can't help it . . . couldn't put off this trip. . . . No, Janin's acting for me . . . of course . . . he's got my instructions . . . well, it can't be helped . . . yes, I know . . . more than a hundred thousand francs . . . just too bad. . . ."

"He's hung up," said Jean-Louis, coming back into the bedroom.

He sat down again by the bed. Yves began to question him. Was it because of him that the deal about which Dussol had been speaking had misfired? His brother reassured him. He had taken all the necessary steps before leaving. It was a good sign that Yves was showing anxiety, that he wanted to know, for instance, whether Joséfa had got the cheque which they had decided to send her.

"Would you believe it, old man, she actually sent it back. . . ."

"I always said it wasn't enough. . . ."

"You're barking up the wrong tree. She sent it back because she thought it was too much. Uncle Xavier had given her a hundred thousand francs in hard cash. . . . She wrote me a letter in which she said that he had felt very guilty about the money, and couldn't get the idea out of his mind that he had deprived *us* of it. She doesn't want to do anything that might be contrary to his wishes. All the poor creature asks is to be allowed to send us her good wishes each New Year's day. She says she hopes I will let her have news of the family and that I will advise her about her investments."

"What securities did Uncle Xavier buy for her?"

"*Lombards Anciens* and *Noblesse Russe*, three and a half per cent. There's nothing for her to worry about. . . ."

"Is she living at Niort with her daughter?"

"Yes . . . and, oh, by the way, she wants to keep our photographs. Marie and Danièle don't quite like the idea, but she has promised not to display them, but to keep them in the glass-fronted wardrobe. . . . What do you think?"

It was Jean-Louis's opinion that the humble Joséfa had entered into the Frontenac mystery, and now formed part of it. Nothing, he thought, from now on, could break her connexion with it. Beyond any doubt, she was entitled to her photographs and to her New Year's wishes. . . .

"Look here, Jean-Louis, when José has finished his military service, I'm all for our living together, snuggling up like puppies in a basket. . . ." (He knew that this could never be.)

"Like when we used to put our napkins on our heads, and play at 'Communities', in the small room, remember?"

"How extraordinary to think that that room still exists. Life marches on . . . but Bourideys, at least, hasn't changed."

"A lot of timber has been cut," said Jean-Louis. . . . "In the Lassus direction there's been quite a clean sweep . . . and all along the road, too. . . . Try to imagine the mill, with not a tree standing. . . ."

"There'll always be the pines in the park."

"They're rotting where they stand. . . . Every year a few of them die."

Yves sighed:

"The Frontenac pines, wearing away like human flesh and blood."

"Yves, what d'you say to our going back to Bourideys together?"

Yves made no reply. He was trying to remember what Bourideys would be looking like at that moment. The evening breeze must be clashing the high tops of the pines together, then tearing them apart, then once more making a tangle of their branches, as though the shackled trees had private things to say to one another, and secrets to shower upon the earth. . . . After the shower, the forest would be filled with the sound of rain-drops. . . . They would go out upon the terrace to sniff the autumn evening. . . . But, if Bourideys, for Yves, existed still, it was only as his mother, while he lay dreaming, had existed. She had seemed to be living, though he knew her to be dead. In Bourideys today nothing was left but the abandoned chrysalis of childhood and of love. How could he express such feelings even to the brother who dwelt so deeply in his heart? He protested lamely, that it would be difficult for them to remain long together.

"You couldn't wait until I was cured."

Jean-Louis did not ask – "cured of what?" (He knew that he should have phrased it, "cured of whom?") It amazed him to think that so many young and charming beings, like Yves, could know love only in the form of suffering. For them it is no more than a tormenting fantasy. . . . But to Jean-Louis love seemed a simple and an easy thing . . . yet, if God did not command his highest loyalty! . . . He was deeply fond of Madeleine, and took Communion every Sunday: yet, twice already, once with a girl in the office, once with one of his wife's friends, he had felt that a rather special link existed . . . had been conscious of something to which he was only too ready to respond. . . . He had had to pray hard, but even so was not at all sure that he had not been guilty of the sin of desire . . . for how is it always possible to distinguish temptation from desire? Holding his brother's hand in the lamplight, he gazed with sad surprise at the face so seamed with pain, at the clenched jaw, at all the tell-tale marks of exhaustion and fatigue.

Perhaps Yves would have been pleased if Jean-Louis had questioned him. But the shyness between them was too strong. Jean-Louis would have liked to say – "your work . . ." but to have done so would have been to risk wounding him. Besides, he felt confusedly, that his brother's work, if it were to flower into supreme achievement, must ever be the expression of despair. . . . He knew by heart the poem in which Yves, when little more than a child, had told how, if he were to be torn from silence, he would need, as did the pines of Bourideys, the wild West wind, and an infinity of torment.

Jean-Louis would have liked to say: "a home . . . a wife . . . other Frontenac children. . . ." Above all, he would have liked to speak to him of God, but dared not.

A little later (darkness had already fallen), he leaned over Yves, whose eyes were closed, and was surprised to see him smile, to hear him murmur that he was not asleep. Jean-Louis was rejoiced to see the tenderness and calm which lit the gaze that held his own so long. He would have liked to know what it was that Yves was thinking. He could not know that what produced that smile was the happiness Yves felt that he was not to die in solitude. No, never would he die alone. Wherever it might be that death would find him, he believed, he knew, that his elder brother would be with him, holding his hand, and going with him as far as it is possible for another human being to go, to the brink of the great darkness.

Far away, in the country of the Frontenacs and the Péloueyres, beyond the lost lands where the tracks end, the moon was shining on the drenched and spongy heath. It kept its state especially in that clearing of the trees, left free by the resinous growths, around some five or six huge oaks, very old and very gnarled, giant children of the earth. There it was still possible for the slashed and wounded pines to raise their heads Heavenwards. Drowsy sheep-bells were tinkling at intervals in the pastures, known as the "parc de l'Homme", where one of the Frontenac shepherds was spending the October darkness. But for the occasional cry of some prowling animal of the night, and the jolting of a passing wagon, no sound broke the murmur of the breeze as it passed on from pine to pine, from the distant brink of ocean, travelling along the dense network of their branches. Within the hut, empty of sportsmen till the dawn should break, blinded pigeons, set there as decoys, fluttered their wings and suffered pangs of thirst and hunger. A flight of cranes creaked its way across the lighter spaces of the sky. From within the dark mystery of the Téchoueyre marshes, with their reedy, turf-ringed pools, sounded the whirring flap of water-birds. Old Frontenacs and Péloueyres, waking from the sleep of death in that corner of the world, would have seen no sign of change. The old oaks, fed for two centuries on the secret juices of the soil, were enjoying, at this very moment, a second, and more ephemeral, life in the mind of a young man lying in a Paris room with his brother fondly watching him. It was under the shade of those trees, thought Yves, that a great pit should have been dug, and in it piled and jumbled the bodies of all the Frontenac wives and husbands, of the Frontenac brothers and uncles, of the Frontenac sons. Only thus could the family have won the solace of one vast embrace, could have been mixed for ever with that much-loved earth, could have lain at home in nothingness.

Around, bent all in the same direction by the sea-wind, and offering to the West their rain-black bark, the pines would ever reach towards the sky, and strain and stretch. Each would have its wound – different from the wounds of all the others (each one of us knows why he bleeds). And he, Yves Frontenac, like them, wounded, and rooted like them in the drifting sand, but a free being with full liberty to tear himself adrift, should he so wish, from the world of the living, had chosen vainly to moan, to stay as one in the confused tangle of the human forest. Yet all his gestures were of supplication, and all his cries were still addressed to somebody.

He remembered his mother's worn face on one September evening at Bouirdeys, and how her eyes had sought for God behind the topmost branches. "Tell me, Yves, you who know so much . . . do the spirits in Heaven still think of those they have left behind upon the earth?" Since she could not imagine a world in which her sons had ceased to be the very heart of her heart, Yves had promised her that all separate loves would be perfected in one perfect love, single and absolute. And now, tonight, after many years, the words which he had uttered for her comfort, came back into his memory. Jean-Louis was sleeping. The night lamp shed a glow upon his gracious face. Oh, bond of the divine! Oh, mark of God's parentage! Never would the Frontenac mystery know corruption, for it was one beam of the Eternal Love refracted through the prism of a Race. The impossible union of wives and husbands, of sons and brothers, would, before long, be consummated. The last pines of Bourideys would see moving, not at their feet along the ride that led to the Great Oak, but far above their highest branches, a mother and her five children now made for ever one.

A WOMAN OF THE PHARISEES

I

"COME here, boy!"

I turned round, thinking that the words were addressed to one of my companions. But no, it was to me that the one-time Papal Zouave had spoken. He was smiling, and the scar on his upper lip made the smile hideous.

Colonel the Comte de Mirbel was in the habit of coming once every week into Middle School Yard. On these occasions his ward, Jean de Mirbel, who was almost always in a state of being "kept in," would move away from the wall against which he had been made to stand, while we, from a distance, watched the arraignment to which his terrifying uncle subjected him. Our master, Monsieur Rausch, called upon to act as witness for the prosecution, replied obsequiously to the Colonel's questions. The old man was tall and vigorous. On his head he wore one of those caps known as a "cronstadt," and his coat, buttoned up to the neck, gave him a military air. He was never to be seen without a riding-switch, probably of raw-hide, tucked under his arm. When our friend's conduct had been particularly bad, he would be marched away across the Yard between Monsieur Rausch and his guardian, and the three of them would disappear into a staircase in the left wing of the building, which led to the dormitories. We would stop whatever game we were playing and wait until a long-drawn wail struck sharply on our ears. It sounded like the yelp of a beaten dog (though that may have been due to our imaginations). A moment later, Monsieur Rausch would reappear, accompanied by the Colonel, the scar showing livid in his purple face. His blue eyes would look faintly bloodshot. Monsieur Rausch was all attention. He kept his head turned towards his companion and his lips were stretched in a servile grin. That was the only occasion on which we ever saw that pale, terrifying face, topped by its red, crimped hair, distorted into a grimace of laughter. Monsieur Rausch, the terror of our lives! Whenever we went into class and found his seat still empty, I used to pray: "O God, please let Monsieur Rausch be dead! Blessed Virgin, please let him have broken his leg, or make it so that he's ill—not seriously, but just a little!" . . . But he had an iron constitution, and his hard, dry hand at the end of its skinny arm was more to be feared than a slab of wood. Jean de Mirbel, fresh from the mysterious punishments inflicted upon him by his two executioners (vastly exaggerated, no doubt, in our boyish fancies), would come back into the form-room with his eyes red and his grubby face streaked with tears, and make his way to his desk. The rest of us kept our eyes fixed firmly on our note-books.

"Do as you're told, Louis!" barked Monsieur Rausch. It was the first time he had ever called me by my Christian name. I stayed hesitating on the threshold of the parlour door. Jean de Mirbel was standing inside the room, his back towards me. On a small table there lay an open parcel containing two chocolate éclairs and a bun. The Colonel asked me whether I liked cakes. I nodded my head.

"Well, tuck into those, then . . . go on; what are you waiting for? It's young Pian, isn't it?—know his family well—doesn't look as though he'd got more spunk than his poor father. . . . Brigitte Pian, his stepmother, now there's a woman for you—reg'lar Mother of the Church. . . . You, there! stop where you are!"—this he shouted at Jean, who was trying to slink away. "You're not going to get off as lightly as that! You've got to watch your young friend having a good time. . . . Come on, make up your mind, you little fool!" he added, his two eyes fixing me, from either side of the short, firm nose, with a stare in which a glint of anger already showed.

"He's shy," said Monsieur Rausch; "don't wait to be asked twice, Pian."

My friend was looking out of the window. His turn-down collar had come unfastened, and I could see his dirty neck above it. No one in the world had such power to frighten me as the two men now bending down and smiling into my face. I knew from of old the harsh, animal-like smell which hung about Monsieur Rausch. I stammered out that I wasn't hungry, but the Colonel retorted that a boy didn't have to be hungry to eat cakes. Seeing that I was persisting in my obstinacy, Monsieur Rausch told me to go to the Devil, adding that there were plenty of others who wouldn't be so stupid. As I was making my escape into the Yard, I heard him call to Mouleyre, an unnaturally fat boy who always ate anything on which he could lay his hands in the dining-hall. He ran up at the summons, sweating. Monsieur Rausch shut the parlour door, from which Mouleyre emerged later, his mouth smeared with cream.

It was a June evening, and still swelteringly hot. When the day-boys had gone home we were allowed to remain outside for a bit because of the heat. Mirbel came up to me. We could hardly be described as friends, and I am pretty sure that he despised me because, in those days, I was a rather spiritless and well-behaved boy. He took from his pocket a pill-box and half raised the lid.

"Look!"

It contained two stag-beetles, of the kind we called capricorns. He had given them a cherry for food.

"They don't like cherries," said I. "They live on the rotten bark of old oaks."

We used to catch them on Thursdays, near the School Lodge, on our way out. These particular insects always start flying at sunset.

"You can have one of them. Choose the biggest, but be careful, they're not tame yet!"

I couldn't tell him that I didn't know where to put the capricorn. But I was pleased that he should speak so kindly to me. We sat down on the steps that led to the main block of the school buildings. Two hundred boys and about twenty masters were crowded into what had once been a beautifully proportioned town-house.

"I'm going to train them to pull a cart," said Jean.

He took from his pocket a small box which he fastened with thread to the beetle's claws. We played with it for a while. During these special recreation periods on summer evenings no boy was ever kept in, and there was no insistence on community games. Elsewhere on the steps other boys were busy spitting on apricot stones and polishing them. This done, they made a hole in them and took out the kernels, using the empty husks as whistles. The heat of the day was still intense within the space surrounded on four sides by buildings. Not a breath of air stirred the leaves on the sickly plane-trees. Monsieur Rausch, his legs apart, was in his usual place over by the lavatories, to see that we didn't stay too long in them. They gave off a powerful stench which fought a losing battle with the smell of chlorine and disinfectant. From the other side of the wall came the sound of a "fly" bumping over the rough cobbles of the Rue Leyteire. I was filled with envy of the unknown passenger, of the coachman, and even of the horse, because they were not shut away in school, and didn't have to go in fear of Monsieur Rausch.

"I'm jolly well going to thrash Mouleyre," said Jean suddenly.

"I say, Mirbel, what's a Papal Zouave?"

He shrugged his shoulders:

"I'm not quite sure, but I should say he was one of the chaps who fought for the Pope before 1870, and got beaten."

He was silent for a few moments, and then added:

"I don't want him and Rausch to die before I'm grown up."

Hatred made him look ugly. I asked him why he was the only one of us who was treated as he was.

"My uncle says it's for my good. He says that when his brother was dying, he swore by God that he'd make a man of me. . . ."

"And your mother? . . ."

"Oh, she believes everything he says . . . or maybe she doesn't dare contradict him. She didn't really want me to be a boarder here. She would have liked me to stay at home at La Devize with a tutor. . . . But he wouldn't allow that. He said my character was too bad."

"*My* mother," said I proudly, "has come to live in Bordeaux for my education."

"But you're a boarder just the same."

"Only for these two weeks, because Vignotte—he's the Agent over at Larjuzon—is sick, and my father's got to do his work. But she writes to me every day."

"Madame Brigitte Pian isn't your real mother, is she?"

"It's the same thing, though . . . it's just as if she were."

I stopped at that and felt my cheeks burning. Had my real mother heard? Are the dead always listening to find out what the living are saying about them? But if mamma knew everything, she would realize that no one had ever taken her place in my heart. . . . It didn't matter how kind my stepmother was to me. It was quite true that she wrote to me every day, but I hadn't even opened the letter which had come from her that morning. And when I cried that night, in the stifling dormitory, before going to sleep, it would be because I was thinking of my father, of my sister Michèle, or of Larjuzon, and not of Brigitte Pian. Still, my father would have liked me to be a boarder all the year round, so that he could have gone on living in the country. It was my stepmother who had insisted. They had taken a little flat in Bordeaux, to make it possible for me to go home every evening. My sister Michèle, who hated our father's wife, always maintained that she had used me as an excuse for breaking the promise she had made when she married, that she would live at Larjuzon. No doubt Michèle was right. If my stepmother was never tired of saying that I was "too nervous and too sensitive to be sent to boarding-school," it was because that was the only argument which could persuade my father to stay on in Bordeaux. I knew that well enough, but it didn't make any difference. The grown-ups could settle their own affairs. It was enough for me that my stepmother had had the last word. But I knew that papa was unhappy when separated from his woods, his horses and his guns. He must be enjoying himself now. . . . That thought was a great comfort to me during this fortnight of trial. Besides, it would soon be Prize-Day, and then Brigitte Pian would have to resign herself to going back to Larjuzon.

"Prize-Day soon!" I exclaimed.

Mirbel had a beetle in each hand and was pressing them together.

"They're kissing!" he said, and added without looking at me: "You don't know what a beastly trick my uncle's thought up if I don't get a good report. I'm not going to be allowed to spend the holidays with my mother. . . . I'm not to go to La Devize at all. I'm to be sent to lodge with a Priest, the Curé of Baluzac—it's actually only a few miles from where you live. He's been told to make me work six hours a day and to break me in. . . . I gather that's his line."

"Then why not try to get a good report?"

He shook his head. It couldn't be done; not with Rausch. He'd often tried.

"He never takes his eyes off me. You know my desk's just under his nose. You'd almost think he'd nothing to do but watch me. I've only got to glance out of the window . . ."

It was true enough, and nothing could be done to help Mirbel. I promised that if he spent his holidays at Baluzac I'd see a lot of him. I knew Monsieur Calou, the Curé, very well. There was nothing specially terrible about him. As a matter of fact, he was very decent. . . .

"No, he's horrible. Uncle says that bad boys are sent to him to be broken in. . . . I've heard that he drove the two Baillaud boys nearly wild. . . . But I shan't let him lay a finger on me. . . ."

Perhaps the Curé of Baluzac was kind only to me? I didn't know what to say to Mirbel. I suggested that perhaps his mother, who never saw him, wouldn't give up the chance of having him home for the holidays.

"She will, if he says so . . . she does everything he wants!" replied Mirbel in a fury. I realized that he was very near to tears.

"How about letting me help you with your lessons?"

He shook his head. He had too much lee-way to make up. Besides, Rausch would spot it.

"Whenever I show up a decent copy he always accuses me of cribbing."

At that moment Rausch put a whistle to his lips. He wore a long frock-coat with stains down the front. In spite of it being summer, he had still got his feet stuffed into padded felt slippers. His crinkled, carroty hair grew well back from a bony forehead covered with pimples. His eyes were of different colours and blinked from beneath reddened lids. We marched off in a long line towards the dining-hall. I hated the smell of greasy soup which came from it. It was still broad daylight but no sky was visible through the dirty windows. I noticed that Mirbel was the only boy at our table who did not eat ravenously. The Papal Zouave had hit on the one punishment which could get under his ward's skin—spending the holidays with the Curé of Baluzac, away from his mother. I should be able, with my bicycle, to see him every day. I felt a little stab of happiness. I would speak about Jean to the Curé who was so kind to me and let me gather nuts in his garden. . . . True, I was "young Pian," the stepson of Madame Brigitte his "benefactress." . . . But that made it all the better. I would ask my stepmother to intercede on Jean's behalf. . . . I told him as much on our way upstairs to the dormitory. Twenty of us slept in a room which was ventilated by one window only which gave on to the Rue Leyteire. At the foot of each bed stood a wash-hand stand with a basin. In this we put our tooth-glasses in such a way that the man who came round with a jug could fill both glasses and basins at the same time. In five minutes we were all undressed and in bed. The usher, Monsieur Puybaraud, lowered the gas, and in a trembling voice recited three prayers which brought the tears to my eyes. I cried because I was lonely, because some day I should have to die, because I was thinking of my mother. I was thirteen. She had been dead for six years. She had vanished so quickly! One evening she had kissed me, so full of life and sweetness, and the next day . . . the horse had bolted and brought home the trap empty. I never knew how the accident had happened. No one had told me much about it, and my father, now that he had married again, never mentioned his first wife's name. As though to make up for that, my stepmother often exhorted me to pray for the dead woman. She used to ask me each evening whether I had a thought for her. She seemed to believe that mamma had more need of prayers than other dead people. She had always known my mother, who had been her cousin, and had sometimes invited her to the house during the holidays. "You ought to ask your cousin Brigitte to come to Larjuzon," said my father. "She can't afford a holiday: she gives away all she has. . . ." My mother would do her best to stand out against this appeal, although she professed to admire Brigitte. Perhaps she was afraid of her. That, at any rate, was what my sister Michèle thought. "Mamma saw through her: she knew only too well what an influence her cousin had got over papa. . . ."

I attached little importance to such statements. But my stepmother's exhortations produced an impression on me. It was only too true that mamma had had no time in which to prepare herself for death. The sort of education I had had helped me to understand Brigitte's insistence. It was indeed necessary that I should intercede for that poor departed spirit.

That evening, snuffling beneath the sheets, I had begun to tell my beads for mamma while the usher, Monsieur Puybaraud, lowered the gas until he had reduced the butterfly of flame to no more than a bluish flicker. He took off his frock-coat and started on a last round of the beds. The rhythmic breathing of the sleepers was already audible. As he passed close by me he must have heard the sob which I was doing my best to smother, for he came close and laid his hand on my tear-stained cheek. With a sigh he tucked me up as mamma used to do, and then, bending down suddenly, kissed me on the forehead. I flung my arms round his neck and kissed his bristly cheek. He crept away very quietly to his cubicle. I could see his shadow moving behind the thin curtain.

Almost every evening Monsieur Puybaraud consoled me in the same way. "Much too soft-hearted, and dangerously over-sensitive," said my stepmother, who had a good deal to do with him, since he acted as general secretary to the Charity Organization.

A few days later, when my parents returned to Bordeaux, and the butler fetched me about six to take me home, I ran into Monsieur Puybaraud, who seemed to have been on the look-out for me, in the Yard. After smoothing back my hair from my forehead with his rather damp hand, he gave me a sealed letter which he begged me to post. This I promised to do, astonished that he had not given the letter to the Censor, whose business it was to take charge of the school correspondence.

I waited until I was in the street before reading the address. The envelope bore the name of Mademoiselle Octavia Tronche, teacher at the Free School, Rue Parmentade, Bordeaux. I knew her well. She used to come to the house between her classes, and my stepmother employed her on various tasks. On the reverse side of the envelope, in a fair round hand, Monsieur Puybaraud had written: *Go little letter, and bring to my heart a gleam of hope. . . .* Walking a few paces behind the butler, who had put my satchel under his arm, I read and re-read this strange invocation. I pondered over it there on the pavement of the Cours Victor-Hugo, just where it joins the Rue Sainte-Catherine, in the dusk of the evening before Prize-Day. And in my nostrils was the faint smell of absinthe.

II

IT was then that I was guilty of the first bad action of my life, of an action, I mean, the thought of which even now fills me with a sense of remorse. Monsieur Puybaraud had made no attempt to extract from me any promise about the letter, but I knew, nevertheless, that he regarded me as more deserving of his confidence than any of my comrades. I tried, later, to persuade myself that I had not, at thirteen, realized what was at stake for the usher. That is not true. I understood perfectly well what was involved, and had a pretty shrewd idea of the dramatic touch which his semi-religious state of mind gave to the incident. It was a matter of common knowledge that he belonged to a lay Society (now long dispersed), to a sort of Third Order, the members of which were bound by no vows. Sometimes, indeed quite frequently, one or other of the so-called "Brethren" would, with the consent of his superiors, leave the Community in order to marry. But Monsieur Puybaraud's position was rather peculiar. His work kept him in close contact with the diocesan officials of the Charity Organization Society, and with several of the boys' parents. Everyone in the town knew him, and not only the higher clergy and the rich middle-class families. He was a familiar figure in the poorest slums, where the children flocked round him as soon as he appeared at the corner of a street: for he always brought them sweets and fruit-drops. His frock-coat and the curious high beaver which he affected drew no surprised glances. His kindly face looked longer than it was by reason of the short whiskers which stopped at the level of his cheek-bones. In summer he held his hat in his hand, and continually mopped his bald forehead and the sparse, silky hair which he wore long behind. His small features were almost too "pretty" for a man. There was about his eyes something of the look of a wounded animal, and his hands were always damp. My stepmother was loud in praise of his virtues, though she held strong views on the subject of his "excessive and morbid sensibility." I, of all people, should have kept myself from mentioning to her the secret of his letter, but it was precisely to her that I burned to impart my knowledge. The possession of it filled me with a sense of self-importance. Young as I was, I longed to be the means of shocking and astonishing her. Nevertheless, I was too frightened to say anything so long as other members of the family were present.

I have a vivid recollection of that evening. The flat which my father had consented to lease was situated on the second floor of a house in the Cours de l'Intendance. On summer evenings the noise of traffic on the cobble-stones, and the clang of the electric trams—which had only recently begun to operate in the city—made conversation difficult. A fortnight spent in the country had brought the colour back to my father's cheeks, and the prospect of the approaching holidays had put him in a good humour. At a word from his wife, however, he left the table to put on a bow tie and a black coat. She could not bear the untidy clothes which he always wore at Larjuzon.

In spite of the heat she had on a high dress and a lace collar which swathed her neck to the ears. Her large face, with its heavy, lustreless cheeks, was surmounted by a mass of hair puffed out with curls, and kept in place by an almost invisible "net." Her black, staring eyes had a hard look, but her mouth was always smiling, though she scarcely ever opened it wide enough to show her long yellow teeth which were generously stopped with gold and stood out firmly from the gums. A double chin gave her an air of dignity which was accentuated by the way she carried her head, by the way she walked, and by her deep voice which was never heard to better advantage than when she was engaged in issuing orders. The right place for her would have been at the head of some Community. After the death of her father, Baron Maillard, who had been Prefect of the Gironde at the time of the Empire, Brigitte had devoted the bulk of her fortune to the purchase and reconditioning of a small convent in the outskirts of Lourdes, where it was her intention to house young women of fashion under a new Rule inspired, in part, by her Director, the abbé Margis. The material part of the work was completed, but nothing more was ever heard of the scheme.

Brigitte Maillard had more than once, in connexion with this undertaking, consulted my father who, in his youth, had worked as an unpaid clerk in the office of a Bordeaux solicitor, and knew a good deal about the ins and outs of legal business. He dissuaded her from bringing a suit which would have caused a good deal of scandal and could not possibly have succeeded. He, on his side, valued the advice which she gave him about the domestic difficulties in which he was, at that time, involved, though they were later to be solved so tragically by the death of my mother.

Those who knew nothing of the events which, at a certain period of my father's life, had led to the forming of a deep intimacy between him and Brigitte Maillard, found it hard to imagine how two such dissimilar characters had come to link their destinies. Seen in company with this tall, bilious-looking Madame de Maintenon, my poor father aroused feelings of pity. His appearance was eloquent of weak good-nature. He spoke hesitatingly, there was a greedy look about his mouth, and his drooping moustache seemed as though it should be for ever trailing in little "nips" and rich gravies. Overfeeding had given him a red face, and his eyes were prominent.

I can see my sister now, as she sat, that evening, between husband and wife, when the Puybaraud affair came to a head. Michèle was at that time fourteen. The general opinion was that her skin was too swarthy. The lower part of her face was abnormally heavy, and her hair grew too low on her forehead. But her really beautiful eyes softened all hearts, and she had very fine teeth which she showed whenever her wide mouth parted in a smile. Some might think that her arms were rather too muscular, but the same could not be said of her legs. They were a matter of great pride to her, and she did her best to show them in spite of the semi-long skirts which our stepmother insisted on her wearing even then.

As a matter of fact Brigitte was always extremely patient with her, and was careful, as a rule, not to get herself involved in arguments with the headstrong little girl. She was never tired of saying: "Since I can exercise no sort of influence over the child, it is my duty to keep peace in the home at all costs." She derived a feeling of triumph from the fact that the Ladies of the Sacred Heart failed equally to elicit any sort of response from Michèle. "The girl is filled with a spirit of contradiction and bad temper," she would remark to our father. But against this sentence he protested. "You are quite wrong, my dear. You do so love to dramatize things! She is wilful, that's all, and flares up quickly like my poor mother. . . . But a good husband will settle all that."

Brigitte shook her head with a sigh. She looked on life from a higher standpoint. Her mission, her glory, was to view the world from the highest possible point of vantage. The evening on which the Puybaraud complication burst into flame was a Saturday. We were listening to the sound of the crowds on the pavements of the Cours de l'Intendance where the garrison tattoo was in progress. Michèle and my father were leaning on their elbows at one end of the balcony. I was some little distance off with my stepmother. The sharp-winged swifts were skimming the roof-tops. The flow of traffic was continuous. The walls still held the heat of the day. An occasional gust brought the sweet scent of limes and, with it, that smell to be found only in big cities before the days of motor-cars—a rich mixture of horse-droppings, wet roadways and circus tan. I was still wrestling with the temptation to reveal Monsieur Puybaraud's secret. But I knew that I should succumb. My stepmother was questioning me methodically about the end-of-term examinations. She wanted to know all about the papers in each subject, and how I had answered them. I knew that this interest came only from a sense of duty, and that her thoughts were elsewhere. But she said what she had to say. Always, in every circumstance of life, and in all her relations with other people, she knew precisely what her words, what her attitude, ought to be.

I made up my mind.

"Mother," I said, "there's something I want to tell you. But" —I added with a touch of hypocrisy—"I'm not sure whether I ought."

A spark of attention began to glow in the black eyes which, till then, had shown no interest in me.

"My dear child, I have no idea what you have to say. But there is one rule which you would do well to follow blindly, and that is, never to keep anything from your second mother. For on her has devolved the duty of bringing you up."

"Even when it is a secret involving others?"

"If it involves others that is all the more reason why you should tell me," she replied sharply. Hungry for my revelations, she asked:

"Whom does it concern?—your sister?"

She already suspected the worst of Michèle, although the girl was only fourteen years old. I shook my head. No, it wasn't about Michèle: it was about Monsieur Puybaraud and Octavia Tronche.

She choked back an exclamation:

"What's that?" (she grabbed my arm)—"Monsieur Puybaraud, Octavia?"

I was too ignorant as yet about love to have noticed that my stepmother could never approach the subject calmly, but, that as soon as it was mentioned, she became, as it were, all worked up. No sooner had I mentioned the letter, and the sentence written on its flap, than she interrupted me.

"Give it to me, now, at once."

"The letter?—but I posted it."

She seemed to be disappointed.

"That was very wrong of you. You should have given it to me. I am responsible for Octavia's moral well-being. She holds an important position at the Free School, and hopes one day to be headmistress. It is not only my right, but my duty, to know everything about her. . . . Never mind, I shall manage to have a look at the letter, somehow or other," she added more calmly.

She saw that I was worried. Monsieur Puybaraud was so fond of me. What on earth would he think? She made it clear to me that I need take no action in the matter. She felt sure that she could persuade Octavia to tell her what it was all about.

"It is not, my dear child, that I suspect anything *wrong*. So estimable a person as Monsieur Puybaraud deserves my complete confidence. After all, if he wishes to leave his Order and go back into the world, he has a perfect right to do so. We must not hold him guilty of anything worse than imprudence. Not, that is, unless we have proof to the contrary. I have always thought that his rather over-emotional form of piety might lead him to act rashly. Thanks to you, I can now intervene while there is still time."

In a low voice, from behind clenched teeth, she added, with sudden violence: "Octavia, of all people! But they're all the same —all bitches, every one of them!"

The sound of the brass band playing the tattoo came from the direction of the Rue Vital-Carle. The people of Bordeaux were delighted with a recent innovation in the ceremony. The bandsmen had electric bulbs in their caps instead of pom-poms. My stepmother went back into the drawing-room, while I remained, leaning on my elbows above the heads of the crowd. Boys and girls were marching in step with the soldiers. They walked arm in arm and made a living chain across the pavement. They were shouting and laughing. I struggled no longer with my sense of shame and with the agony of spirit which oppressed me. What was going to happen to poor Monsieur Puybaraud? I was too young fully to understand the paternal instinct which had made him to lean over my bed, tuck me in, and kiss me on the forehead. But I did feel that I had betrayed a man whose loneliness was such that he had turned to a boy of thirteen for comfort. I remembered Alphonse Daudet's *Enfant Espion*, and what the German soldiers had said to young Sten: "Not nice that, not nice." Had I done wrong? My stepmother said that I had done my duty . . . why, then, should I feel so remorseful?

I joined her in the room. She was seated close to the window, trying to read. (We could not have any light because of the mosquitoes, and it was too hot to close the windows.) A vague longing to "make up" for what I had done made me feel that I wanted to perform some kind action. So I spoke about Mirbel, begging her to speak to the Curé of Baluzac on his behalf. I watched her large pale face in the dusk. It was much too dark to read. She was sitting there quite motionless and very upright. Her early convent training had taught her never to lean back in a chair (nor do I remember that I ever once saw her cross her legs). I knew that she was only half paying attention, and that her thoughts were busy with the Puybaraud-Tronche affair.

"The Curé of Baluzac?" she said at last. "Poor abbé Calou!—it can't be very easy for him to pose as an ogre! . . . well, I suppose the extra money helps him to buy a few books. . . . I wonder whether I ought to tell the Colonel how misinformed he has been?"

I begged her to do nothing of the sort. Her words confirmed me in my feeling that the abbé Calou would not be a very terrifying gaoler, and I was particularly anxious not to be deprived of the pleasure of having Jean de Mirbel as a companion during the holidays. But she added that, on second thoughts, she felt sure that the young good-for-nothing could get only what was good from living in the company of Monsieur Calou, and that God's will must be done.

All the next week I watched Monsieur Puybaraud with considerable apprehension. But I was still his "favourite" (as the other boys called me), and up to the end of term he was as kind to me as ever. The examinations were almost over, and the heat became too oppressive to make much work possible. Even Monsieur Rausch relaxed and read *Le Soldat Chapuzot* to us in form. In Senior Yard the carpenters were busy putting up stands for the Prize-giving. Every day we rehearsed Mendelssohn's Choruses from *Athalie*:

> *All the world is filled with His glory:*
> *Oh, come, let us adore Him!*

But for Michèle I should probably have known nothing of the opening rounds of the Puybaraud-Tronche scandal. Though her nature was of the frankest, and she, of all people, would be the last to dream of listening at key-holes, her attitude towards our stepmother was defensive. She watched Brigitte Pian with a clear-sighted mistrust which she never, for one moment, relaxed. Besides, Octavia Tronche was devoted to her, and could not for long hold out against her questions. Consequently, I was kept informed about the deplorable results of my indiscretion.

Octavia Tronche worked at my stepmother's on Thursdays and Saturdays—the only times at which she was free from school classes—from eight to eleven in the mornings. She had thin, lifeless hair, but, though without any freshness of youth, was not wholly devoid of charm. This she owed to her eyes, though they were small and of an indeterminate colour, and to the very sweet smile which hung about her rather bloodless lips. The children adored her, and, because of this, she was constantly exposed to the malicious pin-pricks of her jealous colleagues. Her clothes drooped from thin shoulders, and no one could well have had less indication of a bosom. Below the waist, however, she was more markedly feminine, and even her nun-like skirt could not altogether conceal the fullness of her hips and the other indications of her sex.

When, on that particular morning, she entered the small drawing-room where Madame Pian—"Madame Brigitte"—was sitting, Octavia was greeted with an unaccustomed smile.

"I am afraid you are feeling the heat, my dear: I can see it in your face."

Octavia assured her patroness that she was not at all tired.

"And in your work even more than in your face." Brigitte Pian's voice had taken on a sudden note of sternness.

"You made several mistakes in addressing when you sent out the last number of the *Bulletin*. I have had complaints from a good many ladies that it arrived late."

Octavia, in some confusion, began to make excuses.

"That, in itself, would not be very serious," went on my stepmother: "but the circular which I dictated to you, and neglected to read over (yes, *neglected*: please observe that I do not spare myself when I have been worthy of blame)—was full of errors and omissions. . . . Some of the sentences did not even make sense. . . ."

"I am afraid that my head has not been very clear these last few days," Octavia stammered.

"Your head or your heart?" asked Brigitte, in a voice whose sweetness was belied by her severe and haughty mien.

"Oh, Madame Brigitte! . . . what *can* you mean?"

"I am not asking you to tell me your secrets, my dear: confidences cannot be forced."

And then, as Octavia began to protest that she had no secrets from Madame Brigitte:

"You know how scrupulous I am in respecting the consciences of others. You are one of our old girls. I trust you—not blindly, but with my eyes open, and with a sense of almost maternal responsibility. We all have difficult times to go through, my dear."

This was more than Octavia could stand. Falling on her knees, she hid her face in Madame Brigitte's lap. The latter looked at the thin neck beneath the tight little bun into which the girl's hair was drawn, at the pale skin, and at the topmost vertebra which the gaping collar of her dress left exposed. It was as well that the poor creature could not see the expression of disgust which came over the older woman's face. 'Even she is no exception, ill-favoured though she is' (it seemed to say). Out loud, but quite gently, Madame Brigitte said:

"And so, my poor Octavia, you too think that you have a lover?"

Octavia Tronche looked up, protesting:

"That I have a lover? Oh no, Madame: I am not quite such a fool. It is not that!"

In those few seconds her face had become transfigured. Shyness had given to it a delicate loveliness, something of the adorable charm which comes from utter humility.

"All I ask is that *he* should let me live for him alone and for the children which God in his mercy may see fit to give us."

"Naturally, my dear Octavia, naturally," said my stepmother, helping her to her feet. "Come and sit down beside me and control yourself. That I once looked on you as one called to a higher vocation is no matter. It will make me very happy to think of you with a home and a Christian family of your own. What could be more natural, more simple? The excess of your emotion surprises me."

"But it is not simple at all, Madame: far from it. If you only knew. . . ."

I imagine that my stepmother realized, at that moment, what it was to be completely happy. She was tasting the pleasure that belongs, of right, to God alone: the pleasure of knowing to the full the destiny of someone who thought that she was imparting a piece of unsuspected news; of feeling that it was in her power to mould that destiny as she willed. For she did not doubt her hold over the scrupulous conscience of Monsieur Puybaraud. Had she been tempted to do so, Octavia's attitude would have restored her confidence. With masterly skill she let her tone range through every shade of expression from that of confidential friendship to suspicion. At last she said: "I feel your trouble as keenly as you do yourself," and then went on to ask the poor girl, with every mark of anxiety, whether the man in question was married or divorced. At that, her victim hid her face and struggled to conceal her tears. When next Madame Brigitte spoke there was a note almost of horror in her voice.

"Wretched girl! Am I to understand that this man is already bound to somebody whose claims are absolute? Are you setting yourself against the ordinances of God?"

"No, Madame, no!—he is free. His superiors have raised no difficulty. Monsieur Puybaraud (you must have guessed already that it is he) has arranged to leave the College at the end of this week. As soon as he has done so, we have permission to consider ourselves as being engaged."

My stepmother rose, cutting her visitor's protestations short:

"You need say no more! I do not wish to *hear* more. The responsibility lies with your respective spiritual directors. It may be that I should not see eye to eye with them in this matter. . . ."

"But that is why I am so upset, Madame Brigitte!" cried Octavia between her sobs. "You see, Monsieur Puybaraud will not let himself be convinced that he has the right to act as he wishes. He keeps on saying that you alone can clarify his mind, that you alone are sufficiently instructed to give him peace of mind. But please, please, understand, Madame, that the situation is not as you think it. . . . You have only got to look at me to see that. Monsieur Puybaraud is not the slave of mere physical desire. He says the thought that he may one day have a son like your Louis makes him almost sob with joy."

"That I can quite realize," responded my stepmother in gloomy tones. "The Evil One always employs tricks and subterfuges when he sets out to attack men of a frank and upright nature."

"Oh, Madame, surely you are not going to persuade him that this is a trap set by the Evil One?"

Impulsively she seized the hand of my stepmother, who was seated in her usual chair in front of a desk littered with circulars and files.

"Unless he asks me, I shall say nothing at all to him, my child. . . . If he does ask, I shall say only what I feel moved by the Holy Spirit to say. But whatever that may be, I shall speak out fearlessly and directly, as it has ever been my rule to do."

Octavia clasped her hands and gazed at the expressionless face with eyes that resembled those of a defenceless lamb.

"But surely there is nothing wrong in his wish to be a father? His director doesn't think so. For years Monsieur Puybaraud has fought against his feelings. May it not be that his failure to overcome them is in itself a sign that he is called upon to follow this particular vocation?"

My stepmother nodded her head:

"We should do wrong altogether to dismiss such an hypothesis," she remarked; "though it is not God's way to set the feet of His servants on the heights only to cast them down into the valleys. I shall need more definite evidence before I can bring myself to believe that Heaven has asked of Monsieur Puybaraud such an abandonment of his post, so dire a retreat, so sad a return to a less austere way of life. Nothing should be allowed to shake our faith."

"He says that he has been guilty of the sin of pride, that he has overestimated his strength. It is a blessing vouchsafed him by Heaven, he thinks, that he should have been permitted to see his way clearly before it was too late," urged Octavia in a voice of supplication.

"If he is so certain"—my stepmother interrupted her dryly—"what need is there for him to seek further? Why should I be brought into the matter at all?"

Octavia realized that this was precisely where the trouble lay. He was *not* certain: his mind changed from day to day. Bursting into tears she declared that she could see how it was: Madame Brigitte's mind was made up, she would be inexorable.

At this my stepmother became more human. "You are wrong, Octavia. You must not think that I am hostile *in principle* to these promptings of nature. There are others concerned, besides Monsieur Puybaraud. It would, indeed, make me very happy to know that you, at least, had been called upon to fulfil the duties of a wife and mother. Yes"—she went on, her gaze fixed upon her humble suppliant (and perhaps seeing already in anticipation the swollen figure beneath its smock, the plain face made plainer still by the physical symptoms of pregnancy)—"it may be that the intentions of the Almighty on your behalf have made necessary this deviation of Monsieur Puybaraud from a higher vocation. I realize that he may have to be humbled if you are to be saved."

Thus it was that Brigitte Pian attributed to our Father in Heaven the complexities and perversities of her own nature. But Octavia Tronche, snatching at this straw of hope, was already recovering like a flower in water. She raised her gentle, suffering face.

"Oh, Madame Brigitte!" she exclaimed in tones of exaltation, "now indeed you are speaking with God's voice. You know everything, I admit everything. Unworthy though I am, it is for me that Monsieur Puybaraud is willing to renounce the joys of a higher vocation, to turn his back on the peace which might await him within the walls of an institution on which he has already brought so much credit. . . ."

"And you would quite calmly accept such a sacrifice, my child?" asked Brigitte Pian sharply.

Octavia was nonplussed.

"I am not saying that you ought to refuse it. All I wish to point out is that, all other considerations apart, you have to ask yourself this question: have you, or have you not, the right to accept such a sacrifice? Are you willing that a man like Monsieur Puybaraud, who is infinitely superior to you in spiritual gifts and in the degree to which Grace has been accorded him, should, for your sake, abandon the fruits of his apostolic mission, and lose the glory he enjoys in the sight of God as well as the honour he has won in the eyes of men? For it is no good disguising the fact that if he deserts his present post he *will* suffer a loss of credit, even (and especially) in the opinion of his neighbours. You must face the facts. Every door will be closed to him. No one could well be more helpless than he in all that pertains to the day-to-day struggle for existence, and you must realize that, owing entirely to you, he may find himself condemned to a life of care and even of poverty. . . ."

Octavia Tronche's face was irradiated, not for the first time, by a smile of pure humility.

"*That* does not trouble me, Madame Brigitte. I am strong and healthy. So long as there is breath in my body he shall lack for nothing, no, not even if it means my taking a place as a daily woman. . . . He shall want neither for the necessities nor yet for the luxuries. . . ."

"You know perfectly well that you are *not* strong. Why, even your secretarial work here (which amounts to practically nothing) is almost too much for you when added to your duties at school: though I don't want you to think that I am complaining."

It was true enough that Octavia Tronche could not stand up to long hours, and that the work of organizing charity sales, coming on top of her teaching, very soon exhausted her. My stepmother repeated that it was her duty to face that aspect of the problem, however painful she might find it to do so. When Octavia shyly suggested that they had hoped he might get some appointment on the staff of the Charity Organization, in which for years he had been doing unpaid work, Brigitte expressed surprise that she should have been guilty of such an offence against all tact and propriety. How could she dream that any such thing was possible? There are certain facts, surely, that need no explanation.

"You must be out of your senses, my poor child. . . . Quite apart from anything else, it is not customary to use the money of the poor to pay for work which can be performed by almost any priest, to say nothing of pious laymen. No, the most we shall be able to do will be to recommend Monsieur Puybaraud—so far, that is, as we can recommend *honestly* any man who has sunk so low through no fault but his own, and who, so far as I know, has no particular qualification and holds no diploma."

Whenever my stepmother cast a fellow human creature into the depths of affliction, it gave her pleasure to raise the victim by a spontaneous act of mercy. Since, in her view, Octavia had been driven to the lowest level of despair, she was now at pains to bring her slowly back again and to give her grounds for hope. It was only later, on the evening before Prize-Day, and from the lips of Monsieur Puybaraud himself, that I learned what had been decided between them.

We had been working hard all day, hanging banners and grouping the Papal and Republican flags. Monsieur Puybaraud appeared, walking across the Yard, and I hastened to join him. This I always did. It was a special privilege which none of the other boys ever thought of disputing. He made me sit down on the steps of the platform, and told me that he was on the point of making a very grave decision. Madame Brigitte, "who, like all real saints, conceals much true goodness of heart beneath a forbidding exterior," realized that he needed a period of calm and solitude in which to collect his thoughts and decide what it would be best for him to do. She had had the great kindness to suggest that he should spend the holidays at Larjuzon. . . .

"At Larjuzon!" I exclaimed in amazement. There are places into which certain persons do not fit. I found it impossible to think of one of my schoolmasters in the country surroundings which were the background of my summer holidays.

The official explanation of his presence at Larjuzon would be that he was there to coach me in Latin.

I tried to imagine what Monsieur Puybaraud would look like in his frock-coat and high-hat on a blazing summer's day walking the garden paths at Larjuzon. I asked him whether he would wear the same clothes that he always did. He told me that he would have to invest in a country outfit, and that, consequently, he might not arrive for a few days.

Monsieur Rausch had moved from his usual position near the lavatories. In his shirt-sleeves, perched on a ladder, and armed with a hammer, he was at present expending his natural ferocity on a nail. The boys were exchanging addresses. The school orchestra was busy in the Hall rehearsing the opening bars of *Travels in China*. Jean de Mirbel, leaning as usual against the wall, though punishments were over for the term, even for him, had his eyes fixed on the ground. His hands were in his trousers pockets, and he wore his cap untidily (his appearance did no credit to the school) on the side of his head. The slight down on his cheeks made him look much older than the rest of us (he was two years in arrears in his school work). It was probably his age even more than his bad behaviour that cut him off from his companions. He lived alone in a stormy world, with no one to give him a helping hand, the victim of some mysterious fate which seemed to hang over his future. What it might be he did not know, and there was no one whom he could take into his confidence.

III

THE hired victoria from Langon stopped in front of the Presbytery garden. The Colonel was the first to get out. The luncheon which he had just devoured had had the effect of heightening to an unusual degree the mottled purple of his face, so that the scar looked white by comparison. His cap was tilted slightly over his left ear. The short fawn top-coat, reaching only to his thighs, which he called his "bum-shaver," had a faded red rosette on its lapel. His skinny legs, clad in very tight trousers, were like those of a cock. He wore white spats.

Jean, encumbered with a suitcase and a haversack, followed him into the garden, where it was almost impossible to tread without stepping on serried rows of vegetables. The Presbytery was surrounded, jostled is the better word, on all sides by potatoes, beans, tomatoes and green-stuff of every description. Currant bushes and peach trees lined the narrow path which led to a low doorway which was surmounted by a St. John's cross made from the pith of an elder tree.

Neither the nephew nor the uncle had the slightest idea that from behind a dusty window on the ground-floor somebody was watching them. As soon as the abbé Calou heard the sound of the knocker he opened the front door. He was a head taller than the Colonel. He wore over his soutane a blue gardening smock. He had not shaved for several days and the stubble on his face reached as high as his cheek-bones. His forehead was low, and his wide blue eyes gave him the look of a child. He had a cleft tip to his nose and strong, healthy teeth. But the only thing that Jean de Mirbel noticed on the occasion of this first meeting was that the priest's huge hands, with their square-tipped fingers, were covered with hair.

"I've brought you your young boarder. Can't say he's a present most people would like to have. . . . Take your hat off to the Curé! . . . Come on, quicker than that! I don't want to have to tell you twice. . . . True to type, you see, from the word go!"

Jean, his béret in his hand, bowed his head without so much as uttering a word.

"A reg'lar young hooligan! I'm not sorry you should see him in his true colours—gives you an idea of the sort of ill-conditioned cub you've got on your hands. . . . Won't get a how-d'ye-do out of him without a flogging!"

"We've plenty of time to get to know one another," replied the Curé.

There was something cold and impersonal about his tone. Without another word he led them upstairs to the boy's room on the second floor. It was a whitewashed attic, with the bare minimum of furniture, but very clean. The window looked on to the church and the graveyard, with, beyond it, a valley through which, behind a screen of pine-trees, ran the Ciron, a minor tributary of the Garonne. The fresh green of willows marked its course.

"I sleep and work just below. There is nothing but these floor-boards between us. I shall almost be able to hear him breathing."

The Papal Zouave expressed his complete approval of the arrangements. The boy, he said, was up to all sorts of tricks. "Doesn't do to let him out of your sight for a single moment, day or night." They went downstairs again to the large apartment on the ground-floor which the Curé dignified with the name of drawing-room. It was furnished with a small table and four armchairs. The lime, working out of the walls, had eaten away most of the paper. The Colonel whispered to their host:

"'Sh'd like a word with you in private. Run along, you, and stay in the garden till I tell you to come back—now then, quick march!"

At this point the Curé interrupted very quietly:

"If you don't mind, Colonel, I would rather he remained here and heard our conversation. It is part of my system that he should do so. You must have complete confidence in me. I consider it important that the young man should know precisely what it is in his behaviour of which you complain, and what it is that we have to correct."

"I warn you that such a step may have serious consequences. . . . You don't know him. . . . I should feel free-er."

The Colonel was displeased, but the Curé would listen to no objection. Jean, therefore, remained standing in the middle of the drawing-room floor, his eyes fixed upon his uncle.

"Don't quite know how to tell you what I want to say. Young hooligan's about the length and breadth of it. Incorrigible, no other word for him—in-corr-ig-ible," he repeated in an acid tone.

It was perfectly true that he could find no other word. Like many people who regard themselves as being above the common herd, he had a very limited vocabulary which he enriched with dumb-show, the use of clichés, intonation and gesture.

"Rather be killed than do what he's told. . . . Usually gives in in the long run, though . . . gets sick of being flogged. . . . No fool, though . . . got abilities. . . . Trouble is, won't do as he's told . . . won't learn his lessons."

"What does he like doing? I mean, what are his special tastes?"

"Like doing?"—the Colonel seemed to be taken aback. "Well, what *do* you like doing? Nothing, eh? I know all about that. But what else?—come on, answer, now. . . . You see, not a word—just like him. Answer me, boy, or I'll box your ears!"

The Curé laid his hand on the arm raised to strike.

"Let him be: I'll find out soon enough what his tastes are."

"Well, yours are sound enough, I'll be bound. He'll find out what your system is in double-quick time . . . nothing very mysterious about it. I don't mind betting"—and he gave the Curé a wink. "Only two ways of getting the better of a vicious horse—spur and whip. At least, *I* don't know any others. . . . And when I say vicious, I know what I'm talking about. . . . There are one or two things I'd have liked to tell you in private. . . ."

Jean de Mirbel's face had become scarlet. So low did he hang his head that the Curé could see nothing but his hair.

"Need I add that I speak as his guardian and in the name of the Comtesse de Mirbel, the young scoundrel's mother? You are at liberty to use any means you may think proper, provided you break him in, *any*—you understand me—short of injuring his health."

"I quite understand," replied the Curé, his eyes still fixed upon the shamefaced object before him.

"To go back to what you were saying about his tastes. He likes reading—and not unnaturally his choice in books is pretty low. Young though he is, he knows a thing or two. Don't think I need say more about that. . . . And he's not always as dumb as he is now—can argue the hind legs off a donkey when he likes. D'you know what he was brazen enough to maintain last Easter to Monsieur Talazac, our Curé at home?—that not only oughtn't Combes to be blamed if he acted sincerely in kicking the Religious Orders out of France, but that he had acquired merit in the eyes of God by doing so!"

"Did he really argue that?" asked the Curé with a show of interest.

"Should dam' well think he did. . . . Fine state of affairs, eh? And nothing would budge him—not Monsieur Talazac's reasoning, not the shocked looks of the ladies, nor yet the thrashing I gave him!"

"So you actually argued like that?" repeated the Curé. And he fixed a thoughtful gaze upon the little fox imprisoned there, with staring coat, within his own four walls, darting frightened glances here and there to see whether he could find some way of escape.

"If you have some private recipe for getting brains to work as they should, the family will be eternally grateful. You see, our name, our fortune and the future of our line are all dependent on this young devil. He says he'd rather be seen dead than take the St.-Cyr entrance exam, or volunteer for service with the colours, as the Mirbels have always done. Anyhow, he's so behindhand with his work that it's too late now for him to start thinking about the professional Army. He has the cynical effrontery to say that he'll do nothing, that he doesn't want to do anything, not even to look after his estates. You see, not a word of denial from him!—just a grin. You, there, stop grinning, or I'll let you feel the weight of my hand!"

Jean had retreated towards the wall. His lips were parted in a smile that showed his side-teeth which, though white and pointed, were irregular. He put up his arm to protect himself—the familiar gesture of a boy who knows what it is to be frequently beaten.

"Please don't get worked up, Colonel. From now on this lad is my concern. You can leave him here with an easy conscience. I will send regular reports on his progress to you and the Countess, and he shall write home himself."

"Not if I know it!" exclaimed Jean. They were the first words that he had uttered.

"Till our next meeting, then, young feller-me-lad. I am leaving you in good hands"—he shook the Curé's enormous fist, and added —"in good, strong hands. I am told that they have done wonders in other cases."

He burst into one of his surprisingly shrill guffaws of laughter.

The Curé went with him as far as the carriage. "And no coddling, mind," was the Colonel's final injunction. He handed the priest an envelope containing the first instalment of fees. "You're not dealing with a young girl. He's got a hide like a rhinoceros. You needn't be afraid of treating him rough. I'll back you up. Whatever happens, just ignore anything that my sister-in-law may write. I'm captain of this ship, and it's for me to decide what's to be done."

The Curé went back into the drawing-room. Jean had not moved from where he had been standing. He started back as the priest approached, and once again his arm went up as though to ward off an expected blow.

"Come and help me lay the table," said the Curé.

"I'm not your servant!"

"In this house everyone is his own servant . . . except in the matter of cooking. Maria looks after that, but she is seventy-one and suffers from rheumatism. When I said lay the table, I meant for your tea. I never take it myself. Your friend Louis Pian and his sister are bicycling over to see you. They'll be here any moment now."

He opened the dining-room door.

"There's a fruit-tart and some plums in the sideboard, and an opened bottle of orange syrup. If you want some water, you'll find a jug in the scullery. See you again this evening, my boy. . . . One thing more. My study, as you know, is just under your room. There are plenty of books, though probably not the kind you like. Still, if you look carefully, you may come on something. . . . You can rout about there to your heart's content. You won't disturb me."

Jean listened to the Curé's heavy footsteps on the wooden stairs. Then he heard the sound of a chair scraping on the floor above his head. There followed an interval of complete silence broken only by the noise of grasshoppers, the cluck of fowls and the buzzing of flies.

"If he thinks he's going to get round me like that! . . ."

Nevertheless, he pushed open the dining-room door and sniffed the odour of fruit-tart. The room was better furnished than the rest of the house. It contained an old-fashioned clock, a long,

Louis-Philippe sideboard, a table of waxed cherry-wood, and several wicker chairs. It felt cool and the air was filled with the faint scent of fruit. Beyond the French windows there was a view on to the low roofs of outhouses and, beyond them, to a sloping field in which the hay stood ready stacked.

Someone will be sure to ask: "But how do you know so much about events of which you were not a witness? What right have you to reproduce conversations which you cannot have heard?" Well, if the truth must be told, I have outlived most of my characters, several of whom played an important part in my life. Besides, I am the sort of man who keeps old papers, and I have at my disposition not only a private diary (Monsieur Puybaraud's), but various notes made by Monsieur Calou which Mirbel found after the priest's death. At this very moment, for instance, I have before me the very letter which the abbé was reading—not for the first time—while Jean, alone in the dining-room, was wandering round the table and yielding to the temptation to take an occasional bite at a plum . . . and while I and my sister Michèle were bicycling to see him along the white and dusty roads which, in those days, were still innocent of tar. . . . (At Vallandraut we had seen the Comte de Mirbel driving home in the Victoria, his cap perched over one ear, his thin legs crossed. Michèle had drawn my attention to his scar, and to the faded red rosette on the lapel of his fawn top-coat.)

I don't deny that I have exercised my right to arrange my material, to orchestrate the reality which it records—that cross-section of existence which will live for as long as I live, with memory unimpaired, and upon which the passing years have had no effect. I may have given literary form to the talk that went on, but at least I am guiltless of changing so much as a syllable of that letter from the Comtesse de Mirbel which the abbé Calou had received the day before Jean's arrival. It was signed, in a spidery hand, "La Mirandieuze-Mirbel" and was written in blue ink. It ran as follows:

I am venturing to write to you direct because I understand from Madame Baillaud that your methods of educating the young are very different from those attributed to you by my brother-in-law, the Comte Adhémar de Mirbel. I thank God that it did not occur to him to pay the Baillauds a visit, and that he still believes in the reputation you have gained for taming difficult boys and, as he puts it, of using an iron hand with them. Unlike him, I did not stand upon ceremony. It is not easy for me to be on calling-terms with the family of a retired chemist whose forbears were *my* forbears' servants. Nevertheless, I did not hesitate to get into touch with them, and any effort it may have cost me has been amply rewarded by the knowledge I have gained of the kind of man I am dealing with, and by the certainty I now possess that I can have complete confidence in you. . . .

. . . It is essential that I should tell you certain things which will help you to get a clear picture of my unfortunate son. In the first place, you should know that his love for me is very much more violent than that which a boy of his age usually feels for his mother. . . . Jean is convinced that I do not return his affection. He believes that I judge him in the light of his uncle's attitude. To be perfectly frank, he has some reason for so thinking, since it must look as though I were abandoning him without a struggle and handing him over to the tender mercies of a butcher! I trust that you will forgive my choice of phrase. When you have seen the Count you will understand what I mean.

And at this point, I think, I must make a rather painful confession. I do so with the greater readiness because I realize that I am addressing a priest, a man, in other words, long trained in the duty of forgiveness. I am powerless where my brother-in-law is concerned, partly because by the Will of my husband he was given complete charge of my son, but chiefly because he has a hold over me. My husband, during his last illness, put into Adhémar's hands certain documents which are terribly damaging to me in more ways than one. I will not go so far as to say that I was ever a "guilty" wife. In whatever I have done my conscience has been clear. I have but exercised my rights as a woman. Imprudent, incapable of deceit or calculation, I may have been. It would have been easy for me to trick my husband, and it is only fair to myself to say that I should have had every excuse for doing so. What I suffered as a young woman, the bullying and incarceration to which I was exposed as a result of my husband's jealousy, the secret punishments and acts of vengeance which were wreaked upon me with impunity in the solitude of our Armagnac Chateau, would make a novel in themselves. I don't say that one day I may not perhaps write it. For I *can* write. In a sense writing has been my undoing. Adhémar has in his possession a number of unfortunate letters sent to me by a certain person, together with my replies. I was a fool not to have destroyed them, because, egged on by the demon of literary composition, I expressed on paper, and in extremely passionate terms, sentiments to which, in the eyes of the world, a woman may be forgiven for yielding, though never for putting into words.

That is my secret. Though I no longer believe in the mysteries of religion, I still trust in the virtue and discretion of its ministers. It is necessary that you should know all this. Adhémar has complete power over Jean only because my honour has been betrayed into his hands. If I so much as stumble on the road in which he has set my feet, I am lost. My saying this will show you what manner of man he is. But he fears that his hold over me is insufficient. He would like me to be his wife. My very considerable fortune is an added temptation, but it is only fair to say that it was my husband's dying wish that he should marry me. It was one of his favourite maxims that a woman can be tamed only in marriage. It never occurred to either of them that a Mirbel who was also, on her mother's side, a La Mirandieuze could ever so much as dream of divorce. Adhémar exercises over me a sort of indirect blackmail. He hints that in the event of my consenting to become his wife, he would give his permission for Jean to be brought up at home, here, at La Devize. I gather that if such a course were taken, I should have the deciding vote in all matters affecting his education, and be free to spend part of each year with my parents. Madame de La Mirandieuze, as you probably know, has influential connexions, nor have I abandoned the idea that I might even now be able to take a staggering revenge for everything I have suffered through the medium of a literary success. . . .

What am I to do? I have not given my brother-in-law a definite "no": I am playing for time. Adhémar is over sixty and gets very red after meals. The irregularities of his present way of life—over which I am generous enough to draw a veil—would be sufficient to encourage in me certain definite anticipations, were it not for the fact that I am not that sort of woman. I may have been foolish, but I am incapable of baseness. I have told you all this because I thought it necessary to do so. I venture to hope that you will judge me, not by those narrow standards which I know are abhorrent to you, but by the touchstone of an enlightened and humane religion, and that you will not withhold from me the forgiveness which you alone can confer. It is my dear wish that you should prevail upon Adhémar to allow me to pay a visit to Jean while he is at Baluzac. If you write to him that in your opinion it would be good for the boy, he will not refuse. Tell him that you can let me have a room in your house. Not that I intend to impose myself upon you. Rather than cause you any inconvenience, I will sleep in the Inn at Vallandraut. I have a mother's heart, and it waits impatiently for your reply. I beg you to believe that I am already deeply grateful to the benefactor of an only and much loved child.

The Curé took a red pencil and underlined the words—*I will sleep in the Inn at Vallandraut.* Those marks of red chalk, scarcely faded by time, lie before me as I write. . . . Did the Curé, even then, realize that those words formed the very heart and kernel of the letter?—that all the rest of it was merely an elaborate preliminary? I thought so once, but, truth to tell, I very much doubt whether he could have had so prophetic an insight. I am inclined to believe that the words were underlined later, after the events had occurred which gave them such significance. But he must have realized at once that nothing would ever have induced Adhémar de Mirbel to use against his sister-in-law a document which would inevitably have brought disgrace upon his family. Nor was it very probable that the Colonel, at the age of seventy, and the possessor of a handsome fortune of his own, should be playing with the idea of marrying the Countess.

Monsieur Calou took from a drawer a folder on which were written the two words—"False Women." In this he placed the letter, put it back, and closed the drawer. He listened for a while to our voices in the room below, to our laughter, to the clink of plates. He stood there motionless, his elbows resting on the top of the desk, his face hidden in his enormous hands.

IV

"KIDS' stuff," said Jean, emptying his glass of orange syrup: I want something stronger than that."

He started rummaging in the sideboard. I felt pretty sure that it was just swagger meant to impress us, but I was shocked for all that. Might it be true, after all, that Mirbel really was the kind of boy with whom nothing could be done? He brought out several half-empty bottles, uncorked them, and sniffed their contents.

"Probably black-currant or angelica cordial or nut wine—old maid's tipple. . . . But the Curé's not the man to drink that sort of muck. . . . Ah, this is more like it! Here's what he fills himself up on !" he exclaimed suddenly, brandishing an already opened bottle of Armagnac—"1860 too" (he made a clucking noise with his tongue), "the year Uncle Adhémar got his wound at Castelfidardo."

Michèle protested. . . . Surely he wasn't going to drink Armagnac in the afternoon?—you drink it with dessert.

"But when the dessert comes in the Curé will be here."

"Jean, you *can't* do that!"

"Can't I!—and no liqueur glass for me, either!"

I found it difficult to decide just how much was mere play-acting. This noisy boaster was so different from the sullen schoolboy who was always in trouble with the authorities. I did not realize at once that his foolhardy mood was the result of having Michèle as an audience, for he hardly addressed a word directly to her, and answered her when she spoke in monosyllables only. He scarcely seemed to be aware of her presence.

"It's too much, Jean: you'll make yourself ill!"

"And at one gulp, too: just you watch!"

He tilted back his head, but choked and started to cough. Michèle slapped his back. The room was filled with the smell of spirits.

"Monsieur Calou will notice," said I.

"We'll fill up the bottle with water: he'll just think the stuff has gone flat."

"But the smell, Jean. You stink of it, and so does the whole house."

We heard the scraping sound of a chair being pushed back, and then the abbé Calou's heavy tread upon the stairs. As soon as he entered the room he sniffed and looked sharply at us.

"So the young rascals have discovered my Armagnac, have they?" he said in high good-humour. Then, turning to Jean—"You must admit it's not bad, eh?—and you ought to know. I don't mind betting there's good brandy at La Devize—the best of it comes from round there. . . . Louis, you ought to take your young friend down to the Ciron. Does he like fishing?—He does?—Well then, show him the good pools. The pike are doing a lot of damage, but I expect you'll find something."

He opened the French window which led straight out to the back of the house. We stood for a moment looking out, then started across the half-mown meadow. The storms of this wet summer had interfered with the hay-harvest. We walked towards the line of willows. Darting blue dragon-flies announced the proximity of the stream even before we could see it. We trudged on across the marshy ground. It was an afternoon of moist, stifling heat. The brandy must have made Jean bold, for he walked beside Michèle, and far enough behind me to be out of earshot. I led the way. I was conscious of a vague uneasiness. It was the first symptom of that mental and emotional pain which was to infect my whole existence. But I am not telling the story of my own life, and I have no intention of isolating its single thread from the woof of the various destinies with which I am concerned. Still, I can scarcely pass over in silence that consciousness of being hurt of which, as a child, I then became aware. Nothing is so common as ordinary jealousy. But the jealousy which swept over me that day as, a boy of thirteen, I walked through the sodden fields, straining my ears to catch what my friend and my sister were saying, was not of the common kind —at least, I hope not, if only for the sake of humanity in general, whose shoulders already have to bear more than enough of the curses to which flesh is heir.

I did not know then which of my emotions was mainly concerned —my love for my sister or my friendship for Jean. It was hateful to realize that she was talking to him in the low, intimate voice which, till then, she had kept for me alone. Michèle belonged to me. So far I had never shared her with anyone, and now, here was Jean taking her away from me, making her laugh; Jean whom, for the last fortnight, I had loved to picture in imagination on the roads about Larjuzon; Jean, who had played a part in all my holiday plans, whom I had dreamed of having to myself. He, no less than my sister, had suddenly broken away from me. Why hadn't I realized that things would turn out like this?

'They're treating me like a kid: they're hiding from me' . . . Sometimes I had to stop to let them catch up. Now and again, at a twist in the path, I lost sight of them altogether and had to turn back.

"What are you two talking about?"

They looked at one another, laughing but saying nothing. Jean was chewing a piece of grass. Michèle was rather red in the face. The brim of her straw hat was so broad that she had to tilt her head back in order to see me. I pressed my question: what were they talking about? Things that couldn't possibly interest a little boy, Michèle said. Jean's lips approached her ear. This time I caught what he said. "D'you think he *knows*?" he asked.

Now, to "*know*" meant, in our language, to be informed about the facts of life, the mysteries of generation. My face flushed scarlet, and I stalked on ahead, turning over this further grievance in my mind. They were hiding from me in order to discuss forbidden things. Their guilty secret was another barrier between us.

My stepmother had given me permission to ask Jean to lunch with us next day at Larjuzon. I had looked forward to this, but now decided suddenly not to pass on the invitation. I was terrified at the thought that the day was approaching when either Michèle would take Jean from me, or Jean would take Michèle. Rather than that should happen I would deprive myself of Jean's company. Let him stay alone at the Presbytery and be bored stiff! After all, his uncle probably knew what he was doing when he put the screw on. The general view at school was that Mirbel was a dirty beast. He was allowed to stay on only because his guardian had been one of the heroes of Castelfidardo. Probably at this very moment he was telling Michèle what I called "one of his dirty stories." Michèle mustn't be allowed to see him. I would warn my stepmother. It would be far better for me to give him up, never to see him again, than to experience this tightness in the throat, this feeling in the pit of the stomach, this pain, this misery for which there was no cure, since any possible cure was beyond my power to control, and lay within the will, the heart, the hidden thoughts of my friend and my sister who were now in league against me! The torments I was suffering were more acute than any words of mine could express. To be sure, here beside the Ciron, looking down on the swirling stream, leaning against the trunk of a pine tree which had grown to a great height by reason of the water which nourished its roots, I did not fully realize that I could find no words for all that I was feeling. It was pride alone, I thought, that compelled me to hide my vexation. Without waiting for them to come up with me, and in the hope of putting them off my trail, I had walked quickly. I dried my tears, got back my breath and composed my features. They were laughing, and I could hear their laughter long before they came in sight. I caught a glimpse of Michèle's straw hat above the bracken which their movement had set waving. At last I saw them. My sister asked me how Jean de Mirbel was going to get to Larjuzon next day, seeing that he hadn't got a bicycle.

"That old beast has confiscated it!" he said.

The old beast was his uncle. I answered coldly that there was nothing I could do about it.

"I was thinking of lending him mine," said Michèle. "I could ride yours this evening and take you back on the frame."

"Five miles on the frame—thank you for nothing! I have no intention of having my bike smashed up. Mirbel will jolly well have to walk from Larjuzon. If he's so keen on coming, five miles will be nothing."

"I knew he'd say that!" cried Michèle in a sudden fury. "His wretched old bike's sacred. He'll kick up no end of a fuss!"

"Oh no he won't," said Jean, taking my arm, half coaxing, half bullying; "you'll do it for me, won't you, Louis?"

I shook myself free and sat down on a root. "He's sulking," said Michèle: "it'll be ages before we can get him to say yes."

But I wasn't sulking, I was suffering. I watched the water-spiders struggling against the current. Long weeds were swaying in the clear stream. Minnows were darting about near the banks. I could see their shadows on the sandy bottom. Till my dying day I shall have in my nostrils the smell of trodden mint and river plants. They symbolize for me the memory of that moment in which I said good-bye to the happy summers of my childhood, when I made acquaintance with sorrow and the torment of a boy's love. No, I was not sulking, I was wrestling with the miseries of a grown man. The others must have sat down too, some way off, for I could still hear them whispering though the bracken hid them. Suddenly I heard Jean's voice raised. I realized that he was talking loud on purpose.

"Don't worry: he'll come round all right. If he doesn't we'll take matters into our own hands. . . ."

I got up and ran over to them.

"How are you going to do that, you great brute? Just you try!"

He seized my wrists. He was hurting me, but I clenched my teeth so as not to cry out.

"Are you going to lend your sister your bike, or aren't you?"

"Let me go, you're twisting my wrists!"

"Don't want to ride home on the frame, eh?"

Suddenly I was free, Michèle had attacked my tormentor. In a furious voice she shouted:

"Leave my brother alone!"

"All right, all right, I wasn't going to hurt him!"

They glared at one another. I was conscious of a sudden sense of calm. They were quarrelling, they were going to be enemies. Michèle liked me better than him, and he wasn't in love with her after all. It was because of me that they were fighting. It was lovely to feel the tightness in my chest loosen. As always happens with me, as soon as the trouble grew remote, I thought that it had vanished for good. I no longer hated them. My old affection for them both returned. Of course Michèle and I would go back on my bike. But I wasn't going to give in at once, wasn't going to deprive myself of the pleasure of seeing them walk with a space of enmity between them. Now it was Mirbel's turn to go ahead, chewing his piece of grass, while I followed some distance behind, holding my sister by the hand. So on we went, I clutching Michèle's hand and looking at Jean as he marched ahead. It was pure happiness. The grass was wet. A great storm-cloud darkened the sky above the trees, but there was no thunder. Several men and women were busy round a waggon half piled with hay.

"Really, you know, Mirbel *is* just a great brute," I said.

"Still, he's rather nice. . . ."

"Doesn't alter the fact that he's a brute. . . ."

"But we'll fix it up, won't we, so's he can come over to lunch to-morrow?"

Again I felt that tightness in my throat. I asked Michèle whether she was terribly keen that he should come.

"Larjuzon's a bit queer these hols., don't you think, with that Puybaraud of yours looking like a great white worm, and Brigitte always fussing round him?"

"Oh, Michèle!"

"If she's not careful, she will make life at Larjuzon impossible, even for papa. Of course I'm going to lend my bicycle to Mirbel."

"Then you'll jolly well walk back!" I said with a flare of temper.

Jean had turned. This sudden storm of words between Michèle

and me gave him a sense of triumph. That was what came of not letting him show me who was who. *He* knew how to treat kids. . . .

We walked round the Presbytery, all shouting at the same time.

"Well, it's my bike, isn't it?" I protested.

"I call it frightfully nice of you to have asked his permission at all," said Jean to Michèle. "Just you jump on it before he can do anything. If he doesn't want to ride on the frame, well, he can do the five miles on foot, that's all!"

I got in before them and seized my bicycle. But Jean did not let me get far. He hung on to the handle-bar and stuck his foot in the wheel, so that I fell off. Monsieur Calou, who must have seen us, came hurriedly out of the house, ran towards us and picked me up. I had merely grazed my arm. He turned to Mirbel.

"Go up to my room and bring down the tincture of iodine and the packet of cotton-wool which you'll find on the wash-hand stand."

He issued this order in his usual quiet way, but his voice held a threat of thunder, and he kept his eyes fixed on Mirbel, who stood there with his great fists half clenched. Still, he obeyed at once. When he came back again the abbé proceeded to bathe my injury at the pump. Without turning to Jean he said:

"Dab it with cotton-wool. . . . Now, put on some iodine—not too much. Stings a bit, doesn't it? What's been happening, Michèle?—tell me."

She embarked on a confused story. She said we were both to blame. Mirbel had been rough, but I had gone out of my way to irritate him.

"Shake hands," said the abbé.

I took Jean's hand and he made no effort to withdraw it. Monsieur Calou then said that he would settle the matter. He wouldn't hear of two of us going back on the one bicycle. He said that he'd lend Jean his next day so that he could get over to Larjuzon. It could be spared for a few hours, for there was no one seriously ill among his flock. But something unexpected might turn up, so he asked Jean to be sure to be back before four. "And you two can come with him. In that way you'll be able to spend the rest of the afternoon together."

The threat of thunder had gone from his voice; there would be no storm. The wind had swept the sky clean. He asked us to water his vegetables for him, and advised us to do it barefoot so as not to get our shoes wet. As a reward, he said, we could take as many currants as we liked. Maria had finished her jam-making.

As soon as the abbé had gone back into the house, Jean said that he hadn't come there to do manual work, and wouldn't be treated like a servant. But no sooner had Michèle and I taken off our shoes and stockings than the temptation was too much for him. He got out of his sand-shoes and took one of the watering-cans which my sister was carrying. Such is the power of happiness, that I remember that summer's day when we ran shoeless over the gravel which hurt our feet, and did all we could to splash one another as much as possible, as a time of calm, unclouded happiness. But all the same, my pleasure was streaked with pain because it was Michèle whom Jean splashed. She had tucked her skirt up to her knees and, though pretending to be angry, gave vent to little shrill gusts of laughter which were quite unlike any sound I had heard her make before. But I refused to let myself suffer. Deep within me I carried a load of dumb agony which a trifle would have served to waken, and I shouted louder than either of them to keep it from my mind. When the sun disappeared behind the pines it was time for us to think of going. Jean asked what o'clock lunch would be at Larjuzon.

"Twelve, but come early," said Michèle; "we get up at eight. Come as soon as you can get the abbé's bike."

I protested that he mustn't be deprived of it for too long. He might be called to some sick-bed. Jean replied in his "nasty" voice that "people could die without the help of a curé." Michèle seemed shocked at this, and I noticed that there was a certain coldness in her tone when she said good-bye. But she turned round twice to give an answering signal to his waving béret. He was wearing a sailor's pea-jacket over a striped red-and-white jersey. His feet were bare, his trousers rolled above his knees and kept in position by an elastic.

Later, he told me about his first evening at the Presbytery. For a while he had wandered round the house, not knowing what to do with himself. Baluzac could hardly be called a village. It consisted of a single inn and a chemist's shop kept by a man called Voyod, with whom the Curé did not wish his charge to have anything to do. In fact, the only order he had issued was that he should keep clear of the place. The abbé Calou had also spoken about the books in his study. In Jean's life books occupied a place which no one who had had to do with him suspected. On his father's side he belonged to a family which would have viewed a taste for reading in a young boy as a disquieting symptom. His guardian and his mother were convinced that he was interested only in scabrous and obscene publications, and, to tell the truth, their suspicions were not wholly without foundation.

Jean could not resist his desires. The knowledge that the house was full of books, even if they were only books for a priest's reading, that there was a library of which he had been given the free run, exercised over his mind a power no less than many worse temptations. But he stood out against it. He did not want Monsieur Calou to think that he could be won over so easily. He was cautious about putting his head into so obvious a trap. Nevertheless, he went upstairs to the first floor, taking care not to make the stairs creak.

There was a strong smell of pipe tobacco. Jean hesitated to approach the door. His pride held him back. He felt quite sure that the Curé had been listening, had caught the sound of his padding footsteps, and was waiting with as keen a sense of expectation as any fisherman watching the trout circling a waiting snare.

Monsieur Calou could contain himself no longer, but opened the door.

"Anything you want, you young scamp?"

Jean shook his head.

"A book, perhaps?"

The boy entered the thick haze of smoke. He had never seen so many books. They were ranged in rows from floor to ceiling: they lay scattered over chairs and on the mantelpiece. There were books everywhere, bound in paper covers. There was a set of steps mounted on wheels for reaching the upper shelves, and a desk at which a man could read and write standing. Never had he seen so many marvels! The books must be pretty boring, of course; still, one never knew, and no book, thought Jean, could be wholly boring.

The Curé went back to his table without taking any further notice of him. Jean climbed on to the steps. How tiresome it was that he felt so sick, and had such a pain at the back of his neck. . . . The Armagnac which he had drunk out of bravado was giving him a lot of trouble, and the smell of the Curé's pipe was the last straw. Hurriedly, he returned to the floor, picked up a volume at random and read the title: *A Treatise on Concupiscence—A Letter and Some Maxims on the Theatre—Logic—A Treatise on Free Will*, by Bossuet. Was he going to be sick? Was he going to faint, here in the Curé's study? At all costs he must keep his end up! In an effort to forget his qualms, he opened the book and forced himself to read.

The woman in Proverbs who boasted of the perfumes scattered about her bed, and of the sweet odours that regaled the visitor to her chamber; who said, "Let us take our fill of love, let us solace ourselves with love," showed by her words whither may lead those cunning scents which are prepared with an intent to ensnare the Will, and lead it to an indulgence of the senses through an employment of that which seems not directly to attack the stronghold of our modesty. . . .

"You're very pale, my boy: almost green. Don't you feel well?"

Jean protested that it was nothing, just a little attack of sickness.

"Lie down."

The boy refused. It would pass off of itself. He felt better already. He made another effort to concentrate his thoughts on the open page. . . . The abbé heard the sound of Jean's body striking the floor, though not violently, for the sufferer had kept hold of the steps. The boy felt himself lifted by two strong arms, and retched uncontrollably. The Curé, without showing the slightest sign of disgust, handed him a basin and supported his head with his great hand. Jean opened his eyes and asked to be allowed to go down to the garden. He was in despair at the thought that he had been betrayed, unexpectedly like this, into the hands of the enemy.

"I'm coming down too," said the abbé. "I want to finish reading my breviary in the church. You can join me there. It's a lovely little church, built by Bertrand de Gouth, who afterwards became Clement V. I don't suppose you know that he was a 'fellow countryman' of ours—born at Vallandraut, though there are some who say it was at Uzeste, where he is buried. . . . It wouldn't do to have many Popes like him."

Jean replied that he was not interested in old stones.

"Never mind, come along, anyhow, and pay our Lord a little visit."

Aha!—so the nigger was peering out of the wood-pile! Jean, without daring to look the other in the face, muttered that he didn't believe in all those old wives' tales.

"Really?—that's interesting." There was no hint of outrage in Monsieur Calou's tone.

"Does it surprise you?"

There was a self-satisfied air about Mirbel.

"Why should it?" said the Curé. "The really surprising thing is that a man *should* believe. . . . The really surprising thing is that what we believe should be true. The really surprising thing is that the truth should really exist, that it should have taken on flesh, that I can keep it a prisoner here beneath these old vaults which don't interest you, thanks to the strength in these great hands of mine which your uncle Adhémar admires so much. Yes, you little oddity, I can never get over feeling how absurd, how utterly mad, it is that what we believe should be precisely and literally true!"

Was the Curé laughing at him? Jean tried another fling:

"Oh, well, anyhow it doesn't mean a thing to me!"

He tried to carry off his attitude with a swagger, staring his adversary straight in the face. But, in spite of himself, he had to lower his eyes.

"That may be so now, my queer little scrap of humanity, but you may feel different later."

"You shan't get me!" cried the boy defiantly.

"It's not a question of my getting you. How could it be?"

"Well, who else could? There's no one else here, is there, except you and Maria?"

The Curé said nothing. He seemed to be thinking.

"How do you manage at school? I don't suppose you're allowed to trifle with Confession or Communion there?"

Jean replied complacently that he had never let that bother him. They had Confession every Saturday. He just said anything that came into his head. And every Sunday they had to go to Communion. But what did it matter whether one believed or not? It didn't make the slightest difference.

He had expected an outburst, but it did not come.

"You really think so?" asked Monsieur Calou.

Jean presented an insolent face to his gaze. But he felt shamed by its gentle sadness.

"Every Saturday and every Sunday, for Heaven knows how long .... two years at least, O Lord!"

Monsieur Calou looked at the handsome face, at the unsullied brow beneath the mop of dark hair in which one lighter lock shone like a flame. He could say no more than:

"Lie down a little before dinner, my boy." Then he hurried off towards the church without looking back. His bent shoulders made him seem less than his real height.

V

I FIND it difficult, looking back, to distinguish the first occasion on which Mirbel lunched at Larjuzon from those that came later. All through August we were constantly together. When he didn't come to us, Michèle was for ever hanging about him at Baluzac, and nothing would have induced me not to go with her, since my peace of mind would have been utterly destroyed had I known that they were together away from me. My whole life centred round the need I felt to be always the third party in their meetings.

Nor, at first, was it very difficult for me to be with them. The bad days, when they managed to give me the slip, were far fewer than those on which Michèle railed against us two boys and had to protect herself against the tricks which we invented at the expense of my "kid sister." There was never entire harmony between all three of us. Either she or I had to be the victim. I was never happy unless I was defending Michèle against Jean and his often ill-natured teasing. But almost always, just when I thought that they had quarrelled for good and all, they would quite suddenly make it up. It was precisely when I felt myself most safe from any possible hostile coalition of my sister and my friend that inexplicable scenes would occur which had the effect of putting me to the torture, such, for instance, as the occasion on which we sent her off into a temper by alluding to the "story of the cakes" which, as Mirbel said, had united him and me till "death should us part."

"What story of what cakes?" asked my sister. We winked at one another, put our fingers to our lips, and swore our most solemn oath that never, no never, would we let her into the secret. We began to run round her in circles, pulling her hair, snapping our fingers, and chanting: "Cowardy, Cowardy Custard! . . ." I was careful to keep my distance, but Jean jumped about like a dancing Dervish, touching her and then springing back out of reach. . . . Suddenly Michèle leaped at him, her fingers clawed, and made a dash at his face. He did not attempt to defend himself, but stumbled and measured his length on the grass. When he got up we saw that his cheek was bleeding from a scratch. We stood there appalled. Michèle looked quite pale.

"Oh, Jean, wipe your face! I haven't got a hanky." But he did nothing to stanch the blood. I thought he was going to rush at her, but instead, he stood there grinning. It was so unlike him to act in that way that it seemed almost as though he had some hold over her, and she over him, as though he didn't mind her hurting him. Children though they were, they had become, unconsciously, free of that world in which blows mean the same thing as kisses, and insults may express more of love than the tenderest endearments. A sort of curtain seemed to drop between us. They passed from my vision, leaving me, an outsider, on the wrong side of the folds; a small boy lost in a universe peopled by that inconsequent race of monsters whom we knew as "the grown-ups."

If Mirbel showed signs of becoming less wild, the credit was due entirely to my sister, and not to Monsieur Calou (at any rate, until the end of August, when an event occurred which I shall describe in due course). True, the Curé had won a signal victory over his charge on the very day of his arrival, but, during the weeks that followed, he made no noticeable progress in his campaign.

'I have a cat here with me in the house,' noted Monsieur Calou in his diary that summer: 'a cat that slinks in and out of the library without so much as moving a chair, sniffs round the books, pads into the dining-room, settles itself at the table and gobbles its soup. It never shows fight, works an hour each day without complaining, and, on Sunday, goes to Mass. I showed my hand too soon. The boy hates my gentleness . . . that "professional gentleness of yours" —as the young spark from Bordeaux put it one day in accents of repulsion. I don't want there to be anything in my looks or speech to put him off. The great thing is not to sicken him by the slightest hint of unctuousness. How harsh the unction of Christ is! To cleave their hearts one must be as hard as a diamond! Jean would have felt far less dislike for me if I had been rough and stern. He expected that, and was ready armed against it. . . .'

It may be that the abbé Calou had stumbled on Jean's secret: but of mine he had no suspicion. Could anyone really have understood it and explained me to myself? No man can bear a child's cross. It is something beyond the comprehension of the fully grown.

Monsieur Puybaraud watched over my studies and the good of my soul with an ardent singleness of mind for which I was not at all grateful. That he loved me there could be no doubt, and the accepted view at home was that I adored him. To this game of make-believe I willingly lent myself. "Louis swears by Monsieur Puybaraud: he takes no notice of anyone else. . . ." As a matter of fact, I shouldn't have cared greatly if I had been told that I was never going to see him again. The degree of indifference shown by children to grown-ups, even to those to whom they seem to be most attached, is seldom realized. Except for Jean and Michèle and, in quite a different way, for my father and my dead mother, no living creature was altogether real to me. Those who could be collectively described as "the others" were, for me, a mere anonymous crowd. They served to fill the stage. They stood about the centre of my heart when it leaped with happiness or wallowed in despair according to my relations of the moment with Jean and Mirbel, but its condition meant nothing to them.

When I walked in the park with Monsieur Puybaraud, and he talked to me in a moral or a learned strain, I answered him in proper wise, responding to his advances with that rather knowing gentleness which served so well to win me the affection of others whenever I took the trouble to employ it. The poor man had no idea that my heart was suffering a thousand miles away, that the words I uttered had no connexion with my thoughts or real feelings, that effortlessly, and without the faintest sense of shame, I hid my true self from him, substituting for it the mere image of the solemn and attentive child on whom he lavished the treasures of his kindly spirit.

I was in the advantageous position of knowing all about his private life. Not that it really interested me. That summer was Monsieur Puybaraud's moulting season. He was half-way back to the world. He wore a panama instead of his top-hat, a short jacket in place of his frock-coat. But he was loyal to his black trousers and his starched shirts, no matter how stiflingly hot the day might be. His attitude to me was that of a Christian schoolmaster, though he was led to confess more intimate matters than are usually thought fitting for young ears. To-day, after such a long interval of time, when Monsieur Puybaraud has long been dust, I can read his diary and find excitement in the struggle he was waging, in the drama of which I was then the disinterested spectator, because it touches on problems with which I become the more obsessed the older I grow.

During the first week of Monsieur Puybaraud's stay, Brigitte Pian had plenty to occupy her. The days were too short for her happy task of helping a man to straighten the tangled skein of his private problems. She felt that she was not wasting her life, that she was not running counter to her true vocation, which was to make clear to others what God had planned for them from the beginning of time. Here, at her very door, was an unrivalled opportunity for her to show her mettle, though she fully realized the dangers involved. She was, perhaps, too satisfied in the part she felt called upon to play. Not that she was guilty, even in the smallest degree, of self-indulgence: still, at first she did seem to be deriving too much satisfaction from Monsieur Puybaraud's way of listening to her as to an oracle. But, alas, his meekness was superficial only. Very soon it was borne in on Brigitte Pian that she was dealing with a less submissive sheep than she had at first supposed. 'He is a wandering soul . . .' she told herself in the course of the second week. She even went so far as to accuse him of deliberately setting his face against the operations of Grace—by which she meant her own advice.

It was Brigitte Pian's way to drive reluctant souls on to the mountain tops (that was how she phrased it), and she made it her duty to open Monsieur Puybaraud's eyes to that especial trick of the Devil which takes the form of enlisting against a Christian sinner the very sense he has of his own humility. My master was convinced that previously he had had too high an idea of his own strength when he had felt himself called upon to eschew the normal destiny of mankind. He felt that it was his duty, while there might yet be time, to find his way back to the beaten track marked out by those who had gone before him and, like them, to take to himself a wife, have children and watch over them as a bird watches over its brood. But Brigitte Pian knew well that it is sometimes necessary to tear from human souls that mask of spurious humility behind which they take refuge. She declared, as though she had been the very mouthpiece of God, that Monsieur Puybaraud had been taken from his school work only because, from all eternity, he had been destined for the life of the Cloister. She assured him that he had to face one problem and one alone—at what door should he knock? to what Order should he make his submission?

Not only, however, did Madame Brigitte fail to make progress in her struggle with Monsieur Puybaraud, although she was fighting him on ground of her own choosing; she was forced to admit that she was at grips with an influence considerably stronger than any which she could bring to bear—and what an influence! for what was defeating her was the persuasive power exercised by Octavia Tronche, who inspired in my stepmother a feeling which the world would have described as contempt. But she knew that we should feel contempt for no human creature, and that even the soul of Octavia Tronche had value in the sight of God.

It was a matter for astonishment to my stepmother that Octavia at a distance had a greater hold over Monsieur Puybaraud than when, back in the city, she had been seeing him every day. The reason for this was that though separated from my master she wrote to him daily. Madame Brigitte devoured the outside of these letters with her eyes. Monsieur Puybaraud read them in her presence at breakfast-time, bringing to the task a degree of concentration which had to be seen to be believed. The truth was that his former occasional dissatisfaction with Octavia's rather homely appearance (responsive though he always was to the spiritual charm which shone out from her) yielded wholly a feeling of admiration and tender respect during this time of her absence, when her contact with him was confined to the pages that she wrote each night before going to bed.

Their correspondence—which I found among Monsieur Puybaraud's effects—could not possibly be published here, not because it does not deserve publication, but because I doubt whether there are many readers capable of appreciating the charm of true humility, of that particular manifestation of humility, which takes no heed of itself and seems completely ignorant of its effect on others. I cannot, however, pass it by in silence, seeing that Octavia's victory over my stepmother had tragic repercussions on more than one person.

Although Octavia thought highly of Madame Brigitte, she was encouraged by distance to resist her influence, and to warn her lover against indulging in an excessive distrust of the dictates of his own conscience. "No matter how superior in virtue another person may be," she wrote, "her views cannot supersede your own vision of the Divine Will, since that is the fruit of complete surrender to God. . . . My own opinion is that we should most certainly pay attention to the advice of others, but that we should never let it divert our attention from the ever watchful respect which we owe to our own inner voice. Don't you agree, my dear, that it is in the secrecy of our own hearts that we most truly hear the bidding of God? I find it impossible to believe that what I feel for you so strongly can be contrary to His will. Light, for me, is where you are. If I struggle against the instinct which leads me to you, I see nothing but darkness. I am the more convinced that what I say is true, because I know that if your temporal or spiritual welfare depended upon my giving you up, I *could* give you up, not, indeed, without pain and suffering, but certainly without a struggle. Selfish though I am (and God alone knows how selfish that is!), I love you too much to consider my own feelings. So wholly do I love you, that I would not, no, not for a single moment, fight against the influences to which you are exposed at Larjuzon, if I were sure that they are making for your happiness, if I did not feel that too much subtle reasoning may be brought to bear upon what is really a perfectly simple and very ordinary situation. Perhaps a poor creature like me has no right to judge, but I *do* think that there is one point in particular about which Madame Brigitte is wrong. She does not realize, as you and I do, that all flesh, imperfect and corrupt though it may be, is holy; that, in spite of original sin, the birth of a child is still God's loveliest mystery. I have heard her say things on this subject which I may, perhaps, have misunderstood. What I love most in you, my darling, is that fondness for children which God has implanted in your heart, for those little children like whom we must become if we are to gain the Kingdom of Heaven. We cannot become like them, but at least we can bring them into the world, and that is no small thing. No doubt there are higher vocations . . . still, I do not believe that in becoming your wife I shall be resisting Christ's summons to His flock, His insistence that we should leave all and follow Him. For in you, and through you, beloved, in and through the children who may be born to us, I submit to that Will which it is our chief delight to honour. . . . The mere thought that this is so sets me trembling with happiness. . . ."

Monsieur Puybaraud did not show these letters to me, and I could judge of my stepmother's defeat only by the increasing gloom of her demeanour, especially at meal-times, the atmosphere of which soon became almost intolerable.

I had a feeling that his affairs were going badly, that his relations with Madame Brigitte were becoming embittered, but I was far too unhappy myself to pay much attention to what was going on. Ever since Michèle had scratched Jean's cheek, the friendship between them had grown closer and closer. Gone were the happy times when my friend, a child once more, had plotted with me to tease my "kid sister." Whenever Jean came to the house they thought of one thing only—how to be alone together. They were as clever in their efforts to avoid me as I was in trying not to let them out of my sight. I was ashamed of my persistence: it became hateful to me. Yet I dogged their footsteps, pretending not to notice the glances of irritated impatience which passed between them.

If my stepmother called me, if Monsieur Puybaraud had a corrected exercise to give back, if I had to be absent for no matter how short a time, I knew that when I got back Michèle and Jean would have vanished. In the garden path where, but a moment earlier, Michèle's laughter had echoed, or my friend's loud and breaking voice as he called to the dog, I now heard nothing but the sighing of wind in the branches left dripping by the recent storm. I cried their names, "Michèle! Jean!—where are you?" and then fell silent, knowing full well that even if they had heard, the only effect of my appeal would be to make them lower their voices still further, walk on tip-toe, and hide their tracks.

I had no clear idea of the nature of the attraction which held them in thrall. My senses were not yet awakened: I had felt nothing of the kind myself. What causes jealousy is a vision of the delight which a beloved person gives to, and receives from, another. I do not think that I was capable then of any such emotion. But their happiness, conditioned, as it was in part, by my absence, hurt me to such an extent that I could have cried aloud.

I remember the day on which Monsieur Puybaraud suddenly decided to leave us. At luncheon scarcely anybody said a word except Monsieur Calou, who had come over to Larjuzon with Jean. Monsieur Puybaraud answered his questions, but Madame Brigitte never opened her lips. Her great face was gloomy enough to have frightened me. Opposite her, my father sat huddled over his plate, chewing his food and paying not the slightest attention to anybody. Jean and Michèle, with the whole length of the table between them, exchanged wordless speeches with their eyes. I, sitting next to Monsieur Puybaraud, pretended to be absorbed in his remarks. But I was aware of nothing but that silent interchange between my sister and my friend, was conscious of nothing but the happy peace of mind which I knew Michèle was feeling just because Jean was there. For her, I was merely one person the more, which meant that I didn't really exist at all. I was a part of nothingness.

Because of the storm we could not drink our coffee under the trees. My stepmother apologized for her silence. She had a headache, she said, and asked me to fetch an antipyrin tablet from her room. The two minutes during which I was away sufficed for Jean and Michèle to make their escape in spite of the bad weather. I wanted to follow them, but the rain had come on heavier, and my stepmother forbade me. "If Michèle wants to get wet, that is her affair. You will stay indoors."

Could it be that she had noticed nothing? Michèle's behaviour ought to have filled her with horror. But she had eyes for no one but Monsieur Puybaraud. Her headache, which was genuine enough, forced her to go to her room. No matter what the company, my father would never give up his siesta. So I was left alone in the billiard-room, watching the drenched countryside through the french windows. In the drawing-room Monsieur Puybaraud and the abbé Calou were talking. At first they kept their voices low, but after a while I could hear every word of their conversation. Monsieur Puybaraud was complaining of the tactless tyranny to which he was being exposed. Monsieur Calou, I gathered, was laughing at him for being so timid, and was advising him to slip his moorings without any further delay.

'They must be hiding,' I told myself, 'in the derelict farm.' I conjured up a picture of Michèle and Jean in the kitchen where only an occasional shepherd ever lit a fire, and where the walls were scribbled over with pictures and with words which made Jean laugh, but which I did not understand. They were kissing. They were delighting in one another. Michèle was never gentle with me. Even when she was kind there was a rough quality in her kindness. Jean, even when he was in a good mood, always spoke to me as though he were my master. A hulking great brute, but not to Michèle. He would say to her, "Your hands are cold," and hold them in his for a long while. He was never kind to me. I have always wanted people to be kind. . . .

Looking out on to the rainy fields, I suffered.

Monsieur Calou wanted to take advantage of a break in the clouds to go back to Baluzac. He asked me to call Jean. I rang the great bell, but in vain. There was no sign of Jean. The abbé Calou decided at last that his charge was old enough to get home alone. He rode off on his bicycle after saying good-bye to Madame Brigitte. Her headache had gone, and she took a stroll in the Avenue with Monsieur Puybaraud. Standing on the steps, I could see them pacing up and down. My master was doing all the talking. There were only the briefest of interchanges between them, and, although I could hear no high words, something told me that all was not well. Monsieur Puybaraud, on his way back into the house, stroked my hair. He was very pale.

"I am going away tomorrow morning, Louis. I must see to my packing."

I scarcely heard him. Where were Michèle and Jean? They had not come back to tea. I could remember no previous occasion on which they had been alone together for so long. It was not annoyance that I most felt now, but anger, a desire to hurt them. I became a prey to all the nastiest instincts which flourish in us at that period of life when the man we are to be is already fully formed and fully dowered with his individual portion of inclinations and passions.

The rain had left off. I walked quickly beneath the dripping trees. Now and again a raindrop splashed on my cheek or ran down my neck. It was a sunless summer and the grasshoppers were silent. If only there had been some other boy or girl at Larjuzon with whom

I could have played on my own. . . . But no face, no name came to my mind. At a turn in the path I saw my stepmother walking towards me. She saw me standing there, my hand pressed to my forehead. I could not restrain my tears, and, for a while, could make no answer to her questions.

"They're running away from me," I managed at last to stammer.

She thought that I was referring to some childish game.

"Pretend not to notice. Then they'll have to be 'out.' . . ."

"No, no—that's what they want."

"What *are* you talking about?"

"Yes," I insisted, almost whispering, "to be alone."

She frowned. "What do you mean?" she asked. Her suspicions had been awakened, but as yet they had no definite object. She was too much preoccupied, too wholly confined within her own circle of pain. Still, the seed I dropped had fallen on good soil. Sooner or later it would put forth shoots.

"One is always punished when one attaches too much importance to other people," murmured Brigitte Pian on a note of bitterness. "I sometimes wonder, dear child, whether I don't give too much of myself when I work for the salvation of my neighbours. Oh, I know that the least among them is of infinite worth. I would give my life that one might be saved. But there are moments when I am frightened to think how much time I have wasted (at least, it *seems* wasted, but of that God alone is judge) over insignificant, nay, evil persons. It is the cross laid upon the great-hearted that they shall exhaust themselves in darkness and uncertainty on behalf of the spiritually mean and inferior. . . ."

She hissed the last word from between closed lips. I realized that when she spoke of the spiritually inferior she meant Monsieur Puybaraud. Why was she so interested in him? Was she in love with him? If she wasn't in love with him, thought I, why did she get in such a state at the mere mention of his name? How can those whom we do not love affect us either for good or ill?

I caught sight of Michèle in the distance seated on one of the stone steps. Without waiting for me to ask her what she had been doing, she said that she had been for a ride on her bicycle, and that Jean had gone back to Baluzac without returning to Larjuzon. She must have come straight from her room. She had tidied her hair and washed her face and hands. She looked at me, trying to guess what I was thinking. But I pretended not to be interested. I found pleasure in feeling at once acutely miserable and completely master of myself.

I went upstairs early, meaning to read in bed, but this I could not do. Through the floor I could hear the rumblings of a violent dispute. Michèle told me next day that my stepmother had lost control of herself and had been most unkind about Monsieur Puybaraud. He too, finally, had lost his temper, exasperated by the fact that when he tried to explain to my stepmother why it was that he had decided to marry Octavia, she had replied, raising her eyes to Heaven, that this was the cross she had always known was reserved for her, and that she willingly accepted the sacrifice.

"But, Madame Brigitte, there is no question of your being sacrificed. . . . This is my affair, and mine only. . . ."

But Madame Brigitte would not listen. She had been wounded, but forgave the hand that held the weapon. She always behaved like this when people told her that she had been wrong or had committed some injustice. Instead of frankly admitting her fault and sitting in sackcloth and ashes, she turned the other cheek, protesting that it was well she should be thus misunderstood and vilified. In this way she added another link of mail to the armour of perfection and merit in which she went clad from head to foot. On such occasions her interlocutor was driven to speak angry words, and this gave her a feeling of still greater excellence at the bar of her own conscience and in the sight of God.

On this particular evening, however, she had given full rein to her fury. She must have exceeded all decent limits, for next day, at breakfast (which was earlier than usual, because my master was taking the eight o'clock train), she humbled herself to the extent of apologizing to him in my presence.

"Such behaviour was unworthy of me," she said, not once, but many times, in an access of humility, "and I want Louis to hear me acknowledge my fault. When I have reason to believe that a fellow human soul is straying and in danger of damnation, I can contain myself no longer. . . . But excess of zeal is no excuse for the violence of my words. He who would tame the old Adam must never sleep. I realize, in all humility, that I have an ardent temperament." This she said with every sign of satisfaction: "My friend, you must forgive me."

"No, Madame Brigitte" Monsieur Puybaraud protested, "I cannot bear to see you abasing yourself in this way. I am not worthy."

But she would not listen. She wanted to revel in the grandeur of her attitude. She had paid the price asked of her, and it cost her nothing now to tread the path of humiliation to the end, since, by so doing, she forced her adversary to lay down his arms, and increased her own sense of personal merit (one link the more added to the armour of perfection).

"My conduct to you and to Octavia shall prove that I bear you no grudge. What I have said, I felt in conscience bound to say. But that is all over now, and I confide you both to God. You will have no trustier friend than me in the new life, so beset by snares, so full, I fear, of ordeals, which is opening before you."

Monsieur Puybaraud seized her hand and kissed it fervently. What would they do without Madame Brigitte? Octavia's position at the Free School, and his own in the Charity Organization, depended upon her. One word from her . . . He raised his eyes to the face of his benefactress, which suddenly emptied itself of all expression. Brigitte Pian's words became vague. She spoke of the necessity of trusting in Providence, that ever sure protector which wrapped us in its loving care when we suffered most and felt ourselves abandoned by the world. And then, since Monsieur Puybaraud insisted on mentioning the subject again, she said that she could decide nothing as yet. She had, she remarked, only one vote in the Organization, like every other member of the Committee.

"Oh, but Madame Brigitte," he urgently replied, "no one knows better than you that if only you would espouse our cause . . ."

But my stepmother this morning was in humble mood, and the more Monsieur Puybaraud assured her that she was all-powerful in the matter of assuring continued employment for Octavia and himself, the more she retreated, taking a delight in minimizing her influence and stressing her utter worthlessness.

VI

AFTER Monsieur Puybaraud had gone, Larjuzon knew peace for several days. My stepmother scarcely ever left her bedroom. She both wrote and received a great many letters. It had now turned hot and fine, but though the thunder had ceased to crack and crash behind the trees, it still rumbled deep down in many hearts. That week Jean bicycled over only once. He spent the whole afternoon with me, but I got no pleasure from his companionship. That sixth sense of suffering which I have never yet found misleading warned me that he was not following his own inclinations, but was acting in conformity with some plan of action drawn up in advance by him and Michèle.

She made no effort to come with us when we set off intending to idle our time away on the bank of the stream. Jean was kind to me that afternoon, just as kind as I had long wanted him to be. But in spite of this I had never felt so sad, the reason being that his kindness derived from the same source as my own sense of irritation—from the influence, namely, that Michèle had acquired over him. That he who but yesterday had been a misunderstood and tormented child, should now be basking in a diffused warmth of happiness, was, for me, a cause of suffering.

We talked very little. He was deep in a daydream and I was brooding over my suspicion that he had arranged to meet Michèle somewhere else. Almost every day now Michèle went off alone on her bicycle while I was working. There must be some place on the road between Baluzac and Larjuzon where they met. . . . He had come with me to-day merely in order to put me off the scent. I watched him whittling away at a willow branch. He said he was making a whistle. His swarthy face was radiant with good humour.

"Monsieur Calou is really pretty decent, you know. He's actually written to my uncle suggesting that Mamma should pay me a visit, and uncle's given his consent. She's coming next week. She's going to stay at Vallandraut."

"Oh I say, I *am* pleased!"

And I was. It was the thought of his mother's visit, then, that had caused his happiness. Michèle had something to do with it, of course, but it wasn't only because of her.

"You've never met Mamma, have you? She's lovely"—he made an appreciative noise with his tongue. "Lots of well-known artists have wanted to paint her portrait. But you'll see for yourself. She's planning to call on your stepmother to thank her. And she wants to see you: she said so in her letter. She'll enjoy it here, though she isn't one for calls as a rule. I've told her a lot about you and Michèle. I'm sure she'll like Michèle. Mamma loves natural people. There's only one thing I'm afraid of, and that is that Michèle will be too careful: you know what she's like when she wants to be thought a perfect young lady, the way she minces when she speaks—and it's not her style, really. I don't think her hair ought to be too tidy, do you?"

I said nothing. Actually, he was talking to himself. I didn't really mean a thing to him. He looked at his watch, yawned, suddenly grasped my arm, and gave me a hug. He was overflowing with tenderness, and I had come in for a drop of it because I happened to be available. But I knew that the hug had been meant for Michèle.

That day they said good-bye to one another with a decidedly frosty handshake. But when he had mounted his bicycle they exchanged a few words in a low tone. At dinner my stepmother talked of the Comtesse de Mirbel and her coming visit. To hear her speak one would have thought that Jean's mother represented in beauty of soul and loveliness of body all that was fairest in contemporary society. Of course, she *had* given occasion for a good deal of gossip, but charity should forbid us to believe everything we hear, and certainly she, Brigitte Pian, gave no credence to the abominable stories that were going round. No one should say things like that except on the evidence of his own eyes. Besides, however great the scandal may have been, it could not be denied that, ever since her husband's death, Julia de Mirbel had lived a very retired existence at La Devize. Except for the few months which she spent in Paris with her Mirandieuze relations, she had never left it. Her general conduct had been a perfect example of quiet dignity.

From what was said it became perfectly clear that the daughter of the former Imperial Prefect attached considerable importance to the behaviour of a lady whose parents would not have condescended to recognize the existence of her own. The coming visit stood, on the worldly plane, for the only piece of snobbish gratification which, in those days, was available to my stepmother. For no one could deny that she belonged to the highest circle of local society, less by reason of her family background and considerable wealth, than of the mysterious power which she wielded among church-going folk, and of her reputation for shining virtue. There could be no doubt that it was the name of Mirbel that had opened the doors of Larjuzon to Jean. Normally, my stepmother would have been loud in her disapproval of him, and certainly the boy had always been spoken of in our family as both headstrong and undesirable.

After dinner the moon rose, and Michèle wanted to go for a walk in the Park. My father woke from his doze for just long enough to repeat, word for word, the phrase which our mother had always been in the habit of using on such occasions: "Cover up well: there's a damp chill from the river."

I noticed in Michèle the same sort of happiness as that with which Jean had been overflowing that afternoon, the same excitement, the same appearance of intoxication. The moon lit up her face with its slightly underhung jaw. The full, projecting lower lip gave her a hungry, an almost animal, appearance which was, to some extent, a true symbol of her character. Nowhere have I ever met with anybody who had so ravenous an appetite for happiness. It had been marked in her ever since she was fifteen, and showed itself by the greedy way in which she bit into fruit or buried her face in a rose; by a complete surrender to sleep, which seemed to act upon her like an enchanter's spell, and came upon her at times as she sat beside me on the grass, striking her suddenly into unconsciousness. But she never waited passively for happiness to come. She was constantly tormented by the urge to fight, to conquer, and of this she gave me proof that evening when she spoke of Jean. For it was in order to speak to me of Jean that she had suggested taking this walk in the Park. Just before we began to skirt the mist-drenched meadows, she decided to broach the subject. She put her bare arm round my neck, and I could feel her breath on my ear. What she had to tell me was quite mad, so amazing indeed that I could scarcely believe her.

"We're engaged, you know—I mean it, honestly I do. It's terribly serious, though he's not yet seventeen and I'm only fifteen. . . . I know everyone'll just laugh and not believe it . . . so we're not telling anyone except you—only you, dear, darling Louis. . . . Why are you crying? Don't you think it's marvellous?"

Marvellous!—it was her favourite word. I hid my face against her shoulder, and she let me cry, not asking me anything. For she was accustomed to my tears, which were apt to come on the slightest pretext. I was conscious of a feeling of peace. No need to ask more questions: everything was settled now; there was nothing left for me to hope for, nothing for me to look forward to except playing the rôle of confidant for which they had cast me. Never again should I be the only, the prime, concern of Michèle's heart. From the meadows came the quiet, cold gurgle of water. Michèle smelt of warm carnations. She wiped my eyes with her handkerchief, talking all the while in her low voice.

I had guessed right. They were in the habit of meeting several times a week behind Monsieur Du Buch's mill. They were terrified lest my stepmother should discover them. Michèle made me swear to say nothing that might put her on their track. When she said that, I remembered what I had told Brigitte Pian about Jean and Michèle hiding from me. I had spoken with no thought of making mischief (was that really true?). Perhaps her suspicions had already been aroused.

"I'm frightened of her, Louis. She hates people to be happy. I have a feeling that she's always got it in for me because I don't look miserable. We must be very careful. But Jean is so reckless!"

She spoke to me of him with a freedom of which I should never have been capable. She knew perfectly well the risk she ran. He was much, much worse even than his uncle imagined. I ask myself to-day why she thought that, because he has told me himself that he would have regarded as sacrilege any attempt on his part to give her more than the most chaste of kisses. . . . Perhaps it was that she knew he would not always be so lamblike. . . . Whatever the reason, she was not frightened of him. She would marry him and nobody else. She had chosen him, and he her, children though they were. If she lived to be a hundred no other man would ever mean anything in her life. That was a truth on which there could be no going back. He was so intelligent, so strong.

"And so handsome, too—don't you think?"

No, I did not think that he was handsome. What meaning can a child attach to the word? He knows strength, of course, when he meets it, physical power. But the question must have made an impression on me, because now, at the end of a long life, I can still remember that spot in the path where Michèle asked me about Jean. Am I in any better position to-day to say precisely what I mean by the word handsome, beautiful? Can I say by what signs I recognize it in a human face, in a landscape, in a stretch of sky, a colour, a word, a tune? All I know is that beauty troubles the senses, for all that it concerns the spirit, that it breeds in one a sort of despairing happiness, leads to a contemplation that never wholly finds its object but is worth a world of kisses. . . .

"Look here, Michèle," I said. "I suppose you know that the boys at school say that Jean is a dirty beast?"

"Yes, I think I do. . . . But Monsieur Calou doesn't think so. What I am going to say may startle you, but *I* think it's better to be a dirty beast than to have Brigitte Pian's brand of virtue!"

"Oh, Michèle!"

"I mean it. I'd rather be in Hell without her than in Heaven with her!"

"But, darling Michèle, it's blasphemous to say things like that," I protested. "It'll bring you bad luck. Ask to be forgiven, now, at once; make an act of contrition."

Obediently she made a quick sign of the cross, and murmured a few words: *I repent with all my heart the sin which I have committed against Thy adorable Majesty*—then she burst out laughing.

"D'you know what Monsieur Calou said to Jean about Brigitte Pian? He said that there are some people who choose God, but that perhaps God doesn't choose them. . . ."

"Monsieur Puybaraud," said I in shocked tones, "thinks that Monsieur Calou has too much wit for a priest: that he is too mordant, and that his ideas smell of the stake."

Michèle did not know what the expression "to smell of the stake" meant. She asked me, but I did not answer, for my whole attention was fixed on an idea that had just occurred to me.

"Dearest," I said sharply, "there's something I want you to tell me. . . . Don't be angry, will you? . . . Does he kiss you?"

"Of course he does . . . passionately," she said. "You wouldn't understand, but it's marvellous. He doesn't do anything else, though, Louis . . . not anything. . . . You mustn't imagine . . ."

Gracious Heaven! what worse could they do than kiss? My cheeks were on fire. I looked at Michèle, who was my senior by just a year (but she was already a woman, I, still a child), and thought how old she was, how heavily burdened with experience and sin!

"You *are* a silly, Louis: haven't I just told you we're engaged?"

She, too, was trying to reassure herself. Her conscience was far from easy. But a fresh wave of happiness swept suddenly over her and she started humming in that voice of hers which was as yet "unplaced," was still capable of astonishing breaks. The tune was an air of Gounod's which our mother used to sing on just such summer nights as this:

"*The darkness brings the silence back. . . .*"

It was a long while before I could get to sleep: not that I was more unhappy than usual, but that I was tormented by a sense of remorse. I tried to remember the expression on Brigitte Pian's face when I had complained that Jean and Michèle were hiding from me. I knew her too well to feel comforted because she had shown no overt sign. I was not without experience of her self-control, and was aware that she never yielded to sudden impulses. She buried her grievances and dug them up weeks later when no one remembered what had caused them. I was often scolded for something I had done in such and such circumstances a year earlier, and about which she had never spoken until then.

Certain slight changes in my stepmother increased my anxiety, and I warned my sister. I pointed out to her that Madame Brigitte kept less often to her room than was usual, despite the heat; that one was liable to come across her at all hours of the day on the stairs or even in the Park. She would enter the drawing-room unheralded by any creak of footsteps. Michèle did her best to reassure me by pointing out that our stepmother no longer had Monsieur Puybaraud to get her teeth into. But the very first day that Jean came over to Larjuzon again, I knew, from certain signs, that he had entered the world of Brigitte's preoccupations. One morning she expressed surprise that Michèle should walk about on the roads during the hours of siesta, when even the farm animals stayed in their lean-to's.

Such remarks were the sharp flashes of lightning which announced the coming storm. But I, at least, had the consolation of being able to tell myself that my fears had been groundless, that so far as the present unease was concerned, I was without guilt.

I have not yet had occasion to speak of the Vignottes. He was the Estate Agent at Larjuzon, where he had been installed with his wife for only a short while. They had been imported by my stepmother, and it was about them, I feel pretty sure, that my father and she had had their first serious disagreement. Very shortly after her marriage Brigitte had fallen foul of old Saintis, who had been born on the place, and with whose outspokenness, inebriety and dishonesty my father put up uncomplainingly. People who settle in the country after having spent all their lives in cities soon find themselves at odds with the local folk and make enemies of them. The theme is as old as the hills. Balzac made use of it. But in this case the story had not followed the usual course of fiction, for the country dwellers of Larjuzon had been worsted by the lady from the city. One day, when Saintis had been drinking heavily, he was so rude to my stepmother that my father was compelled to get rid of him. But he never forgave his second wife for having driven him to take this step.

The Vignottes, who regarded Brigitte as their benefactress, were very grudgingly accepted by my father. He could not abide his new agent and regretted old Saintis for all his drunkenness and his thieving propensities.

Ours was a part of the country where all wagging tongues were feared, but those of the Vignottes most of all. Madame Vignotte, with her lips and cheeks sucked inwards over her toothless gums, looked like nothing so much as a walking proboscis straddled by a pair of spectacles and surmounted by shiny strands of false black hair. She never returned from her shopping expeditions without having some morsel of gossip for Madame Brigitte. She rarely made direct assaults upon the reputations of our neighbours, but delighted in hints and sly jokes at their expense. The odd thing was that nothing ever seemed to disconcert the pietistic old dame, who had never in her life been a step from the village. Adultery, needless to say, she took in her stride. But she knew all about, and was quite willing to discuss, incest and every kind of sexual aberration, not excluding the crime of sodomy, chuckling and winking the while.

The market was her happy hunting-ground, and she left the woods and fields to the tender mercies of her husband who, from the vantage-ground of his pony-trap perched high on its big wheels, dominated the countryside as he drove from farm to farm. Many were the couples philandering in fancied security during the heat of the day or when darkness fell who were singled out by his hawk-like eye. Sometimes the actual prey was hidden from view, but the sight of two bicycles, symbolically entwined beneath a bush, would fill him with a wicked joy.

Now it so happened that one day, not far from a hut used for pigeon-shooting, he noticed a tall, dusty bicycle, and, close beside it, looking tiny by comparison, the very machine which Mademoiselle Michèle had asked him, the day before, to oil (as though it was his business to oil bicycles!). True to her usual methods, Brigitte Pian at first made no use of what Vignotte told her. She pretended not to believe him and, by so doing, put him on his mettle. The more she refused to be convinced, the coarser became his charges. He went so far as to say that Mademoiselle Michèle and the young fellow over at Monsieur Calou's . . . All this he asserted to an accompaniment of resounding oaths. He had seen them with his own eyes, or as good as. Nothing was going to persuade him that a young scamp like that would stay for over an hour with a girl in a shooting-hut without . . . Still, one mustn't be too hard. After all, one had been young oneself, and these things happened . . . even to young ladies . . . why, one had only got to look at her to see . . . Abeline Vignotte had got wise to it all right, not that it much surprised her. "B it I said, 'No, Abeline, fun and games, perhaps, but . . .' 'Get away with you,' she replied; 'just you look and see how her figure's developing! . . . It's sad, all the same, a girl like that, with the example of Madame Brigitte always before her eyes. . . .' "

Brigitte had decided to do nothing until Madame de Mirbel should have paid her expected visit. But the situation was serious from more than one point of view, and extremely delicate. Monsieur Pian adored Michèle, and it was difficult to foresee the nature of his reactions. I gather from a note-book kept by Monsieur Calou, which is relevant to this incident, that my stepmother had certain scruples (for at this time she searched her conscience with avidity, though never to the point of fanaticism). What troubled her was that she could not disguise from herself the fact that she found considerable pleasure in the thought of a disaster which ought to have brought her nothing but shame and consternation. For was she not as a second mother to Michèle? But faced by a difficulty of this complexion, Brigitte Pian set herself to apply the only solution to which she attached any value. She must conquer her scruples by force of logic, must find some reason which would make her pleasure seem legitimate and fit it into the pattern of her moral perfection.

She was helped, on this occasion, by letting her mind dwell, for the space of a few seconds, upon the alluring prospect of a marriage into the Mirbel family—though such a prospect, it is true, was distant and by no means certain. Given the age of the young man it would have been foolish to attach too much importance to it. Madame Brigitte rejected the temptation without much difficulty, but she gloried, all the same, in her renunciation, and wove it diligently into the mail corslet of her merits. Had she been a worldly woman, she told herself, she would have taken full advantage of a scandal of this kind. But no, she would turn it into a weapon with which to achieve the wretched girl's salvation. That the child should have come as close as she had done to the edge of the abyss was disaster enough, even if she had not actually taken the final plunge into the depths, but a rescue was still possible. The situation should be painted in its true colours. The scales would fall from Monsieur Pian's eyes, and the whole spiritual atmosphere of the house would be transformed. There would be nothing but profit for Michèle in being made to drink this cup of humiliation to the dregs.

Where Michèle was concerned, Madame Brigitte did her utmost to encourage thoughts of mercy in herself, for mercy is a virtue that must not be neglected. How could she help feeling indulgent when she remembered whose daughter the poor child was? The first Madame Pian had been precipitated into outer darkness as the result of a sudden and terrible death over which had hung the only too well founded suspicion of suicide. Brigitte had in her possession a file of documents which only a sentiment of charity had prevented her from opening in the presence of her husband, who insisted on remaining so wilfully blind to the truth. So far she had not done so, in spite of the odious, the actually insulting, comparisons which he allowed himself at times to draw between her and her predecessor. Only the highest kind of virtue—heroic virtue, as God well knew—had kept Brigitte silent. But perhaps the time was coming, was even now at hand, when, for the sake of the girl, she would have to display to the eyes of the outraged father and husband written proofs that the wife whom he mourned had been far from deserving of his tears. But if the papers proved that, they would prove, too, that the foolish rather than blameworthy daughter should be pardoned because of the heavy legacy that lay so crushingly upon her.

In this way did Brigitte Pian colour the pleasure which she savoured in anticipation. She was a logically minded woman who kept to a straight road marked out by clearly labelled principles. She never took a step that she could not immediately justify. Later she would yield to the onset of those obscure anxieties which now she put from her without excessive difficulty, would leave the high-road to beat the undergrowth of guilty motive.

A day was to come when the memory of deeds which could never be undone would prove her torment, when she would recognize in herself for the first time a countenance till then undreamed of and beyond words horrible. But that time was far off. Many were to be her victims before the true vision dawned on her of that love in whose service she thought herself enrolled, but of which, in fact, she was wholly ignorant.

VII

THE only thing that I remember at all vividly about the Comtesse de Mirbel's day at Larjuzon is that Jean appeared to my eyes in an entirely new light. Up till then I had always seen him as the bad boy of the school who knew rather too much about "life" for his age; as the dunce on whom Uncle Adhémar and Monsieur Rausch had to use physical force; as a dangerous sort of chap, albeit he could be kind enough when he liked, almost gentle in fact, in his dealings with me. That was the trouble. I was fond of him but could not respect him. As the result of a logical contradiction which I can't say worried me a great deal, I thought the less of my sister when I knew that she was in love with him. But when his mother was there, Jean seemed a different person. His eyes never left her face except when he glanced round at us to see whether we were sufficiently admiring. Every time the Countess produced a verbal sally, he looked at me with a laugh, as though fearful that I might have missed the point, or might not show myself responsive to wit of so pure a water. From the very moment of their arrival he showed how pleased he was at our surprise on finding that the mother of this great lout of seventeen was both elegant and young. To-day there is nothing particularly miraculous about the preservation of a youthful figure. Examples are to be found everywhere. It is a thing that can be had by all who are willing to pay for it. But at the time of which I am speaking, it was a matter for astonishment to find a mother who still retained the outlines of a young girl. At first, therefore, we were more struck by the apparent youth of the Countess than by her beauty, which, though almost perfect so far as features went, was lacking in brilliance. She was nervous of the sun, and went to as much trouble to avoid it as she would to-day to expose every inch of her body to its rays. The veil in which her face and straw hat was swathed did not, in her opinion, afford sufficient protection, and whenever she had to cross the tiniest patch of sunlight she was most careful to open her elegant parasol. She never so much as half removed her gloves, except at luncheon. In her anxiety to produce a good impression on us she achieved an effect of rather affected simplicity.

When coffee had been served under the trees, Jean took her off for a stroll along the path which made the circuit of the Park, that she might have an opportunity of talking to Michèle. During the short time that they were away the abbé Calou and my parents exchanged a number of acid remarks.

"In her own way she's a very superior sort of person, of course," said my stepmother; "but I need hardly add that it's not a way I particularly like, even judging by worldly standards. Don't you think there's something almost idolatrous about the cult of the body when it's carried to quite such extremes?"

Although at that time she still regarded Monsieur Calou as a good and learned priest, though rather on the simple side and quite without ambition, she held that his judgments were both childish and eccentric. She kept, as she said, "a careful eye" on him, for she regarded it as her privilege to watch over every soutane that came within her orbit.

"The Comtesse de Mirbel," said the priest, "is a lady of letters"—and he gave vent to a guffaw of laughter out of all proportion to the very mild humour of his remark. "Did you know that she has written novels?"

"Has she ever had any of them published?" I asked.

"No," snapped my stepmother in her most sarcastic tone; "she finds it sufficient to live them."

Heavens!—backbiting, and in front of a child too, who might well be scandalized by such a remark. One link—two—started from the carefully wrought armour of her perfection. But almost immediately she set herself to repair the damage. She spoke, she said, without any real knowledge, and regretted that she had not resisted the temptation.

"I give you absolution, Madame," said the abbé Calou.

"There are some things about which a priest ought not to joke," replied Brigitte, frowning portentously.

We could see the Countess in the distance, coming towards us flanked by Michèle and her son. Jean had his face turned towards her as he walked. He was laughing and leaning forward in his anxiety to hear what my sister was saying. He did not see us: the two adored creatures at his side completely blotted us out from his consciousness. I suffered, but there was no jealousy in my suffering. I felt I wanted to cry. Jean was not what we had thought him. He was good, though at times he might give the impression of naughtiness. Brigitte gazed at the group as it moved towards us. The corners of her mouth were drawn slightly downwards: her great face was like a mask, and I could learn nothing from its carefully assumed expression of composure. The abbé Calou, like her, never took his eyes from them. He seemed to be preoccupied and sad. By the time they had come within hearing, an argument had broken out between mother and son.

Jean was begging to be allowed to go back with her to Vallandraut. She shook her head. They must be careful to observe every detail of the arrangements made by Uncle Adhémar. It had been agreed that she should have an early dinner with Jean at the Presbytery, and then go back in the carriage to Vallandraut in time to get early to bed since she had to be up betimes on the morrow. The train left at six, which meant that she would have to be ready at dawn. They must say good-bye at the abbé Calou's.

But Jean would never give up anything on which he had set his heart. His mother's arguments went in at one ear and out at the other. They made no impression on him. Nothing mattered to him except his longing to spend part of the night with her. He had secretly planned to sit up in her room and watch the day break.

"But we're *always* apart: I never see you: and now, when I've *got* a chance, you grudge me an evening—a night."

He was speaking in the obstinate tones I knew so well, and his face had assumed the mulish look which Monsieur Rausch found so exasperating. But his mother was as determined in her refusal as he was in his request. Michèle tactfully left them to themselves. The argument grew noisier. We could hear Madame de Mirbel's last words, uttered with a dry finality.

"I said no, and I mean no. You always ask for more than you are given. You're spoiling the whole day for yourself. No . . . I'll not listen."

She came towards us with a smile. Though it seemed to light up her whole face there was something about it that was strained and tremulous. Jean watched her surreptitiously, a look of defiance in his eye. The Countess, after my stepmother had entertained her with currant syrup and barley water, went back to the carriage, telling her hostess once more how *very* kind she had been, though we got the impression that she was more distant and more preoccupied than she had been when she first arrived. I watched the victoria out of sight. Jean occupied a little let-down seat, and had his back to the horses. He looked obstinate and far from happy, but his face was soon hidden from us by the parasol which the Countess suddenly opened.

What I am now going to relate owes nothing to my imagination, though Jean rarely spoke of it to me. But one whole volume of the abbé Calou's diary is taken up with the details of what happened.

Scarcely had the victoria reached the main road than Jean returned to the attack. At such times he was like a hound on the scent. But it was no good. His mother maintained her refusal with an air of irritated firmness. When she had exhausted all her arguments, she half turned to the abbé Calou, who was looking on in silence.

"You're in charge of Jean: please make him be sensible."

He answered her dryly that to-day he had "transferred his responsibility." To this she replied, with something of insolence in her tone, that now if ever was the time to show that strong hand about which she had heard so much. At this Jean, white with anger, sprang up and, taking advantage of the fact that the horses had slowed down for a hill, jumped from the carriage and narrowly escaped falling under the wheels.

The driver tugged at his reins, the horses reared. By the time the Countess and the priest reached Jean, he had got up. He was unhurt. For a few moments mother and son glared at one another in silence, standing there on the deserted highway. It was an overcast day with occasional bursts of sunlight. The grasshoppers were scraping away at a sort of intermittent prelude. The coachman had the greatest difficulty in holding in his team, and kept slashing with his whip at the horse-flies which were proving troublesome.

"I am forced to agree with your uncle. There's no doing anything with you."

But Jean started to argue again. He hadn't seen her for three months: she had made this trip for his sake, and now she wanted to spoil the one evening that they might have spent together.

"My dear boy," she said, "I promised your uncle, I gave him my word. . . . Next time I will keep a whole night for you . . . and I won't wait until the end of the holidays, either. But we mustn't set your uncle against us. Now, get back into the carriage and sit between us. If that won't be too uncomfortable for *you*," she added, turning to the priest. Then she put her arm round her son. "Snuggle up to me . . . like a baby," she said.

He stopped fighting, gave up the battle. He had surrendered at last! The shadows of the pines grew longer, spanning the road from verge to verge. The abbé Calou turned away his head.

"This is the best time for catching grasshoppers," said Jean; "they come down the trunks when the sun sinks, and start making their noise when they're about a man's height from the ground."

The Countess heaved a sigh of relief. He was talking of other things. He had loosened his grip. When they reached the Presbytery, she told the coachman that it was not worth while taking the horses out, because she was going to start for Vallandraut before eight. But the man would not listen to her. He meant to feed and water his animals. In hot weather like this they needed a rub-down, too. All the Countess could get from him was a promise that he would leave their harness on.

When they sat down to dinner she complained that Madame Pian's too lavish luncheon had made it impossible for her to do honour to Maria's chicken. It was only seven o'clock, and the level light was flooding the small Presbytery dining-room although the blinds were drawn.

"How pleasant it is here!" she said. "Jocelyn's dining-room must have been just like this."[1]

She took scarcely a thing on her plate, and kept glancing towards the kitchen. The service was slow because Maria had no one to help her. More than once the Curé had to get up and go into the kitchen for a dish, but this he did gloomily and with a grudging air. Perhaps he was still upset by what had happened in the carriage. Jean was not surprised that the priest should remain proof against his mother's charms. It was only to be expected. 'They could never get on together,' he thought. And then, she made no effort to conceal her anxiety to be gone. She was aware of this herself, and tried to find some excuse. The coachman, she said, had made her feel nervous: he had the look of a gaol-bird.

"I don't want to be out late on the roads with a man like that."

Jean interrupted her:

"I'll ride back with you, mamma, on my bicycle."

[1] The reference is to Lamartine's novel in verse, "Jocelyn."—TRANSLATOR.

She bit her lip:

"You're *not* going to begin that all over again! You promised me. . . ."

He hung his head. Maria brought in the "pastry" which was her masterpiece.

"You won't taste many better," said the Curé.

The Countess did her best to swallow a few mouthfuls. That was the best she could manage. But she liked making herself popular, and did not want to leave with a feeling that she had disappointed her host. She tried, therefore, to be friendly with him, and gentle to the boy. But the gloom on the Curé's face remained unlightened. As soon as dessert had been served, he left the room in order to read for a short while in his breviary. The Countess realized that he had done this in order to give her an opportunity to be alone with her son before she took her departure. Jean realized it too, and came closer. He could have given a very accurate account of her thoughts at that moment. He knew that she was in a hurry to be off, yet was ashamed to let her anxiety be seen. She forced herself to stroke his hair, but kept on glancing surreptitiously at the clock which hung over the chimney-piece. Jean caught her doing this, and reassured her. "It's fast," he said. She replied eagerly that she could spare him a few more moments. She embarked on some advice, speaking in a rather preoccupied tone of voice. The abbé Calou was quite nice, really. . . . Jean wasn't unhappy, was he?

"No, mamma, no . . . I'm happy . . . honestly I am—very happy," he added with shy warmth.

She did not see the blush that came into his cheeks, nor feel him tremble. The day before he had made up his mind to confide in his mother, hoping she would not laugh, would not mock him, would treat the matter seriously. . . . But he had let the right moment slip, and it was too late now to pour out his feelings. . . . Much better to keep Michèle's name from this last-minute conversation. Thus he argued to himself, but there was another reason which he dared not admit—namely, that it was no use giving himself away to someone whose mind was elsewhere. Many years later, when we were seated by my fire in the Rue Vaneau in Paris, and Jean was telling me about the saddest moments of his life, he could still remember those few minutes of twilight after the stifling day, with himself sitting in the Presbytery dining-room at the side of his adored mother, their knees almost touching, and watching her as she kept on glancing at the clock. Through the glass door he could see the Curé moving up and down in the kitchen garden, intent upon his breviary.

"I'll come back before the end of the holidays, darling: that's a promise. And next time you shall have a whole evening."

He made no reply. She told the coachman to close the hood of the victoria. Jean jumped on the step and touched her neck with his lips.

"Get down! Don't you see he can't hold the horses in? . . ."

A cloud of dust rose and then subsided. Jean waited until the carriage had disappeared round the last bend, and then went back into the garden. He took off his shoes and stockings, fetched a watering-can, and began to water the chicory which he had transplanted the day before. Monsieur Calou said not a word, but went off to the church to make his devotions. When he returned, Jean had gone to bed, and called out "good night" sleepily through the door. The Curé, before himself retiring, went down again to make sure that he had bolted the front entrance. Contrary to his usual custom, he did not leave the key hanging on its nail in the passage, but put it under his pillow. Then, kneeling down beside the bed, he prayed at greater length than on other nights.

Monsieur Calou thought at first that it was the wind that had woken him. It was blowing hard, though the night was fine and moonlight lay along the floor. Somewhere a shutter was banging. Leaning out of the window he saw that it belonged to the room above his own, where Jean slept. The fastening must be broken. He slipped on his soutane, reached the attic landing, and opened Jean's door as quietly as possible, meaning to shut the window. A violent gust overturned a vase filled with heather picked by Michèle, standing on the table. The abbé saw at once that the bed was empty. He waited a few moments to get his breath, then went downstairs and tried the front-door. The bolt had not been drawn, nor the lock forced. The young lunatic must have got out through the window by hanging on to the gutter. The Curé fetched the key from under his pillow and went out.

The night was given over to wind and moonlight. All about the house was a great murmuring of pines. It was not like the intermittent moaning of the sea. No wave, no crash of foam broke the green swell and surge of the trees. He went first to the shed where the two bicycles were kept (he had hired one for his pupil at Vallandraut), and found that only his own was there. At the corner of the house, where the gutter ended, he could see in the sandy soil the marks of a fall. Jean must have jumped from a fair height because the trace of his two heels was clearly defined.

The abbé went back to the shed, took out his bicycle, and then hesitated.

It was almost midnight—too late now to do anything. The worst had happened! What worst? . . . No use letting himself get into a state. Why make a tragedy of the furious midnight scene which was probably taking place in the inn at Vallandraut? What, in any case, had it to do with the Curé of Baluzac? True, he was in charge of the boy, had made himself responsible for him: but the truant would return before morning, and the simplest thing would be to notice nothing. There were some things were better ignored. The really wise man never let himself be forced into the position of having to take disciplinary action which might destroy at a blow all the advantages he had previously gained. . . . But that was precisely the problem! The Curé paced for a while among the currant bushes, pushed open the gate, and gazed down the road which lay empty beneath the moon.

There was no way in which he could be of help to the boy whom he loved so dearly, who, perhaps at that very moment, was receiving a mortal blow. His mother had had good reason for wishing to be left alone at night. Her opposition to Jean had been obstinate, fierce, almost, it had seemed, inspired by hate. The abbé Calou tried to make himself believe that his thoughts were nonsense. . . . But he knew the type too well! The exigence (which Jean had inherited), the frenzy which would not stop, if need be, at trampling a son into the mud. . . . Perhaps, though, he was exaggerating the danger just because he loved Jean so dearly.

It was the first time he had ever become attached to one of his pupils. Since he had begun to specialize in "difficult cases" no such opportunity for affection had come his way. He had not taken on the work because he had to. His brother, a landed proprietor in the Sauterne country, to whom he had surrendered his share of the family estate, sent him each year a sum of money, the amount of which varied according to the state of the harvest, though it was never more than six thousand francs. This, with his stipend and the small sums that came to him from parishioners, was a great deal more than he needed, for he lived off his own poultry and vegetables augmented by occasional gifts from the neighbours.

If, then, he had decided to undertake the training of boys whom their parents could not manage, it had not been from any desire to make money. No, he just spread his nets and patiently waited, never abandoning hope that some day the one wild bird who might really prove worthy of his care would drop plumb into his house. If that should happen, he would make a man of him. He thought he ran a better chance of finding the right one if he confined himself to the unruly. This predilection for "bad lots" was doubtless due to the strain of romanticism which still remained in him, to the heritage which he had brought with him from the Seminary. But it responded, too, to some deeper and more secret yearning, to a desire to help young creatures who might be threatened, who might already have been hurt, by life, who did not care whether they were saved or not, who needed a sponsor at the Father's throne. It was not a matter of virtue so much as of preference and inclination.

Until now he had put up with his charges because he was in love with young life and adolescence. But in every case, so far, the ephemeral charm of youth had overlaid a solid bottom of vulgarity, stupidity and boorishness. A superficial grace often lent a glow to the most ordinary and insensitive little middle-class oaf. In Jean de Mirbel the abbé Calou had found, for the first time, what he had always hoped that God might some day send him. At last a child had come his way who had a soul.

But that soul was hard to reach. Not that it mattered. The abbé Calou was one of those people who, from their earliest days, are vowed to a life of disinterested labour, whose affections ask nothing in return for what they give. The trouble was that Jean would not let himself be loved or protected. Though he had had the boy there under his hand, and just a little watchfulness would have served to make all well, the abbé had not been able to avert the danger of this nocturnal meeting between mother and son. What would happen to Jean when he had left the Presbytery and was at large upon the highways of the world? (for the abbé could not imagine that he would ever be content to vegetate in a country chateau). Even when he had left his roof, the abbé would feel himself still bound by the responsibility which he had undertaken. . . . Where was he now? How follow him? How reach him? Doubtless he would be home before morning. If he were not, the abbé would just go out and look for him. Meanwhile, there was nothing to be done but to make some hot coffee. He went back to the kitchen, and, after opening the shutters to let the moonlight in, lit a few twigs. This done, he sat down in Maria's low chair, took from his pocket a rosary made of olive stones, and stayed there motionless. The moonlight touched the back of his head and shone upon his rough, untended hair. He sat there with his arms resting upon his thighs. The enormous hands, hanging down between his legs, took on a strange, exaggerated significance.

VIII

JEAN had waited to put his plan of escape into action until he heard the sound of the Curé's regular breathing through the floor. The clock had not yet struck eleven when he started off down the moonlit road. The wind was at his back, and he rode without effort in a state of tranquil intoxication, certain now that nothing in the world could keep him from accomplishing what he had set his mind upon. He would see his mother this very night, would watch by her pillow until break of day. He was as sure that this would be so as that one day he would hold Michèle in his arms. Never before had he ridden at dead of night by the light of a moon spun by the wind above an empty world. He felt no nervousness about the result of the coming interview with his mother. In the presence of a third person she had seemed to be the stronger: alone with him she would be at his mercy.

He travelled swiftly and was soon enveloped by the river mist where the road dropped into a hollow, just before it reached the first houses of Vallandraut. At once he lost his self-assurance. He conjured up a picture of the locked and bolted inn. How could he explain his presence there? how manage to have his mother wakened? What excuse could he contrive? Not that it much mattered. He would just say that the thought of not seeing her again had made him ill, and that Monsieur Calou had advised him to take a chance. At dead of night, and in a public inn, his mother could scarcely scold him overmuch, for fear of scandal. He would attack her hard hostility; yes, in the long run, he would soften it. He would not fly into a rage, whatever happened. He would hide his face in her skirt and cry: he would kiss her hands.

He reached the market-square where a few carts with uptilted shafts cast on the ground a shadow as of horned animals. The waning moon shone straight on to the flaking plaster of the Hotel Larrue, picking out the black lettering of a sign that said: "Lodging for Man and Beast." There was still a light in the bar, and he could hear the click of billiard balls. He lent his bicycle against the wall, and asked the plump young woman who was dozing in a chair by the deserted counter for a glass of lemonade. She answered him with an ill grace that it was too late, that the hotel ought, by rights, to be shut, and that no drinks were served after eleven. Then he put to her the question he had long prepared: was the Comtesse de Mirbel staying there? He was the bearer of an urgent message.

"Countess?—what Countess?"

The girl was suspicious and obviously thought that her leg was being pulled. She said that she had other things to do than listen to tall stories, and added that, at his age, he'd be better off at home than wandering the roads.

"But I know there is a lady staying here" (perhaps, he thought, she had not given her name). "A fair lady, wearing a straw hat and a grey tailor-made suit. . . ."

"A fair lady?—wait a moment. . . ." A flicker of intelligence showed in the stupid eye.

"In a tailor-made costume . . ." she went on, "and a spotted veil, and carrying a handsome dressing-case which she left here to be taken care of?"

Jean interrupted her with some impatience: where was her room?

"Her room?—but she's not sleeping here. She only came in to leave her luggage. She's staying at Balauze"—the girl was insistent "she gave me a telegram this morning addressed to the Hotel Garbet, reserving a room."

Jean reflected that Balauze was the county town, and that probably his mother had thought she would be more comfortable at the Garbet than here. But then, why had she told him that she would be sleeping at Vallandraut? He asked how far it was to Balauze. Seven miles? . . . less than an hour's run on his bicycle.

"She meant to sleep at the Garbet," went on the girl, who had suddenly become talkative (and was probably moved by an instinct of hostility towards a lady who had scorned the Hotel Larrue). "But I shouldn't be surprised to hear that she'd spent the night in a ditch. . . ."

Jean became anxious.

"Why? did she have bad horses?"

"Horses!—I like that! She was fetched in a motor-car. The whole town turned out to see the sight. You've no idea the row it made, and what a stink of petrol and oil and dust there was. . . . And it ran over Madame Caffin's chicken, though it's only fair to say that they paid her much more than it was worth. . . . You ought to have seen the gentleman in a pair of goggles that almost covered his face, a regular mask it was, enough to frighten one to death, and a grey dust-coat down to his heels. . . . The things they invent nowadays!"

"Then she's at the Hotel Garbet at Balauze, close to the church?—you're quite sure?"

He thanked her, jumped on his bicycle, and turned right from the Baluzac road. The wind, now, was in his face, and he struggled against its unseen strength, against the hostile power (or was it pity, perhaps, and not hostility that inspired it?) which was doing its best to slow down his approach to Balauze. Had he been with the young Pians he would never have dared confess his weakness, but since he was alone, he dismounted as soon as the road began to rise. In spite of the cool night wind, his face was running with sweat, and his backside was sore. He could think of nothing but how tired he was. For all his boast of manhood, he was still a child about anything that concerned his mother. It would never have occurred to him that she could have any connexion with what he vaguely thought of as human crimes and passions. Both his father and his uncle figured in his imagination as brutes. From his earliest years at La Devize he remembered his father's shrill voice, could see him now, looking like an angry little turkey-cock strutting round his mother where she sat, an image of silent martyrdom. Uncle Adhémar, who had the same kind of voice, had always shown a certain amount of courtesy in his dealings with his sister-in-law. Never, for a moment, had Jean entertained the idea that she might have deserved their hatred. But, for all that, he had scarcely ever spent a whole day with his mother without being made aware that she was not in the least like his private idea of her. He was constantly noticing her lack of warmth, her insincerity. The way she had deceived them all about spending the night at Balauze ought not to have surprised him. At La Devize, as in Paris, where she always stayed with her grandparents, the Mirandieuzes, from January to June, Jean, home for the Easter holidays, had more than once caught her out in a contradiction, for the Countess never bothered to give plausibility to her various lies. She would say, for instance, that she was simply *longing* to go to some play of which everyone was talking, quite forgetful of the fact that she had been one evening the week before ostensibly to see it and, the next day, had given them an enthusiastic, if rather vague, account of its plot. Often and often had Jean, with the terrible logic of childhood, disconcerted her by his never-varying comment—"But mummy, you *said*"—never dreaming of taking her words at other than their face value. What she had said did not always, did not, indeed, very often, agree with the story she was telling then. But she never troubled to think up an explanation. "Did I *really* say that?—you must have dreamed it, darling. . . ." But if ever Jean had been visited by the hint of a suspicion, it did not survive their separation. How should he have dreamed that her soul was less lovely than her face? In his memory of her the idea of sin must ever be a stranger to that serene brow, to the set of her rather too short nose, to those heavy lids veiling eyes that held the colour of the sea ("glaukopis": he had underlined the Greek word in his lexicon), to the thrilling contralto voice, above all, with its occasional hoarseness: that unforgettable voice which casts its spell over me even to-day whenever I go to see the old lady whose hand alone seems to show the ravages of time, for the structure of her face has remained unaltered beneath the flaccid skin, like some marvel of Greek statuary which has survived the centuries, and her eyelids are as the trampled verge of those same green pools with their reflections of sea anemone and weed.

Jean pushed his bicycle up the last hill on the road to Balauze, in no wise worried by what he had heard, but nervous at the thought that the interview between him and his mother would have a witness at the Hotel Garbet. Which of his mother's friends had a motor-car? It must be Raoul . . . for that was how the famous dramatist was known to the Mirandieuzes, who, like all people of fashion, enjoyed being on familiar terms with so well-known a man. He was not in fact called Raoul, but I am not going to set down the real name of a man who was once as celebrated as Donnay, Bernstein or Porto-Riche, though to-day it is entirely forgotten. If nothing now remains of a body of work which was once highly considered, if the very titles of his most famous plays have passed from human memory, it remains true that he once exercised a profound influence on many who are still alive and who, like the Comtesse de Mirbel, are dragging out the fag-end of their existence before taking the final plunge into nothingness.

It would never have occurred to Jean that there could be any bond between his mother and this fat gentleman in his forties. 'She probably thought it would be amusing as well as convenient to do the journey by motor-car,' he reflected. 'But it was not nice of her to deprive me of a treat which I should have enjoyed so enormously. . .'

He rode down a dark, narrow street which debouched on to the Cathedral square with its arcaded pavements. It was empty. He went round it and had some difficulty in making out the hotel which stood in the shadow of the church. It had been contrived from the outbuildings of the former bishop's palace, and only a narrow alley separated it from the Cathedral. The front-door and the entrance to the stable-yard were both closed, and all the shutters were fastened, except on the first floor where two windows seemed to be half open. Should he ring, knock at the door, wake the household in the middle of the night? What excuse could he give? He might ask them to take him in, but he had scarcely any money. . . . Would his mother pay for him? He stood hesitating. Though his mind was innocent of all suspicion, something told him that he had better do nothing of the sort, that it would be wiser to advance no further down the path on which he had so foolishly set his feet. But he couldn't go back to Baluzac: that would be tantamount to admitting that he was beaten, and for nothing in the world would he have done that. He decided to lie down on a sort of low ledge which he could see between two of the buttresses of the Cathedral, and to wait for morning. The alley was so narrow that this meant he would be as good as directly under the windows of the hotel. When his mother came out, he would give her a hug and say nothing at all. She would be so surprised that it would not occur to her to question him. The fact that he had ridden all that distance through the darkness, that, worn out and hungry though he was, he had kept his vigil there just in order to be able to give her one more kiss, would prove how much he loved her. Within these walls she was sleeping now, doubtless on the first floor, behind those unfastened shutters—she always kept her bedroom windows open.

By this time the moon had disappeared behind the apse of the Cathedral, but its diffused light still cast a pallor on the sky, so that only an occasional twinkling star was visible. Jean was cold, and the stones hurt him. He lay down on the grass, but some nettles which he had not noticed stung him, and he got up again with an exclamation of pain. A dog which had been keeping late hours was wakened by the sound and barked, but soon left off again. The hour of cock-crow was still far off. Jean began to think of Michèle, and his thoughts were chaste, no matter what his life may have been. In imagination he held her in his arms, though seeking no other pleasure in the contact than that of finding peace in the nearness of a faithful heart. And all the time, close to him, on the other side of the road, behind the half-closed shutters . . .

Later, he was to know everything about his mother. All this man's affairs were public property, all were marked by the same horrible character. There are many novels that bear, or might bear, the title: "A Woman's Heart"—more than one professional psychologist has plumbed the secrets of the feminine mind. . . . The man who was sharing, to-night, the Comtesse de Mirbel's bed at the Hotel Garbet, lived for no other object than to reduce this mystery to its true and rather squalid proportions. His victims knew precisely what they might expect of him. Those whom he had possessed all bore about with them the same indelible sign—the sign of a lust that could know no satisfaction. They became moral wanderers on the face of the earth, creatures wholly detached from all human responsibility, obsessed by the experiences which they had shared with him. "You don't know yourself," he would whisper to each in turn; "you are ignorant of your potentialities and limitations: you have no idea what perspectives lie before you. . . ." Though he might leave them later, they still retained from their contact with him the rudiments of that dangerous science of bodily pleasure which is more difficult to learn than the virtuous think, since beings who are genuinely perverse are almost as rare in this world as saints. One does not often meet a saint by the roadside, but neither does one often come across anyone capable of dragging from one's vitals that particular kind of groan, that cry expressing horror no less than delight, which becomes sharper as time lays its hand upon a body already threatened by decay, already undermined as much by desire as by age, by the passage of the years, and by passions that can no longer be assuaged. No one has ever written of the torment which old age brings to women of a certain type. In it they taste of Hell before death touches them.

Jean slept for a considerable while, his head resting against the corner made by the wall and the buttress. The discomfort of his cramped position woke him, or, maybe, it was the cold, or perhaps the sound of a man's voice speaking at the window above.

"Come and look. I don't know whether it's the moon or the dawn that makes the sky so pale."

He was speaking to someone in the room behind him, whom Jean could not see. He was standing a little back from the window, with his face turned sideways to it. He wore a dressing-gown of dark-coloured silk.

"Put something on," he added, "the night is chilly."

He leaned his elbows on the bar of the window, and made room beside him for the woman. But he occupied most of the opening, and the white, light figure could barely squeeze between the wall and his powerful torso.

"What a wonderful sense of loneliness!—how still it is. . . . No, darling, I'm not cold."

"But you must be: throw my overcoat round your shoulders."

She disappeared and came back wearing a man's ulster. It made her body look larger and her head very small. The two of them remained there for a long time without speaking.

"How unimportant it makes one feel," said the man. "Do you think that the people now asleep in all these houses have ever seen one of my plays?—that they so much as know my name?"

"They've probably read them in *l'Illustration*."

"That's true," he said more cheerfully; "the Supplement to *l'Illustration* goes everywhere. . . . They must have seen it, if only at the hairdresser's. . . . What a stage-set this square would make, eh? But the open air's not really my line. The stuff I write needs four walls."

She made her answer in a low voice, choking back a little laugh. He, too, laughed, and added:

"With one of the four walls cut away. That's what a play ought to be, the masterpiece of which I dream. . . ."

"And with no dialogue: isn't that what you're thinking?"

They whispered. Jean could hear nothing but the throbbing of the blood in his own ears.

One o'clock sounded.

"No, no . . . really, we must get some sleep."

Once again there was the sound of a choked-back laugh. The woman leaned her head against the shoulder at her side. Jean looked at the gable that crowned the front of the building. The door of the stable-yard must be very old. A horseshoe was nailed to one of its sides. He read: *Hotel Garbet. Weddings and Banquets Catered For.* He compared in his imagination the man standing at the window, every note of whose voice he recognized, with the middle-aged individual with the dyed hair combed across a bald, white pate, whom the Mirandieuzes knew as Raoul. The comfort which a child seeks instinctively deep down within itself when threatened by some terrible pain, he now expressed out loud. "It's comic!" he said in mocking tones; "it really is . . . just too comic!" And then: "All right, my fine lady!" He heard the faint sound made by the window being closed. "Oh, well, I suppose it amuses you, and it doesn't do anyone any harm. . . ." And suddenly he was seized with panic at the idea that he might be discovered, might have to listen to her explanations. How awful! He had a sudden vision of his mother's face, could see her look of shame, could hear her stammered words. . . . He jumped on to his bicycle, crossed the square, unconscious at first of his fatigue, so happy was he at the idea of increasing the distance between himself and that room at Balauze. But at the first hill his legs felt weak. He dismounted, dragged his bicycle to a nearby mill, dropped into some hay, and lost consciousness.

How hot it was in the hay! He felt as though he were on fire in spite of the cold dawn wind. His head ached. That must be a lark singing there above him in the mist. Close by his ear a hen and her brood were scratching the earth and clucking. He tried to get up. He was shivering. 'I'm feverish,' he told himself. He took his bicycle and tried to resume his journey. About a hundred yards further on, at the crossing where a road led off to Uzeste, a pine-branch over a door announced an ale-house. With great difficulty he reached it and ordered some hot coffee. An old woman looked at him curiously, muttering something in the local dialect. The sun was hot upon the seat beside the door on to which he dropped. What if the motor-car suddenly appeared? But no, they would get up late. They had the whole day before them, the dirty beasts! . . . Because they *were* dirty beasts . . . not because they were lovers, but because they were so horribly mincing and affected. . . . Well, that was the last time he'd make a fool of himself . . . for anyone. Everyone slept with everyone else: that was what life was. With whom did Uncle sleep? and Monsieur Rausch? and Monsieur Calou? . . . It'd be fun to see the old Curé on the job. He'd ask them, all of them . . . that's to say, if he didn't die before he got the chance.

He moistened his lips with the coffee, swallowed a few mouthfuls, and then turned round and was sick. He leaned his head against the wall and closed his eyes. He no longer had sufficient energy even to brush the flies away from his burning face. A bicycle passed and slowed down. He heard an exclamation, and then the sound of his own name repeated several times. The huge, anxious face of Monsieur Calou was close to his own. If he made an effort perhaps he would be able to understand and answer. But the Curé was there; so why struggle any more? why not just let himself go? He felt himself lifted like a little child, put into a bed in a dark room which smelled of manure. Monsieur Calou wrapped him in his old black cloak, after which he had a long argument with the landlord, who didn't want to hire him his cart because it was market-day at Balauze. "I don't care how much you charge," said Monsieur Calou in an impatient voice. At last came the clip-clop of a horse on the cobbles of the yard. Some straw had been laid in the cart. Jean was asleep when the Curé lifted him, and his head bumped against the old man's shoulder. The priest laid him in the straw and covered him with his cloak. He took off the knitted jersey which he had put on under his soutane in the chill of the dawn, and rolled it up under the boy's head.

The attack of pleurisy was serious. For a fortnight Jean was in danger. The Papal Zouave spent forty-eight hours at the Presbytery and agreed with Monsieur Calou that it would be better not to say anything to the Countess. If she were told that the boy had a bad attack of bronchitis she wouldn't worry. Mountain treatment was not then in vogue, and was only very rarely prescribed. The doctor summoned from Bordeaux said that the smell of pines was the best possible thing in such cases, and advised the Colonel to accept Monsieur Calou's offer. The Curé had undertaken to coach the boy for his examination, and to get him through in two years without any danger of overworking him. But what ultimately decided the Papal Zouave was his dislike of the idea of sending his nephew back to a school which had recently been dishonoured by "the scandal of Monsieur Puybaraud's marriage."

The evening on which it was decided to leave Jean at Baluzac, the Curé wished ardently that God was still incarnate, so that he might have kissed His hands and embraced His feet in token of gratitude. Jean maintained a hostile silence, and never opened his mouth except to ask for what he wanted in a hard, overweening tone. Monsieur Calou knew nothing about what had happened at Balauze, but he could see that the boy had suffered a terrible shock. How the wound had been inflicted, and with what weapon, he would learn later. Or perhaps he wouldn't. It did not matter. What mattered was to prevent the infection from spreading. At dusk he sat by the dozing boy and asked him whether he didn't dread a winter spent at Baluzac. Jean replied that anything was better than Monsieur Rausch, but that he was sorry he couldn't "bash his face in," as he had meant to do.

The Curé pretended to think he was joking. "Just you wait till you see what a lovely blaze I get going when we're working and reading in the evenings. We'll take notes and drink walnut juice, while the west wind roars in the pines and flings rain against the shutters. . . ."

In a voice quite unlike his own, Jean said that "there wouldn't be much love knocking around."

Monsieur Calou replied very gently that what was important was to love in one's heart.

"You don't say so!" (the voice was still the voice of another, of a stranger).

Without showing any sign that he was put out by this reply, the Curé returned the rosary to the pocket of his soutane, took out his pipe, and set to sniffing it (he wouldn't let himself smoke in Jean's room).

"I'm an old man," he said, "and I've found my way into port."

"Oh, of course: God and all that. You needn't tell me."

The priest got up and laid his hand on Jean's forehead.

"Yes, God first, last, and all the time, naturally."

It was as though he had a son of his own, a naughty son, or rather, a son who would have liked to be naughty, but *his* for all that.

Jean threw himself back on his pillow and exclaimed:

"Don't go getting ideas. If you want to know, I loathe and detest everything you stand for!"

"You'll make your fever worse," said the Curé.

How terribly the poor boy was suffering! 'He takes it out of me because I happen to be at hand and there's no one else he can snap at. . . .' The abbé sat plunged in thought, his elbows on his knees, deliberately keeping his face in shadow because Jean, from the depths of his pillows, was trying to see the effect of his outburst. But even if the lamp had been shining full on it, the sick boy would have seen nothing, so empty of expression was it. Suddenly he felt ashamed of what he had said.

"I didn't mean that as an attack on you," he muttered, and hung his head.

Monsieur Calou shrugged his shoulders.

"Much better to get it off your chest. . . . Very soon, you know, you'll be able to have visitors."

"I don't know anyone."

"What about the Pians?"

"They haven't come near me: they haven't even written."

"They've sent over every day for news."

"But they haven't come," Jean said again, and turned his face to the wall.

One of our farmers who lived at Baluzac and brought us milk every morning, did, in fact, give us news of Jean. But the Curé was surprised that we hadn't made any more definite sign of life. He was pretty sure that Mirbel felt hurt by this neglect, though he could not know how deeply wounded he had been by our seeming indifference. The Curé of Baluzac, however, firmly convinced that "that Brigitte woman" was behind it all, made up his mind to go over to Larjuzon as soon as his patient was a little better, and have it out with her.

IX

AT Larjuzon the postman always arrived while the family was gathered round the breakfast table. My stepmother, whether she had come back from Mass or had only just emerged from her room, was invariably, even at this early hour, dressed and buttoned up to the neck with formal precision. The morning on which I read out the letter from Monsieur Calou announcing Mirbel's illness she was in one of her bad moods. Her face was set and hard, and she was frowning. At eleven o'clock she was due to take a Confirmation class in its catechism, and, to judge by the way she spoke of the children, they were, without exception, stupid, incapable of learning anything, and interested only in pinching one another's behinds. In addition to which they were dirty, given to making grubby marks on the floor, and they smelt. As to the least sign of gratitude—well, one might wear oneself to the bone for them and not get so much as a word of thanks. If their parents only got the chance, they would think nothing of looting the house and murdering everyone in it.

We knew that on these catechism days the least shock was enough to set a spark to that inflammable temperament with which Heaven had seen fit to endow Madame Brigitte.

"We must go over to Baluzac at once!" cried Michèle, as soon as I had come to the end of the letter; "and I'm not dressed yet."

My stepmother's voice broke in on a high note:

"Am I to understand that you are proposing to go over to Baluzac this morning?"

"Of course I am!"

"I forbid it!"

"Why shouldn't I go this morning?"

"You'll go neither this morning nor this afternoon!" snapped Madame Brigitte, white with anger.

We looked at one another dumbfounded. Strained though her relations with my sister were, she had always, till now, avoided an open breach.

"What's the matter with you?" replied Michèle, stung to insolence. "There's no reason why I should wait until to-morrow."

"Nor to-morrow either. You're never going to Baluzac again!" said my stepmother. "And don't look as though you'd no idea what I mean, you little hypocrite!"

My father glanced up nervously from his newspaper.

"Brigitte, dear, what are you in such a state about?"

"I ought to have asserted myself sooner" (her voice had become solemn).

Michèle asked of what it was she was being accused.

"I am accusing you of nothing. I never believe evil of anyone until I see it with my own eyes."

My father got up. He was wearing an old brown dressing-gown. A few tufts of grey hair showed through the unbuttoned collar of his shirt.

"All the same, you seem . . ."

She fixed upon her husband a look of angelic patience.

"It hurts me to hurt you: but it is necessary that you should know the truth. I am told that she is in the habit of meeting young Mirbel behind Du Buch's mill."

Michèle replied in a firm voice that it was perfectly true that she did sometimes meet Jean. What harm was there in that?

"Don't look so innocent: it ill becomes you. You have been seen."

"*What* has been seen? There was nothing *to* see."

My father drew her tenderly to him. "Of course there is no harm in your meeting young Mirbel at Monsieur Du Buch's mill. But though you are still only a child, you look older, and the people of this town, especially the women, are a lot of poisonous snakes."

Brigitte cut him short.

"Poisonous snakes, indeed! . . . Don't you go taking Michèle's part against me! I am interfering now, before it is too late, simply and solely in order to protect her from idle gossip—though I am prepared to admit that it may have no foundation. Young Mirbel is a bad lot. May God forgive me for ever having had him in the house!" In a lower voice, she added: "The important question is, how far has it gone?"

She had become very gentle all of a sudden. My father took hold of her by the wrist.

"Come on now, out with it! What *is* all this nonsense?"

"It's . . . let me go!" she exclaimed. "You seem to forget who I am! . . . If you want the truth you shall have it."

She was furious, and moved back to the other side of the table where, entrenched behind the china and the silver, she stood with her hands on the back of a chair. Her eyes were closed, and, under cover of their veined lids, she seemed to be concentrating her thoughts.

"Michèle is a young girl who is in love with a young man. There you have it in a nutshell."

In the silence which followed these words we none of us dared to exchange a glance. Madame Brigitte, suddenly sobered, fixed her eyes with a look of pain on father and daughter.

Octave Pian had risen. He looked very tall, and more as I remembered him before mamma's death. He had been wounded in his tenderest feelings—the affection of a father for his daughter, in which respect plays a large part, as well as a modesty so sensitive that the least affront to it is unforgivable. He had been jerked out of his normal mood of black gloom, and the memory of his dead wife had, for the moment, been driven from his mind by the presence of that other woman who was so terribly real, so horribly alive.

"A child who is not yet fifteen?—how ridiculous to talk like that! You ought to be ashamed of yourself!"

"Ashamed of what? I am not accusing her of anything," replied my stepmother with an obvious effort at self-control. "I want to believe that she is innocent—or comparatively so: I said it before, and I say it again."

But girl-mothers of fourteen and fifteen *had* been known. It was only necessary to visit the poor to realize that!

I can still hear the sound of her voice as she pronounced the words "girl-mothers." Never had two words contained such a concentrated accent of disgust. In a low voice I asked Michèle what girl-mothers were. She said nothing (perhaps she did not know). With her eyes fixed on her father she said:

"You don't believe her, do you?"

"Of course I don't, my dear, dear child!" and he drew her to him again.

"Do you wish me to produce her accusers?" asked my stepmother; "the people who say that they saw her with their own eyes?"

"Yes, produce them!" cried the girl.

"I can make a pretty shrewd guess: it's the Vignottes," said my father, suddenly quite calm. "We all know what the Vignottes are like! . . . So you're ready to swallow the tittle-tattle of a pair like that, are you?"

"Who says that I'm *ready* to do anything of the sort? As I said before, I am accusing no one. I am performing a painful duty. I am repeating something that was told me—no more. It is your duty to satisfy yourself whether it is true. *My* task finishes where yours begins."

Brigitte Pian folded her arms. She stood there, impartial, invulnerable, justified in the sight of God and all His angels.

"And what, may I ask, do the Vignottes say that Michèle was doing?"

"You must ask them that yourself. You can hardly expect me to soil my lips. . . . It is bad enough to have to listen to such things. But if it is absolutely necessary, if you insist on my being present, I will find the needful courage in that love which I have vowed to all of you, and especially to *you*, Michèle. . . . Oh, you can laugh if you like! But I have never loved you so fondly as at this moment."

A few tears started to her eyes. She was careful to wipe them away only when she was sure that we were looking.

My father, without the slightest show of heat, told me to go and fetch the Vignottes.

Vignotte came in holding his béret in his hand. His right eye, which had received a charge of slugs out shooting, was closed. The other had a sort of look of concentrated stupidity. Round his mouth with its few stumps of decayed teeth was a growth of untrimmed beard. He was bandy-legged. He had left his wooden clogs in the hall, and padded through the half-open door, his feet encased in list slippers which flapped as he walked. No one had heard him enter. We just turned our heads, and there he was, obsequious, grinning, stinking of sweat and garlic.

He realized what was in the wind as soon as he had crossed the threshold. My father ordered me out of the room, and told Michèle, very gently, to go upstairs and wait until she was summoned. I went to the drawing-room, but stayed near the door in a state of considerable excitement. My chief sensation, I remember, was one of rather shamefaced hope. Michèle and Jean were going to be separated. My function would be to act as the link between them. They would be able to communicate only when *I* was willing, and under *my* supervision. I had no very clear idea of all this: I just felt it, sensed it with extreme vividness. I had run like a mad creature to find Vignotte, and had hurried back with him. Though haste was no part of that prudent man's make-up, I had made him follow me at once without giving him time even to put on his "overthings" (as he called his jacket). Now I could hear him through the door.

"I never said no such thing. . . . I sees what I sees. . . . Not but what I was in that there 'ut all right. . . . I can't tell 'ow long *they'd* been there not saying a thing . . . and what was they doin', all silent like? That's what I asks meself. . . . Didn't 'ave to use my eyes to know as they was there. . . . S'pose they was just *lookin'*. . . . Well, I only 'opes they was. . . . Though it don't matter to me."

My father asked some questions which I could not properly hear. He did not raise his voice, but spoke in his normal slow drawl. Every now and then he used some word of local dialect, stressing it in an odd sort of way. Those parts of his talk I understood better than the rest. He had become once more the master who has no need to shout, who can make himself feared by the turn of an inflexion. He interrupted my stepmother, cutting her short in the middle of a sentence.

"Let me finish what I have to say to Vignotte."

It was not an argument, not even a discussion, but a summing-up. When my father had finished speaking, I heard no more save the trumpeting sound made by Vignotte when he blew his nose. Then my stepmother opened the door, and I had only just time to get out of the way. She never so much as glanced at me. With her garden hat stuck well at the back of her head, her hands concealed in white mittens, she reached the hall, took a parasol and went down the front steps, looking not so much angry as plunged in thought. I learned shortly afterwards from my sister that our father had just shown some of the firmness which had marked him in the old days, but which we children had quite forgotten.

He had apparently given in to his wife to the extent of forbidding Michèle, not only to go to Baluzac, but to exchange letters with Jean. I was staggered to learn that this ruling was to apply to me as well. As a safeguard against its possible violation, our father confiscated our bicycles for the time being. Sister Scholastique, the Superior of the Free School, who was under a sense of considerable obligation to my parents, was to be asked to superintend Michèle's studies during the holidays, when she would have a certain amount of time at her disposal. Actually, my father did not suspect his young daughter, and told her as much, kissing her tenderly. But he knew how merciless the people round Larjuzon could be, and wished to protect her against possible gossip. The whole affair, therefore, would have represented a victory for Madame Brigitte, had it not been for the fact that my father had told the Vignottes that they had better look out for another place. This decision struck directly at their patroness. She argued, but in vain, that her husband was running considerable risks by making enemies of such people, armed as they were. But my father assured her that he had a hold over the Vignottes and could find ways and means of stopping their mouths.

This scandal, then, which was destined to have serious consequences for so many of us, did, at least, produce one happy result, though it was, unfortunately, of short duration. It roused our father from the state of apathy in which he had been living for the past ten years. Brigitte suddenly saw herself opposed by an adversary with whom she had long ceased to reckon. Her husband's love for Michèle derived from the passion he had felt for the first Madame Pian. The real struggle was being fought over a dead woman's body. This, no doubt, my stepmother knew perfectly well—which explains her behaviour during the days that followed.

In every circumstance of her life Brigitte Pian was sincerely anxious to do good. Or that, at least, was what she believed. That fact must never for a moment be forgotten by readers of this chronicle. I could have painted quite a different portrait of her than the one on which so pitiless a light is shed in these pages. I was made too clearly aware of her victims' sufferings to be altogether fair to her. But I feel that even when recounting what may seem to be some of her blackest acts, I ought not to yield to the too easy temptation of showing one side only of her forbidding character.

It is important to remember that when, before her marriage, Brigitte Pian used to spend the summer months at Larjuzon, she found herself involved in one of those marital dramas which may well go on, quite silently, for years without any violent arguments or outbursts of nagging, until one or other of the actors is safely dead. My father had always before his eyes the vision of his dearly loved wife, Marthe. He had known that she was suffering because of someone else, had realized that he could do nothing to help, and had seen that the spectacle of his own pain merely had the effect of making her own sense of remorse the more acute. He was a simple man, not much given to introspection, and he had found comfort in Brigitte's clear-sighted analysis of the situation. A close tie had grown up between them. But when the circumstances in which it had had its origins no longer existed, it inevitably grew slack. Brigitte always claimed that she had saved him from suicide. However that may be, it cannot be denied that, when things were at their worst, he did relieve his feelings by confiding in an affectionate companion who had never been far from him, had even guided his footsteps, during the most terrible moments of his ordeal. In her, too, he had found the only means he had of communicating with his wife, whose cousin and childhood friend she was.

But when Brigitte Pian became he second Madame Pian, she quite honestly felt it to be her duty tot finish the good work she had begun by delivering her husband from the obsessive influence of the dead—all the more so, since he had consented to this second marriage only in the hope that some such cure might result from it. Possibly, at some later date, her actions were dictated by a sense of personal grievance, by feelings of jealousy which she would not admit even to herself. But at first she had a perfect right to believe in a mission to which no less a person than her husband had called her. When, after a few months, she realized that the influence of Marthe was still in the ascendant, that my father still believed that her virtue, in spite of all temptations forced upon her by an overwhelming passion, had never, never yielded, that the dead woman was still in his eyes a heroine who might have died for love but would never have been false to her plighted word, Brigitte thought it incumbent on her to make sure that this halo of sanctity had been truly merited. If only she could confront her husband with definite proof that the first Madame Pian had been guilty of adultery, that she had assumed the appearance of virtue only after her lover had abandoned her, and had finally taken her own life in an access of despair, then, and then only, she thought, would he be freed from the shameful spell. For a long while before any real evidence came her way, she had felt quite sure, as a result of what she had heard, that Marthe had, in fact, been guilty. Maybe her ardent desire to step into her shoes was, in some sort, influenced by her wish to discover this evidence. She knew that it would be easier to find once she was free to come and go as she chose through all the rooms of the house, and to rummage in desks and drawers unseen by others.

This she did with a pleasure that one finds it difficult to credit. A very few weeks after her marriage she laid hands on a document which so far exceeded her wildest hopes that she thought it better, for the time being, to say nothing about it. This reluctance to make use of so tremendous a weapon shows that Brigitte was capable of pity. So long as any hope remained of effecting her husband's cure without opening his eyes, she resisted the temptation of telling what she knew.

Once the Vignottes had gone, it did seem as though, perhaps, he might be cured. Defeated on that issue, Brigitte got full satisfaction on every other. She could not but applaud a decision which my father took a few days later. From the beginning of the following term, Michèle was to go as a boarder to the Ladies of the Sacred Heart, whose school she had hitherto been attending as a day-girl. (Octave Pian did not look on this as a punishment, but only as the best way of ensuring that his young daughter would be removed from the influence of her formidable stepmother.)

Madame Brigitte ought now to have declared herself satisfied. But she was far from feeling so. In defending his daughter, her father had, in reality, been defending his dead wife. His sudden return to the world of action had put the coping-stone, not on Brigitte's victory, but on Marthe's; had proved that he was still possessed, mind and soul, by the image of the dead woman. That, I have very little doubt, was the truth which my stepmother glimpsed in the dark recesses of her conscience, and it urged her to spring the mine which had been lying so long concealed, which, for so many months, she had refrained from detonating.

My sister and I were still, however, very closely watched. Unfortunately for us, the local postmistress was completely under Madame Brigitte's thumb, and must have received very precise instructions on the subject of our letters. Everything at Larjuzon intended for the post had to be put in the study each evening, to be collected next morning by the postman. Not an envelope could leave the house without our stepmother knowing all about it.

Michèle, therefore, had to rely on me for getting messages to Jean. She had no wish to break the promise made to our father that she would not write to him, but she badly wanted to send him a little gold locket, made in the shape of a heart, which she wore on her breast. In contained a piece of our mother's hair. I was shocked that she should give away such a relic to Mirbel, and showed no very great enthusiasm about making on foot a journey which would be all the longer and more tiring since I should have to go a roundabout way if I was to avoid being seen in the town and promptly denounced. Besides, so prolonged an absence would have aroused the suspicions of Madame Brigitte, who was keeping a more than usually watchful eye on me, though without any appearance of ill-will. At times she would give me a hug, would stroke the hair back from my forehead, would murmur, "my poor child!" and heave a deep sigh.

The more insistent Michèle became, the more clearly did I show my dislike of undertaking such an adventure. And so it came about that the last weeks of the holidays were spoiled by a series of fruitless arguments. I was deprived of the fun of long days spent with my sister, free of any third person to spoil our intimacy. I had so looked forward to them. As for Mirbel, I should see him again, I thought, when term began, for I did not then know that he was to spend the rest of the year at Baluzac. The fate awaiting me—the worst I could possibly have imagined—remained hidden. At school it was my pleasure to feel that I had to share Mirbel with nobody else. To be sure, it was as Michèle's brother that I should find favour in his eyes. But at least they would not be seeing one another, and would have no means of communicating, while I should always be at hand, the only one among all that tribe of boys whom he would deign to recognize.

One September day, about four o'clock, a priest riding a bicycle turned into the Avenue. Michèle cried: "The abbé Calou!" Brigitte Pian told us to go to our room, and, when Michèle began to protest, she was backed up firmly by our father. On this occasion, too, he stayed where he was, though as a rule, whenever a visitor was announced, he hid himself in the study. I am pretty sure that he wanted to make certain that his wife would say nothing about Michèle beyond what it had been agreed between them should be said. Since I was not present at the interview, I will here reproduce the notes which Monsieur Calou jotted down the same evening in his diary. I give them, succinct and dry, precisely as I found them.

"An extraordinary woman—quite a miracle of perversity. In her eyes the appearance of evil is as important as evil itself—when it suits her purpose. A deep nature, but she reminds me of those aquariums in which the spectator can see the fish from every side. Each one of Madame Brigitte's most secret motives, the intention lying behind her every act, is plainly visible. If ever that gift of judgment and condemnation which she now exercises at the expense of others is turned against herself, she's in for a bad time!

Much shocked that I should plead the case of these young people, and should anticipate nothing but good for Jean from this first love affair. She pursed her lips at me. Obviously thinks me a second 'Vicaire Savoyard.' I ventured to warn her against being over zealous in her desire to act as the mouthpiece of the Divine Will. It is a fault to which pious persons are only too prone. But how unwise of me to include the clergy in my criticism! It was just asking her to hit back at me with some comment about my denying the rights of the Church to instruct its children! She's quite capable of denouncing me to the Archbishop—I can see her doing it! She's not so much concerned to find out what I think as to remember enough of what I *say* to incriminate me with the authorities. She would have no hesitation about ruining me if she thought it necessary to do so. I said as much, and though my attitude, when I took my leave, was respectful enough, hers was decidedly dry—not to say rude.

Just as I reached the door on the way out, Michèle emerged from behind the bushes. She was very flushed and wouldn't look me in the face. When I got to the bottom of the steps, she said:

'Do you believe what they told you?'

'No, Michèle, I don't.'

'I should like you to know that . . . if I were making my confession to you . . . I should have nothing to say about Jean.'

She was crying. I just stammered out—'God bless the two of you!'

'Tell him that I can't see him or write to him, that I'm going to be a boarder from the beginning of next term. I shall be closely watched. Can't you imagine the instructions that will be given about me? . . . But, please tell Jean that I'll wait just as long as is necessary. . . . You will, won't you?'

I tried to turn the whole thing into a joke. 'That's an odd sort of mission to give to an old priest, Michèle,' I said.

'I don't care whether you're an old priest or not. Except for me, you're the only person in the whole world who loves him.' She said this as though it were the most natural, the simplest, the most obvious thing that could be imagined. There was nothing I could say in reply. I had to turn my head away. Then she held out a little parcel addressed to him.

'I swore not to write to him, but I didn't say anything about not giving him a little remembrance. Tell him it's the most precious thing I have. I want him to keep it until we meet again. Tell him . . .'

She made a sign to me to go, and jumped back into the bushes. Sister Scholastique's coif appeared between the trees. . . ."

The abbé Calou found Jean just where he had left him, lying on a chaise-longue under the west wall of the house. A book was open on his knees, but he was not reading.

"Well, *you've* started a hornet's nest at Larjuzon, my poor boy."

"Have you just come from Larjuzon?" Mirbel tried, though in vain, to assume a detached and indifferent expression.

"Yes. That Brigitte woman is up to her old tricks again. Just imagine, Michèle . . ."

At the Curé's first words Jean could contain himself no longer:

"She ought to have sent me an answer," he burst out. "When one's in love, walls don't mean a thing. One takes any risk. . . ."

"She's only a little girl, Jean . . . though I've never met a braver one."

Without looking at Monsieur Calou, the boy asked whether he had spoken to her.

"Yes, for a few minutes. I've remembered everything she asked me to tell you. She can't see you or write to you: from the beginning of next term she's going as a boarder to the school of the Sacred Heart. But she will wait—for years, if necessary."

He spoke like someone repeating a lesson learned by heart. In this way he gave the maximum weight to each word.

"Is that all?"

"No, she asked me to give you this . . . it is her most sacred possession, and she wants you to keep it until you see her again."

"What is it?"

The Curé did not know. He laid the little object on Jean's knees and went into the house. Through the half-open shutters he could see the boy holding the little golden heart at the end of its chain in the hollow of his hand. He raised it to his lips as though he would drink it down like a draught of water.

Monsieur Calou sat down at his desk, opened the manuscript of *Descartes, and the Theory of Faith*, and read over the last paragraph he had written. But he could not concentrate, and went back to the window. Mirbel's face was hidden in his two hands. No doubt the locket lay there, imprisoned between them and his lips.

For the past two days Jean had been taking his midday and evening meal in the dining-room. About seven o'clock, once more shut away in his old black mood of silence, he sat down at table opposite the Curé. (Monsieur Calou had taken to keeping a magazine or a newspaper beside him while he ate.) It was obvious from the moment the soup was brought in that the boy was shooting covert glances at his host. If he still maintained silence, that was because he was shy and embarrassed and did not know how to start on what he wanted to say. Nor was the Curé wholly at ease. He was afraid that a clumsy word might ruin all. He confined himself, as always, therefore, to keeping a watchful eye on Jean's rather capricious appetite. When, after the meal, they went out into the garden, he asked him what he would like to eat next day. Jean replied that there was nothing he had particularly set his heart on, but he spoke with rather less ill grace than usual. Suddenly he asked a question:

"Are you really bothered about my health?"

"My dear boy, what a question!"

Murmuring, "No, honestly, I mean it," in a childlike tone, Jean sat down in his chaise-longue and took the abbé's hand. The latter was still standing. Without looking at him, Jean said:

"I've been pretty beastly to you . . . and then . . . you went and did a thing like that for me."

He started to cry, as a child cries, making no attempt to hide his tears.

The abbé Calou sat down beside him. He had not withdrawn his hand.

"You can't know what it means. . . . If Michèle had given me up, I should have killed myself. I suppose you don't believe that?"

"Yes, my boy, I do."

"Honour bright?"

He longed to be reassured, to have his word believed.

"I knew from the very first that this was serious."

But when Jean murmured in a low voice—"Was I dreaming? Did I really see what I thought I saw, at Balauze?"—the abbé interrupted him:

"Don't tell me anything if it's going to hurt you too much."

"She lied to us. Do you realize that? It was all my eye about her sleeping at Vallandraut. . . . They had booked a room at Balauze, at the Garbet. . . ."

"It is the way of women to say one thing and do another . . . it's a well-known fact. . . ."

"She wasn't alone . . . there was a fellow with her. I saw them at the window of their room, in the middle of the night."

He had seen them, and his staring eyes could see them still.

Monsieur Calou took his head between his hands and shook it gently, as though to wake him.

"It's no use trying to force one's way into other people's lives, if they don't want one there: remember that, my boy. Never push open the door of another person's life, for it can be known only to God. Never turn your eyes upon that secret city, that place of damnation, which is the soul of another, unless you wish to be turned into a pillar of salt. . . ."

But Jean still went on, his gaze fixed on some invisible picture. He described what he could still see by the light of memory, what he would go on seeing until his dying day:

"He was almost an old man. . . . I recognized him—a chap from Paris who writes plays. . . . Dyed hair, a paunch . . . and . . . and . . . that mouth. . . . Oh, it was horrible!"

"You must tell yourself that in her eyes he represents wit, genius, elegance. To love another person means to see a miracle of beauty which is invisible to the rest of the world." A moment later, he added: "We must go in. It soon gets dark at this time of year, and you haven't got enough on."

Mirbel followed him without protesting. The abbé held him by the arm until they reached the library where the boy was now sleeping. Jean lay down on the bed. Monsieur Calou lit the lamp and went over to his armchair.

"And did they," he asked, "see you?"

"No, I was standing against the wall of the church, hidden in the shadow. I had gone before it was light. I slept in a mill. If you hadn't searched for me I believe I should have died like a sick dog. When I think of all you have done for me . . ."

"You could hardly expect me to sit here with my slippers on waiting for you to come back, could you? You are in my charge, and I am responsible for your welfare. Think of the trouble I should have got into. . . ."

"That wasn't the reason, was it?—not the only reason?"

"Little silly!"

"Because you do like me, don't you—just a bit?"

"As if there were no one else but an old curé to care for Jean de Mirbel!"

"I don't believe it's possible: it can't be!"

"Look at that golden heart . . . where have you put it? Ah, hung it round your neck, as she used to hang it round hers . . . against your heart. That's the right place for it: like that, you can always feel it. When things get bad you've only got to touch it."

"But she's such a little girl. She doesn't know me, anything about me. She's so pure that she wouldn't understand me, no matter how hard I tried to explain. Even you don't know some of the things I've done. . . ."

Monsieur Calou laid his hand on the boy's head.

"You're not one of the virtuous, I know. You're not of that kind. . . . You are one of those whom Christ came into the world to save. Michèle loves you for what you are, just as God loves you because you are as He made you."

"Mamma doesn't love me."

"Passion blinds her to the love she has for you in her heart . . . but it exists all the same."

"I hate her!"

This he said in the rather forced and artificial voice which he sometimes affected:

"You think I don't mean it. But it's true: I hate her!"

"Of course you do, as we all of us *can* hate those we love. Our Lord told us to love our enemies. It is often easier to do that than not to hate those we love."

"Yes," said Jean, "because they can hurt us so frightfully."

He leaned his head against the Curé's shoulder, and went on in a low voice:

"If only you knew how terribly it hurt, and still does. It's as though I were touching an open sore. It hurts so much that I want to shriek—to die!"

"My poor child—we must forgive women a great deal. . . . I can't yet explain to you why. Perhaps you will understand later: I think you will, because you have it in you to hurt them too. Even those among them who seem to have everything they want deserve our pity . . . not a corrupt and furtive pity, but the pity of Christ, the pity of a man and of a God who knows well from what imperfect clay He has made His creatures. But this is not the time to speak of such things."

"I'm no longer a child. You must realize that."

"I do realize it: you are a man. You have reached the age at which suffering begins."

"Ah, *you* can understand!"

They went on talking for a long time, the priest and the boy, even after Jean had gone to bed. And when weariness lay heavy on his eyes, he asked Monsieur Calou to say his prayers beside him there, and not to leave the room until he was asleep.

X

THE crowing of a cock woke me. Was it dawn already? I struck a match: it was not yet five. I decided to wait a bit. Though Michèle had never succeeded in making me promise to take that journey to Baluzac, I had made up my mind to go this morning on my own account. The evening before, after Monsieur Calou had gone, I had been told by my stepmother that Mirbel would not be going back to school for the rest of that year. Had she seen me tremble? Had she realized what a mortal blow she was striking at the pale little boy who pretended so hard not to mind? She added that it would make a great difference to her own plans, that she and my father had agreed to look for another school, so that I might be removed from the influence of so black a sheep. Now, however, that would not be necessary. I should find Monsieur Puybaraud gone, but about that, too, she was glad. I was quite sensitive enough, as it was, and Monsieur Puybaraud had been altogether the wrong sort of master for me—a dangerous man.

Jean at Baluzac, Michèle at boarding-school . . . what on earth would become of me? On that day I looked for the first time straight in the face of loneliness. He is an old enemy now. We have learned to rub along together, to know one another. Loneliness has struck me every imaginable blow. There is no spot in me left to strike. It has set me many traps, and I have fallen into every one. But it torments me no longer. We sit, now, one on either side of the fire, on winter evenings, when the fall of a fir-cone and the sobbing of the night wind mean as much to me as the sound of a human voice.

Whatever happened I must see Jean again for the last time. . . . We must arrange to write. . . . It would be easy for me, but how should I address my letters? How does one have letters delivered *poste restante*? I must see him once more, must be convinced that I still existed for him, that Michèle had not entirely taken my place.

The roses on my curtains grew faintly pink: the day was breaking. I dressed, holding my breath the while. Not a creak did I make on the floor. A single wall stood between me and the huge room in which the two mahogany beds of Monsieur and Madame Pian stood as far as possible from one another.

I opened my door without a sound. The stairs, it is true, creaked a little, but Brigitte was no light sleeper. I would go out by the kitchen door so as to make sure of not being heard. . . . The key was hanging in the scullery.

"Where are you off to so early?"

I choked back a cry. There she stood, at the turn of the stairs, upright in the dawn light that fell from the skylight. She was wearing an amethyst-coloured dressing-gown. A great coil of hair, looking like a fat snake with a red ribbon round its snout, fell to her waist.

"Where are you off to? Tell me now!"

It did not occur to me to lie. She knew everything before I so much as opened my mouth. Besides, despair had sapped my courage. In a panic of escape I flung myself into its waiting arms. I sought safety in that very over-sensitiveness which had only to show its face to terrify any aggressor, however formidable, and compel him to help rather than to punish me. I screamed, I choked: I went further than I intended, and could not stop. Brigitte lifted me in her strong arms and took me to her room, where my father, suddenly wakened, sat up in bed thinking that he was in the throes of a nightmare.

"Quiet, quiet . . . I'm not going to eat you. Drink a little water. It's flavoured with orange."

She had laid me on her own bed.

"It was because I was never going to see him again," I stammered. "I wanted to say goodbye to him."

"It's that Mirbel boy all the trouble's about," said Brigitte to Octave. "See what a state he's in. I sometimes wonder whether it is not too late to do anything about these fits of his. He's so morbidly sensitive." And then, in a lower voice; "Poor child!—what an inheritance!"

"What do you mean, talking about inheritance with him here?" asked my father in the same low tone; "what are you hinting at?"

"Hinting is not one of my failings."

"Oh, isn't it?" He chuckled, shook his head, and said: "Oh, that's rich!"

I had never seen him looking so pale. He was sitting on the edge of his bed. His legs, all covered with black hair, did not reach the ground. Large swollen blue veins showed in his feet with their malformed toes. A mat of grey hair sprouted from his open nightshirt. His thighs were terribly thin, almost emaciated. Brigitte, standing there in her ecclesiastical-looking robe, her hair drawn forward on her prominent forehead, with one long, fat, shining tress hanging down, brooded over him with an eye that was at once hostile and watchful.

My father got up, took me in his arms and carried me back to my own bed. I sobbed into his nightshirt. He tucked me in. A misty sunlight entered through the fleur-de-lis openings cut in the shutters. I can still hear the tone of his voice as he said: "Wipe your eyes, you little fool; blow your nose and go to sleep." While he was saying this he brushed the hair away from my eyes with his hand, and stared—stared as though he had never seen me before.

I ought never to have known what I am now going to relate (I write it with an overwhelming sense of shame and embarrassment, but it must be done), and, in fact, I did not know it until immediately after the Great War when I became reconciled with my uncle Moulis, one of my mother's brothers from whom I had been separated all my life as the result of a family quarrel into the details of which I need not enter here. He had been devoted to his sister Marthe, and wanted to get to know me before he died. He was an architect, like my grandfather, practising in the city, a Bohemian, artistic sort of man, of the kind that Brigitte Pian loathed. She always maintained that he was responsible for the influences which had surrounded my mother's early life and had led to her undoing. This cynical old bachelor, speaking more than twenty years after the events he was describing, told me about the circumstances which had attended my birth. He could not actually prove that I was not Octave Pian's son, but he thought it more likely that I owed my existence to a first cousin of my mother's, Alfred Moulis—"a regular Adonis," said my uncle. I could see no trace of charm in the photograph he showed me, and the idea that I may be the son of the curly-headed and rather sheepish-looking individual there portrayed gives me no sort of pleasure. From childhood he had adored his cousin, and she responded without reserve. I will not expatiate on this odious subject. I intend to say only what is absolutely necessary to an understanding of the document which my stepmother discovered very soon after her marriage.

According to my uncle Moulis, it was a sort of memorandum written in my mother's hand: a series of calculations and comparisons of dates, from which it seemed clear that, if Octave was really my father, I must have been born two months too soon. It is true that at the time of my birth I was considerably under the normal weight, that I had to be wrapped in cotton-wool, and that I was reared only with the greatest difficulty. But what had been the purpose of this paper? There seems little doubt that it formed part of a letter. That, at least, was what my uncle thought, though he could not be sure.

But Octave Pian had a reason, which he thought was known only to himself, for doubting whether I could really be his son, and to this the document in question lent strong support. Uncle Moulis had had the facts from his sister. . . . It is an extremely delicate subject, and I can broach it only in the most roundabout manner. What I gathered was that Octave belonged to that by no means rare species of men who, when desperately in love, are afflicted with impotence. Such a state of affairs must lead to atrocious suffering, especially when the love is not mutual, and the ridiculous despair of one partner is observed by the other with a cold and mocking eye.

I hope that the reader will realize how very repugnant it is to me to put all this down in words. But it does, at least, prove that what I am relating is true and in no wise invented. Subjects of this kind are, as a rule, instinctively avoided by the professional novelist, because he knows that most people find them repellent. But those who turn their backs on fiction, and set out to follow up the destinies of persons with whom they have actually been connected, are for ever coming on the traces of these miseries and aberrations of the flesh. And even worse than the aberrations are the insufficiencies. For those are just the things about which we do not wish to hear, because so many of us may have been, to some extent, their victims. Renan once said that the truth may well be depressing. He was thinking in terms of metaphysics. On the level of human affairs it may be not only depressing but ridiculous and embarrassing—so much so that decency forbids us to put it into words. Hence the silence in which such things are usually shrouded. Only when they result in a divorce or a suit for annulment at Rome, does the glaring light of publicity beat upon them.

When, in October, I went back to the city with my stepmother, Octave Pian stayed on at Larjuzon. The separation of husband and wife had now become an accomplished fact, even though they had never discussed it in so many words. Everything happened quite naturally. My father had not yet seen the revealing document (though it had been left behind, as by accident, in a drawer of his room where he must, sooner or later, come upon it), but he had been sufficiently prepared and worked upon by Brigitte to see me go without any real feelings of regret. He preferred winter solitude in the depths of the country to life with a woman whom he hated and a son the very sight of whom opened old wounds. My last memory of him is of a man who had sunk back into the apathetic stupor from which he had roused himself for a brief spell in order to take up the cudgels on Michèle's behalf. It must have been about this time that he started drinking again: but it was only after our departure that the habit grew upon him.

Michèle was now a boarder at the Sacred Heart, and I was left alone with my stepmother. The two years which elapsed before I took my final examination were bleak and dreary, but I suffered a good deal less than I thought I should. Work came easily to me, and Brigitte had little cause to anticipate trouble from the silent schoolboy who spent his evenings mugging up his home-work and doing his essays without any need of supervision. During the first year my father came into town once every month on Michèle's free day, and took both of us to lunch at a restaurant. I can still remember vividly the peculiar pleasure which it gave me to choose my favourite dish from the menu—oysters, jugged hare or duck hash. The certain knowledge that Michèle and Jean were separated, probably for ever, had the effect of diminishing not only my jealousy, but also my affection, though spasms of both would occasionally recur for a few brief moments. I have never been able fully to realize that I love anybody unless the emotion is accompanied by some degree of suffering.

Here, I think, I ought to recall two incidents which proved to me, once and for all, that my friendship for Mirbel was a thing of the past. One evening, during that first winter, when I got back from school, my stepmother said, without raising her eyes from her book: "There's a letter for you." I was not taken in by her assumed indifference. "It's from Mirbel," I remarked, after one glance at the envelope, and immediately, with that instinctive cunning which certain children show when they have to deal with difficult relations, added, with seeming frankness, " D'you think I ought to read it?"

At first Brigitte Pian appeared to hesitate, but almost at once decided to leave it to me whether I thought I ought to show it to her. She never so much as glanced at me as I opened it. Jean de Mirbel, after describing the "deadly existence" he was leading at the Baluzac Presbytery ("and it's enough to make a fellow want to blow the lid off," he wrote), begged me to send him news of my sister. . . . "Perhaps you could persuade her to scribble a few words at the end of your reply. It would make me awfully happy, and it wouldn't really be breaking her promise. Tell her that no one can imagine what it's like to live in a scrubby little country town tucked away in a pine forest, cheek by jowl with an old priest—though I don't deny he's a decent enough chap and does what he can for me. The trouble is that *I'm* not decent. Tell her that three lines would make all the difference to me. She can have no idea how it would help. . . ."

I can remember my feeling of anger when I read on and found that the letter contained nothing whatever about my own affairs. I was more irritated than hurt. If that was how things were I felt I'd much better think no more about him, but wipe the slate clean. How often, in the course of my life, have I felt a similar need to terminate some relationship, to throw some person or persons overboard!

I held the letter out to Brigitte, who read it at once, but without any display of haste. When she had finished, she folded it up, baring her large, horse-like teeth in a smile. "The Reverend Mother," she said, "has forwarded me a whole packet in this young man's handwriting. He had the impudence actually to send a number of letters to your sister at the Convent. Each one began, though you'd hardly believe it, with an appeal to Reverend Mother—or to whomsoever might first open the envelope—to deliver it to Michèle! Which goes to prove," she added sententiously, "that corruption of mind may walk hand in hand with stupidity, and that the two things are by no means incompatible." Saying which, she threw the pages into the grate, where they fell a prey to the flickering flames.

I am not sure that the second incident belongs to the same period. I have an idea that my meeting with the abbé Calou took place during the winter of the following year. One Thursday, just as I left the house, someone called my name. I at once recognized the abbé, though he had grown much thinner. His old soutane flapped round his bony shoulders. He must have been watching for me to come out. I told him that I was on my way to Feret's bookshop, and he fell into step beside me.

"How pleased Jean will be when I tell him this evening that I have seen you."

"Is he all right?" I asked with an air of indifference.

"No," he said; "no, the poor fellow is very far from being all right."

He waited for me to question him, but in vain, for I had stopped at the door of Feret's shop and was turning over the pages of several second-hand books which were ranged there in the open. Was I really so hard? I don't think I can have been, for I was vividly aware of the poor old priest's distress as he leaned over my shoulder, and am even now conscious of the remorse which assailed me at that moment.

"Actually, I'm very worried about Jean. Do you know, he hasn't been home to La Devize once this year? His mother is spending the winter in Egypt. Of course, he's working very hard, and he gets a certain amount of shooting. I took him out after pigeon last October. He bagged a hundred and forty-seven. I've found a horse for him, too, at Du Buch's mill, a sorry old screw, but rideable. It's the lack of companionship that's so bad for him."

"But what about you?" I asked with the ingenuousness of youth.

"Oh, me. . . ."

He made a vague movement with his hands, and said no more. He must have realized for a long time how helpless he was. He had none of the qualities which a boy of Jean's age needs for happy companionship. His pupil had no more use for his erudition than for his gentleness. What else could he be but a gaoler in the eyes of a young man whom he would find, of an evening, curled up in a wicker chair by the kitchen fire, in precisely the same position as that in which he had left him after luncheon, with his book open at the same page. On these occasions Jean never so much as raised his eyes to the abbé's face. Nor did he find much amusement in going out alone on his old hack. When he was not in the house the abbé knew only too well where he had sought refuge. I was not, at that time, aware of this latest cause for anxiety. The truth was that Jean frequently stayed late in the enemy's camp—namely, at the chemist's shop kept by that very Voyod who was the abbé Calou's declared foe. The master and mistress of the local school would join the party after school hours. There would be much drinking of coffee in the back shop, and much discussion of articles by Jaurès and Hervé.

Although I knew perfectly well what the abbé was after, I gave him no assistance. He had to launch into his subject without preliminaries.

"I much regret that I have had words with Madame Pian," he said. "I believe her to be quite incapable of yielding to any emotion of bitterness, and I am sure that only the highest motives led her to act as she has done towards Michèle and Jean. I have no wish to discuss her decision, and am perfectly willing to yield to her superior wisdom. But don't you think, my dear boy, that Michèle might occasionally write a few lines to the Curé of Baluzac? What harm could there be in that? I am not suggesting that she should send Jean any direct message, but she could tell me something about her life. That would be an enormous source of comfort to your young friend. I am prepared to go even further, Louis, and to say"—he almost whispered the words into my ear—"to say that it might prove his salvation. For things have got to that pitch now—he has got to be saved. Do you understand what I am talking about?"

I could see his childlike eyes close to mine, could smell his sour breath. But I did not really understand what he was talking about. Still, this time, I was touched, and it was for his sake, rather than for Jean's, that I agreed to do what he asked. I gave him a promise that I would pass on his suggestion to Michèle, and I spared him the embarrassment of having to beg me to say nothing to my stepmother. I gave him that assurance unasked. He enveloped the back of my head in his great hand, and pressed my face to his stained soutane. I went with him as far as the tram. The men standing round him on the rear platform looked like a lot of midgets.

The correspondence between the abbé Calou and Michèle, which might, perhaps, have prevented, or at any rate retarded, much unhappiness, was interrupted after the third letter. Michèle had been foolish enough to give it to one of the weekly boarders, because she had not been able to resist the temptation to address it directly to Jean, though the name and superscription on the envelope were those of the abbé Calou. The letter was impounded by one of the nuns, who sent it to Brigitte Pian. She related the whole incident to me, though without attaching any blame to Michèle. "It was the priest who led her into temptation," she said; "there can be no doubt of that. Your sister has been guilty of a grave fault, but I thought it my duty to ask Reverend Mother to overlook it, and I must say that she has behaved in the whole affair with exemplary charity. But the account against the Curé of Baluzac grows daily"—she spoke with involuntary satisfaction—"and this letter is the last straw."

In some such words she spoke out her thoughts in my presence. Did she love me? For a long time I was quite convinced that her show of affection was due to the fact that I was the living proof of the first Madame Pian's sin. But I have since changed my mind. I am inclined to believe now that she lavished on me all the love of which she was capable, and that I had, in some way, managed to touch that maternal instinct which is to be found even in the most insensitive of women.

XI

FROM then on my existence was closely bound to that of Brigitte Pian. The small drawing-room where she worked and in which she received visitors separated my bedroom from hers. The door was always left half open until someone was announced, when she would close it. But no matter how low she kept her naturally vibrant tones, I could follow all conversations easily enough, especially in winter, when the windows were kept shut, and only a dull rumble reached the flat from the Cours de l'Intendance.

Occasionally, when I recognized Monsieur Puybaraud's voice, I would go and say how-d'you-do to him, though not always. It was usually he who made the move. He would come into my room and give me a hug just before taking his leave. My behaviour to him had changed in proportion as his position in the world had deteriorated. The poor, frail creature whose shoddy ready-made overcoat offered little protection against the wind, whose boots were never polished, could not inspire in me the same deference as the frock-coated schoolmaster whose favourite pupil I had been.

I owe it, in justice to myself, to add that his appearance moved me to a sense of pity, or, at any rate, produced in me the sort of moral discomfort which is always excited by the sight of another's poverty, and which we are tempted to call by the nobler name. But when I thought about Monsieur Puybaraud's misfortunes I could not but feel myself in agreement with Madame Brigitte. I found it difficult not to despise him for having yielded to an attraction which, though I had never yet felt its power myself, I was already inclined to view with suspicion and disgust. I should not have felt quite so keenly repelled by the outward signs of his deterioration had they not stood in my eyes for a spiritual equivalent; had he not, by marrying, made himself deliberately guilty, in my opinion, of disloyalty to a higher vocation. My views on this matter have not greatly changed. I believe that all the miseries of our human state come from our inability to remain chaste, and that men vowed to chastity would be spared most of the evils that weigh them down (even those that seem to have no direct connexion with the passions of the flesh). From the lives of a very small number of human beings I have derived an idea of what happiness might be in this world if it were based on generosity and love. Wherever I have found it, the movements of the heart and the promptings of the flesh have been kept under a strict discipline.

Monsieur Puybaraud came once every fortnight to receive from the hands of my stepmother the small allowance on which his household depended. The rest of the time he spent in running all over the city in search of an employment which he never found. Octavia, now pregnant, but threatened with a miscarriage, had to stay on her back until the child should be born, and could be of no help to him. I heard it said that a Little Sister of the Assumption went in every morning to do their housework. That was all I knew about the domestic arrangements of the wretched couple, and I was too incurious to ask many questions.

I did notice, however, that if the bi-monthly interviews between Monsieur Puybaraud and my stepmother always ended with the passing of an envelope from one hand to another, they usually involved a long, low argument diversified by occasional muted outbursts. On his side the tone was that of an eager beggar, while my stepmother's replies were given in a voice which I knew only too well. She was obstinate in her denials, undeviating in her refusals. Suddenly his tone would dwindle, and she would be left speaking alone, in the manner of one expounding the law to an inferior who had been talked down and reduced to silence.

"You know perfectly well that things will happen like that because I mean them to, and the sooner you reconcile yourself to the fact, the better."

This she said one day loudly enough for me to hear every word.

"When I say 'I mean,' I express myself badly, because we should do not what *we* will but what God wills. It is no use your hoping that I shall back you up in this matter any longer."

Whereupon, my former master, in spite of all that he owed to my stepmother and his utter dependence on her good-will, accused her of abiding by the letter of the law rather than the spirit, and so far forgot himself as to say that her neighbours always had to pay for her scruples, that it was always at somebody else's expense that she displayed her spiritual delicacy and the rigours of her conscience. He added that he would not go away until he had got what he was asking for. (I had not been able to make out through the door what all this was about.) My stepmother, by this time quite beside herself, exclaimed that if such were the case she had better leave him, and I heard her go out of the drawing-room, not without considerable commotion. A few seconds later Monsieur Puybaraud came into my room. His face was dead white. He held in his hand the envelope which she must almost have flung at him. His trousers were mud-spattered to the knees. He was wearing no cuffs. His black tie and starched shirt-front were the left-overs of his old school outfit.

"You heard?" he asked. "Louis, dear boy, you shall judge between us. . . ."

I don't think that many youngsters can have been asked to referee between older persons quite so often as I was. The trust which I had inspired in my master on that evening, now long past, when he gave me a letter to post to Octavia Tronche, urged him once again to have recourse to my good offices. It was a rational trust which derived from that cult of the young which he had always professed. According to him (and he had been foolish enough to develop his views in my hearing) boys between the ages of seven and twelve are the privileged possessors of a remarkable clarity of mind, of something that amounts, at times, to the inspiration of genius, though older persons find it hard to believe this. It vanishes, however, with the approach of puberty. In spite of the fact that I was now fifteen, I had retained, in his eyes, all the glamour of childhood. Poor Puybaraud! Marriage had not improved him physically. He was now almost bald. A few sparse strands of fair hair waged a hopeless struggle against the encroaching nakedness of his skull. His flushed cheek-bones alone gave colour to his bloodless face, and he was continually coughing.

He drew a chair up to mine as he used to do when he explained some Latin text to me in the old Larjuzon days.

"*You* will understand. . . ."

He used the second person singular. This he did only in moments of emotional outpouring, and when he was speaking to one of those young persons whom he regarded as the possessor of an infallible genius. He told me that the doctor believed that Octavia could have a child in the normal way only if she were assured of complete rest, both mental and physical. He had thought it best, therefore, to calm her most harrowing anxieties by keeping from her the origin of the small sum of money which he brought back to her each fortnight. She did not know that it came from my stepmother, but believed that her husband was earning his living and had succeeded at last in getting some post in the diocesan organization.

"Yes, I lied to her, and I do still, every day, though at the cost of how much shame and moral agony God alone knows! But surely fibs we are obliged to tell a sick woman can hardly rank as lies? I refuse to admit that they *are* lies, in spite of anything that Madame Brigitte may say!"

He gazed fixedly at me, as though expecting some oracular pronouncement.

I shrugged my shoulders.

"Surely it doesn't matter what she says, Monsieur Puybaraud, so long as you are easy in your own conscience? . . ."

"It's not so simple as all that, Louis, my boy. . . . You see, Octavia is surprised and worried that Madame Brigitte has never been to see her since she has been confined to bed. . . . Up to now, your stepmother has always refused to come. She won't come—so she had the effrontery to write—until I have repudiated what she calls my 'offence against the truth.' Consequently, I have been led into a series of explanations to Octavia of which I will spare you the details. Lies beget lies. I know that I ought to give way. I am in a maze from which I can find no way out. But so far I have managed, more or less, to save my face. . . . Now, however, Madame Brigitte is beginning to use threats. She says that her conscience forbids her to remain my accomplice any longer in this deception. She insists that I tell Octavia where the money comes from. . . . Can you imagine such a thing?"

I could, very easily, and I told Monsieur Puybaraud that what really astonished me was that my stepmother should have consented to keep Octavia in the dark for so long. I made it pretty clear that I admired this scrupulous honesty on the part of my stepmother, though I did not say so in words. I was just then beginning to make the acquaintance of Pascal in the little Brunschwig edition. The

Brigitte Pian type appealed to me. I found it beautiful. It reminded me of Mother Agnes, of Mother Angélique, and of those other proud ladies of Port-Royal. I can see myself now, implacable in my youthful fervour, seated beside the log-fire in front of a little table loaded with dictionaries and note-books with, opposite me, that poor, worn-out figure stretching two small, grubby white hands to the blaze, his uncobbled shoes smoking in the heat. There, in the flames, his gentle and defeated eyes could see the image of a woman lying in bed with her precious, menaced burden. That was a reality which Brigitte Pian refused to recognize, a reality which he could not make me see. My stepmother had said to him, more than once—"I warned you before it all happened: you have no cause of grievance against me. . . ." It was true that everything was turning out precisely as she had foreseen, that in the light of events she could feel no doubt of the illumination which had descended from God upon her spirit.

"She left me with a threat. She warned me that she would call on Octavia late to-morrow afternoon," said Monsieur Puybaraud in a gloomy voice. "She is going to bring her some broth, but she insists that between now and then I shall prepare Octavia for the news of my real situation. What am I to do? I want to spare my poor wife the spectacle of my shame. As you very well know, I am incapable of self-control. I shall not be able to keep myself from crying. . . ."

I asked him why he didn't get some pupils. Couldn't he do some tutoring? He shook his head. He had no degree, and his marriage had closed most of the houses against him in which he might have found some chance of employment.

"What a pity that *I* don't need a tutor," I said in a self-satisfied voice; "but you see, I am always top of the class."

"Oh, you!" he answered on a note of tender admiration; "you already know as much as I do. Pass your examination: get as many diplomas as you can, my boy. You don't need them now, but one never knows. . . . If only I had a degree!"

Child of a poor family, and educated out of charity by his future colleagues because they saw great possibilities in him, Léonce Puybaraud had found no difficulty in learning, and might have gone far, had he not been asked, when he reached the age of eighteen, to deputize for some of the teachers when the school happened to be short of staff. He had to continue his own education while acting as a form-master, and knew no more of literature than what he had managed to pick up from anthologies and school text-books. On the other hand, he had read more deeply than most University students in the great classic writers of Greece and Rome. But to-day all his erudition could not help him to earn the three hundred francs a month which was the minimum on which his family could live.

I longed for him to go, and began turning over the pages of my dictionary in an effort to make it clear that I had no time to waste. But he allowed himself to relax in the warm, cosy atmosphere of the room, in the presence of the youth to whom he was devoted. He sat there, wondering and wondering what he could do to disillusion Octavia without causing her too great an emotional disturbance.

"Why tell her yourself?" I suggested. "Couldn't you get somebody else to do it for you?—the Little Sister of the Assumption, for instance, who comes every day?"

"What a good idea, Louis!" he cried, slapping his skinny thighs. "No one but you would have thought of such a solution! She's a little saint, that girl: Octavia is devoted to her, and she to Octavia. It is quite curious to see two human beings each so convinced that she is inferior to the other. . . . I only wish that Madame Brigitte could share the spectacle with me. . . . It would teach her the nature of true humility. . . ."

He stopped because I pursed my lips. He felt that I was more completely under the influence of Madame Brigitte than he had ever been.

Next day, about the middle of the afternoon, Brigitte Pian descended from a landau in front of the house in the Rue du Mirail where the Puybarauds lived in furnished rooms which she had chosen for them and the rent of which she paid. Her arms were so loaded with a variety of parcels that she could not lift the hem of her skirt as she climbed the appallingly squalid staircase. The water from the household sinks ran in an open gutter. The smell was not unfamiliar to her: she met it constantly in the course of her charitable visits. The prevailing stench of urban poverty is always the same: a mixture of kitchens and privies. But it is not my intention to underrate what was best in Brigitte Pian's life, tempting though it is to do so. Whatever her true motives may have been, she was always a great giver of alms, and at times, when visiting the genuinely sick, showed herself capable of real personal devotion. She worked on the principle that it was better to provide solid help for a few than to spread inadequate relief over a wide field. I remember that when I accompanied her on her shopping rounds, she would buy cotton-wool or groceries at out-of-the-way shops kept by protégés whom she had helped out of their difficulties, and would send her friends on similar errands. She spared these petty tradespeople neither advice nor criticism, and was for ever complaining of the ingratitude of those who resolutely refused to make a success of their lives, no matter how much pecuniary aid she might bring them.

She had been less generous than usual with the Puybarauds, and, though she kept them alive, left them to struggle along as best they could. I find it hard to say whether this was deliberate policy on her part. It is conceivable that she did not know the full facts of the case. I am inclined to think that she thought it a good thing that they should remain in the state of penury which she had always predicted for them; should so obviously suffer the punishment which had come upon them as a result of their refusal to follow her advice. She never ceased to find a source of triumphant satisfaction in her knowledge that they were entirely dependent on her. Had she recognized the true nature of her feelings for Octavia, they might have caused her a passing tremor.

The first object that caught her eye as she entered the sick-room was an upright piano standing at right angles to the bed, close to the pillow. It took up so much space that it was difficult to move freely between the wardrobe, the table and the dresser, on top of which lay a litter of bottles, cups and dirty plates. (Each morning Monsieur Puybaraud would make a hurried effort to get a little order into the confusion which the young Sister of Mercy left behind her.)

While the first courtesies were being exchanged, and their visitor was enquiring about the patient's health, the Puybarauds noticed—with what anxiety may be imagined—that the piano had already "caught Madame Brigitte's eye." They realized that at any moment she might begin to ask them about it. The shop from which they hired it had promised to fetch it away, but had not done so. That very morning Monsieur Puybaraud had started another hopeless discussion on the subject. How were they ever going to explain to Brigitte Pian that they had been guilty of so absurd an act of self-indulgence?—absurd, because neither of them could play a note, although they both loved picking out hymn tunes with one finger on the keys. Even had they not been in the last extremes of poverty, their hiring of the instrument would have been difficult to excuse: but dependent, as they were, for the very means of life on another's charity . . .

Octavia hurriedly embarked on a subject designed to divert Madame Brigitte's attention. She thanked that lady from the bottom of her heart for not having allowed Léonce to deceive her any longer about where the money came from which he brought home every other week. He had acted as he had with the best possible intentions, and out of consideration for her. But for some time now she had suspected a trick, and had thought, at first, that it was of Madame Brigitte's own devising, since, as all the world knew, she would do good by stealth as others did evil. (Octavia was not wholly innocent of a fault, so widespread in the circles in which she had been brought up, where flattery causes few pangs when it is addressed to rich and influential patrons with the power of life and death over those around them.) She added that she understood and shared Madame Brigitte's scruples of conscience. That lady listened with but half her mind. Her eyes kept constantly returning to the piano. She interrupted the invalid to say how sorry she was that she had caused Monsieur Puybaraud any distress of mind. She might, she said, have been weak enough to yield to his representations had she been dealing with one of those worldly persons (and life was full of them) who know nothing of the ways of God. But she had decided that a Christian like Octavia ought not to remain ignorant of the consequences of her acts, that she ought to face the trials which it had seen fit to Providence to lay upon her. "Since it was clearly part of the Divine plan that you should live on the charity of a devoted friend, and that Monsieur Puybaraud should be unable to find suitable employment in the workaday world, I felt that I had no right to spare you the effects of so salutary a lesson."

Monsieur Puybaraud, having noted these words in his diary, and stigmatized them as "damnable," adds: "I won't swear that she spoke them with conscious irony, but I am pretty sure that she felt considerable satisfaction at being able to find a water-tight excuse (from the religious point of view, I mean) for the pleasure it gave her to know that she had such a hold over us: that nothing stood between us and starvation but the little envelope which I had to accept from her twice a month."

"It is odd," she said, "but somehow I don't remember that piano in the inventory which was sent me when I took these rooms for you."

"No," replied Octavia in a voice that trembled; "it is a piece of silliness for which I alone am responsible."

She looked at the elder woman with that sweet, disarming smile which few could resist. But the expression of hauteur on the face of her patroness showed no sign of softening.

"Forgive me, darling," broke in Monsieur Puybaraud; "it was I who suggested it, and I was thinking more about my own pleasure than yours."

It was foolish of him to call his wife "darling" in front of Brigitte Pian. She had always hated the lack of reserve in married couples who, presuming on the legitimacy of such endearments, stressed by word and gesture the fact of their squalid intimacy. In the case of this particular pair it was quite intolerable.

"Am I to understand," she enquired in tones which were suspiciously gentle, "that you have hired this piano?"

The accused nodded.

"One of you, then, must be capable of giving music lessons. I had an idea that you were both so ignorant of the art as not even to know your notes."

Octavia explained that they had agreed to give themselves this small indulgence.

"What indulgence?—picking out tunes with one finger as I often used to see you doing at school, though it made you ridiculous in the eyes of the girls?"

Madame Brigitte, who scarcely ever laughed, emitted a sort of sharp bark.

Octavia hung her head. Her faded yellow hair was parted in the middle and drooped low on either side of her face. Her breast rose and fell rapidly beneath her coarse cotton slip.

"I know that it was wrong of us, Madame Brigitte," said Monsieur Puybaraud; "but please do not distress Octavia"—he sank his voice to a whisper—"we will discuss the matter, if you don't mind, on the occasion of your next visit. I will explain it all. . . ."

"Yes"—she had adopted the same low tone—"we will go into it another time. You can tell me then where the money came from. . . ."

"It is yours: I am not denying that. . . . I realize that for people who are living on charity it is unpardonable to spend twenty francs a month on a piano which neither of them knows how to play. But I'd rather not discuss it now. . . ."

"What is there to discuss? You have already made the whole matter abundantly clear." Brigitte was still speaking in the same low voice (but Octavia had not lost a single word). "There is nothing you can add. You neither of you seem to realize that you have done anything at all out of the ordinary. It is not the money I am worrying about. . . . It is not a question of money. . . ."

Monsieur Puybaraud broke in by reminding her that she herself had remarked that there was no more to be said. He put his arms round Octavia, who was choking back her sobs. But Brigitte Pian, alarmed by the woman's tears, was in the grip of one of those fits of temper which she found it extremely hard to control, and regarded, in all humility, as a sign of that volcanic temperament with which it had pleased Heaven to endow her. Though she tried hard not to raise her voice, the fury of her mood came from behind clenched teeth in a spate of words:

"Well, I suppose I've got to make the best of it, but there is a limit beyond which the highest virtue can hardly be expected to go! It is my duty not to be weak: however charitable I may have been towards you, I am not going to push kindness to the point of idiocy!"

"I beg of you either to stop talking or to go! Can't you see that you are distressing Octavia?"

Monsieur Puybaraud so far forgot himself as to seize her by the arm and push her towards the door.

"How dare you lay a finger on me!" This attempt at physical interference with her movements had had the immediate effect of once more seating Brigitte Pian on the familiar throne of her perfection.

"No, Léonce!" groaned Octavia, "she is our benefactress. It is me you hurt when you fall short of the behaviour which she has a right to expect from us."

At this, Monsieur Puybaraud allowed himself to be carried away by one of those sudden outbursts of temper to which weak natures are prone. Seeing that Brigitte was already on the landing, he exclaimed rather too loudly:

"After all, darling, this is our house, isn't it?"

My stepmother, framed in the doorway, drew herself to her full height.

"*Your* house, indeed!"

Such an easy triumph enabled her to recover an almost divine complacency. The statement with which she had just silenced her wretched adversary stood in no need of being elaborated. But she could not resist the temptation of levelling a parting shot.

"Would you like me to send you the lease? You will find, I think, that the name in which it is drawn up is not yours!"

Monsieur Puybaraud slammed the door and went across to the bed where Octavia lay with her face in her hands, sobbing.

"It was wrong of you to act so, Léonce. We owe everything to her . . . and, really, you know, that piano . . ."

"Calm yourself, beloved: you'll do some injury to our child. . . ."

They always spoke of "our child" when referring to the still unborn life, the adored baby, which might never come into the world. Holding his wife's head pressed close to him, he said, more than once: "Horrible creature!"

But Octavia protested. "No, Léonce, no; it is wrong to speak like that. Temperament is a stumbling-block to us all. It is easy enough to resist the crimes for which God has seen fit to spare us the opportunity. But only a special gift of Grace can enable us to overcome in our daily lives the real weaknesses of character with which we are burdened. It would have been better, perhaps, if Madame Brigitte had lived under the discipline of an enclosed Order."

"If she ever had become a nun she would soon have bossed the whole Community. They'd all have gone in dread of her, and she'd have had plenty of time to pick out her particular victims. We ought to rejoice, rather, that she is not in a convent where she would have had complete authority over the lives and thoughts of the sisterhood. A woman like Brigitte Pian would be in her element there. We, at least, are free to starve, free never to set eyes on her again! . . ."

"I agree with you that she would have made it her business to ensure the sanctity of the Sisters," said Octavia, still tearful, but with the faint glimmer of a smile. "You must have noticed that the history of the great Orders is full of instances of Superiors like Brigitte Pian. They have always pointed the Community along the stony way to Heaven—and the shortest, for people submitted to that sort of discipline do not live long. . . . But I oughtn't to talk like this," she added; "after all she *is* our benefactress. . . . Oh, it's wicked of me!"

For a while they said no more. Monsieur Puybaraud, seated on the bed, began to nibble one of the biscuits that Brigitte had brought with her. At last:

"What's going to become of us?" he asked.

"You must go and see her to-morrow morning," replied Octavia.

"I know her. She will spend to-night wrestling with her scruples, and will be the first to ask forgiveness. In any case, things will be different when little Louis arrives."

He could not share her conviction. Never, no never, would he expose himself to such treatment again!

"It is hard to have to humble oneself, darling; for a man, and a really good man like you, it's the hardest thing in the world. But it is what God asks of us."

"What I find hardest to bear is her assumption that God has justified her belief that things would turn out exactly as they have. Do *you* think we are being punished for what we have done?"

"No," she exclaimed with eager passion. "Not punished but tested. We were right in what we did. Our lives belong together. Madame Brigitte does not understand that we were meant to suffer together."

"You're right. From our suffering has come all our happiness."

She flung her thin arms round his neck.

"You regret nothing?"

"I suffer because I cannot support us . . . but once the child is born, nothing else will matter. Our happiness will be complete."

She whispered in his ear: "Don't set too much store on it, don't be too hopeful."

"What makes you think . . . Has the doctor said anything you haven't told me?"

He pressed her with questions, but she shook her head. No, the doctor had said nothing; it was only that she had an idea that the ultimate sacrifice might be asked of them. "No," said Monsieur Puybaraud again, as she went on to say that he must be ready to accept whatever God might think best for them, must acquiesce whole-heartedly in the possible ordeal, as Abraham had acquiesced, and that then, and then only, their Isaac might be given back to them. Monsieur Puybaraud continued to say "No," but more gently now, until at last he slid to his knees, pressed his forehead against the bed, and in a strangled voice made the responses to the evening prayer which Octavia had begun to recite.

When it was over she relapsed into silence and closed her eyes.

Then her husband lit a candle, went over to the piano, the keys of which reflected the light, and, with one hesitating finger, tried to pick out her favourite hymn, the hymn sung by little children at their first Communion. As he did so he whispered the words:

"Heaven has come down to earth, beloved: do thou rest in me."

XII

BRIGITTE PIAN was no sooner in the street than she turned what remained of her anger against herself. How could she so utterly have lost control of her temper? What would the Puybarauds think? They did not, as she did, see her perfections from within, nor could they measure the height, breadth and depth of her virtue. They would judge her in the light of an outburst which, if the truth were told, had made her feel thoroughly ashamed. How could human nature be relied upon, she thought as she walked up the Rue de Mirail towards the Cours Victor Hugo, if, after a whole lifetime spent in the conquest of herself, at an age when she might reasonably expect to be exempt from the weaknesses which disgusted her in others, the mere sight of a piano was enough to break down all her self-control?

Though the maintenance of her armour of perfection was one of her most constant preoccupations, there was nothing so very extraordinary in a link occasionally working loose. She could always console herself for such an occurrence—provided no witness had been by. But the Puybarauds, and especially Octavia, were the last people in the world before whom she would willingly have shown signs of weakness. 'They'll take me for a beginner,' said Brigitte to herself, and the idea was painful, because she measured her progress in the spiritual life very much as she would have done in the study of a foreign language. She was made furious by the thought that the Puybarauds should be in ignorance of the way she had "moved up" in class during the last few months; should, on the evidence of a moment's ill-humour, rank her among the ragtag and bobtail of ordinary church-going females. Just how far Brigitte Pian had been "promoted" it was not for her, conscious of the need for humility, to say, but she would gladly have climbed all the way upstairs again to the Puybarauds' rooms just to remind them that even great saints have sometimes been the victims of bad temper. Was she a saint? She was making great efforts to be one, and, at each step forward, fought hard to hold the ground that she had gained. No one had ever told her that the closer a man gets to sanctity the more conscious does he become of his own worthlessness, his own nothingness, and gives to God, not from a sense of duty, but because the evidence is overwhelming, all credit for the few good activities with which Grace has endowed him. Brigitte Pian pursued an opposite course, finding each day ever stronger reasons for thanking her Creator that He had made of her so admirable a person. There had been a time when she was worried by the spiritual aridity which marked her relations with her God: but since then she had read somewhere that it is as a rule the beginners on whom the tangible marks of Grace are showered, since it is only in that way that they can be extricated from the slough of this world and set upon the right path. The kind of insensitiveness which afflicted her was, she gathered, a sign that she had long ago emerged from those lower regions of the spiritual life where fervour is usually suspect. In this way her frigid soul was led on to glory in its own lack of warmth. It did not occur to her that never, for a single moment, even in the earliest stages of her search for perfection, had she felt any emotion which could be said to have borne the faintest resemblance to love: that she had never approached her Master save with the object of calling His attention to her own remarkably rapid progress along the Way, and suggesting that He give special heed to her singular merits.

Nevertheless, here, on the pavement between the Rue de Mirail and the Cours de l'Intendance, as she made her way up the Rue Duffour-Dubergier and the Rue Vital-Carles, all blanketed in their customary fog, Brigitte Pian found herself yielding to a mood of spiritual discomfort which was far more profound than could be accounted for merely by the fact that she had cheapened herself in the Puybarauds' eyes. A sense of suppressed anxiety (which, though it was sometimes in abeyance, never wholly vanished from her consciousness) made her aware that the balance-sheet of her soul had not been truly audited, and that she too might one day be weighed in those unchanging standards of the Infinite by which, so she had always understood, the Uncreated Being was in the habit of judging the world of men. There were days—more particularly those on which she had been to see Octavia Tronche—when a flash of lightning would tear holes in the mists that shrouded her soul, and show her to herself as she really was. When that happened, she realized, beyond all possibility of denial (the mood never lasted for more than a moment), that her way of life was not the only way of life, nor her God the only God. The sense of satisfaction in being Brigitte Pian, which, as a rule, was so overpowering, fell away from her suddenly, and she shivered, feeling herself naked and miserable, cast upon an arid waste of sand beneath a copper sky. Far away she could hear angelic choirs, and, mingled with them, the hateful voices of the Puybarauds. The feeling soon passed, and she always managed, by dint of certain impromptu prayers of proved efficacy, to recover her spiritual equilibrium. When the need for such rehabilitation came on her, she would pause before an altar somewhere (as now in the Cathedral) until silence once more filled her heart. She not only felt the silence, but adored it as a sign sent to her from her hidden Master that she had again found grace in His eyes. But to-day, first before the Holy Sacrament and, later, before the statue of the Virgin which stands behind the choir (looking for all the world like the Empress Eugénie), she was conscious of a voice within her that spoke in tones of disapproval. 'It has been sent to try me,' she thought; 'I must submit in all humility,' which was her way of saying: "Notice, I beg, O Lord, that I do not kick against the pricks, and enter my acquiescence, please, on the credit side of the account." But since peace of mind still would not come to her, she went into a Confessional and accused herself of violence of thought, though not of injustice (for her anger had been fully justified), of having failed to keep her legitimate indignation within the bounds of a duly disciplined charity.

If, after luncheon on the day following, Monsieur Puybaraud had paid a visit to Brigitte in her own home, he would have found himself in the presence of a woman now utterly defenceless and only too willing to exhibit herself as an object-lesson in humility. In the matter of humility she feared competition with none.

But when my master, pale with emotion, asked the servant whether her mistress was at home, he was told that she had been summoned back to Larjuzon by telegram, and that the young people had gone with her. Monsieur Pian had been taken suddenly ill, and the wording of the telegram had been sufficiently alarming to set Madame packing at once. She had taken "all the mourning she happened to have."

There was nothing suspicious about my father's death. Saintis (who had been re-established in the vacancy left by the dismissal of Vignotte) had found him, early in the morning, lying on his face by the side of his bed and already cold. Like many of his comfortable country neighbours, Octave Pian had always eaten and drunk too much; but after he had been left alone in the house, his drinking had taken on frightening proportions. The evening before his death he must have surpassed himself, for the bottle of Armagnac which he had opened that day was found empty in the study, where it was his custom to sit smoking by the fire until the stroke of midnight.

I know to-day that Brigitte Pian's scruples had crystallized around the paper to which I have already referred. Rightly or wrongly, she held that it must strike a final blow at my mother's memory. I long believed that when she went from Larjuzon she had deliberately left that document in a drawer where she was certain that sooner or later my father must find it. That was, doubtless, to let my imagination outstrip events. Knowing what I do to-day, I can read their true meaning into the phrases which my stepmother endlessly repeated as she lay in her bedroom through the long nights which preceded and which followed my father's funeral. Lying wide-eyed in the dark, I listened in a state of terror, firmly convinced that Brigitte

Pian had gone mad. Beneath the door, the woodwork of which had been gnawed by rats, the light showed, obscured at regular intervals by the passage of her body as she paced up and down. Though she was wearing bedroom slippers, the floor creaked beneath her tread. "I must think, I must think," she kept on saying in a loud voice. I can hear the words still, words spoken by someone intent, at any price, on getting order into the confusion of her mind. She could have shown him the paper, but she had not done so. She had always hesitated to cause him anxiety, although it would have been a simple matter for her to destroy the kind of worship with which he surrounded the memory of Marthe. But she had never allowed herself to do so. It was far from certain that he would open that drawer. The only thing for which she can be truly blamed is that she did not burn the paper. . . . She never did, but it was not because she still had a lingering hope that one day he would discover it. "Into Thy hands, O Lord, I commit myself." God must be the judge. Whether or no Octave opened the drawer must depend on God, and even if he did, it must still depend on God whether the poor man would understand the meaning of what he read, would attach any significance to it. There is nothing to prove that he *would* have caught its drift. "I know, of course, that the document is no longer in the drawer, and that the stove in the hall is full of the fragments of papers which he burned. But he got rid of everything that had belonged to his first wife, and of that paper along with the rest. . . . He didn't know what he was doing. He was drinking hard at the time, had made up his mind to get as drunk as possible. . . ."

I am not, I need hardly say, reporting any actual words of hers. I have compounded those I have written down from memory, giving full weight to what I have learned since, but did not know at the time. I have set myself the task of getting to the heart of her scruples. The only ones to which I can bear witness are "I must think," which expressed the eager necessity to which, during the long night, her wandering mind still clung.

Michèle pretended not to see Brigitte—poor Michèle, who had to face the torment of her own remorse, a remorse which I shared with her, which, for some time, had been a part of both our lives, but of which, now, in the evening of my days, I can recapture no trace. However genuine Michèle's sorrow may have been—and she had loved her father dearly—her chief preoccupation just before the funeral, when she was at Larjuzon, was to wonder whether she would see Jean at the service. And when it was all over, her grief as a daughter was dominated and, so to speak, eclipsed by her disappointment at not having caught a glimpse of Mirbel in the congregation.

Because she was afraid that the thick crape which veiled her face might prevent her from noticing him, she had given me the task of telling her the moment I caught sight of Jean de Mirbel. So wholly had I identified my wishes with hers, that my own personal feelings counted for nothing in the curiosity with which I scrutinized the faces of the local shopkeepers and country-folk who crowded the church. Among all these animal faces, with their ferrety noses, their foxy or rabbity masks and cow-like expressions, some of the women's eyes looking dead or vacant, others bright, glittering, bird-like and utterly stupid, I sought for the familiar features, the powerful brow beneath its shock of short, curly hair, the eyes, the laughing mouth—but all in vain. No doubt Jean had been afraid that he might have to file in front of my stepmother, but, since it was not customary for the widow to accompany the coffin to the graveside, I still had hopes that he might pluck up courage and join us.

The morning had promised well, but later, a mist had blown across the face of the feeble sun. Up to that very last moment when we stood by the open grave, while the trowel was passing from hand to hand among a crowd of living persons who looked, in the shrouding fog, as though they were already half dead themselves, while skimpy handfuls of earth were falling on the coffin of that Octave Pian who, perhaps, had never been my father after all, I still hoped to see Jean's figure emerge from the ghost-like figures that surrounded me. More than once Michèle thought she had seen him, and pressed my arm. For years afterwards we shared a feeling of shame when we remembered that day. Still, the very pain it caused us was in itself a proof that we had genuinely loved our father. I no longer feel indignant now at the thought of that convention which claimed my sister's obedience in the little cemetery of Larjuzon. She was one of those human beings whose temperaments are so surely balanced, their hearts so pure, that their instincts are almost always at one with their duty, so that their natural inclinations lead them to do precisely what God expects of them.

In the afternoon my stepmother retired to her room, where we could hear her pacing up and down until the evening. Contrary to custom, we none of us appeared at the funeral meal, but the din reached us up on the first floor where we had taken refuge. In the absence of any near relation, our guardian, Monsieur Malbec, the local solicitor, did the honours. He came up to us after coffee, red in the face and almost merry. We knew that there were clients waiting for him, and that we should not have to endure his presence for long. If I were writing a novel, I should find it amusing to sketch in the character of Malbec, who was the sort of man of whom it is said that "he might have stepped straight out of the pages of Balzac." But he played no other part in our lives than that of a man who relieved us of all those responsibilities which might have served to divert our attention from what was going on in our hearts and minds. He bored me to extinction. Whenever I had to visit him in his office to hear him read documents which I then signed with my initials, I used to tell myself stories in an effort to alleviate the tedium. During all the period of my youth I believed (or behaved as though I believed) that people like him, with their bony skulls, their pince-nez and their whiskers, middle-aged men of business who looked as though they were "made-up" for a part, knew nothing of the human affections and were utter strangers to the emotions of every day.

When Monsieur Malbec had left us, and the last carriages had driven off, we gave ourselves over to what, at that moment, seemed to us no less than sacrilege—to a discussion, in fact, of de Mirbel. We sat there talking of him and smoking, in a room that was separated only by a partition from the one from which our father's body had been so lately taken. We realized then that we should have no difficulty about going over to see Jean at Baluzac. The cemetery, which we were to visit again next day, lay beyond the village and directly on the Baluzac road. We could easily make the journey to the Presbytery on foot. Brigitte Pian seemed to be in no state to keep an eye on us, and the death of her father had released Michèle from her promise.

When the next day came, the fog was thicker than ever. If we kept to the woods it was most unlikely that we should meet anybody. At the grave, with its panoply of already faded flowers, Michèle insisted on saying the *De Profundis* twice over. I thought she was never going to finish. Then, with a strong sense that we were abandoning our poor, dead father, we began walking so fast that, in spite of the mist, the sweat began to stand out on my forehead in great drops. Michèle led the way. She was wearing a white béret (the only mourning hat she had was the one she had worn at the funeral), and a short jacket cut close to her waist which, in those days, most people would have thought was rather thick. Her shoulders were too high. Those physical blemishes are still vivid in my memory. But her dumpy little figure radiated strength and an overmastering sense of vitality.

The few houses which formed the township of Baluzac seemed stricken with death. They were not arranged in the form of a street, and there was nothing which bore the slightest resemblance to a market-square. The Presbytery was separated from the church by the graveyard. Beyond it was the new school; opposite, an inn-cum-grocery-store, the blacksmith's forge and Voyod's chemist's shop which, on this particular day, was shut. Two-thirds of the abbé Calou's parishioners lived in isolated farms lying some miles outside the hamlet.

The nearer we approached the more infectious did Michèle's nervousness become. We felt, we breathed, as one person. I had turned up the bottom of my black trousers to clear my funereal button boots.

The kitchen-garden appeared to be abandoned. "Wait till I've got my breath before you knock," said Michèle. She did not make the gesture which she would certainly make to-day. She had neither powder nor lip-stick. For that matter, she had not even a handbag, but only a pocket beneath her skirt.

I lifted the knocker. The sound echoed through the house as though it had been an empty sepulchre. Half a minute passed, and then we heard the sound of a chair being pushed back, followed by the noise of dragging clogs. The door was opened by what might have been a ghost. It was the abbé Calou. He was already much thinner than when I had met him last in the Cours de l'Intendance.

"Ah, my dear young people . . . I was just going to write to you. . . . I ought to have come to the funeral . . . but I didn't dare . . . because of Madame Pian, you know."

He led the way into the drawing-room and opened the shutters. It was as though an icy cape had fallen about our shoulders. When he asked us, rather hesitatingly, whether we weren't afraid of catching cold, I said that, as a matter of fact, we had got very warm, and that perhaps it would be wiser if we went upstairs. He seemed put out by the suggestion, begged us to forgive the untidiness we should find there, and then, with a faint shrug, signed to us to follow him to the first floor.

I could feel Michèle go all tense in anticipation of the longed-for meeting. Jean would appear, leaning over the banisters. He was, perhaps, behind the very door which the abbé Calou was even then in the act of opening—still to an accompaniment of muttered apologies.

"The bed is not made. Maria is growing old, and I never feel really up to the mark in the morning. . . ."

What a mess! Books were scattered all over the grey-looking sheets. On the mantelpiece, in a confusion of papers, stood a plate with the remains of a meal. The coffee-pot was wedged in the dead ashes of the grate.

The abbé Calou pulled two chairs forward and himself sat down on the bed.

"I should like to be able to tell you that I share your sorrow, but, for the moment, I am incapable of thinking of others. I am the prisoner of my own misery. Perhaps you know where he is? There must be rumours going round. I know nothing at all, and it looks as though I never shall, because it is not very likely that his family will keep me informed of the result of their search—as you may well imagine! Forgive me for talking like this. . . . Since the whole wretched business started, I have not exchanged ten words with a single living soul. . . . The people here turn their backs on me, or, worse still, laugh at me. . . ."

"What wretched business?" I asked. But Michèle had understood.

"What has happened to him? Nothing serious?"

The abbé Calou kept hold of the hand which she had stretched towards him. He repeated that he was the last person in the world to be able to give her an answer. He was the one person who must expect to be told nothing. . . . At length he became aware of our amazement.

"You didn't know that he had gone? You weren't told? . . . It'll be a week ago to-morrow."

We exclaimed with one voice:

"Gone? but why?"

The abbé raised his arms and let them fall again.

"Why? . . . boredom, of course. . . . Living here with a priest, an old priest. . . . But the idea would never have occurred to him if someone hadn't started meddling. . . . No, I can't speak out to you . . . you're both of you only children. . . . Ah, Michèle! . . . you alone could have . . . you alone. . . ."

I had never seen a man of his age, let alone a priest, cry. His tears were not those of a grown-up person. His drowned blue eyes were just like those that his mother must have wiped sixty years before, on some occasion when he was terribly unhappy, and there was a childlike air about the way in which his mouth was twisted all awry by grief.

"I thought I had done everything possible. . . . I ought to have run after you, Michèle, got hold of you by hook or by crook, brought you here by force. But my judgment was at fault. What an idiotic arrangement that was of mine that you and I should exchange letters. Naturally, you couldn't resist the temptation of slipping a note to Jean into an envelope addressed to me. I ought to have foreseen that. You probably don't know that, so far as my part in the affair is concerned, a complaint has been made to the Archbishop. That dear woman, your stepmother, has lodged a formal charge against me. Fortunately, Cardinal Lecot is not so formidable as he looks. I have no doubt that His Eminence has had a good laugh at my expense. He referred to me as "Love's messenger," and quoted some Latin verses. But that was because he wanted to treat the whole thing as a joke instead of taking it seriously. The Cardinal is a hard man, and his mockery is terrible, but he has the heart that usually goes with a fine intelligence. I realize that he has behaved very well. . . ."

Monsieur Calou hid his face for a moment in his two enormous hands. Michèle asked him what she ought to do. He lowered his hands and looked at her for an instant. A smile spread over his tear-stained face.

"Oh, it's very simple for you, Michèle. So long as you and he are still alive nothing is lost. Do you know what you mean to him?—really know? But it is different for me. I can suffer: I know that. One can always suffer for others. . . ." Then he muttered, as though to himself: "Do I really believe that?" He seemed to have forgotten our presence. "Yes, I do. What an appalling doctrine it is that acts count for nothing, that no man can gain merit for himself or for those whom he loves. All through the centuries Christians have believed that the humble crosses to which they were nailed on the right and left hand of our Lord meant something for their own redemption, and for the redemption of those they loved. And then Calvin came and took away that hope. But I have never lost it. . . . No," he said again, "No!"

Michèle and I exchanged glances. We thought that he was going out of his mind, and we were frightened. He had taken from his pocket a huge handkerchief of purple check. He wiped his eyes, and made an effort to steady his voice.

"You can write to La Devize, Louis," he said to me. "It is natural that you should ask the Countess for news of your friend. You'll have to read between the lines of her reply, of course, for no one can lie as she can. . . . Perhaps he's home back there already. . . . They can't have got far," he added.

"Then he wasn't alone?" asked Michèle. The abbé kept his eyes on the fire to which he had just added a log. I pointed out that one couldn't travel without money, and that Mirbel was given practically nothing by his family.

"He was always complaining of that . . . you can't have forgotten, sir?"

The abbé went on picking red-hot embers from the fire as though he had not heard my question. We stood there waiting, while he, obviously frightened of being interrogated, hoped that we would go. Michèle brought no pressure to bear on him. She gave one last look round the dirty, untidy room, and then slowly went downstairs, her hand touching the rail on which Jean's must so often have rested. The paper on the wall showed damp patches, the very tiles of the hall floor were wet.

"Please," said the Curé, "write to me as soon as you hear anything, and I will do the same."

"I'm not asking you the name of the person he went away with," said Michèle suddenly. (I heard later that she had picked up from Saintis the rumours that were going around about Hortense Voyod and the odd young fellow who was living up at Monsieur Calou's.) "Though it's not hard to guess," she added with a laugh.

I remember that laugh very clearly. The Curé had opened the front-door, and the mist had drifted in, smelling of smoke. Monsieur Calou began talking very fast, without looking at us, and still keeping his hand upon the latch.

"What has that got to do with you? It is a matter of no importance, Michèle, because he cares about no one in the world except you. You were his despair. What has it got to do with you?" he repeated, "if another woman took the chance that came her way simply because you were not on the spot? Have some pity on me and don't ask questions. . . . You'll hear all you want to know from the people round. You won't even have to ask them. It is not for a poor priest to speak of such things. You are a couple of children. All I am permitted to say, Michèle, is that if Jean is to be saved, it will be through you. No matter what happens, he will never forsake you. He has not in any real sense betrayed you. . . . He was to me as the son of my old age, but I made no attempt to force his confidence. The office of fatherhood, which I had myself assumed, put no obligation on him. He is guilty of an offence against God alone, that God whose presence I so signally failed to make him feel, of whom he knew no more, after all these months spent under my roof, than he did on that first day when the three of you were quarrelling in the garden: do you remember?"

Yes, I remembered. Young as I was, the past had already become for me an abyss in which even the most trivial events of my childhood showed now as lost delights.

It may have been on this very evening, after we had closed the door behind us and had plunged into the fog, that Monsieur Calou wrote the lines which are now lying before me.

"If we want to know in what relation we really stand to God, we cannot do better than consider our feelings about other people. This is peculiarly the case when one person above all others has touched our affections. If he is seen to be the source of all our happiness and all our pain, if our peace of mind depends on him alone, then, let it be said at once, we are separated as far from God as we can be, short of having committed mortal sin. Not that love of God condemns us to aridity in our human friendships, but it does lay on us the duty of seeing that our affection for other human beings shall not be an end in itself, shall not usurp the place of that utterly complete love which no one can begin to understand who has not felt it. During the retreat which I made before I was ordained, I sacrificed to Thee, O God, all hope of human fatherhood. I sought to find it again in my feeling for this boy. How could I hope to overcome in him, and conquer, those natural instincts of the young animal, if I found them so attractive? It is easier to hate the evil in ourselves than in those whom we love."

Michèle led the way. Each time I tried to catch up with her she quickened her pace as though she wanted to be left undisturbed. She held her head high and gave no sign that what she had just heard had beaten down her high spirit. All that really mattered to me was that we should get home before our stepmother should have noticed our long absence. This anxiety blotted all other considerations from my mind.

As we crossed the hall on the way to our rooms, Brigitte opened the door of the small drawing-room and called to us.

"Wouldn't you like some tea? It will warm you after your long walk."

Michèle replied that she was not hungry, but, faced by the insistence of our stepmother, she felt, I think, that she mustn't seem fearful or anxious to conceal anything. We entered the room, therefore, and found the tea-things laid. Brigitte Pian's face was void of the expression which I knew so well when she was girding herself for battle. I was pretty sure, however, that she knew where we had been, and found it hard to square with her actual appearance of fatigue and defeat the mood of anger which should normally have been hers. She set herself to fill our cups and to butter some slices of bread. These she offered first to Michèle, after which she asked us, as though it had been the most natural thing in the world, whether we had seen the abbé Calou. Michèle nodded assent, but the crash of thunder which I fully expected to follow never came.

"In that case," said Brigitte in a sad and sympathetic voice, "I suppose you know . . ."

Michèle, keen to carry the fight into the enemy's camp, interrupted the sentence. We knew all that there was to know, but she would rather not discuss it. . . . As she moved towards the door, my stepmother called her back.

"Please stay here a little longer, Michèle."

"If you are going to preach to me, I tell you plainly that I am in no mood . . ."

The note of defiance in the girl's voice seemed to make no impression on Brigitte Pian who, doubtless, was pursuing her own train of thought. What was it?

"You need not worry. I haven't the heart to preach to you. I only want you to be fair to me. But I want that very much."

Michèle, her face set in hard lines, was wondering how the attack was going to develop. She raised her cup to her lips and slowly sipped her tea, thus avoiding the necessity of answering Brigitte, and forcing that lady to show her hand.

"You will tell me that it is useless to look for justice to our fellow men, and that the approval of our own conscience should be sufficient for us. But, like all other human beings, I am weak. I have no wish to triumph over you, my poor child, but, for my own peace of mind, I want you to admit that I was right in scenting danger for you. You do see that, don't you? This young man has turned out to be worse even than I feared. I knew how to protect you as well as, if not better than, your real mother. . . ."

We were so used to the fact that Brigitte Pian never spoke aimlessly, that our first instinct was always to wonder what lay behind her words. I think she had never been more sincere than she was at that moment. There was nothing to tell us that the question which she had put to Michèle was the expression of an agony of mind which had not left her for a single instant since our father's death. We knew nothing of that. What she wanted was to be reassured. She did not see how Michèle could possibly avoid the necessity of admitting that she had been right. My sister had no idea of the strength of the blow she was levelling at her enemy when she exclaimed:

"You want me to recognize that you were stronger than I was. Well, I do. It was you, and you only, who separated us. It was you who drove him to desperation. If he is a lost soul, you are the cause of his damnation, and if I . . ."

The sky did not fall. Brigitte Pian remained seated in her chair: or rather, contrary to her usual habit, she lay slumped in it. She scarcely raised her voice.

"Misery has unhinged your mind, Michèle. Either that, or you have not been told all. If anyone is the cause of his damnation, it is that Voyod woman."

"A letter from me would have sufficed to turn him from his intention, just one letter. If only I had been able to speak to him, if only you had not put yourself between us with the same merciless obstinacy which has led you to ruin the abbé Calou in the eyes of his Superiors. . . ."

Sobs prevented Michèle from going on. It was the first time that she had ever cried in her struggles with Brigitte. It was as though some instinct, prompted by hatred, had told her that tears would spoil the older woman's triumph and leave her beaten and bewildered.

"Come now," said Brigitte Pian, "come now." She spoke in the same voice that she had used during the night when I had heard her muttering to herself. "You can hardly deny that the young man has shown himself to be a black sheep, an evil-liver. . . ."

"An evil-liver because at eighteen he has let himself be led away? . . ."

Michèle hesitated to add "by a woman."

"Yes," Brigitte insisted with the concentrated passion of someone seeking to gain peace of mind. "I mean what I say—an evil-liver. We will leave the woman out of it, if you so wish. The fact remains that this young man of good family has behaved like a ruffian, and that if there was any justice in this world, he would be behind bars at this moment."

Michèle shrugged her shoulders. This kind of talk seemed utterly absurd to her. Its very excess did something to disarm her indignation. She replied that, as everyone knew, Brigitte Pian was quite unable to control herself when she had to deal with a matter of this kind. The prisons would have to be enlarged if all the young men guilty of such crimes were to be locked up.

"It isn't every young man," retorted Brigitte, "who breaks open desks and runs off with his benefactor's savings."

She had flung this remark at my sister with no definite intention, thinking that we knew all the circumstances of Jean's flight. The look of horror on Michèle's face warned her too late of her mistake. She jumped up and hurried to the girl's assistance, but Michèle pushed her away and sought comfort on my shoulder. I was standing close to the wall.

"That's a wicked lie!" She spoke so fast that the words tumbled over one another: "an invention of the Vignottes!"

"Hadn't they told you, my poor dears?" She fixed on us a long gaze of happy astonishment. Never had she addressed us in tones so quiet, so almost gentle. She felt reassured. We should have to admit that no mother could have acted otherwise.

Evening was deepening into night. Brigitte stood there illuminated only by the flickering flames.

"I should have realized that that wretched abbé wouldn't have the courage to tell you of his pupil's villainy. I am sorry that I gave you such a shock, Michèle. But now do you understand? It was my duty to protect you against a criminal. I knew what I was about. The necessary information had been given me by the Comte de Mirbel . . . but too late, alas, and for that I ask your forgiveness. My great fault lay in ever letting you associate with that young ne'er-do-well. I should never have regarded the presence of Monsieur Calou as providing a sufficient guarantee. I fear that I was wrong, too, in my estimate of him. . . ."

She read acquiescence into our lack of words and proceeded to yield utterly to her craving for self-abandonment and surrender.

"There are moments in one's life," she went on, "when one fails to see clearly. More than once I have questioned myself, have felt myself oppressed by doubts. . . . Your father's death had a greater effect on me than you will ever realize. We are responsible for every one of the souls with which God brings us into contact on our way through life. 'What hast thou done to thy brother?' That question, put by God to Cain, I asked myself when I looked at the dead body of the man whose life had been so suddenly required of him. Sudden death is a fearful warning. . . . Each day I become more aware of all those for whom I shall have to answer. There may have been times when my judgment was wrong, but God is my witness that I have ever striven for His greater glory and for the welfare of men's souls. . . . What was that you said, Michèle?"

My sister shook her head as a sign that she had said nothing, moved away from the wall, and left the room. I made as though to follow her, but my stepmother kept me back.

"No, better leave her alone with her thoughts."

Time passed. Brigitte Pian poked the fire, and every now and again a flame leapt upwards setting her large face in a warm glow, and then died down, until nothing but her forehead and the pale mass of her cheeks was visible in the gathering dusk.

"No," I said suddenly, "it would be better not to leave her alone."

I went out and climbed to the second floor where Michèle's room was situated. I knocked, but there was no reply. I opened the door, thinking that she was lying in the dark as it was so often her habit to do. I called to her in a low voice, for I was frightened of dark rooms. But she was not there. I looked for her high and low, scouring the house from the kitchen to the linen-cupboard. But no one had seen her. I went out on to the steps. The cold darkness was lit by an invisible moon. I went back to the small drawing-room.

"I don't know where Michèle is," I cried; "I have looked for her everywhere."

"Well, she's probably gone out—into the town, perhaps: what is there so tragic about that, you little silly?"

My stepmother had risen from her chair. With the tears pouring down my cheeks, I replied that there was nothing to take Michèle into the town at this time of night; at which, in a wild sort of voice, she murmured that these children would drive her mad. But already she had hurried before me to the steps. Someone was walking along the path.

"Is that you, Michèle?"

"No, ma'am: it's Saintis."

Saintis, her enemy, had been reinstated, and she could not, with decency, dismiss him until some further time should have elapsed. He was out of breath, and we could hear him panting in the darkness. He told us that Mademoiselle Michèle had borrowed a lamp from him for her bicycle. She had asked him to tell Madame not to wait dinner, as she had something very important to see to.

"Where can she have gone?"

"Gone?—to Baluzac, I don't mind betting."

"I suppose it is just as well," said Brigitte Pian when we had returned to the little drawing-room, where a lamp was now burning. "She probably hopes that the abbé Calou will explain everything satisfactorily, will be able to gloss matters over. . . . Still, theft with breaking and entering is theft with breaking and entering: nothing will alter that."

She started to stroke my hair: "What an example for you, my poor boy," she sighed. "At your age you should know nothing of such horrors. But what a lesson, too, Louis. Look at your sister, a good girl if ever there was one . . . yet nothing can keep her from roaming the woods and fields on a winter's night. That is what passion does to human beings—just swallows them up. Promise me that you will be different, that you will never let yourself be changed into a wild beast."

She tried to kiss me, but I turned away my face and went to the other end of the room, where I sat down out of reach of the circle of lamplight.

XIII

I SAID nothing that could betray the hatred with which she filled me. But she must have felt its presence there between us as we sat together at dinner, and later still, while we waited for Michèle. It was eleven o'clock before she got back. This time Brigitte called to her in vain. Michèle went straight upstairs without pausing at the drawing-room. I replied in monosyllables to the remarks which my stepmother made as she gave me my candle.

Just as I was bracing myself to stretch my legs beneath the icy sheets, she came into my room. She was wearing a purple dressing-gown, and her hair was without lustre. One heavy coil lay like a fat snake between her neck and the collar of her gown.

"It's a cold night: I've brought you a hot-water bottle," she said.

She slipped it into my bed and touched my feet. For the first time in my experience she kissed me good-night and tucked me up.

"The poor child didn't dare to admit that Monsieur Calou had finally opened her eyes to what really happened. I think I know how she must be suffering. We must be gentle with her. She will realize later that I was right. . . . Don't you think she will?" she asked, raising the candle above her head the better to see me.

Sheer exhaustion offered me a way of escape. I closed my eyes and turned my face to the wall, taking refuge in a state that was half waking, half sleeping, like a swimmer struggling between conflicting currents.

She sighed.

"Asleep already!" she murmured; "how lucky you are!" and went back to the loneliness of her own room.

I was awakened in the night by the creaking of her floor. I told myself that she was brooding over her scruples, and the thought gave me an unworthy sense of pleasure. I did not realize then the full horror of the torment which those servants of God inflict upon themselves who do not know the true nature of love.

Next day, at breakfast, Michèle, looking pale and heavy-eyed, avoided my questions.

"According to Monsieur Calou it is ridiculous to say that he stole anything," she told me. "The abbé was in the habit of making small advances to Jean when he wanted money. This time, Jean helped himself, but he knew that his mother would pay it back at once. He left a note in the desk, and the abbé knew perfectly well that he would be reimbursed."

I asked whether it was true that Mirbel had broken open the lock. My sister was forced to admit that he had, but she was annoyed by the face I pulled, and turned her back on me, refusing to say any more. The odd thing was that though I regarded such an act as monstrous, it somehow reawakened my feeling of affection for Mirbel. I could never willingly turn from him or deny him, and I trembled to think that I was thus indissolubly bound to a boy who could wallow in crime.

It was only much later, and then very scrappily, that the details of this adventure were imparted to me, not by Monsieur Calou but by Michèle herself. Even to-day, the old Countess sometimes talks of that time, when I go to see her, but without the slightest sign that she finds the memory of it in any way embarrassing. "It would make a good subject for one of your novels," she says, savouring her words as though they were something good to eat. "I might have kept it for myself, but you can have it. I'd only spoil it. It's not really my line of country. It has nothing to do with love, you see. . . ." For her, only fashionable adultery has any right to the name of love.

The origin of this theft and of this flight which lay so heavily on Michèle's destiny was to be found in a "good action" which the abbé Calou had performed many years earlier, during his first few years at Baluzac. He was suffering at that time from the worst form of spiritual discomfort to which a priest can be exposed. He felt convinced that the great mass of the people with whom he was brought in contact had no need of him. It wasn't that they just laughed at the Kingdom of God: they did not even know that it existed, had never been stung to awareness by the good news of the Gospel. For them the Church was merely an organization which carried out certain prearranged rites suitable for special occasions, using for the purpose a class of men called priests. That was the most they would admit. What, then, was there left for a priest to do but turn in upon himself and tend in his own heart the flickering flame that lit his footsteps, and those of a very few others, until such time as God's intentions for His world should be manifested with glory?

Such was the abbé's state of mind when, after twelve years spent in a seminary, he had to give up the Chair he occupied because of certain charges that had been levelled at his orthodoxy. Very humbly he had accepted the cure of souls at Baluzac, a place situated in the remote confines of the heath country, and one of the most dreaded livings in the whole diocese. Study and prayer made up the tale of his days. He decided that he would devote himself entirely to the small flock entrusted to him without looking for any results. On the very first Sunday after his installation he spoke as simply as he could—and such was always his habit—to about forty faithful parishioners, but without any deliberate attempt to put himself on their level. The subject with which his sermon dealt was the priest's mission. What he really did was to meditate out loud, speaking to himself rather than to them. The next day he found, slipped beneath his door, an anonymous letter of eight pages. A woman had heard him and had understood. She must be someone of education. She had come to church, she said, out of curiosity, and because she had nothing else to do. She had gone away completely overwhelmed. But she complained that priests had fallen into the error of waiting until the lost sheep came to them. They should imitate their Master who sought them out and carried them home upon His shoulders. She alluded to something shameful that could not be put into words, to a state of despair from which the human soul could not free itself unless God took the first steps towards achieving its release.

That morning, the abbé Calou believed that a sign had been vouchsafed to him. He was, by temperament, inclined (like Pascal) to expect from God sensible marks of His intentions, the provision of material evidence. This cry which, on the very first day of his new life, had reached him from the wastes of a forgotten countryside, he interpreted as an answer to his prayer for comfort, it is true, as a reply to his questing heart, but also as a gentle reproach. He prepared his sermon for the following Sunday with all his usual care, but, while couching it in general terms, he weighed its every word so that the unknown writer of the letter might hear in it an answer designed for her in particular. As he glanced round the congregation, he saw two brown eyes fixed on him from behind a pillar, and noticed that they were set in a young, fresh face that lacked something of firmness in its contours. Later that same day he discovered that it belonged to a schoolmistress from Vallandraut who came frequently to Baluzac for reasons which his informants would not specify, though they shook their heads a good deal and chuckled. The abbé Calou noted in his diary how fierce a struggle he had had to wage with himself before delivering his sermon, but after that single entry there are no further references to the incident, or only such indirect and obscure hints as would have meaning for no one but himself. This was due to the fact that the schoolmistress had almost at once become his penitent, and that he felt himself bound by the secrecy of the Confessional.

I will set down, as discreetly as possible, what I know of the affair. This young and innocent woman had, very early, fallen under the fascination of Hortense Voyod—a type of amazon not wholly unknown, contrary to general opinion, in country districts. There are people who set their toils and are prepared to go hungry for a very long while before any prey lets itself be caught. The patience of vice is infinite. One single victim will content such people, and a brief moment of contact will ensure them long years of happy repletion. When at the end of September Monsieur Calou entered on his cure at Baluzac, the chemist's wife had just completed a different kind of cure at Vichy. Though she was fully aware that her new young friend would be a difficult catch to land, since she was a girl with an excessively scrupulous conscience, she was far from supposing that her influence would be seriously menaced. She could think of no one within a radius of ten miles whose intervention she need fear. Consequently, she attached little importance to the letter she received one morning putting an end to the friendship, though it did have the effect of making her hasten her return. No sooner had she got home than she discovered the identity of her adversary. She told herself that it would be mere child's play to get the better of him.

Here, once again, if I am to be faithful to my promise to invent nothing, I cannot describe a struggle about the progress of which I have no precise information. It must have been hard, since the abbé Calou, who never asked favours and hated meddling, managed to get his penitent transferred. The young girl, in spite of the fact that she was sent to another school, was still exposed not only to Madame Voyod's letters, but also to her frequent visits, that lady having recently bought a car, the first to be owned by anyone living in Baluzac. But on the very eve of the day which she had chosen for her second trip, the post brought her a short note dated from Marseilles. In it the girl announced that she had entered the novitiate of a Missionary Order, and said farewell to her friend until such time as they should meet in another world.

Although no scene ever took place between the chemist's wife and the abbé, he realized, before very long, that he had roused in her a degree of hatred which no mere passage of time would serve to allay. The knowledge did not much worry him on his own account, because it seemed impossible that she could get any hold over him, but it did on hers, for he was a man who could well understand the depths of her misery, no matter how shameful its causes might be.

He had always had an eye for the unforeseeable repercussions, the mysterious consequences, of our actions when we intervene in the destinies of others, for no matter what good reasons.

His adversary was not slow in opening her attack. At first it was confined to the only field in which she could come to grips with him. Anti-clerical feeling was running high at that time. Together with the schoolmaster of Baluzac and his wife, Hortense Voyod set up a sort of committee of propaganda the activities of which very soon extended to the whole neighbourhood. But in Baluzac itself her reputation was so bad that the offensive made very little headway. For the space of two or three years the Curé seemed to be justified in his belief that he had very little to fear. For all that, he never felt comfortable when he had to pass the chemist's shop, and, if he happened to meet the woman in the street, it was he who looked away, so violent was the effect upon him of her cold, implacable glare.

She had waited years for her victim. Her opportunity for revenge was not so long in coming. The abbé had every excuse for being caught off his guard, since she was known not to be interested in young men, and was not likely to be physically attractive to them. She often showed herself arrayed in the "bloomers" which, at that time, were fashionable among female cyclists. She sported a low-cut bodice confined by a belt which was adorned in front by an enormous clasp engraved with her monogram. Her hair, arranged "à la Cléo," was parted in the middle, arranged in two shining bandeaux over her ears, only the lobes of which were visible, and caught, at the nape of her neck, into a huge yellow "bun" which rained innumerable pins. Her face was a mass of freckles which were thickly clustered on her nose and cheek-bones, thining out above. A few seemed to have strayed into the substance of her wild and voracious eyes, where they showed like pieces of wreckage in a waste of sea.

The abbé Calou had profited by Jean's convalescence to complete his conquest of him. Or that, at least, was what he thought. He was, in this, the dupe of an illusion from which we all suffer in spite of the lessons of experience. In dealing with human beings, no position is ever permanently won either in love or friendship. Jean de Mirbel, betrayed by his mother and weakened by illness, was in the mood to feel a shock of passing gratitude and to surrender before a show of tenderness. But from his very first day at Baluzac, a hard core of resistance to the priest had grown up in his mind. It was still there, though Monsieur Calou did not realize it. The relation of priest to layman is never a neutral one: he either attracts or repels. Mirbel was always conscious of an instinctive repulsion, a feeling of disgust for the man who was "professionally" chaste. Against this instinct he struggled as hard as he could, but was unable to keep himself from hating the very smell of a house which had no woman in it. He held it as a grievance that Monsieur Calou should think it natural for a young man of his age to subscribe to the same rule as himself, and his brooding rancour was the greater since neither in mind nor in heart was he susceptible to the attractions of piety, purity and divine love. Those who live by the light of the latter find it hard to understand that the majority of mankind are complete strangers to it. They can form no idea of a state of mind in which it plays no part. The monotony of his solitary life, his losing fight against seeming to be ungrateful to a man who had done so much for him, combined to reawaken in Jean de Mirbel the old slumbering devil. The very affection which Monsieur Calou showed to him played into the enemy's hands, for Jean was by nature just the kind of young man who instinctively sets himself against any display of tenderness. Many and many a time in after life I have heard him say: "How I hate being loved!"

As the result of an inward contradiction which he never attempted to resolve, Mirbel resented the fact that the abbé seemed willing to relax in his favour the rigours of a moral and religious rule which he nevertheless hated. The priest shut his eyes to a number of things, and refrained from bothering the boy where the mere letter of the law was concerned. Far from feeling grateful for this latitude, Jean drew strength from the old man's weakness, and began to "run wild." On several occasions he went to the local inn, but he was not naturally sociable, and he made no friends there. On the other hand, he was definitely attractive to women, and had had his first "adventure" before the winter was out. The girl's parents complained to the abbé, who intervened, though in rather a tactless way. Like most chaste men he believed that a serious love affair was the best way of protecting a young man from the passing temptations of the flesh. He had no doubts about Jean's loyalty to Michèle, and felt sure that he would never be false to her. Now, however true it may be that a great many young men are capable of remaining faithful to the young women whom they love, there are plenty of others, and Mirbel was one of them, who think of "being in love" and indulging their senses as two totally different things. They really care for one woman and for one woman only, and it exasperates them to think that the same standard should be applied to the genuine adoration of true love and to the trivial affairs in which the body is all that matters.

This subject was the occasion of the first real quarrel that took place between the abbé and Mirbel. In the course of it the latter let himself go with a violence which, until that moment, he had kept under strict control. He at once established himself in a position of advantage by making a mock of the fact that the priest did not dream of condemning him on grounds of Christian morality, but appealed rather to an outworn code of sentiment in which no one outside the walls of a seminary any longer believed. He went so far as to exclaim that he forbade him to speak of Michèle, adding that he would let no one mention her name in his presence. The angrier Mirbel became, the less did the abbé press his argument. But Jean felt no gratitude for this consideration, and resented the other's obvious, if unspoken, grief. "He makes it a point of grievance that I behave to him much too like a complacent father," the abbé noted in his diary that evening. "However little of a Christian a man may be, he wants to be loved in and for God alone—even though he does not believe in God."

Though Mirbel has never confessed to me precisely what it was that he said in the heat of anger, I imagine that this sentence of the abbé Calou's had reference to something very cruel which he had let slip that evening. Jean knew that he had been cruel, and though part of him was horrified by the realization, he drove ahead along the same road with a sort of fierce intensity, and went on to display a needless spitefulness. It was, however, neither of malice aforethought, nor with any intention of dealing his benefactor a stunning blow, that he became entangled with the chemist's wife. It was the couple from the school who first took him to visit Hortense Voyod. On that rainy February day when the young man whom she had watched for so long from behind her window blinds crossed the rain-soaked little courtyard wrapped in his schoolboy's cape and hood, and entered the shop, she could at last heave a sigh of relief, even though her revenge was as yet far from complete.

Many were the discussions held by the light of an oil lamp and in the warmth of a roaring stove, with Armagnac loosening the assembled tongues. Jean would have found it impossible to say precisely what satisfaction he derived from the presence of this pallid woman and from the sound of her voice which, for all its hoarseness, was gentle and quite unmarked by any local brogue. While the schoolmaster's anti-clerical passion, when it was expended on the politics of the moment, had no manner of interest for Mirbel, the mocking sallies of the chemist's wife roused an immediate response in him. She spoke a language which he had never heard till then, but which he at once recognized.

On that first evening she insisted that he should come to her shop only after nightfall, and should never enter the door until he was quite certain that no one had seen him. For, said she, the Curé, with whom she had had several passages of arms, would certainly not approve of their friendship. There was no reason, however, why it should not be kept secret. He protested against being involved in his tutor's quarrels. During the next few days they began to realize how deep was the sentiment that bound them together.

The ruling passion of this woman (who was without any real education, though she had read a number of modern books both good and bad) was a hatred of, a sense of grievance against, the God whose very existence she denied. The lack of logic in such an attitude did not bother her in the slightest degree. Against an unknown Being in whom she did not believe she levelled the reproaches of a class of creatures for whom, in this world, there can be no release save in complete destruction.

It is most unlikely that she ever spoke to Mirbel of this private and festering sore. But it so happened that, though there was no particular reason why he should share the special bitterness of a woman twenty years his senior, he did suffer from a wild sense of anger against the Fate that had made him what he was. That he was a Mirbel, the heir to a patrician name, made it all the stranger that he should be animated by so hostile, so stubborn a feeling of resentment against all ordered living, against all constraint where his own happiness was concerned. Hortense Voyod was well aware from what poisoned source her own hatred proceeded, but for no consideration in the world would she have imparted this knowledge to Jean, though she could have done so had she wished. The young man, on the other hand, had no idea why it was that everything in life seemed hateful to him with the exception of one young girl whom he would probably never see again, and a priest who represented the very object of his detestation.

Perhaps Hortense Voyod would have reached her goal less easily had not Jean been an instrument ready to her hand. But the understanding which grew between them from the occasion of their very first meeting, the link that bound them so tightly together, facilitated her manœuvre. No longer was it necessary for her to feign a sympathy, which, in fact, she genuinely felt. The youth had walked willingly into her spider's parlour and seemed to take pleasure in the consciousness of his imprisonment. No trickery on her part had been necessary to attract him thither.

It was the abbé Calou's habit to go into the church each evening with the object of finishing the reading of his breviary before the Holy Sacrament, and he stayed there until dinner-time. As soon as he was out of the way, Jean used to leave the Presbytery by the door which faced away from the main road, and make his way round the outskirts of the village. It was not necessary to go into the shop at all. He could reach Hortense's house by jumping over the fence which surrounded the kitchen garden.

Even had he not wanted to avoid meeting stray customers,

Mirbel would have been careful to keep out of the way of the chemist, who was a little old man for ever occupied in wrapping up bottles of medicine as though the lives of all the invalids in the neighbourhood depended on him. His manners were excessively humble, but his way of laughing and the expression of his eyes gave them the lie. He looked after his wife's property (that he should do so formed the essential clause of their secret compact: he made no claim on her person, but, in return for this concession, had insisted that her property be consigned to his charge). Consequently he was absent every afternoon, and, on returning home, never ventured into the back shop when what he called "the club" was in session.

Scarcely a fortnight passed before Monsieur Calou got wind of these secret meetings. This time he did not yield to his first impulse, and, when at last he mentioned the subject to Mirbel, did so without any show of anger, and only after giving much thought to the problem of how best to deal with the situation. Far from reproaching the boy, he realized that solitude is a vocation which can hardly be expected to appeal to youths of eighteen. But he had good reasons—reasons which he could not mention to Jean—for holding that Hortense Voyod was a woman bent on his destruction. What he did, therefore, was to make an appeal to his loyalty. To enter into close relations with such a woman while he was living under her enemy's roof would be tantamount to treachery. If Jean felt it impossible to remain at Baluzac without paying constant visits to the chemist's shop, they had better face the fact, and the abbé would make arrangements for the boy to go home. But this was what Jean dreaded above all else, since it would mean that he would be sent to board at some Jesuit college. Moreover, his master's tone in mentioning the subject had touched him. He could not deny that Hortense Voyod wanted to injure the Curé—not that she had ever attacked him in Jean's hearing (he would never have permitted such a thing), but her sentiments were obvious in every word she spoke; so much so, that each time he left the back shop and found himself again in the Presbytery dining-room, looking across the steaming tureen at the abbé's childlike gaze, and returning his smile, he felt deeply ashamed. He gave his word that he would discontinue his visits. He told me later that he spoke in perfect good faith and fully meant to keep his promise.

It was about this time that Monsieur Calou arranged for him to have a horse, and stopped me in the street with the proposal that he and Michèle should exchange letters, with what disastrous results I have already explained.

Separated, as he was, from Michèle, and forbidden to correspond with her, Jean had been suffering from a sense of being exiled even before he made the acquaintance of Hortense Voyod. He felt it still harder to endure his isolation when he was deprived of the distraction provided by the discussions to which he had grown accustomed, and those readings aloud by the schoolmaster of articles by Hervé, Gérault-Richard and Jaurès. (On these occasions Hortense would toss off her glass like a man, light a cigarette, and hold the company by those bursts of bitter, lively talk which, as Mirbel told me many years later, still remained in his memory as having been curiously exciting.)

The abbé Calou would far rather have faced some active show of resentment by his pupil. How could he deal with this sullen gloom, as of some caged beast?—especially after the Superior of the Sacred Heart had dryly intimated that all epistolary communications between him and Michèle must cease? Jean no longer occupied his time with reading, but roamed the woods on foot and on horseback until darkness fell. After some weeks he took to paying frequent visits to the schoolmaster. The abbé shut his eyes to all this. He had a pretty shrewd suspicion that the boy found a letter from Hortense Voyod awaiting him each time he went there, and that he left one for her when he said goodnight. But nothing had been said about writing. Without these almost daily exchanges, it is probable that their relations would never have taken a passionate turn, and that it was the young man's romantic effusions which gave Hortense her great idea. She began to think that certain developments might be possible of which, hitherto, she had never even dreamed; for Jean was young enough to be her son.

She proceeded with the utmost caution. At first she confined herself to the language of friendship, a sentiment which she was an adept in using for her own purposes, though quite incapable of feeling in fact. Since her days at boarding-school, where she had remained until she got her diploma, friendship had never been anything for her but an alibi for desire. And now it was her desire for revenge that was at stake. She had no illusions about the kind of feeling which she inspired in Mirbel. He had not confided in her, but she knew perfectly well that he was very unhappy, and that his heart belonged to another. But, more clear-sighted than the abbé, she soon realized how strong the animal was in him, and how wholly dominated he was by the blind and irresistible cravings of his senses.

Hortense Voyod had begun by getting a clear picture of this side of his nature. The two or three letters from her which Jean kept, and which he showed me later, were not so much sentimental in tone as carefully composed with the sole object of stirring, without any touch of coarseness, a young imagination condemned to loneliness. One of the few notes left by the abbé on the subject of Hortense shows the extent to which the priest was preoccupied, even obsessed, by the thought of this woman. "It is difficult to account for such knowledge of the human mind in a mere country-bred woman," he wrote; "the explanation is, I suppose, that vice itself has a certain educational effect. It is not given to all of us to look evil in the face. Our petty individual weaknesses, to which we give the name of "evil," have nothing in common with this violent determination to destroy the soul. . . . The spirit of evil, as the eighteenth century knew it and expressed it in the *Liaisons Dangereuses*, exists, as I know now, actually within a few miles of my Presbytery, behind the shutters of a chemist's shop. . . ."

Spring came early. Jean, though he would have to face his finals before the year was out, continually played truant. Hortense knew that she could contrive a meeting with him as soon as she thought that the right moment had come. All she had to do was to take a walk along the banks of the Ciron. But she was in no hurry and wanted to avoid all unnecessary risk. First of all, she must so arrange matters that the boy was haunted by the thought of her, obsessed by dreams in which she was the central figure. Her plans were beginning to extend further than the mere satisfaction of a desire for vengeance. It was not enough for her to deal the abbé Calou a mortal blow. Ever since she had lost her girl friend she had been seeking a pretext to get rid of her old chemist husband, whose days of usefulness were over. She reckoned that this young Mirbel could not only help her to her revenge, but could serve as a stage in her fight for freedom, provided he was willing to face the scandal. But she was still uncertain what steps to take.

As soon as the first fine weather came, the abbé Calou, as was his custom, made a tour of the district and the outlying farms, on his bicycle. He had to round up the children for his catechism classes and visit the sick, especially the old men whom their sons kept hard at work until they dropped down dead. Very often, as they lay helpless in bed, there would be some virago of a daughter-in-law to grudge them the very black bread which they mumbled with their toothless gums. Here was to be seen humanity with very little pity for itself and none whatever for others. The general view in such houses was that all priests are sly and lazy. . . . "What's the use of the clergy, anyway? . . . much better . . ." What it would be much better to do with them was never clear in the speakers' minds, but it had some connexion with an idea, so familiar at that time to the abbé Calou, of what that stationary cross bearing the figure of the nailed God really meant. The priest, fastened to the same instrument of torment and exposed to the same derision, confronts mankind with an enigma which it makes no effort to solve.

One afternoon towards the end of April, when the Curé got home before dusk, he was met by Maria who had been on the look-out for his return. She told him that Monsieur Voyod, the chemist, had been there for half an hour. She had thought it her duty, she said, to light the fire.

This was the first time that Hortense's husband had crossed the threshold of the Presbytery. The abbé, much moved by curiosity, found his visitor seated beside the smoking grate. As the priest entered he rose from his chair. He was wearing his Sunday best. A narrow black ribbon failed to conceal his shirt stud, and it would not have been difficult to insert a hand between his collar and his skinny neck. When he smiled he showed a mouth entirely empty.

He apologized for not having come before this to pay his respects to his parish priest. He had feared that he would not be too well received. Most people, however, knew that he did not share all his wife's ideas. When his first wife had been alive he had always gone to church on feast-days, and had sung in the choir until he was nineteen. He was very anxious that the Curé should not look on him as an enemy, and hoped that he would be good enough to give him his custom. It was a nuisance to have to go into Vallandraut every time one wanted a few lozenges.

All this was spoken glibly, like a lesson learned by heart, and the abbé could not think what it was that the man really wanted. He referred once again to the principles expressed by Madame Voyod, which, he said, he was far from approving. Things weren't any too easy for him, as the Curé might well imagine. He had sacrificed much in order to be a father to the daughter of his old friend Destiou when she was left alone in the world with no one to look after her property. The chemist knew, he said, that people had imputed interested motives to him . . . but what advantage had the marriage brought *him*?—all the troubles of ownership without any of the rewards. The ideas of Madame Voyod had lost him quite a number of customers. She had been a trial to him from the beginning, and now the cloven hoof was beginning to show. It wasn't for him to give the Curé advice, but he couldn't help feeling rather surprised that that young pupil of his should be allowed to see so much of a woman who was known to be an enemy of the Church. However that might be, he, as her husband—though he was more a father to her than a husband—was getting a trifle worried about the meetings between the two. . . . All Baluzac was talking. He knew that the boy was just a young scamp, and that at his age such things didn't seem to be of much importance . . . still . . .

At this point the Curé interrupted him with an assurance that his pupil would pay no further visits to the shop; but the old man went on to talk of meetings in the woods, which couldn't do the young man much good, and which she'd be a great deal better without, as was shown by the fact that she had taken his remarks on the subject with a very bad grace. As though he had forgotten that he had already represented his marriage as an act of disinterested devotion on his part, he began to snivel, and to say that it was very hard that, after a lifetime of work for others, he should find himself threatened in his old age with the loss of everything that he had struggled to build up. When a man has spent years looking after a property, has got it into good fettle, has sown the waste land, cleared the brush, and fought off encroaching neighbours, it's a bit rough, just when everything is going smoothly, to find himself threatened with dismissal like a servant.

Monsieur Calou pointed out that all this had nothing to do with his pupil. The chemist admitted that it was hard to believe the situation had taken so serious a turn. It was the last thing that would ever have entered his head because, after all, it was only fair to Hortense to say that she had never run after men, and no one could say there'd ever been any reason why she should . . . (here the old chemist shot a quick glance at the Curé, but hastily veiled his eyes behind their inflamed lids).

The abbé had taken up the tongs and was paying very self-conscious attention to the fire. He said that the chimney was cold, that they hadn't burned so much as a handful of twigs there all winter. The smoke was making the old man cough. He urged the Curé to give a word of warning to his pupil. . . . Of course there was nothing in it all . . . but why arouse unnecessary gossip? . . . Hortense was getting to the difficult age. . . .

The tongs shook in the priest's large hands. He got up. He had to bend his head in order to see his visitor's face.

"You can be perfectly easy in your mind, Monsieur Voyod. There shall be no more wandering in the woods—from to-morrow: I give you my word for that."

His visitor was of the opinion that the Curé was not in the best of tempers. He said later that he had never seen a man look so "mad," so capable of giving someone a bad half-hour. He felt very glad not to be in that young man's skin when he came in for supper.

As soon as Monsieur Calou was alone he went up to his room, poured some water into the basin, and bathed his face. Then he knelt down, but the words got no further than his lips. Thoughts swarmed in his brain like dead leaves in a high wind. In his brother's family there was a saying: "That was during the holidays in 1880, the year when Ernest saw red. . . ." The last of these terrible fits of temper had delayed his ordination as Deacon by twelve months, and, since that time he had always managed, aided by the gift of Grace, to keep his outbursts within bounds.

On this particular evening he knelt at his *prie-Dieu* and held his head in his hands. "'Ware danger . . . you may do him irreparable harm. . . ." But stronger than this appeal to his sense of prudence was an angry longing to take the boy by the scruff of the neck and force him to his knees until he begged for mercy. That done, there should be an end to this business of not taking things seriously. He should be treated as Uncle Adhémar had always hoped he would be. Since he would obey nothing but superior strength, and yield to nothing but fear, the Curé of Baluzac would find some way of breaking his will and making him as obedient as a whipped cur. "Go on praying, give yourself time," went on the tireless inner voice.

Suddenly he heard the well-known footstep on the stairs. He went to the door and opened it.

"Come in here: I've got something to say to you."

And when the other replied, "Later," he remained stern and insistent.

"Now, at once."

Jean shrugged his shoulders and started up the second flight. But a hand gripped his collar, he felt the pressure of a knee in the small of his back, and found himself lying on the divan-bed where he had been thrown like a parcel, all among the books and pamphlets.

Staggered by what had occurred, he sat here, conscious of two enormous fists in close proximity to his face. He could do nothing but stammer: "What on earth's up?"

The abbé was breathing hard and wiping his damp brow with the back of his hand. Thank Heavens! he had not given way to violence. For the time being, at least the worst was over.

His voice was icy but completely under control. He told his pupil that he had been within an ace of getting a sound thrashing. He added that in future he would keep a watchful eye on him until such time as the Mirbel family should see fit to relieve him of his responsibilities. He hoped, he said, that the boy would not compel him to have recourse to physical violence, because he was apt to lose control of himself, and was a hard hitter.

Having delivered himself of this warning, he ordered his pupil to his room, and remarked that supper would be sent up to him.

"All the time he was behaving like a bargee," wrote Jean to Hortense Voyod. "The Curé kept his eyes shut. Perhaps he was praying, though his lips did not move. . . . Priests always manage to get away with things in that way!"

The abbé kept his word. He never let Mirbel out of his sight except when duty called him away, and then he left Maria in charge. No doubt Jean managed to slip away quite often, and not for a moment did he discontinue his correspondence with Hortense Voyod. This he managed thanks to the visits of the schoolmaster who came to coach him in mathematics. But, for all that, he was completely dominated by the priest, and was forced to bow to his inflexible will. Besides, the moment of examination was approaching, and he had to keep his nose to the grindstone, which meant that he must postpone until later any plans of revolt which he might have formed. He satisfied the examiners on his written work, but was ploughed on his *viva voce*. He did not return to Baluzac until September, having spent a month with the Countess at La Devize. It was the first time that he had met his mother since the terrible revelation which had come to him at Balauze.

"My Jean has changed," wrote the Countess to the abbé Calou. "He was always a handful, but he never used to be cynical. Now all that has changed! I can't utter a word of advice, or even try to raise the tone of our conversations (hard though I try to do so), without the little wretch laughing in my face. I don't want to question the excellence of your methods, but I hope you won't mind my saying that they seem to have misfired entirely in the case of my son."

Almost every day during the vacation Jean got a letter from the chemist's wife. No sooner had he returned to the Presbytery than her plans began to take shape. In October a fresh cause of frustration occurred, and he hesitated no longer. The necessity of making his Retreat had obliged the abbé to be absent for some days. During all that time Jean was constantly in the company of Hortense. The abbé found on his return that the boy seemed much calmer, almost mild, in fact, and consequently he somewhat relaxed his watchful attitude. Relations between the two had become merely those between master and pupil. They hardly ever spoke except about work, and avoided all controversial subjects. The priest was giving himself with renewed confidence to his little flock. The children were beginning to talk freely to him and even showed some signs of affection. He failed to notice the new barrier which had arisen between Jean and himself. Illogical and hard to believe though it may seem, the young man was irritated and hurt by Monsieur Calou's attitude of detachment, and this fresh wound had a good deal to do with the fatal resolution which he was so soon now to take. Its gravity was cunningly concealed from him by Hortense Voyod.

It is by no means uncommon for human beings to set great store by the affection of those for whom they themselves feel no love, and may even think they despise. Jean was quite incapable of understanding how it was that the abbé Calou should keep for him the first place in his heart and mind, though for no consideration in the world would he have admitted as much. Mystics obey the law of an economy which they find it impossible to explain in words to those who are not themselves initiates. How should the priest not feel easy in his mind about Jean? How could he help believing that they were quits, seeing that he had already offered his life for the boy, and daily renewed his sacrifice? The discipline of exchange, of compensation, of transference which Grace imposes on the true believer, was far removed from the world of the flesh into which the adolescent was slowly being introduced. Jean felt that he had been rejected by the one man who held the key to all his secrets, who knew what he had suffered, and was still suffering, because of his mother and because of Michèle. If *he* deserted him, what was there left but flight from a hateful world that held no place for him? He knew, of course, that his relations with Hortense would not last for very long . . . but he had vowed himself to the vocation of misery, and what most attracted him in the whole of this adventure was the thought that it was so utterly hopeless, so completely beyond any power to solve; that it would compel him to set sail from his sheltered harbour and commit himself to a course from which there would be no turning back.

XIV

WE were to stay at Larjuzon until the celebration of what, in the Gironde, is cal'ed the Mass of the Octave. On the very day before it occurred my stepmother received a letter from the Sister who was looking after Octavia. It had been found impossible to prevent a miscarriage, and double phlebitis had set in. The patient's temperature remained high, and her heart was growing weaker. The doctor feared the worst. There was a complete lack of everything in the Rue de Mirail. Though Monsieur Puybaraud had forbidden her to make any appeal to Madame Pian, the Sister felt compelled to disobey him, because the baker and the chemist were turning nasty.

This news seemed to overwhelm my stepmother. She could, no doubt, have managed to get to Bordeaux and back before the Mass of the Octave, but she felt that my old master would, in all probability, not welcome her. So with her customary generosity, she telegraphed a money order in the name of the Sister, and had it addressed to the Convent.

Brigitte asked my advice, and thought her thoughts aloud in my presence, as though she had quite failed to notice the coldness of my attitude. "If they hadn't had *me*!" she kept on saying, and then proceeded to rehearse all that she had already done for the Puybarauds. "I warned them how it would be. Everything is turning out exactly as I said it would. I didn't dare say anything about this final mishap, to warn him that Octavia would almost certainly die, though God knows I felt that something of the kind was bound to happen. . . . It wasn't for a poor weak woman like me to dot their i's for them. Their spiritual director has been very lax. He was the only person who might have been able to keep them from the abyss, instead of doing which he pushed them over the edge! . . . But Monsieur Puybaraud will hold *me* responsible: you see if he doesn't! . . . . Your sister, as it is, thinks that I was the cause of your father's death, as well as of the flight and house-breaking escapade of young Mirbel. . . . Really, it's hard to believe."

She gazed into my face, and the anxious laugh with which she wound up this catalogue of grievances was an invitation, a piteous invitation, to me to say something, to offer her some crumb of comfort. But I remained obstinately silent, and, by so doing, showed clearly enough that I was on the side both of Monsieur Puybaraud and of Michèle in every single instance that she had quoted. She had no one to fall back on but herself. She spent her time dragging from room to room or wandering aimlessly round the table, strengthening her defences against an attack that could come only from herself. Should I, I wonder, be quite so ready to-day to put the weight of responsibility for so much unhappiness on the shoulders of a woman so chivied by the Furies of the new dispensation, so torn by those scruples which, ever since the coming of Christ, have been the stock-in-trade of tortured consciences? Brigitte Pian's urged her to return as soon as possible to town in order that she might see Monsieur Puybaraud in person and so be reassured. But since there was only one train a day, we had to wait until the Mass of the Octave was over.

It meant getting up in pitch darkness. During the whole journey Brigitte had to submit to the presence of Michèle who, at Larjuzon, was for long periods out of her sight. During the whole three hours which we spent cooped up in a second-class carriage, the young girl, swathed from head to foot in crape, played a wicked game. Not once did she so much as look at our stepmother, although she knew that she was being wordlessly implored to do so. To-day I am filled with pity for the poor woman who has been dust these many years. But at the time I felt none. The train, a slow one, was insufficiently heated by hot-water tins which the porter had given us, and I had to kneel on the seat to get a little warmth into my frozen feet. But I began to be aware of what was passing in Madame Brigitte's mind. I fixed my eyes with keen curiosity on the imposing presence, on the great brazen statue whose shadow had darkened my childhood, but now, before my eyes, was toppling on its base. Cracks were opening here and there. Perhaps in a moment I should see it fall. When she got up to leave the carriage she gave me the impression of a small woman. I was astonished. It never occurred to me that it was I who had grown.

She gave the cabman not our address but the Puybarauds'. It was a gloomy morning, and the noise of the conveyance filled the melancholy Rue de Mirail. We glanced up to the floor on which my old master lived, and saw that the shutters were closed. The concierge poked her bony face out of the lean-to which served her as a lodge. From her we learned that the end had come on the previous evening, that Monsieur Puybaraud would not see anybody, and that no one knew when the funeral was to be. We were informed that he had issued very harsh instructions about us. "Misfortune very often makes folk ungrateful," she said, as no doubt we had often noticed. When we were once again in the cab, Michèle's attitude underwent a sudden change. She no longer kept her eyes averted, but stared so long and so relentlessly at our stepmother that the latter was compelled to turn away her own and look out of the window. Though her lips scarcely moved, I knew that she had already begun to recite the prayers for the dead. I am pretty sure that she could not resist the temptation of crying across the spaces of eternal silence: "Well, my poor Octavia, who was right?"

No doubt she surrendered to the temporary satisfaction of finding her views and those of Providence in such complete agreement. But by the time we reached the Cours de l'Intendance an air of gloom had settled on her face. Michèle went to her room and we saw her no more that day. Brigitte Pian came into mine to plague me with questions, but I scarcely answered her. She left the communicating door open. Even though I was in a hostile mood, she found my presence necessary to her peace of mind. After a few moments she came back, and once again went over the whole story of her relations with the Puybarauds during the past two years, making a point of praising her own conduct except on the occasion of her last visit to Octavia's sick-bed. She only hoped, she said, that Monsieur Puybaraud would not run away with the idea that the little argument they had had then had been injurious to the patient! She rehearsed all its ins and outs: she even tried to remember the actual words that she had used. I listened with icy politeness, and gave her not one sentence either of comfort or approval.

At last she could stand it no longer, and begged me to go back alone to the Rue de Mirail. Monsieur Puybaraud would be sure to receive me, and would say when the funeral was to be.

But the concierge would not let me go up, no matter how hard I begged, and I had to get the information I wanted from the Church of St. Éloi, where I was told that there would be no Requiem but only the Absolution. This would be given at eight o'clock next day.

Our stepmother had fully expected that we should be the only people present: but we were not. A great many of Octavia's old pupils had come, and several of the mistresses from the Free School. Almost everyone was crying, and so thick was the air with prayers that I felt something like a sense of physical oppression. Monsieur Puybaraud, wearing the old black overcoat which had been so familiar to me on winter days in the school playground, stood stiffly upright. He neither knelt nor wept. His face was as white as

Octavia's must have been within the four wooden walls of her coffin. Since he appeared to see no one, we might have been able to persuade ourselves that there was nothing hostile in his attitude to us. At the gate of the cemetery he seemed not to notice the hand which I held out to him, and I had to take hold of his. He withdrew it at once. As to my stepmother, she did not dare even to make the gesture, for he bowed his head without giving her a glance or making the slightest movement with his arm.

That evening, after dinner, in my room, whither she had followed me, she said that she feared that Monsieur Puybaraud had listened to the promptings of rebellion. It was much to be regretted that she had not been able to have a word with him, for she might have succeeded in softening his hard heart and helping him to achieve a mood of resignation and submission. To this I objected that the enmity he had shown us was no proof that he felt in the same way towards God, and I added hypocritically that, since he had been the husband of a saint, my stepmother could ask her intercession for all those particular manifestations of grace of which Monsieur Puybaraud stood in need.

"A saint?" said Brigitte Pian; "a saint?" She looked at me without anger, but with a sort of concentrated gaze which might have been taken for stupidity. For a moment or two she moved about the table, and then withdrew, taking with her, doubtless, an added load of trouble and anxiety upon which to brood during the night.

All through the days that followed Octavia's funeral she made no attempt to see the widower again, though she continued to help him surreptitiously, with the connivance of the Sister. Michèle had gone back to the Sacred Heart, and my stepmother and I resumed our old life of shared solitude. She did everything she could to please me, showing an eagerness in the task which might almost have deserved the name of humility. It was as though her sole hope of succour lay in a young man whose attitude to her was one of frightening correctness.

Following the suggestion made to me by the abbé Calou, I wrote from Larjuzon to the Comtesse de Mirbel asking for news of Jean. I found her answer awaiting me in Bordeaux. Every word of her letter had been carefully weighed, with the sole intention of minimizing the scandal.

"I am not at all surprised, my dear young friend, that you should be anxious about Jean, or that you should have been influenced by the ridiculous tittle-tattle that has been going the rounds. He has returned to us here much surprised and considerably disturbed by all the talk there has been about his little escapade. The Curé and the chemist are the two persons chiefly responsible. Both are guilty of having stirred up public opinion. For the second of the gentlemen in question there is some show of excuse, but the former has shown a lack of judgment and moderation which is really quite intolerable in one of his cloth, to say nothing of the fact that he claims to be an educator of youth! I said as much when I went to pay back the money which he had advanced to my son. It has been the subject of fantastic gossip. I can only hope that if it came to your ears you refused to believe a word. The priest had nothing to say to my charges, and I must admit that my feelings as a mother led me to express myself with what may have been rather excessive warmth."

(Much later I was able to realize how sublime the abbé's silence had been. With a single word he could have crushed the woman who was hurling insults at his head, for she did not then know that her son had spent a whole night shivering beneath the windows of the Balauze hotel, that he had very nearly died as a result of that adventure, and that his mind had been permanently scarred and poisoned by what his eyes had seen on that occasion, and by what his ears had heard.)

The Countess told me, in conclusion, that Jean was to spend the rest of the year in England, and that he would have to be in Bordeaux for a few days before starting on his journey. She hoped that he would be permitted to come and say good-bye to us.

This letter left me with a feeling of embarrassment and uncertainty. Ought I to send it on to the abbé Calou in accordance with my promise? I had to relax my attitude of reserve towards my stepmother in order to ask her advice on the point. As a matter of fact, I anticipated a certain amount of pleasure from watching her reactions. But if I had expected her to rail violently against the Curé of Baluzac, there was a surprise in store for me (as there had often been on previous occasions). She adopted an entirely unexpected attitude. She gave it as her considered view that I should do nothing which might unnecessarily wound a man who had recently been so sorely tried. Since, on the other hand, the document might be useful to him, she advised me to forward it, but with a covering note to the effect that we none of us believed the Countess's allegations. This was the first time, so far as I knew, that my stepmother had ever gone back on a verdict once given, and when I wrote to the abbé Calou I did not hesitate to draw his attention to this extraordinary change in her. I allowed myself to indulge in an expression of irony which he did not at all approve. His answer reached me only a week later. I insert a copy of it here with feelings of respect and admiration. I can truly say that, having read it, I was never quite the same again.

"Dear Boy: I have delayed replying to your letter because it arrived after I had left Baluzac, and was forwarded to me at my brother's house where I shall be for some time to come. I shall not beat about the bush with you. You know too much about what has happened for me to be able to deceive you successfully. I am no longer Curé of Baluzac. I am no longer even permitted to live there. I was told to leave the parish as soon as possible, and to retire into the bosom of my family. The long and the short of it is—I am in disgrace, and circumstances compel me to attach rather more significance to that phrase than it usually bears. The Mirbels and old Voyod have agreed to saddle me with full responsibility for the scandal. But that is not all. The report which Madame Brigitte did me the honour of compiling some months ago and of sending to the Vicar-General appears to have anticipated in every detail precisely what did in fact occur. Events have fully justified the weighty and truly remarkable survey which your dear stepmother then prepared of my character and general tendencies. I write this in no spirit of irony, my dear boy, and I will take this opportunity of saying that I did not greatly care for the tone which marked your letter to me. As you know very well, I do not believe in chance, and I do not believe that it is mere chance that all Madame Brigitte's prognostications were borne out by the facts. I will not go so far as to say that her interpretation of the facts or of the motives of others is always very judicious, but she does have a sort of gift for unearthing evil intentions. She would probably be quite genuinely surprised if I told her that my mistake and hers are at bottom identical. They pursue different roads, only to reach the same end. Both of us, she ruled by her reason, I by my feelings, have been inclined to believe that it is our duty to interfere in the destinies of those around us. I do not deny that it is the first duty of the sacred office conferred by priesthood—as, indeed, it is part of the duty of every Christian—to preach the Gospel: but that does not mean that we should try to turn our neighbour into a replica of ourselves, nor force him to see with our eyes. Of ourselves we can do nothing. Our concern should be limited to walking before the Divine Grace as the dog goes in front of the invisible hunter. This we can do with greater or less effectiveness in proportion as we are more or less attentive and obedient to the Will of our Master, more or less willing to let ourselves be moulded by it, more or less ready to ignore our own. So far as I am concerned, Madame Brigitte has been perfectly justified in her attitude. What she condemns in me is the lack of any sense of proportion, of any genuine power of judgment. She points out, with striking truth, that this lack, when found in a priest, and in the highly developed form which it has assumed in my own case, is apt to produce worse disasters than any low, criminal passion. It led me to interfere rashly, heatedly and ill-advisedly, in the concerns of others. Naturally, these activities of mine have, to some extent, served the purposes of Grace, because such is the Love of God that it turns all things to the greater good of those on whom it is lavished. But when it comes to measuring the havoc that accumulates about what we conceive to be our mission, we must give full weight to all those unadmitted interests, all those secret desires the existence of which in our hearts we scarcely realize. That is why we should allow full play to the spirit of compassion.

I am afraid, my dear boy, that all this will seem very obscure to you. We will talk about it again some years from now, should the Father not have seen fit meanwhile to call unto Himself his very useless, nay, his sometimes actively dangerous, servant. For the moment, let me give you the following word of advice in regard to Madame Brigitte. You must not sneer at the way her spirit moves nor look on her ordeal as something petty and unimportant. Up to now she has seen only the edifying aspect of her activities. Suddenly, and without any warning, her eyes have been opened on to a new and horrible view of herself. When Christ makes us see clearly, and we become aware of our actions pressing in upon and surrounding us, we are as much astonished as was the man born blind who, in the Gospel story, saw 'men as trees walking.' But it is important that Madame Brigitte should understand the truth of what I have discovered for myself as a result of my present condition of degradation, which is a great deal worse than you can possibly know. There is no form of calumny that has not been heaped upon me. People believe of me what they will, both in the Archbishop's palace and out of it. I can say without fear of contradiction that now, in my old age, I have lost every scrap of that honourable reputation I once enjoyed in men's eyes, that, in my own person, I have allowed outrage to be done upon that Jesus who has marked me as His own. My family is humiliated and fretted as a result of the shame which I have brought upon it, to say nothing of the material embarrassment which my constant presence in this house has caused to its inmates. My youngest nephew has had to give up his room to me, and share with his brother. I need hardly say that they are all very kind to me. But my sister-in-law is just a little too insistent with her questions. What am I going to do with myself? she asks, and I can answer only that I do not know, for, truth to tell, I am good for nothing, and can be of use to none. . . . It would be foolish to deceive myself further. I stand now in the presence of my

God, as naked, as much stripped of all merit, as utterly defenceless as a man well can be. Perhaps that is the state in which those of us should be whose profession it is—if I may so express myself —to be virtuous. It is almost inevitable that the professionally virtuous should hold exaggerated ideas of the importance of their actions, that they should constitute themselves the judges of their own progress in excellence, that, measuring themselves by the standards of those around them, they should at times be made slightly giddy by the spectacle of their own merits. I should like to think that Madame Brigitte is drawing from her present testing-time an assurance that her feet are set upon the road to a great discovery. . . ."

Some may think that the abbé Calou, by thus addressing a young man of seventeen, was merely showing that he had not made much progress towards bettering his judgment. I did not dare to show this letter to my stepmother, though she no longer made any effort to keep her state of mind from me. I lived continuously now in the intolerable atmosphere created by her condition of spiritual torment. About this time, an anarchist weekly rag called *The Battle*, which flourished on scandal, published a number of poisonous paragraphs about the "abduction of a chemist's wife." I was amazed when Brigitte Pian asked me to get this scurrilous production for her each week. She would never have dared to buy it for herself, nor would she have sent a servant to buy it for her. I could not understand the curious pleasure which she seemed to get from reading it, especially after learning at school that Monsieur Puybaraud had been taken on as editorial secretary, and that, rightly or wrongly, the general view was that all the anti-religious muck which it contained came from his pen.

She spent the whole of each Saturday evening reading this paper. I know, for I was always there, and I suspect that she carried her perusal of it far into the night. It was as though she wanted to saturate her mind in the vileness of a man whom she had herself driven (or thought she had) by despair into a state of rebellion and hatred. Children (and adolescents too, for that matter) are not as a rule conscious of the physical changes which take place in the grown-up persons with whom they live. But I did become aware that Brigitte Pian was growing a little bit thinner each day. The amethyst-coloured dressing-gown hung loosely now upon her body, as though the thick, bloated snake of braided hair were indeed feeding on the very substance of her flesh. The oddest thing of all was that after the lapse of a few months, Monsieur Puybaraud not only left the paper and shut himself away in the Trappist Monastery of Septfonts for a Retreat, but that he stayed there for good and all, and, in the habit of a novice, accomplished that destiny which my stepmother had always urged on him. Once again the views of Brigitte Pian had coincided with those of Providence. . . . But she could not, at the time of which I am speaking, have foreseen such an unhoped-for issue, and if at moments her anxious mind ceased to concern herself with a renegade, it was only because she was obsessed by thoughts of her other victims—of her husband, of Octavia, both of whom might still have been alive, or so she believed, had they not met with Brigitte Pian on their way through life. She thought too of Michèle, of Jean, and of the abbé Calou whom she had denounced.

On one point I am still not clear—whether she could have derived comfort, during her time of crisis, from a spiritual director. I did not know who hers was, and was not even certain that she had one. I have an idea, moreover, that even at the period of her life when she was deriving most satisfaction from the thought of her progress in virtue, and when there was no reason to suppose that she would one day become a prey to the furies of scruple, she did not take the Sacraments as often as might have been expected of so convinced a church-goer. The quarrel centring about the question of "frequent Communion," which had been loosed upon Christendom two and a half centuries before, was, in my childhood, still very much alive. There are, to-day, few Christians, however devout, who have recourse to the Eucharist as often as they might. Forty years ago a spirit of fear and trembling still ruled the minds of certain persons in their relations with the Incarnate Love, who, so they had been taught by Jansenism to believe, was implacable.

One thing is beyond doubt. All through Lent that year, and the closer we drew to Easter, Brigitte Pian's worries took on more and more the character of sheer terror. One evening she came into my room without knocking. I was already in my bed, reading *Dominique*, and the eyes I turned on the intruder were still full of the imaginary sights from which I had been snatched.

"Aren't you asleep?" she asked in a shy, imploring tone.

She saw from my face that I resented being disturbed. If I had not been in bed, I should have clasped my head in my hands, stuck my fingers in my ears, and buried myself in my book in such a way as to discourage her from persisting in her interruption. But there, beneath the sheets, I was, as it were, quite defenceless.

"I want your advice, Louis. . . . It may seem odd to you that I should say that, but there are moments when I can no longer see my way clear before me. Which do you think is worse: to disobey the Church by not Communicating at Easter, or, by obeying, to expose oneself to the risk of receiving the Eucharist in an improper state of mind? . . . No, don't answer at once: take your time and give me a considered reply. Remember what St. Paul said when he spoke of those who do not fully realize the presence of our Lord's body. . . ."

I told her that my answer didn't need much thought, and that there was really no dilemma at all, because the confession of her sins to a priest would ensure her recovering a state of Grace. . . .

"That may be true for you, Louis, my dear: true enough for the heart of a child. Indeed, I am sure it *is*!"

She sat down heavily on the edge of my bed. I was in for a long visit! I must give up all thoughts of *Dominique*. Instead, I had got to listen to the outpourings of a haggard old woman.

"For that to be true, the sins must, in the first place, be simple, easily recognized and defined, capable of being fitted into a formula. But how do you think I could ever make intelligible to a priest the problems which are tormenting me? How could he understand my relations with your father, with the Puybarauds, with Monsieur Calou, with Michèle? I have tried three times already. I have been, in turn, to a Secular, to a Dominican and to a Jesuit. All three regarded me as one of those over-scrupulous females who are the bane of Confessors, and against whom they use the one weapon most calculated to increase the torments of their penitents by speaking as though they did not take their self-accusations seriously. On such occasions one leaves the Confessional convinced that one has not been understood, that one cannot be pardoned for a sin which has made no real impression on the priest. . . . Well, that is *my* position," she added suddenly, after a moment's silence. "The whole problem is to know whether one's scruples are justified. Surely, the mere fact of suffering as I am suffering *must* mean that my sins are real."

"In such a case," said I priggishly, "scruple is the wrong word. What you mean is remorse."

"You have put your finger on the sore place, Louis. We try to comfort ourselves by using pretty words. It is true that I am tormented, not by scruples but by remorse: yes, remorse. You, with that quickness of mind which poor Monsieur Puybaraud so much admired, have understood me at once. But I despair of making myself clear to those inexperienced men who look on sins as so many easily defined gestures; who entirely fail to grasp the fact that evil can sometimes poison a whole life, that evil may have many shapes, may be invisible, incomprehensible and, consequently, incommunicable—impossible to put into words. . . ."

She stopped speaking. The weight of her body was crushing me. I could hear her heavy breathing.

"I have an idea," I said. (I now felt as excited as I used to do in the old days when Monsieur Puybaraud asked me questions as though I had been an oracle, and I tried to dazzle him by an answer that should be at once unexpected and full of wisdom.) "The only priest who can restore your peace of mind is one who not only has known you for many years, but is well versed in the events which are causing you so much uneasiness." I warmed to my task, while she watched me with the same kind of eager attention which the seriously ill show as soon as the doctor opens his lips. "The abbé Calou knows everything already. In his last letter to me he described all the details of the trouble from which you are suffering. Scruple or remorse—the name does not matter. He will know what is on your mind and, because he knows, will be in a position to give you absolution."

"The abbé Calou? Do you really think so? Do you think I could make my Confession to him after everything I have done?"

"That's just the point: after all you've done *to him.*"

She got up and began to pace about the room. She kept on groaning that she could never bring herself to do it. . . .

"It will be hard, of course," I said (I was becoming crafty); "but by so much the more will you acquire merit."

That word "merit" made her raise her head.

"It would be beyond the strength of most people, but you . . ."

She straightened up still more. "After all . . ." she muttered, and then went on: "I should have to seek him out in the bosom of his family. But is it certain that he has the right now to hear Confessions?" She addressed the question to herself rather than to me. "Yes, surely he has, provided it is within the limits of the diocese."

She started walking up and down again. I yawned noisily and urrowed down under the sheets.

"Sleepy, aren't you? Lucky you: nothing will keep *you* awake."

She leaned over me, and her cracked lips touched my forehead.

"It *is* a good idea, isn't it?" I asked in a self-satisfied voice.

She made no reply, but stood turning the matter over and over in her mind. She put out the light, but I lit it again as soon as she had closed the door. Once more, *Dominique* drew my thoughts far from the concerns of that hag-ridden woman.

XV

WHEN she left the train which had brought her back from the abbé Calou, it wanted still two hours to dinner-time. Instead, therefore, of taking a cab, she walked back along the gloomy Rue Saint-Jean. It was foggy and she was jostled by the crowd. But to-day she was indifferent to all that usually she most disliked, for she carried within her the assurance of pardon. She pursued her way with a light heart and, for the first time, the impulse of gratitude which set her in the presence of God had in it something of a tenderness that was at once humble and very human. Her evil had been taken from her. She no longer suffered, no longer found it difficult to breathe. Occasionally, as a sharp reminder, the prick of her old anxieties returned. Had she confessed everything? Yes, of course she had: and anyhow, he who had listened to her had known it all before.

She let her mind dwell on what had been said in the fireless, whitewashed, almost bare room in which the abbé Calou had received her. He had offered her no words of comfort. Instead, he had made her feel ashamed because she had attached so much importance to her faults, as though she didn't know that it is God's way to turn even our sins to His own purposes. The abbé had begged her to dwell on her own insignificance, and not to substitute for the illusion that she was a person well advanced along the way of perfection, that other, no less vicious, illusion that she was a noted sinner. He had added that she could do much for those to whom she thought she owed reparation; for the dead, naturally, but also for the living. "As, for example," he said, "you can be of great help to me with the Cardinal. . . ." (She realized that he was saying this to help her, from a feeling of charity. . . .) To be taken back into favour was not what he desired, but to be allowed to settle, at his own cost, somewhere between Bastide and Souys, in the poorest, most solitary part of the country he could find, there to take premises where he might be permitted to teach the catechism and to say Mass. Brigitte Pian, walking so light-heartedly along the pavements damp with fog, decided that she would shoulder the expenses of this enterprise. Already she saw in imagination a new parish arising around the abbé Calou.

She had just time to go into the Cathedral before the doors were locked, and remained there for a few minutes, motionless, like some-one who has been blessed by a miraculous cure and can find no words of gratitude. Then she set out again and reached her own front-door, scarcely conscious of what streets she passed along.

In the hall an unusual smell of tobacco brought her back to earth. Who could it be who dared to smoke in her house? She recognized a voice, Michèle's, mingled with another which she could not identify. Yet, for all that, she knew at once who had penetrated, had dared to penetrate, into her drawing-room. The Countess's letter had hinted that young Mirbel might pay us a visit, but Brigitte had not seriously believed that the young thief would have the effrontery to show himself. But he had come! We had actually received him! There he was, behind this very door, talking freely to Michèle.

Brigitte Pian drew herself up. There, in the hall lit by a single gas-burner in a frosted globe, she became once more her old self, a woman strong in her assurance of Grace, convinced of her right to interfere in the lives of those over whom she had authority. At the same time she heard within herself the low rumblings of that righteous anger which she found it so difficult to resist, which showed itself whenever her orders were flouted and anyone dared to question or avoid something which she had determined and laid down. With her hand on the latch, she hesitated once more. In spite of her anger, in spite of this blow administered to her newly acquired sense of peace, the deep call of her spirit was still operative. She knew that the people there in her drawing-room felt that she had done them a wrong. On that point, however, her conscience did not reproach her. What else could she have done? She had protected Michèle, who was still a child, and any mother would have done the same. The abbé Calou, however, saw things in a different light. She knew what young Mirbel meant to him, even though he had never once, that day, mentioned his name in her hearing. But certain words that he had spoken came back now into her memory, and doubtless put her in mind of the lost sheep. Each one of us, he had said, has his own peculiar destiny, and it is, perhaps, one of the secrets of that compassionate Justice which watches over us, that there is no universally valid law by which human beings are to be assessed. Every man inherits his own past. For that he is to be pitied, because he carries with him through life a load made up of the sins and merits of his forbears to an extent which it is beyond our power to grasp. He is free to say yes or no when God's love is offered to him, but which of us can claim the right to judge what it is that influences his choice? It was while talking of the Puybarauds that the abbé had said: "We must not interfere blindly between two persons who love one another, even when they do so in sin. The important thing is that we should understand what their being brought together means, for the ways of human beings do not cross by chance. . . ."

As Brigitte Pian listened outside the door she could hear two voices intermingled: that of the young girl, which sounded depressed; the other, virile, uncertain in its register, with occasional rising passages which were muted by distance. No longer annoyed, but still uncertain, she sat down on the wood-chest. That it might not be thought that she was listening at key-holes (though she could not hear what was being said in the drawing-room), she went up to her room a few minutes later, and remained there a long time alone and on her knees in the darkness.

Jean de Mirbel had chosen Thursday for his attempted meeting with Michèle, because he knew that she would be free in the afternoon. It was me whom he asked to see. My first thought was to tell Michèle, and I saw at once that she knew that Jean was there. Her school uniform made her look plain. Her hair, half caught up into a "bun," was tied with a mauve ribbon. Her high button-boots gave her ankles a thick appearance. I was not taken in by her assumed air of calmness. It was essential that this visit should not be made an excuse by our stepmother for a show of malevolence, and we agreed that even should Jean ask me to do so, I must not leave them alone together at any time during his visit.

That settled, we went down into the drawing-room. It was not yet four o'clock, but the heavy, fringed lace curtains made the room dark, and the wall-lamp had been lit. A smell of paraffin hung about the "occasional tables" with their poker-work tops, and the painted screens. The gilded chairs caught the light. Mirbel was taller than of old and had filled out, but his face was thinner. His hollow cheeks threw into relief the nose which had always been aquiline, though we had thought of it as small. His forehead was more lined that befitted his eighteen years. He was wearing a new, ready-made suit the shoulders of which were too much padded.

The two young people who had fallen in love before the lines of their physical development had become fully determined, looked at one another with astonishment. There was what seemed to me a long interval of silence. The poor human insects had to trace backwards the stages of their metamorphosis before each could see once more in the other the child whom he and she had loved. But their eyes had not changed, and it was they, I am sure, which first gave them the clue to their identities.

My boyish jealousy had long ago vanished. I wanted only to get away, to make myself invisible. It was no difficult task, for as soon as they began to speak, they were conscious only of one another. But their conversation dragged. It was as though they did not know what to talk about. Michèle sat down, but Jean remained standing with his back to the window. He had lit a cigarette without asking her whether she minded. From my corner I could not hear them very well, especially Jean, who kept on saying in angry, impatient tones, "But that's not the point . . . that's not of the least importance," to which Michèle replied with an air of mockery: "Really?" I gathered that they were discussing the chemist's wife. Jean, his hands in his pockets and his shoulders hunched, was rocking backwards and forwards on his feet. It was obvious, he said, that she did not want to have anything more to do with him, that she was taking the first excuse that came to hand to send him packing. Not that it wasn't perfectly natural. The only surprising thing was how she had ever come to believe that she cared for him.

Michèle interrupted the flow of his words. She spoke as she used to do in the days of their old childhood's quarrels.

"So *you're* accusing *me*! I must say, I like that: after all, you started it!"

To this, Jean in a fit of exasperation replied:

"Why must you harp on that idiotic story? I do wish you'd try to understand that it meant absolutely nothing to me. It was merely my way of smashing things up and breaking loose. . . . I just had to get out of that house . . . because of you, because life had become intolerable. . . . Yes, it was you who were the cause of it all. . . . What about the woman? you say. Well, you'd have laughed if you could have seen us in the hotel at Biarritz. Why, everybody thought I was her son, and she didn't dare to say I wasn't. As a matter of fact, she didn't much mind . . . she was laughing at me the whole time . . . but I can't explain. . . ."

And when Michèle struck back with, "I wouldn't try, if I were you!" he assured her that it was the Curé and no one else who had mattered to Madame Voyod from beginning to end of the business. "She kept on talking about him: 'He'll be just about getting home now,' she would say. 'He must have been told by this time. What will his first reactions be? D'you think he's capable of crying? Have you ever seen him cry?' Those were the questions she asked me. She wanted to play him a dirty trick, or to revenge herself on him."

"But what for?"

"Oh, I suppose the mere fact that he wears a soutane makes her want to hurt him. . . . However that may be, *I* didn't count for much with her."

Michèle replied that she was quite prepared to believe that the woman had been laughing at him. But what she could never forgive was that he had allowed himself to be caught like that.

To this burst of temper Jean replied with a show of tenderness. It gave the measure of his exhaustion. "What's the good of arguing?" He realized, he said, that everything was over between them. She didn't know what he had had to put up with. There were things he couldn't tell her. He had trusted her, believed the promise she had made to be faithful to him whatever happened. . . . But naturally he understood now that she had overestimated her strength. A young girl shouldn't get mixed up with a fellow like Jean de Mirbel. If she did, she ran the risk of being lost for ever.

"You're getting away from the point," insisted Michèle, who kept on mulishly returning to the subject of the Voyod woman.

Jean groaned:

"You don't understand. . . ."

But I, sitting there alone, and more or less outside the arena, could see clearly into both their minds. Michèle was the victim of the same sort of evil mood which used to afflict me, on their account, when I was little more than a child. She could never have been sure that she had loved this emaciated young man whom she scarcely recognized, were it not for the fact that he had caused her so much pain during the last few weeks. And he, indifferent to her jealousy, was calling from the depths of his loneliness: "Take me as I am: I am sick; I am only a boy; take me, look after me!" But she was deaf to his appeal. She had become a woman, the kind of woman who cannot see beyond the outrage done to the craving of her senses, a woman practical and positive.

"I'm really very sorry for you," she said. "To hear you speak, one would think you were an outlaw . . . you, Jean de Mirbel."

He could find no answer to that, or rather, he could not find the only words which might have broken down her obstinacy. He was amazed that she should speak to him of his birth and fortune. . . . How could he make her see what was going on inside him? that he was repudiating something, longing for something, and had no idea what it was all about? . . . After a fairly long silence, he said:

"Tell me, Michèle, why was it that I was always in trouble at school, always being pointed at? Why did my brute of an uncle want to break my spirit? . . . As I said before, there are things you know nothing about. . . ."

"What things?" she asked.

He shook his head: not, as I supposed, as a sign that he couldn't answer, but to free himself of an image by which, as he told me later, when we had become inseparable, he was obsessed at the time of which I am writing: of a picture of a narrow street in Balauze, of nettles growing against the wall of the Cathedral, of the stocky figure of a man at a window, of the white, wraith-like form of a woman who could scarcely find room to slip between his shoulder and the wall.

After another silence, he went on: "I must give you back . . . you know what, surely?"

He was thinking of the locket; she protested:

"No, keep it!"

But he had already undone his collar, and was trying to take off the chain. After a bit of fumbling he gave up, sat down, and remained, saying nothing, his head drooped forward.

I did not notice at once that he was crying, but it was to his tears that Michèle at last surrendered. They had moved no nearer to one another. This visible sign of a misery at whose cause she could not guess overcame Michèle's resistance, though she had stood out against everything else. She had not forgotten a single one of her grievances. She would have a whole lifetime in which to brood on them. She would add many others to them, storing up ammunition for future quarrels. But he was crying, and she found it impossible, physically impossible, to bear.

She went close to him and, bending down, wiped away his tears with her diminutive handkerchief. At the same time she laid her hand on his head.

Though I had turned away, I could see what was happening in the mirror. I saw, too, the door into the hall open. It remained open. No one came in. Jean de Mirbel had got up from his chair. Then, Brigitte Pian appeared, carrying a tray loaded with cups and bread and butter. I realized that she must have put it down on the wood-chest in order to open the door.

Only her lips smiled, and she looked at us from a pair of sombre eyes.

XVI

SHE served tea with an eagerness of humility very different from the eagerness which she had displayed when it was her object to edify us in the old days. Or, perhaps I should say, that if some concern for our edification was still discernible in her attitude, it made less impression on me than did my feeling, which increased as time went on, that her nature was, as it were, turning back upon itself. People do not change. At my age one can have no illusions on that point: but they do quite often turn back to what they were once and show again those very characteristics which they have striven tirelessly, through a whole lifetime, to suppress. This does not mean that they necessarily end by succumbing to what is worst in themselves. God is very often the good temptation to which many human beings in the long run yield.

This was not at once the case with Brigitte Pian, although we were to see her, under the abbé Calou's influence, rid herself in the course of a few weeks of her old tendency to dominate. Clearly, she was seeking the sources of a deep, personal religion. But it was precisely in those things which she was now trying to suppress that she had formerly found that religion, in all that could satisfy her craving to direct others, to rule. She had always been unwilling to take second place to no matter whom in purity of intention or perfection of virtue.

I can see her still, upright in the middle of that hideous room, a cup of tea in each hand. During the few moments in which she imposed the fact of her presence on us, everything which separated Jean from Michèle and from me vanished. We formed a compact block of youth confronted by an ageing woman. Three stars which are separated by vast distances of space may seem to be quite close to one another when seen in relation to a fourth, more distant, star.

She looked at us with a sort of hungry concentration. At first I did not understand its full significance.

"We're on top all right now, she'll have to knuckle under!" exclaimed Michèle as soon as our stepmother had left the room. But no, that was not what chiefly emerged from this incident. It is true that Jean was asked, in the most friendly tone possible, to remember us to his mother. Brigitte even went so far as to express a hope that he would let us hear from him when he got to England, which was tantamount to admitting his right to correspond with my sister. . . . This seeming defeat showed its true significance only in the course of the two or three years which elapsed before I went off to Paris. During all that time Jean wrote regularly, several times a week, to Michèle from Cambridge. To say that our stepmother acquiesced in all this is to put the matter too mildly. Every day she studied the girl's face, trying to read in it whether she had received a letter, and whether it had told of pain or happiness. Not one detail of this love affair, of this interminable succession of storms and stresses, the story of which I must some day tell, was lost on Brigitte Pian.

"She is pleased when I suffer," complained Michèle. But that was not true. Brigitte was not pleased, only interested, passionately concerned.

Another thing that Michèle said was: "Now that she can no longer torment anybody she has become like those people who find their only sexual satisfaction in watching others making love. . . ." And that I found nearer to the truth. The whole centre of Brigitte Pian's interest in life had shifted. She no longer worked at her old task, adding link by link to the armour of her false perfection. Consequently, she had time now to study others, to observe the strange game they played under the name of love, that game from which, for so long, she had averted her gaze in horror, without attempting to fathom the mysteries which the word conceals.

Michèle, so far from being touched by the interest which our stepmother was showing in her, suspected every kind of evil intention, and was careful not to reveal anything which concerned her relations with Jean. But Brigitte interpreted in her own way the girl's fits of ill-temper, and drew her own conclusions from her least sigh, and even from her periods of silence.

Doubtless she was more regular now than she had been in her religious duties, and may even have taken the Sacrament more often, for her scruples had at last vanished. But from now on she led two lives. When she was not in church, she spent her time exploring a world which had no connexion with the one illuminated by Grace. At the age of fifty she had suddenly discovered the joys of imaginative literature, and I often came on her in my room taking down some book from the shelves. Her method of reading was more like eating—like the greedy eating of a child who stuffs its mouth with food. She had to make up so much time that she had wasted on printed nonsense, the worthlessness of which she was too intelligent not to have realized at the time. I remember the way in which, in the old days, she used to open the regular parcel of "Good Family Reading." She would pick out some volume at random, turn several pages at once, sigh, shrug. Now she showed a similar eagerness in her approach to *Adolphe*, the *Lys dans la Vallée*, *Anna Karénina*. I indulged her taste for books that dealt in the precise analysis of sentiment. All love stories appealed to her, provided they did not falsify reality. In just such a way will a man, condemned to lead a sedentary life, cram himself with tales of travel, but always with a keen eye for the veracity of the writer. She scarcely ever saw the abbé Calou now. The attempt to get permission for him to occupy himself with a "cure of souls" at Souys had come to nothing. Already he was suspected in high places (though quite wrongly) of being responsible for certain venomous comments in *The Battle* on the subject of diocesan administration. He was one of those innocent souls who cannot always resist the temptation to say something amusing, the kind of man who would rather be hanged than miss the chance of some biting rejoinder. Unfortunately for him, the man who had succeeded Cardinal Lecot in the office made illustrious by the Primates of Aquitaine was a cleric of limited intelligence, who, therefore, became an implacable foe. One of these days I may, perhaps, tell the story of the sainted abbé Calou's road to Calvary. He was already on the point of being suspended, and wore out Brigitte Pian with the tale of his miseries. But it was to talk of herself and not of him that she made the necessary train journey. She who knew that art and literature represented no bad investment. . . . Even in those days they were taking a chance on Matisse. But was I a sound proposition? They could not make up their minds, were suspicious of my impatience, and regarded me as, on the whole, a great hobbledehoy—which I was. They did all they could, therefore, to keep me hanging on. When I threatened to give up the whole idea, they redoubled their friendliness. My stepmother had picked up some disturbing rumours about their medical history, and they went so far as to beg me to go and see their doctor, whom they had, so to speak, released for the occasion from his oath of professional secrecy.

That ridiculous, rather sordid, errand of mine seems now like a dream. I have a picture of myself facing, from behind his desk, the eminent practitioner who waited, icily polite, to answer the questions which I wanted to put to him. The whole business ended in a final family conclave from which I emerged definitely engaged, and received from the young woman a rapturous letter. But by the next day the whole situation had changed, and I found myself cast off without a word of excuse or explanation. I blamed myself. The fact was clear to me, that in spite of all the solid proofs of my worthiness which I could produce, she did not like me. In view of this check to my hopes, every other encouraging sign went for nothing. Something about me, I did not know what, had come between me and the Angelic Being. Was it a sign in me of the incurable romanticism of youth? The men of my generation were born with a sense of personal guilt. They imagined that they were destined for a life of solitude and despair.

I told my stepmother, without going into details, that my engagement had been broken off. I had expected a letter of condolence from her, but what was my surprise to see her arrive in person on my doorstep! She seemed to have taken my misfortune very much to heart. She carried her attitude of pity to excess, and gave me to understand that she feared I might have contemplated some desperate act. Her tactless efforts at cheerfulness bored me. They also had the effect of making me realize that I was considerably less unhappy than I had seemed to be in the first moments of disappointment. I saw that what I was really suffering from was wounded vanity. Brigitte took me back with her to Larjuzon. I felt that she resented the fact that I was being so reasonable. But all through that tropical summer of 1911 the evidence was too plain for her to mistake. Far from being mortally wounded by my disaster in love, I found it a stimulus, and was driven by a wild desire to get what compensation I could from life. That summer I found a wonderful antidote in the prolonged reading of Balzac. An author is neither moral nor immoral in himself. It is our own attitude of mind that decides what his influence on us is to be. In my then state of mind, Balzac put me in love with life, though at the same time he infected my still childish mind with a strong dose of cynicism. I was enchanted by the coldly calculating tricks and subterfuges of his young heroes.

It was about this time that Brigitte began to cut herself adrift from me. I had disturbed the idea of love which she had built up for herself. There was nothing that she had come to dislike more in anyone than an absence of passion. She could not bear to think that I had recovered from my disappointment so quickly. She did not dare admit this to me, but I could feel that she suspected me of not belonging to the true race of tormented lovers. I did not then know how far her self-deception had gone.

Michèle spent the summer holidays of 1911 with the Mirbels at La Devize. The only resource, therefore, left to me and my stepmother was reading. Her gloom deepened. Already she had begun to grow slack in the performance of her religious duties. Her talk was more and more concerned with one subject only. Human passion had become an obsession with her. Occasionally she spoke to me of my mother in a tone of hostility which betrayed both admiration and envy. But for the most part she remained silent, lying on the veranda, a faint flush staining the dead white of her face.

I have always had a horror of neurasthenics, and that year I welcomed the necessity of having to go back to Paris. It was a way of escape. I still wrote to my stepmother, but our letters were always came back from these trips in a disappointed frame of mind. But by next day she had forgotten all about it, and would concentrate her attention once again on Michèle's love affair, or become completely absorbed in some book which she read far into the night.

Not that the pharisee was dead in her. She took pride in the very clarity of mind which enabled her to sit in judgment upon herself and condemn her own conduct. She did not believe that there were many instances of a Christian woman capable, at fifty, of realizing that her feet had been set on the wrong road. Not that she ever admitted in so many words that she would like never again to meddle in the affairs of her neighbours. Sometimes she would be caught up into a mood of deep nostalgia when she remembered the years gone by. One day it happened that we had just come back from the funeral of my old trustee Maître Malbec. He had been carried from the house of his mistress with his mouth twisted sideways. His affairs were much compromised, for, unknown to all, he had led a very dissipated life. "All the same," said Brigitte as we were driving home, "he did live." I protested. Was that what she called living? My stepmother seemed to be embarrassed by my question, and assured me that I had mistaken her meaning. One said of a man that he had lived when he had done things on the grand scale. That was all she had meant to say. I do not doubt for a moment that she was sincere. My studious existence was a matter of surprise to her. "All men are beasts" she said more than once, not in her old, bitter tone, but with a smile. When I settled in Paris to read for a degree in Political Science, I had to endure endless sessions of acute, subtle questioning whenever I returned to Bordeaux for a short visit. She was convinced that I was leading an existence of intrigue and smouldering passion, and she kept up a regular correspondence with the Comtesse de Mirbel of which Jean and I were the constant theme (for, from 1910 on, my old friend had joined me in the capital). Here, too, I must refrain from anticipating the story of these Paris years, though I may tell it later. I will mention one incident only, and that because Brigitte was mixed up in it, and because it illustrated the sudden flowering of the extraordinary change that had come over her.

Very early my mind began to play round the idea of marriage. The thought had obsessed me ever since the days when I was quite a boy, and it still did so at that time of my life when I was better placed than thousands of young men to try my hand at winning happiness. It was due to my fear of losing my way in the chaotic wilderness of my sensibilities. I might well have applied to myself the wise words of Nietzsche which he wrote about the French seventeenth century: "It contained much of wildness, much too of that will to asceticism which was so necessary if it was to remain master in its own house. . . ." One day a friend spoke to me of his cousin, a young woman of wealth, who had spent all her childhood in a world inhabited by writers and painters. He extolled her charms, and I snapped at the hook almost as soon as it was dangled before me. Living, as I did, in such close communion with God, believing, as I did, that nothing ever happened to me which did not spring from the direct purpose of the Uncreated Being, and that no one could cross my path without being, in some sense, a delegate of the Infinite, I was prepared to find in this young woman an angel of liberation. *Their eyes all full of light, they walk before me. . . .*

As it turned out, this girl, whom I saw as a sort of combination of Madonna and Muse, hesitated a great deal longer, and was far less easy to capture, than I had either expected or wished. She was anxious not to make up her mind until she had travelled extensively in Europe. My love was, on the whole, flattered by the thought of our coming separation, and by my knowledge of her perplexities, which I regarded as a merit in one who lived ever in the regions of the sublime.

So taken up was I by this idea of sublimity that I quite failed to see her as she was, a rich, middle-class young woman who was in no hurry to bind herself by a definite engagement, who carefully weighed the pros and cons of the situation, with a wary eye on me. it was known that I had money, but my family came from the provinces and was no more than decently respectable. Was I a good "buy"? Her parents belonged to a world of sophisticated Parisians trivial and colourless. Michèle, who was planning to marry Jean after he had done his two years of military service, was still living at the Cours de l'Intendance. In her letters to me she mentioned "something quite unbelievable that has happened to Brigitte," but waited to tell me what it was until she should come to Paris, where she was due to stay with the Mirandieuzes.

When at last I heard the details, the whole thing did, in fact, seem so unbelievable that I could do nothing at first but shrug my shoulders. I thought that Michèle was giving rein to her imagination when she told me that my stepmother had fallen in love with her doctor, a man well on in his sixties. But at Bordeaux I was confronted by evidence which would not be denied. It was not just a question of a sick old woman developing a liking for her medical attendant. No, she had fallen a prey to a fierce, exclusive, and (what was really odd) a thoroughly happy and reciprocated passion. Not that there was anything "wrong" in their relations. Dr. Gellis, a fervent Huguenot with a practice which included all the best Protestant families of the city, was beyond the reach of any scandal. But, separated from a wife who had dragged his name in the mud, and plagued by a horde of children, most of whom were married, embittered and needy, it had been a matter of delight for him to discover, in the evening of his days, that he had become an object of exclusive concern to a woman who was far stronger-minded and better fitted to face life than he was. He saw her every day, and took no decisions without first consulting her. The two lonely old things were perfectly unashamed about talking of their mutual attachment, and it never seemed to occur to them that they were making themselves ridiculous. They found in one another's faces not the signs of old age, but of tenderness. They lived for one another like two old innocents, blissfully unaware that their irritated relations were laughing at them, and that the neighbours were gossiping at their expense.

It was the last year of Jean's military service, and his marriage was to take place in October. The families exchanged dinners, and the contract was drawn up. Brigitte Pian had to act to Michèle as a mother, but did so with a bad grace. Her stepdaughter's passion no longer interested her. What chiefly worried her was the imprudent promise she had made to divide the family estate during her lifetime. This was a sacrifice which she had once gladly envisaged as, in some sort, making up for the wrong she had done the girl. Brigitte's personal fortune was less than ours. She scarcely had enough capital left (though she realized it too late) to enable her to buy a small property adjoining Dr. Gellis's Clinic. The Comtesse de Mirbel expressed it as her view that this "entirely changed the whole situation. . . ." In her eyes, the loss of half a million francs only underlined the fact that her son was making a mésalliance. Brigitte played deaf, pretended not to understand the hints, but avoided any open warfare and anything which might have disturbed her strange, deep happiness. This happiness, seen in terms of the human figure, was a stout gentleman of sixty-odd years, with short legs. He wore a tight-fitting frock-coat and had a dyed beard which, taken in conjunction with his austere gestures and bald head, gave him a certain resemblance to the Chancellor Michel de l'Hôpital. He talked a great deal and listened to no one except Brigitte, though she preferred to stay silent so as not to lose a single word that might drop from the lips of the beloved. Most of their conversation was concerned with serious subjects, not excluding theology. She showed herself responsive to the logic of Calvinism, though neither gave the least sign of wishing to convert the other, either because of a mutual tenderness for their respective beliefs, or because they were no longer greatly interested in the matter of creeds. Age made them conscious of the value of every fleeting moment. Not a minute must be diverted from the one essential thing—their love for one another.

From now on Brigitte's life and ours lay apart. I got out of the habit of dropping in at the Cours de l'Intendance when I visited Bordeaux. My room had become a pied-à-terre for Dr. Gellis on those evenings when he took Brigitte to the theatre or to a concert, and slept in town. Their love of music was a great bond. The doctor had no car, but sported one of those ancient broughams which say "doctor" a mile off. It took a long time to cover the distance between the town and his Clinic.

It is not always the case that greybeards fall for young girls, or ageing women for growing youths. It sometimes happens that a man and a woman who have vainly sought one another through a long life, meet by chance when the shadows begin to fall. When that happens, their passion takes on a peculiarly intense quality of isolation. Nothing else seems to matter. There is so little time left! The world may laugh, but, then, the world knows little of the secrets of the heart. When I did pay one of my infrequent visits to the Cours de l'Intendance, Brigitte's attitude to me was one almost of pity. I, not she, was the one who stood in need of sympathy. The old, formidable side of her character still showed at times when she conjured up the memory of my mother or of the Puybarauds; of all those people whom she no longer needed to envy, who, unlike her, had never known the delights of a love that was truly shared. The sight of that cruel flame flickering beneath the thick eyebrows which almost met across Brigitte's forehead got on my nerves, and I was goaded into dropping allusions to the kind of love that she would never know. I had discovered a chink in the armour of her proud and throned emotion. Passion, I hinted, is but the ghost of itself when it cannot take bodily form. So long as we cannot lose and find ourselves again in the beloved, we merely intoxicate ourselves with words and with the gestures of love, but we can never know whether what we have is the reality.

Brigitte broke in upon my monologue: "You don't know what you're saying, what you're talking about. . . ."

Her face had assumed the old, familiar expression of disgust which had always shown in the old days whenever the forbidden subject was mentioned in her hearing. I have a feeling of remorse now when I think that I may have spoiled their happiness with these insinuations of mine because, about the time that I was indulging in these bouts of rhetoric, I learned from Michèle of occasional stormy scenes between Philemon and his Baucis. Could it be that Brigitte was conscious of regret? Could it be that she made certain demands upon her lover? One dare not attempt to visualize the squalid little efforts and contortions of those two bodies whose powers had not kept pace with the sentiments which stirred them. When youth suffers (as I was suffering then) it cannot bear the sight of age's placid contentment.

Dr. Gellis had his children and the parents of his grandchildren for ever yapping at his heels. The purchase of the little property adjoining the Clinic, which Brigitte concluded on the day before Michèle's marriage, set a match to the powder barrel. One of the pastors of Bordeaux made representations to the doctor, while his family begged Michèle to persuade her stepmother to see some priest in whom she had confidence, and to whose criticism she would listen. This was just about the time that the abbé Calou had been deprived of the right to say Mass. Since, however, he was merely suspended and not excommunicated, his poor, humiliated soutane could be seen among the black dresses of the old women each morning when Communion was administered in the small chapel that stands close to the Faculty of Letters. He would go back to his seat followed by the curious or pitying glances of the congregation, and his face was as the face of an angel.

The Gellis family had no time in which to enlist his help. To use one of the cruel and futile sayings of which the Comtesse de Mirbel was so fond—"the whole thing was taken out of their hands." One evening, close to the Clinic, a motor-car struck the doctor's brougham a glancing blow. He was killed on the spot. My stepmother saw the news next day in the paper. A number of no doubt highly coloured stories spread through the town to the effect that Brigitte Pian had arrived, haggard and hatless, at the house where the Gellis children were living. It was said that the eldest son had tried to keep her out of the room where the body lay, but that she had thrust him aside, had broken through the defences erected in her path by the rest of the family, and had thrown herself upon the corpse with never a tear or a cry, and that she had had to be pulled away by main force.

I was living at that time with friends at Cap Martin. I did not feel that so unofficial a case of mourning necessitated my presence. I merely wrote a letter. It was a difficult letter to compose, and it remained unanswered. But Michèle and Jean were away in Algeria on their honeymoon, and the thought of Brigitte haunted me. It was not in my power, just then, to make the trip to Bordeaux in order to assure myself that my stepmother had not gone out of her mind. I was due back in Paris. I therefore postponed the difficult duty until the beginning of spring.

The servant did not know me, and I was left waiting in the hall. I could hear my stepmother's exclamation: "But of course! Show him in." I was much relieved to find that her voice sounded as usual. She was sitting in her accustomed place by the writing-table, which was no longer, as of old, littered with circulars and invitations to charity sales. She had grown no older in appearance. I noticed, after the first few minutes, that she had gone back to the old way of doing her hair—raised high, puffed out with numberless little curls, and so arranged as to leave her large ears and well-modelled forehead free. A photograph of Dr. Gellis stood on the mantelpiece, surmounted by a bunch of lilac. There was nothing about Madame Brigitte to indicate nervous disturbance or mental unbalance. Her shoulders were covered by a knitted woollen shawl. As I came in, she had just put back on her desk the rosary which she had always used when I was a child. She began the conversation by apologizing for not having answered my letter. She made no attempt to deceive me, but said that for several days she had been in a condition of prostration from which she had recovered only with considerable difficulty.

"And now?" I asked.

She looked at me thoughtfully:

"If Monsieur Puybaraud were here, he would insist that you were the only person capable of understanding. . . ."

There was calm certainty in her smile. "You see, the real, secret truth is that I have not lost him . . . but there is no one I can tell. . . . Dear Monsieur Gellis was never so close to me as he is now, not even when he was alive. He had already embarked on his mission to me while he was in this world, but we are all of us poor mortal flesh, and our bodies were a barrier. But there is nothing between us now."

She spoke much on this theme, and at first I suspected a trick of sorrow seeking to cheat death of the dear doctor. But at the end of a few days I realized that the sun of human love had not risen too late on the arid destiny of this woman of the Pharisees, that the "whited sepulchre" had been unsealed and stood open at last. Perhaps it still contained a few dried bones, a trace of corruption. Occasionally the formidable eyebrows met in a frown above the smouldering eyes. Some grievance, long chewed over, brought, now and then, a bitter word to her lips. But "dear Monsieur Gellis" was never far away, was always there at the critical moment to lead Brigitte Pian into the calm ways of God.

An urgent letter from the Comtesse de Mirbel called me to La Devize where Michèle and Jean had just arrived, some considerable time before they were expected. This hurried return of theirs worried me. I set off without delay, and was at once caught up into their drama, the story of which I shall some day tell. I became the satellite of their system, and was whirled about in the constant eddy of strife and reconciliation which made up their existence. I had no leisure in which to think of the old woman whom I had left in the Cours de l'Intendance, embalmed, as it were, in the posthumous adoration of "dear Monsieur Gellis." It was my strange destiny to become the go-between for Jean and Michèle—continually warding off the blows which they blindly aimed at one another—a rôle especially strange for a young man who had his own private misery and suffered in a solitude which no one in the world could break.

The mobilization of 2nd August, 1914, woke us from our dream. That thunder-clap disturbed thousands of personal dramas, all of them much like our own. We struggled up from the depths of our dark passions, all our saps destroyed, stupefied and dazed by an appalling disaster which was so infinitely greater than the one we were inflicting on ourselves. I left Jean and Michèle, who, now that they were to lose one another, could do themselves no further hurt, and faced the full extremity of my loneliness when I realized that there was no one in the world, except Brigitte, to whom I could even say good-bye.

She looked small now, and had grown thin. She drew me to her, and her tears surprised me. The name of Dr. Gellis was never once mentioned between us. She looked after me as a mother might have done. I found out later that she was seeing a great deal of Monsieur Calou at this time, and was doing much to help him. He had been taken back into favour by the Diocesan authorities, but was already near his end.

All the time I was at the Front I was overwhelmed with parcels and letters and with enquiries about my health and my needs. I spent my first leave with Madame Brigitte. A few days before it fell due, Monsieur Calou had died in her arms. She told me about it quite unemotionally, and without making any attempt to point a lesson. Monsieur Calou, she said, had certainly not grown less in spiritual stature, though, towards the end, he had scarcely been of this world. He had suffered from agonising attacks of angina pectoris—the kind that drive the sufferer to the open window in a terrifying struggle for air. But as soon as he had recovered his breath, he would say that he was ready for still greater suffering. He had on his table a photograph which I had taken long ago in the kitchen garden at Baluzac. It showed Jean and Michèle, bare-footed, their eyes screwed up against the sun, clinging to the same watering-can. Brigitte added that, in spite of the pain he had to endure, he never gave one a feeling of pity.

When I alluded to past events, she talked of them quite openly. But I could feel that she had become detached even from the consciousness of her faults, and that she had decided to lay everything at the throne of the Great Compassion. In the evening of her life, Brigitte Pian had come to the knowledge that it is useless to play the part of a proud servitor eager to impress his master by a show of readiness to repay his debts to the last farthing. It had been revealed to her that our Father does not ask us to give a scrupulous account of what merits we can claim. She understood at last that it is not our deserts that matter but our love.

THE END